BROKEN CROWNS

Lauren DeStefano earned her BA in English with a concentration in creative writing from Albertus Magnus College in Connecticut. She is the author of *The Chemical Garden* trilogy. She lives in Connecticut.

Visit LaurenDeStefano.com to learn more about Lauren.

ALSO BY LAUREN DESTEFANO

The Chemical Garden Trilogy
Wither
Fever
Sever

The Internment Chronicles E-novellas
No Intention of Dying
The Heir Apparent

The Internment Chronicles
Perfect Ruin
Burning Kingdoms

Broken

Crowns

LAUREN
DESTEFANO

Book 3 of The Internment Chronicles

HARPER
Voyager

Harper*Voyager*
An imprint of HarperCollins*Publishers*
1 London Bridge Street
London SE1 9GF

www.harpervoyagerbooks.co.uk

A Paperback Original 2016
1

A catalogue record for this book
is available from the British Library

ISBN: 978-0-00-754128-7

Book design by Lizzy Bromley

Printed and bound in Great Britain by
Clays Ltd, St Ives plc

acknowledgments

Thank you, always, to my parents and my family for always being my first supporters and fans. And for enduring the poems I wrote in high school. Thank you to my little cousins, especially, who are growing into such brilliant young readers and who are forever asking me to tell my stories to them whenever there's a lull in the day.

Thank you to my agent, Barbara Poelle, whose faith in me has somehow yet to falter even after all these years; you are the reason people think I'm a well-oiled writing machine when I'm actually the source of the weeping in the bathroom stall. Thank you also to Rachel Ekstrom, for her help and editorial insights when I needed it most, and for spending so much time helping me sort things out; thank you to the entire team of Irene Goodman, for the overwhelming support, not just for this story, but for the entirety of my career—not just at the beginning, but before even then. And thank you to my editor, Jaime Levine, without whom, believe me, this book wouldn't be happening right now; thank you for the infinite patience, the vegan dinner and subsequent frozen yogurt, and the countless conversations that reignited the flame for this story every time I thought it was dimming down for good.

Thank you to Harry Lam, professional know-it-all

and genius extraordinaire, for always questioning my ideas and encouraging me to see them through; you are the great constant of my life, and I am thankful beyond words. Thank you to my work wives and confidants, Beth Revis and Aprilynne Pike; you are the humor in the hollow void and all the sappy gushy things I quit writing down when I kicked my poetry phase. So all I'll say is thank you again. Thank you to Laura Bickle and Aimée Carter, for the copious support, and Tahereh Mafi, whose brilliance inspires me to be better. Thank you to Leigh Bardugo, whose books were my self-set reward for meeting my daily writing goals. Thank you to Alexandra Cooper and Amy Rosenbaum, who believed in this story at its beginning.

Thank you to my publisher, Simon & Schuster BFYR, for taking a chance on an unknown writer all the way back at the start, and for teaching me so many valuable lessons about the industry that I will carry with me for the rest of my life.

Thank you, always always always, to my readers, for their loyalty and warmth and laughter that I carry like a lantern in the darkest hours of writing.

We shall not cease from exploration

And the end of all our exploring

Will be to arrive where we started

And know the place for the first time.

—*T. S. Eliot*

1

"The city is falling out of the sky," Professor Leander said. They were his last words. The medicine of the ground was not enough to cure an old man of the sun disease. He refused most of the efforts anyway. He told me that he'd already accomplished what no one else had been able to do. He'd gotten us to the ground. He was quite curious, he said, to know if his spirit would be taken to the tributary, or if he'd go to whatever afterlife the ground believed in, or if there was nothing at all.

Amy was with him when he died, and she called it a peaceful death. A fitting death.

Down a labyrinthine set of hallways in the same hospital, Gertrude Piper opened her eyes after a month of sleep. It was as though the two gods had made an even trade—the life of a man from the sky in exchange for the life of a girl on the ground.

Before that, we all thought that Birdie Piper would die. After I landed in Havalais at the dawn of winter, she was the most vibrant thing in her strange world. She offered her friendship to Pen and me without question; she snuck us through our bedroom window and showed us the wonders of Havalais. The mermaids in the sea. The glittering lights cast upon the water at night. The spinning metal rides in her family's amusement park.

And then the cold war between Havalais and its neighboring kingdom of Dastor advanced on us all at once, in the middle of the spring festival. I watched as an explosion swallowed Birdie. I saw her body, broken and bleeding and burnt, being kept alive by some coppery machine. Even worse than my brother had been when he'd come too close to the edge.

But nothing is certain, not even death when it's hovering over a girl. Not in my world, and not in this one. Birdie came back slowly. It took a month for her to open her eyes, and even longer for her to speak, serene in her delirium.

She told us about a spirit that would come into her room late at night to sing to her and to tend to the flowers on the table by the window.

When she had faded back to sleep, Nim slouched forward in his chair and rubbed his temples, anguished. "It wasn't a spirit," he told us. "Our mother's been here."

Mrs. Piper disappeared some years earlier to see the world. The same madness that brings so many to the edge of Internment haunts the people on the ground as well. One place is not ever enough for anyone, it seems.

It's August now, and Birdie no longer talks about her spirit. Instead she has returned to solid ground along with the rest of us. She asks her brother about the war. She wants to visit the grave of her other brother, Riles. She is getting well and she is ready to face the grimness that often comes with being awake. She doesn't wallow in her despair, and does not mind that her soft face has been forever scarred.

Pen is different. She doesn't seem ready to face anything these days. It has been months since King Ingram left for Internment, taking Princess Celeste with him, and in that time, Pen has been prone to more and more moments of distance. Jack Piper's guards surround the premises, and we are scarcely permitted to leave unescorted. Not until King Ingram returns with his instructions for us. But every week, Pen gives Nimble a new list of books she'd like from the library. Physics. Calculus. Philosophy. She is drowning in pages and pages of things she never shares with any of us. And that's when she isn't off someplace where none of us can find her, even within the confines.

The sun is starting to set, and after nearly an hour of searching, I find her at the amusement park. It would normally be thriving in August, the Pipers have told us, if not for the king's absence and the war. Now it's locked. But Pen and I sneak in sometimes.

"Pen?" I step onto one of the metal bars, preparing to climb over the locked fence.

She's standing high up on the platform with the telescopes that face Internment, and she turns to me.

"What are you doing?" I say.

She shrugs. She presses a piece of paper against the telescope and writes something down, then tucks the paper into her dress. "Nothing. Don't climb up. I was just leaving."

She descends the staircase, the steps reverberating under her stacked leather heels that make her taller than me. A girl our age would never be permitted to wear such things back home.

She comes to the fence and grips the bars and leans close, so that her forehead is almost touching mine.

"What are you doing all the way out here?" she says.

"Looking for you. You didn't come in for dinner."

"Who can eat?" she says, and hands me her shoes and hoists herself up over the fence. "The food in this place is nauseating. A different animal a night. I'd rather chew on grass." She lands on her feet with a thud, and goes about straightening her skirt. She takes the shoes but doesn't bother putting them back on.

I hate myself for trying to smell the tonic on her breath, but it must be done. She finds ways to steal gulps of it. We've fallen into an unspoken understanding that I will dispose of anything she tries to hide, and it will never be mentioned.

But if she's had anything to drink, I can't tell. Her eyes seem bright and alert when she looks at me. "Has Thomas been trying to find me?"

"Isn't he always?" I say.

She tugs my hand. "I don't want to go back inside just yet. Let's go to the water. Maybe there are mermaids."

Birdie told us that the mermaids never come close to the

4

shore. They prefer to stay where the water is deep, where they cannot easily be captured or get their hair ensnared on a fishing line. But I don't mind pretending we'll spot one. I try to keep pace with her as she runs.

With my other hand I hold my hat to my head. But eventually I let it go, and it escapes. When I'm with Pen, it seems I must always leave some small thing behind.

We are in a valley of green, with shy bright flowers poking their way through. In the wind I see dotted lines. I see red lines and blue lines. I see the maps that my best friend is always drawing as she moves, as she thinks.

"Maybe if we hold our arms out, the wind will carry us up," she says, and I think she believes it to be true.

Eventually we stop to catch our breaths somewhere along the ocean's shore. Pen rests her elbow on my shoulder and laughs at my wheezing. I have never been a match for her.

The wind is so loud that I can scarcely hear her laughter.

She drops onto the grass and pulls me down after her. Once I've caught my breath, she leans back on her elbows and looks at me. "What is it?" she says. "What's that worried look for?"

"I don't like all this wind," I say, over a roar of it. "It doesn't feel right." This time of year is so mellow on Internment. It is surely beautiful back home, the pathways all traced with bright flowers.

"A lot of the breeze comes from the sea," Pen says. "That's all."

"I know."

"Morgan, we aren't on Internment. Things are bound to be different. We've been here for months. We survived all that snow; this is just a little wind."

"I know." What I don't say is that I'm afraid she'll be swallowed whole by this whirling sky. This world already tried to kill her once, and Pen is fearless and foolish enough to let it try again.

A flock of birds flies high above us, in a uniform formation. Pen stretches her arms straight up over her head, her fingers arranged like a frame. I rest my head next to hers and try to see through that frame from her perspective.

After the birds have gone, she says, "Suppose Internment were to fall out of the sky."

"What?" I say.

"Suppose it couldn't stay afloat any longer and it came down all at once, hard and fast. I think it would coast at an angle, rather than straight down. I've been looking at the way the birds come down from the sky, and it's sort of a sixty degree angle most times."

"I don't give it any thought," I say.

She turns her head in the grass to look at me. "You've never thought about Internment falling from the sky before?"

"I have, I suppose." I stare up at the graying sky, where shades of pink and gold still cling to the sparse clouds. "But more as a nightmare, not something that will happen. I don't weigh the probability or try to picture what it would look like."

Pen stares up at the sky again.

"I think it would fall on King Ingram's castle," she says. "I think it would kill him and all his men. But the impact would destroy Internment, too. The foundations for all the buildings would shift. They'd likely collapse."

"Internment won't fall out of the sky," I say. I am gentle with her, but firm. I have heard Amy wonder about Internment coming down. I wondered myself, as a child. But Pen is different. She gets ideas like these in her head and they become real to her. She forgets what's in front of her and sees only what's in her mind, and just like that she's lost.

A mechanical growling from somewhere high above us disturbs the tranquil gray sky, and I flinch. Not even the largest beast on Internment could make a sound like that. The sound comes from the king's jet, descending from Internment for its monthly fuel delivery.

At the start of each month, the king's jet returns to Havalais to deliver more phosane that it has mined from Internment's soil. A refinery was built in Havalais to process that soil into fuel. In the mornings when I step outside, I can see the plumes of black smoke billowing out into the air, and sometimes I can smell it, too—like compost and metal.

But in six months, King Ingram has yet to return with his men, and after the delivery is made, the jet flies back to Internment for more. It's a wonder there is any city left up there at all.

The warring kingdom of Dastor has seen the jet's comings and goings. Nimble tells us that the war has moved to the home front. Boys even younger than he is are being recruited to fight. If Dastor means to have Internment and its fuel source, it will have to take ownership of Havalais itself.

"It won't happen," he's told us. "Havalais is bigger, more advanced."

I'm not so certain. I see nothing of the war from the confines of this sheltered world where Jack Piper raised his children, but sometimes when the air is still, I think I hear gunfire.

Pen puts her hand over mine, and I realize that I've been holding my breath. I know she's trying to keep me calm. She has heard me tossing and turning in my bed at night as I worry what news this king will bring when he returns from Internment. Only, I don't feel worry now. I don't feel anything, not even the dread that King Ingram usually ignites in me.

"We should go back and tell the others," I say.

Pen gnaws her lip, and even as she sits up, her face is still angled skyward. "It's probably just another delivery," she says, and she is likely right. Five times before this, the jet has returned, and five times we have all waited in silence for word of the king's arrival, and it never comes.

I pull Pen to her feet, and we make our way back to the hotel, both of us looking over our shoulders as the jet moves at an angle. Like a bird. Like a city falling from the sky.

Basil and Thomas arrive at the front steps moments before Pen and I do. Back on Internment, Pen's and my friendship was the only bond between them, but since coming here they've forged something like an independent friendship of their own, perhaps because if nothing else they have home in common.

They wouldn't have been able to go very far. Jack Piper has forbidden us to leave the grounds, for our own protection, all on the king's orders that we are to be kept away from anyone who may have sinister intentions for us now that it's revealed that we come from the magical floating island above this world. Though, the people of Havalais have more cause to distrust their king than to harm us.

Truth be told, I don't mind the restriction half the time. It makes me feel safe. Reminds me of the train tracks that surrounded me back home.

Other times, my wanderer's spirit comes out for a visit and I wonder at when this will all be over.

"We were walking back from the theme park when we saw the jet," Thomas says. "Did you see it?"

"Yes," I say.

Princess Celeste became a pawn when King Ingram needed access to Internment. King Furlow up in his sky has only two weaknesses, and those weaknesses are his children. He would allow King Ingram to have anything he asked for in exchange for Celeste's safe return.

I have worried for her in silence. Pen would be angry if I so much as brought her name up. But I do hope that she's well, and that her decision making abilities have improved.

Basil's standing close. His eyes are on me, and whether or not he knows it, he still sets my stomach fluttering.

Another gust of wind comes, and even the fearless Pen hugs her arms across her stomach and shivers.

Thomas frowns at her. "I've been looking all over for you."

"Not all over, clearly, or you'd have found me," she says.

He stands at a pace's distance from her, and I can see the worry in his eyes. I can see that he is trying to get a whiff of tonic on her breath. When he can't find one, he looks to me, and while Pen isn't watching I give a slight shake of my head. She's sober.

The jet has quit rumbling in the sky; presumably it has landed.

"Come on," I say to Pen, and hold the door open. "Let's see if we can find something in the kitchen you're willing to eat."

She follows me into the house, past the smallest Piper children, who are playing a war game in the living room. Annie is a soldier whose legs were blown off in an explosion, and Marjorie is a nurse applying a tourniquet. I have seen them play this game a dozen times, and it is anyone's guess whether Annie will survive her wounds. Last time, an explosion hit their pretend medical tent and all the nurses and soldiers were killed.

I hate this game, but I think it makes them feel closer to Riles.

Up at the top of the stairs, Amy watches them from between the bars of the railing, not quite ready for human interaction. She has been quiet since her grandfather's death, and she's added another cloth around her wrist beside the one meant to symbolize her sister.

"Let's say I lost my arm too," Annie says.

"Which one?" Marjorie asks.

"The left."

"Would you girls like to help me in the garden?" Alice calls down from the top of the stairs. She cannot bear this game of theirs.

Annie sits up from her deathbed on the hearth. "Why do you tend to the garden? We have a gardener."

"It just makes me happy, I suppose," Alice says. She reaches the bottom step and holds her hands out to them, and they forget their game and happily follow her outside.

In the kitchen, Pen and I sit at the small table reserved for the maids, and Pen bites into a raw carrot from the cold box.

"I wish you'd stop looking so worried," she says.

"I can't play it as cool as you, I suppose."

She stares at me for a long moment, and then she says, "You're not the only one who has nightmares about what's happening back home. Just because I don't talk about it doesn't mean I don't care."

"I know that you care. That's what's so frustrating," I say. "We've hardly spoken in months."

"What are you going on about 'we've hardly spoken'? We share a room. We speak every day. We're speaking right now."

"You know what I mean."

She takes another bite of the carrot, with a crunch I swear is meant to be pointed. "You'll forgive me if I don't entirely trust you with my secrets these days."

I know just what she means. It has been a source of

contention that's never fully gone away these past several months. She discovered that Internment's soil contains the very fuel source King Ingram wants for his kingdom, and she confided this secret to me. But after she nearly drowned, I told the princess everything, hoping an alliance could be forged between Internment and Havalais, giving us all a chance to return home.

Instead, King Ingram used the princess as a hostage and has been depleting Internment of its soil as he pleases.

I don't know the enormity of what's already happened and what's to come, but even so I wouldn't take back what I did. I'm still holding out hope that I'll be able to return Pen home to her family, to the city that she loves so much that she's been going to pieces without it.

So I say nothing, and Pen can see that she's wounded me. "Nim says Birdie has had her last surgery, and can come home soon," she says to change the subject. "She'll still be confined to her wheelchair, but I doubt that will last for long."

I push my chair away from the table. "I'm going to make some tea for Lex."

"Oh, Morgan, don't be cross. I didn't mean it. I'm just on edge because of that bloody jet."

"I know," I say softly.

I hope that this time the king has returned, and the princess as well, alive and safe. Whatever news they bring will surely be better than all this wondering and fear.

I don't know what sort of mood Lex will be in when I reach the top of the stairs, but he's been especially sour lately. He's running low on paper for his transcriber, and soon he will no longer be able to spend his days hiding in his fictional worlds.

I knock when I reach his door.

"Alice?" he says.

"No, it's me." Back home he always knew when I was the one approaching him, but something about this house and its noises disorients him. "I've brought some tea."

"Oh," he says, rather unenthusiastically. "Come in."

He's sitting in a wing chair near the open window, and the worry on his face mirrors my own from earlier. He doesn't care for the wind; perhaps it reminds him too much of the edge. "The weather down here takes some getting used to," I say. I press the teacup into his hand, not letting go until I'm sure he's got a grip on it.

"I have a bad feeling," he says.

"Me too."

I hesitate, standing before him, debating with myself whether to tell him what I saw in the sky.

But in the end I'm not given a choice. Even without his sight, Lex is clever at sensing when anything is wrong. "What is it, Little Sister? What's happened?"

I wring my skirt in my hands. "We saw the jet about an hour ago. Pen, Basil, Thomas, and I. We've been waiting for someone to come home and tell us what it means."

Lex is silent for a long moment. "I heard." He takes a sip of his tea and then with minimal fumbling he sets it on the window ledge. "So it begins," he says.

"There's no need to be so theatrical," I say. "It may be good news."

"A greedy king in a wasteland of wealth holds a princess hostage so that he may invade a tiny floating city, and you still think he may return with good news. My sister the optimist."

I am tired of being called an optimist as though it were a bad thing. Pen has used this word against me as well. "I'm merely trying not to panic, Lex." I hold myself back from saying anything too combative. I don't want to fight, and it has taken me so long to stop hating my brother for lying to me about our father being dead. I would like for us to be reasonable with each other.

"Where is Alice?" he asks. Maybe he wants to avoid an argument too.

"She's in the garden."

"And she knows about the jet?"

"I told her when we came back inside. We're all waiting now. Drink your tea, all right? Alice will be up to check on you in a bit."

As I cross the threshold, he says, "Morgan?"

I turn.

"Be careful."

"I'm only going downstairs."

"I never know what mad and wild adventures you'll get off to on a whim."

I can't help but smile at the thought. Mad and wild adventures. It's not something he ever would have accused me of back home, when I was tucked safely in our little floating world.

They never exhale, the trees. It was the same on Internment; on a very windy day, the trees rustle and inhale, and then the leaves and the branches all tremble as though something were trying to strangle the life from them. The dark sky watches on, filled with anticipation, wondering if this will be a great night, or a horrible night, or the last night of the world.

"Morgan." Basil's voice pulls me out of my trance. He joins me at the window, and when his arm brushes mine, my skin swells with tiny bumps. "You've been standing here for an hour."

My body releases some of its tension and I lean my head toward his. "I have a bad feeling. Lex does too. Like something big is about to happen."

"Suppose something is about to happen," he says. "Then what?"

I shake my head. "I'm tired of being driven mad by the 'what if' game. I just want to know. I want King Ingram to come back and tell us what's happening. Good or bad. So all the wondering can stop."

Basil is quiet for a few seconds, and then with some difficulty he says, "I've been playing that same game, wondering about my parents and Leland."

I look at him.

"I think they must be okay," he says, and nods straight ahead at the sky, where our floating city is hiding somewhere in that darkness beyond our sullen reflections. "They would follow the king's orders. They've always been smart about that."

"Which king's orders?" I say.

"Whichever king is in charge these days," he says.

"Maybe King Ingram and King Furlow really are forming some sort of alliance," I say. "Maybe there will be good news."

He glances sidelong at me, and a smile comes to his lips. "I've always loved your optimistic side."

"You're the only one. Everyone else seems to think I'm foolish for harboring it."

He puts his arm around my back, and the last of the tension in me dies. I rest my temple against his shoulder. "I'm tired, Basil. And so worried that the decisions I've made were the wrong ones."

"The wrong decisions have been made by these kings," he says. "And for what it's worth, I would have done the same thing you did. If I'd known about the phosane, I would have told."

"Really?"

"If what's happening to Pen had been happening to you, if I'd thought this world were killing you, yes. I'd do anything it took to bring you back home."

"You've always understood me, Basil."

His arm tightens around me and I close my eyes. The anxiety feels so distant when he's around. Farther away and smaller in the sky than our long-lost floating city.

Then I hear the front door open, and my stomach drops.

The younger Pipers have long since gone to bed, and everyone else has been in the lobby for hours, waiting for word. All eyes are at the front door when Nimble steps inside, his shoulders dropped, his eyes weary. He is always the first to run to the tarmac when the jet returns, hoping for word about Celeste. And he is always heartsick when no word comes.

We all wait in silence. Nim raises his head and looks at each of us, settling on me. "King Ingram has returned. My father is with him now. I don't know what any of this means yet. I'm sorry."

He moves toward his bedroom, and by the heaviness of his steps I can suspect what the answer will be. But still I have to ask, "Was Celeste with him?"

He pauses, his back to me. "No," he says. "My father told me only that the king has brought a special visitor, but it isn't her." He takes a deep breath, and his voice is so tight, I think he may be fighting tears. "I doubt my father will be back tonight. You might as well all go to bed."

He can't get away from us fast enough.

Pen is standing by the couch, Thomas at her side. She's staring worriedly after Nimble, though, and she doesn't hear Thomas until the third or fourth time he's said her name. "Pen." She flinches, startled.

"We'll know more tomorrow, surely," Basil says.

The hotel falls into its nightly silence. I soak in the tub long after everyone else has gone to bed. The mornings in this place can be so noisy, with the Piper children running about, shrieking with laughter as they play their games, most of which involve explosions. And footsteps going this way and that, and voices, and silverware on plates.

But the nights are still. I can feel everyone's silence just as surely as I can hear their voices during the day.

Someone knocks at the door. "Morgan?" Pen's voice. "Are you all right? You've been in there forever."

"I thought you were in bed," I say.

"I couldn't sleep, and I wanted to make sure you hadn't drowned."

"I'll be out in a minute." The water's gone cold anyway. I wring out my wet hair, dry off, and slip into my nightgown.

When I open the door, Pen is waiting in the hallway, holding a lantern. Its orange glow picks up the bags under her eyes, and I can see all at once how troubled she's been, despite her best efforts to conceal it.

"I'm not tired," she whispers. "Are you?"

"No," I say, although it's a lie. I will stay awake all night if there's a chance she'll finally be honest with me. She is much more likely to reveal her secrets at night, when the sleeping world will be undisturbed by her whispering voice.

She smiles. "Do you want to go for a midnight walk?"

We don't bother with our shoes. We tiptoe barefoot down the steps and through the front door.

Unlike earlier, the night's wind is mellow and warm. The moon outshines our lantern, nearly full and bright white.

As soon as we've stepped into the grass, I can feel the cool earth under my feet, astoundingly like the ground back home. Pen moves forward, and when I don't follow, she turns to face me. "Aren't you coming?"

I wriggle my bare toes in the grass and stare down at it. I have never seen the heaps of soil being flown down from Internment. I've only heard about it from Nim. I imagine Internment filled with craters so wide that you could look through them and see the ground below.

"I was just thinking about home," I say. "About what King Ingram is going to tell us, if he plans to tell us anything at all."

Pen takes my hand, leads me away from the hotel. "Come on. There's something I want to show you."

She leads me to the amusement park, and I climb the fence after her without question, happy to see whatever it is she wants to show me. Maybe it will be something other than tonic this time. Maybe it will give me some insight into this distance she's built between herself and everyone else in this world.

I expect her to lead me to the telescopes. That's where I find her sometimes. But instead she leads me to the giant teacups, sitting inanimate in the moonlight. She is still clutching the lantern when she kneels beside one of the saucers—chipped but still bright green—and reaches beneath it, somewhere in the mechanism that would cause it to spin.

Eventually she finds what she was looking for: several pieces of paper folded together. Whatever is on those pages must be important, if she would keep them all the way out here.

Is this because I discovered her request paper all those months ago? Does she think I'll go rifling through her things when she's not in our room? I haven't. I would never. But sometimes, when I hear her tossing and turning, muttering through her nightmares about the harbor, I would do anything to know what is happening in her mind.

"Here." She hands me the lantern, and then she swings one leg over the teacup's rim, then the other. She takes the lantern back so I can climb in after her.

Inside the teacup is a metal wraparound bench, and she sits so close to me that my wet hair dampens her shoulder.

She spreads the papers open on the small table before us—the one that we would twist if we wanted the teacup to spin. "Now that the king is back, we have to find a way to stop him," she says. Her eyes are on the pages. "If we don't, I think we're in real trouble."

I stare at the pages, lit up by the moon and the lantern, and as always, I don't understand. I see Pen's steadily drawn lines. I see a circle and a small floating silhouette that could be Internment. I see numbers drifting around it like birds.

Pen shuffles through the pages like a madman. "I've been reading up on the sunsets. The sun goes down about a minute earlier every day, except about once a week or so when it goes down two minutes earlier."

She looks at me to be sure I'm following along. "Okay," I say. I've never paid too much attention to the sunset, but I know that we're at the time of year when we lose a bit of light each day. "So?"

"So," she says. "For the past few months, I've been keeping a grid of where Internment sits in the sky, and where the sun should be. Every day I look through the same telescope at the same angle."

She points to Internment's shape on each of the pages before us, as though I should know what we're looking at.

"I don't understand."

She looks at me, and I can see how tired her face is, how worried. But her eyes are bright, the way they always are when she's onto something important. "Internment is sinking. Not very much, but a bit each month. Enough that it's bound to be a problem if this keeps up."

I can only stare at the pages as these words sink in. In her ever steady hand Pen has drawn the outline of the clock tower, protruding above the mass of apartment buildings. Scraggly roots jut from the torn underbelly of the floating city. The sun, a perfect circle, is at a distance, held in the pure white sky by tiny equations I can't decipher.

There are two versions of Pen. There is the silly,

spontaneous, and brutally blunt girl I know, and then there is the side of her that can ingeniously solve these mysteries. It is frightening what she is capable of.

"Can you be sure?" I say.

"The professor helped me with the algorithm." She gnaws on her lower lip guiltily. "I'd been visiting him before he died."

I suppose she expects me to feel betrayed. And I do, in a way, but I am also relieved. I knew she was off somewhere; I'm only grateful it wasn't with a bottle.

"It must be all the mining," I say. "We don't know how much soil King Ingram's men bring back on each shipment."

"It would have to be a lot of soil to affect Internment's weight," Pen says. "More soil than could possibly be fitting into those jets. Internment is thousands of times their size. I don't think it's that."

"What, then?"

Pen shuffles through the papers until she finds a full-page drawing of Internment. The accuracy and scale is stunning, as though she'd sat in the sky and sketched its likeness. She has drawn a bubble around the city in rough overlapping lines.

"When your brother went to the edge, it was the wind that threw him back. The wind was moving sideways, like a current around the city. Have you ever noticed the way clouds that get too close to Internment seem to zip past us?"

"Those clouds get caught up in the wind that surrounds

the city," I say. "And you think that wind is part of what's keeping Internment afloat?"

"I have several theories about what keeps Internment afloat, but I do think the wind is a big factor," Pen says. "When we left the city in the metal bird, we went under the city, through the dirt. But King Ingram's jet lands and departs from the surface."

"It flies through the wind," I say, understanding.

She nods eagerly. "And disrupts it. Maybe even weakens it. It's a slight change for now, but over the course of years, it could knock Internment from the sky completely."

Her voice is excited, the way it always is when she is explaining things. But in the silence that follows, she remembers the magnitude of what she's said, and I feel it too. Internment is not only being ravaged by this world's greedy king; it could be knocked right out of the sky.

"King Ingram wouldn't care if he knew," I say.

"No. Why should he? He'll have what he wants. Even if Internment crashed right into Havalais, he'd stand clear and let people die like he did at the harbor."

I look at Pen. "How do we stop it?"

She shrugs. "I say we kill King Ingram."

"Be serious."

"I am, rather."

"Yes, okay," I say. "We'll just walk right up to his castle, and we'll knock on the door, and then we'll stab him with the knife you keep under your pillow. I can't find any fault in that. But suppose we come up with a backup plan."

"There's only one person I trust who has access to the

king," Pen says. "And I'd trust him with a secret, too. After all, he's lived his entire life never letting anyone know he's third in line to the throne."

"Nimble?" I say. One night after too much drinking, Birdie confided in us that her father was the king's secret bastard, and that she and her siblings were princes and princesses. Later when she was comatose after the bombings, Nim confirmed it.

"He hates King Ingram as much as I do," Pen says. "The king is the reason his brother is dead. The king is the reason the princess was taken away from him. He has no reason to care about Internment, but he cares about her, and she's up there. He'll want to help us."

A light breeze coasts along the ground, bringing the salt of the endless ocean, rustling the grass and causing some rusted metal thing within the park to squeak.

The papers rattle, and Pen organizes them with affection and folds them along their crease.

"Should we talk to him tomorrow?" I say.

"We won't have to wait until then." Pen nods up at the telescope at a distance. In the moonlight I can just see a dark outline clutching one of the telescopes aimed at Internment. "He comes here every night and drops coin after coin into that thing so he can stare up at the city. He would never be able to see her, though. At best those lenses make a blurry faraway view bigger and blurrier."

I feel a pain in my chest, watching him. He lives in this vast world that goes on forever until it wraps around to where it started again. There are trains and biplanes and ferries and elegors that can take him anywhere. But he cannot reach the girl he loves up in her kingdom in the sky.

"I hear him sneaking out sometimes at night," Pen says. "The poor fool." She heaves a deep breath then blows out the lantern.

We climb one after the other from the teacup, through the man-made labyrinth of gears and metal pieces until we reach the stairway to the telescopes.

It is here that we hesitate. As pressing as the matter is, neither of us wants to interrupt this intimate sadness.

But we don't have to. He heard us approach, and after a few seconds, when the telescope must have expired, he comes to the top of the staircase and looks down at us.

"Bit late for a stroll, isn't it, girls?" he says in his breezy Havalais accent.

Pen is clutching the papers to her chest. "We have something to tell you," she says.

We sit on the wooden planks beside the telescopes, Pen's drawings spread out between the three of us like a deck of morbid cards.

Throughout Pen's explanation, Nimble said nothing and asked no questions. He only stared with that pensive expression he gives when his father is discussing politics. Now he reaches forward to touch Internment's outline on one of the sketches. "So much detail," he says. "There must be an atlas in your head. It must be so exhausting."

He looks up at us, smiling grimly. "Celeste and I predicted something like this happening. Not exactly this, per se, but that King Ingram's greed about the phosane would make him reckless. We knew Internment was in jeopardy."

"We already have the riddle, then," I say. "What's the answer?"

"You girls aren't the only ones unhappy with King Ingram," Nim says. "It isn't just the people of Internment who have cause to hate him. There's been a lot of unrest down here since the bombing at the harbor. I have a boy who works as one of the king's guards who has been feeding me intelligence. His niece was killed in the bombing."

"That's awful," I say.

"What kind of intelligence?" Pen says.

"So far it's all just been a lot of angry chatter," Nim says. "The refinery has caused some people in the heart of the city to become sick. Water comes out of the pipes smelling like sulfur. After the bombings, this phosane was supposed to make everything better, and it has only caused more problems. King Ingram has the phosane, but he doesn't know what to do with it. He's a politician, not a scientist. The scientist who initially discovered its usefulness is dead now, and there's speculation that Dastor would know a thing or two about refining it, but as for our kingdom, Havalais has yet to see this miracle fuel in action and they're beginning to doubt it exists."

"It exists," Pen says. "Down here you call it phosane, but up on Internment we call it sunstone, and it's a powerful fuel source if it's refined properly." She sits up straight, stricken with a new thought. "What if the engineers on Internment are refusing to help them refine it? Or what if they're giving faulty instructions?" She looks between Nim and me, giddy and proud. "What if they're up there fighting?"

I struggle to suppress my smile. It's bad luck to hope for such a thing, but I could believe it. I do believe it. "If that's true," I say, "King Ingram needs Internment. He can't just take all he pleases and then dispose of its people. It took decades for our engineers to perfect the glasslands and harness our fuel. Your king may have all the riches to build and employ a refinery, and all the raw materials, but if he doesn't know how to use them, it's all for nothing."

"Clever little city," Nim says, looking up. He does not share in our joy, though. "If that's true, it's surely an ugly scene up there right now. Think torture. Think homes being burnt down. Your people can be as stubborn as you please, but no one down here can hear them scream from up there."

Pen shakes her head wildly. "It doesn't matter. Don't you see? Being tortured, deprived—it's the lesser evil. Our people would withstand anything to keep the city afloat."

"She's right," I say. "Down here, if you don't like where you live, you can pick up and leave. If you don't like the weather, or your children—you can just go. But on Internment, our home is all we have."

The people of Internment are resilient if we have to be. We don't value property or money the way they do down here; often our secrets are the only things of worth to us. I think of, but don't say aloud, the time the prince and princess held us hostage in their clock tower's dungeon. All they wanted was a way to the metal bird, and proof that it existed, but I would have died before I'd have let them have it.

"Your king underestimated Internment," I say. "But that's good. Isn't it? We can work with that. We can—I don't know."

I look at Pen, hoping she'll blurt out a solution. But she foolishly expects the solution to come from me. "Go on," she says.

"We can try to get sent to Internment, and then we'll know for sure what's happening up there. If they're not telling King Ingram how to refine the phosane, maybe there's a rebellion being organized."

"If that's true, there's plenty of intelligence here on the ground that would be of use to them," Nimble says. "There are men in King Ingram's court who are disgruntled enough to help. It's just a matter of finding who to trust, and I know those boys. You could leave that to me."

"How would we get ourselves sent back to Internment, though?" Pen says.

"We could go to King Ingram and pretend we'd like to help him," I say. "We can make him think that he can use us the way he used Celeste. As leverage or a sort of hostage. And he'll send us back home." I look at Nim. "Do you think he would do that?"

Pen laughs and grabs my face in her hands and kisses my temple. "Brilliant," she says.

"Really?"

"Really," Nim says. "That might work." The hope in

his eyes is too much to take. I don't tell him that if the people of Internment are as stubborn as we're hoping, King Ingram may have gotten desperate and gone for the jugular. And there are only two things on Internment that could be taken from King Furlow that are of any value: his children. Prince Azure, and Princess Celeste. They may already be dead.

Pen is not ready to divulge her findings to Thomas or the others, but she understands when I insist on telling Basil. If I'm going to attempt to return to Internment, he deserves to know.

In the morning I meet him in his room as everyone else is going to breakfast. I close the door behind me. We sit on his bed and I tell him everything in a hushed tone. Through it all, he doesn't say a word, listening patiently to my eager, harried rambling.

When I get to the end, it takes all my willpower not to look away from him when I say, "And Pen and I want to convince King Ingram to send us back. If we make him think we're on his side, and that we want to try to talk the engineers back home into helping him, we're hoping he'll go along with it."

He is the first to break our gaze. He looks down at my

hand as he covers it with his own and then he looks back at me. "When we were back home, your mind wandered toward the ground. But now that we're on the ground, your mind wanders back home. Sometimes I think what you want is to be away from wherever it is you're standing."

"Maybe there's some truth to that," I admit.

"I think about home, too." He speaks with great caution. "Not just my parents and Leland, but the life I had there. The sounds. The future I might have had." He shakes his head. "It was enough for me, staying there. I didn't mind it. But for as long as I can remember, there has been this current leading me away. You," he says.

"I tried, Basil. I tried to stay within the train tracks, to do what was expected of me."

"I know you did. I was there with you."

I stare down at our hands. "I didn't want to be the current pulling you away from all the things that you loved."

"Morgan," he says, in that practical way of his. "You were the thing I loved."

The words feel both wonderful and painful at the same time. "The truth is that I had to pull you along with me," I say. "I couldn't untangle myself from you if I tried. We've always just sort've gone together. It's as though someone mixed us up until we were a secondary color, and there's no way to tell which one of us started out which color."

I am terrible with words. My brother's the writer. I'm only clumsily trying to come up with words for things I'll never have the skill to say.

Basil laughs, but he isn't making fun of me. I know he understands.

"I am going to live my life worrying about you," he says. "But I do think you're right that there is unrest on Internment. It's a peaceful city. It has nothing to protect itself against a kingdom like Havalais, much less the ground itself. If nothing is done, and Pen's calculations are correct, Internment will crash-land on the ground before King Ingram ever has a way to refine his phosane."

"A lose-lose," I say.

"If you were to go back home, you would need something that would give Internment a fighting chance against King Ingram. Do you have anything like that?"

"Nim thinks he can get us some allies on the ground. A lot of King Ingram's men are disgruntled after the bombing. And on Internment we'll have an ally in Princess Celeste. If she's still alive."

"She'll be alive," Basil assures me. "If King Ingram wants something from Internment, he won't go killing King Furlow's children before he has it."

"I hope you're right."

"What if I go with you?" Basil says. "No matter what information or power you may be able to gather, the fact remains that both Havalais and Internment are patriarchies."

Pen would hate him for saying it, but I know that he's right. Kings are more reasonable with men than they are with girls. King Ingram is more likely to believe that Basil could influence the engineers.

"But is that what you want?" I say.

"I could never sit idly by while you disappear into the clouds, leaving me to wonder if you're alive each day," he says, and despite everything, I can't help but indulge in that beautiful thing he's just said to me. He goes on, "I also don't want Internment to come crashing down on our heads, killing us all and my family too."

"Nim is hoping to get an audience with the king this afternoon," I say. "Let's hope he can come through. Oh, and, Basil, about all this. Pen doesn't want Thomas to know about it."

He frowns. "It isn't our business to get involved, then. But I do wish she'd be more forthright about things. It would be healthier for her."

"You and me both," I say. "But for now I think it's best we keep this to ourselves until we know more."

"Agreed," he says.

Nim is gone after lunchtime, off to King Ingram's castle to play the good son to Jack Piper for once, in an attempt to stay in his graces.

Pen and Thomas are playing a board game. They're leaning toward each other on opposing sides of the coffee table, the crowns of their blond heads almost touching.

It's a beautiful day, and Alice has taken Amy and the youngest Pipers outside. Through an open window I can hear them laughing in the garden. This Havalais air has had a positive effect on Amy; she hasn't had one of her fits in months.

Basil is trying to engage me in a game of cards. The decks

they use on the ground are similar to our own, and with a bit of compromise we can duplicate most of the games we played back home. But I am having the hardest time sitting still. My leg shakes anxiously. My mind is spinning out dozens of scenarios about Nim's efforts at the castle.

Should I tell Judas and Amy any of this?

The thought of Judas brings a rush of heat to my cheeks. We've barely spoken in weeks, and I don't see him anywhere now, but somehow I feel his presence hiding nearby, as always, just out of frame. We have scarcely spoken since our kiss, save for a few benign polite exchanges—*good morning; yes, please; thank you*—but time has done nothing to extinguish my curiosity about him. Time has not assuaged my guilt, and the sight of him still confuses me. I do not know what it will take to rid myself of that kiss, but I would pay any price to undo it. I would pay any price to stop wanting another.

Basil lays his stack of cards on the table and then gently takes the cards from my hands too. I blink dumbly at him.

"Would a walk help take your mind off it?" he says.

I shake my head. "I don't want to be gone when Nim gets back."

"We won't go far," he says. "Come on. The air will do you some good."

He's right. As soon as we've stepped outside, I feel less anxious. There's some comfort in hearing the living things in the grass and in the sky. A blue bird shoots from one tree to the next, and I wish I could capture a perfect image of him to take back home. There are no birds on Internment, only speculation as to what they must be like.

Basil and I walk a lap around the hotel, past the charred altar where Nim burnt his beloved car in offering so that his sister might live. Whether or not it was an answered prayer, Birdie did pull through. It makes me wonder if their god is real. It makes me wonder if any god is real, or if it's only easier to believe in that than in the arbitrary series of events that make up all our lives.

"What do you think it's like back home?" I say, to break the silence.

Basil is not one to lie about the way of things. "Ugly. I wonder what King Furlow is doing to reassure everyone. If he's able to do anything at all."

"I never realized how small Internment was until we came here," I say. "From down here it just looks like a big clot of dirt in the sky. If I had lived down here all my life, I would never have suspected there was any life up there. I would think it a mistake of nature, something small enough to fit into my palm if only I could reach out and take it."

How strange that I've lived so much of my life on a clump of dirt in an infinite sky. After all these months, I can feel myself starting to forget how alive it was up there, how bright and cheerful.

We've stopped walking, and as I shield my eyes and stare up at Internment, I can feel Basil watching me. My heart is fluttering in my chest, anxious and frightened and strangely thrilled. It is an act of bravery for me to look at him when he makes me feel this way.

"I was wrong, all those times I said your eyes might be

the same color as the sea down here," he says.

"No?"

"No," he says. "They're still the brightest blue I've ever seen."

I look at the ground, flustered, smiling. Without looking at him, I can feel his victorious smirk.

"You're being too kind," I say.

"Ridiculous accusation. When have you ever known me to be kind?"

"It's true; you're a real beast most days. Flat-out tyrannical."

He laughs. Somehow my arm ends up around his back, and his around my shoulders, squeezing me close. The sun burns the crown of my hair, and despite the warmth, my blood is running chills up and down my spine.

I want to tell him everything. About Judas kissing me in the grass, and the way he still haunts my thoughts even though he is surely using me to quell his loneliness. I want to tell Basil that I'm sorry, that I've made a mess of everything, that I'm scared.

But here beside him, insects hopping around our feet, all the worlds have gone still. This planet has stopped rotating around its sun. Everything is calm. We're safe here. We'll be okay.

After dinner, I help Alice with the dishes. For security purposes, Jack Piper has dismissed most of the hotel's staff, and chores like these are supposed to fall to his children, but Alice always gets to them first. Years of being married to my brother have left her restless and with an endless desire to make things clean.

She hands me a clean white plate, and I go over it with the dishrag. "Do you want to go back home?" I say.

She shakes her head. "I couldn't leave your brother, and he's told me he won't return. Not after what the king did to your parents, and especially to you."

"I didn't ask you what Lex wants. I asked what you want."

She smiles. It is a kind, wistful smile. "Should there be any difference?"

"What a thing to say. Of course there's a difference."

She hands me another dish. "After your brother jumped,

one afternoon while he was still in the hospital, I came home to tend to the plants, and there was a letter waiting for me at the door, from my parents. I was welcome to return home if I estranged myself from Lex. But if not, they felt it best for me not to associate with them anymore."

I suspected as much. Alice's parents stopped coming around, and jumpers carry a stigma. With the exception of Pen and Basil, I lost virtually all my friends. Still, to hear it said out loud disgusts me. There is no one kinder than Alice, and no one who deserves kindness more.

"That's the thing about marriage, love. You hope you won't ever have to choose, but if there's a choice to be made, it's the one whose blood is in your ring. It doesn't matter how many worlds there are; our place is with each other."

"Lex doesn't deserve you," I say. "Truly."

She smiles. "But there is nothing left for me up there," she adds. "Since you asked. Everything I need is here."

I don't know that there's much left on Internment for me either. I tell myself that my father is still alive up there, and that I'll be reunited with him. But when that happens, will he want to leave Internment behind? He risked his life trying to do just that.

After Alice and I have finished with the dishes, I slip outside unnoticed, and I walk to the ocean's edge, where the boats bob along lengths of rope. This place is asleep, like all of Havalais, lying in wait for a solution to this war. I lie in the sand for what feels like hours, fixated on that dark shadow of earth in the sky.

Long after the sun has set, Nim still hasn't returned. The smallest Pipers are asleep.

I lie in bed while Pen reads one of Birdie's catalogs by candlelight. She's got a drawing pad resting on her knee, and she keeps returning to a sketch she started earlier this evening of Ehco, a divinity that lives in the sea and contains all the world's sadness. It's Birdie's favorite story from *The Text*, and I suppose the drawing will be a gift for Birdie when she returns home.

"Pen?"

I can hear the rapid strokes of the pencil on the page. "Mm? Sorry, am I keeping you awake?"

"No." I turn onto my side so I'm facing her. "It's just that you've been so guarded with your secrets lately. Why did you tell me your theory about Internment sinking?"

She goes on sketching. "It wasn't the right time before now. No sense making you panic until King Ingram was back and we could do something about it."

"It's just . . . After I told Celeste about the phosane, and she went to the king, I thought you hadn't forgiven me. I thought I'd been locked out of your head."

The pencil stills in her hand. She stares down at the page as she speaks, with difficulty. "I thought about everything," she says in a soft voice. "I thought about what it would have done to me to pull you out of the water, with you the one not breathing. I . . ." She draws a line on the page, feebly. "I saw it all very clearly, and I understood why you did it. I can't say I'd have done something different if the tables had been turned."

She clears her throat. "And besides, you could strike a
match and set Internment on fire. You could lose your wits
and destroy it all. I'd still be here. There's nothing in the
worlds that I couldn't forgive you for."

The words are so sincere and candid that I'd like to get up
and embrace her. But I don't move for fear of breaking this
fragile moment between us. I have known Pen since before
we were old enough to speak, and perhaps that is why so
much of our friendship is built on what goes unsaid. But it
feels so good to hear her say those words.

"I could never turn my back on you, either," I tell her.

"I know what I'm like, Morgan. I know it's not easy."

"So it's not easy," I say. "What is?"

She smiles briefly, and then allows herself to be distracted
anew by her drawing.

I close my eyes, and eventually I feel myself fading into
sleep, soothed by the sound of pencil on paper and catalog
pages turning.

But it isn't a very sound sleep, because when there's a
knock on the door, I'm startled awake.

"You girls awake?" Nim whispers through the door.

Pen is still sitting up by the candle. "Come in," she says.

I comb my fingers through my hair and wipe away the
drool in the corner of my mouth, hastily trying to make
myself presentable.

Nim opens the door and peeks his head in. "I didn't see
the king. Or my father. I wasn't permitted into any of the

meetings. My father isn't exactly happy with me these days."

"But you were gone all day," Pen says. "What were you doing?"

Nim smirks. "I was speaking with a few of the king's men. You remember how I said they were unhappy with things since the harbor? One of the men is assigned to guard King Ingram's special guest, come down from Internment. My contact is escorting the guest to a meeting spot for us, but we have to go right now."

"Him?" I say, trying to keep myself from hoping that the guest from home could possibly be my father. The disappointment would be unbearable if I were wrong.

"I think you'll love this," Nim says. "Hurry on and get dressed. I'll meet you outside."

I'm on my feet as soon as he's closed the door. I'm finished changing before Pen. "I have to get Basil," I say. "He'll want to come."

Pen sighs theatrically. "Must you?"

I stare at her flatly. "He's my betrothed."

"So?"

"You said you were fine with my telling him about all this. He's coming."

"Fine. But if you wake Thomas, I'll strangle you."

"Noted."

I turn the knob to the boys' room very slowly, wincing as I push the door away from the frame. I tread lightly past Judas's and Thomas's beds.

"Basil," I whisper, as quiet as breathing.

He murmurs something, tries to embrace me when I lean

in. It's my breathy laugh that wakes him. "Morgan?"

I put my finger to his lips, nod my head at the door in gesture.

He climbs out of bed and follows me out to the hallway. In whispers I tell him that Nim is taking us to see King Ingram's guest from Internment.

"'Hostage' may be more accurate," Basil whispers.

"Perhaps, yes." There are many people on Internment who secretly dream of life beyond the edge of the city, but most would be too terrified to ever leave. Especially now that King Ingram and his men have likely taken over the city.

We meet on the front steps, and Pen shivers excitedly. She has been carrying this information about Internment sinking in her head for months, and now finally she will be able to put her knowledge to use.

"Are you going to tell us who this mystery guest is?" she asks as we start walking.

"I don't think you'd believe me if I did," Nim says. "I'm not sure I'll believe it myself until I see him."

"How trustworthy are the men at the castle you've been speaking with?" Basil asks, the most practical of us all.

"Extremely. I've grown up in and out of the castle walls. I know which men are good and which are bad news."

"How can you tell which are good and which are bad?" Basil asks.

"The bad ones are friends of my father's."

Despite the grim sentiment, Nim is the most upbeat he's been in months. After the bombings and after Celeste's departure, he became despondent. I've been worried about him, but Pen's theory and the hope it brings has put light back into his eyes.

We can't fail. I run the words in my head over and over as we walk through the darkness and into the woods. We can't fail.

We walk for miles in fields and wooded areas off the main road. We must be near the city, because I can taste the burnt metallic quality to the air and I'm sure it's from one of the fuel refineries. Whatever King Ingram is doing with that phosane, it can't be right. I have never been inside the glasslands, but I have been near them, and there was never any smoke, never any horrid fumes.

Pen's father works in the glasslands. He's one of their top engineers. But Pen has not brought him up since our fight several months ago, when I found her request paper and she reluctantly confessed that he had hurt her in some way she wouldn't share with me. I have wondered in silence since then, hoping for and dreading her confidence in the matter. But Pen cannot be pushed. She cannot even be coaxed. I know this.

I walk between her and Basil, and for the next several paces it almost feels as though we're still back home, returning late from a play at the theater. We're just ordinary schoolchildren and our world is intact.

I have yet to see the outside of Havalais. Annette and Marjorie go into Birdie's room sometimes, and one afternoon they found a shoebox under her bed filled with all the post-cards their mother had sent from the farthest reaches of this world. Watercolor paintings of sprawling cities and barren deserts and long slender boats coasting over still waters. There is still so much to see, and confined as we are by King Ingram and his rules, I wonder at whether I'll ever have the chance.

Nimble leads us into the thick of some woods. We move guided only by the moonlight through the trees, and I can't help asking, "How do you know where we are?"

"Birds and I used to play here," he says. "The castle is less than a mile away. In the summer our father would send us outside so he could convene with the king. I know all the trees and roots by heart."

"Morgan and I used to have a spot in the woods," Pen says. "There was a cavern."

"It's still there," I say.

"Maybe."

"It is," I say. It is important to me that she believes this. That she believes there is still a safe place for us in our own world, hidden from all the warfare.

A whistle pierces the air. Something rustles in the brambles ahead of us, and Basil advances protectively at my side.

Nim is unconcerned. "This way," he says, and leads us toward the sound.

The trees are very tall here, blocking out most of the moonlight. But I can make out the dark silhouettes of two men standing side by side. I know it's unlikely. Unrealistic. But I hope that one of those men is my father. In this darkness they could be anyone.

"You're on time, but we won't have long," one of the men says. "The king is an insomniac since his return. He got up several times last night to wander the halls. No telling if he'll want to check in on our guest."

This guest, whoever he may be, doesn't say a word, leaving me to agonize.

"Is this him?" Nimble says.

"I'm standing right here," the other man says. "You could just ask me yourself."

My blood goes cold. Pen is in a dead silence beside me. I think she's stopped breathing. We know that voice, and it doesn't belong to my father.

Nimble reaches into his pocket for his matchbook, and then he strikes a match and brings the flame to a lantern the first man is carrying. And I see the face of King Ingram's guest. Prince Azure.

"May I present our honored guest," the man says, rather unenthusiastically, as though he must appease some imaginary court, "Prince Azure of the magical floating city."

"Internment," Prince Azure corrects. "There's nothing magical about it. We aren't a bedtime story."

"Prince Azure of Internment, then," the man corrects.

Nimble is frozen in place for a moment. Here in the lantern light, Azure bears a striking resemblance to his sister. He has the same clear, sparkling eyes, the rounded cheeks, the gold hair.

Nim snaps out of it after a few seconds and falls into a bow. "Your Highness," he says. "I'm—"

"Yes, I know who you are," the prince says with impatience. He grabs the lantern from the man beside him and holds it to Pen, Basil, and me.

He is wearing a pin-striped suit with a ruffled lace ascot that I recognize from his appearances back home. He stands tall and regal, nothing at all like the dying boy he was when I left him.

"I hope you're not expecting us to curtsy," Pen says.

"Pen!" I whisper.

Prince Azure chuckles, but even with that cocky grin he's wearing, I can see how tired he seems, how frightened. I am sure he wasn't brought here of his own will. King Furlow would not have happily relinquished another of his children to this place.

"Don't curtsy, don't bow," he says. "I think we're well past formalities now." He turns to Nim. "Don't let these girls fool you, what with their dresses and this one's curls. They tried to kill me."

"You were holding us hostage," Pen says through gritted teeth. "Your insane sister kidnapped my betrothed, held a knife to his throat—"

The prince puts his fingers to her lips. "Shh."

Pen's face goes red with rage and I can hear the crack of her knuckles. I put my hand over her fist, a silent plea for her to be calm. She can hit him with another rock some other time. There are more pressing matters to attend to now.

I am trying not to stare at Prince Azure, but I'm so taken aback by the sight of him. When I saw him last, he was limp and lifeless, bleeding from the head and being carried up the stairs by medics. And before that he had been a maniacal, childish young prince scheming with his sister to pry out of Pen and me information about the metal bird that would bring us to the ground.

But like his sister, he has grown since then. "Your Highness," I begin cautiously. "You've surely noticed by now that Internment is in trouble, and we'd like to do what we can to help."

Prince Azure looks to Basil. "It's unfair to be male, isn't it? We're betrothed to these unreasonable things, and for what? Just for being born."

Basil swallows whatever unkind response he'd like to give to that, and instead he says, "Morgan and Pen have some information about Internment that I think you'd be interested in. Perhaps you should ask them what it is."

"They have information about Internment?" Prince Azure says, sneering. "From all the way down here? That's a laugh. I'm the one who's been made to watch as foreigners fly up onto my kingdom in a metal beast of a machine, terrorizing everyone, stealing our soil. I haven't been down here very long"—he looks up at the sky and then sharply back at us—"but the view from down here hardly seems accurate."

Pen is steeling herself beside me, and I fear what she may say next, so I speak first. "Be that as it may, Your Highness"—the honorific is sour on my tongue—"from down here we've been able to see that Internment is sinking."

At that, the prince regards me as though I may be of some use to him after all. "How?" he says. "How can you see that?"

"It was Pen who made the calculations. She was able to compare its location in the sky against the sun. It began sinking bit by bit when the jet started to make its comings and goings."

I don't think I am doing the explanation any justice. I lack Pen's finesse. But the prince seems to believe me. He advances on Pen and says, "How much has it sunk?"

"Not terribly much," she says with surprising civility. "Equal to about an arm's length, which isn't enough to disrupt things. But if the jet keeps passing through the wind surrounding the city, I believe it will weaken the current that helps hold Internment in place. It may continue to sink bit by bit over time, or it may come crashing down all at once. I don't know."

I always thought the prince to be a fool, but he's smart enough to be troubled by all this. He paces with the lantern in his hands. His shadow dances in the fragile light.

"We have to stop the jet," he says. "I already knew that. King Ingram's arrival has brought nothing but chaos to Internment, but if what you say is true, we will have to stop him soon."

Pen looks startled by this. "You believe me?" she says.

The prince stops pacing and looks at her. "By the time I woke up, after you'd hit me, you were long gone. My sister had disappeared, too, and I knew that she had found her way to that contraption of yours that was headed for the ground. I was alone, bedridden, with nothing but free time. I wanted to know everything I could about the girls who'd tried to kill me. The girls my sister had followed to the ground." He waves his hand at me. "You were boring, Stockhour. Yes, your brother was a jumper, but you were as dull as dirt. A nobody."

I know it isn't meant to be a compliment, but somehow I

am flattered that my attempts to blend in and hide my daydreams convinced someone up there.

The prince turns on Pen. "But you, Atmus. The daughter of the top engineer at the glasslands. A perfect student. You have the lights on up in your head, don't you? You're just like your father. A budding engineer."

"I'm not like him," she says feebly. "Having a brain in my head doesn't make me like him."

He narrows his eyes at her. "But you know things. You figure them out. Who else in this bloody world down here would have thought to calculate Internment's position in the sky? Nobody but you."

Pen has nothing to say to this. People who figure things out on Internment are likely to end up dead for treason. If her father knows as much as she does, he's not foolish enough to say it aloud while he's in the city.

The other man clears his throat. "Your Highness, we should be getting back before King Ingram notices that you're gone."

"We want to go back to Internment," I say. "The three of us. We want King Ingram to send us under the pretense of helping his cause, and then we want to help your father overthrow King Ingram's men however we can."

The prince gives a sad smile. "You want to help my father? Our world is being drilled apart, bled dry, and my father has been reduced to nothing. He cannot save us."

"So who can save us, then?" I say. "You?"

"No," he says softly. "Not me."

He allows the other man to lead him back toward the

castle. Down here, he is not a prince, but a prisoner.

"Wait!" Nim calls after him. "Your sister, Celeste, is she all right? Is she alive?"

The prince stops but doesn't turn to face us. "Celeste is a silly princess with silly ideas that she can think the way a king thinks. She fancies herself the political sort. But she only ever makes things worse. You would be wise to forget about her."

Nim's shoulders sag with what may be despair or relief, or both. The prince spoke of Celeste as though she were still alive and well, and that's something.

"I can't stand that little nit," Pen mutters.

"But he listened," I remind her.

Nim is staring off into the darkness. The lantern has been blown out, and the prince and his escort have disappeared from view. Even in the frail bits of moonlight, I can see the pain in Nim's eyes.

"Are they twins?" he asks. "Celeste and her brother."

"No," Pen says. "But they are equally annoying."

"Stop," I whisper to her.

She softens. "Don't let what he said get to you," Pen says to Nim. "You'll see her again. You can try to come back to Internment with us."

Nim shakes his head. "I can't leave Havalais. Someone will have to keep an eye on things here once you've gone. I don't trust my father, or the king."

Two kings who can't be trusted. What a fabulous predicament we're all in now.

We walk back to the hotel, all of us silent, knowing there are no words that could reassure any of us.

5

It's a week before Jack Piper returns home. Nimble plays a contrite role that is painful to watch, but it pays off. He convinces his father that we could be of some help to the king.

Jack Piper, whether it is arrogance or exhaustion, mistakes our scheme for gratitude for Havalais's hospitality. Over dinner he tells us that he's arranged a meeting with King Ingram in the morning.

I stare at my plate, trying to ignore Judas's and Amy's stares. True to my promise to Pen, I have not told anyone about our encounter with the prince. Not even Alice or my brother.

If things go as I hope, I'll tell Lex that I'm leaving. He may wish to stop me, but he won't be able to. He knows that he owes me that much, after letting me think our father was dead. I have to try to find my father as well.

Thomas clears his throat. "Pen?" he says. "Can I speak with you privately?" His calm tone is a mirage.

"It'd be rude to leave the table before dinner is over," Pen says, mirroring his tone.

Basil and I exchange worried glances but say nothing.

When the Pipers begin clearing the dinner plates, I have never been so relieved in my life as I leave that dinner table. Pen, poised and cool, follows Thomas outside. Basil and I go upstairs.

Once we're in my room, I close the door behind us and drop onto the edge of my bed.

Basil sits beside me. "That's going to be an ugly fight the two of them have."

"I wish she had just told him," I say. "He would have been happy. He wants her to go home. He begged me to find a way to get her back to Internment."

"Unless she means to go without him," Basil says.

"I believe that's it," I say. "She's forever evading him. It's been that way since we were children."

"They'll work it out eventually," Basil says. "They always do."

I think of Pen's drawing, the ugly word she wrote over and over on that scrap of request paper, and I wonder if I will ever fully understand her. I wonder if she would want anyone to.

And am I any better than she is? I've got secrets of my own. Even now, the words are on my tongue: Basil, I kissed Judas.

I almost say it. I let it replay in my head over and

over as this loaded silence exists between us.

But I don't. Selfishly I rest my head on his shoulder and I think about the jet breaking through Internment's atmosphere. I think about what will await us when we arrive, if we arrive, and I wonder if any of it can be undone.

Pen is gone for most of the evening, and she returns just as I'm turning down the covers. I'm only going through the motions; I know I'll be too nervous to sleep.

"Well, that was brutal," she says, and falls onto her bed.

"What happened?"

"He was upset that I didn't clue him in to what's going on. It's just that he worries about me, and I feel how much he worries about me." She squirms against the mattress. "All his doting can make me so itchy."

"Did he go along with it?" I say.

"Ultimately, yes. He hates this world. Maybe he's foolishly hoping that we can go back to Internment and it will be as we left it. I don't know." She wriggles under the blanket. "He's going to try to come with us if the king will allow a fourth. I suppose I owe him at least that much."

"Mind if I turn out the lights?"

She shakes her head, closes her eyes.

It's only after I've gotten into my bed and we've settled into the darkness that I'm brave enough to say what's on my mind.

"Do you think I'm a detestable person for kissing Judas?"

"From what I saw, he was the one who kissed you."

"Even so."

I hear the sheets rustling as she moves. "You're not a detestable person, Morgan. I mean, if you were—what does that make me? I'm sure if we kept a tally of our sins, I would be in the lead."

"It's not the quantity of sins in this instance, but the magnitude."

"I don't think it was right," she admits. "But I know you, and I know you wouldn't have done something like that at home. It's this mad world that's made us all feverish."

I think of the night I saved Judas from the patrolmen who were coming for him. I pushed him into the lake to hide him, and after that he tried to scare me off. I still remember the fresh grief in his eyes, the severe angles of his face. He was nothing at all like Basil, and yet he stood so close to me that I could feel his breath. I was terrified with intrigue.

But Pen is right. I wouldn't have kissed him, because back home I did all I could to follow the rules, to be what was expected of me.

"I spent my life thinking all those little things mattered back home. Those rules. But five minutes in this world and it all came undone."

"Stop punishing yourself," Pen says. "Everything I ever loved about you is still intact. I'm sure Basil feels the same way."

We don't speak after that, and eventually her breathing changes, and somehow she has found a way to sleep.

I'm still lying awake when the sun begins to lighten the sky. Nimble knocks on the door and says, "Ten minutes."

It's still early enough that the rest of the house is sleeping. The night's insects are still singing.

Nimble is waiting for us at the door, weaving the car keys between his fingers anxiously. He watches as Pen, Basil, Thomas, and I convene before him. His eyes are sympathetic. "Sorry, kiddos. The king sent word this morning that he'd like to speak with only you and you." He nods to Basil and me.

"What?" Pen says. "But I thought—"

"Prince Azure's request," Nim says. "We should be grateful that he convinced King Ingram to meet with you at all."

Pen looks from Thomas to me, fury in her eyes. "That royal terror is trying to ruin everything."

"He must have a plan," I say, trying to calm her. "Let Basil and me go. We'll see what it's all about, and I'll tell you everything once I return."

Her teeth are gritted, but she knows no good would come from arguing and she gives in.

Nimble is our driver, and as usual, Jack Piper is nowhere. "I visited with Birds yesterday," Nim says, trying to sound cheerful to lighten the mood. He glances at us in the rearview mirror. "Father finally got around to visiting her, and wouldn't you know, they spent the whole time arguing."

"Why?" Basil asks.

"She's got scars," Nim says. "In particular, this deep continuous gash that runs down the side of her face and her arm. Father says it ruins her. He says no man will ever marry her and that he'd like to send her overseas to this surgeon in the north who can fix it. Only, she doesn't want it fixed. She wants to keep it. She says it's a part of her now."

"She should keep it, then," I say.

"Father hates the reminder. I dare even to say that he feels guilty for what's happened to her. Maybe he has a conscience in there after all."

Like burials, this is another custom I don't understand. We wear our scars where I come from.

I meet his eyes in the mirror for an instant before he looks back to the road. "If that's what it's about, don't let him send her off to that surgeon," I say. "If her scars remind him of what he did, he should have to look at them every day. Maybe it will change his mind the next time he goes along with the king's warfare."

"It's a nice thought, but nothing can change his mind once he's made it up. Especially not when he's working for the king." He glances at me in the mirror again. "What's your king like?"

"Celeste didn't talk about him?"

"She did," Nim says. "But with a sort of hopefulness. I got the sense that she was idealizing things when she said he could be reasoned with."

The king's castle has begun to emerge from the distance, and I'm getting a queasy feeling in my stomach.

"Whatever you do," Nim says, "don't let on to the king that you know anything about the phosane. He doesn't think much of broads anyway, so all you have to do is act dense. You don't know anything. You just want to help."

That shouldn't be hard. King Ingram makes me so uneasy that it's hard to speak around him anyway. Maybe it's a good thing Pen isn't here; she isn't intimidated by anyone.

It's a perfectly sunny day, but when we reach the castle, it doesn't glimmer as much as it has in the past. A shadow seems to loom over it.

Nimble brings the car to a stop. He turns in his seat and looks between Basil and me. "Say as little as you can," he says. "Be dumb. If the king realizes you know more than he does about the city sinking, you'll never get what you want. You'll be trapped here working for him."

Two of the king's guards have been waiting for us, and they open the car doors so we can step out.

"King Ingram and his guest are expecting the three of you," a guard says. "Right this way."

I have come to hate this castle. The waste of it. How many bricks were laid, and how much money went into this sprawling palace filled with empty rooms? On Internment, children dream about whether castles exist. I used to dream as well. But in my grandest dreams, the castle was not half the size of this one, and every room was filled with parties and food and dancing girls in sweeping dresses, not a gleaming stone gone to waste.

I'm grateful that Basil is here beside me. When I begin to feel that I'll drown in this world and its strange luxuries, he makes me remember who I am, where we come from.

"You're here, you're here!" King Ingram is clapping as he greets us in the hallway. He walks straight to me and takes my hand in both of his and kisses my knuckles with enthusiasm. "Now I've seen your brilliant little kingdom for myself. It's magnificent!"

"Thank you," I manage, startled by his energy.

"And your friend the princess was kind enough to give me the grand tour. Your people were so happy for her return that there were parties daily. Parades. A marvelous festival."

The only celebration we have on Internment is the Festival of Stars in December, and it both worries and intrigues me to think of the celebration he's describing. King Furlow must have been frightened if he was willing to expend the city's resources to throw such an affair.

But when I realize that King Ingram is waiting for me to speak, what I say is, "And how is Princess Celeste?"

Nimble stands beside me now, and I see his face come alive at the mention of her name, but he quickly hides within himself before the king might notice.

"The poor thing has taken ill. The festivities were a bit much for her. But she is back at home in her charming clock tower castle getting the rest she needs. The journey back to Havalais would have been too much for her, but she sends her love. And I've brought a surprise for all of you, sent from your King Furlow himself."

King Ingram leads us to his parlor, saying "Come, come!" as he goes, like a child excited to receive a gift rather than a king about to give one.

He throws open the heavy wooden doors, and Prince Azure rises up from the wing chair. He is dressed in the fashions of this world: a plaid sport jacket with a silk handkerchief in his pocket, and gray pants with sharp creases. But even in the foreign fashion, something about his posture makes me think of home.

"May I present to you Prince Azure of Internment," King Ingram says.

Basil and I feign surprise. He nods into a bow, I into a curtsy.

"Your Highness," Nim says. "Welcome to Havalais."

"Such formality!" King Ingram says. "It's nice to see young people with a regard for custom. Refreshing. But please sit. Sit!"

I sit on the same couch cushion as I did the very first time I met the king, Basil at one side and Nimble at the other.

It has been mere hours since I saw Prince Azure, but he looks the worse for wear. Or perhaps it's only that the lantern light concealed his true condition. He is pale, with light purple bags under his eyes that have been dabbed over with cosmetics. He seems smaller in the daylight, regal but still frail. His hair has grown a bit longer, and a lock of it is doing little to conceal a series of pink scars at his right temple.

He meets my eyes but offers neither a smile nor a frown. A politician's neutral gaze, so much like his father. "I've heard quite a bit about this world, and I'm glad for the opportunity to see it myself," he says.

"Yes, yes, we have quite the itinerary planned," King Ingram says. "Tomorrow afternoon, we'll be presenting our Prince Azure to the rest of the kingdom. My staff is already at work organizing the festivities. There will be radio announcements broadcast today at the top of every hour."

"Plans?" Nimble says.

The king looks to Basil and me. "Well, yes, of course. Our Havalais has fallen on some dark times, I think you'd agree.

Warfare, bombings, deaths, and devastation. Of course the phosane mining will fix that, and soon enough peace will be restored. That's all well and good, isn't it? But all of that is a lot to take in, and the people will need a bit of a morale boost, yes? Someone to cheer for."

"Morgan and Basil have expressed a willingness to help, of course," Nim says. "Father said he spoke with you about that."

"Yes, yes, of course, and I'm so glad. And I know just how they can help." King Ingram reaches out and grabs Basil and me each by the left hand, and holds up our ring fingers like a pair of identical trophies. "Love," he whispers excitedly. "It's the biggest thing our two worlds have in common. You two are the perfect representatives for your world. You are young, vibrant, hopeful, in love. You're a prime example of what life on your floating city is all about."

My mouth and throat have gone dry, and I can see my hand paling in the king's grasp. On the surface, he's correct. Basil and I have always been what we were expected to be. Basil still is. I'm the one who has strayed. I'm the one who daydreamed about the edge and admired the sharp angles of another boy's face and throat in the moonlight. I'm the one who has left the pair of us in limbo, wondering what we are and what we will be.

The king releases our hands, and we withdraw.

Nimble senses our trepidation and does the asking for us. "What is it they're expected to do?"

"Well, obviously the pair of you will not be involved in anything dangerous. No. You'll only be asked to appear before a crowd, read a few prepared speeches, and smile."

"We'd be honored," Basil says, without any resentment at all. I'm proud of him for that. I know how much he hates the king; I saw it in his eyes after the bombing at the harbor. It is the same hatred he has for our own king, who has taken the same liberties with the lives of his own citizens. This whole ordeal has made us all quite wary of kings.

But if Basil can fake it, so can I. If wearing a pretty dress and speaking some pretty words will keep us all safe, I will happily oblige. We're getting off quite easily, I think.

And then King Ingram says, "And after the festivities here, the pair of you will return home."

I open my mouth to speak, but words don't form. I can only try to subdue the alarm that is surely washing over my face. Only the two of us?

Basil is once again the steady one. "We're going back to Internment?"

"You'll meet with my father," Prince Azure says. "You'll oversee the phosane mining and speak to the workers."

I look at Prince Azure and just for a moment I see it—a glimmer of fear in his eyes. Worry. Dread. He, too, is a captive of King Ingram.

But it is not safe to ask my questions, and I may never have all my answers anyway. What I do know is that Basil and I are in for something much bigger than festivities. And home will not be as we left it.

King Ingram's staff works quickly. By the time we make the drive back to the hotel, the capital city of Havalais is already hanging banners welcoming the Sky Prince. A stage is being set up before the library.

I look away, down at my betrothal band. It is made of glass and a bit of the phosane this world so desires. It is identical to all the other betrothal bands on Internment. I wonder at the factory worker who crafted this exact ring. That person would never have dreamed what trouble a little ring could cause.

Tears threaten in my eyes and I force them away. Now is not the time to show weakness. I make myself feel nothing.

The driver brings us to the front door, and I do not want to get out of this car. I do not want to face Alice and my brother, and especially Pen, to tell them that I will be returning home without them, and I do not know for how long, and I do not know if I will be back.

Nimble exits the car first, and then he opens the door for me, and reluctantly I step out into the calm, tepid air.

He pats my shoulder in some small gesture of reassurance. "I'm going to walk into the city and visit with Birdie," he says. "I'll tell her you said hello?"

I smile. That does lift my spirits a little. "Yes. Thank you."

"Attagirl," he says. "See you later."

"We don't have to go inside," Basil says once we're alone. "We could stay out here for a little longer."

I look at him. "We got what we wanted, didn't we? I should be happy."

"It's still rather a shock to hear it. And I know that you were expecting Pen to come along." He glances at the sky and then back to me. "I've spent all these months trying to decide if I'd go back, given the chance. It was foolish of me to think I'd have a choice. That any of us would."

"You'll get to see your parents and brother again," I offer, trying to be optimistic. But I worry the words sound bitter. My own mother is gone, and I have no way of knowing whether my father is still alive, or if he's being tortured by the king for his treason.

"Whatever we face, we'll get through it," is all Basil says.

"I'm not scared to go home," I say. It's the truth. Whatever dread I might harbor for that jet ride back home is less than the anticipation and the not knowing. "It's Pen I'm worried about. I've got to go in there and tell her I'm going to leave her behind."

Basil has nothing to say to this. He has always had words of comfort for me in the past, no matter how bad things were, and no matter how undeserving I may have been of his patience at the time. But for this one thing there are no words of comfort.

Tears threaten again. I ball my hands into fists and I refuse to let them free. I take a deep breath. "Best to get this over with, then," I say, and climb the steps and push open the door.

6

Everyone is in the lobby with questions for us. Everyone but my brother, who never leaves his room, and Pen.

Basil offers to tell everyone what's happened, freeing me to look for Pen so that I might speak to her alone.

I find her upstairs on her bed, staring at one of Birdie's old catalogs.

"These drawings are magnificent," Pen says without looking up. She traces the outline of a plumed hat. "They could almost be images. I'm envious of the realism."

"I much prefer your drawings," I say. "Pen?"

She turns the page.

"Pen, there's something I need to speak to you about."

"I will say I don't understand all the plaids," she says. "It's all the men wear. It gets boring. Do they not see that? Back home I always thought Thomas looked more handsome in pinstripes. Well, not handsome, but, you know—acceptable."

I sit on the edge of her bed, and she winces. "Pen."

She closes the catalog and places her hands down on the cover, as though she is trying to keep something trapped within the pages. With difficulty, she says, "What is it?"

Now it's my turn to look at the cover of the catalog in her lap. The drawing of the woman is lifelike. She has dark lips and white teeth, and she's wearing a coat that looks three sizes too big, with pockets big enough to smuggle melons. But in her own way she's glamorous, without a care, much like the Piper children's mother hiding behind the cemetery trees at Riles's funeral. "Do you think Birdie would mind if I kept that?" I ask.

In answer, Pen tosses it into my lap.

"Thank you," I say. I trace my index finger from corner to corner. "Pen, King Ingram is sending Basil and me back to Internment alone."

She is very still, the way she gets some nights when Thomas looks in on her and she pretends to be sleeping. After a moment she reminds herself to breathe, as though waking from a trance, and it's a sharp painful sound.

"I knew it was going to be that," she says.

"He means to use Basil and me as war symbols. He thinks people in Havalais and Internment will be more trusting of two young people in love. He thinks it will give everyone something to hope for."

"Are you in love now?" Pen says. "That's news to me."

"I don't know. That isn't the point."

"Isn't it?" she says coolly. "If two kingdoms are going to rest their hopes on two young people in love, shouldn't they be in love?"

"I love Basil, you know that I do."

"But that's not quite the same thing as being in love, is it?"

I press my lips together, hard. I don't want to fight with her.

I don't think Pen wants to fight either, and in the silence that falls between us, I feel her anger melting away. "When will you leave?"

"The king is planning festivities this week for Prince Azure's arrival. I suspect it will be after that."

"When will you be back?"

"He didn't say."

"Will you be back?"

I don't want to say the words, but I have to, not just for Pen, but for myself, so I can accept what is happening. "I don't know."

There is no color left in Pen's cheeks, no life in her eyes. There was a single day back on Internment when I disappeared and she was told I was dead. She was broken when I found her again, but this is worse than that. She betrays no signs of life now, save for a bottom lip that has begun quivering.

"You know that all of this young-lovers nonsense is a lie King Ingram is telling you and the rest of the two kingdoms," she says.

"Yes," I say.

"You know that he's probably done something horrible to the princess. Maybe she's even dead."

Sickness in my stomach. "Yes. I know."

Her voice cracks. "You know that whatever he's done to the princess to make her disappear, he's going to do the same to you and Basil."

"We're not going to play this game," I say. "We're just going to see what happens."

"No, you'll see what happens. I'll be down here wondering. I'll always wonder and I'll never know if you're hurt, or—or dead, or—"

"Or perfectly fine. Stop it."

There are tears glittering in her eyelashes, and she draws one quick breath after another. I grab her hands, clammy, ice cold. It takes all my strength not to fall apart too, not because of what horrors may or may not await me in the sky, but because I don't want to leave her on the ground in this state.

She nods at the floor. "Okay," she says. "Okay, this is what we wanted, isn't it? A way to go back. So I wasn't invited. You'll just have to cause a big enough commotion for the both of us."

I smile at her. "There's my girl," I say. "See? It will all work out. You and I can go over all of your notes. I'll memorize as much as I can. They can't confiscate plans that are in my head, yes? And whatever happens up in the sky, Basil and I will handle it."

There's a knock on the open door, and Pen turns away, sniffling.

"Hey." It's Judas, standing on the threshold. "Did I come at a bad time?"

"It's always a bad time in this awful place," Pen says.

"I just heard about the king's plans to send you back," he says. He's looking right at me. "I wanted to make sure you were okay. That's all."

Pen laughs incredulously. "You really have some nerve," she says. She gets to her feet and paces out of the room, making a big show of avoiding him as she passes through the doorway.

"Sorry," I say, even though I understand Pen completely. As far as we've fallen from home, she still believes in our traditions. She may think less of me for it, but she still disapproves of Judas taking the liberty to kiss me. Down here in this world, sins are contagious, but someone from home should know better.

A frown tugs at the corner of his mouth. "Be careful, okay?" he says. "Be more than careful. Be clever. Be aware. This king is no more a friend to you than the one who had you poisoned."

I nod. "I know, and Basil knows it, too."

I drop my eyes to the catalog in my lap. I will keep it with me when I go home, a token of this world. Maybe I'll be able to show my father and tell him of the things I've seen.

It hurts to let myself hope.

Judas stands there for a long time. "I wanted to say good-bye."

My heart is pounding. "I'm not leaving yet. There will be time for good-byes later, I'm sure."

"I wanted to say it now. Sometimes you think you'll get a chance later, but then you don't."

I understand. Daphne. And now he's got me thinking about the enormity of all this. Leaving. Possibly never coming back. All the good-byes I have the opportunity, but not the courage, to say. I push it all down, away, out of sight. It's the only way I can bear to keep myself breathing.

But there is one thing I'm bold enough to ask, since I may never get another chance. I look at Judas. "Do I remind you of her? Is that it?"

"Is that it?" he retorts, offended.

"Is that why you kissed me? Is that why you always look at me when you think I'm not paying attention?"

"No, it's not—" He lowers his voice to a whisper, steps into the room. "No it's not why I kissed you. Does there have to be a reason?"

"Customarily when you kiss a person, there is a reason, yes."

Judas shifts his weight uncomfortably. He is tall and thin, and always seems astonished by his limbs, as though he finds the very concept of having a body perplexing. "I don't want you to think I betrayed Daphne," he says. "It isn't like that. She would want me to go on living. She would be proud to know I was defying betrothal laws after her death, rather than dooming myself to never feel anything for another person again. And it isn't that you remind me of her at all. It wasn't about her. She wasn't there. In that moment it was just you."

I'm finding it difficult to breathe. All this time, I felt

certain that Judas's attraction to me was brought on by the madness of being alone. He still mourns her; I know he does.

"I didn't expect that to be your answer," I manage.

"Please believe me, if you never believe another word I say."

"I do. It's just, I—" I clear my throat, turn myself on the bed so that I'm away from him. But that doesn't ease the anxiety or the guilt. It doesn't make this any easier, and I know that I must face him. I stand and take a few steps toward him. "While Daphne may not have been in that moment, Basil was." I press my hand against my chest. "He's very much a part of me. I can't betray him. I won't. Not again."

Judas is looking into my eyes, and I question what I've just said. Was Basil with me in that moment? The real truth is that everything in the worlds fell away. He kissed me, but I kissed back. And now, if he cares for me at all, he will go along with my lie. He will let me pretend that there is nothing between us, until one day it's the truth.

"Okay," he says. Scratches the back of his head. Turns for the door. "Just—okay."

As he crosses the threshold, I say, "Good-bye, Judas."

He pauses, his back to me. Then he walks away without a word. He has already said good-bye.

In the span of a single day, everything has begun to fall apart. I spend much of the day outside, avoiding everybody. And it's only when I'm alone in one of the teacups at the empty amusement park that I allow myself at last to cry. I lie back, sobbing, and stare at Internment's pale purple form in the cloudless sky. I sob for my mother, whose body was likely burnt in secret with all the other victims of the king, without a proper send-off and without anyone to say so much as a few final words. Is her spirit still trapped there, looking for my brother and me? Does she wonder why we've left her?

It is not a pain I've allowed myself to feel. I was so caught up in the danger and the mystery of our journey. I have worn this cloth of grieving tied around my wrist all this time—it is tattered and dirtied—but I have not truly grieved.

Now it comes all at once.

And my father—I have to believe he's alive and whole and safe. I have to.

I shall have to speak to Thomas about Pen. She and I have never been apart for more than a day, and I've seen what loss can do to her. I don't want to return to the ground and find that she has drunk herself into illness. That's what I'll tell Thomas. Make sure she isn't hoarding bottles. Make sure she isn't going off alone. She can be quite deceitful, so be vigilant. I want to see her well when I get back.

When I get back.

That's what I'll say.

The festivities are a blur. The king's seamstress and tailor have created clothes for Basil and the prince and me that are a mix of what we wore back home and what people wear in Havalais.

Prince Azure goes up to the podium before us, and he reads the words that have been prepared for him in neat typewritten letters on small squares of paper. Words about joining the kingdoms and ending the war with Dastor. But it is not Prince Azure's war, and it is not Internment's war, and I know that there is anger behind the prince's dazzling smiles.

I never get a chance to ask him about that anger. Nor do I get a chance to ask why he has denied Pen her chance to go to Internment with me. She is the one with the knowledge he needs. The moment after his speech, he is whisked off into the crowd, escorted by two of King Ingram's men, to reassure the people.

Charming the people is nothing new for Prince Azure. Back on Internment there was little else for him to do in public. He is tall and attractive and rather eloquent, even if all his words have been prepared for him.

I sit up on the stage, holding Basil's hand, doing my best not to look terrified.

Eventually the king sends us out into the crowd. He has not given us an exact script, but we know what he wants us to say. Everything will be well. Internment is happy to help. The war will be over soon. Dastor is the enemy but soon they'll leave us alone, once the phosane makes us the more powerful kingdom.

The others don't approach us. Pen and Judas and Amy and Nim. But I see them sometimes in the crowd, watching Basil and me. I see Judas's expressionless face that hides so much, and I see Pen's worried eyes.

I swallow a lump in my throat, and I go on speaking lies.

On our last night in Havalais, Basil and I arrive at the castle for a feast being held in our honor. A send-off. Roasted animals of every variety and vegetables that weren't cut out of a can, for once in this world. I force myself to eat. Everything tastes like paste. All I want is to go home, and I'm not sure where that is anymore.

"Ghastly party, isn't it?" Prince Azure says, stepping up from behind me. He's holding two long-stemmed glasses of sparkling tonic and he hands one to me. "I think that's an entire pig on that table over there with—what is that in its mouth?"

"I don't know," I say, because I'm too nauseated to look.

"Tomorrow's the big day," the prince says. "I have been waiting all week to have a moment alone with you. Looks like now's our only chance." He nods to the opened glass doors that lead to the balcony.

I look to Basil, trapped in a conversation between the king and one of his guests.

"Hurry, before the king forces us to recite another line from one of his scripts." Despite his glibness, I can hear in his tone that he's serious, and I let him lead me onto the balcony.

The hot and humid air is hardly better than that of the stale party, but Prince Azure seems relieved. He pauses for a moment to breathe it in.

"So that was him?" Prince Azure says. "That boy with the glass over his eyes? The one my sister is so in love with?"

"Nimble Piper," I say. "That was him."

Prince Azure huffs. "I expected something more extraordinary, to hear the way she spoke on about him. He hardly seems like a prince, although I'll hand it to him, he is doing a brilliant job concealing his lineage."

"For what it's worth, he's kind," I say.

Prince Azure stares out at the sky. "That is worth something."

"Is Celeste—is she all right?" I say.

"She's taken ill," Prince Azure says. "She was in no condition to be flying between worlds. King Ingram meant to drag her to Havalais anyway, but Father put his foot down and sent me instead."

"But she's alive," I think aloud.

Prince Azure throws me a frosty glare. "Yes. And she had all manner of kind things to say about you. For that and so many other reasons, I think the ground caused her to go mad."

"Is that why you've advised the king to send Basil and me back to Internment?" I say. "Pen would be valuable to Internment, and if you're trying to keep her down here out of spite—"

"I am trying to keep her alive," he says. "Do I care for her? No. She tried to kill me and I don't especially like what she does with her hair. But her value is not lost on me. I know that she is the one who figured it all out about the phosane, or as we call it back home, sunstone. I know that she has an engineer's head on her shoulders. And if my father knew this, she'd be on her way to the clock tower as soon as you touched ground, and she would spend what's left of her life there, working for him."

"Pen would never," I say.

"She would, or she would be tortured. Drowned within a sliver of death. Cut. Hung by her wrists."

I force the imagery from my mind and keep my steady gaze on him. "Is that the sort of torture you saw at the attraction camp? For people who are attracted to the same sex?"

He pales at that. Swallows a hard lump in his throat and goes on, "When King Ingram asked which one of you should be used as symbols, I chose the pair of you because of your dumb expressions. Look at you—you're utterly harmless. Nobody would suspect you had a valuable thought in your head. But that friend of yours is another story. My sister told me all about how brilliant she is and on this front, I believe her."

"Why did you choose me, then? If you want to save Internment so badly and Pen's so valuable?"

Prince Azure closes his eyes for a long, painful moment. "Because I do not want her helping my father. Or King Ingram. I no longer believe either of them can do what's best for Internment."

"We agree, then," I say. "Your father is doing more harm than good."

Prince Azure waves his hand. "Fine. Let's be candid. Yes, I agree with you. My father's way may have been sinister at times, but it worked when Internment was self-contained. He had people killed in the interest of suppressing riots that would have destroyed the city. But now things have changed. I need you and that betrothed of yours to go up there with your dumb expressions and play the part of two harmless idiots. I need you to talk to my sister. She'll know what needs to be done. And moreover, I need you to look after her."

I blink. "I thought you were coming back with us."

"You don't get it, do you?" he says. "I'm not here by choice, Stockhour."

King Ingram has spotted us, and from across his party he calls our names, waving us enthusiastically back into the party.

I follow after Prince Azure, with a lead anchor in the pit of my stomach.

When I return to the hotel, I fall into bed without bothering to unpin my hair or scrub the cosmetics from my skin.

Pen climbs into the bed with me and for the longest time we don't speak. My back is turned to her, and I'm watching the curtain arch around the open window like a force field when the wind comes.

"I've been thinking about the gardens of stones," she says.

"The graveyards?"

"Yes. Those. I've been thinking about all those bodies beneath the earth just rotting and feeding the worms and the soil. On Internment we burn everything away—the skin and the bones, the brain, the heart, until there's just dust."

She rests her chin on my shoulder. "But down here, what's left inside these people who are buried? Do they still hold on to the secrets that people have told them? Where does it all go?"

"I don't know," I say.

"I think we have a lot in common with the dead," Pen says. "We're filled with things we won't say out loud. Things that get trapped inside us that nobody will ever hear."

When I leave, is she going to go on having thoughts like this? "We aren't dead," I remind her. "What we say or don't say, the secrets we do or don't keep—those are all choices. Conscious choices we get to make while we're alive."

"I thought you'd see it that way." She lies back against the pillow. "If there's anyone I can tell my secrets to, it's you, Morgan. You'll keep them if I ask, won't you?"

"Of course I will."

I understand now what is about to happen. Several months ago, I discovered one of her secrets on a piece of paper that was meant to be burnt at the Festival of Stars. It was the most desperate, hateful thing I'd ever seen her draw: buildings with the word "die" making up their bricks and plumes of chimney smoke. We fought each other to the ground over that bit of paper and she never fully explained what it meant.

That secret has taken on a body of its own. It sits between us all the time, this thing we don't acknowledge.

She turns away from me and settles with the back of her head against mine. "It started the day my father took me to the glasslands," she says. "It was evening and we were alone. He said we were going to share a secret, he and I. I knew that something was wrong, because he'd never so much as talked about his work with me, much less taken me to see it." She is very still as she talks.

I don't understand but I don't ask. I know that if I interrupt, she will stop this story and never begin again. "I don't even remember if I looked at him. I remember the spire filling up with orange light as the sun went down. I remember reciting a poem in my head. You know, the one we read in kinder year about the flowers being the eyes of the god in the sky, spread out to keep watch over us. I recited it over and over until the words didn't seem like words anymore.

"That was the first time."

I close my eyes tight against the words she is about to say.

"After that, he started coming to my bedroom when it was late. Usually just as the sky was changing before the sunrise. I told Mother about it. She was still good back then. She still had her wits. She went right to the clock tower, to speak to one of the king's advisers.

"But what could be done when my father was so important to the glasslands? He's one of their top engineers. He was in the middle of a project to outfit older buildings with electricity. The king didn't want a scandal. So it was decided that I was mistaken, then. I had to speak to a specialist and explain, once a week, why I wouldn't stop telling these lies.

"Do you know what I remember most, though? All the lines that started appearing in my mother's face. You'd think I'd be the one crying about it, but it was never me. It was always her. Breaking into hysterics while she was washing the dishes, or going for these long walks and not returning until after my father had gone to sleep. She never slept herself, and she was prescribed tonic. As much as she wanted. As much as it would take to drown her thoughts."

My nails are digging into my palms, and I hold my breath for long stretches, exhaling slowly, silently. I always blamed Pen's mother for her battle with tonic. Vilified her at times for spreading that toxic addiction to her only daughter like a terminal disease. I never once thought that there might have been a cause.

"There are dozens of men like my father on Internment. Maybe even hundreds. Even if you look, you won't see them. Every king knows what happens in his kingdom. He knows how to hide things. I'm not afraid of my father anymore. I don't know that I ever was. I've been afraid of what would happen to my mother and me if anyone found out.

My mother can't handle herself the way that I can. She's like a train car that only goes backward. Around and around all the time in the wrong direction, and there's nothing I can do to even slow her down. It wasn't always that way, I think, but it has been for as long as I've been alive. I suppose I can't blame my father for all of her madness. I don't believe in that. I don't believe in letting other people be the reason we turn out the way that we do.

"Thomas doesn't know. He absolutely can't. He may not seem like much, but if he found out, I know that he would do something as violent as it is stupid." She's right. The boy has no sensibility when it comes to her, he loves her so. "I've found ways to handle it myself. I've started keeping a knife under my pillow, and the last time he came into my room, I pretended to be asleep until he came close, and then I had the knife at his cheek and I asked him how he would explain his injuries at work tomorrow. He does so value his charming smile. That's how he gets everyone to trust him."

The curtain falls limp as the wind leaves it. Insects impassively go on with their songs.

For the first time all night, Pen's voice loses its cool detachment and she sounds small. "Say something."

Say something.

After Lex's incident I modeled myself after her. I wanted to be as strong for my parents as she was for her declining mother. I foolishly believed that we had something in common, something we didn't have to talk about. Every night while I slept safely in my bed, while my greatest problem was that I didn't have the attention I craved, the light was being stolen from Pen's spirit, and I saw nothing, did nothing. And rather than bonding over our tragic little lives, the real truth was that our childhood was disappearing behind our footfalls as we walked, hand in hand, down very different paths.

"I remember this one December, we must have been seven or eight," I say. "We were at the Festival of Stars. My brother was supposed to come and light our papers for us, but you had been bouncing all day; you had thought of something really important to ask for, and you couldn't wait any longer. So you climbed onto one of the picnic tables so you could reach the flame lantern. I couldn't have stopped you if I'd tried. The fire burnt right down to your fingers before you let the paper go and it spiraled away from you. You stood there in your white dress, the hem and ribbons already stained by the grass, and you watched your flame disappear into a sky that was already on fire."

The sun was deep orange, like it was bleeding into the sky, and everything—our whole world—had seemed ablaze.

"You were beautiful. You were the bravest and most powerful thing in the sky."

I turn to face her in the darkness. The moonlight clings to the curve of her cheek. "I still see that girl when I look at you," I say. "I always will."

Pen closes her eyes, and her stoic expression melts.

"No one has ever seen me the way you do," she says.

8

It's early when Nim knocks at my door. The sun itself is still sleeping. "We'll be leaving in a half hour," he says, and then he's gone. I'm uncertain whether or not I've slept. I didn't dream, and spent most of the night in silence, with Pen just as silent beside me.

I light a candle so I can see what I'm doing, but I don't turn on the light as I slip into a dress from the closet. It's satin with a drop waist, and a sequined collar. The fashion will startle the king, if he bothers to notice.

I thought Pen was sleeping, but she sits up and watches me attempt to brush the tangles from my hair. "I told you not to go to bed with all those pins in it."

"What do you think everyone back home will say about this dress?" I say, and can't help but grin.

"It's positively scandalous," Pen says, dropping back against the pillows with a flourish. Staring up at the ceiling, she says, "Are you nervous about flying in the jet?"

"After tumbling to the earth in the professor's metal bird, it's a relief to be flying in something with a proper engine."

"That bird was quite impressive, though," Pen says. "It had a full kitchen. I think we could have lived there if things had gone differently. For a while, at least."

"You should draw it," I say. "Not like a map, but a full rendition, with the bolts and gears and everything."

"I don't know if I remember it clearly enough now."

"Of course you do. Your mind works that way. You capture images of things and they stay up in your head forever."

She sits up again, turns on the lamp, and looks at me. "I hope you're right."

It's painful to take in the sight of her. Twin braids. Sleepy green eyes. Defiant smirk that never really leaves her lips. I saw it even after her body was pulled from the water, taunting death itself.

She squints curiously at me. "What is it?"

"I'm just thinking is all."

"Yes, thank you, I gathered that much."

Everything has changed. That's what I'm thinking. The way I saw the world has changed. The way I saw life. But Pen still looks the same. My beautiful Pen, who has given me her ugliest secret.

"Do you really want the truth?" I ask.

"Yes, I really do."

"I'm thinking that when I go home, I don't know what will be waiting for me, but I hope that I can find your father—in your apartment or just leaving the glasslands. I'm thinking I'd like to stop his heart. It isn't right. What he did. It isn't right that Daphne and my mother and how many others had to die such awful deaths, but he goes on as though he's done nothing wrong."

Her face softens. Her eyes have awoken now.

"You don't have to kill my father," she says, her voice gentle. "But I can't tell you how much it means to me that someone else wants him gone as much as I do."

"Maybe I'll only trip him, then."

She laughs. It's an explosive laugh, and she throws her hand over her mouth, and in the next instant she's sobbing.

I go to her, sit across from her on the bed. "Don't cry," I say, but my own eyes are filling. "Don't."

"Nothing bad can happen to you, Morgan. Do you understand? There are pieces of me—important pieces— that stop existing when you're not around."

Shuddering, she grabs my hands, but then changes her mind and throws her arms around me.

"When I told the king about the phosane, I was thinking of what would be best for you," I remind her. "So I want to find the same Pen when I return. Sober and alive."

She nods. Furiously, desperately, because she will tell me anything I want to hear in this moment. Anything that will make me happy. It is our way of protecting each other, filling each other's heads with these silly illusions that neither of us will change a drop while we're apart, and that we will see each other again.

When I leave the bedroom, I close the door behind me, holding the knob so as to make as little noise as possible. Most of the house is sleeping, and I'd like to avoid a teary good-bye.

But someone is waiting for me at the top of the stairs.

Alice's hair is bright red even as the rest of her is shadowed by the darkness of the hour. I hold my breath. It is the only way I won't fall to pieces and change my mind about going.

I can just see her sad smile. "I wanted to say good-bye before you left. Lex asked me to wake him, but it seemed for the best if I didn't."

My brother and I had come to an understanding of sorts. He had lied about our father. If I was choosing to return home, he owed me enough to let me go. But he didn't have to like it. If he were standing here now, he would try to stop me, and being my brother and knowing me as he does, he would play to my sympathies. He would know just what to say, not to stop me, but to make me feel lousy enough about going.

"Don't worry," Alice says. "I'll look after him."

"Look after yourself, too," I say, my voice tight. I will miss them both terribly.

"I'm working on him," she says. "I think I've almost convinced him to come around to this world. When this war is through, we can get a new apartment. He can write his novels, I can work."

"Just like home, but entirely the opposite," I say.

She laughs. "Yes."

I take her hands. "Tell him that there are different freedoms down here," I say. "Tell him that no one will stigmatize him for being a jumper—the people down here don't even know what that is. Tell him you can have a family."

She squeezes my hands. "That one will take more time, love. There's so much healing to do."

"Healing can only happen once you begin the process. Tell him."

"Yes," she says, and her voice cracks with tears. I think it's because I brought up that awful memory again, and I hate myself for being so hasty. I'm so desperate for them to be happy that I lose my own patience. But Alice puts her arms around me, kisses my cheek with such force, I can still feel her lips even after she's drawn back. "Come back to us alive," she says. "Whatever you have to do."

I can't bear another promise I'm not sure I can keep. Instead I hug her and I tell her I love her, and I remind her again to combat Lex's stubbornness and get him to rejoin the living. They're both still so young. I can't stand the thought of my brother squandering all the decades they both have left to live. "There's still a life for you down here," I say. "Don't let him go on harping about the terrible things when there's still so much good."

She hugs me again. There are no more promises to be made, and neither of us wants to say good-bye. When we at last let go, I offer a smile before I turn away and descend the stairs.

Basil is wearing what I think is one of Nim's suits. He looks striking in it, I think, even if the shoulders are a bit snug. Nim is considerably thin and willowy.

Basil gives a somber smile when he sees me. There are tears in my eyes.

"Hi," I say, keeping my voice low. The rest of the hotel is sleeping, or pretending to be asleep. Nimble says we're running a few minutes early. He says we can go say good-bye to the others if we like. "Until next time," he quickly adds.

I look at Basil. "I don't want to. But you should go on if there's anything you need to say."

"What about your brother?" he asks.

I especially don't want to say good-bye to him. If there is anyone in this hotel whose words are powerful enough to change my mind, it's Lex.

Even if my father's death were a certainty, I would go. I still belong to Internment. It's still a part of me. I have to see this through. I want to.

"I've said all my good-byes," I tell him.

Jack Piper is nowhere, nor is his driver. Nim leads us to one of the black cars used by the staff here, and he drives us himself.

We reach a turn in the road, and the hotel is no longer visible when I look back, and I break into a fresh round of tears. They fast become hysterical, and I am a mess of incoherent whimpers that are meant to be the names of the people in that hotel.

Basil puts his arms around me, rubs my back and whispers that it's okay, let it out, go on, I've been incredibly brave. He understands that this is harder for me than it is for him. We are returning to his family and leaving mine behind.

He kisses the crown of my head. "Oh, Morgan."

I shake in his arms the way that Pen shook in mine. I think she was what held me together for so long. "I wanted to be strong for her." I gag on saliva. "And Alice and—" I can't speak.

Basil holds me steady against the jostling of the car. He has to be the steady one when I can't be. Alice was right. Things change. People leave. The one whose blood fills your ring is the one who never leaves your side.

I tighten my fists around his shirt.

For all its hype, the send-off is unspectacular. Nim stops the car in what at first seems to be the middle of a field. Then, in the approaching sunlight, I see the long stretch of concrete that leads like a road to a multilevel building with a large, closed door making up its front.

"Take a minute to dry your eyes," Nim says. "We're running early anyway." He turns in his seat and gives me the handkerchief from his pocket. It's embroidered with a black *JP*, for "Jack Piper." The real name he never uses.

I sniff. "Thank you."

His lips are pressed tightly, not quite a smile. I am going to miss him, and his sisters, but I can't think about that now if there's any chance of holding myself together. I watch him step out of the car and close the door behind him.

I dab at my eyes, blow my nose, and let out a shuddering breath.

"Why didn't you tell me this is how it felt when you left your family behind?" I say.

"It wasn't quite the same." Basil uses his sleeve to dab at my persistent tears. "I knew that I was making the choice they'd want me to make. I knew that their best chance at staying safe was for me to leave them behind."

I shake my head. "This isn't what my brother or Alice want. That's why I couldn't say good-bye to my brother. I want it to seem as though—as though I just stepped out for a walk before he woke up, and I'll be back soon." I look at him. "And Pen. I need her. I need both of you in my life. I don't know who I am without the two of you beside me."

"You're Morgan," he says. "The girl I could never keep up with in kinder year, who was always chasing flutterlings and even bramble flies—anything with wings. You're the girl who dove into that ocean when Pen didn't surface. You're the thing that calls me back when my thoughts have begun to tread into darkness."

I sniffle dumbly. "I am?"

He tilts my chin so that I'm looking at him. "Yes."

"You always know the exact thing to say." I blow my nose again and fold the handkerchief in my lap. "I don't suppose Nim will want this back."

Basil laughs. "He probably meant for you to keep it."

"Shall we go, then?"

"I'm ready if you are."

Basil opens the door, and I follow him out into the dark morning air. It's chilly, although last night was quite warm.

I hug my arms across my stomach. "Your weather is unpre-dictable," I say to Nim.

We begin the walk down the concrete, and to keep myself rooted in the moment, I tell Nim about the long seasons and the short back home. There is no real weather. No snow. A slight change in the leaves sometimes, a slight dip in the temperature when the days get shorter, but nothing like this.

"I imagine all of our seasons must be a nuisance for someone like you," he says.

"No. I think they're beautiful."

"What do you call this road?" Basil asks. "It's strange. On one end it just stops in the grass."

"It's a runway," Nim says. "The plane will come out of that carriage house there, and pick up momentum by speeding down the runway, and then it'll take flight."

I turn to him as we walk. "Do you wish you were coming with us?"

"The idea is intriguing," he admits. "But I have my sisters to look after." He brightens a little. "Birds will be excited to know you've gone home. She'll expect all sorts of stories when you return." He says it with such confidence, and I cannot tell whether he believes it himself or is just a convincing liar for my sake.

I play along. "I'm looking forward to seeing her up and about."

I look ahead to see that the carriage house that holds the plane is much closer. I can hear voices echoing inside its brick walls.

"Morgan," Nim says. "Your kindness meant a lot to Celeste. She told me that you were someone she could trust. One of the only people that she could trust, actually. I was wondering if maybe—if you could give this to her. When you see her, that is." He has extracted a folded envelope from his breast pocket and he puts it in my hand. It's sealed shut, and I can feel the heft of several pages inside. "It's very important that she's the only one who reads that."

I meet his eyes. "Of course," I say.

"And if—" He cuts himself off and then begins anew after he's summoned some courage. "And if what the others have feared is true, and she's no longer alive, I need you to destroy that for me."

I'm amazed by his bravery, saying those words and accepting them as a possibility.

"Okay," I say, and repeat something I've heard Birdie say so many times, copying her accent and emphasizing the four syllables. "Absolutely."

Nim smiles, punches my shoulder lightly. "Thanks, kiddo."

He bangs on the wooden door to the carriage house: once, pause, three times, pause, once.

There's a stirring and a metallic sound from within, like ropes being fed through a pulley, and then the door begins lumbering upward, arching back into the carriage house itself.

As the door rises and I begin to get a good look at the jet in the early morning light, a painfully bright flash blinds me. Too late, we shield our eyes. "There they are, our lovely young beacons of hope!" the king says. He's holding a heavy-looking metal device in front of his face, and he lowers it to smile at us. "That will look lovely on the front page of the paper. I'll be sure to reserve a copy for you when you return."

If you don't call upon your men to kill us, I think. That's what my own king tried to do to me.

As the burning dots fade from my vision, I see Prince Azure standing behind the king, outfitted on either side by two of King Ingram's men. *Hostage,* I think. He is dressed in more of this world's fashions; if he were to return home like this, it would take mere seconds for the schoolboys back home to mimic this foreign image. Internment would begin to resemble the ground. The thought frightens me more than I was prepared for.

The prince's weary eyes are on Nim, the boy from a strange land who stole his sister's heart.

Nim notices and tips his cap in greeting, but this gets no response.

Beside the prince, the jet sits like a giant metal creature I'd expect to find in one of the oceans here. If the professor's contraption was a bird, this is a creature of the sea. A whale with an arched back and pectoral fins spread out at either side. The metal is dark with "001" painted on the side in chipped white letters.

I turn to Basil, who is staring at the thing with worried eyes. I'd like to console him, but it doesn't seem wise to speak candidly in the king's presence. And besides that, I don't want to lie to him.

The king positions Basil and the prince and me at the jet's nose for photos. I'm made to stand between the two of them with my arms up around their shoulders. Through his teeth, Prince Azure says to me, "It'll go a lot faster if you smile." He glances at me. "Not like you're facing execution. Like you mean it."

I force my best smile. The king seems pleased with the lot of us and he hands the horrid flashing device to one of his men. They call it a camera, I know, but it's a much more crude version of the image recorders we have back home. This world has many advances compared to Internment, but Internment has much better technology. I suppose Havalais harnessing the phosane would change all that.

"This is the part where I wish you all safe travels," the king says. He hands Basil and me each a thick stack of papers. "I've prepared some notes—scripts, information, itineraries, what to say when you are asked certain questions. There will be someone waiting to receive you when you return home."

Home. He shouldn't be allowed to use such an intimate word to describe the place he's so cheerfully willing to destroy.

His delighted grin does nothing to ease my mind. I am more sure than ever that some horrible fate awaits us back home. He has used us as symbols of hope, and now that we're leaving, he can tell his kingdom all sorts of brilliant stories about what we're doing up there. No need for us to be alive for that.

One of the men opens the jet's door. It unfolds from the body of the jet like a bit of orange peel. Our shoes make hard noises on the metal steps as we climb up to the door. Basil goes first and I follow. Just before I step into the jet's doorway, I look back over my shoulder at Nim, who gives me a pitying smile. Beside him, the prince mouths the words "my sister." I give the slightest of nods so that the king, giddy about his plans, won't see it.

As I step onto the jet, two men wheel away the ladder. Basil grips my arm as though he thinks I might fall in the open space. And then the same two men swing the door shut behind us with a jarring slam. I tense. The jet's shudder never leaves my body, instead running up and down my bones, trapped inside me.

It's dim inside the jet. The only light comes from the rows of small windows on either side of the tiny chamber.

The ceiling is low and arched. Basil can't stand fully upright and must duck his head as we make our way to the seats. The seats are very similar to the ones on the trains back home. There are four of them, made of polished brown leather, in pairs of two that face one another beside a small oval window.

My legs are shaking as I bend into a seat beside the window. Basil sits beside me and puts his hand on my knee.

I notice two buckets under the seats across from us. "What do you suppose those are for?" I say, desperate for a distraction.

"In case we need to get sick," Basil guesses. I don't feel any better. I didn't get sick when we fell out of the sky, but now the thought has been put into my head, and I purse my lips together.

A roar begins from seemingly within the jet's walls. Our seats rattle and shake. I grip Basil's hand that's on my knee. I can feel the last breath he draws before he holds it all in. The jet lurches forward, and the darkness of the garage outside the window becomes the lightening sky. I see Nim with his hands in his pocket for less than a second before he has been ripped from view. The grass flies past us, an endless field, and then suddenly that grass is far below us. We are moving up, leaving my stomach below us.

My hand, squeezing Basil's, is slick with sweat. My face is hot and then cold.

Basil exhales, and his next breaths are shallow and light. He's staring at the tiny window.

I take a deep breath and exhale hard. "Maybe it will distract us if we read these papers King Ingram left with us."

Basil shakes his head lightly. "I can't look at words just now."

I don't think I'm much in the condition for reading, either. I roll my head back against the seat and try to find my bearings.

Several minutes of quiet pass, and as soon as I realize I won't need the bucket under my seat, I do feel better.

We don't speak, either because we fear being sick, or because this week of being paraded about has exhausted us.

An hour into the flight, my head feels as though it were being compressed in a vise. I lean against Basil, who draws patterns on my knee, pausing occasionally to rub the satin of my dress between his fingers.

I think of the grim alternate reality Prince Azure painted for Pen. Shackled and tortured in the clock tower, prodded for information. Her mind has always been a commodity, and I think she's always known it, because she has kept her brilliance hidden. She whispers her secrets aloud only when we're alone. Never trusting anyone. She knew it was unsafe.

And despite trying not to, I think of what Pen endured at her father's hand. I think of all those mornings back home when she dabbed herself with cosmetics or struggled to stay awake on the train and carried the scent of tonic. All those times I held her hair away from her face when she was sick, wondering what this affliction was that caused her to drink as much as she did. How stupid I was, and how useless.

"Are you all right?" Basil asks, leaning forward to see my face.

I nod. Whether I see Pen ever again or not, this is one secret of hers that I will keep. I say, "Prince Azure pulled me aside at the party last night. He's afraid, Basil. He's a hostage."

Basil nods. "King Ingram is using him for some sort of leverage, to be sure."

"Do you think King Ingram will kill him if Internment goes on refusing to comply?" I say.

"It's possible. But if that's the case, do you think he's willing to die for Internment?"

"It wouldn't do much good," I say. "If Internment goes

on being useless to King Ingram's plan, what's to stop him from bombing the entire city right out of the sky?" I stare out the window at wisps of clouds. The ground is a faraway patch of green. "Prince Azure told me to speak to his sister. He didn't have a chance to explain, but I think the two of them have something planned and they seem to think we can help."

"I hope they're right," Basil says. "Resistance is fine and well, but a tiny floating city can avoid a king's wrath for only so long."

Our fingers have become intertwined, and I stare down at his betrothal band, empty of my blood. I wonder if we'll live long enough to speak our vows. I wonder if we will still choose each other if we're given the luxury of that time.

"Look." Basil nods to the window, and I follow his gaze.

There at a distance, floating in the still blue, is a swirling sphere of clouds, a perfect dome. And below that I see the jagged earth, and I realize at once that this is home. A small cloud drifts toward it and immediately gets pulled into the current of wind, zipping into fast motion.

"It always looks so much calmer from within the city," I say.

"It's something, isn't it?" Basil says.

We're approaching rapidly, huddled around that small window as we watch our world from the outside. These clouds are swirling in the wind that threw my brother back against the earth when he got too close. It nearly killed him. Amy too. It changed them irreparably. It killed so many others.

We slice through that wind like through water. The jet wobbles and shakes and I think that surely we will be propelled back into the sky, away from the city, from the force of it.

The jet holds steady, though, and the window fills up with white for a moment before I see dirt.

We touch ground and I can hear the furious squealing of the jet's wheels, and I begin to worry that we'll career into the train tracks in the distance.

I brace myself, gripping the edge of the seat. Basil's arm, pressed against mine, is so tense, there could be steel under his skin.

When we finally stop, my head and stomach are still speeding off ahead of me somewhere. I can feel myself breathing, but I am not in control of my own body as it struggles to understand that I've stopped flying.

It takes several seconds for me to focus, and when I do, I wish, not for the first time, that Pen were here. She would somehow know exactly where we are.

When my vision settles enough that I can see what's on the other side of the window, I realize that we are just outside the train tracks, on the long stretch of unused land between the tracks and the road. The grass here grows scraggly and wild, scarcely tended to.

I have time to give Basil only a worried look before the door is opened and we're pulled out by a group of King Furlow's patrolmen. I hear a low growl in Basil's throat when one of the guards pulls me down the last step. In an instant Basil is at my side, keeping pace.

I hold nothing but contempt for these patrolmen after what they've done to my family. Which of them are to be trusted? But even as they're telling us to step outside and move quickly, I hear the cadence of their voices—Birdie called it an accent—like my own, and I know that I am once again home.

The air is perfect, warm and still. The sky is calm.

I count five patrolmen, and they lead us over the train tracks, back to within the city's limits. I'd never been on the wrong side of these tracks before, but I no longer fear that being too close to the edge of the city will drive me mad. I have seen madness in a king who would allow an attack on his own city for political gain. I have seen bodies cracked open like fruit fallen from a tree and left to rot in the sun. There's no god in that wind, warning me away or calling me closer.

Even more unnerving are the men in clothes that are not from this world. I recognize the drab gray of their coats. I saw them in the dozens after the explosion at the harbor. Soldiers from King Ingram's army.

I look to the workers ahead of me. I recognize some of them from my section or Basil's. There's a woman who worked as a seamstress and who repaired my coat sleeve when I tore it on a loose scrap of metal jutting from the train's wall. Now she is glistening with sweat. She spears the dirt with a shovel, searching for the clumps of soil that glimmer with that invaluable mineral that can be refined.

With all this open land, we must be in Section Seven, a broad field in which animals are bred and free to roam.

Only, there are no animals here now. The land is being torn apart. Ruined. The grass has started to brown and thin, as though it would rather die than be a part of what's being done here.

The workers all seem to be going out of their way to avoid looking at us. They've been instructed not to, I think.

I look for my father in the crowd. And then I look for his face among the patrolmen standing guard. He is nowhere.

Basil walks in silence beside me, but I note the nearly imperceptible change in his next breath and I follow his gaze. He's looking at a woman who is waist-high in one of the holes, brushing at the dirt with her fingers, looking for specks that will be of use. His mother.

At first I think she hasn't seen us yet. But then she looks at him. Sharpness and longing in her eyes. She goes right back to her task.

I touch Basil's arm to bring him back to me. I fear what will happen to him if he's caught staring, or if any of the guards realize he's related to one of the workers. I do not know what our presence means, if we're hated or loved.

It's hard to think we would be loved.

We walk for what feels like an hour, until the workers are behind us and we eventually come to a cobblestone road. There aren't many shuttles in this section, nor is there a train platform nearby—it would startle the livestock. There is a shuttle bus waiting for us here now, though. The patrolmen guide us inside.

It's just Basil and me, and a patrolman who stands by the door, watching us even as the shuttle begins to move.

The man driving the shuttle is dressed in the gray of King Ingram's soldiers.

We are all silent, but I know Basil. I look at his face and I can see that something has changed. The sight of his mother working with the mining effort, unable to so much as speak to him, has proven to us that things are not as we left them.

I don't ask where we're going. We drive on the outskirts of Section Seven, far from any buildings. I never knew Internment had so many trees. I never knew the section for livestock was so vast. We could almost be on Havalais, I think. I've become accustomed to the idea that a patch of land can go on forever, never stopping at all, but rather looping back around to itself.

When I begin to recognize where we are, my skin prickles. Through the window I can see the clock tower in the distance.

"Out," the patrolman says after the shuttle has come to a stop.

As I follow Basil down the aisle, my body thinks, for just a moment, that I am moving for the train that will take us to school. It is a normal day. It is all the same inside the shuttle—the metal walls, the cushioned seats, the smell of it. It is the same and not the same.

A train hasn't gone by since we landed. Even this far from the tracks, I would still be able to hear it. I would still feel the rattle under my feet. One surely should have passed by now.

It's been hours since we left Havalais, and I force myself not to think of what the others might be doing on the ground now that they're surely awake. But the clock tower does not make for a pleasant distraction.

Nim's letter to Celeste sits heavily against my chest, where I've folded it in half and tucked it under my dress for safekeeping and to hide it. As unique and glamorous as the fashions of the ground are, women's clothing in particular isn't very practical. If I were wearing my uniform or one of my old dresses, there would be pockets. There would be more modesty as well.

I'm feeling very conscious, suddenly, of the short hem of this dress, the straps that do nothing to cover my shoulders. This feeling only intensifies when we reach the clock tower and I realize that we are surely on our way to see King Furlow.

The main floor of the clock tower is a public lobby. I was here a few times with my parents when they were collecting their weekly wages, and once on a tour in first year. The last time Alice was here was when she appealed directly to the king about allowing the birth of her child. After that, neither she nor Lex could stand to come back, and I would often collect their wages for them so they wouldn't have to.

I find myself once again looking for my father. But he isn't here; hardly anyone is. Most of the citizens must be out there mining for fuel. Internment has become a labor camp, just as we all feared.

Two patrolmen lead us down a hallway that's always restricted from the public, and it leads to a single door I've never seen. The door is unlike the others on Internment. Rather than wood, it is made of steel. There are two locks above the doorknob, and each patrolman holds just one of the keys to open it.

The door opens, revealing an archaic staircase made of carved stone. Parts of the steps have crumbled into pebbles, and I can tell the staircase has never been repaired and is probably as old as the clock tower itself.

We move single file, with a patrolman ahead of us and a patrolman behind us, for what seems to be a thousand steps spiraling up the walls of the clock tower.

When at last we reach a landing, one of the patrolmen stands to attention while the other unlocks the door. I wonder if there has always been this much security surrounding the king, or if this is all in light of the hatred he must be facing for what Internment has become.

The patrolman moves through the open door, and looks over his shoulder at us. "Come on, then," he says. "The king will be expecting you."

I'd like to take hold of Basil's hand, but I don't dare. Neither of us betray fear or emotion of any kind as we step forward, clutching only the stack of instructions King Ingram doled out to us this morning.

No wooden floor covers the original stone of this tower, and our footsteps and breaths echo as we move. We pass several closed doors along the wall, and then, at last, we come to the end of the hallway, and the patrolman opens a final door.

When I last saw King Furlow, he was coming undone. It was the middle of the night and his son was dying before him, his daughter in hysterics at his side. Now he stands straight at a window that overlooks the workers in the distance. His pudgy frame has thinned somewhat, and when he turns to us, his eyes are tired, the skin purpled beneath them.

Near the window there is a large wooden desk, its surface free of any papers, I suspect because he has nothing to read through or to sign. No one is seeking his approval. He has lost control of his kingdom.

He waves dismissively to the patrolman, who remains out in the hallway and closes the door behind us.

"Ms. Stockhour, Mr. Cowl," King Furlow says with forced spirit. "I am glad you've returned."

Like the rest of Internment, I was raised to show respect to my king. Even after Alice's baby was taken from her womb at his command. Even after Lex went to the edge and condemned us all to the king's scrutiny.

But I am so very tired of it all. The false cheer. The curtsies. The polite nods. Pretending I should admire this cracked hollow shell of a king. And yet he seems to expect it, staring at us the way he does.

"Are you?" I say.

Basil tenses beside me. He could bow. I wouldn't blame him for it. He is, after all, the one who wants to play it safe. He wants us to survive whatever awaits us. I can feel how frightened he is by my candor.

But he doesn't bow to the king who ordered my death and the death of my family. And I must keep myself from smiling.

King Furlow's troubled face does not register a reaction to our small insubordination. He says, "When King Ingram said he would be returning two of my citizens, I couldn't be sure what his word was worth. I didn't know that he would allow you to come, and alive at that. I suppose it was too much to hope that my son would be returned. He did arrive on the ground in one piece?"

"The prince is well," Basil says. "He saw us off."

"Good, good," King Furlow says. "Please be seated. What is that you're holding?"

"Scripts," I say as Basil and I sit in the cushioned chairs opposite the king's desk.

No sooner do we sit, than the ground rumbles under our feet. The legs of the desk rattle against the stone floor. Basil and I start, but the king is unfazed.

"That would be the engine as the jet takes off. Ingram did say he would be taking it back as soon as he returned you two."

I have lived on this floating city my entire life with no way out, and yet for the first time I feel panic at the idea that my ride has left without me. My brother and Alice and Pen are off in a place where I cannot reach them. Sweat is pooling in my palms, and I clench my fingers into fists.

"Now then," King Furlow says. He paces the length of his desk before sitting in the chair behind it. He gestures to the papers Basil and I hold. "You say those are scripts?" The king seems to have gotten comfortable in his chair, but Basil and I are rigid, like two tightly wound toys ready to go off in motion once the string is released. "I shouldn't be surprised. I suppose King Ingram has sent you back here to convince the people of our city that they should do as he commands."

"Yes," I say.

"We find ourselves in a jam, don't we?" the king says. "It would seem that the sunstone in our soil contains a substance those on the ground refer to as 'phosane,' and King Ingram would like to use it for his own purposes. And my daughter, too trusting as she is, told King Ingram about our sunstone, hoping for an alliance between our two kingdoms.

"King Ingram has men camped throughout the city. I do not know how much he plans to drain our resources. But we are a small kingdom. My daughter tells me that our entire city is hardly bigger than King Ingram's castle. If we don't cooperate, what's to stop them from destroying us entirely, killing us all, and taking our dirt as they see fit?"

He's looking at Basil and me, and after a long silence I realize he means for us to answer the question.

Basil looks at me. I am the one who witnessed the bombs at the harbor. I am the one who knew about the phosane. I am the one who met with King Ingram when Princess Celeste was present. I am also the one who knows the most about Pen's theory about Internment sinking and something needing to be done.

But I am also thinking of what Prince Azure said, about my talking to his sister. He didn't seem to trust his own father, and I certainly don't either, so I must limit the information I give him.

"I do not believe that King Ingram will destroy us," I

say. "Not right away, at least. Down on the ground he's having trouble utilizing the phosane. He doesn't know how to refine it. I suspect he's ruining it in the process, which may be why he's taking as much of it as he can fit into the jet and then coming back for more." I swallow hard, steady myself. It is very taxing just to be in the presence of this king, trying to be civil after all he has cost me. "Havalais has bombs. They could destroy Internment in an instant. But—they are at war with their own neighboring kingdom, Dastor. The people of Havalais are tired and in mourning. They have lost faith in King Ingram, and I believe—I believe King Ingram means to use Internment as a way to regain their hope. If he destroys us, there will be chaos. His own people might overthrow him. It isn't like it is up here. There are thousands more citizens. There are thousands of places to run to. A riot could destroy the kingdom."

The king folds his hands on the desk. "How refreshing," he says, "to hear from a young lady who is not so idyllic as my daughter. You may have a head for politics."

I don't want a head for politics. I want my family back. I want to be at peace, whatever "peace" may mean now that so many things have happened that can't be undone.

"What I propose, Your Highness, is that we offer to be that symbol of hope for King Ingram. If his people love us and value us, he won't destroy us. And perhaps, rather than showing him how to refine our fuel, we could give it to him in small doses."

"You mean work for him," King Furlow says. "Slave labor."

"It's the only suggestion I've been able to come up with," I say.

The king looks at me for a long while with an unreadable expression, and then he looks to Basil.

"You must be tired," the king says. "Rest up now. This building is rather old, I'm afraid, and there's no running water. Someone will be in with water basins for you to get cleaned up." He claps his hands together and there's an eerie sparkle in his eyes as he adds, "There will be a party for your return. King Ingram's men will be present, so you would be wise to read up on his notes."

I would rather set my hair on fire than attend another party by now, but when the patrolman opens the door to escort us to our chambers, we follow. Though we are at the top of the clock tower, it doesn't feel much different from the dungeon, as far as design is concerned. The hallway is lit by small windows and candles that burn in sconces. It's a modest kingdom, nothing worthy of comparison to King Ingram's castle.

"You'll be staying here," the patrolman says, leading Basil and me to a small room that is modestly furnished. The stone floor is covered by a large woven rug, and the walls have been plastered and painted white. A single window overlooks the woods that surround the clock tower, and I can see the train tracks in the distance.

Above the bed, a small, framed picture hangs on the wall, of a long-stemmed purple flower open in a ray of sunlight.

"The chamber pot is behind that screen in the corner, and there are clothes for you in the wardrobe. The seamstress will be by later to make any adjustments if they don't fit. In the meantime, do make yourselves comfortable."

He closes the door behind us, and I hear a lock sliding into place.

I spend the rest of the afternoon sitting on the window ledge, staring out. Basil paces and then eventually goes still. When I finally look away from the window, I find him propped up on the bed, asleep, with the stack of papers in his hand.

I don't believe he's gotten much sleep this past week. I have been so worried about what will become of Pen in my absence that I haven't paid Basil much attention. Not that he has complained. All patience and understanding, he has worried in silence as we prepared to return home.

Carefully, I sit on the bed and slide the papers from his hands, set them on the night table, and lie down beside him. I close my eyes and I listen to his soft measured breathing, and as my own exhaustion takes me over, I beg myself not to dream.

9

The seamstress comes sometime in the evening to adjust our clothes, but they are a perfect fit. Basil in pinstripes, me in a simple blue dress that laces up the back. It is the color of the sky on a clear day, and the roughness of the familiar sheep-shaving fabric tells me that I have grown too used to the satin linings and softer fabrics they make on the ground.

"Better the evil king you know, right?" I say to Basil when our seamstress has left.

"Morgan, that's treason," he whispers fiercely. "Be careful."

He's right. I hate it, but he's right. We're not safe to speak freely anywhere.

A patrolman arrives to take us to whatever horrible affair King Furlow has prepared for us, and Basil takes my arm. I find comfort in the strength of his hold, him ever sturdy at my side.

Our footsteps echo throughout the old stairwell, which smells faintly of mold. What a juxtaposition: two kings from two different nations, one living so modestly while the other is perched on a sparkling throne, each of them menacing in their way.

Basil and I walk in silence, afraid to speak before these guards.

When we reach the lobby, through the windows I can see that the sun has begun to melt at Internment's edge. I begin to think of Alice, coaxing my brother to take a break from his fretting and have some tea, maybe eat something. And Pen, in Thomas's charge, fighting for sobriety. And Judas, who kissed me once in the endless grass, who loses every girl he dares to care for.

Without them, and without a home to return to, Internment feels like another foreign city on that round planet below us. It isn't home anymore.

I wonder in silence about Celeste, who has yet to reveal herself to us. And her dying mother, whom Celeste flew to the ground to save. I wonder if either of them is still alive.

By the time we reach the bottom step, I can hear the people talking just outside the clock tower. I can smell— almost taste—the warm air. I hear songstresses still chirping; the insects hold no grudge about having their land torn up. Or maybe it's just that they don't have a choice.

When we step outside, the chatter stops. Glass lanterns hang on wires between tree branches, flickering and alight with flames. The crowd turns to watch us step out into the night air, and I recognize so many of their faces. People from my building, students from the academy. All of them watching us now with hope on their tired faces, as though we can save them with some great answer.

"There they are!" King Furlow cries, arms outstretched for us as he moves through the crowd. Panting from the effort, he stands beside us just outside the doorway. "Morgan Stockhour and Basil Cowl. The ones who have been to the ground."

The applause is nervous and contrived, conducted by the king's exuberant gesturing.

Around the perimeter of the crowd, I see patrolmen, and also soldiers in gray—King Ingram's men. As long as they're here, King Furlow will of course have to play along. So will Basil and I.

The party is a dull and dreary affair. King Furlow parades us about, forcing us to tell stories about the things we've seen on the ground—the mermaids, the elegors, the rain.

It's clear that this is just a political move King Furlow is playing with King Ingram's guards. Nothing of substance is being said, and the workers and students in the crowd all seem exhausted and afraid. Basil and I try to find his parents, but they aren't here.

An hour into the affair, King Furlow leaves us to mingle.

Basil and I hang back against the clock tower's outer wall, away from the crowd, to catch our breaths. One of the guards in gray grabs my arm, startling me.

"Ms. Stockhour," he says. Before he's even gotten the words out, Basil has stepped between us. The guard is unfazed. "Both of you, come with me," he says.

"Where are we going?" Basil says.

"There is someone who requested a private audience with you."

"Who is it?" I ask. Why would one of King Ingram's men be working for anyone on Internment?

But he doesn't answer, only starts walking behind the clock tower. Basil and I exchange glances, and then I make the decision to go ahead. Whatever it is, it can't be worse than this party and what King Furlow has planned for us next.

We're led through a small garden, and then the plum court, which I recognize from the night Pen and I escaped our makeshift dungeon prison.

I hear something rustling in the shrubs that frame the perimeter of the court, and then a voice says, "Morgan?" and my heart skips a beat. There at a distance, hidden up to her shoulders by greenery, is Princess Celeste.

I'm too stunned to speak for a moment, and then all I can get out is, "You're alive." She looks well. Unharmed. And she's smiling.

"I knew you'd return," she says. She nods to the guard in gray. "Thank you, Curtis." She looks back to me. "He's a friend of Nim's. A lot of the guards are. From what I hear, there's a lot of unrest on the ground."

I walk over to her, all the while battling a suspicion that something isn't right. Why is she hiding here? Why hasn't her father mentioned her, much less forced her to make an appearance at his party?

She stays on her own side of the shrub. "Things on the ground are a mess," I say quietly. "King Ingram has no idea how to use the phosane, and the people are upset. The king has set up a factory, and all it's good for are the fumes."

"What about the Pipers?" she says. "Nim?"

"They're doing fine," I say. "And Nim sent this along to give to you." I reach into my dress for the folded envelope. I didn't want to leave it up in my room, where anyone could come in and find it.

I hand the envelope to Celeste, and she presses it between both hands, as though she can feel Nim's words throbbing like a pulse. "Thank you," she says, and her eyes begin to water. She dabs at them with her lacy sleeve. "It's been difficult spending all these months apart. He must be so worried about me. I know he must be wondering how I am, but my father has made it impossible for me to get word to him about what's happening up here."

"Is your father using you for some political strategy? Because there has been no word about you on the ground for months. The jet comes and goes with more soil, but none of us have known whether you've been alive or dead."

"My father is trying to protect me," Celeste says. "He has always treated me as a sort of . . . well, a pet. Azure is the one who will inherit the throne, and I'm just a spare of sorts. So when I returned from the ground with talk of uniting Internment with Havalais, he didn't want to take me seriously. I told him that King Ingram wasn't to be trusted, but that I had a plan. Nim and I had a plan to unite our kingdoms, in a way that couldn't be disputed or overturned."

"A plan?" I say. "Nimble hasn't told us anything."

"I was rushed back home in such a hurry, we couldn't be sure that it would take. And it's too dangerous for me to send word with one of the guards. If the wrong person knows about it, I'll be killed and it will all be for nothing. All I can hope for now is that my brother will find a way to tell Nim for me. He deserves to know."

"I'm confused," I say. "What is this plan? What does Nim deserve to know?"

Celeste looks to the guard in gray, who does a sweeping glance of the perimeter. Then he nods at her.

Daintily, Celeste walks the length of the brush until she has found a clearing. She meets my eyes and for once she seems uncertain, nervous.

And then she steps out into the plum court, and I see her pregnant stomach.

My breath catches in my throat, and for an instant I think it's some sort of trick—a costume. But her worried stare as she gnaws on her lip tells me that this is quite real. I must sway a bit on my feet, because Basil puts his hand against my back to steady me.

"You and Nimble planned this?" I get out.

Her eyes brighten. "Don't you see? Whether it's a secret in his world or not, Nim is a prince. The king is his grandfather. And I'm a princess. Our child is going to be born of two worlds. The first ever! Just think of it."

"I . . ." There are so many questions, I scarcely know where to begin. "What does your betrothed have to say about all this?"

She waves her hand. "I told you, he doesn't care about me. My only worth to him is all for political gain. He came by to see me once, when I first returned, and I suspect my father arranged the entire thing for show, just so the kingdom would believe he was worried about me. But he doesn't know about this."

I'm trying not to stare. It's just that I've never seen anyone pregnant as young as she is. And out of the queue, at that. "But your father didn't arrange for you to have a termination procedure?" The words are sour on my tongue. That's what would have happened to anyone else.

"I have a good understanding of how these things go," Celeste says, seeming quite proud of herself. "I kept it a secret for as long as I could. Months. By the time he caught on, it was too late to do anything about it. Around the fourth month or so, there are too many risks. He was livid, of course, but he doesn't want me to be killed. Oh, Morgan, you look so pensive."

"I'm surprised," I amend. Though, really, should I be? This is exactly the sort of reckless plan she would come up with. I'm only shocked that Nim—cool, practical, level-headed Nim—would agree to it.

She reaches forward and grabs my hand. She's still holding Nim's envelope, and something about it seems to have energized her anew. "There will be more. You should go back to the party before anyone knows you're missing, but

I'll visit you as soon as I can—tonight if I can manage it. I'm so glad you're the one King Ingram sent back."

She's gone before I can think of anything else to say to her.

The guard in gray brings us back to the party. He leans between Basil and me. "There are those of us who are on your side," he says. And then he's gone.

I wish Pen were here. Undoubtedly she would say the wrong thing about Celeste's situation. The unkind thing. She would fill this silence with words, easily. That's just one of her many talents.

But she isn't here, and I'm left to face my own thoughts about it, and they frighten me. My anger frightens me.

The party is over and the door has been closed behind us. Basil lights the oil lamp and sits on the edge of the window and watches me.

I pace.

"Are you all right?" he says.

"Yes," I say. "No."

"Tell me," he says.

If Pen were here, she'd speak for me. I wouldn't have to say it. "I have no right to be angry," I confess. "It isn't my decision. Maybe she's got a coherent plan this time."

"But you are angry," Basil says.

I drop onto the edge of the bed. "Alice didn't get to keep her baby," I say, and I keep my voice low in case anyone might overhear. We've surely got guards keeping watch over us somewhere. "I saw what that did to her, and to Lex. It ruined their lives, and the king knew it would, but he didn't care. But Celeste can do as she pleases because she's a princess?"

My hands are shaking. I lock my fingers together and press them into my lap.

"Would you feel better if the king had forced her to terminate it?" Basil asks, and he knows me well enough to already know my answer. He just wants me to admit it.

"No, that isn't it. I just think it's unfair is all." I think back on what Celeste told me about the attraction camps, how scared she was that her brother might end up there if the king found out. I thought that being prince and princess didn't immunize them to our world's rules. But Celeste, cleverly and foolishly, slipped through somehow. Just this one time. I hate the unfairness of it, and I hate that, in spite of everything, it gives me hope. "I don't want her to terminate it," I say. "But I didn't want Alice to have to, either. And she's hardly the only one. My brother told me that there were lots of procedures when he was a medical student. Lots of people who didn't want to."

Basil is quiet for a long while, and then he gets up and he makes his way over to the bed. He sits beside me, stares down at my hands that are so tightly clinging to each other that my knuckles are white.

"Lots of people would find it unfair that she's having a baby out of queue," he says. "Some might be as angry as you are, but others might be less understanding. Don't you think there are even some out there who might want to terminate it themselves?"

I wince. I know he's right. "The whole point of the queue is to keep things fair," I say, repeating something I've heard countless times in class. "To abate jealousy. I do think there are people who would want to kill it—kill her if they had to. And with things being what they are, people are more likely to snap."

"Which is why the king is hiding her from the city," Basil says.

I nod. "The prince told me to find her when I returned home. Whatever her plan is, she needs my help. And I will help. For Internment, and to make sure she's safe. It's just . . . unfair."

"I know," Basil says. He puts his arm around me, and I lean against him. "Prince Azure knew what he was doing when he convinced King Ingram to send you back home. He knew you'd be just the one to help."

"What a foolish idea," I say. "Pen is the genius. Why me?"

"Pen is a logical thinker and a problem solver," he agrees. "But you've got a cooler head. You care about people."

"I've been told I'm diplomatic," I say, mockingly.

"You are," he says. "It's one of my favorite things about you. Don't undersell yourself. You're here to do something important."

"Oh yeah?" I look at him, and I'm startled by the

sincerity in his eyes. "And just what is that?"

He tucks a bit of stray hair behind my ear. "I don't know," he says. "We'll see." There's a bit of a grin tugging at the corner of his lips. He's worn this expression since we were children, whenever he had something kind to say to me.

"I don't understand you," I say, my voice nearly a whisper. "I cause you nothing but trouble, but still, you just— love me. Why?"

He tucks my hair back again, and this time he keeps his hand at my cheek. "Don't know," he says. "I'm out of my mind, I guess."

I lean closer. "Me too," I say, and I see his eyes close an instant before mine, and then I'm kissing him.

I can feel the rumble of the jet in my bones, and smell the fresh cut grass that spluttered from the blades on the ground, and I can hear the songstresses chirping outside the open window. He's everywhere and nowhere, his fingers moving down the length of my arm.

I forget about Princess Celeste and Prince Azure and the painfully desperate eyes of the people at that party. I forget about untrustworthy kings and spinning round planets, and I know that of all the places, and of all the people in this world and the one below, I am right where I'm meant to be.

Somehow, one of his hands has made it to my thigh, and I feel the fabric of my dress moving up and up as he knots the fabric in his fist.

"Basil?"

He kisses my jaw, and then right under my ear. "What?"

"I want to be honest with you." My dress has reached my hip and I roll my head back. He kisses my neck, and I wrap my arms around his neck to draw him nearer still. And suddenly I'm afraid to speak, afraid to ruin whatever has brought us to this moment. We have both lost so much and stand to lose so much more, but we still have each other, and maybe that's the only thing left that's certain.

"Honest about what?" He draws back just enough to look at my face. "Is this too much? Do you want to stop?"

"No," I say. "No, I want this. But you might not, after you know what I've done."

His hand is still on my thigh, and I'm sorry that I've said anything, that I may have put a halt to things. But no, he should know the truth. "I kissed Judas," I say. "Or—he kissed me, but I didn't stop it."

It's as though he has just absorbed a punch. His eyes are dark. "When?"

"Months ago, on the ground, right before the jet took off for the first time." My skin feels cold where he was kissing me.

"Do you love him?" Basil asks.

"No." I shake my head. "And he doesn't love me. That's not what it was."

He sits back, away from me. "What was it, then?"

"I don't know," I say. "It isn't about love on the ground. People our age just don't think that way. It's all about—about just being in the moment."

"Yes, I've been to the ground," he says. "I know that they all live without consequences down there. I've seen how that kingdom is run. But I assumed we were different."

"Better, you mean."

"Yes, better. I thought our way was better. I thought you agreed."

"We aren't better than anyone, Basil. Look at our king. He's no better than theirs."

"I'm not talking about kings," he says, and his voice is frighteningly low. He's never been so angry with me. "I'm talking about you and me."

"You asked me if I wanted to take off my ring," I remind him. "You said, 'You can call what we have a betrothal, or not, but I'll still be here.'"

I know he remembers. It was after the bombing at the harbor, and I'd just said I loved him as we walked past the charred remains of Nim's car at the fire altar.

"You said it," I tell him, desperate to wipe that look of pain from his face. "You said you'd still be here."

He stands and paces to the window. Maybe he'd walk away if he thought he could get out the door without being accosted by guards. "You didn't tell me for months. Part of you must have wanted him. Even if it was just one kiss, he's lived on in your mind, in secret, for all these months. You must have been replaying it over and over."

He knows me better than anyone else could. Better than even Judas could. And he's right. My knees are shaking. "You're right," I confess. "All my life I've known what to expect. Lex couldn't take it. He went too close to the edge, and even after I saw what happened to him, even after all that pain he suffered, I was jealous, because he did something brave. He broke an important rule that our world had laid out for him. Not a lot of people do that. I wanted to do that, and I was afraid. Even after we left Internment, I told Pen over and over that I was going to marry you, and I tried to keep her from drinking too much, and I was polite, and I was still living my life according to these rules."

My voice cracks. "And then Judas kissed me. That was the one thing I never expected to happen; I never saw myself kissing someone other than you. I didn't think I was capable of something like that. It surprised me that I was. And yes, I wanted it for myself. Not Judas, not even the kiss, but the bravery of it. "

"Well, I'm truly glad you got to experience your rebel moment," Basil says bitterly.

"I wanted to share it with you," I say. "Basil, please. I want you to understand."

"You can't share it with me," he cries, turning to face me. "That's the whole point!"

I look at my lap. Tears are blurring my vision. "I'm sorry." I shake my head. "I can't undo it."

"Would you even want to?" he asks.

After a long pause, I whisper, "No."

"Well, at least you're still being honest."

He turns back to face the window, and the silence between us is so painful, I can't stand it. I know that he's right to be angry, but I can't undo that kiss with Judas. I can't even bring myself to regret it.

I stare at the door and I contemplate using it. I know I

can't go far. But maybe I could just sit on the other side of it, put some distance between us.

Ultimately I'm not brave enough to move. I only sit on the edge of the bed, tears blurring my view of the floor, as the silence goes on.

I don't know how long it is before a soft knock at the door jars me from my thoughts. "Morgan?" Celeste whispers. The door creaks open and she peers into the room. "Oh, I'm so glad you're still awake. I saw the light under the door."

She has no idea what sort of tension she's walking into. Basil doesn't move from the window as she comes in and sits on the bed. She sinks back against her arms with a groan. "I've never realized what a chore all these stairs are, all my life running up and down them. Some of the newer buildings have lifts, but Papa refuses to install one here. He says it will ruin the structural integrity or some such."

She's barefoot, and with a glance I can see how purpled and swollen her feet are.

"Where do you sleep?" I ask.

"Our apartment is up one more flight, on the top floor," she says. "It's quite nice, actually. Mother has been too ill to leave for a year now, but she's got everything she needs up there. I've hardly been able to come down myself. I can't tell you what an ordeal it was coming back up after I met you in the plum court." She waves her hand over her head. "But I didn't come here to complain." She grabs my hands. "You've seen my brother, yes? How is he?"

"Travel agrees with him," I say.

"He wasn't happy about being made to go to the ground," Celeste says. "He's convinced that being down there so long has caused me to go mad. But as I'm sure you gathered, King Ingram forced my father's hand. He needs a prisoner. That's how he works."

"Isn't your father worried about your brother?" I say.

"Well—yes," Celeste says. "But the way he sees it, Azure is next in line to be king. And it's a king's duty to protect his kingdom. He should be willing to put himself in a bit of peril if that's what Internment needs." She squeezes my hand. "But Az and I aren't planning to do things our father's way. We've got a plan that we know he'd never go for."

"The baby, you mean," I say.

She pats her stomach. "The baby is more of a long term plan. It'll be born of two worlds and inherit both thrones, but not anytime soon. No. In the short term, before he left, my brother and I spoke with several of the guards and patrolmen. We learned which ones were to be trusted. We've been gathering intelligence about King Ingram and the ground. In fact, that letter from Nimble was stuffed with information about King Ingram's failed attempts to refine the phosane."

"I thought it would be all love letters," I say.

"Well, yes." She grins. "There was a bit of that, too. But that's neither here nor there." She turns her head to Basil, who has been listening in silence. "This isn't all girl talk, you know. Come over and join us."

Without a word he pulls up the footstool and sits across from us. He doesn't meet my eyes.

"You've come at just the right time," Celeste tells us. "As much as I can trust a few of the patrolmen and guards, I can't exactly go broadcasting my condition to the city. When my condition became . . . well, more obvious, my brother began doing all the speaking with the engineers. But in his absence, it'll be your turn."

"You want Basil and me to speak to engineers?" I say.

"Yes. Well, one engineer. He's head honcho over at the glasslands and you'll want to update him about what's going on with the ground. My father will send you there on some frivolous pretense of giving them a morale boost. He doesn't expect you to accomplish anything—it's all so the guards will have something positive to report back to King Ingram. But really, I've already arranged for you to speak to the head engineer. He'll tell you his plans, and then you'll report back to me." She bounces in her seat, and I wish I had the optimism to mimic her enthusiasm. "It's all very covert."

There's a sick feeling in my stomach, and I know the answer even before I ask. "Who is the head engineer?" There are several engineers, but there's one in particular who seems to be in charge of things, and whom I know to be brilliant, the way that his daughter is brilliant.

"That's the best part," Celeste says. "You've been acquainted. The head engineer is Nolan Atmus—Pen's father. He's a genius, of course. Several years ago he played a key role in the refining system that Internment uses to this day. He found a way to mine our soil more efficiently, so that we no longer need steam power. I can see now where that girl gets her brains, but I wish some of his diplomacy had rubbed off on her."

"Diplomacy," I echo hollowly.

Basil catches my grim tone, even if Celeste doesn't, and he raises a brow at me but says nothing.

"Listen to me going on," Celeste says. "I swear I haven't been this chatty all these months. Things up here have been looking rather grim." She smiles, and I can see how worn she truly is. "It's so good to have you back." She gives me a hug before she leaves. "Get some sleep. Tomorrow will be a big day."

The door closes, and I can hear her shuffling up the steps. Every little sound carries within all these stone walls.

Basil is watching me. I told him about Judas, the secret that's been nagging at me for months. But I won't tell him about Pen's father and the monster he truly is; that secret is not mine to tell.

"I'm going to sleep" is all I say. I move to the changing screen and change into the nightgown that's been laid out for me. I leave the dress rumpled on the floor, and without another word I climb into bed and close my eyes.

It's a long while before I feel the weight of Basil getting into the bed beside me. He turns off the oil lamp.

We maintain our distance, and eventually, somehow, I'm able to fall asleep.

11

All morning, I think about Alice. I've known her since the day I was born, and she has been in love with my brother all that time. Miraculously. He isn't an easy person to love, and I know that. I've seen the way that they argue, and it's always his fault, but it always gets fixed.

I've never fought with Basil. We have, despite our flaws, found it easy to love each other.

Until now.

I don't know how to fix this. I need Alice to tell me what to do when one of us has broken something this important.

Basil and I don't speak. Celeste is the one to bring us a tray of breakfast—fresh fruits and bread—and she is all chatter about the day's plans. She can't wait for us to speak to Nolan Atmus, the head engineer over at the glasslands. Maybe we'll even get a tour, she says. "That's a rare privilege," she says. "My brother and I have seen it, of course, but for a normal citizen it's a high honor. You're so lucky!"

Pen has seen the inside of the glasslands, but I don't say that.

Celeste slips a stack of folded papers into my hand. "Keep these hidden. Do you understand? They're for Nolan Atmus's eyes only. Top secret information from Nim."

I tuck the papers into my dress pocket.

After breakfast, a patrolman comes to our room to take us to the glasslands at King Furlow's request, just as Celeste predicted. He stops Basil in the doorway. "The invitation has been extended only to Ms. Stockhour.".

"I'm sure my invitation was implied," Basil says with uncharacteristic boldness. "We go everywhere together."

"King Furlow has requested a private audience with you," the patrolman says. "Someone will be along to escort you shortly."

Basil and I exchange glances. He seems worried. "It'll be fine," I tell him. It's the first thing spoken between us in hours, and my voice sounds strange.

He nods.

There are two more patrolmen and a guard in gray waiting for me when I step outside the clock tower. I suppose they think I'll run away, but it isn't as though I have many options. Maybe they think I'll fling myself over the edge and hope for death.

Or maybe they aren't worried about what I'll do, but rather what someone might mean to do to me.

I'm led to a shuttle, which is empty aside from the guards

and me. We drive over grass, away from the train tracks, and through the windows I can see that the city itself has changed. There aren't many people, and the shops appear to be closed. I wonder if children are in class, or if they've all been forced to mine for sunstone as well.

The glasslands appear in the distance, and the shuttle slows to a stop.

"Up," one of the patrolmen tells me. I recognize him. After the fire at the flower shop, he was assigned to my building. I remember him holding open the door for Pen and me, telling us to be safe.

But if he recognizes me, he gives no sign. And without Celeste here, I don't know whether he's one of the patrolmen to be trusted.

I've never been this close to the glasslands before. I can see the beveled edges of the panes of glass, see the bolts holding the panels in place. The fence that surrounds the area is buzzing like a swarm of bramble flies, making my skin prickle.

Surrounded by a cloud of guards, I approach a gate where patrolmen seem to be waiting for us. "Ms. Stockhour?" one of them asks me.

I nod.

"Come with me," the patrolman says. And to the others, "None of you are permitted. You may wait for her here if you wish. This is the only entrance or exit, so there's no need to worry about an escape."

Escape? I could laugh. Where would I go? I suppose I could be like Judas and roam the wilderness for a few days, never staying in one place long enough to get caught. Only, this time there's no metal bird waiting for me underground.

The guard in gray tries to protest. He wants to see what's on the other side of this fence. But if there's one thing that makes the people of Internment bold, it's protecting our fuel source. Otherwise, what's to stop King Ingram from stripping us of our resources and blowing us right out of the sky?

I'm led inside by the patrolman from the gate. Once we have put some distance between ourselves and the others, he says in a low voice, "What is it like? On the ground? I've heard that there are thousands of kingdoms and that they shoot at each other for fun."

"You're not too far off," I say. Now that I've seen the ground, I'm no longer awestruck by the thought of it. Sometimes I even wish I could go back in time to before I left Internment. But then I remember that the king murdered my mother and quite possibly my father as well, and that I didn't have a choice.

"Are they barbarians down there?" the patrolman asks.

"People are people, regardless of where they are," I say. It isn't a yes or a no, because I don't have the answer. I used to think I did. I used to think that by living in the sky I had evaded some vengeful god's curse. I used to think that the ground was mysterious and intriguing. But as it stands, I've lost any sense of enchantment for either place.

"Mr. Atmus has been looking forward to meeting with you," the patrolman says. And again he lowers his voice. "He's going to help you."

"Is he?" I say. I hope my face doesn't betray the nausea I'm starting to feel, not only at the thought of facing Pen's father, but as a result of all the constant humming in this place. And there's so much heat. This place is meant to absorb the sunlight, and I suppose it stands to reason that it absorbs a lot of heat as well.

And despite everything, I am in awe of what I see. It's as though we are walking in a giant gemstone, or a betrothal band.

I see a few men and women working in the distance, taking notes, fiddling with knobs and steering wheels that are built right into the glass. Sun engineers. Internment's elite, the ones who give us the fuel for our trains and our lights.

When we've reached what looks to be the center of the glasslands, I see a small building made of brick, scarcely bigger than a water room, with a door but no windows. There's a glowing red lightbulb, and a sign that cautions people not to enter while the red light is on.

The patrolman steps forward and knocks on the door. "Sir?" he says. "You told me to inform you when Ms. Stockhour was here."

There's a long pause, and I hear shuffling within the building, the clink of something metal. And then the door swings open.

Pen's father stands in the doorway, wearing a denim jumpsuit, just like many of the other sun engineers. He looks from the patrolman to me with a distracted, almost deranged, stare that I know all too well. I hate how much he reminds me of Pen. She's even got his smile.

"Morgan!" he says, and makes room for me. "I've been waiting for you. Come in, come in." And then, to the patrolman, "Wait outside. See that no one disturbs us."

I will myself not to tremble. Whether the feeling is from hatred or fear, I can't tell. I don't want to be alone with him. I don't trust him, but more important, I don't trust myself. I'd like to take that pencil that's tucked behind his ear and stab him in the jugular.

But it's because of Pen that I don't. If I killed her father, I would be arrested, probably executed, and what good would that do her? And besides, we made a promise to keep ourselves safe and alive so that we'll see each other again.

I force a smile and follow him into the brick building. The door closes behind us, but despite being windowless, this tiny room is filled with lights. There's a wall made up entirely of glowing buttons in a gradient of colors. On an adjacent wall there's a small, flickering screen that shows a gray, aerial image of the glasslands.

"Sit, sit," he says, gesturing to two wooden stools beside the wall of buttons, next to a desk littered with papers, maps, and pencils. "I know it isn't very much to look at. It certainly isn't as spectacular as the rest of the glasslands. But it's the only place on Internment where I feel confident no one will hear us."

That hardly puts me at ease. Is this the place where he lured Pen when she was a child? Is this where it all started?

I fold my arms across my stomach and I wish desperately that Basil were here. Suddenly the air feels very warm.

"First things first." He runs his hand through his blond hair. "How is Margaret? Her mother and I have been beside ourselves all these months. When I heard that the king of the ground was sending someone back home, I had hoped she would be in the group."

He is the only one to call Pen by the name she was born with. Margaret. She's always hated that name with a vitriol I never understood until now.

"She's doing well," I say.

"Is she truly?" he says. "I know that she can be sort of . . ." He trails off. "I know that she takes after her mother, in some regards."

"The ground has suited her," I say.

I see a bit of her in his smile, and I force myself to look at the papers on the table instead. "What are all these?" I ask.

"Boring paperwork, I'm afraid. We gather daily reports from all posts to ensure that things are running smoothly. King Furlow is very particular about this place. Without electricity, the whole city would fall into chaos. Although I suppose an argument could be made that it's in sort of a chaotic state right now."

He leans forward on his knees, closer to me.

"What I really need from you is information about the ground. The princess said that you would be coming back with something for me."

"I suppose she means this," I say, and hand him the stack of papers from my dress pocket.

He unfolds the top page and reads it, and his eyes

brighten. "It's as I thought," he says. "That king down there on the ground hasn't got a clue what to do with our sunstone. His people are about ready to overthrow him."

"That's what I gather," I say. "So what are you planning to do?"

"Oh, let it happen, of course. We hardly need to concern ourselves with that greedy world down there. No, when it comes to the ground, we just wait for King Ingram to be assassinated. Believe me, it will happen. He thinks that he's holding Prince Azure as his hostage, but I guarantee that the prince has got a plan up his sleeve. I spoke to him myself before he left."

"But those notes are from Nimble Piper. He's the son of one of King Ingram's advisers." He's also King Ingram's grandson, but I don't say that, as I'm not sure whether Celeste has shared this with anyone up here. "You're telling me Nimble is part of a plan to assassinate his own king?"

Nolan Atmus slaps the papers against his knee in triumph. "That's what I'm saying. You seem surprised."

"I suppose it does make sense," I say. Murder hardly seems like something Nim would go for; he's so peaceful by nature. But then I think of the lost look in his eyes in the weeks following the bombing, after he'd buried his only brother and burned an offering to save Birdie. Maybe he's still trying to save her, and his other sisters too, from a king who would hurt them a thousand times over for his own gain.

"If that's Nimble's plan, I'm okay with it," I say. "He knows what he's doing."

"That's what the princess said as well. She seems to have a lot of faith in his politics. Splendid. Now we can discuss what to do while we're up here in the sky."

I can smell whatever redolence he's wearing. I smelled it every time I was in Pen's apartment. He has been everywhere all her life, and somehow I never noticed. He was always polite to me, pleasant. Much like the way he is now. How did I never see him for what he really is?

"For now," he says, "you should go along with King Furlow's plans. I suspect he'll parade you around for a bit. Let King Furlow's men have the illusion that you are trying to convince all of them down on the ground to aid his dying little kingdom. Let him watch your every move and believe you're under his thumb."

"That's it?" I say. "Just wait?"

"Just wait," he says. "I suspect King Ingram will be dead by the end of the month."

I walk back to the shuttle in a daze. I knew that Nimble would have some plan brewing, but murdering his own grandfather? Now I see why he was so adamant about my delivering that envelope to Celeste directly.

The shuttle begins to move.

I wonder how he'll do it. Will he stage an accident? Will he march up to the palace and cut the king's throat?

I wonder if Birdie knows. I think, after everything, she would want to help. It took weeks for her to emerge from her coma, and even longer for her to regain awareness of her surroundings. When she learned that Riles was gone,

I worried that the news would destroy her. She cried for days. She said that she hated the king, and her father too. Nim tried to quiet her, but only because he didn't want anyone to overhear her spouting treason.

I understand. My king killed someone that I love, too. I wouldn't object to someone killing him either. Maybe that's a good plan. Kill both kings and just start over.

The shuttle comes to a stop. I'm led back into the clock tower, smiling at the thought of King Ingram and King Furlow both dead. Justice.

I feel guilty for this thought when I see Celeste. Vile or not, King Furlow is still her father, and I know that she loves him, in her way.

She closes my bedroom door behind her, and her eyes are bright. "So?" she says. "Did you meet with Nolan Atmus?"

"Yes," I say. "He told me we're waiting to hear about King Ingram."

Celeste sits on the edge of the bed beside me. "Oh good," she says. "We can't discuss it here. You understand. For your own safety, it's best we don't talk about it in great detail." She giggles giddily. "But it will all work out, won't it? And I was so happy to hear from Nim and know that he was willing to help. Our child is going to be an heir to two kingdoms one day. Just think of it."

"Your plan for King Ingram seems . . . drastic," I say. "But perhaps necessary."

"There are two kingdoms at stake," she says. "Desperate times." She puts her hand on mine. "Listen, Morgan.

You've seen how brutal things can get on the ground. All that land, all that greed. There are two kingdoms at war over a fuel source that we offer to people on Internment for free. Money talks down there. It's terrible. And I tried to reason with King Ingram; you know that I did. But the truth is that he has no regard for anyone's life, not even the people in his own kingdom. If we let him go on, he'll strip Internment of its resources and then do away with us all if it suits him."

"I know," I say. "I do know that. But—" I cut myself off and think better of what I was about to say.

But Celeste already knows. "You're going to say that my father is the same way."

"What I was going to say is that I imagine every king is that way."

She gives me a weak smile. "I don't blame you if you hate my father, and certainly you're smart not to trust him. I don't always trust him myself. It's hard knowing that my father would send Az off to one of those torturous attraction camps if he knew the truth. And he would have made me have a termination procedure if he'd known about this baby in time to stop it." She takes a deep breath, composing herself. "But he means to do right by his kingdom. He loves Internment. He doesn't pose a threat to the city."

Maybe not the whole city, but certainly to those he's killed.

"Morgan," she says. All the joy and lightheartedness have left her tone. "I know what my father did to your family. I'm not asking you to forgive him. I'm not asking you to trust him. But you've got me on your side, and I promise that no harm will come to you or Basil. You trust me, don't you?"

"Yes," I say, and it's the truth. I do trust her. But I don't believe she understands everything that her father is capable of, and I don't believe she can truly give me the protection she's promising.

"Good." She pats my knee. "Now all we do is wait for chaos to break out."

"How will we know?" I say. "Once it's happened. How will word get to us?"

"Before he left, Azure said he'd work with Nim." She grins, and leans close to me, her voice barely a whisper. "They're going to kill the king, and before anyone can know what's happened, they'll have the pilot fly my brother back to the sky."

"But what about the others?" I say, panic bubbling up in my stomach. "What about my brother and his wife? Pen? Judas and Amy?"

"I'm sure Az will try to bring them along."

"Try?" I say. "Try? You can't very well kill King Ingram and then leave them behind. They could be killed in retaliation to prove some sort of point. Or arrested, and who knows what. You don't know what could become of them!"

"Lower your voice," she hisses. "I know how my brother can come across sometimes, but he isn't completely without a heart. He will do all he can to protect them."

"What if he can't?" I stand and pace to the window and back, my heart thudding.

"Morgan, if it does come to that, I think you need to be honest. Your brother was a jumper, and he and his wife ultimately took part in a plan to betray the government and escape the city. Judas is a fugitive. Pen—well, she'd do anything to keep Internment safe. I may not know a lot about her, but I do know that."

She's right. "What's your point?" I say.

"Morgan, sit down. Be calm. Think about it. If they can't be saved, don't you think they would find a way to be at peace with it? Don't you think they would die for Internment?"

"That can't be part of your plan," I say. My mind is going into such a panic that my vision is clouding. "You can't just sacrifice them like that."

"I've already told you that my brother will do all he can to save them."

"You don't sound too certain."

"Nothing is ever certain."

"You don't sound certain enough."

She frowns. "It was the only way. I hope that you can see that. My brother is down there, too. And the father of my child. They're at risk as much as everyone you care about. I'm worried. Do you think I'm not worried? But worry doesn't help. We've got to think positively. Have some faith."

"Faith," I echo miserably. "What choice do I have now?"

"That's the spirit," she says, undeterred by my glare. Pen once accused me of having a delusional sense of optimism, but the princess has certainly surpassed me there.

"I have to return to my mother," she says. "It's almost time for her lunch, and if I'm not there when she wakes up, she'll worry." She stands, and puts her hands on my shoulders. "King Ingram promised he would help her, you know. He promised me that he would fly her down to that big bright hospital in Havalais and the doctors there would make her better. He lied about that, and now she may not have much time left. So you see, we've all lost something in this mess, haven't we?"

I don't know what to say to that, but she doesn't seem to require a response. She drops her hands from my shoulders, and she leaves me with that.

And all I'm left to do is hope.

Basil returns shortly after the arrival of our lunch cart. He seems troubled, but he won't tell me what happened during his meeting with the king. Instead, he wants to know what happened at the glasslands. In whispers, I tell him everything. The plan to let Havalais murder King Ingram, Prince Azure's intention of returning on the jet, the potential danger to everyone from Internment. "She had the audacity to tell me that Pen and my brother would be willing to die for the cause."

"Pen would be," Basil admits. "You know she'd do anything to protect Internment."

"You're not helping."

"I'm sorry," he says. "I agree with you. It's terrible. But, in a way, it's the only plan that's got a shot at working. If King Ingram is dead, maybe Internment will be safe."

"Safe may be asking for too much," I say. "We're never going to be safe. We probably never were safe, not even before all this. We only thought we were."

He stares distractedly at his plate.

"Are you going to tell me what you and King Furlow talked about?"

He shakes his head. "It was nothing important. More rambling about what's expected of us in the coming days. That's all."

"Basil, I don't think I can survive all of this if we're going to be mad at each other. I can't stand the thought of fighting with you."

"I don't want to fight, either," he says. "I just can't get the image out of my head. And don't tell me it didn't mean anything; clearly it did, or you would have told me sooner. But it happened. It's done."

"It's done," I agree. "He came by to say good-bye to me before I left, and I told him that you were a part of me. I told him that I couldn't betray you again. I suppose that may not be worth much to you now, but—"

"It's worth a lot," Basil says.

"I meant it."

"I know."

He stares at his plate, forces himself to eat one of the grapes. When he looks up again, he offers me a smile, and I know that he wants to let this be the end of it. But I also know that something has changed between us. I don't know what it means, but I know it can't be undone.

The rest of the afternoon is a blur. The king sends us out

to the field where our jet first landed. A patrolman tells us about the sunstone mining process, but his words are very rehearsed. The guards in gray are listening to everything we say.

It isn't until after dinner, when the sun has just set, that Basil and I are granted a few moments of reprieve. We walk a narrow dirt path in the garden behind the clock tower. There are guards and patrolmen along the way, but if I ignore them, it feels a bit like Basil and I are alone.

"You've been wearing that worried expression all day," I tell him. "Is it because of what we talked about?"

"No," he says, and in a show of devotion he takes my hand. "No, it has nothing to do with that."

"Well, are you going to tell me? I was never good at guessing games."

He hesitates. "If I don't, you'll find out soon enough. May as well hear it from me."

"Hear what?"

He stops our walking, and as I face him, he takes my other hand. "I've loved you my whole life," he says. "Even when we were children, before 'love' was the word I'd use to describe it. And you were always running over the boundary lines, wherever we were. If there was a line to the shuttle, you had to move ahead. If there was a butterfly, you had to run after it and see where it was flying. And as we got older, your boundaries broadened. I've always sensed your need to wander."

I don't know that this is appropriate talk with patrol-men in such proximity, but I don't try to stop him.

Somehow I know that what he's trying to say is big, and I want to hear it.

"You loved to explore," he says. "So I wanted that for you. It doesn't surprise me at all that you found a way to the ground." He squeezes my hands. "I love that about you; you have to know that. I've never wanted to be the thing that held you in place."

"Of course you haven't. Basil, what are you trying to say?"

"This morning, when I spoke to King Furlow, he told me that our return to Internment may or may not be permanent, but he emphasized how important it is for us to give our people hope. And the way he means to do that is to make examples of us. Show everyone that even though we went to the ground and came back, and even though all of this mining is going on, things can be normal. They can turn out happily."

I search his face. I can see sweat forming at his temples. "Turn out happily?" I say.

"In marriage," he says. "King Furlow wants us to get married."

My mouth is dry and I can't feel my heart beating. I am hollow. "When?" My voice feels far away.

"In another week, on the first of September. He wants to hold a big ceremony."

"But there's never a big ceremony for weddings," I say, though none of this feels real. When Alice and Lex were married, I think he gave her a bouquet of flowers, and we had a small party for them in our apartment, but weddings happen often enough, and it would be impractical to turn them into a big affair.

"He says I'll get to see my parents and Leland there," he says lamely.

I nod. "Good. That's—that's good."

He frowns. "Morgan, if you don't want to, maybe we can reason with him."

"No," I say, because we both know there is no reasoning with King Furlow, and I don't want Basil getting killed because of me. "No, I think we should do it."

"Really?"

"It isn't as though we weren't going to get married eventually anyway," I say practically. "It'll be a little sooner than we expected, is all."

He tries to smile, and I can see how frightened he is. Of the king. Of this new plan. Of everything.

"I'm only sorry Pen can't be there," I say. "When she finds out I got married without her, she's going to throw a fit of epic proportions." When I laugh, Basil laughs too, both of us trying to make light of this bizarre situation.

All around us, the stars are bright and still in their sky.

I don't allow myself to wonder what's happening on the ground below our floating city. I can't afford the pain.

12

Celeste is surprisingly sympathetic when I tell her about the wedding. She tells me that I can pick any of her long season dresses and the seamstress will alter it to fit me. She can't allow me into her family's private apartment upstairs, but she sends the seamstress down with armfuls of dresses for me to choose from. Celeste shoos Basil from the room and sends him down to the garden with a patrolman.

"This is girl stuff," she tells him. "It wouldn't interest you."

He gives me a worried look but I nod, and he allows the patrolman to lead him away.

I drop onto the stool by the bed, deflated.

"He really is a sweet boy," Celeste tells me. "You should see the mess that I'm betrothed to. He has an unusual nose, you know, and I didn't quite know how to describe it until we got to the ground and I saw all those birds up close. Wouldn't you know it, his nose is exactly like a beak."

Despite everything, I laugh. "Now you sound like Pen," I say. "She's always saying things like that about Thomas, even if none of them are true."

"Oh, believe me, it's true," Celeste says, and holds up a paisley pink dress that only a girl with her confidence could ever pull off. "Not that his nose is the real problem. It's who he is. He's truly one of the most awful people I've ever encountered. Cocky, self-serving, and the way he looks at me—like I'm a buffet. Just the thought of being married to him makes me shudder."

"What does your father say?"

"Papa adores him," Celeste says. "His mother and father are both doctors, very motivated. Apparently they were both at the top of their class as students. And Papa was so impressed with the pair of them that he selected them from dozens of other couples in the queue to birth my future husband. It was sealed before the boy was even conceived, and months before I was born."

She holds up a bright green dress the color of grass. "Here, try this one on." As I move to the changing screen, she goes on. "I guess it went to his head, knowing that his sole purpose in the world was to marry the princess of Internment. Maybe he would have grown up to be a decent person if he hadn't had his destiny sealed, but I doubt it. And anyway, who cares? I'm not going to marry him now."

"What's to stop your father from claiming the baby is your betrothed's?" I say.

"He won't do that," Celeste says. "I won't let him. He won't have his way, not about this. Oh! Come into the sunlight. That looks so pretty on you. But it clashes with your eyes. I'm sure I have something with more blue in this pile somewhere. . . ."

"Do you have anything white?" I say.

"Lots of white. And pure white, too. Not that cream or beige stuff everyone else wears."

"Birdie told me that people wear white when they get married on the ground," I say.

Celeste begins plucking choice dresses from her collection and making a separate pile. There are a dozen of them, at least. Some with fake feathers, others with fluffy petticoats, others simple with straight hems. "I think a ground wedding would be nice," Celeste says. "Nim says that when we get married, we won't have to go to a church. That's what's popular down there—churches. But he says we can get married in a garden if I like, or on the ferry."

"Celeste." I sit on the edge of the bed and stare at the fabric of all the dresses. "Be honest with me for a minute. Are we really going to make it back to the ground? Can you say that with any certainty?"

"Not with any certainty," Celeste says. "One can never promise that. There could be a fatal virus pandemic tomorrow. Internment could fall out of the sky. The sun could explode. Nothing is certain."

"Is it probable, then?"

She heaves a deep breath, lays her dress down, and looks at me. "Here is what I believe. You will marry Basil in a few days, and maybe it will be sooner than both of you expected, but you'll treat each other well, and you'll be happy. Nim will find a way to"—she lowers her voice to a whisper—"kill that awful king of his." She clears her throat. "And then he will find his way back to me. He'll supersede his father and take over as the new king of Havalais; believe me, nobody wants his father in charge. They blame him for all of King Ingram's bad decisions."

"What happens then?" I ask. I'm trying to make her see that it may not be as easy as she believes, but she's determined not to.

"Then this baby is born and we all live happily ever after. The end."

"What about your father?"

"He'll see that it's for the best, once this all plays out."

She truly believes what she's saying, or at least she's trying hard to believe it. What I see is a big mess that's going to end with all of us dead and Internment a big scorch mark in the sky.

"Try this dress," she says, and hands me a simple white gown with billowing lace sleeves. "I wore it only once, to some ribbon-cutting ceremony at a new hospital wing or some such."

A year ago I would have been over the moon—marrying my betrothed and wearing one of the princess's dresses. A white dress, at that. Usually they are worn only by members of the royal family. If all this were happening under normal circumstances, I would be happy. Basil would be happy, too.

Instead, both of us are fumbling around trying to make this work somehow.

I try on the dress and then I stand before the small mirror on the dressing table. Celeste stands beside me, her stomach so swollen, it's surreal. "I love this one," she says. "What do you think?"

"I'm frightened I'll dirty it," I say. "I've never worn white before."

"It's only for one afternoon," Celeste says. "Just gather the skirts if you go into any high grasses."

"It'll do," I say. "Thank you."

"'It'll do'?" She pinches my cheek. "Come on. You can give me something better than that."

I smile. My reflection in the mirror seems strange. I've never seen myself in all white before, and I don't know who this girl is, about to get married when she ought to be at the academy learning about why the god in the sky loves her so much. "Do you think Basil will like it?" I ask.

"If he doesn't, he's an idiot," Celeste says with confidence. "If you were wearing this, I'd marry you."

I stare at my collarbone, framed with lace. So much like a woman, my mother told me several months back, before all this. She knew then what I didn't know. She knew all about the metal bird hiding in the soil below our feet, and she knew that something big was coming. I don't believe she asked for any of it. All she wanted was for her children to be safe, and to hang on to some semblance of the life she and my father had built for us.

But if she were alive, even with our world in ruins, she

would want to be here for this. She would want to see me get married.

Celeste frowns at my reflection. "You look as though you're about to cry," she says. "Oh, Morgan, don't. It won't be such a terrible thing. You're marrying someone you're truly in love with."

"It isn't that," I say. I take a deep breath, straighten my back, and steady myself. "If I have to be married at all, I'm glad it's to Basil. I was only thinking that I wish my family could be here." I look at Celeste. "I don't suppose you were able to find out what's become of my father."

She purses her lips together and then says, "I wish I had been able to find out. If Papa knows, he won't tell me. I did plead a case on your behalf. I told him all you had done for me, and that if he knew where your father was, and if your father were alive, to spare him. But that's all I was able to do. I'm sorry."

This news just gets absorbed into the existing numbness I've felt since my return. I nod.

"Here." Celeste pulls the stool up to the mirror and guides me to sit. "Let's work on hairstyles, shall we?"

In the week leading up to the wedding, the only time that Basil and I get alone is in the evening after dinner. The king has made a point to keep us busy, sending us to talk to the miners and the hospitals like we've done something that's made us famous.

The hospital is the worst of it. We're brought to see only the newborns, but the sterile smell is the same in every room.

When we at last step outside, I feel as though I can breathe again.

"Are you all right?" Basil asks me as we walk for the shuttle. My legs are trembling.

There are guards ahead of us and patrolmen behind us, and I keep my voice low, but I don't really care if they hear me anymore. "That place always makes me think of Lex. I hate it. I hate it, and I miss him, even though he infuriates me most of the time."

"He's okay," Basil reminds me. "He's with Alice, and he's infuriating her for the time being, until you get to see him again." He forces a smile, and for his sake I return it.

"Wherever he is now, I'm sure that's just what he's doing," I say.

"He's with the Pipers and Alice," Basil reassures me. "He's safe."

I know he's trying to console me, but I suddenly wish he would stop talking. His parents and brother are here in the city, and he'll see them at our wedding. I don't know if Lex or my father are truly safe. I don't know if I'll ever see them again.

We sit across from each other on the shuttle, and I'm filled with so much jealousy that I can only stare out the window. It's so strong that I'm certain he can sense it.

He reaches out and puts his hand over mine.

We ride back to the clock tower in silence.

The night before the wedding, I can't sleep. The clock tower strikes midnight and I can feel its chime rattling the walls. I stare at a patch of stone ceiling that's illuminated by starlight.

Basil stirs beside me. It's been nearly a week since our fight about Judas, and even though we've made amends, we haven't gotten very close to each other since then. I can still feel that argument hovering in the air around us, filled with the things we wish we hadn't said, and the things we wish we had.

"Can't sleep?" he says.

I shake my head against the pillow. "I'm thinking about the city lights in Havalais. If I looked out my bedroom window at night, I would see them in the distance, and sometimes I wouldn't be able to tell which lights were stars. It was strange at first, but after a while it was comforting to know that someone else was always awake, going about their business somewhere out there. But here there's just insects and stars."

He turns so that he's facing me. "Those lights are still on. We just can't see them."

After a long pause, he says, "When you think about Havalais, are you thinking about Judas, too?"

I turn my head to look at him.

"It's all right if you are. I'd rather the truth than have you try to spare my feelings."

"Yes, but not in the way you might think," I say. "I think about what it must be like for him to be living in a world Daphne wanted so badly to be a part of. I wonder if he's thinking about her, what those thoughts are. And I think that they'll always belong to each other, and how painful that must be, to have the other half of your destiny murdered."

In the starlight I can make out Basil's face, but not clearly. All I can really see are his dark eyes watching me as he listens.

"And then I think that if you had been murdered in that way, I would walk around every day feeling like I was half-dead. I would be just like him, in a way. I would look for you in other people, knowing the whole time I'd never find you. Or even anyone like you.

"He says otherwise, but that's why he kissed me. He was just looking for Daphne. And in a way, I was looking for you. I was thinking about you."

After a long silence he says, "If I ever lost you, I would be lost, too." He puts his hand on my cheek, and his thumb brushes over my lips.

My lips part, and I can taste his skin on the tip of my tongue. "It's you," I murmur. "It was always going to be you. I don't know how you could think it would be anyone else."

He moves forward and kisses me, and I feel at last as though he understands what happened in the field with Judas. Understands me.

"You never had to look elsewhere for me," he says. "I've always been here."

I close my eyes against the darkness. I don't want to think about what tomorrow will bring. I only want to know that he's here with me now, and that whatever we face, it will be together.

That much, the decision makers got right.

13

I have been told that more than a hundred people will attend my wedding. Honored specialists and patrolmen and even students from my academy. And Basil's family, of course.

I don't even know a hundred people. I can count on both hands the ones who ought to attend, and with the exception of Basil, none of them will be there.

It is strange to think that so many people will be in attendance for what should be a simple, ordinary affair.

Basil has been taken to a separate room somewhere to be fitted into his suit and dressed.

The seamstress has brought a standing mirror into my bedroom, and at Celeste's instruction she is pinning cloth flowers around the waist of my dress.

Once that's done, Celeste lights a fire in the fireplace and uses the flames to heat up an iron hair curler. She sits me on the stool before the mirror and sets about rolling curls.

"I saw that smile," Celeste says brightly. "Admit it. You're at least a little bit excited."

"I'm nervous, mostly," I say. "What is this going to accomplish?"

"Hope," Celeste says.

"Everyone keeps using that word."

"Well, it's all we've got for now," she says, twirling the curler so close to my scalp, I can feel the heat of it.

I stare at my reflection in the mirror. If Pen were here, maybe she would have some glib remark about what should happen on my wedding night. Or even some advice. She's the only one I'd want to talk to about it. But her first time was stolen from her; it was violent, and not what it was intended to be. I suppose that she felt changed by it, and I didn't notice. How could I not have noticed?

I feel a burn at the back of my head and I wince.

"Sorry," Celeste says. "It's my stupid stomach, getting in the way of everything."

"Does it hurt?" I ask.

"What—being pregnant? No, I wouldn't say that 'hurt' is the right word. But sometimes I feel like I'm in the body of a seventy-year-old. Once I sit down and get comfortable, it takes ages to stand back up again. My back aches, my knees. I never know what's going to give me heartburn anymore. And I can't get enough of the color blue."

"Blue?" I say.

"Yes. The other day, for example, I was looking for something to read in the library upstairs, and I came upon this old book with a bright blue cover. It didn't even have a title printed on it. It was just pure blue, and I wanted to take a bite right out of it."

"Colors don't have a taste," I say. "It would have tasted like paper, I should think."

"I didn't say it made sense."

"Did you?" I ask.

"Did I what?"

"Did you bite into it?"

"Please. I'm not quite that insane. Though I admit it's becoming a battle between what I know is logical and what I want. My mother says I've always been that way, though." There's a moment of melancholy at her mention of her mother; she wanted so desperately to save her, and now her chances are slimmer than ever. Even if the queen were to survive this ordeal and find a way to the ground, I don't think they would be able to cure her sun disease. Professor Leander died of that very thing.

Celeste slides the curler away from my hair, watching with satisfaction as the new curl bounces into place. "I so wish I could come. Papa told me I'm not even allowed to watch from the windows. He's got the entire kingdom thinking I've contracted some fever from the ground and that I'm all but dead. Meanwhile I'm trapped in this tower going out of my head, ready to start eating books."

She walks around me and begins curling the hair on the other side of my head. "Thank goodness you're back. I've been so bored and now it's like I have a living doll to play with. Before Azure left for the ground, his hair had grown longer. You may have noticed, it's almost to his shoulders. I asked if he'd let me style it for him and he about bit my head off."

"It's not that I mind letting you play with my hair, but how much longer am I going to be in the clock tower?" I say. "Basil and I get married and we just stay up here? We don't get an apartment? Do something other than be paraded around Internment?"

"You'll get an apartment," Celeste says. "A nice one with actual electricity, unlike this ancient place. It will just take a while. Once King Ingram is dead, I'd bet. Things will be better then."

With all this talk of dead kings, I wonder whether Celeste has ever admitted to herself, even once, that this kingdom would be better off if King Furlow were dead, too, and surely she's wise enough to know he'll never change his ways, but I don't think she's capable of admitting it.

She finishes with my hair and then sits on the edge of the bed, admiring me.

"You truly are lucky," she says. "I never believed betrothals were for the best until I met you and Pen and saw for myself that sometimes they are. Even your brother and his wife seem to get on rather well."

"Sometimes betrothals work," I say. "But sometimes not." I look at her reflection.

"It's not as though Az were going to get a fitting match, no matter what the decision makers decided," she says, and grins, but sadly. "You could line up the most beautiful girls in the city. You could even find a few who would put up with his ego. The heart wants what it wants, I guess."

I hope the prince is able to find what he wants, at least.

Celeste is pouting when the patrolmen come to take me to the courtyard. "It isn't fair that Morgan must be escorted by patrolmen to her own wedding."

"I don't mind," I say. Although that's not true. This isn't at all how I wanted my wedding to go.

"I'll be there for the ring ceremony," Celeste insists. "Papa won't be able to keep me away."

The stuffy heat of the stairwell smothers me, and as I follow the patrolmen down into the darkness that will end at the courtyard, Pen's words find me: *Our people would do anything to keep the city afloat.*

That was what she told Nim that night in the empty amusement park as the three of us lamented what we'd lost.

With each step down, I feel as though Internment is sinking below my feet, and I know that Pen is right. I don't know why this task has fallen to Basil and me, but we must do whatever it takes to save our city. Even if it means playing along with the king's silly plan.

I hear the music a moment before I step outside. The sun is high and blinding, the grass and flowers a perfect brightness that Havalais for all its wonder can't claim.

There's a trail of multicolored petals making a path to the garden. The trail ends at a field of poppies as red as a lake of blood. And there Basil stands in a black suit, a hard shadow against all the red.

He must surely be burning under this hot sun in such dark clothes, but if he is, he doesn't show it. This is the most elegant he has ever been. The brass music moves between us, the only breeze in the still air, and he turns his head just as I step onto the cobblestone clearing.

The corner of his mouth raises into a reassuring smile meant only for me.

People line the path between us. Old classmates from a lifetime ago. Citizens. People I've seen but seldom spoken to.

I don't have to look into the crowd to know that Basil's family isn't among them. I can see the sadness in his eyes, buried where only I could notice it glimmering like a fleck in a stone.

I approach him, and as I reach him, I glance up at the clock tower, wondering if I'll find Celeste spying from one of the windows. But all I see in the high windows is the cloudless sky reflected back.

The king himself is standing between us when I finally reach Basil, and he's holding a sheet of paper with the standard vows. He means to officiate this ceremony, then. Usually it's a patrolman. My father was the one to officiate Lex and Alice's wedding. I wanted him to officiate mine one day. It's just another thing that has been stolen from my family by King Furlow.

As he begins to read the words, the promises Basil and I must keep to each other, I imagine King Furlow lying dead in his own blood.

I don't hear the words that are being said. Basil takes my hands, and I know we're approaching the end of this thing, that a few words of consent uttered by each of us will make it official. And then while the others are celebrating, we'll be taken to the blood room and our rings will be filled.

"Morgan," King Furlow says. It's so bizarre to hear him speak my name so informally that I don't realize right away that it's my turn to speak.

I raise my head and look at him, cursedly alive and well. "Do you consent to these vows?" he asks.

"I . . ." Basil's expression is steely, unreadable. In a single word he'll belong to me.

And then the ground rattles under our feet, and there's a roar like thunder. The wind pushes all those heavy curls in front of my eyes, and I bat them away so that I can see what is happening.

Basil's grip on my hand tightens, and I'm not sure whether it's fear or hope that makes the laugh bubble up in my throat. There on the horizon is King Ingram's jet, tearing through the sky.

The alarm on King Furlow's face says that this arrival was not planned, and that the jet is not returning for its routine shipment of sunstone-rich soil.

The jet is also not landing in its usual spot, far in the outreaches on the other side of the fence. It's close to the city, too close.

"Come on," Basil says, and we run past the king and through the field of poppies. I lose one of my shoes as I go, and kick the second one away.

The king doesn't come after us. He has his own chaos to contend with. All his wedding guests are running away from the jet. Basil and I are the only ones running toward it.

"What about Celeste?" I yell over the roar of the wind. It smells like exhaust and fire and all the ever-advancing mechanical devices of the ground.

"She'll be safer where she is," Basil says.

I stop running, and, still tethered by my hand, he stops too. We're both breathing hard. I meet his eyes. "If this is an attack and they've come for King Furlow, we have to go back for her. Promise."

He nods.

The jet crash-lands at the fence that surrounds the city, causing it to collapse onto the tracks with a shrill whine and the sound of engines dying.

I double over to catch my breath, both of us choking on the fumes. There's a satchel abandoned on the ground. Everyone has fled in fear. They have perhaps grown accustomed to the jet's arrival at a safe distance, but something is clearly amiss this time.

The wind begins to settle, and after a long pause, the door to the jet swings open. "You nearly killed us!" Thomas yells. He is the first to stagger down the metal steps, with Pen holding the back of his shirt in her fist to steady him as they both stumble dizzily into the daylight.

"There are no scratches on any of you, so quit yapping. You all volunteered me to fly this thing in the first place," Nim says, following after them. The frame of his lenses is dented.

Basil and I run to them, and Pen sags gratefully against me. "Oh, thank goodness, a welcome committee that isn't wielding weapons."

"Give it a minute and there will be," Basil says. "What are you doing back here?"

"That's the problem with this city—its utter lack of communication." We all turn to see Prince Azure leaning in the doorway, not a hair out of place. "You haven't heard? The king of Havalais is dead."

Pen rolls her eyes as she looks from him to me. "He's been rehearsing that line for the entire flight."

"How'd I do?" the prince asks. He descends the steps as though they were flanked by adoring fans. He's looking at Basil and me. "Did our arrival interrupt a wedding?"

I ignore him. "Is King Ingram really dead?" I ask Pen.

"He is. It's a bloody mess down there." Her shoulders drop. "I tried to go back for your brother and Alice, but there wasn't time."

"They'll be all right," Nim assures us. "They're with my siblings someplace safe."

It's doubtful that Lex would have come along anyway, he's so insistent on never returning. Maybe it's just that he couldn't face what this city has become since we first left it. I couldn't blame him for that.

"I had hoped my father would be here to greet us," Prince Azure says, and I'm not sure whether he's serious.

"He is probably trying to quell the hysterical crowd," I say.

"Yes, well," Prince Azure says, and steps over the tracks and begins walking. "Shall we?"

The prince of Internment taking a casual stroll through the city is a rare sight, but if people are watching, they are doing so from the other side of windows, terrified of what fresh horrors this jet will bring with it.

"It was poison," Pen whispers to me as we all cross the tracks.

"Who did it?" Basil asks.

"I'm not sure," Pen says. "One of his own men, I suspect. So many have cause to hate him. All I know is that Nim saw it coming, and he woke us from our beds in the middle of the night and packed us into the jet. There wasn't time to get everyone." She gives me a reassuring smile. "Lex and Alice truly will be safe. Nim had to leave his siblings behind, too. This was less safe for them. And I did check on him every day since you left."

"How is he?"

"As stubborn as ever. Disgruntled—you know."

"I do."

"But he misses you. Truly."

I walk between Basil and Pen, and I'm so relieved to see her, I could almost forget the wars happening far below our feet and here on this floating city.

"We didn't really interrupt your wedding, did we?" she asks.

"You did, actually. But that's all right. I'd rather you were in attendance anyway." I catch her glancing at my ring. "We never had a chance to make it official."

"Good," she says, trying to sound as though she's taking this lightly. "Plenty of time for proper weddings after the dust has settled."

Being married is the least of my concerns, and I know Pen shares this sentiment, but the distraction takes us from the fear of what's to come. King Ingram is dead. That must mean that Jack Piper has assumed leadership. He isn't a better candidate. He's a man with horrors of his own to unleash.

The prince looks back at Basil and me. "Where is my sister?"

"In the clock tower, last I saw her," I say. "The king wouldn't let her outside."

"But you did see her? Talk to her? She's well?"

Nim also glances at me, and beneath his cool exterior I see someone who is tired and fearful himself. I hold his gaze for a moment before I look back to the prince. "Yes."

Thomas is trying to keep up with Pen, who won't look at him.

There's no smell of tonic, and she is alert and sober, which is all I need to know for now. "There's much to talk about," she whispers.

Prince Azure leads us back to the clock tower. Our wedding guests have either fled or are hiding in the offices behind closed doors. They have been trained to fear an ambush from King Ingram.

"Papa?" the prince calls. "Celeste?"

Silence. He opens the door to the stairwell and we follow him up.

"What has happened to this city?" Thomas breathes, horrified.

Pen shushes him, but the pain is all over her face. She loves this city more than our king ever could.

Azure calls out for his father and sister, and when we reach the door to the royal family's apartment, it swings open and Celeste is the only one there to greet us. "Az!" Her voice is a mix of fright and relief. She pulls him into her arms, trembling. "When the jet came, I thought it meant you might have been killed and King Ingram was coming to finish us all off."

"King Ingram is dead," he tells her, and in his gratitude to be reunited with her, he shows himself to still be human under all that pomp and conceit. "Where are Papa and Mother?"

"Mother is—she's been asleep through all this. She's gotten so much worse, Az. And Papa is off with his patrolmen trying to make sure everyone stays indoors."

She at last breaks their embrace and draws back to look at him. "I'm just so happy you're alive."

When she at last looks away from her brother and sees Nimble on the staircase behind him, it sends her into tears.

He is so weary and drained by whatever it is he's seen, and at last he has made it back to the girl he loves. "Leste," he says, and gratefully catches her when she crashes into him.

As they murmur quietly to each other, I hear her say, "I love you, I love you, I love you."

Pen jabs her elbow into my ribs. "When did that happen?"

I shush her.

"Oh." Celeste sniffles, wipes her wrists over her eyes. "I'm being rude. Where's my head? You are the first citizens to see the royal apartment. Ever, I think, isn't that right, Az?"

"It's never been allowed before."

"But we may as well allow it now."

"Clinging to the rules is pointless, given the state of things."

I forgot their bizarre ability to continue the other's sentences. What a set the pair of them are, with such similar mannerisms, the same blond hair and bright eyes.

Azure takes a deep breath, bracing himself before he says, "Mother?"

"In her room. She's refusing to let the nurse in anymore. She'll eat only if I beg her myself. Az, it's . . ." She fights off another sob and then she takes his hand and leads him down a dark and narrow corridor, calling back for us to have a seat and apologizing for having to step away.

I expected the royal family's apartment to possess some sort of luxury, but now I see that it's rather ordinary. Perhaps even smaller than my own was. Though the sofa looks newly upholstered, its wooden frame is antiquated, probably handed down through the generations of royals.

Now that Nimble has had time to find his bearings, he's fascinated. He sits up straight in a wing chair upholstered the same blue as the sky, and he cranes his neck to see out the window.

"It's so . . . bright up here," he says. "The air tastes better. I didn't know air had a taste at all."

Pen sighs and falls back against the couch. "Yes, well, enjoy it while it lasts. It'll all be ashes and a bit of folklore for your city soon enough."

"King Ingram—my grandfather—is dead," Nim reminds her. "I promised you I wouldn't let your city be destroyed, and I won't let anyone else in Havalais be harmed over this either."

"I don't see how you can promise that," Pen fires back. "There is still the small matter of your father to deal with. As I recall he's just as merciless, and next in line to the throne."

Nim has nothing to say to this. He only stares down the corridor where the prince and princess have disappeared. After a while he says, "I did speak with the oncology specialist at the hospital. For your queen. But if what she has truly is a cancer, it progresses in stages and by now I don't know that there's anything we can do. Celeste tells me she's been ill for more than a year, with no treatments whatsoever."

Even Pen, who holds no sympathy for the prince and

princess, looks sorry for this. She knows what it's like to be powerless to help her own mother.

Just before the corridor, there's an old clock, and in our collective silence, each ticking is a small explosion. I try to drown it out, the sound of moments passing as we wait for King Furlow, and wait to learn what's to become of us.

When Celeste returns, she's alone and all traces of tears are gone from her eyes. She clears her throat and makes room for herself on the wing chair beside Nim. She doesn't explain her brother's absence, but presumably he's visiting with his mother. There is a faint medicinal smell to the air, which is stagnant and warm. Beads of sweat are glistening on Celeste's face, but somehow on her they look like cosmetics.

Nimble is watching her with fascination and caution, as though she may turn out to be a figment of his imagination.

She looks at him with resolution. "All right," she says. "Tell us what's happened."

"King Ingram was found dead in his drawing room. The troops weren't seeing results with the phosane, and after burying their loved ones following the harbor explosion, they were restless for revenge. I knew it was coming. I just didn't know when."

"So what Pen said is right, then," Basil says. "Your father is king."

"Not exactly," Nim says. "My father is dead."

Celeste lays her hand over his. "Oh, Nim," she says.

"It had to be done."

Pen leans forward. "You *planned* it?"

"It had to be done," he repeats, though there's a quaver to the words this time. "What you said was correct. My father was merciless. He served as the king's adviser. The bombings at the harbor were as much his fault as they were the king's." He looks at the floor, but then thinks better of it and raises his chin, meeting none of our eyes. "Birdie and I talked it through. We took no pleasure in it, but we agreed it had to be done."

"You're . . ." Celeste is watching him. "That makes you the king of Havalais."

"If you'd like."

"It's not 'if I'd like.' It's a fact. Your grandfather was the king, whether or not he cared to claim your father as his son. Your father was first in line; you were second."

"I don't know that patricide makes me worthy of the throne."

"Worthy?" Celeste asks. "The people of your kingdom will probably hoist you onto their shoulders and have a party in your honor." At his dead expression, she drops her shoulders. "Sorry, Nim."

"Whether or not I'm king, I'm the one who needs to speak with your father now about the state of things."

"Az and I will go with you," Celeste says. "We know how to talk to him. He can be unreasonable."

"Kings always are."

The city is silent beneath us. The window is open, letting in only the sound of air moving through trees.

It feels like ages pass before there's the sound of movement in the stairwell. Voices. Celeste straightens in her seat and listens. "Papa is back. He'll be going to his office. I'll get Az, and the three of us will go together."

She struggles to her feet, and Nim rises to help her. They steal a moment to look at each other. Only a moment. That's all they can afford right now.

My heart breaks for the pair of them. Beside me, Basil is frowning, and I know he's also wondering how this can possibly end well for us all.

An hour passes, and we sit in absolute silence, as though the walls themselves might reprimand us for daring to disrupt the royal air. The queen is bedridden down the hall, and I wonder if she knows we're here, or if she is too far gone to care either way.

Finally, Pen turns to me and says, "How long before it stops being inappropriate for me to ask what has happened to the princess?"

"It seems fairly obvious," Thomas says.

"It's her latest great idea," I say, too tired and anxious to be cynical. "She can't take all the credit, though. Nim went along with it—obviously. They wanted an alliance between their two worlds, and what's more solid than a new heir to two thrones?"

"It isn't all that stupid," Pen concedes. "They're both royalty. Still, with all the forced terminations in the city, there's bound to be some outrage."

"The king has kept her hidden away for months," I say. "The kingdom thinks she's ill. I fear what would happen if they knew the truth."

"I'm sure this will all go horribly wrong," Pen says, with forced cheer. "But it's a valiant effort, I'll give them that."

I put my hand over hers. I truly believed I might never see her again. There is much I want to say to her, but for now, Basil and I tell Pen and Thomas about the wedding they interrupted, and the time we've spent trapped in this tower, and the forced pleasantries in a city that knows something big is about to happen, and that Basil and I cannot possibly be the thing that saves it.

15

In a few minutes there will be a citywide broadcast to announce the death of King Ingram. So Celeste tells us, at least, as she frets and paces in the royal apartment.

"Isn't it a bit hasty to make that announcement?" Pen says, with no hostility for once.

"Yes," Celeste says. She's chewing on her knuckle. "But it gives our city the upper hand. My father's men have gathered all of King Ingram's men. They're being held in interrogation in the basement cells. Their loyalty to Havalais will be determined. Anyone who poses a threat will be executed. Harsh, I know, but I suspect that most of them will stand on our side. What other choice do they have?"

"We're on Internment," I say. "There's only one side to stand on. The other side is over the edge."

Her laugh is nervous and a bit hysterical.

"Sit down," I tell her. "There's no sense working yourself up while we wait."

"Wait," she spits back. "All I've done for months is wait. I'm so tired of it. Aren't you?" She shakes her head. "I can't leave this to my father, Morgan. He's the king, yes, and he's in charge of this city, but he's so . . . outdated."

"I would have opted for 'psychotic,'" Pen says.

"My mother is dying because of his fear of expanding our medical technology," Celeste goes on, ignoring her. "It isn't just medicine, though; it's all technology. This bloody clock tower doesn't even have electricity. Up until now we've had only so much room to grow on this patch of land, but now we have the entire ground. If we handle this properly, we can make Havalais into an ally, but Papa will make them into an enemy. He's scared of them and he's hateful, and he'll do the wrong thing, I just know it."

She walks for the door, and I reach her just as she's put her hand on the knob. "You can't go out there," I remind her. "Be reasonable. No one in this kingdom knows about the state you're in."

"Well, it's time that they do," she says. "Isn't hope our best ally? King Ingram is dead. What's more hopeful than a child who can bridge two worlds? What could be stronger than that?"

"Injustice," I say. I move between her and the door, and the knob is pressing into my back. I lower my voice. "You know a lot about this city, but its rules have never entirely applied to you."

"That's absurd. I—"

"Do you know what happens when people conceive children outside of the queue?"

"Of course I do," Celeste says. "They have a termination procedure. That rule would have applied to me, too, under the right circumstance. But—"

"There's never a right circumstance," I say. "Believe me. You may go out there bearing all the hope in the world. You may even have the means to solve all of the city's problems, appease all of its fears. But it won't matter. They'll hate you. They'll riot. That's the reason your father is keeping you out of sight. Don't you understand?"

Celeste is looking into my eyes, and I can see that she believes me. Much as she tries to be a diplomat, there will always be a divide between the kingdom's rulers and its citizens. We each represent a different view of the same world.

She's quiet for a moment, and then with renewed spirit she says, "Then you have to go." She nods over her shoulder at Basil. "Both of you. You have to force your way into the broadcast. The city loves you. Of course they do. You both represent the citizens better than my father or brother or I ever could. And Nim is an outsider; they'll be wary of him no matter what he says."

"I—" My voice catches. "And say what?"

"The truth. That you've been to Havalais. That the people there are not greedy like their king. Tell them it's a wonderful place, and that Havalais would make a strong ally, not an enemy. I don't have to tell you what to say. You're so good at seeing the best in people."

I look to Basil, who is walking toward me. "I think she's

right," he says. "We've lived in both worlds now. And you especially, after what you lived through at the harbor."

I hope I won't be made to speak about that. It still haunts me, and if I'd never left Internment and seen the ground for myself, the stories of bombs would scare me all the more. Havalais is recovering now, though its harbor will never be the same, but Internment would have been obliterated completely.

"All right," I say. "I'll see what I can do."

There isn't time for Basil or me to change, so Celeste runs her fingers through my windswept hair in an attempt to make me presentable, fits Basil's jacket onto his shoulders, and pushes us out the door.

"Wait!" Pen runs after us and meets us on the first step. She grabs my shoulders. "Tell them what I told you that night in the theme park."

"Do you really think that's wise? Now?"

"They need a bit of fear to keep them listening. They need to know that we'll help them."

She has been right about so many things before. I nod. "You should be doing this instead of me," I say.

"She doesn't have the social graces," Celeste says. "Hurry now."

Basil and I are left to make our way down the spiraling staircase, guided only by flickering sconces. "We'll be lucky if we aren't thrown in with the other prisoners for this," I say. "It's treason."

"Is it treason to intercept a king's broadcast if you're doing it under the order of the princess?" Basil says.

"Maybe 'treason' is the wrong word. There probably is no word for what we're doing, because it's that insane."

"All of this is," Basil says. "But you must agree that the princess made some good points."

"Yes, which adds to the madness. Celeste Furlow, the voice of reason."

We follow the directions Celeste gave us, through the lobby and down another stairwell belowground. The smell of mold and dust is overwhelming, but I hear the faint whine of something electrical. Light is flickering through the cracks in the door. There are voices on the other side.

The broadcast room. Normally there would be patrolmen guarding restricted areas, but with all the hostages from Havalais, the patrolmen have their hands full.

"Do we just barge in?" Basil says.

"No one's here to stop us," I say, and reach for the knob. King Furlow is standing in a sea of wires, looking flushed and fatigued. Behind him hangs a painted mural of Internment as seen from the outside. It was used for a festival some hundred years before, and it often serves as one of his backdrops.

He was in the middle of a sentence when we barged in, but now he has stopped to watch as we pace toward him and take a place at his side. There are three patrolmen—one of whom is operating the camera—and when they try to stop us, King Furlow waves them off. I was prepared for outrage, but he seems relieved that we're here to shoulder some of the burden. Nim and Prince Azure aren't with him.

"Citizens," he says, "you remember our bride- and

groom-to-be. Their own wedding was interrupted by the jet's arrival. So you see, this has hurt us all, but it's to a good end. My son, the prince, has brought word that King Ingram is dead."

"The wedding doesn't matter to us," Basil says. He casts a quick glance my way, as though he fears I might take offense, but if anything I'm relieved. He straightens his back and goes on. "The wedding was merely a distraction from Internment's hardship. But now King Ingram is dead, and you won't have to worry about more of our soil being taken. You can stop digging. Morgan and I have spent time on the ground. We've met its citizens. They never wanted to take so much from you; it was their king all along."

He's right, but I fear that no one will believe him. The people of Internment have been conditioned to fear the ground, and this nightmare has only fueled that fear, and even hatred. I gather my strength and say, "The ground is not very different from us at all. The city below us is beautiful. Its people were welcoming and kind. And they've been suffering too." I begin to describe the bombings at the harbor, going into such detail that the awful memory draws itself within my mind, brushstroke by brushstroke, revealing a coloring I never wanted to see again.

I stand bathed in the bright lights and I stare into the camera lens the whole time, never letting myself think that anyone is on the other side of it. I have no way of knowing if they'll agree with what I'm saying. Now that I've seen the ground, lived there, I hardly remember what it was like to be so uncertain.

"There's more," I go on. "Since the beginning of Havalais's efforts to mine our fuel, Internment has begun sinking in the sky. One theory is that the frequent arrival and departure of the jet is weakening the wind barrier that keeps us in place." I do my best to sound scientific, wishing all the while that Pen could be here to explain.

But a scientific explanation is not needed. The worry registers on King Furlow's face. "Sinking," he breathes. Then, "Cut the cameras."

The buzz of electricity dies away, and the king steps forward and turns to face us. "Is that true? Internment is sinking?"

"Yes," I say.

"How can you be sure?"

I hesitate. I do believe what Prince Azure said about Pen being in danger if the king were to know how truly valuable she could be to his cause. I have never been a good liar, but for Pen's sake, the lie slips out, "I was measuring it." I do my best to explain the sphere of wind that surrounds the city, and the threat that the jet's activity will pose to us over time. "I don't think it's too late," I say. "If the jet stops coming and going, Internment will stay put."

The king paces the length of the room, stepping over wires, pondering. "You," he says to one of the patrolmen standing by the door. "Escort these two back to their quarters while I mull this over."

"Are you sure you should have told him all of that?" Basil whispers once we're back in our room and we're alone. "What will he do with that information?"

"It was Pen's secret and she wanted it told," I say. "She must believe it will serve some purpose. She's never been wrong."

Basil frowns worriedly at the window, and I reach forward to put my hand over his.

We don't mention my father. The thought of him hangs heavily in the silence that falls between us, along with the many fears we don't confess.

Our meals are brought to us without a word. Night begins to fall, bringing with it the familiar trill of hopping songstresses.

Basil lights the candle in our lamp, and we talk in low voices, ever mindful about being overheard.

"I think he's dead," I say. I'm sitting on the window ledge, hugging my knees. I stare at my faded reflection in the glass. "My father. I think he's dead."

"Morgan—"

"The worst part will be the not knowing. The never knowing." I steal a glance at him. "He wanted Lex and me to leave this city. He and my mother wanted us to be someplace safe. I don't even know if such a place exists."

Basil has been sitting on the edge of the bed, and now he stands. "If you want to find out what happened to your father, now is the time to look for him. The patrolmen and the king and everyone else are busy dealing with the aftermath of King Ingram's death."

I laugh bitterly. "Where would you propose I start?"

"The basement cells," he says. "That's where everyone's being kept, isn't it?"

"We'll be seen," I say. But I feel that cursed hope creeping up in me, putting an ache in my chest, and I know that I can't let this opportunity slip by now that it's been introduced to me. "Okay," I say. "Okay. I've been to the basement only once before, but it's like a labyrinth and there isn't electricity. We may be able to move in the shadows."

I know it's foolish to embark with any optimism. I see the state that Internment is in. From the moment the first explosion hit the harbor in Havalais, we have all been trapped in a dream of a world that is covered in old roots and dead vines. We dig for traces of our old lives. We think we hear our loved ones calling beneath the rubble, so we clear it away, hearts pounding, breathing quickly. But time and again we unearth nothing. Nothing but bits of sunstone that go to waste.

The clock tower, like the night itself, is silent and still. I could almost believe that there was no life beyond Basil and me moving in the darkness. There isn't even the distant thrum of the train speeding by; there hasn't been for hours.

We reach the door that will lead us to the basement and I stop and take a steadying breath.

Basil is watching me. In the faint glow of a candle sconce that accents the wall, his eyes are round and dark. I don't need to ask the question that's plaguing me, because he already knows it, and I know his answer.

What if we don't find him?

We look elsewhere. We keep looking. That's all we can do.

I turn the knob; there's a staircase leading down. I swear this building is nothing but stairs and echoing walls. I can hear voices farther down, murmuring. Metal rustling—shackles? The prince and princess held Pen and me hostage using string, but it would surely take more than that to restrain a hundred men from Havalais.

I'm so fixated on the dim light at the bottom of the stairs, I don't notice the body coming up behind me until it's too late, and he's grabbed my arm. "Stop right there."

I don't struggle. Too easy to fall down these steps. He's got Basil, who also obliges but shoots him a venomous glare. The man prods us down the steps and I struggle to keep up. I should have foreseen this; of course I should have. I'm not frightened at all, only disheartened. My heart sinks like a stone in my chest.

Did I really believe I could walk down here and find my father among the prisoners? I was raised to believe that things could be so easy, so attainable. Everyone I ever loved lived within the confines of a train track. My world was laid out so neatly before me. How could I have wanted more? I didn't know the consequences of more.

"Your Highness! I've caught two break-ins trying to get downstairs. Where should I put them?"

We've reached the bottom of the stairs, and my shoulders drop with relief when I see Prince Azure standing before us. "Let them go, you bloody idiot. They're not break-ins. They're *guests*. Haven't you heard about the wedding that was interrupted by the jet?"

The man unhands us, and my arm throbs from the ghost of his grip.

"I'm sorry, Your Highness. I couldn't see them in the darkness."

"Don't apologize to me. Apologize to them."

He nods to me, then Basil, muttering his apologies, and it's strangely gratifying. After he's left, Prince Azure regards us. There are candle sconces lining the corridor of closed doors, and the light traces the sharp angles of his face. "What brings you down to my humble hovel?"

I hesitate, and Basil answers for me. "We were looking for a specific prisoner."

"Ah, yes," the prince says. "Let me guess. Your father, is that right? My sister told me all about that when she first returned, and for her sake I investigated. She feels truly indebted to you, Morgan. But, sadly, nothing came of the search. Your father isn't here, and if he's still alive and has any brains, he won't let himself be found."

If he's still alive.

I bury the enormity of those words. I cannot afford to open that pain anew.

"Best to focus on those we can help, yes?" Prince Azure says, and I do believe he is trying to console me, in his way. He claps a hand on Basil's shoulder and mine and steers us down the hallway. "You aren't allowed down here normally, but since you've found your way, there's something you should see."

All of the doors are guarded by patrolmen. There's talking going on behind some, and eerie silence behind others. "Internment has been in a state of madness for months, hasn't it? My father is quite overwhelmed. My mother doesn't have much time, let's be honest. And my sister is madder than usual."

"Hard to tell what's usual with her," I say.

The prince laughs. "Yes, I suppose. She was always a crazy thing. Maybe we both were. But then, that's the price of growing up in this place, with only each other and the spiders in the cracks to keep us company. And don't mistake my candor; she's a fool, but I will take her side always, even when she goes off and gets herself into predicaments like the one she's in."

I can't help feeling jealous. My brother and I care a great deal about each other, but he's never seemed to agree with a thing I've done, and I don't understand his decisions either.

"I don't know what to make of this boy she's dragged into our lives," the prince goes on. "Nimble Piper. I know only that he's important to her, which means I've been tasked with protecting him."

"Protecting him?" I say. "From the people of Internment?"

"The people of Internment don't know he exists, and besides they're no threat to anyone," the prince says. We've been walking down a long hallway that's been narrowing with each step. The stone floor has given way to raw earth, and the patrolmen stand guard in the glow of candles, several paces away from the only door in this primitive hall. Prince Azure raises a key to the lock and pushes the door open. "The thing I must protect him from is my father."

A candle flickers on the wall, nearly dead. Below that, slumped and beaten, is Nim.

17

My breath catches in my throat, and as I struggle for words, Basil says, "You can't treat him like this. He hasn't done anything!"

"My father is the king. He can do whatever he likes," the prince says. "It was stupid for this boy to come back here after what he and my sister did. Papa has spent these past months wanting to murder him. If I hadn't intervened, he might have."

I rush across the dirt floor and kneel at Nim's side. He's lying on his back with his wrists bound before him, his eyes bruised and swollen. When I touch his cheek, he sucks in a pained breath. It takes a moment for me to realize that the word he's trying to get out is "Celeste."

"No," I say. "It's Morgan. Can you hear me?"

He swallows hard. "Leste."

"She's all right. She's just upstairs." Though from where

he lays, upstairs might as well be a world away.

"I doubt he can hear you," Prince Azure says. "He's been muttering for hours." He closes the door behind us, entombing us all in this room with stale air rife with mold.

I look up at the prince standing over Nim's lifeless body. "We have to get him out of here."

"Believe me when I say that will make it worse. There's nowhere to go. The jet is under heavy guard, and where could we possibly hide him that he won't be found when my father realizes he's gone?"

"Then what's your plan?" Basil asks, venom in his tone. "Even if you can stop your father from laying a hand on him again, he'll die if he isn't cared for."

"I am—" The prince lowers his voice, kneels beside me. "I am caring for him. I've put salve on his wounds, and earlier I brought him some water, as much as I could sneak in."

I lift the hair from Nim's face and find a bloody gash that's been coated with a thin line of cream.

"Does Celeste know?"

"No," the prince says, "and she can't. In her condition, something like this would kill her."

"She isn't as fragile as all that," I say.

The prince laughs. "Fragile? No, she isn't fragile. But as I said before, she's a fool. She would hatch some half-baked rescue mission, be caught, *of course*, and be lynched by all those citizens with bleeding hearts about the queue. Even the king himself couldn't save her then." At my startled expression he says, "Oh yes, I'm well aware how much the people hate the termination procedures and the queue. There's much my father should change but is too stubborn to. He's the one they should lynch, but that won't matter. They'll trample my sister to death in a riot, and that's if they don't cut the bloody thing out of her first." He says this so simply, as though it's a science. "No, you and your husband-to-be are to go back up to your room, and when you see my sister, tell her that all is well and that Nimble Piper and our father are discussing strategies, or whatever it is she expected to happen."

"I can't just leave him," I say.

"If you want what's best for him, you will," the prince says. He and his sister both fancy themselves expert politicians, and from what I've seen they both make poor decisions with amazing ease, but still, just this once I believe he's right.

I lean close to Nim and say into his ear, "Hang on."

The prince escorts us back to the main level, and before he turns back into that awful basement, he says, "Look after my sister. She needs someone who will do that for her."

"I will," I say, and frown as he closes the door behind him. I turn to Basil, helpless.

"For what it's worth, I think he's right," Basil says. "We're in dire straits when one of the royal children is the voice of reason, aren't we?"

When we return to the darkness of our room, I climb under the covers and face the window. The moon is an eye that's suspended midblink. I cannot face Basil. I cannot face anyone. I keep seeing Nimble's wounded face, his bleeding mouth. Another Piper broken.

Birdie survived her wounds, I tell myself. Nimble will too.

After a long silence, I whisper, "Are you still awake?"

"Yes," Basil says.

"King Furlow has to die."

Celeste is in high spirits. Basil and Thomas have been whisked away by a patrolman to help motivate those assigned to clean the mess made by the jet so that the trains can resume soon. Celeste, Pen, and I spend the morning in the living room of Celeste's apartment, sharing bowls of strawberries and grapes. It isn't the arrival of the jet that has reinforced her optimism. It isn't the broadcast or the death of King Ingram. It's Nimble's presence.

"How did he seem when you talked to him? Was he worried? I bet he was worried. He's always so concerned about me; it's sweet, really." Mercifully, she doesn't wait for me to answer. "Hold that thought; I've got to use the water room."

After she's gone, Pen leans toward me and says in a low voice, "All right. Tell me what's really going on. I can read your face like a book. Is he dead?"

I glance down the hallway after Celeste. "Not yet," I whisper. "But it's bad. He's in one of the cells. If I didn't know better, I'd think an animal had attacked him."

Pen winces. "What's the plan to get him out of there?"

"The prince is going to keep him alive while his father figures out what to do next."

Pen sits back against the couch, fretting. "Do you think

the prince will truly keep him alive? I wouldn't trust him as far as I could spit."

"I wouldn't either," I say, "but I believe he will, for Celeste."

Celeste returns and drops unceremoniously beside me. She looks as though she's just been ill.

"Are you all right?" I say.

"Oh, yes, fine, just getting toward the end is all," she says. "Truthfully I'm glad the baby is going to be born here. Medicine on the ground is more advanced for sure, but if there's one thing our doctors do well up here, it's this." She gives a weak laugh. "But then, our population is such an issue, I suppose they have to regulate it the way they do."

Despite her upbeat tone, she doesn't look well. I put my hand on hers. "Maybe you should rest."

"How can I?" she says. She shivers excitedly. "Knowing King Ingram is dead and that an alliance between the two kingdoms is coming, I hardly slept a wink last night."

"Yes, and it shows," Pen says, without malice. I dare to say she sounds sympathetic; perhaps the knowledge of Nim's state has made her take pity. "You'll be no good to either kingdom if you drop from exhaustion. Take a nap."

Celeste blinks, surprised by the concern. "I suppose there isn't much else to do until my brother comes back with an update."

Hesitantly, she retires to her bedroom, leaving Pen and me alone.

"I truly believe she's going to kill herself with stress," Pen says. "What's the king's plan? He can hide Nim from her for only so long. She's going to want to know where he is when she's giving birth."

"I think he's hoping she'll forget about him."

"He must not know much about love, then," Pen says. "Or his daughter."

"I would believe that."

Pen moves to sit beside me, rests her head on my shoulder, and weaves her arm around mine. "Whatever happens now, I'm just so glad you're okay. I didn't know what would become of you after you left."

"I spoke with your father," I say. I feel her body tense. "I didn't tell him what I knew. But, Pen, he's valuable to King Furlow. And to Nim. He knew about the plans to assassinate King Ingram."

"That doesn't surprise me," Pen says, and it's as though she's speaking about a stain on her skirt. "He is head engineer and all that. The king has always favored him."

"You won't have to go back to him. Not ever again. Things are different now."

She pulls away from me and sits upright. "I'm not afraid of my father. I told you." She's focused on a crease in her skirt, and she works to smooth it.

"Pen—"

She looks at me. "The royals don't drink tonic, did you know? Internment's king must be ready to make a decision at a moment's notice. The queen and their children must also be ready, in case there's a death that leaves them in charge. So there's not a drop of tonic to be found in this apartment, and this isn't a conversation I wish to have unless I am very drunk."

I put my hand over hers. "All right. I'm sorry."

"Besides," she says with more verve, "we have enough problems to contend with, don't we? For starters, I nearly missed your wedding." She laughs at the absurdity of it and I do too.

I tell her about the fight Basil and I had after I told him about Judas, and the clumsy reconciliation. It's nice, really, to have normal problems and to pretend a fight with my betrothed is the most harrowing thing in my world.

"I'm relieved that the jet landed when it did," I blurt. "It isn't that I want to be with anyone other than Basil; it's just, after all of this, I want it to be my choice. And I know him; I know that he didn't want it to happen that way, either." I look uncertainly at the floor and then back to her. "Does that make me sound awfully selfish?"

She gives a wan smile. "No," she says. "Internment is frozen in time. Down on the ground, girls have already broken free. That's why we saw all those brilliant night clubs, and why the harbor was so alive at night. Marriage is fine and safe and nice, but there's so much else to do with our youth."

"I never thought I'd hear you say that Internment is frozen in time," I say. "Whenever I would talk about the ground before all of this, you'd try to shut me up."

"I was frightened," she confesses. "I love this city and I always will. It's my home. But I thought that if I under-stood its laws and I believed hard enough, no matter what I endured in life, things would always settle right side up in the end. I see now how small this place is. I was treating it like a god, but it's only a city."

"A magical floating city," I say, and we both laugh.

"I thought that being away from Internment would kill us. I thought it would make me question the god in the sky and everything we've been taught—and it has. I do question everything. But I want to have my questions. I want to have more thoughts than my mind can hold, so many that I have to write them in fragments like a madman."

"How much madder do you want to get?" I say.

She only smiles.

It takes nearly two weeks for the trains to resume running. The fence is repaired, and patrolmen are stationed all along it at every section to deter trespassers. Basil, Pen, Thomas, and I are free to roam the kingdom again, and though we're frequently bombarded with questions about the ground, no one seems to wish us harm.

Basil and Thomas are reunited with their families. I tell Basil that he should return home to them, but while he spends much of his days with his family, still he chooses to spend his nights with me in the clock tower. I want to look after Celeste, who is homebound and desperately lonely.

Pen doesn't return home at all, not even to see her mother, despite all her worrying. She doesn't say as much, but I know that she's afraid of being pulled back into that place again, and that this time she won't be able to leave. Pen's mother should have been the one protecting her, but it was always the other way around.

When I'm not being asked about Havalais, people ask me about the princess. They want to know if the rumors that she's dying are true. I smile and say that she's on the mend.

This is my only lie. Even Celeste's spirits have begun to drop, and she looks worse than ever. She has not been allowed to so much as step outside, not even within the confines of the royal gardens, since the jet returned, because the king is so terrified that someone will spot her. Her own mother's rapid decline and the months of isolation have begun to break her spirit, a spirit I once thought impenetrable.

One afternoon, when she's too exhausted to be up and about, I sit at her bedside and read to her. There must be a storm below us, because the clouds are especially thick and gray. Her still-bright eyes focus on the window and I know that she's missing the rain; it's one of her favorite wonders. She's tethered to that world below us forever now.

"Morgan." She interrupts me, and the words I was reading fade away. "Nim is in trouble. Isn't he?"

"No," I say. "I saw him just last night. Your father won't allow him to see you, and he is quite angry you both went over his head, but that's what you expected, isn't it?"

"I'm not that blind," she says, and pushes herself upright, her hands smoothing over her stomach like it's a globe filled with all the places she wishes to see. "My father has a cruel side. My brother and I have known since we were children. But we thought, 'Papa loves us, so he must be a good man. We'll understand one day.'"

"Don't you still believe that?" I say.

She shakes her head. "I'm not a child anymore," she says.

"I don't believe things simply because I want them to be so."

She winces at a stab of pain. They've been happening now for days. She should be in a hospital; even Prince Azure has told his father as much, but the king refuses. Whether it's for fear of his daughter's safety or fear of losing control of his own kingdom if anyone finds out about this child of two worlds, I don't know. But I suspect the latter. I fear he would let her die in childbirth from lack of care if it meant keeping the child a secret.

"Is there anything I can get you?" I say. "Have you had anything to drink today, at least?"

She closes her eyes for a long moment, and I can see that she's still in pain. "Find my brother," she says. "Make sure he's alone." As I stand, she grips my arm. "Don't let my father know."

"I won't. I'll be right back, I promise." She tightens her grip before she releases it. "I promise," I say again, to convince myself as well.

She doesn't ask me to find Nimble. She knows it would be no use. He would already be by her side if he were free.

I hurry down the steps, through the lobby that is only sparsely populated by people collecting their wages, and make my way down the set of halls that leads to the basement. The prince has been busy these past two weeks, playing his father's politics and overseeing the prisoners. He interviews the men from the ground every day, testing their potential loyalty. I can see all the while that his heart isn't in it. He and his sister have lost whatever respect they held for their father, and have even come to fear him.

While Celeste has begun evading her father, Prince Azure has grown disdainful of him. He doesn't say as much, but I can see it in the way he speaks to the prisoners, as though he sympathized with their anger at being trapped here, as though he knew of a less barbaric way to handle this if only he were king.

But I see it especially in the way he cares for Nimble Piper, spooning water into his mouth when his jaw is clamped shut, whispering that he must get better for the sake of his own kingdom.

When I open the basement door, I find the prince sitting on the top step, pale, exasperated, staring down into the darkness. He barely offers me a glance.

"They never tire of orders," he says. "Our patrolmen. They can't live without someone telling them what to do. It's all so exhausting, having to think for them."

I would love to argue against this. My father, at least, was one who did not accept orders without question. But there's no time. "You have to get to Celeste," I say, trying to catch my breath. "She's in pain again. I think—" I look around to be sure we're alone, and then I whisper, "I think it's time."

He's on his feet in an instant, his self-pitying fatigue gone. He rushes past me, and I follow him up the stairs and into the apartment.

Celeste has tumbled out of bed and she's standing with her hands pressed against the window ledge, head down, struggling to draw even breaths. Her bedsheets are dampened through.

"Leste." The prince is gasping for air, but he's gentle when he wraps his arm around her shoulders and brings her back to the bed. "I'm right here. What do you need?"

She shakes her head. "I don't know! I thought Nim would be here for this. I thought I would be prepared." She shudders with pain.

"Leste, listen to me. I'm going to send for our doctor. It's going to be fine. The doctor will know exactly what to do."

"You can't," she sobs. "Papa will try to take the baby away. He'll put it wherever he's put Nim."

"I won't let him. I won't." He's speaking so calmly, like he's reading a bedtime story to a child. "I'll be right back."

"No!" She's clinging to his arm as he stands. "Please!"

"Don't be stupid," he says. "I've gone along with this plan of yours—not that I've had any choice in the matter— but I won't let you do this without a doctor."

Her fingers are digging into his skin, and he has to wrench himself free. "Az!" She doubles over with pain, and I see the anguish on his face as he rushes past me. I could swear there were tears in his eyes.

I have never seen Celeste so hysterical. It's the fear, not the pain, that's doing it. I sit beside her at the edge of the bed, and I don't speak in dulcet tones, I don't try to console her. I know that she won't believe me.

It's an eternity before the prince returns, a doctor in tow. He's a small man with hair that's severely slicked back, and he's much older than any doctor who would be allowed to practice. The prince surely pulled him out of dodder housing.

"Strip the bed," he tells me, and his tone is so icy and

authoritative, I oblige quickly and with shaking hands. He opens his medical bag and produces a flame generator used for cooking in apartments without electricity. He sends me away to fill a pot with water.

My mind is spinning. After I've brought the water, I'm not allowed back into the room. I sit on the floor in the hallway, staring at an oil coloring of the prince and princess as children, arm in arm in their finest white dress.

"Doctor O. has been with our family for years," Prince Azure says as he comes out of his sister's room. Exiled as well, no doubt. "He's the doctor who saw to our genders before we were in the womb. He's the one who delivered us."

The prince is known for his poise, but now he drops to the floor across from me, his arm draped over his angled knee, and he looks as though he could melt into the floorboards. "A curious thing, isn't it? Our genders being determined even before we're born. The king and queen wanted an heir and a spare, and they knew just how we should be assembled. They ordered us as though we were items on a menu."

He nods to his sister's closed door. "Sometimes I think we were born all wrong, my sister and I. Sure, we know how to dress the part, but we have our own wild ideas about what we would do if the kingdom were left to us.

"I'm better at playing along. I pretend I'll be the king my father wants me to be. I say yes and I go along, knowing I can rule my own way once it's my turn. My sister has no patience for that. No sense of strategy. She's always been stupidly impulsive. But I never thought she would take it this far."

I say nothing. He isn't seeking words of comfort. There's a pained cry from the other side of the door, and he bows his head.

"This baby will merge two worlds, won't it?" he says, with a humorless laugh. "But it has to get here the same grotesque way the rest of us did."

Celeste shouldn't be alone on that soiled mattress. She should be in a hospital, surrounded by electricity and nurses. Nim should be beside her. She was so small and frightened when I left her.

I strain my ears to listen, but I can hear nothing on the other side of the door now.

"This is typical of her," the prince says. I can hear the worry under his cool tone. "She doesn't think things *through*. How am I supposed to pull her out of this one?"

"I think the whole point is that you can't," I say. I pause to see if my boldness has offended him, but he's listening. "She didn't want you to save her. She's never wanted to be saved. She had it in her mind that she was going to do this, and it can't be undone."

"I think you're right about that," he says. I have seen the prince dozens of times in regal sketches, at festivities, and on broadcasts, and this is the first time I look at him and truly see an equal. A person as powerless as the rest of us.

"My sister thought that our father would come around, that he would see what she was doing for the kingdoms and accept this child of two worlds. She's always believed he loves us more than he does."

"Perhaps he will, with time," I try.

"No," he says. "Papa was livid. The only reason he didn't hold her down himself and force her to have a termination procedure is because it was too late by then. She'd have bled to death." The words are horrible, but he's so utterly drained that he can speak only frankly. "Once the child is born, he has asked me to drown it like a double birth. And then it will be as though this never happened. There's to be no love story for my sister and that boy from the ground. She'll be lucky if she sees daylight again before her eighteenth birthday, when she's married off to her betrothed."

Though I suspected something like this, it nauseates me. My heart is pounding. "You can't let that happen."

He looks at me, that trademark royal brightness in his eyes. "I have a plan I've been working out, but I'll need you to prove to me that you're competent," he says, and I should be offended but I find his familiar cockiness to be a sign that things will be all right again. "I'll need you to go to the prison and create a diversion. Get Nimble Piper out of there through the back entrance."

"The one that leads to the plum court?"

"Yes, the very same. Here—" He hurries down the hall and returns with a scrap of paper and a pen. He sketches a crude map of the woods surrounding the clock tower. "There are several stone caverns off the trails. Hide him there. Stay with him and wait for me."

"How long?" I ask.

"I don't know how bloody long. However long it takes babies to be born."

"But Basil and Pen," I say.

"What about them?"

"If you're asking me to betray the king, and I'm certain you are, I need to know that they won't be punished on my behalf."

"You do this for me, and I'll make certain they're someplace safe. You have my word."

A scream from beyond the closed door makes us both wince. "What about Celeste?" I say.

"What about her? She can't very well go sneaking away into the woods right now, can she?" His face has paled considerably. "I'll look after her. But I can't be everywhere. Morgan, I need you."

There's a set of words I never expected to hear from him, but all I say is, "What kind of diversion?"

"It will have to be something that requires the attention of every patrolman. Tell them—tell them my father has been wounded. Say that he's been stabbed by a citizen who's been maddened by the edge or some such. After weeks being cooped up down in the cellar, they're all just itching to be heroes. Go on now, go." He fumbles with the key ring and extracts the key to Nim's cell. "Don't get caught. I can't afford to save you too."

I nod. I hurry through the apartment before I'm made to listen to another scream. I couldn't bear it. The prince is left rooted to the hallway, his sister struggling behind one door, his mother dying behind another.

His diversion works. The patrolmen are so lost and desperate for their leader that when I tell them the king has been harmed, they are eager to rush to the king's side. They pay me no mind as they hurry past.

My hands are shaking as I work the key into the lock. I drop it twice. When I finally get the door open, I find Nim sitting up against the wall. He was dozing in a fitful sleep, but his face registers alertness when he sees me.

"Morgan?" His voice is hoarse, his lips cracked and bloody. But he does look better than he did the last time I was down here. "Is it really you? Is Celeste—"

"Can you stand?" I work the key through the lock on his restraints, and they fall away. He clenches his fists. "Come on. There isn't time." I pull him to his feet and position him so that he can rest on my shoulder as we walk. He stumbles dizzily.

"Wait," he says. He's delirious. I can feel the heat of his fever when he drops his face against my neck.

"We can't wait. We have only a few minutes before the patrolmen realize they've been tricked. They'll be combing the entire city looking for us."

I don't think he hears my explanation. He's scarcely conscious.

All I am thinking as I drag him from the clock tower and into the woods is that I won't allow him to die on the day when his child is born.

I sit huddled in a cavern much like the one Pen and I claimed as our sanctuary. This place feels familiar even though it's the royal family's private property, where the prince and princess do their hunting for sport.

Or they used to, at least.

Nim weaves in and out of consciousness. In his brief lucid moments, I tell him that we're someplace safe and that the others will be with us soon. I tell him over and over, reassuring myself as well.

Before the ground was ever introduced to our city, these woods would have been lined by patrolmen keeping trespassers away, but now there's only the rustle of leaves and a chilly breeze that comes along with the short season.

It was sometime past noon when I left Celeste at the hands of that doctor with the soulless eyes. Now the sun has melted below the city's edge and stars have begun to show themselves.

I wonder if her child has been born. I wonder if Prince Azure has managed to keep it alive.

Nimble stirs. He reaches out and touches my arm. "Birdie?"

"No," I say. "It's me. Morgan."

He struggles to sit upright and I help him. The prince was giving him sedatives to help with the pain, and now he's starting to emerge for the first time in weeks. Awareness is starting to show in his eyes. "Do you know where you are?" I ask.

He looks over my shoulder, at the darkening sky. "Internment," he says. "I was in prison."

"Yes." Hope fills me. "Yes, and you're out now."

"Where's Celeste?" he says. "I have to go to her. You have to take me."

"Soon," I say, uncertain whether I'm lying. He's already in so much pain, I don't want to add to that the pain of uncertainty.

But after weeks of a medicated haze, Nim isn't having it. He's awake now. "What's happened to her?"

He tries to climb out of the cavern, and I hold his shoulders down. "She's having the baby now. Or maybe she already has—it's been hours since I've seen her. Prince Azure is with her."

"I have to get to her." His voice is desperate. For all his injuries, he's found the strength to fight me off when I try to keep him down. He scrambles out of the cavern and starts pacing furiously through the trees.

"Nim," I whisper harshly. "You can't. The king will have patrolmen looking for us. If we're caught, it's all over."

"She needs me!"

I grab his arm, and he stumbles, still dizzy. "Yes, she needs you. She needs you outside of a prison cell, and more important, she needs you alive. I can't promise either of those things if you go bursting into the clock tower demanding to see her."

He looks helplessly into the distance. He wouldn't know how to get to the clock tower even if I did let him go. "The prince won't let anything happen to her."

Nim shakes his head. "She wanted to believe the best of her father, but I knew—I knew he would put her in danger. Her and the baby."

I drop my arms to my sides. "What did you expect, Nim? You've got royal blood; you've seen how kings are. They don't like having their position challenged, much less by an infant."

He stumbles forward and catches himself against a tree. He's breathing hard, teeth gritted. In his urgency to get to Celeste he forgot about his injuries, but the pain has reminded him now.

"All we can do is wait for word from the prince," I tell him. "I'm sorry."

He limps back to the cavern, utterly defeated, and hits the rock face in frustration. Almost in tandem with the motion, there's a sound within the depth of the woods. A creak. I push Nimble into the shadows of the cavern and follow after him and hold my breath.

It was foolish of us to speak as loudly as we did. Patrolmen will be looking for us by now.

I hear the noise again, not so much a creak as a whimper. A figure emerges from the trees, and it whispers my name.

Prince Azure. His steps were silent, not so much as a rustle of leaves or the snap of a twig, expert hunter that he is, but that whimpering persists, and as he gets closer, I realize that he's holding something in his arms.

"Morgan!" he whispers.

I crawl out of the cavern. "I'm here."

Nim is rushing to get past me, but before he can make it to his feet, the prince has knelt down before us. The bundle in his arms is moving, and it gives out a feeble croak.

Nim gasps. "It's—"

"Yes, yes," the prince says, like he's bored with the whole thing. "It's a girl, born just a few moments ago. Perfectly healthy from what I can see, but I'm no doctor."

"Is it safe for a newborn to be outside like this?" I say, marveling despite myself at its pale face like a faded little moon in the darkness. "There's a chill in the air."

"Safer outside than inside," the prince says. "My father thinks I've taken her outside to drown her in the ravine."

Nim is shaking when he reaches for the infant, but the prince hands her to me. He's perhaps still too untrusting of this boy from the ground.

I hold the infant, feel her slight bit of weight. The next generation of an ancient royal lineage in my arms.

Instinctively I raise the blanket up past her ears to keep out the chill.

"I'll escort you to the jet," the prince says. "I've been interrogating men from the ground and there are three whom I trust to fly you back to the ground."

"The ground," I echo dumbly. "But Basil—"

"He's already there waiting for you. Your loudmouthed blond friend too. See? I keep my promises."

Nimble is staring at the child. His child. He surely has a million questions, but all he says is, "What about Celeste?"

"What about her?" the prince says, exasperated.

"Is she coming with us?"

"No, she's not coming. Don't be a moron. She's so heavily sedated, she wouldn't know her own name if you asked her."

"I'm not leaving without her," Nim says.

"Suit yourself." The price rises to a stand. "But that baby is leaving this city tonight, if you want it to survive."

I move to follow the prince, and Nim grabs my sleeve. "Morgan."

"He's right," I say, with all my sympathy. "I can't make you come along, but I think you should. Celeste would want you to take care of your kingdom. You'll find your way back to each other again; of course you will."

Nim looks up at the prince. "You claim to keep your promises. I need your word that Celeste will be safe."

"She's not the one in danger," the prince says.

Hesitantly, Nim moves to follow, and in a rare display, the prince helps pull Nim to his feet. Prince Azure doesn't wait for us, though, before he moves forward into the darkness.

The prince has a hunter's stride. Silent, graceful. Nim struggles to keep up, panting and clutching his wounds.

The infant is mercifully quiet, unfazed by the ordeal of her birth and the great trouble it has caused.

We move through the agriculture section, away from the city's lights. We cross the train tracks, and Prince Azure cuts through the fence with his hunting knife and makes an opening that I can duck through.

"There was nowhere to hide the jet," the prince says. "My father had it moved out here. Everyone's afraid of the thing, even his patrolmen, which is silly if you ask me. It's only a machine."

There was once a time when I feared this side of the tracks. Now I see that it's only grass and starlight. No maddening song on the wind to lure me over. I still remember exactly who I am and what's worth fighting for.

Nim stops to catch his breath, and I let him lean on my shoulder for support. For all his panting and cringing, he stares in awe at the stars, as though he could reach out and pluck them from the sky.

"This is your world," he says, breathless. "This has been floating above me all my life."

"Yes," the prince says. "It's a pity you can't see more of it, but we really must be going."

"Come on," I tell him. "I can see the jet just ahead."

And I can, though there is nothing but starlight to illuminate its dusky, tarnished body. It's hard to believe this battered thing will have enough life left in it to take Nimble and his new child home, but I have to believe it will.

The metal door swings open, revealing a mouth of darkness. But the darkness isn't complete; I can see the outline of blond curls. As we move closer, I can see Pen more clearly. She's standing as still as a statue in the doorway, with her hand gripping the doorframe.

Her eyes move to the infant, and then to Nim. Her lips part, and I can see the faint tremble in her lower lip. She glances sidelong into the jet as though someone is speaking to her.

This isn't right.

"What in the world are you gawking at?" the prince asks her.

"Pen?" I say.

Her mouth forms a word. She whispers it at first, and then she yells it, "Run!"

Only then do I see the king standing behind her in the darkness. He brings his face close to hers, and I can see his pale, tired complexion. He says something to her through gritted teeth, and she yells again, "Run, Morgan. He'll kill you!"

They're the last words she's able to say. Before I can move in one direction or the other, the king has slashed her throat.

19

My scream could surely wake the dead in the tributary.

A clean line of blood appears, thin and even, then dripping. Pen drops to the ground, and I can swear I see her chest rising with a breath when the king kicks her away, into that unyielding blackness.

In my arms, the infant has begun screaming, a shrill cry that's scarcely human. All I can think is that I want her to stop, so I can listen for Pen's breathing, and for Basil, who is surely calling for me. He must be in that jet. He must be injured, or he would come to me now. He would never have let that happen to Pen.

I don't let myself think that either of them could be dead. I won't, until I can see them for myself. I run for the jet, and Nimble is the one to stop me, only as long as it takes for him to grab his daughter from my arms. He no longer has the strength to stand, and he collapses into a kneel, clutching her like life itself.

The prince stands before the two of them protectively.

The king comes toward him like a mad beast, but we're madder, Nimble and the prince and I. The king of Internment, for all his schemes and ploys, may love this city with all his decaying heart, but he will never know the power of loving more important things.

I have seen too many killed, I have lost too much, and I will not lose another thing at his hand. He is brandishing something in his grip—another weapon perhaps. I try to grab it, but I am of no interest to him and he shoves me out of his way.

I'm insubstantial, like his foolish daughter. His son is the one he means to subdue. When the king reaches Prince Azure, he raises something that I believe at first to be the knife. But when he plunges it into the prince's neck, there is no blood.

The prince drops to the ground, his eyes still open and blinking, a tranquilizer dart jutting from his skin.

Perhaps the king truly does love the prince more than the prince could believe. He didn't kill him.

Prince Azure's eyes are on me, and as I meet them, I see what I could swear is permission. The king pays me no mind. Now that he's removed his most immediate threat, he wants the thing he's come to kill—his grandchild.

Nim is struggling to get to his feet. He's broken and tired, and he's just walked hundreds of paces, but whatever is left in him, he'll give. The king knows it isn't much.

It's almost done. He can toss the infant into the edge and she'll bounce back, broken and dead. What's to stop him? There's nothing here. Just me, sobbing and shaking.

When I lunge for the knife that's still in his hand, he isn't expecting it and he gives a startled cry. He's got such a firm grasp on the hilt that I have to grab it by the blade. I feel it slicing into my skin.

He elbows me in the stomach, but to my own surprise I'm laughing, even as the pain hits. He has ruled this floating city for all these years, and all he has to defend it with is a knife.

Blood has made my palm and wrist sticky, and I don't know whether it's his blood or mine. With a punishing shove he manages to throw me to the ground.

The struggle has given Nim enough of an advance. He's gone, but the persistent wail of the infant tells me that he's in the jet. I get a glance and see that the door has been pulled shut.

Nim and that infant may be it, the only ones who will survive this night.

I'm in the dirt, and if the king didn't pay me any mind before, he certainly does now. He's straddled over me, blood smeared on his shirt. Pen's, perhaps, or mine. It could be Basil's, for all I know, but my mind won't allow me to believe it. For all I've been made to believe in the past year, I will not believe that my betrothed and my best friend are gone.

I grab the king's wrist, and the knife is hovering over my face, shaking uncertainly, as though the blade itself isn't sure which of us to kill.

The king drives his knee into my stomach and I see it for just a moment—the fear in his eyes that I may have something in me after all, that I won't die so easily.

The jet's engines splutter and then roar to life. Dirt splashes my face, and the king raises his head. While he's been busy with me, the boy he wounded has gotten away. Nim is going to make it. He's going to fly to the ground and take his place as king, him and his child of two worlds.

The moment's distraction is all I need. I grab the knife from the king's faltered grip and I plunge it into his throat.

Blood rains onto my face, some of it landing in my mouth, and I splutter and cough as I push myself away from him. Despite my hatred, I cannot look at him as he dies. I hear him struggling in the grass, and I turn to the stars. They are oblivious to my existence on this small, floating rock, and yet I've known them all my life. If they cared at all for living things, I believe they would understand what I have done.

The king ceases to struggle. I don't know that I believe in the tributary anymore, if I ever did, but if there is any good in him at all to go there, it's the part that loved his children and his kingdom. Though he betrayed them, though he did deplorable things, it was the best he had to offer.

The taste of his blood makes me vomit in the grass, and even after I recover, I'm still trembling when I get to my feet. I'm only distantly aware of a pain in my hand and chest. No matter. There's no time for that now. The jet is still here, and there's still a chance that Prince Azure and I can be on it.

"Your Majesty," I say when I kneel at the prince's side. His eyes are dull and glassy, but he's breathing and I know he can hear me. I remove the tranquilizer from his neck. "You have to wake up," I tell him. "You're the king."

The words feel very far away. The prince-turned-king blurs, and a pair of arms catches me as I fall back.

My eyes close, and I don't have the strength to open them, but that's no matter. I'd recognize Basil's touch anywhere.

Motion. He's bringing me to my feet. My mind registers the feel of the metal steps reverberating under my shoes. I double over, sick in the grass a second time. He picks me up again when I'm through. I hear my own heavy breathing, taste the blood. Something is screaming, screeching like the seagulls that flew along the shoreline of Havalais.

Darkness.

When I am able to open my eyes again, I'm certain that days have passed. But the starlight is still streaming through the jet's window, and I realize, heart sinking, that we have not gone anywhere.

"Hey." Basil's voice is eager. He holds my arm, keeping me steady. I'm in one of the jet's seats and everything spins when I try to move. "You need to be still. You've lost a lot of blood," he says.

"Where's Pen?" I don't dare look at his face. Before he can answer, I force myself to ask, "The king killed her, didn't he?"

A laugh, weary yet assured. That's when my vision

comes back into focus and I see that Pen is sitting across from me, her blood-soaked shirtsleeve tied around her collar. "It's going to take more than that," she says.

I open my mouth to speak, but a sob comes out instead. I lean against Basil, who frets and smoothes back my hair. "I thought you were both dead," I say.

"Please. He hardly got me," Pen says, panting from the effort of speaking. "Couldn't find an artery if there were an arrow pointing to it. Suppose that's why his men did all the killing for him."

"But I saw you go down," I say.

"A tip, Morgan: If someone tries to slit your throat, and you're fortunate enough that they've failed, you let them think they've succeeded."

I reach out and take her hand. Sometime later, after we are all safe and rested and bathed, I should like to collapse into a good and relieved fit of tears.

"He tranquilized me and propped me up against the wall there," Basil says. "He said he wanted me to see what happened to traitors and bastards born outside of the queue, that men needed to learn about death before they could be of any use."

Pen scoffs, but I see the wince of pain she tries to hide.

"Nim?" I say. "The baby?"

"Both asleep at the helm, remarkably," Pen says. "He wasn't going to leave without you. He wanted to create a diversion by starting the engines."

"Prince Azure?" I say. "Or I suppose he's the new King Furlow now."

"Still out cold. I couldn't move him," Basil says. "His dart must have been stronger."

The thought of Prince Azure lying paralyzed in the grass, mere paces from his father's body, is too much for me to take. With great effort I pull myself to my feet. My hand is wrapped in scraps that are presumably from Basil's torn sleeves.

A pain in my shoulder flares to life. So the king did manage to wound me after all. Basil does not try to stop me, but rather stands behind me, steadying me when I sway one way and then the other, like one who's had too much tonic.

I descend the stairs slowly, Basil's grip on my arm the strongest thing I've ever known.

"It's bad, isn't it?" I say. "Pen's wound."

"I'm convinced she's immortal," Basil says.

"She needs to see a doctor, and Nim, and that baby. Basil, a newborn shouldn't be out like this."

"Nor should you, in this shape," Basil says. "But we're all strong to the point of being stupid, aren't we?"

I laugh, and the pain in my shoulder intensifies. I don't look at the king's body as we pass it, but Basil does, though he says nothing of my gruesome handiwork.

I drop to a kneel at the prince's side. "Your Majesty," I say, for the second time. His eyes open and his fingers twitch. He struggles to speak, opening and closing his mouth and groaning before he gets the word out. "Havalais."

I think he means it to be a question. "No," I say. "You're still on Internment."

He falls unconscious again, for once a victim of those

tranquilizer darts the royal family so favors.

"Should I try to drag him onto the jet?" Basil asks.

"No point," I say. "He needs to stay here and assume his place as king, and we ought to hear his ruling, shouldn't we?"

"Do you suppose it would be in our favor?" Basil asks. "He never did seem to like us. Or Nim."

"No, but he loves Internment. He'll do right by it. I hope."

I stay by Prince Azure's side through the night, weaving in and out of consciousness. Basil sits up in the grass beside me, always awake, keeping watch.

It's the baby's cries that startle us all awake, sometime before dawn. The sound could replace the clock tower's hourly trills, for it's surely being heard through every window in the city.

Prince Azure sits up, wincing, clutching his sore back and neck, shrugging his shoulders. "Are we still here?" he says sourly. "After all that?"

Pen staggers to the door of the jet and has to yell over the baby's cries. "It's not going to shut up, you know. It's hungry." The concept of motherhood has always eluded her and this experience is reinforcing her disdain.

"What do you propose I do about it?" Prince Azure asks her.

"Don't ask me," she fires back. "You're the king."

I don't retain most of the walk back to the clock tower. I black out for moments at a time, but somehow my legs keep moving.

Prince Azure leads the way, saying nothing. The sun is rising now, making the city pink and gold. It's his first day as king, and he does not seem happy to see it.

My knees buckle, and when Basil can't hold me up, he kneels alongside me. The clock tower is in sight now, but as I look up at it, it may as well be a world away. It is Havalais's harbor glittering on the other side of the sea.

"She can't go any farther," Pen says, and drops her arms like dead weight. "She needs to be in a hospital." She needs a doctor as much as I do, but she doesn't say that.

The prince turns to face the lot of us, the infant cradled in his arm. How he managed to silence her is a wonder. Maybe she was born with her own political agenda; it certainly wouldn't surprise me.

"Morgan," the prince says. "You're very tired, and maybe you don't remember what happened back there, so I'll remind you."

I raise my eyes to look at him. My vision is tunneling.

"When we made it to the jet, my father the king was there to see us off. He was sending us to Havalais with his blessing. But one of his patrolmen was maddened from being so close to the edge, and he killed my father. He tried to kill us all, but you managed to wrestle the knife away and kill him instead. You did it to save us. That's what happened, do you understand?"

"Yes," I say.

"I'm glad we're in agreement," he says. "My sister will want a full report and that is what I intend to tell her. Best to leave the details to me. I have the clearest memory of the scuffle."

The infant has begun screaming again. Hungry, cold, nameless. *She ought to be back with her mother,* I think, before my vision goes dark and I fall into silence.

When I sleep, I have a dream that doesn't belong to me. Rather, it's something that has been haunting my brother for years. He told me about it weeks ago, though it all seems like a lifetime away now.

In the dream, Internment is the same as it has always been. I step over the train tracks and suddenly I'm at the edge, staring down at the ground that reveals itself through wisps of clouds.

I don't want to jump. I only want to have a better look. I

lean forward, and my feet are pulled from the ground. Then I'm weightless, careening away from the clouds, away from my answers.

When darkness takes over, it isn't perfect. A heart beats inside it, and I can almost make out the shape of some small and living thing—almost.

"Wait," I say, for it is being pulled out of my reach. "I know who you belong to."

But it doesn't listen. Willing the past to be undone, even in dreams, can't set things right again. All I can say is, "Come back. Come back. Come back," until it is gone.

In the darkness I hear a cry, and I think that I've succeeded, that it has heard me and I will return what has been stolen from my brother. From Alice.

But the cry is not coming from within my dream. It's in the waking world, finding its way to my ears. It belongs to a different life entirely, one that may have a chance yet. We've all fought so hard for it.

I'm in the hospital for the better part of a week. I'm well enough to leave, but I hesitate to leave Nimble and Pen in this awful hospital alone. Though Pen put forth a brave face, she and Nimble bore the worst of it. They've both been scarcely conscious since we got here.

It was only after I began to improve that Basil relented when I told him that his time would be better spent helping the new king and visiting with his family. I know how awful it is to be a visitor in a place like this, and I wish for him to not experience it.

Though Pen was fortunate enough that the king's wound did not prove fatal, it fast became infected and she's been bedridden with fever. I've exaggerated my own injuries just to stay on this floor and be near her. But that can last only so long. A patrolman came to my room to inform me that the king has requested I have an audience with him at noon.

The only consolation is that, under the orders of the king, Pen's and Nimble's rooms are to be guarded at all times, in case anyone may try to cause them harm. No visitors are permitted into this area at all. Not even family or Thomas. Not even Pen's father.

When I visit Pen, her face gleams with perspiration and she's flushed with fever, but determined to stay awake. I think her nightmares of the harbor bombing still haunt her. They surely still haunt me.

I sit in the chair by her bed, and she offers me a wan smile. "You look dreadfully glum," she says.

"I just hate to see you like this," I say.

"Me? I'm fine." She looks to the window, and there are clouds reflected in her green eyes. "I've had plenty of time to think about things."

"You shouldn't be thinking," I say. "You should be resting."

"A girl should never stop thinking," she says. "Otherwise we'll become what our world thinks of us." She's struggling to keep her eyes open. "Dull, simple creatures that must belong to someone lest we hurt ourselves."

I push the sweaty hair from her face. Without her neat curls or glossy plaits, she looks almost like a stranger.

"Oh, Morgan, stop," she pleads. "I can't stand it when you worry so much about me. Really. The look on your face."

"It is taxing being your friend. I worry about you constantly."

She pushes herself upright. "What about you?" She lowers her voice. "You haven't been sleeping. I hear you pass my door a dozen times a night."

"I'm all right," I say.

"Are you, then?" She has a way of staring through me. I've always been a dreadful liar, but I'm trying, for her sake. Her mouth twists, and she looks to the window. "What was it like?" she asks, in a low voice. "Killing him."

"It doesn't matter," I say, all too quickly.

"Of course it matters."

Suddenly the sharp sterile odor of the room turns my mouth dry. My palms are slick and I rub them against my gown as though I could clean it all away that easily.

Pen is looking at me now, offering me no reprieve. She means for me to admit it. "He was going to kill me," I say. "All of us. He was going to kill his own grandchild."

I hate her silence. I stare at the floor. "I had to. That's all. I don't know what more you want."

"You see him when you close your eyes," she says. "Don't you? When you sleep?"

Numbly, I nod. "But I still kill him, even in my dreams," I say. "I have it to do over, and I do, again and again. That's how I know I had to."

The king dies again in the silence that passes just then, the blood black in the starlight, the whites of his eyes dimming like a spent bulb. The only reprieve was the soft sounds of the grass, as though the city wanted to say it forgave me. Thanked me, even.

"I've killed in my dreams, too," Pen says. Her eyes are fixed on the window. She won't look at me, but she won't look down the way that I do. She has had years to grow familiar with the sort of hatred it takes to kill.

"I know that I'm dreaming, in some way, but every time, when he comes into my room and I finally move to kill him, I will it to be real. I think that if I want it enough, I can somehow change the rules about what a dream alone can do." I see the coldness in her eyes that makes me hate the one who did this to her, made her think such things. "Then I wake up, and this world and its consequences race back into my head as though they've been hovering over my pillow waiting for me to come back. And I know that I can't kill him—not without suffering tenfold for it. I learned a long time ago that if I want him to be dead, he's dead. He can't have my thoughts when I'm awake. He can't make his darkness be my darkness."

She runs her hands over the blankets, smoothing the wrinkles. "Still, though. I've wondered how it would feel. If I'd get any satisfaction."

For all the king did, and even though he tried to dispose of me the way he did my parents, I still can't bring myself to hate him as much as I hate Pen's father. The king, in his way, believed he was protecting his kingdom. He believed he was doing something noble. But Pen's father meant only to take something that was not meant to be given. He gave no mind to his daughter, no mind to the way he would change the world as she saw it, even when she was older and stronger. The brilliant thoughts in her head that he pervaded. The tonic forcing itself into her blood the way he forced himself into her, just so she can find solace from him for a few meager hours.

He is a different kind of murderer, and there is nothing in him that can be redeemed.

"I wish your dreams could be real, too," I say.

She moves across the bed and rests her head against my shoulder. I feel all the weight go out of her, and she closes her eyes. For just a moment, she is the little girl I wasn't able to save all those years ago, and at last she allows someone to console her.

I kiss the crown of her head, and she puts her arms around my neck. Both of us killers, both of us murdered and brought back to life.

I'm not the only one pacing the halls of our tiny wing. On my way back to my bed, I find Nimble standing at the tiny window at the end of the hallway, staring at the glasslands in the distance.

He flinches when I stand beside him. "Sorry," I say.

"It isn't your fault," he says. "My nerves are fried." The city is reflected in his lenses. He shakes his head as though he can't believe it. "I expected a war-torn mess when I got here, but if you look away from all the digging and at the city itself, it's beautiful. Hardly what I think of when I imagine a city at all."

"Most of those buildings are hundreds of years old," I say. "We've outfitted them with electricity and plumbing, but the bones are the same. No reason to demolish them and make waste."

"No weather to wear away at them," he says.

I laugh. "I've gotten to know you so well, I almost forgot you're a foreigner here. Still, we aren't very different, are we?"

"No, we aren't," he agrees.

After a long silence, he says, "It doesn't feel real yet that I'm king. All my life it's felt so far away." He shakes his head. "I've always hated them—kings. Wasting away in their castles that could be better used a thousand other ways."

"It's your castle now," I say. "Who says it has to be a castle at all? It could be its own city."

He smiles, and his stare is faraway, as though he's imagining it. "Havalais doesn't know yet that the old king is dead. There are advisers handling affairs for me while I'm gone, and in secret, Birdie is advising them on my behalf. She's the only one I trust. If news got out that there is no formal leader, or that a broad is running the show in my absence, Dastor would be at an advantage. It was irresponsible of me to go, but I felt I had to."

"To see Celeste," I say.

"You make me sound like a lovesick kid."

"No shame in that."

"Maybe it's true," he says. "I did want to see her. I wanted to see her world. To see the city of Internment and the clock tower where she's lived as a princess, I can finally understand her optimism. Her faith in things."

Havalais is quite the opposite of Internment. What it lacks in modesty it makes up for in aggression. Even its beauty is aggressive, with bold music and bright lights and glamorous girls with black lips on silver screens. If Celeste is a product of her world, Nim is a rare creature in his own. All modesty and softness.

"I admit that I have a hard time seeing things the way she does," I say. "But I hope she's right. I hope our two kingdoms really can come together."

"There aren't many things I'm sure of," Nim says. "But I'm sure about that."

The new king is high up in his clock tower, in the royal apartment. He requests to see me alone. Even the patrolman who escorted me waits outside the door.

He's standing at the open window when I reach him, staring into the garden of poppies far below.

"You wanted to see me?" My voice is uncertain; now that he's had time to reflect, I don't know what he makes of his father's murder at my hand. This is the first time we've spoken since the melee.

"There's to be a ceremony," he says hollowly. "I'm king now, of course, living and breathing. But tradition dictates a ceremony. It's what my father did, and his father before him, and so on back to our first king."

"You haven't called me here to advise you on that, have you?" I say. "I wouldn't know how. Parties are best left to someone like your sister."

"Oh, believe me, she's got plenty of ideas about what I should wear." He turns to face me, his hands still braced on the window ledge. "I've called you to share one of my key ideas. Come over here, would you?"

Cautiously I approach the window, not entirely certain whether he means to push me through it.

But as I follow his gesture to look through it, he leans on his forearms and nods to the poppies far beneath us. "That was my sister's favorite place in the world when we were growing up. She was betrothed to a truly dreadful boy who also happened to be deathly allergic to most flowers. She'd run out to the center of the poppies with her skirts gathered, and she'd stand there taunting him as he demanded her affections."

"Sounds quite like her," I say.

"I admired her petulance toward him, and her bravery," he says. "But I also feared it. I thought that if she resisted, she'd be whisked off to one of those camps and that her brains would be scooped out with a spoon until she was nothing but a blubbering mass of compliance."

I look at him. "The attraction camps, you mean."

"Yes, right. I won't startle you with the gruesome details, but needless to say I hate it there—not only for what it is, but because it exists at all. So I'm going to do away with it. And that begins with getting rid of betrothals."

"Completely?" I say.

"I've always hated that tradition," he says. "Perhaps it works sometimes—you and your betrothed seem to get on rather well. But my sister chose that limping, haggard boy from Havalais. And what for? Because, as you've told me, he's kind. He's the opposite of what she was fated to as she fled to the poppies."

"He is," I agree.

"Would you still choose your betrothed if you had the option?"

"Yes," I say.

He gives me a wan smile. "I'm not questioning your loyalty to Internment's laws, Stockhour. It's an honest question. No need to be frightened."

Was I frightened? The quickness of my answer was a reflex, brought on by the interrogation my family endured after my brother jumped.

"It's not an easy question," I confess. "I've known my whole life that Basil and I were meant to be together. I don't know how I'd feel if we met only now for the first time, or if he and I had always just been classmates in a crowd. I can tell you only that I love him now as it is."

"I suspect many will feel the way you do, and that's fine," he says, and raises his chin as though he's come to an important decision that he's quite proud of. "But that shall be my first act as king. Keep your betrotheds if you want, but I'm doing away with that archaic custom."

"What about ensuring everyone gets a match?" I say. "What about the population?"

"Not everyone *wants* a match, and even if they do, they should be free to make that decision. Isn't that what they do on the ground?"

I shrug. "They have more space to roam. They do plenty

of things down there that I find maddening." Like a mother abandoning her children so that she might see the world without them.

"Yes, yes," he says. "I do think Internment could borrow a bit of their madness. I want to talk to your friend Margaret about the risks of opening a regular flight path to the ground."

"If you call her Margaret, she won't help you at all. It's Pen."

"Fine then. Pen. I asked to see her as well. Where is she?"

"She couldn't leave the hospital just yet. She's too ill."

"That won't do." He frowns out at his kingdom. "I'm going to need someone with a head for math and physics giving me counsel."

"Her father is the head engineer at the glasslands," I remind him, and though the idea of Pen's father being put in a position of power frightens me, he does know quite much about how the city is fueled.

"Never cared for him—too pleasant, like he's hiding bodies under the bed," he says. "Never cared for Pen much, either, but I do admire the way she thinks."

"Have you forgiven her for nearly killing you, then?" I say.

"I admire it, really. She's not the sort to hide bodies or make pleasantries; with her one always knows where one stands. If I'm to choose anyone for my council, it's a girl who has no regard for hierarchy." He gives me a sharp look. "But I order you never to tell her that."

"Oh, but of course, Your Majesty."

He turns his back to the window and squints at me. "What do you know of her family? Pen's."

My knees go weak, and I disguise it by leaning beside him against the window ledge. "She's an only child. Her mother is reclusive. Her father works longer hours than most—but you know that already. It's on the record."

"You must know more than that," he presses. "The two of you are as close to each other as I am to my sister. I can tell. It's this nearly psychic connection."

"Like a double birth," I say, echoing something Pen has used to describe us before.

"So you surely must know more than that."

I look at him. "Would you give Celeste's secrets up so easily?"

His smile is fond and sad. "You'd have to cut them from my veins."

"So then you understand."

"Can't blame a king for trying."

"Pen is an only child," I say again. "Her parents didn't reenter the queue. That's about all there is to tell."

"I've been going through my father's records these last few days. You know there's a sheet written about everyone in the city. Medical records, mostly. Allergies. Behavioral mishaps. Pen's mother has quite a few notes."

Yes, I'd imagine she does.

"Her father's sheet, however . . ." He trails off. I think he's waiting to see if I'll interject. When I don't, he says, "There are certain marks in public records to denote repeat offenses and vices—tonic addiction, disturbing the peace, people who have been to the attraction camps, jumpers, what have you. But Pen's father's record is utterly flawless, excepting a black dot by his name."

A black dot. That's all there is to hold him accountable for what he's done. Pen was strong enough to survive it, but there is far more than a dot of ink marking her.

"I don't know what it means," the new king says. "But my father had a way of forgiving crimes if they were committed by someone he deemed useful. And Nolan Atmus is indeed useful, but in a way that I'd like to keep at arm's length. What is your thought on that?"

I take a deep breath. "My thought is that, if you don't refer to her as Margaret, and you don't bring up the black dot, Pen will be happy to help you."

"Splendid!" His sudden cheer is a relief. "Let's go pay her a visit, then."

Pen is weak but entirely lucid when the new king and I enter her hospital room. She gives him a wry smile. "To whatever do I owe the honor, Your Majesty?"

He ignores the jab, and she brightens considerably when she sees the drawing paper he's brought her. "We're to design a flight path between Internment and Havalais, and calculate the impact it will have on our city's new tendency to sink."

She reaches for the paper greedily. "I've already done all the measurements."

As she explains the impact the jet has on Internment's altitude, the new king says nothing of his plans. He asks questions that Pen is all too happy to answer. On a separate sheet, she draws the sunstone itself, explaining how the flecks within the soil are compressed and refined in a way not dissimilar from coal. And when he's had enough, he rolls her drawings up neatly and tucks them under his arm.

"Where are you going?" Pen says as he heads for the door.

"To mull and brood," he says, quite decisively. "It takes a great deal of that to run a kingdom."

Hours later, King Azure summons me outside of the tower. The sun has just set, and he carries a lantern but doesn't light it. Wherever we're going, he doesn't want us to be seen even by the patrolmen meant to protect him.

There's a chill in the air, but it's a relief in contrast to the stuffiness of the clock tower. I don't know how the royal family can stand to live so high up in all that stale air, especially during the long season, when the air is like bath steam.

Once he has led me away from the patrolmen, he lights the lantern. We walk in silence for what feels like an hour before he says, "When we were children, my sister and I would compete for our father's attention. But we did so knowing that I would be the one to inherit the kingdom, and so when Papa confided in me alone, I reveled in it. I did enjoy torturing my sister with knowledge she couldn't have."

"Now you sound like my brother," I say, and brace myself against the pain that fills my chest with those words. I do miss him and Alice quite much.

"One day," he goes on, "Papa led me through the woods. Celeste wasn't invited. At first I was rather smug about it. Important. But the farther on we went, the more I began to worry. I had never been so deep into the woods before, and this sort of . . . dread filled my stomach."

I also never thought the woods ran this deep. It's as though we've stepped into a parallel world that's twice as large as our floating city. He looks at me as though to determine whether I'm afraid. But I've spent years trying to navigate the darkness of my brother's mind. A few trees and a starlit sky are of no concern to me.

"What's out here?" I ask.

"Something my father didn't want the city to see." He raises the lantern, opens the door, and blows out the flame.

It takes a moment for my eyes to adjust to the darkness, and then I see slivers of light up ahead, peeking out from what appear to be buildings clustered together behind a fence.

And I understand.

"These are the attraction camps," I say.

"Yes," King Azure says. "It's the first thing I mean to destroy, as king. Normally there would be more patrolmen standing guard, but they're all preoccupied now, as you can imagine. We can get closer, but we must be quiet. I don't want anyone to know that you've seen this."

He is as silent as a hunter, the way he moves, and I do my best to mimic this.

He crouches before the fence. "Here," he whispers. "You can see into that window there."

I kneel beside him, gathering the skirts of my borrowed dress. I follow his gaze and I see a woman with cloth wrapped around her mouth, spooning liquid to a body lying on a bed. It's hard to believe the body is alive, but I think I see it breathe.

"I've put a stop to the surgeries," he says.

"Surgeries?" When I crane my neck, I'm just able to see the body on the bed. It looks like a child whose head has been shaved. My heart leaps up into my throat. "They do something to their brains," I breathe.

The king's silence is his answer. I'm glad that he can't take me farther than this. I do not want to see what exists in those other buildings without any windows at all.

"It's gone on for more than a century," King Azure says. "As I understand, it began as an experiment to correct the boys who were attracted to boys, the girls who were attracted to girls, and the ones who seemed to be attracted to both or neither."

"Has it ever worked?" I ask, horrified.

"The records say yes, but I think not," he says. "If I had to endure what goes on in that place, I'd be more inclined to lie and say I was healed, wouldn't you?"

I've begun to feel dizzy. I press my lips tightly together and try not to be sick.

"My father took a special interest in this place, even as a boy, before he was king. And its purpose has expanded since then to include criminals and traitors—anyone he means to change. When they recover, they're never quite the same. They have seizures, or memory loss, or they can scarcely walk. In some cases they become entirely dependent on their betrothed to take care of them."

I think of the woman who used to live in my apartment building. Every day she would follow her betrothed to the doorway and then stand there to watch him go. I wonder if she was once here.

"It's awful," I say.

"I mean to have this entire facility demolished," he says. "Let it become a field for livestock. Let it reek of manure. That would suit me just fine."

In the dim light of faraway buildings, I see the fear in his bright eyes. And I know that being a prince would not have spared him this fate, if only his father had known the truth about him.

"Your Majesty," I say, "I'm so sorry."

"Don't be." He blinks and comes back to himself. "I've brought you here to show you that you've done me a favor. This place could never be destroyed while my father was alive. You did what I wish I could have done a long time ago."

I'm stunned that he would see my killing his father as a favor, even if I'm starting to agree. We begin walking, and I look over my shoulder at that horrible shadow of a tiny city. I know what he was trying to tell me. After the king attempted to murder his own grandchild to save the royal reputation, I have no doubt.

I fear speaking, but I know that I have to.

"Was my father in there?"

He looks at me, the candlelight casting long shadows

on his face. "I can't say for certain. After you left for the ground, many patrolmen were killed for their insubordination. Others professed their loyalty. And others, yes, did end up in the attraction camps. The primary purpose is to change—or attempt to change—one's sexual attraction. But that's really only the start of it. My father believed any facets of the mind could be changed with surgery."

I veer around and start pacing toward the camp. King Azure grabs my arm. "Morgan, don't."

I try to break free, but his grip only tightens.

"Let me go!"

"Would you lower your voice?" he says through gritted teeth. "I didn't show you this place so that you could go charging in there causing a scene. I may be in charge of the kingdom now, but I'm still determining which members of my father's council can be trusted, and I can't have you putting yourself at risk."

"He's my father," I bite back. "He's one of the few people I have left. You would go back if you thought Celeste were in there!"

"Yes," he says. "Yes, I would burn the bloody place to the ground if I had to. But Celeste isn't in there, and neither is your father. I checked."

I stop struggling, and cautiously he lets go of my arm, watching and ready to apprehend me if I run again. But I don't. My legs feel rubbery and numb. "You checked? What does that mean?"

"After my father's death, while you were recovering, there was much for me to do. It isn't as easy as just becoming king, you know. I had to assess the damage, so to speak. That included going through the attraction camps and learning the status of each patient—"

"Victim, you mean."

"If you'd rather. And I put a stop to the surgeries and instructed the nurses to return the victims to health. I saw every face in every bed, and there were no grown men left at all."

My breath hitches. "Left?"

He hesitates. "There's an incinerator for the patients who don't make it."

"The ones your father didn't want to make it," I say. I'm struggling to draw each breath, and I can't bear the look of pity in the king's eyes. I lost my parents once already, and I did not think that sharp pain of the initial realization could repeat itself, but now I see that it can. There is no limit to how much pain can be felt in a life.

Lex is the only person in either world who could understand. I wish that he were here. I would even take his cynicism, his "That's the way it is, Little Sister. What did you expect?" if he had no comfort to offer.

But I can't have even that much. All that's left of my family is gone from this floating city. There is no one waiting for me at our apartment. It's only me.

Celeste is not the fool her brother makes her out to be. She has heard the full report of everything that happened the night her father was slain. She has heard that a maddened patrolman killed her father, and that I was the one to fight the patrolman off.

I can tell, however, that she doesn't believe a word of it. We don't speak in the days before her brother's coronation, and the truth lingers in the air between us, something between what she has heard and what she fears.

Hours before her brother is to become king, I find her sitting on the top step before my chamber door, dragging her fingertip across her daughter's face.

"What do they know?"

I stop ascending the stairs and hold fast to the banister. She's just close enough that she could extend her foot and kick me to my death to avenge her father if she wanted.

When I don't answer, she raises her head. It's the first time she's truly looked at me since the ordeal that night, and I'm surprised at the lack of malice in her eyes. She looks only curious.

"What does who know?" I ask.

"The kingdom," she says. "Have they heard about my daughter?"

Strange, I think, that a child with such an important role to play remains nameless.

"There have been rumors about a child," I say. "The night we ran for the jet, some people heard her crying. But they suspect she's the child of a mistress your brother has been keeping. Or that he rescued a fugitive from the ground and the child is hers. It's hard to tell what they think—it changes by the hour."

Her sharp laugh hits the walls of the stairwell like a dozen slaps. "That figures he'd get the credit, even for this. Do you know my brother has been in conference with Nim all morning? 'One king to another' he says. I'm not even invited. Fancy that."

"It's safer for you if the citizens believe the rumor," I say. I mean to console her, and it's also the truth. "There's too much danger if the kingdom finds out you've had a child outside of the queue. It's forbidden."

She shakes her head. "Dead kings dictated our history books, and male appointees transcribed them, Morgan. I wonder how many daughters and sisters and mothers wrote the stories that never made it onto the page."

I know just what she's thinking: She wants to announce

her handiwork to her kingdom. She wants to give them their new child of two worlds, and she believes they'll love it the way she believed her father would love it. I know, also, that she can't be talked out of her ideas once she's had them. But still I'm going to try.

Cautiously, I approach and sit beside her. "Celeste." My voice is soft. "I think what you've done is incredibly brave. I do. And, with time, the two kingdoms will see it as well. Your brother will do away with the queue, and when he opens up a flight path to the ground, everyone will have more freedom than they can fathom. They'll thank you for that."

She looks at me.

"But," I go on, "right now, all they will see is that you have something they can't have. You were allowed a right that would be taken from them. They'll hate you for it."

"Some will," she says. "But I don't care about that. It isn't my mission in life to be liked. It's my mission to do what's right for Internment and Havalais. I'm here to change things. It's why I was born; I've always known that, even before I knew what it meant."

"And you *will*," I assure her.

"Just not today, is that it?"

"Nothing grand can be accomplished in a single day," I say.

"Oh, I beg to differ." She stands, and for all her fire, she must move slowly and cringing all the while. She shouldn't be out of bed at all, if she were to take her doctor's advice.

Her brother told me that it was a torturous labor. After hours of watching his daughter struggle, the king ordered the doctor to render her unconscious and to cut the child from her stomach. He was certain her screams could be heard throughout the kingdom and he wanted it over with. Prince Azure could only listen outside the locked door as his sister fell silent.

That was the most he would speak of it. Celeste said nothing of it at all. She is not the sort of person to acknowledge something so unhelpful as pain.

"We aren't different, you and I," Celeste says. "We don't treat rules as though they're walls. I suppose I was just born surrounded by bigger barriers to climb."

"Sometimes it's wise to pretend to have no interest in climbing," I say.

In her sad smile I can't tell if my words have reached her. I hope that they have.

The coronation ceremony is to take place in the evening. The new king and Nimble have been in conference for days, with Celeste growing all the more anxious.

At last, with three hours before the ceremony, the door to the king's study opens and we're invited inside.

It's a bizarre council for a king. His advisers consist of Pen, Celeste, and myself. He's still determining whether Basil is trustworthy. The table could easily seat a dozen heads. Past kings might have chosen as few as three advisers, though all of them would have been men, and all of them much older and better versed in the old ways than we are.

But this king does not care for the old ways, and we are the only ones on this floating city whom he can truly trust.

"So kind of you to finally invite us in, Brother," Celeste says, breezing past him and taking the seat beside Nimble, who looks at her with concern. Though there's color in her cheeks and she looks well, something has changed. She's aged years in just a few days.

Her hair falls straight before her rigid shoulders, with no braided crown. She's wearing a loose button-up dress that hides her figure, with a lace collar that just brushes her clenched jaw. She looks a decade older than the mischievous princess who stowed away on the metal bird. Nonetheless she still looks the part of the princess Internment loves — pretty and benign.

"Celeste," the new king says, "I've invited you here so that we might get through this bloody ceremony as a team. But for that to work, I need you to trust me without having a tantrum about hierarchy."

"Tantrum?" She looks at him innocently. "Of course not, Your Majesty. I'm only the spare. Here to serve."

He rubs his temples and sighs. To the group of us he says, "None of us has ever been to a coronation ceremony, but throughout history they've been transcribed, and I can tell you from the pages I've just slogged through that they are long and insufferable. This won't be one of those."

"Won't it have to be?" Pen says. "You're declaring so many changes to our law."

"It hasn't been all fun and games behind this locked door," he says. "I've written several new laws and arranged for copies to be delivered to every home. I believe it's better this way. More organized."

The new king sits uneasily at the head of the table, still wearing one of his white ruffled shirts. He looks nothing at all like a king, and I worry over whether he'll be able to command this city.

"The feature of my coronation speech will be with regards to the ground," he says. "Pen has done the math, and it's her prediction that it will take roughly five years for Internment to resurface to its coordinates before the jet began making passage. Knowing that, Nimble—being the king of Havalais now—will head a project to build aircrafts that will travel between the two kingdoms. If all goes well, there will be a larger jet that will carry citizens between the two kingdoms every five years."

Celeste looks between her brother and Nim. "Five years?" she says. "Where will I be during that time?"

Here the new king pauses. No emotion registers on his face, but I can see that he's holding his breath and there's a slight twitching in his thumb. "You and your child will be on the ground," he says. "Someone with royal blood from Internment must be there to oversee the project and to serve as a representative of our kingdom. There's no one better suited than you."

Celeste stares, with wide, dazed eyes, at nothing in particular. She wanted an important role, but I doubt this was what she had in mind.

"Five years." Her voice is a whisper. She looks at King Azure. "When will we leave?"

"Tomorrow morning."

"But what about Mother?"

He can't give her an answer she'll want to hear. No one speaks, and the silence rises up around us like waves. When I can bear it no longer, I say, "King Ingram had a radio that he used to communicate with your father, didn't he?"

"Yes," the new king says, and clears his throat. "Pen has been tinkering with that."

"It's a bit archaic, but functional," Pen offers. "It operates on radio waves, and as long as there's something to pick up the frequency, it will work." She glances at me for an instant and then away. "I've volunteered to return to Havalais and prepare weekly reports, and technology will be one of the things I observe."

A stone-solid weight sinks in my stomach. And suddenly five years feels like a lifetime.

The new king must pick up on my worry, because he leans toward me and says, "Morgan, I'd very much prefer if you stayed here. You know more than I do about the day-to-day life in this city. You've grown up in the public, unlike my sister and me. Your family had a jumper and you've been subjected to specialists. You know more than anyone the importance of changing the way of things. And I dare to say I trust you."

I can't draw a full breath. I hide my hands under the table to conceal their trembling. Though I don't look at her, I can feel Pen's eyes watching me.

"I'd have to think about it, Your Majesty," I say.

"Yes, do," he says.

He goes on talking about the changes he means to make in the city, but I can't retain a word of it. Five years away from my brother and Alice. Five years in this city, where my mother is dead and my father is nowhere to be found. Basil would prefer to stay—I know that. He would be with his family again.

But what do I want?

There's a chill under my skin that won't warm. After the meeting has ended, I am the first through the door. I stumble dazedly down the stairwell and out to the garden, where the poppies pool like blood against the cobbles.

If I focus on the center of all the flowers, I stop seeing the edges of the petals, and it becomes a red ocean. The people of Internment can never know the beauty and the terror of all that water below us, filled with fish and animals that could swallow us whole. And the mermaids, and the lights glittering from the harbor. All my life I wondered what lay below this city, and the truth is so much bigger and more fantastic than I could have imagined.

In five years I could see so much more of it. Without Jack Piper to dictate my every move and exploit me for his gain, I could even leave Havalais. I wouldn't have to report back to any king.

I don't know how long I sit there, mystified by all the possibilities, before Basil sits beside me.

I lean against him, and he wraps his arm around my shoulders. It's one thing to know I love him, but quite another to be reminded in this way of how easily my body fits against his, like coming home.

At last, he says, "Pen told me about your meeting with the king."

I breathe out the weight that's been crushing my chest. "So you know about his offer, then." I look from the poppies to the sky, with its thin wisps of clouds. The sky is always blue here, always calm, even when it's storming below us. "I don't think I can do it, Basil. I don't think I can stay here for five years. Not if I have the chance to leave."

"Then you shouldn't." He says it with such ease, as though he's always known it would come to this. "It's five years, not an eternity. You could always come back if you wanted."

His body is warm and familiar against mine, and I know that for all the wonders the ground holds, there is nothing like this feeling that I belong. I will always want to come back to him.

Though I dread the answer, I ask, "What will you do if I go?"

He's quiet for a long while, and then he says, "I love you for your adventurous spirit, Morgan, as much as I have always feared it. All my life, I've thought that a day would come when you'd hitch a ride on the wind and soar off into the sky."

I sit up and turn to face him. "That isn't what I'm doing. You know that, don't you?"

He smiles. "Yes, I know. But if this opportunity had arisen when we were children, I would have tried to make you stay. I would have thought that it was up to me to protect you. The idea of letting go would have terrified me."

"Basil . . ."

"But I'd rather watch you sail off into the sky than try to keep you here for my sake."

"You think I should go, then."

"You didn't need me to tell you that."

I stare down at my betrothal band, perhaps never to be filled with his blood now that the new king will be doing away with assigned betrothals. These little glass rings have seen thousands upon thousands of marriages. But none has ever been worn by a girl who went off to explore the world alone.

It's only five years, I remind myself. It isn't forever.

I don't have a chance to give the king an answer before the coronation ceremony.

I borrow one of Celeste's dresses—a soft yellow that reminds me of falling leaves—and follow everyone down the stairs. Along the way, Pen takes my hand and holds tight. She doesn't know yet what my decision will be. I wonder if Thomas will follow her to the ground, but I know that it won't change her mind one way or the other. She's going, with or without him. With or without me.

We've both grown so much in less than a year's time. We're less afraid to face life on our own. I know that she won't try to convince me one way or the other, nor will I for her. We will not always be in the same city. We will float off in opposite directions to explore the worlds, and find each other again and again through the years, reveling in the changes we've made while we were apart.

King Azure stands upon a makeshift stage that is centuries old. Its boards creak with his steps. Internment can never compare to the grandeur of the ground. This is no glittering palace the size of a city. But up here, we don't lose ourselves in the illusion of fineries. This king does not mean to dazzle, merely to reign.

Hundreds of people have come to witness the dawning of a new king. It happens only once in a lifetime, and I suspect the entire city would be here if only it were possible to fit them all in front of the clock tower.

A patrolman is managing the camera that will broadcast the event. King Azure is surrounded by a wall of patrolmen as he begins his coronation speech. As always, Celeste stands in her usual place beside him. But unlike in the other broadcasts, the pair of them don't look bored. There is something fierce in their eyes.

When he speaks, he doesn't get deep into the politics. He focuses mainly on the ground, and that his sister will oversee the development of new aircrafts. In five years, he promises aircrafts large enough to transport as many as fifty passengers at a time. And in the future, perhaps a hundred. Perhaps more. The future is all about expansion.

Celeste is regal and as still as a statue, and I wonder if the prospect of returning to Havalais has left her in a daze. All day I've had a horrible feeling that she will announce the birth of her child or something equally damning. But she doesn't, and once the ceremony is through, I'm relieved. I think she is too. She flees from the stage the moment the speech is over. Her brother turns to her for reassurance, and he's met with only the crowd closing in to speak to him.

Someone asks him about the princess's health. She was rumored to be at death's door just a few days ago, after all.

"The king talks to his citizens?" Nim says.

"Of course," I say. "But then, he doesn't have a castle to retreat to. Not like you will once you return."

"Oh, that old thing," Nim says. "Celeste thinks I ought to use it for something public. A shelter of sorts. I think she's onto something." He cranes his neck and searches the crowd. "Where is she?"

"Hiding away somewhere, I'm sure." I nudge him. "You should go inside and look for her."

Once he's gone, I slip through the crowd and begin making my way to the woods. I don't want King Azure to find me. Not yet. Not until I'm ready to answer his proposal.

Just when I've broken free of the ceremony, someone grabs my arm and reels me back. I expect Pen, here to scold me about leaving her to fend for herself in that commotion, but instead I find myself staring into the face of a boy I don't recognize.

He's almost too flawless to be real. A well-colored drawing in one of Birdie's fashion magazines, not a blond hair on his head out of place. "Don't run off so soon," he says, his voice as gentle as it is menacing. "I have so wanted to meet the girl who's been to the ground and back. Morgan, isn't it? I'm Virgil."

In our history book, Virgil was the name of a scribe who fell in love with an uncorrupted who became a star in the sky after she died. Her name was Celeste.

I pull my arm free of his grip. It's all so very on-the-nose. So this is the boy the princess was fated to marry, the one who was conceived just to be her match.

The historical Virgil did not end up with the historical Celeste, and I wonder if this boy has realized yet that history will repeat itself.

"Yes," I say. "Is there something I can help you with?"

His lip quirks into a lopsided smile that might be charming if I didn't know how hated he is by Celeste and her brother. "Eager to please," he says. "I like that."

Eager to be rid of him is all.

"I was hoping you could tell me where my betrothed has run off to. She was gone the moment her brother finally stopped droning on."

"If you'd paid any attention to his droning, you'd know that she's not your betrothed any longer."

He sighs as though this is all a trivial inconvenience. "It will be amusing to watch this child king test the waters. But that's one decree that won't stick, I'm certain. In any case, have you seen her?"

"I haven't, no," I say.

"I've been by several times since her return from the ground," he says. "I was turned away at every instance and led to believe she was at death's door. Imagine my relief to see her alive and well. A miraculous recovery brought on by the excitement of her brother's new role, I suppose."

"It seems that way," I say. With his cool stare he has made me second-guess my decision to go into the woods alone. I look past him, into the milling crowd that seems to be moving, as endlessly as the ocean's waves, in King Azure's direction.

"Would you be so kind as to give her this?" He has extracted a folded note from his breast pocket. "When you see her again."

"All right," I say, and am relieved that this will be the end of it. Even as he turns back into the crowd, he is looking for her, though surely he knows that this will prove futile. She's long gone by now, and half a dozen patrolmen are guarding the only open entrance to the clock tower.

I look at the paper resting in my palm. It has been folded into a perfect square, tied with a length of string. If it's a profession of love, I'm sure that it's insincere.

"Who was that?" Basil has moved to my side.

"Celeste's betrothed."

His eyes widen. "Really. So that's him."

"I wondered why she ran off so quickly after the speech. Now I know."

Basil points to a girl talking to King Azure. From this distance I can just see her light hair pinned atop her head. "That's his betrothed."

"Really?" I stand up on tiptoes to try to have a better look. "How do you know?"

"He introduced her to me. They seem to have a cordial relationship, at least."

I wonder if she knows the full truth about him and his desires. From where I stand, they seem to be laughing as they talk.

"I was just about to run off and hide," I say. "Care to join me?"

He grins. "Always."

We hold hands as we walk. Neither of us planned it; it just seems to happen. We fit together.

"I've made a decision," I say, and though he says nothing, I can feel his body tensing. "Once the ceremony is over, I'll tell the king that he's presented me with a flattering offer, but I must decline." I lean forward so I can see Basil's face. He looks at me. "I'm going to the ground," I tell him. "It's not forever. Only until the next flight to Internment, and then I'll come back. I'll have to. It will always call to me."

He forces a smile. "Good," he says. "I wouldn't have believed you if you'd told me you wanted to stay."

"Basil . . ." I nearly lose my nerve. My heart is beating fast and there's pain tangled up in the fear and excitement. "When we first left Internment, you chose to come with me. You chose to leave your family, and I—I was happy that you did, but it's not a one-way venture anymore. It's not forever. You don't have to choose and neither do I."

He nods. "I was thinking the same." He stops our walking, and he turns to face me. "I need to be with my family now. They're scared, and Leland is so young—I want to be there for him as he grows up. They almost lost me once, I don't want to leave them again."

"Five years isn't forever," I remind him. "And I'll radio in when Pen reports back to the king." I squeeze his hand. "I'll tell you everything."

"I'll be there every broadcast," he says.

"Remind me—remind me of what Internment is like, every time we talk," I say. "While I was on the ground, I think I began to forget bits and pieces of it."

He stares at me a long while, and we say nothing. But when he brushes his hand across my cheek, I fall against him and squeeze my eyes shut to ward off the tears.

"I've loved you all my life," I say.

His arms circle around me. "I've loved you, too."

Later, in the starry silence, Basil and I spend our last night together. We don't guess at what will become of us in five years. We don't imagine the things we'll see or the ways we'll change. We say nothing, absolutely nothing, and in the darkness our bodies find each other, his asking permission, mine drawing him in.

It's painful, and peaceful, and in its own way, freeing. We draw each other as close as we can. And then we let each other go.

23

There's a knock at our bedroom door before the sun has fully risen in its sky. "Morgan?" Pen's voice. She doesn't open the door. "The king wants us downstairs in ten minutes. Are you awake?"

"Yes," I say. "I'll be there."

Basil and I get dressed. I wear another of Celeste's borrowed dresses—white with an eyelet skirt and a red ribbon laced up the bodice—and I realize that it's the only piece of clothing from Internment I'll bring with me to the ground, and it isn't even mine.

The only other thing I carry is my ring, which gleams dully in the early light. Basil and I made no promises to wear them. I don't know if he'll still be wearing his when I return in five years, and I don't know if I'll still be wearing mine. But for now, it comforts me.

We descend the stairs, and King Azure is waiting for us

in the lobby, Celeste at his side, holding her infant in the crook of her arm and rubbing her reddened eyes as though she's been crying all night. After the ceremony, she went into her mother's bedroom and closed the door. She wanted to spend her last hours in this city by her mother's side. After everything, it was the only time they would have left.

Nimble, Pen, and Thomas are talking to one another in low voices nearby. So Thomas has decided to follow Pen. That doesn't surprise me. He wouldn't know how to breathe without her, and I suppose that's a good thing, because she needs him every bit as much, only she's too proud to tell him so. Telling him she was going to the ground was as close as she'd get to asking him to follow.

"Did I tell you?" Celeste says to me when I approach. "I've thought of a name for my daughter. At first I thought 'Riles,' for Nim's brother, but 'Riley' is much more fitting for a girl, don't you think?" She runs her finger against the infant's cheek fondly. "It's a strong name. The name of a girl who won't take an injustice quietly. One who will incite a riot if she needs to."

"I've the feeling she would be willing to do that no matter what her name is," I say. "She's your daughter after all."

Celeste laughs, and it's the first time I've seen her smile in days. "Yes," she says.

There are a dozen patrolmen surrounding us when we make our way to the jet. It will be a crowded flight, as many of the men from the ground will also be returning with us.

"I apologize that it won't be much of a grand send-off,"

King Azure says. "I didn't want there to be a crowd. It's unsafe for you."

"A crowd is the last thing any of us wants," Celeste says. Nim is holding their daughter now, and he looks considerably more rested. He was sent to his chambers early, with a pill to help him sleep. It's his job to fly us home, and King Azure insisted that he not be disturbed until morning.

The jet is waiting for us on the other side of the tracks, and Basil remains by my side until we've reached the metal staircase that leads inside.

This is it. This is where I leave him.

When we first left Internment, and the metal bird began sinking toward the sky, Pen broke into a sudden panic; she would have done anything to remain on Internment, even knowing that to leave the bird was to die.

I understand that panic now. For the first time, I truly understand it. I'm terrified to leave, overtaken by the finality of my decision. In five years, this city will have changed without me. Basil will be older. I'll be older. We'll both have learned who we are without each other.

If I stayed here, I could marry him tomorrow. In five years, without the queue we could even have a child.

I could stay. I could.

But I would never forgive myself. The things I love about Internment would turn into the things I'd resent for holding me back. And so I say, "Good-bye." Not only to Basil, but to all I'm leaving behind.

He kisses me once, briefly. "Good-bye."

The warmth of his lips, I'm certain, will stay with me

the entire way down, just like the dull pain deep within my hips that reminds me of the night before.

Everyone else has said their good-byes and boarded the jet. I'm the last to go.

"Stop!" a voice cries out, just as Pen and Celeste are guiding me into the jet's entrance. For one bereft, dazed instant I think that it's Basil saying that he'll come with me. But no, the voice does not belong to him.

Celeste's eyes narrow and she pushes past me. "What do you want, Virgil?"

Her ex-betrothed is scrambling over the train tracks and running toward us. He doesn't make it far. The patrolmen step into action, but it's King Azure who grabs him and pins his arms behind his back. Virgil struggles. "I knew you would try to sneak off without me. I demand to go with you!"

Celeste rubs her palms over her eyes, exasperated. "If you want to see the ground, you'll have your opportunity in five years. On your own."

"You can't go without me," he calls out. "We're meant to be together. I was born to be your other."

"What's done is done. We're nothing to each other now. I suggest you go on and have your own future. I'm off to start mine."

"There's someone else, isn't there?" he snaps. "I knew that must be it. You've been maddened by lust!"

Celeste stands tall. She is no longer a child who needs to run to the poppies to be free of him. "There's always been someone else," she says. "Me."

She pulls the door shut with a slam, and the latches fall into place.

The engines burst to life, and I rush to the tiny oval window to catch one last glimpse of Internment before it's gone. In seconds we're moving, and Basil is too far away for me to see his face. He stands still to watch me go, even with the dirt and the wind in his hair.

And then we've broken through the wind barrier, and when the clouds have cleared, I can no longer see him.

Pen and Celeste put their arms around me, and together we watch our city become a shadow in the sky, and then nothing at all.

"Once we land, where will you go?" Pen asks me.

"Everywhere," I say.

Liane Moriarty is the Australian author of eight internationally bestselling novels, including the number one *New York Times* bestsellers *The Husband's Secret*, *Big Little Lies* and *Truly Madly Guilty*. Her books have been read by more than fourteen million people worldwide, including two million in Australia

The Husband's Secret was a number one UK bestseller, an Amazon Best Book of 2013 and has been translated into over forty languages. *Big Little Lies* and *Truly Madly Guilty* reached number one on the *New York Times* bestseller list in their first week of publication – the first time this has been achieved by an Australian. Liane is also the author of the Space Brigade series for children. She lives in Sydney with her husband, son and daughter.

You can find out more about Liane's books at her website www.lianemoriarty.com

Also by Liane Moriarty

nine
perfect
strangers

LIANE
MORIARTY

PAN
Pan Macmillan Australia

First published 2018 in Macmillan by Pan Macmillan Australia Pty Ltd
This Pan edition published 2019 by Pan Macmillan Australia Pty Ltd
1 Market Street, Sydney, New South Wales, Australia, 2000

Cataloguing-in-Publication entry is available from the National Library of Australia
http://catalogue.nla.gov.au

Typeset in Bembo Regular by Post Pre-press
Printed by McPherson's Printing Group

MIX
Paper from
responsible sources
FSC® C001695
FSC
www.fsc.org

For Kati
And for Dad
With lots of love from me

You suppose you are the trouble
But you are the cure
You suppose that you are the lock on the door
But you are the key that opens it
Rumi

Just when I discovered the meaning of life, they changed it.
George Carlin

chapter one

Yao

'I'm fine,' said the woman. 'There's nothing wrong with me.'

She didn't look fine to Yao.

It was his first day as a trainee paramedic. His third call-out. Yao wasn't nervous, but he was in a hyper-vigilant state because he couldn't bear to make even an inconsequential mistake. When he was a child, mistakes had made him wail inconsolably, and they still made his stomach cramp.

A single bead of perspiration rolled down the woman's face, leaving a snail's trail through her make-up. Yao wondered why women painted their faces orange, but that was not relevant.

'I'm fine. Maybe just twenty-four-hour virus,' she said, with the hint of an Eastern European accent.

'Observe everything about your patient and their environment,' Yao's supervisor, Finn, had told him. 'Think of yourself as a secret agent looking for diagnostic clues.'

Yao observed a middle-aged, overweight woman with pronounced pink shadows under distinctive sea-green eyes and wispy brown hair pulled into a sad little knot at the back

1

of her neck. She was pale and clammy, her breathing ragged. A heavy smoker, judging by her ashtray scent. She sat in a high-backed leather chair behind a gigantic desk. It seemed like she was something of a bigwig, if the size of this plush corner office and its floor-to-ceiling harbour views were any indication of corporate status. They were on the seventeenth floor and the sails of the Opera House were so close you could see the diamond-shaped cream and white tiles.

The woman had one hand on her mouse. She scrolled through emails on her oversized computer screen, as if the two paramedics checking her over were a minor inconvenience, repairmen there to fix a power point. She wore a tailored navy business suit like a punishment, the jacket pulled uncomfortably tight across her shoulders.

Yao took the woman's free hand and clipped a pulse oximeter onto her finger. He noted a shiny, scaly patch of reddish skin on her forearm. Pre-diabetic?

Finn asked, 'Are you on any medication, Masha?' He had a chatty, loose manner with patients, as if he were making small talk at a barbecue, beer in hand.

Yao noticed that Finn always used the names of patients, whereas Yao felt shy talking to them as though they were old friends, but if it enhanced patient outcomes, he would learn to overcome his shyness.

'I am on no medication at all,' said Masha, her gaze fixed on the computer. She clicked on something decisively then looked away from her monitor and back up at Finn. Her eyes looked like they'd been borrowed from someone beautiful. Yao assumed they were coloured contact lenses. 'I am in good health. I apologise for taking up your time. I certainly didn't ask for an ambulance.'

'I called the ambulance,' said a very pretty, dark-haired young woman in high heels and a tight checked skirt with interlocking diamond shapes similar to the Opera House tiles. The skirt looked excellent on her but that was obviously of no relevance right now, even though she was, technically, part of the surrounding environment Yao was meant to be observing. The girl chewed on the fingernail of her little finger. 'I'm her PA. She . . . ah . . .' She lowered her voice as if she were about to reveal something shameful. 'Her face went dead white and then she fell off her chair.'

'I did not fall off my chair!' snapped Masha.

'She kind of slid off it,' amended the girl.

'I momentarily felt dizzy, that is all,' said Masha to Finn. 'And then I got straight back to work. Could we cut this short? I'm happy to pay your full, you know, cost or *rate*, or however it is you charge for your services. I have private health cover, of course. I just really don't have time for this right now.' She turned her attention back to her assistant. 'Don't I have an eleven o'clock with Ryan?'

'I'll cancel him.'

'Did I hear my name?' said a man from the doorway. 'What's going on?' A guy in a too-tight purple shirt swaggered in carrying a bundle of manila folders. He spoke with a plummy British accent, like he was a member of the royal family.

'Nothing,' said Masha. 'Take a seat.'

'Masha is clearly not available right now!' said the poor PA.

Yao sympathised. He didn't appreciate flippancy about matters of health, and he thought his profession deserved more respect. He also had a strong aversion to spiky-haired guys with posh accents who wore purple shirts a size too small to show off their overly developed pecs.

'No, no, just sit down, Ryan! This won't take long. I'm fine.' Masha beckoned impatiently.

'Can I check your blood pressure, please, ah, Masha?' said Yao, bravely mumbling her name as he went to strap the cuff around her upper arm.

'Let's take that jacket off first.' Finn sounded amused. 'You're a busy lady, Masha.'

'I actually really do need her sign-off on these,' said the young guy to the PA in a low voice.

Yao thought, *I actually really do need to check your boss's vital signs right now, motherfucker.*

Finn helped Masha out of her jacket and put it over the back of her chair in a courtly way.

'Let's see those documents, Ryan.' Masha adjusted the buttons on her cream silk shirt.

'I just need signatures on the top two pages.' The guy held out the folder.

'Are you kidding me?' The PA lifted both hands incredulously.

'Mate, you need to come back another time,' said Finn, with a definite edge to his barbecue voice.

The guy stepped back, but Masha clicked her fingers at him for the folder, and he instantly jumped forward and handed it over. He obviously considered Masha scarier than Finn, which was saying something, because Finn was a big, strong guy.

'This will take fourteen seconds at the most,' she said to Finn. Her voice thickened on the word 'most' so that it sounded like 'mosht'.

Yao, the blood-pressure cuff still in his hand, made eye contact with Finn.

Masha's head lolled to one side, as though she'd just nodded off. The manila folder slipped from her fingers.

'Masha?' Finn spoke in a loud, commanding voice.

She slumped forward, arms akimbo, like a puppet.

'Just like that!' screeched the PA with satisfaction. 'That's exactly what she did before!'

'Jesus!' The purple-shirt guy retreated. *Jesus.* Sorry! I'll just . . .'

'Okay, Masha, let's get you onto the floor,' said Finn.

Finn lifted her under the armpits and Yao took her legs, grunting with the effort. She was a very tall woman, Yao realised; much taller than him. At least six feet and a dead weight. Together, he and Finn laid her on her side on the grey carpet. Finn folded her jacket into a pillow and put it behind her head.

Masha's left arm rose stiff and zombie-like above her head. Her hands curled into spastic fists. She continued to breathe in jerky gasps as her body postured.

She was having a seizure.

Seizures were disquieting to watch but Yao knew you just had to wait them out. There was nothing around Masha's neck that Yao could loosen. He scanned the space around her, and saw nowhere she could bang her head.

'Is this what happened earlier?' Finn looked up at the assistant.

'*No.* No, before she just sort of fainted.' The wide-eyed PA watched with appalled fascination.

'Does she have a history of seizures?' asked Finn.

'I don't think so. I don't know.' As she spoke, the PA was shuffling back towards the door of the office, where a crowd of other corporate types had now gathered. Someone held up a mobile phone, filming, as if their boss's seizure were a rock concert.

'Start compressions.' Finn's eyes were flat and smooth like stones.

There was a moment – no more than a second, but still a moment – in which Yao did nothing as his brain scrambled to process what had just happened. He would remember that moment of frozen incomprehension forever. He *knew* that a cardiac arrest could present with seizure-like symptoms and yet he'd still missed it because his brain had been so utterly, erroneously convinced of one reality: *This patient is having a seizure.* If Finn hadn't been there, Yao may have sat back on his haunches and observed a woman in cardiac arrest *without acting,* like an airline pilot flying a jet into the ground because he is overly reliant on his faulty instruments. Yao's finest instrument was his brain, and on this day it was faulty.

They shocked her twice but were unable to establish a consistent heart rhythm. Masha Dmitrichenko was in full cardiac arrest as they carried her out of the corner office to which she would never return.

chapter two

Ten years later

Frances

On a hot, cloudless January day, Frances Welty, the formerly bestselling romantic novelist, drove alone through scrubby bushland six hours north-west of her Sydney home.

The black ribbon of highway unrolled hypnotically ahead of her as the air-conditioning vents roared arctic air full-blast at her face. The sky was a giant deep blue dome surrounding her tiny solitary car. There was far too *much* sky for her liking.

She smiled because she reminded herself of one of those peevish TripAdvisor reviewers: *So I called reception and asked for a lower, cloudier, more comfortable sky. A woman with a strong foreign accent said there were no other skies available! She was very rude about it too! NEVER AGAIN. DON'T WASTE YOUR MONEY.*

It occurred to Frances that she was possibly quite close to losing her mind.

No, she wasn't. She was fine. Perfectly sane. Really and truly.

She flexed her hands around the steering wheel, blinked dry eyes behind her sunglasses and yawned so hugely her jaw clicked.

'Ow,' she said, although it didn't hurt.

She sighed, looking out the window for something to break the monotony of the landscape. It would be so harsh and unforgiving out there. She could just imagine it: the drone of blowflies, the mournful cry of crows, and all that glaring white-hot light. Wide brown land indeed.

Come on. Give me a cow, a crop, a shed. I spy with my little eye something beginning with . . .

N. Nothing.

She shifted in her seat, and her lower back rewarded her with a jolt of pain so violent and personal it brought tears to her eyes.

'For God's *sake*,' she said pitifully.

The back pain had begun two weeks ago, on the day she finally accepted that Paul Drabble had disappeared. She was dialling the number for the police and trying to work out how to refer to Paul – her partner, boyfriend, lover, her 'special friend'? – when she felt the first twinge. It was the most obvious example of psychosomatic pain ever, except knowing it was psychosomatic didn't make it hurt any less.

It was strange to look in the mirror each night and see the reflection of her lower back looking as soft, white and gently plump as it always had. She expected to see something dreadful, like a gnarled mass of tree roots.

She checked the time on the dashboard: 2.57 pm. The turn-off should be coming up any minute. She'd told the reservations people at Tranquillum House that she'd be there around 3.30 to 4 pm and she hadn't made any unscheduled stops.

Tranquillum House was a 'boutique health and wellness

resort'. Her friend Ellen had suggested it. 'You need to *heal*,' she'd told Frances after their third cocktail (an excellent white peach Bellini) at lunch last week. 'You look like *shit*.'

Ellen had done a 'cleanse' at Tranquillum House three years ago when she, too, had been 'burnt out' and 'run-down' and 'out of condition' and – 'Yes, yes, I get it,' Frances had said.

'It's quite . . . unusual, this place,' Ellen had told Frances. 'Their approach is kind of unconventional. Life-changing.'

'How exactly did your life change?' Frances had asked, reasonably, but she'd never got a clear answer to that question. In the end, it all seemed to come down to the whites of Ellen's eyes, which had become really white, like, freakily white! Also, she lost three kilos! Although Tranquillum House wasn't about weight loss – Ellen was at great pains to point that out. It was about *wellness*, but, you know, what woman complains about losing three kilos? Not Ellen, that's for sure. Not Frances either.

Frances had gone home and looked up the website. She'd never been a fan of self-denial, never been on a diet, rarely said no if she felt like saying yes or yes if she felt like saying no. According to her mother, Frances's first greedy word was 'more'. She always wanted more.

Yet the photos of Tranquillum House had filled her with a strange, unexpected yearning. They were golden-hued, all taken at sunset or sunrise, or else filtered to make it look that way. Pleasantly middle-aged people did warrior poses in a garden of white roses next to a beautiful country house. A couple sat in one of the 'natural hot springs' that surrounded the property. Their eyes were closed, heads tipped back, and they were smiling ecstatically as water bubbled around them. Another photo showed a woman enjoying a 'hot stone massage' on a deckchair next to an aquamarine swimming pool. Frances had imagined those hot stones placed with delightful symmetry down her own spine, their magical heat melting away her pain.

As she dreamed of hot springs and gentle yoga, a message flashed urgently on her screen: *Only one place remaining for the exclusive Ten-Day Mind and Body Total Transformation Retreat!* It had made her feel stupidly competitive and she clicked *Book now*, even though she didn't *really* believe there was only one place remaining. Still, she keyed in her credit card details pretty damned fast, just in case.

It seemed that in a mere ten days she would be 'transformed' in ways she 'never thought possible'. There would be fasting, meditation, yoga, creative 'emotional release exercises'. There would be no alcohol, sugar, caffeine, gluten or dairy – but as she'd just had the degustation menu at the Four Seasons, she was stuffed full of alcohol, sugar, caffeine, gluten and dairy, and the thought of giving them up didn't seem that big a deal. Meals would be 'personalised' to her 'unique needs'.

Before her booking was 'accepted', she had to answer a very long, rather invasive online questionnaire about her relationship status, diet, medical history, alcohol consumption in the previous week, and so on. She cheerfully lied her way through it. It was really none of their business. She even had to upload a photo taken in the last two weeks. She sent one of herself from her lunch with Ellen at the Four Seasons, holding up a Bellini.

There were boxes to tick for what she hoped to achieve during her ten days: everything from 'intensive couples counselling' to 'significant weight loss'. Frances ticked only the nice-sounding boxes, like 'spiritual nourishment'.

Like so many things in life, it had seemed like an excellent idea at the time.

The TripAdvisor reviews for Tranquillum House, which

she'd looked at *after* she'd paid her non-refundable fee, had been noticeably mixed. It was either the best, most incredible experience people had ever had, they wished they could give it more than five stars, they were evangelical about the food, the hot springs, the staff, or it was the worst experience of their entire lives, there was talk of legal action, post-traumatic stress and dire warnings of 'enter at your own peril'.

Frances looked again at the dashboard, hoping to catch the clock tick over to three.

Stop it. Focus. Eyes on the road, Frances. You're the one in charge of this car.

Something flickered in her peripheral vision and she flinched, ready for the massive thud of a kangaroo smashing her windscreen.

It was nothing. These imaginary wildlife collisions were all in her head. If it happened, it happened. There probably wouldn't be time to react.

She remembered a long-ago road trip with a boyfriend. They'd come across a dying emu that had been hit by a car in the middle of a highway. Frances had stayed in the passenger seat, a passive princess, while her boyfriend got out and killed the poor emu with a rock. One sharp blow to the head. When he returned to the driver's seat he was sweaty and exhilarated, a city boy thrilled with his own humane pragmatism. Frances never quite forgave him for the sweaty exhilaration. He'd *liked* killing the emu.

Frances wasn't sure if she could kill a dying animal, even now when she was fifty-two years old, financially secure and too old to be a princess.

'You could kill the emu,' she said out loud. 'Certainly you could.'

Goodness. She'd just remembered that the boyfriend was dead. Wait, was he? Yes, definitely dead. She'd heard it on the grapevine a few years back. Complications from pneumonia, supposedly. Gary always did suffer terribly from colds. Frances had never been especially sympathetic.

At that very moment her nose dripped like a tap. Perfect timing. She held the steering wheel with one hand and wiped her nose with the back of her other hand. Disgusting. It was probably Gary vindictively making her nose drip from the afterlife. Fair enough too. They'd once been on road trips and professed their love and now she couldn't even be bothered to remember he was dead.

She apologised to Gary, although, really, if he was able to access her thoughts then he should know that it wasn't her fault; if he'd made it to this age he'd know how extraordinarily vague and forgetful one became. Not all the time. Just sometimes.

Sometimes I'm as sharp as a tack, Gary.

She sniffed again. It seemed like she'd had this truly horrendous head cold even longer than the back pain. Hadn't she been sniffling the day she delivered her manuscript? Three weeks ago. Her nineteenth novel. She was still waiting to hear what her publisher thought. Once upon a time, back in the late nineties, her 'heyday', her editor would have sent champagne and flowers within two days of delivery, together with a handwritten note. *Another masterpiece!*

She understood she was no longer in her heyday, but she was still a solid, mid-level performer. An effusive email would be nice.

Or just a friendly one.

Even a brisk one-liner: *Sorry, haven't got to it yet but can't wait!* That would have been polite.

A fear she refused to acknowledge tried to worm its way up from her subconscious. No. No. Absolutely not.

She clutched the steering wheel and tried to calm her

breathing. She'd been throwing back cold and flu tablets to try to clear her nose and the pseudoephedrine was making her heart race, as if something wonderful or terrible was about to happen. It reminded her of the feeling of walking down the aisle on both her wedding days.

She was probably addicted to the cold and flu tablets. She was easily addicted. Men. Food. Wine. In fact, she felt like a glass of wine right now and the sun was still high in the sky. Lately, she'd been drinking, maybe not excessively, but certainly more enthusiastically than usual. She was on that slippery slope, hurtling towards drug and alcohol addiction! Exciting to know she could still change in significant ways. Back home there was a half-empty bottle of pinot noir sitting brazenly on her writing desk for anyone (only the cleaning lady) to see. She was Ernest frigging Hemingway. Didn't he have a bad back too? They had so much in common.

Except that Frances had a weakness for adjectives and adverbs. Apparently she scattered them about her novels like throw cushions. What was that Mark Twain quote Sol used to murmur to himself, just loud enough for her to hear, while reading her manuscripts? *When you catch an adjective, kill it.*

Sol was a real man who didn't like adjectives or throw cushions. She had an image of Sol, in bed, on top of her, swearing comically as he pulled out yet another cushion from behind her head, chucking it across the room while she giggled. She shook her head as if to shake off the memory. Fond sexual memories felt like a point for her first husband.

When everything was good in Frances's life she wished both her ex-husbands nothing but happiness and excellent erectile function. Right now, she wished plagues of locusts to rain down upon their silvery heads.

She sucked on the tiny, vicious paper cut on the tip of her right thumb. Every now and then it throbbed to remind her that it might be the smallest of her ailments but it could still ruin her day.

Her car veered to the bumpy side of the road and she removed her thumb from her mouth and clung to the steering wheel. 'Whoops-a-daisy.'

She had quite short legs, so she had to move the driver's seat close to the steering wheel. Henry used to say she looked like she was driving a dodgem car. He said it was cute. But after five years or so he stopped finding it cute and swore every time he got in the car and had to slide the seat back.

She found his sleep-talking charming for about five years or so too.

Focus!

The countryside flew by. At last a sign: *Welcome to the town of Jarribong. We're proud to be a TIDY TOWN.*

She slowed down to the speed limit of fifty, which felt almost absurdly slow.

Her head swivelled from side to side as she studied the town. A Chinese restaurant with a faded red and gold dragon on the door. A service station that looked closed. A red-brick post office. A drive-through bottle shop that looked open. A police station that seemed entirely unnecessary. Not a person in sight. It might have been tidy but it felt post-apocalyptic.

She thought of her latest manuscript. It was set in a small town. *This* was the gritty, bleak reality of small towns! Not the charming village she'd created, nestled in the mountains, with a warm, bustling cafe that smelled of cinnamon and, most fanciful of all, a *bookstore* supposedly making a profit. The reviewers would rightly call it 'twee', but it probably wouldn't get reviewed and she never read her reviews anyway.

So that was it for poor old Jarribong. Goodbye, sad little tidy town.

She put her foot on the accelerator and watched her speed slide back up to one hundred. The website had said that the turn-off was twenty minutes outside of Jarribong.

There was a sign ahead. She narrowed her eyes, hunched over the wheel to read it: *Tranquillum House next turn on the left.*

Her heart lifted. She'd done it. She'd driven six hours without quite losing her mind. Then her heart sank, because now she was going to have to go through with this thing.

'Turn left in one kilometre,' ordered her GPS.

'I don't want to turn left in one kilometre,' said Frances dolefully.

She wasn't even meant to be here, in this season or hemisphere. She was meant to be with her 'special friend' Paul Drabble in Santa Barbara, the Californian winter sun warm upon their faces as they visited wineries, restaurants and museums. She was meant to be spending long lingering afternoons getting to know Paul's twelve-year-old son, Ari, hearing his dry little chuckle as he taught her how to play some violent PlayStation game he loved. Frances's friends with kids had laughed and scoffed over that, but she'd been looking *forward* to learning the game; the storylines sounded really quite rich and complex.

An image came to her of that detective's earnest young face. He had freckles left over from childhood and he wrote down everything she said in laborious longhand using a scratchy blue ballpoint. His spelling was atrocious. He spelled 'tomorrow' with two m's. He couldn't meet her eye.

A sudden rush of intense heat enveloped her body at the memory.

Humiliation?

Probably.

Her head swam. She shivered and shook. Her hands were instantly slippery on the steering wheel.

Pull over, she told herself. *You need to pull over right now.*

She indicated, even though there was no-one behind her, and came to a stop on the side of the road. She had the sense to switch on her hazard lights. Sweat poured from her face. Within seconds her shirt was drenched. She pulled at the fabric and smeared back strands of wet hair from her forehead. A cold chill made her shake.

She sneezed, and the act of sneezing caused her back to spasm. The pain was of such truly biblical proportions that she began to laugh as tears streamed down her face. Oh yes, she *was* losing her mind. She certainly was.

A great wave of unfocused primal rage swept over her. She banged her fist against her car horn over and over, closed her eyes, threw back her head and screamed in unison with the horn, because she had this cold and this back pain and this broken bloody heart and –

'Hey!'

She opened her eyes and jumped back in her seat.

A man crouched next to her car window, rapping hard on the glass. She saw what must be his car pulled up on the opposite side of the road, with its hazard lights also on.

'You okay?' he shouted. 'Do you need help?'

For God's sake. This was meant to be a private moment of despair. How deeply embarrassing. She pressed the button to lower the window.

A very large, unpleasant, unkempt, unshaven man peered in at her. He wore a t-shirt with the faded emblem of some ancient band over a proud, solid beer belly and low-slung blue jeans. He was probably one of those outback serial killers. Even though this wasn't technically the outback. He was probably on holiday from the outback.

'Got car trouble?' he asked.

'No,' said Frances. She sat up straighter and tried to smile.

She ran a hand through her damp hair. 'Thank you. I'm fine. The car is fine. Everything is fine.'

'Are you *sick*?' said the man. He looked faintly disgusted.

'No,' said Frances. 'Not really. Just a bad cold.'

'Maybe you've got the proper flu. You look *really* sick,' said the man. He frowned, and his eyes moved to the back of her car. 'And you were screaming and sounding your horn like you . . . were in trouble.'

'Yes,' said Frances. 'Well. I thought I was alone in the middle of nowhere. I was just . . . having a bad moment.' She tried to keep the resentment from her voice. He was a good citizen who had done the right thing. He'd done what anyone would do.

'Thank you for stopping but I'm fine,' she said nicely, with her sweetest, most placatory smile. One must placate large strange men in the middle of nowhere.

'Okay then.' The man straightened with a groan of effort, his hands on his thighs to give himself leverage, but then he rapped the top of her car with his knuckles and bent down again, suddenly decisive. *I'm a man, I know what's what.* 'Look, are you too sick to drive? Because if you're not safe to drive, if you're a danger to other drivers on the road, I really can't in good conscience let you –'

Frances sat up straight. For heaven's sake. 'I just had a hot flash,' she snapped.

The man blanched. 'Oh!' He studied her. Paused. 'I always thought it was a hot *flush*,' he said.

'I believe both terms are used,' said Frances. This was her third one. She'd done a lot of reading, spoken to every woman she knew over the age of forty-five, and had a double appointment with her GP, where she had cried, 'But no-one ever said it was like this!' For now they were monitoring things. She was taking supplements, cutting back on alcohol and spicy foods. Ha ha.

'So you're okay,' said the man. He looked up and down the highway as if for help.

'I really am perfectly fine,' said Frances. Her back gave a friendly little spasm and she tried not to flinch.

'I didn't realise that hot flashes – flushes – were so . . .'

'Dramatic? Well, they're not for everyone. Just a lucky few.'

'Isn't there . . . what's it called? Hormone replacement therapy?'

Oh my Lord.

'Can you prescribe me something?' asked Frances brightly.

The man took a little step back from the car, hands up in surrender. 'Sorry. It's just, I think that was what my wife . . . Anyway, none of my business. If everything is okay, I'll just be on my way.'

'Great,' said Frances. 'Thank you for stopping.'

'No worries.'

He lifted a hand, went to say something else, evidently changed his mind and walked back towards his car. There were sweat marks on the back of his t-shirt. A mountain of a man. Lucky he decided she wasn't worth killing and raping. He probably preferred his victims less sweaty.

She watched him start his car and pull out onto the highway. He tipped one finger to his forehead as he drove off.

She waited until his car was a tiny speck in her rear-view mirror and then she reached over for the change of clothes she had waiting on the passenger seat ready for this exact situation.

'Menopause?' her eighty-year-old mother had said

vaguely, on the phone from the other side of the world, where she now lived blissfully in the south of France. 'Oh, I don't think it gave me too much trouble, darling. I got it all over and done with in a weekend, as I recall. I'm sure you'll be the same. I never had those hot flushes. I think they're a myth, to be honest.'

Hmmph, thought Frances as she used a towel to wipe away her mythical sweat.

She thought of texting a photo of her tomato-red face to her group of schoolfriends, some of whom she'd known since kindergarten. Now when they went out to dinner they discussed menopause symptoms with the same avid horror with which they'd once discussed their first periods. Nobody else was getting these over-the-top hot flushes like Frances, so she was taking it for the team. Like everything in life, their reactions to menopause were driven by their personalities: Di said she was in a permanent state of rage and if her gynaecologist didn't agree to a hysterectomy soon she was going to grab the little fucker by the collar and slam him up against the wall, Monica was embracing the 'beautiful intensity' of her emotions and Natalie was wondering anxiously if it was contributing to her anxiety. They all agreed it was totally typical of their friend Gillian to die so she could get out of menopause and then they cried into their prosecco.

No, she wouldn't text her schoolfriends, because she suddenly remembered how at that last dinner she'd looked up from her menu to catch an exchange of glances that most definitely meant: 'Poor Frances.' She could not bear pity. That particular group of solidly married friends was meant to *envy* her, or they'd pretended to envy her anyway, for all these years, but it seemed that being childless and single in your thirties was very different from being childless and single in your fifties. No longer glamorous. Now kind of tragic.

I'm only temporarily tragic, she told herself as she pulled on a clean blouse that showed a lot of cleavage. She tossed the sweaty shirt into the back seat, restarted the car, looked over her shoulder and pulled out onto the highway. *Temporarily Tragic*. It could be the name of a band.

There was a sign. She squinted. *Tranquillum House*, it said.

'Left turn ahead,' said her GPS.

'Yes, I *know*, I see it.'

She met her own eyes in the rear-view mirror and tried to give herself a wry 'isn't life interesting!' look.

Frances had always enjoyed the idea of parallel universes in which multiple versions of herself tried out different lives – one where she was a CEO instead of an author; one where she was a mother of two or four or six kids instead of none; one where she hadn't divorced Sol and one where she hadn't divorced Henry – but for the most part she'd always felt satisfied or at least accepting of the universe in which she found herself . . . except for right now, because right now it felt like there had been some sort of cataclysmic quantum physics administrative error. She'd slipped universes. She was meant to be high on lust and love in America, not pain-ridden and grief-stricken in Australia. It was just wrong. Unacceptable.

And yet here she was. There was nothing else to do, nowhere else to turn.

'Goddamn it,' she said, and turned left.

chapter three

Lars

'This one is my wife's favourite.' The vineyard manager, a chunky, cheery guy in his sixties with a retro moustache, held up a bottle of white wine. 'She says it makes her think of silk sheets. It has a creamy, velvety finish I think you'll enjoy.'

Lars swirled the tasting glass and breathed in the scent: apples and sunshine and wood smoke. An instant memory of an autumnal day. The comfort of a large, warm hand holding his. It felt like a childhood memory but probably wasn't; more likely a memory he'd borrowed from a book or movie. He sipped the wine, let it roll around his mouth, and was transported to a bar on the Amalfi Coast. Vine leaves over the light fitting and the smell of garlic and the sea. That was a bona fide happy memory from real life with photos to prove it. He remembered the spaghetti. Just parsley, olive oil and almonds. There might even be a photo of the spaghetti somewhere.

'What do you think?' The vineyard manager grinned. It was like his moustache had been perfectly preserved from 1975.

'It's excellent.' Lars took another sip, trying to get the full picture. Wine could fool you: all sunshine and apples and spaghetti and then nothing but sour disappointment and empty promises.

'I also have a pinot grigio that might appeal . . .'

Lars held up his hand and looked at his watch. 'I'd better stop there.'

'Have you got far to travel today?'

Anyone who stopped here would be on their way to somewhere else. Lars had nearly missed the small wooden *Tasting Cellar* sign. He'd slammed on the brakes because that's the sort of man he was: spontaneous. When he remembered to be.

'I'm due to check in at a health resort in an hour's time.' Lars held the wineglass up to the light and admired the golden colour. 'So no alcohol for me for the next ten days.'

'Ah. Tranquillum House, right?' said the manager. 'Doing the – what do they call it? – ten-day cleanse or some such thing?'

'For my sins,' said Lars.

'We normally get guests stopping in here on their way home. We're the first vineyard they drive by on the road back to Sydney.'

'What do they have to say about the place?' asked Lars. He pulled out his wallet. He was going to order some wine to be delivered as a welcome-home treat.

'Some of them seem a bit shell-shocked, to be honest. They mostly just need a drink and some potato chips and they get the colour back in their cheeks.' The manager placed his hand around the neck of the bottle, as if for comfort. 'Actually, my sister just got a job working in the spa there. She says her new boss is a bit . . .' He squinted hard as if trying to see the word he wanted. Finally, he said, 'Different.'

'I'm forewarned,' said Lars. He wasn't concerned. He was a health-retreat junkie. The people who ran these places tended to be 'different'.

'She says the house itself is amazing. It's got a fascinating history.'

'Built by convicts, I believe.' Lars tapped the corner of his gold Amex against the bar.

'Yeah. Poor buggers. No spa treatments for them.'

A woman appeared from a door behind him, muttering, 'Bloody internet is down *again*.' She stopped when she saw Lars and did a double take. He was used to it. He'd had a lifetime of double takes. She looked away fast, flustered.

'This is my wife,' said the vineyard manager with pride. 'We were just talking about your favourite semillon, love – the silk-sheets semillon.'

The colour rose up her neck. 'I wish you wouldn't tell people that.'

Her husband looked confused. 'I *always* tell people that.'

'I'm going to get a case,' said Lars.

He watched the wife pat her husband's back as she moved past him.

'Make it two cases,' Lars said, because he spent his days dealing with the shattered remnants of broken marriages and he was a sucker for a good one.

He smiled at the woman. Her hands fluttered to her hair while her oblivious husband pulled out a battered old order book with a pen attached by a string, leaned heavily on the counter and peered at the form in a way that indicated this was going to take some time. 'Name?'

'Lars Lee,' said Lars, as his phone beeped with a text message. He tapped the screen.

Can you at least think about it? Xx

His heart lurched as if at the sudden scuttle of a black

furry spider. For fuck's sake. He'd thought they were done with this. His thumb hovered over the message, considering. The passive aggressiveness of the 'at least'. The saccharine double kiss. Also, he didn't like the fact that the first kiss was upper case and the second was lower case and he didn't like the fact that he didn't like this. It was mildly OCD-ish.

He tapped in a rude, boorish upper-case reply: *NO. I WILL NOT.*

But then he deleted it, and shoved his phone back into the pocket of his jeans.

'Let me try that pinot grigio.'

chapter four

Frances

Frances drove twenty minutes down a bumpy dirt road that jolted the car so hard her bones rattled and her lower back screamed.

At last she came to a stop in front of what appeared to be an extremely locked gate with an intercom. It was like arriving at a minimum-security jail. An ugly barbed-wire fence stretched endlessly in either direction.

She had envisaged driving up a stately tree-lined drive to the 'historic' house and having someone greet her with a green smoothie. This didn't feel very *healing*, to be frank.

Stop it, she told herself. If she got into that *I'm a dissatisfied consumer* mode everything would start to dissatisfy her, and she was going to be here for ten days. She needed to be open and flexible. Going to a health resort was like travelling to a new country. One must embrace different cultures and be patient with minor inconveniences.

She lowered her car window. Hot thick air filled her throat like smoke as she leaned out and pressed the green button on the intercom with her thumb. The button burned from the sun and it hurt her paper cut.

She sucked on her thumb and waited for a disembodied voice to welcome her, or for the wrought-iron gate to magically open.

Nothing.

She looked again at the intercom and saw a handwritten note sticky-taped next to the button. The writing was so small she could only make out the important word 'instructions' but nothing else.

For goodness sake, she thought, as she went through her handbag for her reading glasses. Surely a good proportion of visitors were over forty.

She found her glasses, put them on, peered at the sign and *still* couldn't make it out. Tut-tutting and muttering, she got out of the car. The heat grabbed her in a heavy embrace and beads of sweat sprang up all over her scalp.

She ducked down next to the intercom and read the note, written in neat, tiny block letters as if by the tooth fairy.

NAMASTE AND WELCOME TO TRANQUILLUM HOUSE WHERE A NEW YOU AWAITS. PLEASE PRESS THE SECURITY CODE 564–312 FOLLOWED IMMEDIATELY BY THE GREEN BUTTON.

She pressed the security code numbers then the green button and waited. Sweat rolled down her back. She would need to change her clothes *again*. A blowfly buzzed near her mouth. Her nose dripped.

'Oh come *on!*' she said to the intercom with a sudden spurt of rage, and she wondered if her agitated sweaty face was appearing on some screen inside, while an expert dispassionately analysed her symptoms, her misaligned chakras. *This one needs work. Look at how she responds to one of life's simplest stresses: waiting.*

Had she got the damned code wrong?

Once again she carefully punched in the security code, saying each number out loud, in a sarcastic tone, to prove a point to God knows who, and gave the hot green button a slow, deliberate push, holding it for five seconds just to be sure.

There. Now let me in.

She took off her reading glasses and let them dangle in her hand.

The baking heat seemed to be melting her scalp like chocolate in the sun. Silence again. She gave the intercom a fierce, hard look, as if that would shame it into acting.

At least this would make a funny story for Paul. She wondered if he'd ever been to a health resort. She thought he'd most likely be a sceptic. She herself was –

Her chest constricted. This wouldn't make a good story for Paul. Paul was gone. How humiliating for him to have slipped into her thoughts like that. She wished she felt a surge of white-hot anger instead of this utter sadness, this pretend grief for what had never been real in the first place.

Stop it. Don't think about it. Focus on the problem at hand.

The solution was obvious. She would *ring* Tranquillum House! They would be mortified to hear that their intercom had broken and Frances would be calm and understanding and brush away their apologies. 'These things happen,' she'd say. 'Namaste.'

She got back in the car, cranked up the air-conditioner. She found the paperwork with her booking details, and rang the number listed. All her other communications had been by email, so it was the first time she'd heard the recorded message that immediately began to play.

'Thank you for calling the historic Tranquillum House Health and Wellness Hot Springs Resort, where a new you awaits.

Your call is so important and special to us, as is your health and wellbeing, but we are experiencing an unusually high volume of calls at the moment. We know your time is precious, so please do leave a message after the chimes and we will call you back just as soon as we can. We so appreciate your patience. Namaste.'

Frances cleared her throat as wind chimes made their annoying twinkly dinging sounds.

'Oh yes, my name is –'

The wind chimes kept going. She stopped, waited, went to speak and stopped again. It was a wind-chime *symphony*.

At last there was silence.

'Hello, this is Frances Welty.' She sniffed. 'Excuse me. Bit of a cold. Anyway, as I said, I'm Frances Welty. I'm a guest.'

Guest? Was that the right word? Patient? Inmate?

'I'm trying to check in and I'm stuck outside the gate. It's, ah, twenty past three, twenty-five past three, and I'm . . . here! The intercom doesn't seem to be working even though I've followed all the instructions. The teeny-tiny instructions. I'd appreciate it if you could just open the gate? Let me in?' Her message finished on a rising note of hysteria, which she regretted. She put the phone down on the seat next to her and studied the gate.

Nothing. She would give it twenty minutes and then she was throwing in the towel.

Her phone rang and she snatched it up without looking at the screen.

'Hi there!' she said cheerfully, to show how understanding and patient she really was and to make up for the sarcastic 'teeny-tiny' comment.

'Frances?' It was Alain, her literary agent. 'You don't sound like you.'

Frances sighed. 'I was expecting someone else. I'm doing that health retreat I told you about, but I can't even get through the front gate. Their intercom isn't working.'

'How incompetent! How *unsatisfactory!*' Alain was easily and often enraged by poor service. 'You should turn around and come back home. It's not *alternative*, is it? Remember those poor people who died in that sweat lodge? They all thought they were becoming enlightened when in reality they were being cooked?'

'This place is pretty mainstream. Hot springs and massages and art therapy. Maybe some gentle fasting.'

'Gentle fasting.' Alain snorted. 'Eat when you're hungry. That's a *privilege*, you know, to eat when you're hungry, when there are people starving in this world.'

'Well, that's the point – we're *not* starving in this part of the world,' said Frances. She looked at the wrapper for the KitKat bar sitting in the console of her car. 'We're eating too much processed food. So that's why us privileged people need to detox –'

'Oh my Lord, she's falling for it. She's drunk the Kool-Aid! Detoxing is a *myth*, darling, it's been debunked! Your liver does it for you. Or maybe it's your kidneys. It's all taken care of somehow.'

'*Anyway*,' said Frances. She had a feeling he was procrastinating.

'Anyway,' said Alain. 'You sound like you've got a cold, Frances.' He seemed quite anguished about her cold.

'I do have a very bad, persistent, possibly permanent cold,' said Frances. She coughed to demonstrate. 'You'd be proud of me. I've been taking a *lot* of very powerful drugs. My heart is going at a million miles per hour.'

'That's the ticket,' said Alain.

There was a pause.

'Alain?' she prompted, but she knew, she already knew exactly what he was going to say.

'I'm afraid I am not the bearer of good news,' said Alain.
'I see.'

She sucked in her stomach, ready to take it like a man, or
at least like a romance novelist capable of reading her own
royalty statements.

'Well, as you know, darling,' began Alain.

But Frances couldn't bear to hear him hedging, trying to
soften the blow with compliments.

'They don't want the new book, do they?' she said.

'They don't want the new book,' said Alain sadly. 'I'm
so sorry. I think it's a beautiful book, I really do, it's just the
current environment, and romance has taken the worst hit,
it won't be forever, romance always comes back, it's a *blip*,
but –'

'So you'll sell it to someone else,' interrupted Frances.
'Sell it to Timmy.'

There was another pause.

'The thing is,' said Alain, 'I didn't tell you this, but I
slipped the manuscript to Timmy a few weeks back, because
I did have a tiny fear this might happen and obviously an
offer from Timmy before we had anything on the table
would have given me leverage, so I –'

'Timmy *passed*?' Frances couldn't believe it. Hanging in
her wardrobe was a designer dress that she'd never be able to
wear again because of the stain from a pina colada Timmy
had spilled on her while he had her cornered in a room at
the Melbourne Writers Festival, his voice hasty and hot in
her ear, looking back over his shoulder like a spy, telling her
how much he wanted to publish her, how it was his *destiny*
to publish her, how no-one else in the publishing industry
knew how to publish her the way he did, how her loyalty
to Jo was admirable but misplaced because Jo thought she
understood romance but she *didn't*, only Timmy did, and

only Timmy could and *would* take Frances 'to the next level', and so on and so forth until Jo turned up and rescued her. 'Oi, leave my author alone.'

How long ago was that? Not that long surely. Maybe nine, ten years ago. A decade. Time went so fast these days. There was some sort of malfunction going on with how fast the earth was spinning. Decades went by as quickly as years once did.

'Timmy loved the book,' said Alain. 'Adored it. He was nearly in tears. He couldn't get it past acquisitions. They're all shaking in their boots over there. It was a hell of a year. The decree from above is psychological thrillers.'

'I can't write a thriller,' said Frances. She never liked to kill characters. Sometimes she let them break a limb, but she felt bad enough about that.

'Of course you can't!' said Alain too quickly, and Frances felt mildly insulted.

'Look, I have to admit I was worried when Jo left and you were out of contract,' said Alain. 'But Ashlee seemed to really be a fan of yours.'

Frances's concentration drifted as Alain continued to talk. She watched the closed gate and pushed the knuckles of her left hand into her lower back.

What would Jo say when she heard Frances had been rejected? Or would she have had to do the same thing? Frances had always assumed that Jo would be her editor forever. She had fondly imagined them finishing their working lives simultaneously, perhaps with a lavish joint retirement lunch, but late last year Jo had announced her intention to retire. *Retire!* Like she was some sort of old grandma! Jo actually was a grandmother, but for goodness sake that wasn't a reason to *stop*. Frances felt like she was only just getting into the swing of things, and all of a sudden people in her circle were doing old-people things: having grandchildren, retiring, downsizing, dying – not in car accidents or plane crashes, no, dying *peacefully* in their sleep. She would never forgive Gillian for that. Gillian always slipped out of parties without saying goodbye.

It shouldn't have come as a surprise when Jo's replacement turned out to be a child, because children were taking over the world. Everywhere Frances looked there were children: children sitting gravely behind news desks, controlling traffic, running writers' festivals, taking her blood pressure, managing her taxes and fitting her bras. When Frances first met Ashlee she had genuinely thought she was there on work experience. She'd been about to say, 'A cappuccino would be lovely, darling,' when the child had walked around to the other side of Jo's old desk.

'Frances,' she'd said, 'this is such a *fan girl* moment for me! I used to read your books when I was, like, *eleven*! I stole them from my mum's handbag. I'd be like, Mum, you've got to let me read *Nathaniel's Kiss*, and she'd be like, No way, Ashlee, there's too much sex in it!'

Then Ashlee had proceeded to tell Frances that her next book needed more sex, a lot more sex, but she knew Frances could totally pull it off! As Ashlee was sure Frances knew, the market was changing, and 'If you just look at this chart here, Frances – no, *here*; that's it – you'll see that your sales have been on kind of a, well, sorry to say this, but you kind of have to call this a *downward trend*, and we, like, really need to reverse that, like, super-fast. Oh, and one other thing . . .' Ashlee looked pained, as if she were about to bring up an embarrassing medical issue. 'Your social media presence? I hear you're not so keen on social media. Neither is my mum! But it's kind of essential in today's market. Your fans really do need to see you on Twitter and Instagram and

Facebook – that's just the bare minimum. Also, we'd love you to start a blog and a newsletter and perhaps do some regular vlogs? That would be so much fun! They're like little films!'

'I have a website,' replied Frances.

'Yes,' said Ashlee kindly. 'Yes you do, Frances. But nobody cares about websites.'

And then she'd angled her computer monitor towards Frances so she could show her some examples of other, better behaved authors with 'active' social media presences, and Frances had stopped listening and waited for it to be over, like a dental appointment. (She couldn't see the screen anyway. She didn't have her glasses with her.) But she wasn't worried, because she was falling in love with Paul Drabble at the time, and when she was falling in love she always wrote her best books. And besides, she had the sweetest, most loyal readers in the world. Her sales might drop but she would always be *published*.

'I will find the right home for this book,' said Alain now. 'It might just take a little while. Romance isn't dead!'

'Isn't it?' said Frances.

'Not even close,' said Alain.

She picked up the empty KitKat wrapper and licked it, hoping for fragments of chocolate. How was she going to get through this setback without sugar?

'Frances?' said Alain.

'My back hurts a great deal,' said Frances. She blew her nose hard. 'Also, I had to stop the car in the middle of the road to have a hot flush.'

'That sounds truly awful,' said Alain with feeling. 'I can't even imagine.'

'No you can't. A man stopped to see if I was alright because I was screaming.'

'You were *screaming*?' said Alain.

'I felt like screaming,' said Frances.

'Of course, of course,' said Alain hurriedly. 'I understand. I often feel like screaming.'

This was rock-bottom. She'd just *licked a KitKat wrapper.*

'Oh dear, Frances, I'm so sorry about this, especially after what happened with that horrendous man. Have the police had anything new to say?'

'No,' said Frances. 'No news.'

'Darling, I'm just *bleeding* for you here.'

'That's not necessary,' sniffed Frances.

'You've just had such a bad trot lately, darling – speaking of which, I want you to know that review had absolutely no impact on their decision.'

'What review?' said Frances.

There was silence. She knew Alain was smacking his forehead.

'Alain?'

'Oh God,' he said. 'Oh God, oh God, oh God.'

'I haven't read a review since 1998,' said Frances. 'Not a single review. You know that.'

'I absolutely know that,' said Alain. 'I'm an idiot. I'm a fool.'

'Why would there be a review when I don't have a new book out?' Frances wriggled upright in her seat. Her back hurt so much she thought she might be sick.

'Some bitch picked up a copy of *What the Heart Wants* at the airport and did an opinion piece about, ah, your books in general, a mad diatribe. She kind of linked it to the Me Too movement, which gave it some clickbait traction. It was just ridiculous – as if romance books are to blame for sexual predators!'

'*What?*'

'Nobody even read the review. I don't know why I mentioned it. I must have early onset dementia.'

'You just said it got traction!'

Everyone had read the review. Everyone.

'Send me the link,' said Frances.

'It's not even that bad,' said Alain. 'It's just this prejudice against your genre –'

'Send it!'

'No,' said Alain. 'I won't. You've gone all these years without reading reviews. Don't fall off the wagon!'

'Right now,' said Frances in her dangerous voice. She used it rarely. When she was getting divorced, for example.

'I'll send it,' said Alain meekly. 'I'm so sorry, Frances. I'm so sorry about this entire phone call.'

He hung up, and Frances immediately went to her email. There wasn't much time. As soon as she arrived at Tranquillum House she would need to 'hand in' her 'device'. It would be a digital detox, along with everything else. She was going 'off the grid'.

SO SORRY! said Alain's email.

She clicked on the review.

It was written by someone called Helen Ihnat. Frances didn't know the name and there was no picture. She read it fast, with a wry, dignified smile, as if the author were saying these things to her face. It was a terrible review: vicious, sarcastic and superior, but, interestingly, it didn't hurt. The words – *Formulaic. Trash. Drivel. Trite* – slid right off her.

She was fine! Can't please everyone. Comes with the territory.

And then she felt it.

It was like when you burn yourself on a hotplate and at first you think, *Huh, that should have hurt more*, and then it does hurt more, and then all of a sudden it hurts like hell.

A quite extraordinary pain in her chest radiated throughout her entire body. Another fun symptom of menopause? Maybe it was a heart attack. Women had heart attacks. Surely this was more than hurt feelings. This, of course, was why she'd given up reading reviews in the first place. Her skin was too thin. 'It was the best decision I ever made,' she'd told the audience at the Romance Writers of Australia Conference when she gave the keynote address last year. They'd probably all been thinking: *Yeah, maybe you should read a review or two, Frances, you old has-been.*

Why did she think it was a good idea to read a bad review directly after she'd just received her first rejection in thirty years?

And now something else was happening. It appeared and, gosh, this was just so fascinating, but it seemed she was losing her entire sense of self.

Come on now, Frances, get a grip, you're too old for an existential crisis.

But apparently she wasn't.

She scrabbled hopelessly after her self-identity, but it was like trying to catch water rushing down a drain. If she was no longer a published writer, who was she? What was the actual point of her? She wasn't a mother or a wife or a girlfriend. She was a twice-divorced, middle-aged, hot-flushing/flashing menopausal woman. A punchline. A cliché. Invisible to most – except, of course, to men like Paul Drabble.

She looked at the gate in front of her that *still would not open* and her vision blurred with tears and she told herself not to panic, you are not *disappearing*, Frances, don't be so melodramatic, this is just a rough trot, a bad patch, and it's the cold and flu tablets making your heart race, but it felt like she was hovering on a precipice, and on the other side of the precipice was a howling abyss of despair unlike anything she'd ever experienced, even during those times of true grief – and this is *not* true grief, she reminded herself, this is a career setback combined with the loss of a relationship, a bad back, a cold and a paper cut; this is not like when Dad died, or Gillian died – but actually it wasn't that helpful to start remembering the deaths of loved ones, not helpful at all.

She looked around wildly for distraction – her phone, her book, *food* – and then she saw movement in her rear-view mirror.

What was it? An animal? A trick of the light? No, it was something.

It was too slow for a car.

Wait. It *was* a car. It was just driving so slowly it was barely moving.

She sat up straight and ran her fingers under her eyes where her mascara had run.

A canary-yellow sports car drove down the dirt drive slower than she would have thought possible.

Frances had no interest in cars, but as it got closer even she could tell this was a spectacularly expensive piece of machinery. Low to the ground and shimmery-shiny with futuristic headlights.

It came to a stop behind hers and the doors on either side opened simultaneously. A young man and woman emerged. Frances adjusted her mirror to see them more clearly. The man looked like a suburban plumber off to a Sunday barbecue: baseball cap on backwards, sunglasses, t-shirt, shorts and boat shoes with no socks. The woman had amazing long curly auburn hair, skin-tight capri pants, an impossibly tiny waist and even more unlikely breasts. She teetered on stilettos.

Why in the world would a young couple like that come

to a health retreat? Wasn't this sort of place for the over-weight and burnt out, for those grappling with bad backs and pathetic midlife identity crises? As Frances watched, the man turned his baseball cap around the right way and tipped his head back, arching his back as if he, too, found the sky overwhelming. The woman said something to him. Frances could tell by the way her mouth moved that it was sharp.

They were arguing.

How delightfully distracting. Frances lowered her window. These people would pull her back from the preci-pice, bring her back into existence. She would regain her self-identity by existing in their eyes. They would see her as old and eccentric and maybe even annoying, but it didn't matter how they saw her, as long as they saw her.

She leaned clumsily out the car window, waggled her fingers and called out, 'Helloooo!'

The girl tottered over the grass towards her.

chapter five

Ben

Ben watched Jessica walk like a baby giraffe towards the Peugeot 308 – overpriced piece of crap – parked at the gate, engine running. One of the Peugeot's brake lights was gone and the muffler looked like it was bent, no doubt from that dirt road. The lady behind the wheel was leaning halfway out her window, practically falling out, waving wildly at Jessica as if she couldn't be more pleased to see her. Why didn't she just open her car door and get out?

It looked like the health resort was closed. A burst water main? A mutiny? He could only hope.

Jessica could hardly walk in those stupid shoes. It was like she was on stilts. The heels were as skinny as toothpicks. She would roll an ankle any minute.

Ben squatted down next to his car and ran his fingers over the paintwork, searching for stone chips. He glanced back at the road they'd just come down and winced. How could a place that charged eye-watering rates have a road like that? There should have been a warning on the website. He'd thought for sure they were going to bottom out on some of those potholes.

No scratches that he could see, which was a miracle, but who knew what damage there was to the undercarriage? He'd have to wait till he could get it back up in the workshop, take a look. He wanted to do it right now, but he was going to have to wait ten days.

Maybe he should get the car towed back to Melbourne. He could call Pete's guys. It wasn't the craziest of ideas, except that he'd never hear the end of it if any of his former workmates saw that he'd driven *this* car down *that* road. He suspected his ex-boss would cry, literally cry, if he saw what Ben had done.

Pete's eyes had got suspiciously shiny after the scratch incident last month. 'Scratchgate', they all called it.

'Jealous fuck,' Pete said when Ben showed him the long deliberate scratch left by some evil person's key on the passenger door. Ben couldn't work out where and when it had happened. He never left the car in public car parks. It felt like it had to be someone they knew. Ben could name multiple people who might resent him and Jessica enough to have done it. Once he would have found it hard to name a single enemy in his life. Now it seemed they had a nice little collection. He knew Jessica thought it was Ben's sister who had done it, although she never accused Lucy out loud. He could read her mind by the thin fold of her lips. Maybe she was right. It could have been Lucy.

Pete had fixed the scratch with the same care as if he were restoring a priceless painting, and Ben had been vigilant until right now, when he'd put the car at huge, unforgivable risk by driving down that hellish road.

Ben should never have given in to Jessica. He'd tried. He stopped the car and told her, calmly and without swearing, that driving a car like this down an unsealed road was *negligent* and that the consequences could be catastrophic. They could, for example, rip out the exhaust system.

It was almost like she seriously didn't care about the exhaust system.

They'd yelled at each other for ten minutes straight. Proper yelling. Spitballs flying. Their faces red and ugly and contorted. The head-exploding frustration he'd felt during that argument was like something half-remembered from childhood, when you couldn't express yourself properly and you had no control over your life because you were a kid, so when your mum or dad said you couldn't have the new *Star Wars* action figure you wanted with all your heart you totally lost your shit.

There had been a moment there when he'd clenched his fists; when he had to tell himself, *Don't hit her.* He hadn't known he was capable of feeling the desire to hit a woman. He folded right then. He said, 'Fine. I'll ruin the car. Whatever.'

Most guys he knew wouldn't have even stopped for the yelling. They would have just done a U-turn.

Most guys would never have agreed to this crazy idea in the first place.

A *health resort.* Yoga and hot springs. He didn't get it. But Jessica had said they needed to do something dramatic and this would fix things. She said they needed to detox their minds and their bodies to save their marriage. They were going to eat organic lettuce and get 'couples counselling'. It was going to be ten days of pure torture.

Some celebrity couple had come to this place and saved their marriage. They had 'achieved inner peace' and got back in touch with their 'true selves'. What a load of crap. They may as well have handed over their money to Nigerian email scammers. Ben had a horrible feeling the celebrity couple might have got together on *The Bachelorette.* Jessica loved celebrities. He used to think it was sweet, a dumb interest for a smart girl. But now she was making too many life decisions based on what celebrities did, or what it was reported they did; it was probably all crap anyway, they were probably getting paid to support products on their Instagram accounts. And there was Jessica, his poor innocent, hopeful Jessica, soaking it all up.

Now it was like she thought she was one of those people. She was imagining *herself* at those trashy red-carpet events. Every time she got her photo taken these days she put her hand on her hip, like she was doing the actions for 'I'm a Little Teapot', then turned side on and thrust out her jaw with this maniacal smile. It was the weirdest thing. And the time she took setting up these photographs. The other day she had spent forty-two minutes (he'd timed it) taking a photo of *her feet*.

One of their biggest fights recently had been about one of her Instagram posts. It was a photo of her in a bikini top, leaning over, pushing her arms together so her new boobs looked even bigger and pouting her puffy new lips at the camera. She'd asked what he thought of the photo, her face all hopeful, and because of her hopeful face he hadn't said what he really thought – that it looked like she was advertising a cheap escort service. He'd just shrugged and said, 'It's okay.'

Her hopeful face fell. You'd think he'd called her a name. Next thing he knew she was screaming at him (these days she could go from zero to a hundred in a second) and he felt sucker-punched, unable to understand what had just happened. So he'd walked away while she was in the middle of yelling and went upstairs to play the Xbox. He thought walking away was a *good* thing to do. A mature, manly thing to do. To disengage and give her time to calm down. He kept getting these things wrong. She ran up the stairs after him and grabbed the back of his t-shirt before he reached the top.

'Look at me!' she screamed. 'You don't even look at me anymore!'

And it killed him to hear her say that, because it was true. He avoided looking at her. He was trying *really* hard to get over that. There were men who stayed married to women who were disfigured by accidents, burns or scars or whatever. It shouldn't make a difference that Jessica was disfigured by her own hand. Not literally her own hand. Her own credit card. Wilful disfigurement.

And then all her stupid friends encouraged her. 'Oh my God, Jessica, you look incredible.'

He wanted to yell at them, 'Are you blind? She looks like a chipmunk!'

The thought of separating from Jessica was like having his guts ripped out, but these days being married to Jessica was like having his guts ripped out. Whatever way you looked at it: guts ripped out.

If this retreat worked, if they got back to the way they used to be, it was even worth the damage to the car. Obviously, it was worth it. Jessica was meant to be the mother of his children – his future children.

He thought of the day of the robbery, two years ago now. He remembered the way her face – it was still her own beautiful face back then – had crumpled like a little kid's, and the rage he'd felt. He'd wanted to find those fuckwits and smash their faces.

If not for the robbery, if not for the fuckwits, they wouldn't be at this place. He wouldn't have the car, but at least he wouldn't be stuck here for the next ten days.

On balance, he still wanted to smash their faces.

'Ben!'

Jessica beckoned him over. She was all social and smiley, like they hadn't just been yelling at each other. She was so good at that. They could drive to a party and fight all the way, not say a word to each other as they walked up someone's stairs, and then the door of the apartment opens and – bang – different person. Laughing, joking, teasing him, touching him, taking selfies, like they were so having sex tonight, when they were so not having sex tonight.

Then, back in the car on the way home, she'd *restart* the fight. It was like flicking a switch on and off. It freaked him out. 'It's just good manners,' she told him. 'You don't take your fight to a party. It's no-one else's business.'

He straightened up, adjusted his cap and went over to stand beside Jessica to perform like her monkey.

'This is my husband, Ben,' said Jessica. 'Ben, this is Frances. She's doing the same retreat as us. Well, probably not exactly the same . . .'

The lady smiled up at him from the driver's seat. 'That's a very fancy car, Ben,' she said. She spoke as if she already knew him. Her voice was snuffly and hoarse, the tip of her nose bright red. 'It's like something from a movie.' He could see straight down the huge chasm of her cleavage; he couldn't help it, there was literally nowhere else to look. It wasn't *bad*, but she was old, so it wasn't good either. She wore red lipstick and had a lot of curly gold-coloured hair pulled back in a ponytail. She reminded him of one of his mum's tennis friends. He liked his mum's tennis friends – they were uncomplicated and didn't expect him to say much – but he preferred them not to have cleavage.

'Thanks,' he said, trying to focus on her very shiny, friendly eyes. 'Nice to meet you.'

'What sort of car is it?' asked Frances.

'It's a Lamborghini.'

'Ooh la la – a Lamborghini!' She grinned up at him. 'This here is a Peugeot.'

'Uh, yeah, I know,' he said, pained.

'Don't think much of the Peugeot?' She tilted her head to one side.

'It's a heap of shit,' said Ben.

'*Ben!*' said Jessica, but Frances laughed delightedly.

'I love my little Peugeot,' purred Frances as she caressed her steering wheel.

'Well,' said Ben. 'Each to their own.'

'Frances says nobody is answering the intercom,' said Jessica. 'She's been sitting out here waiting for twenty minutes.'

Jessica was using her posh new voice, where she made each word sound as fat and round as an apple. She was using it almost exclusively now, except when she really lost her temper or got upset, like last night, when she forgot to be posh and yelled at him, 'Why can't you just be happy? Why are you *ruining* this?'

'Have you phoned them?' he said now to the cleavage lady. 'Maybe there's something wrong with the intercom.'

'I've left a message,' said Frances.

'I wonder if this is like a test,' said Jessica. 'Maybe it's part of our treatment plan.' She lifted her hair up to cool her neck. Sometimes, when she spoke normally, when she was just being herself, he could forget the frozen forehead, the blowfish lips, the puffy cheeks, the camel eyelashes ('eyelash extensions'), the fake hair ('hair extensions') and fake boobs and there, for just a moment, was his sweet Jessica, the Jessica he'd known since high school.

'I thought that too!' said Frances.

Ben turned to look at the intercom.

'I could hardly read the instructions,' said Frances. 'They were so tiny.'

Ben could read them perfectly well. He punched in the code and pressed the green button.

'I will be absolutely furious if it works for you,' said Frances.

A tinny voice sprang from the intercom. 'Namaste and welcome to Tranquillum House. How may I help you?'

'What the hell?' Frances mouthed in comical disbelief.

Ben shrugged. 'Just needed a man's touch.'

'Oh *you*,' she said. She reached out of the car and flicked his arm with her hand.

Jessica bent down next to the intercom and spoke too loudly. 'We're here to check in.' It was cute, like Ben's grandma on the phone. 'The name is Chandler, Jessica and Ben –'

There was a burst of static from the intercom and the gates began to creak open. Jessica straightened, tucked her hair behind her ear, worried as always about her dignity. She never used to take herself so seriously.

'I promise you I pressed that code correctly, or I thought I did!' said Frances, as she buckled her seatbelt and revved her tappety little engine. She gave them a little wave. 'I'll see you in there! Don't try to race me with your fancy-schmancy Ferrari.'

'It's a *Lamborghini*!' protested Ben.

Frances winked at him, as if she knew that perfectly well, and drove off, faster than he would have expected, or recommended, on this road.

As they walked back towards the car, Jessica said, 'We're not telling anybody, right? That's the deal. If anyone asks, just say the car isn't even yours. Say it belongs to a friend.'

'Yeah, but I'm not as good a liar as you,' he said. He meant it as a joke or even a compliment, but he was leaving the interpretation up to her.

'Fuck you,' she said, though without much heat.

So maybe they were okay. But sometimes the embers of a

dying argument sparked without warning. You never knew. He would stay alert.

'She seemed nice,' said Ben. 'The lady. Frances.' That was safe. Frances was old. There could be no possibility of jealousy. The jealousy was a fun new development in their relationship. The more Jessica changed her face and body, the less secure she got.

'I think I recognised her,' said Jessica.

'Really?'

'I'm pretty sure she's Frances Welty, the writer. I used to be crazy about her books.'

'What sort of books does she write?' asked Ben. He opened his car door.

She said something he didn't catch. 'Sorry, what?'

'*Romance.*' Jessica slammed the passenger door so hard he winced.

chapter six

Frances

That's more like it, thought Frances when she got her first look at the Victorian mansion emerging majestically in the distance. The road was sealed now, thankfully, and the bushland became progressively greener and softer. Tranquillum House was sandstone, three storeys, with a red corrugated-iron roof and a princess tower. Frances had the delightful sensation of time-travelling to the late nineteenth century, although the sensation was somewhat spoiled by the yellow Lamborghini purring along behind her.

How could those kids afford that car? Drug dealers? Trust-fund kids? Drug dealing seemed more likely than trust fund; neither of them had that creamy entitled look of old money.

She glanced in the rear-view mirror again. From here, with her hair blowing in the wind, Jessica looked like the pretty girl she was meant to be. You couldn't see all the procedures she'd had done to her young face. The thick layer of make-up was bad enough, but oh goodness me, the blinding white teeth, the enormous puffy lips and the work, it was such *bad* work. Frances was not opposed to cosmetic procedures – in fact she was very fond of them – but there was something so sad and garish about this sweet child's plumped-up, smoothed-out face.

Surely all that jewellery she was wearing couldn't be real, could it? Those massive sapphires in her ears would be worth . . . what? Frances had no idea. A lot. The car was obviously real, though, so maybe the jewellery was real too.

Up-and-coming mobsters? YouTube stars?

The boy, Jessica's 'husband' (they seemed too young for such grown-up terms), was cute as a button. Frances would try not to flirt with him. The joke might wear thin after ten days. Possibly even bordering on . . . sleazy? *Possibly bordering on paedophilia, darling,* Alain would say. It was awful to think of lovely Ben shuddering over Frances the way Frances had once shuddered over the behaviour of older male authors at publishing parties.

They used to be particularly hideous if they'd recently won a literary prize. Their dialogue was so powerful and impenetrable it didn't require punctuation! So naturally they didn't require permission to slip-slide their hairy hands over the body of a young writer of *genre* fiction. In their minds, Frances virtually owed them sex in return for her unseemly mass-market sales of 'airport trash'.

Stop it. Don't think about the review, Frances.

She'd marched in the Women's March! She was not 'a blight on feminism' just because she described the colour of her hero's eyes. How could you fall in love with someone if you didn't know the colour of his eyes? And she was *obliged* to tie everything up at the end with a 'giant bow'. Those were the rules. If Frances left her endings ambiguous, her readers would come after her with pitchforks.

Do not think about the review. Do not think about the review.

She dragged her mind back to Ben and Jessica. So, yes, she would remember to be age-appropriate with Ben. She would pretend they were related. She'd behave like his aunt. She certainly wouldn't *touch* him. My God, she hadn't touched him already, had she? The review was making her doubt everything about herself. Her hands tightened around the steering wheel. She had a habit of touching people on the arm to make a point, or when they said something that made her laugh, or when she felt in any way fondly towards them.

At least talking with Ben and Jessica had calmed her down. She'd scared herself for a moment there. Loss of self, indeed. What a drama queen.

The road circled up towards the house. Ben politely kept his powerful car at a respectable distance behind Frances, even though he probably longed to floor it on the curves.

She drove up a stately driveway lined with towering pine trees.

'Not too shabby,' she murmured.

She'd prepared herself for a seedier reality than the website pictures, but up close Tranquillum House was beautiful. The lacy white balconies glowed in the sunlight. The garden was lush and green in the summer heat, with a sign helpfully proclaiming THIS PROPERTY USES RAINWATER so no-one could criticise the lushness.

Two white-uniformed staff members, with the floaty, straight-backed postures of the spiritually advanced, emerged unhurriedly from the house onto the wide veranda to greet them. Perhaps they'd been off meditating while she was stuck outside the gate trying to ring them. Frances had barely come to a complete stop when her car door was opened by the man. He was young, of course, like everyone, Asian, with a hipster beard and a man bun, bright-eyed and smooth-skinned. A delightful man-kid.

'Namaste.' The man-kid pressed his palms together and bowed. 'A very warm welcome to Tranquillum House.'

He spoke with a tiny . . . measured . . . pause between each word.

'I'm Yao,' he said. 'Your personal wellness consultant.'

'Hello, Yao. I'm Frances Welty. Your new victim.'

She undid her seatbelt and smiled up at him. She told herself she would not laugh, or attempt to imitate his yogic voice, or let it drive her mad.

'We'll take care of everything from here,' said Yao. 'How many bags do you have?'

'Just the one,' said Frances. She indicated the back seat. 'I can carry it. It's quite light.' She didn't want to let the bag out of her sight because she'd packed a few banned items, like coffee, tea, chocolate (dark chocolate – antioxidants!) and just *one* bottle of a good red (also antioxidants!).

'Leave your bag right there, Frances, and your keys in the ignition,' said Yao firmly.

Damn it. Oh well. Her slight embarrassment over her contraband, even though there was no way he could tell just by looking at the bag (she was normally such a good girl when it came to rules), caused her to hop out of the car awkwardly and too fast, forgetting her new fragility.

'Ooof,' she said. She straightened slowly and met Yao's eyes. 'Back pain.'

'I'm sorry to hear that,' said Yao. 'I'm going to arrange an urgent massage at the spa for you.' He took a small notepad and pencil out of his pocket and made a note.

'I also have a paper cut,' said Frances solemnly. She held up her thumb.

Yao took hold of her thumb and peered at it. 'Nasty,' he said. 'We'll need to get some aloe vera on that.'

Oh God, he was gorgeous with his little notebook, taking

her paper cut so seriously. She caught herself studying his shoulders and looked away fast. *For God's sake, Frances.* Nobody had warned her that this would happen during middle age: these sudden, wildly inappropriate waves of desire for young men, with no biological imperative whatsoever. Maybe this was what men felt like all their lives? No wonder the poor things had to pay out all that money in lawsuits.

'And you're here for the ten-day cleanse,' said Yao.

'That's right,' said Frances.

'Awesome,' said Yao, causing Frances to fortunately lose all desire in an instant. She could never sleep with someone who said 'awesome'.

'So . . . may I go inside?' asked Frances snappily. Now she felt quite ill at the thought of sex with the man-kid, or sex with anyone for that matter; she was far too hot.

She saw that Yao was distracted by the sight of Ben and Jessica's car, or possibly by Jessica, who was standing with one hip cocked, slowly curling a long strand of hair around her finger while Ben talked to another white-uniformed wellness consultant, a young woman with skin so beautiful it looked like it was lit from within.

'That's a Lamborghini,' said Frances.

'I know it is,' said Yao, forgetting to put the tiny pauses between his words. He gestured towards the house, stepping aside to let Frances cross the threshold first.

She walked into a large entrance hall and waited for her eyes to adjust to the dim light. The soft hush unique to old houses washed over her like cool water. There were beautiful details wherever she looked: honey-coloured parquetry floors, antique chandeliers, ornately carved ceiling cornices and leadlight windows.

'This is so beautiful,' she said. 'Oh – and look at that. It's like the staircase from the *Titanic!*'

She walked over to touch the lustrous mahogany wood. Flecks of light streamed from a stained-glass window on the landing.

'As you may know, Tranquillum House was built in 1840 and this is the original red cedar and rosewood staircase,' said Yao. 'Other people have commented on the resemblance to the *Titanic's* staircase. So far we've had much better luck than the *Titanic*. We won't sink, Frances!'

He'd clearly made this joke many times before. Frances gave him a more generous laugh than it deserved.

'The house was built of locally quarried sandstone by a wealthy solicitor from England.' Yao continued to recite facts like a nerdy museum guide. 'He wanted a house that would be "the best in the colony".'

'Built with the help of convicts, I understand,' said Frances, who had read the website.

'That's right,' said Yao. 'The solicitor was granted five hundred acres of good farming land and assigned ten convicts. He got lucky because they included two former stonemason brothers from York.'

'We have a convict in our family tree,' said Frances. 'She was transported from Dublin for stealing a silk gown. We're tremendously proud of her.'

Yao gestured away from the staircase to make it clear she wasn't to go up there just yet. 'I know you'll want to rest after that long drive, but first I'd like to give you a quick tour of your new home for the next ten days.'

'Unless I don't last the distance,' said Frances. Ten days suddenly seemed like a very long time. 'I might go home early.'

'No-one goes home early,' said Yao serenely.

'Well, yes, but they *can*,' said Frances. 'If they *choose*.'

'No-one goes home early,' repeated Yao. 'It just doesn't

happen. No-one *wants* to go home at all! You're about to embark on a truly transformative experience, Frances.'

He led her to a large room at the side of the house with bay windows overlooking the valley and one long monastery-like table. 'This is the dining room where you'll come for your meals. All the guests eat together, of course.'

'Of course,' said Frances hoarsely. She cleared her throat. 'Great.'

'Breakfast is served at seven am, lunch at noon and dinner at six pm.'

'Breakfast at *seven am*?' Frances blanched. She could manage the communal meals for lunch and dinner, but she couldn't eat and talk with strangers in the morning. 'I'm a night owl,' she told Yao. 'I'm normally comatose at seven am.'

'Ah, but that's the old Frances – the new Frances will have already done a sunrise tai chi class and guided meditation by seven,' said Yao.

'I seriously doubt that,' said Frances.

Yao smiled, as if he knew better.

'There will be a five-minute warning bell before meals are served – or smoothies, during the fast periods. We do ask that you come promptly to the dining room as soon as you hear the warning bell.'

'Certainly,' said Frances, with a rising sense of horror. She'd quite forgotten about the 'fast periods'. 'Is there . . . ah, room service?'

'I'm afraid not, although your morning and late-evening smoothies will be brought to your room,' said Yao.

'But no club sandwiches at midnight, hey?'

Yao shuddered. 'God no.'

He led her past the dining room to a cosy living room lined with bookshelves. A number of couches surrounded a marble fireplace.

'The Lavender Room,' said Yao. 'You're welcome to come here any time to relax, read or enjoy an herbal tea.'

He said 'herbal' the American way: *erbal*.

'Lovely,' said Frances, mollified by the sight of the books. They walked by a closed door with the word PRIVATE stencilled on it in gold letters, which Frances, being Frances, felt strongly compelled to open. She couldn't abide member-only lounges to which she didn't have membership.

'This leads to our director's office at the top of the house.' Yao touched the door gently. 'We do ask that you only open this door if you have an appointment.'

'By all means,' said Frances resentfully.

'You will meet the director later today,' said Yao, as if this were a special treat she'd been long anticipating. 'At your first guided meditation.'

'Awesome,' said Frances through her teeth.

'Now you'll want to see the gym,' said Yao.

'Oh, not especially,' said Frances, but he was already leading her back across the reception area to the opposite side of the house.

'This was originally the drawing room,' said Yao. 'It's been refurbished as a state-of-the-art gym.'

'Well, *that* is a *tragedy*,' Frances proclaimed when Yao opened a glass door to reveal a light-filled room crowded with what appeared to be elaborate torture devices.

Yao's smile faltered. 'We kept all the original plasterwork.' He pointed at the ceiling.

Frances gave a disdainful sniff. *Marvellous. You can lie back and admire the ceiling rose while you're being drawn and quartered.*

Yao looked at her face and hurriedly closed the gym door. 'Let me show you the yoga and meditation studio.' He continued past the gym to a door at the far corner of the house. 'Watch your head.'

She ducked unnecessarily beneath the doorjamb and followed Yao down a flight of narrow stone stairs.

'I smell wine,' she said.

'Don't get your hopes up,' said Yao. 'It's the ghost of old wine.'

He pushed back a heavy oak door with some effort and ushered her into a surprisingly large cave-like room with an arched wood-beamed ceiling, brick walls lined with a few chairs, and a series of soft blue rectangular mats laid out at intervals on the hardwood floor.

'This is where you will come for yoga classes and all your guided sitting meditations,' said Yao. 'You'll be spending a lot of time down here.'

It was quiet and cool, and the ghostly smell of wine was overlaid by the scent of incense. The studio did have a lovely, peaceful feel to it, and Frances thought she would enjoy being here, even though she wasn't that keen on yoga or meditation. She had done a transcendental meditation course years ago, hoping for enlightenment, and every time, without fail, she'd nod off within two minutes of focusing on her breathing, waking up at the end to discover that everyone else had experienced flashes of light, memories of past lives and *rapture* or whatever, while she'd snoozed and drooled. Basically, she'd paid to have a forty-minute nap at the local high school once a week. No doubt she would be spending a lot of time *napping* down here, dreaming of wine.

'At one point, when the property operated a vineyard, this cellar could hold up to twenty thousand bottles of wine.' Yao gestured at the walls, although there were no longer any facilities for keeping wine. 'But when the house was originally built, it was used for storage, or as somewhere to secure misbehaving convict workers, or even to hide from bushrangers.'

'If these walls could talk,' said Frances.

Her eye was caught by a large flat-screen television hanging from one of the beams at the end of the room. 'What's that screen for?' It seemed especially incongruous after Yao's talk of the house's early colonial history. 'I thought this was a screen-free environment.'

'Tranquillum House is absolutely a screen-free environment,' agreed Yao. He glanced at the television screen with a slight frown. 'But we recently installed a security and intercom system so we can all communicate with each other from different parts of the resort when necessary. It's quite a large property and the safety of our guests is paramount.'

He changed the subject abruptly. 'I'm sure you'll be interested in *this*, Frances.' He ushered her over to a corner of the room and pointed to a brick almost concealed by the joinery of one of the arched beams. Frances put on her reading glasses and read out loud the small, beautifully inscribed words: *Adam and Roy Webster, stonemasons, 1840.*

'The stonemason brothers,' said Yao. 'The assumption is that they did this secretly.'

'Good for them,' said Frances. 'They were proud of their work. As they should have been.'

They silently contemplated the inscription for a few moments before Yao clapped his hands together. 'Let's head back up.'

He led her up the stairs into the house and to another glass door featuring just one beautiful word: *SPA*.

'Last but not least, the spa where you will come for your massages and any other wellness treatments scheduled for you.' Yao opened the door and Frances sniffed like Pavlov's dog at the scent of essential oils.

'This was another drawing room that was remodelled,' said Yao carefully.

'Ah well, I'm sure you did a good job retaining the

original features.' Frances patted his arm as she peered inside the dimly lit room. She could hear the trickling sound of a water feature and one of those ridiculous but divine 'relaxation' soundtracks – the kind with crashing waves, harp music and the occasional frog – piped through the walls.

'All spa treatments are complimentary, part of the package – you won't receive a scary bill at the end of your stay!' said Yao as he closed the door.

'I did read that on the website, but I wasn't sure if it could be true!' said Frances disingenuously, because if it wasn't true she would be making a complaint to the Department of Fair Trading quick-smart. She made her eyes wide and grateful, as Yao seemed to take personal pride in the wonders of Tranquillum House.

'Well, it *is* true, Frances,' said Yao lovingly, like a parent telling her that tomorrow really *was* Christmas Day. 'Now we'll just pop in here and get your blood tests and so on out of the way.'

'I'm sorry – what?' said Frances, as she was shepherded into a room that looked like a doctor's office. She felt discombobulated. Weren't they just talking about spa treatments?

'Just sit right here,' said Yao. 'We'll do your blood pressure first.'

Frances found herself seated as Yao wrapped a cuff around her arm and pumped it enthusiastically.

'It might be higher than usual,' he said. 'People feel a little stressed and nervous when they arrive. They're tired after their journey. It's natural. But let me tell you, I've never had a guest finish their retreat without a significant drop in their blood pressure!'

'Mmm,' said Frances.

She watched Yao write down her blood pressure. She didn't ask if it was high or low. It was often low. She had been checked out for hypotension before because of her tendency to faint. If she got dehydrated or tired, or saw blood, her vision tunnelled and the world tipped.

Yao snapped on a pair of plastic green gloves. Frances looked away and focused on a point on the wall. He buckled a tourniquet around her arm and tapped her forearm.

'Great veins,' he said. Nurses often said that about Frances's veins. She always felt momentarily proud and then kind of depressed, because what a waste of a positive attribute.

'I didn't actually realise there would be a blood test,' said Frances.

'Daily blood tests,' said Yao cheerfully. 'Very important because it means we can tweak your treatment plans accordingly.'

'Mmm, I might actually opt out of the —'

'Tiny ouch,' said Yao.

Frances looked back to her arm, and then quickly away again as she caught sight of a test tube filling with her blood. She hadn't even registered the prick of the needle. She felt all at once as powerless as a child, and was reminded of the few times in her life she'd had to go into hospital for minor surgeries, and how much she disliked the lack of control over her body. Nurses and doctors had the right to prod at her as they pleased, with no love or desire or affection, just expertise. It always took a few days to fully reinhabit her body again.

Did this young man currently helping himself to her blood even have medical expertise? Had she really done her due diligence on this place?

'Are you trained as a . . .?' She was trying to say, 'Do you know what the hell you're doing?'

'I used to be a paramedic in a previous life,' replied Yao.

She met his eyes. Was he possibly a little mad? Did he mean he was a reincarnated paramedic? You never knew with these alternative types. 'You don't mean, literally, a previous life?'

Yao laughed out loud. A very normal-sounding laugh. 'It was about ten years ago now.'

'Do you miss it?'

'Absolutely not. I'm passionate about the work we do here.' His eyes blazed. Maybe just slightly mad.

'Right, that's that,' said Yao, removing the needle and handing her a cottonwool ball. 'Press firmly.' He labelled her test tube and smiled at her. 'Excellent. Now, we'll just check your weight.'

'Oh, is that really necessary? I'm not here for weight loss; I'm here for, you know . . . personal transformation.'

'Just for our files,' said Yao. He removed the cottonwool ball, pressed a circular bandaid onto the tiny red pinprick and indicated a set of scales. 'On you hop.'

Frances averted her eyes from the number. She had no idea of her weight and no interest in learning it. She knew she could be thinner, and of course when she was younger she was indeed much thinner, but she was generally happy with her body as long as it wasn't giving her pain, and bored by all the different ways women droned on about the subject of weight, as if it were one of the great mysteries of life. The recent weight-losers, evangelical about whatever method had worked for them, the thin women who called themselves fat, the average women who called themselves obese, the ones desperate for her to join in their lavish self-loathing. 'Oh, Frances, isn't it just so *depressing* when you see young, thin girls like that!' 'Not especially,' Frances would say, adding extra butter to her bread roll.

Yao wrote something on a form in a cream-coloured

file marked in black sharpie block letters with her name, FRANCES WELTY.

This was starting to feel too much like a visit to the doctor. Frances felt exposed and vulnerable and regretful. She wanted to go home. She wanted a muffin.

'I'd really like to get to my room now,' she said. 'It was a long drive.'

'Absolutely. I'm going to book you into the spa for an urgent massage for that back pain,' said Yao. 'Shall I give you half an hour to settle into your room, enjoy your welcome smoothie and read your welcome pack?'

'That sounds like heaven,' said Frances.

They walked back past the dining room, where her darling drug dealers, Jessica and Ben, stood with their own white-uniformed wellness consultant, a dark-haired young woman who, according to her name badge, was called Delilah. Delilah was delivering the same spiel as Yao about the warning bells.

Jessica's plastic face was filled with worry, so much so that she was almost, but not quite, pulling off a frown. 'But what if you don't hear the bell?'

'Then off with your head!' said Frances.

Everyone turned to look at her. Ben, whose cap was now the wrong way around again, raised a single eyebrow.

'Joke,' said Frances weakly.

Frances saw the two wellness consultants exchange looks she couldn't quite read. She wondered if they were sleeping together. They'd have such aerobic, flexible sex with all that wellness pumping through their young bodies. It would be just so *awesome*.

Yao led her back towards the *Titanic* stairs. As Frances hurried to keep pace, they passed a man and two women coming down the staircase together, all three in olive-green robes featuring the Tranquillum House emblem.

The man lagged behind to put on glasses so he could closely examine the wall on the landing. He was so tall the dressing-gown was more like a miniskirt, revealing knobbly knees and very white, very hairy legs. They were the sort of male legs that made you feel uncomfortable, as if you were looking at a private part of the body.

'Well, my point is that you just don't see craftsmanship like this anymore!' he said, as he peered at the wall. 'That's what I just love about houses like this: the attention to detail. I mean, think of those tiles I was showing you earlier. What's extraordinary is that somebody took the time to *individually* – hello again, Yao! Another guest, is it? How are you?'

He took off his glasses, beamed at Frances and thrust out his hand. 'Napoleon!' he cried.

It took her a terrifying second to realise he was introducing himself, not just yelling out a random historical figure's name.

'Frances,' she said in the nick of time.

'Nice to meet you! Here for the ten-day retreat, I assume?'

He was on the stair above her, so his height was even more pronounced. It was like tipping her head back to look at a monument.

'I am.' Frances made a tremendous effort not to comment on his height, as she knew from her six-foot friend Jen that tall people were well aware they were tall. 'I most certainly am.'

Napoleon indicated the two women further down the stairs. 'Us too! These are my beautiful girls, my wife, Heather, and daughter, Zoe.'

The two women were also notably tall. They were a basketball team. They gave her the restrained, polite smiles of a celebrity's family members who are used to having to wait while he is accosted by fans, except that in this case it was

Napoleon doing the accosting. The wife, *Heather*, bounced on the balls of her feet. She was wiry, with extremely wrinkled, tanned skin, as if she'd been scrunched up and then spread smooth. *Heather skin like leather*, thought Frances. That was a really mean mnemonic but Heather would never know. Heather had grey hair pulled back in a tight ponytail and bloodshot eyes. She seemed very intense, which was fine. Frances had some intense friends; she knew how to cope with intensity. (Never try to match it.)

The daughter, *Zoe*, had her dad's height and the casual grace of an athletic, outdoorsy girl. Showy Zoe? But she wasn't showy at all. *Not-showy Zoe*. Zoe certainly didn't look like she was in need of a health resort. How much more rejuvenated could you get?

Frances thought about the young couple, Ben and Jessica, who also seemed in sparkling good health. Were health resorts only attended by the already healthy? Was she going to be the least healthy-looking person here? She'd never been bottom of the class, except for that one time in Transcendental Meditation for Beginners.

'We thought we'd explore the hot springs, maybe have a quick soak,' said Napoleon to Yao and Frances, as if they'd asked. 'Then we'll do a few laps of the pool.'

Clearly, they were one of those active families who threw their bags down on the floor and left their hotel room the moment they checked in.

'I'm planning a quick nap before an urgent massage,' said Frances.

'Excellent idea!' cried Napoleon. 'A nap and a massage! Sounds perfect! Isn't this place *amazing*? And I hear the hot springs are incredible.' He was an extremely enthusiastic man.

'Make sure you rehydrate after the hot springs,' Yao said

to him. 'There are water bottles at reception.'

'Will do, Yao! And then we'll be back in time for the noble silence!'

'Noble silence?' said Frances.

'It will all become clear, Frances,' said Yao.

'It's in your information pack, Frances!' said Napoleon. 'Bit of a surprise; I wasn't expecting the "silence" aspect. I've heard of silent retreats, of course, but must admit they didn't appeal – I'm a talker myself, as my girls here will tell you. But we'll roll with the punches, go with the flow!'

As he talked on in the comforting way of the chronically loquacious, Frances watched his wife and daughter further down the stairs. The daughter, who wore black flip-flops, put one heel on the step above her and leaned forward as if she were discreetly stretching her hamstring. The mother watched her daughter, and Frances saw the ghost of a smile, followed almost immediately by an expression of pure despair that dragged all her features down, as if she were clawing at her cheeks. Then in the next instant it was gone and she smiled benignly up at Frances, and Frances felt as though she had seen something she shouldn't have.

Napoleon said, 'It wasn't you who arrived in that Lamborghini was it, Frances? I saw it from our room. That's one hell of a car.'

'Not me – I'm the Peugeot,' said Frances.

'Nothing wrong with the Peugeot! Although I hear those jackals charge like wounded bulls when it comes to servicing, right?'

He mixed his metaphors most delightfully. Frances was keen to talk more with him. He was someone who would answer any question with candour and vigour. She loved those sorts of people.

'Dad,' said his daughter. Not-showy Zoe. 'Let the lady

pass. She's only just got here. She probably wants to get to her room.'

'Sorry, sorry, I'll see you at dinner! Although we won't be chatting then, will we?' He tapped the side of his nose and grinned, but there was a trapped, panicky look in his eyes. 'Lovely to meet you!' He clapped Yao on the shoulder. 'See you later, Yao, mate!'

Frances followed Yao up the stairs. At the top, he turned right and led her down a carpeted hallway lined with historical photos that she planned to study later.

'This wing of the house was added in 1895,' said Yao. 'You'll find all the rooms have original fireplaces with marble mantelpieces of Georgian design. Not that you'll be lighting any fires in this heat.'

'I didn't expect to see families doing this retreat,' commented Frances. 'I must admit I thought there'd be more . . . people like me.'

Fatter people than me, Yao. Much fatter.

'We get people from all walks of life here at Tranquillum House,' said Yao as he unlocked her room with a large, old-fashioned metal key.

'Probably not *all* walks of life,' mused Frances, because come on now, the place wasn't cheap, but she stopped talking as Yao held open the door for her.

'Here we are.'

It was an airy, plush-carpeted room filled with period furniture, including an enormous four-poster bed. Open French doors led to a balcony with a view that stretched to the horizon: a rolling patchwork quilt of vineyards and farmhouses and green-and-gold countryside. Flocks of birds wheeled across the sky. Her bag sat like an old familiar friend in a corner of the room. There was a fruit basket on the coffee table, along with a glass of green, sludge-like juice with a strawberry on the side. Everything except the juice looked extremely appealing.

'That's your welcome smoothie there,' said Yao. 'There are six organic smoothies a day, prepared specifically for your changing individual needs.'

'They're not wheatgrass, are they? I once had a wheat-grass shot and it scarred me for life.'

Yao picked up the glass and handed it to her. 'Trust me, it's tasty!'

Frances looked at it doubtfully.

'The smoothies *are* mandatory,' said Yao kindly. It was confusing because you'd think from his tone that he'd said, 'They *are* optional.'

She took a sip. 'Oh!' she said, surprised. She could taste mango, coconut and berries. It was like drinking a tropical holiday. 'It's quite good. Very good.'

'Yes, Frances,' said Yao. He used her name as often as a desperate real estate agent. 'And the good news is it's not only delicious but brimming with natural goodness! Please make sure you drink the entire glass.'

'I will,' said Frances agreeably.

There was an awkward pause.

'Oh,' said Frances. 'You mean now?' She took another, larger sip. 'Yum!'

Yao smiled. 'The daily smoothies are crucial for your wellness journey.'

'Gosh, well, I want to keep my wellness journey on track.'

'Absolutely you do,' said Yao.

She met his eyes. There was no irony as far back as she could see. He was going to shame that snark right out of her.

'I'm going to leave you to relax,' said Yao. 'Your welcome pack is right here. Please take the time to read it because there are important instructions for the next twenty-four hours. The noble silence that Napoleon mentioned will be beginning shortly, and I know you're going to find that so beneficial. Oh, now, speaking of silence, Frances, I'm sure you can guess what I need next from you!' He looked at her expectantly.

'No idea. Not more blood, I hope?'

'It's time to hand over all your electronic devices,' said Yao. 'Mobile phone, tablets, everything.'

'No problem.' Frances retrieved her phone from her handbag, switched it off, and handed it to Yao. A not unpleasant feeling of subservience crept over her. It was like being on an aeroplane once the seatbelt sign was turned on and the flight attendants were now in charge of your entire existence.

'Great. Thanks. You're officially "off the grid"!' Yao held up her phone. 'We'll keep it safe. Some guests say the digital detox is one of the most enjoyable elements of their time with us. When it's time to leave, you'll be saying, "Don't give it back! I don't want it back!"' He held up his hands to indicate someone waving him away.

Frances tried to imagine herself in ten days and found it strangely difficult, as if it wasn't ten days but ten years she was imagining. Would she really be transformed? Thinner, lighter, pain-free, able to leap from her bed at sunrise without caffeine?

'Don't forget your massage at the spa,' said Yao. 'Oh – and that nasty paper cut!'

He walked to a sideboard, selected a tube from an array of Tranquillum House-branded cosmetics and said, 'Let's see that thumb.'

Frances presented it to him and he placed a dab of soothing cool gel on her paper cut with tender care.

'Your wellness journey has begun, Frances,' he said, still holding her hand, and instead of smirking Frances found herself close to tears.

'I've actually been feeling *very* unwell lately, Yao,' she said pitifully.

'I know you have.' Yao put both his hands on her shoulders and it didn't feel silly or sexual; it felt healing. 'We're going to get you well, Frances. We're going to get you feeling as well as you've ever felt in your life.' He closed the door gently behind him as he left.

Frances turned in a slow circle and waited for that inevitable moment of solitary traveller gloom, but instead her spirits lifted. She wasn't alone. She had Yao to take care of her. She was on a wellness *journey*.

She walked out onto her balcony to admire the view and gasped. A man on the balcony next to hers was leaning so far over it he looked in danger of falling.

'Careful!' she warned, but only under her breath so as not to startle him.

The man turned in her direction, lifted his hand and smiled. It was Ben. She recognised the baseball cap. She waved back.

If they raised their voices they could probably hear each other perfectly well, but it was better to pretend they were too far away to chat, otherwise they'd feel obligated to talk every time they happened to see each other on their balconies, and there was going to be enough obligatory chatting at every meal.

She looked in the other direction and saw a row of identical balconies stretching to the end of the house. All the guestrooms shared this same view. The other balconies were empty, although, as Frances watched, the figure of a woman emerged from the room at the furthest end of the house. She was too far away to distinguish her features, but Frances, keen to be friendly, gave her a wave. The woman instantly spun around and went back inside her room.

Oh, well, perhaps she hadn't seen Frances. Or perhaps she suffered from tremendous social anxiety. Frances could handle the dreadfully shy. You just needed to approach slowly, as if they were little woodland creatures.

Frances turned back to Ben, and saw that he'd also gone back inside. She wondered if he and Jessica were still arguing. Their rooms were adjoining, so if things got heated Frances might overhear. Once, on a book tour, she'd stayed in a thin-walled hotel where she had the pleasure of overhearing a couple argue passionately and descriptively about their sex life. That had been great.

'I don't get the obsession with strangers,' her first husband, Sol, once said to her, and Frances had struggled to explain that strangers were by definition interesting. It was their *strangeness*. The not-knowing. Once you knew everything there was to know about someone, you were generally ready to divorce them.

She went back inside her room to unpack. It might be nice to have a cup of tea and a few squares of chocolate while she read her information pack. She was sure it was going to have rules she would prefer not to follow; the 'noble silence' that was beginning shortly sounded foreboding and she would need sugar to cope. Also, she hadn't exactly followed the suggestion about reducing her sugar and caffeine intake in the days leading up to the retreat so as to avoid withdrawal symptoms. Frances couldn't be dealing with a headache right now.

She went to pull out her contraband from where she'd carefully hidden it right at the bottom of her bag, underneath her underwear, wrapped in her nightie. She'd laughed at herself for hiding it; it wasn't like they were going to be checking her bag. This wasn't rehab or boarding school.

'You've got to be kidding,' she said out loud.

It wasn't there.

She emptied all her clothes onto her bed with a growing sense of fury. They wouldn't, would they? It was unconscionable. Illegal, surely.

It was *very* bad manners!

She turned the bag upside down and shook it. The nightie was still there, neatly folded by invisible hands, but the coffee, tea, chocolate and wine were most definitely gone. Who had been through her bag? It couldn't be Yao; he'd been with her the whole time from when she arrived. Someone else had rifled through her underwear and confiscated her treats.

What could she do? She couldn't ring reception and say, 'Somebody took my chocolate and wine!' Well, she could, but she didn't have the requisite chutzpah. The website made it clear that snacks and coffee and alcohol were all banned. She'd broken the rules and she'd been caught.

She would say nothing and they would say nothing and on the last day they would hand it all back to her with a knowing smirk as she checked out, like returning a prisoner's personal effects.

This was *deeply* embarrassing.

She sat on the end of her bed and looked dolefully at the lovely fruit bowl. She laughed a little, trying to turn it into a funny story her friends would enjoy, and selected a mandarin from the bowl. As she plunged her thumb into its fleshy centre, she heard something. A voice? It didn't come from Ben and Jessica's room. It was the other room adjoining hers. There was a thud, followed immediately by the unmistakeable sound of something breaking.

A male voice swore, loudly and forcefully. 'Fuck it!'

Indeed, thought Frances, as the malevolent beginnings of a headache crept slowly across her forehead.

chapter seven

Jessica

Jessica sat on the four-poster bed and tested the mattress with the palm of her hand while Ben stood on the balcony, one hand shielding his eyes. He wasn't enjoying the beautiful view.

'I'm sure they haven't stolen it,' she said. She meant to sound funny and light-hearted but she couldn't seem to get the tone of her voice to come out right these days. A hardness kept creeping in.

'Yeah, but *where* have they parked it?' said Ben. 'That's what I don't get. I'd just like to know where it is. Have they got an underground bunker somewhere? Did you notice that when I asked if it was parked undercover, she sort of avoided answering the question?'

'Mmm,' said Jessica noncommittally.

She couldn't bear another fight about the car, or about anything. Her stomach was still recovering from the last screaming match. Whenever they fought she got instant indigestion, and that meant that these days she nearly always had indigestion. Their arguments were like submerged rocks they kept crashing up against. They couldn't be avoided. *Wham. Wham. Wham.*

She lay back on the bed and looked at the light fitting. Was that a spider web near the globe? This house was so old and dark and depressing. She'd been aware it was going to be a 'historic' house, but she thought they might have, you know, *renovated*. There were cracks all over the walls, and a kind of damp smell.

She turned on her side and looked at Ben. Now he was leaning dangerously over the balcony railing, trying to see the other side of the house. He cared about that car more than he cared about her. Once, she saw him running his hand along the bonnet and for just a moment she'd felt *envious of the car*, of the way Ben was touching it so gently and sensuously, the same way he used to touch her. She was going to tell their counsellor that. She'd written it down so she wouldn't forget. She felt like it was a really profound, powerful thing to mention, quite significant and *telling*. It made her eyes prickle with tears when she thought of it. If the counsellor ever wrote a book about her experience as a marriage counsellor she would probably mention it: *I once had a patient who treated his car more tenderly than he treated his wife.* (No need to mention the car was a Lamborghini; if they did, all the male readers would say, 'Oh, well, then.')

She wished the 'intensive couples counselling' part of this retreat would hurry up and start but 'Delilah', their 'wellness consultant', had been annoyingly vague about when it would begin. She wondered if the counsellor would ask them about their sex life, and if she (Jessica assumed she would be a *she*) would be able to hide her surprise when she heard they were down to having sex, like, *once a week*, which meant their marriage was officially in dire trouble.

Jessica didn't know if she could talk about sex in front of

the counsellor anyway. The counsellor might automatically assume that she was sexually unskilled or that there was something wrong with her, in a very personal, gynaecological kind of way. Jessica was beginning to wonder that herself.

She was obviously prepared to get more surgery (even down there) or do a course. Read a book. Improve her skills. She'd always been prepared to improve, to listen to the advice of experts. She read a lot of self-help books. She Googled. Ben had never read a self-help book in his life.

Ben came back inside from the balcony, lifting up his t-shirt to scratch his stomach. He didn't bother with crunches or planks and his stomach still looked that good.

'That author we met is in the room next to us,' he said. He picked up an apple from the fruit bowl and tossed it from hand to hand like a baseball. 'Frances. Why do you reckon she's here?'

'I expect she wants to lose weight,' said Jessica. Like, duh. She thought it was kind of obvious. Frances had that *padded* look middle-aged women got. Jessica herself would never allow that to happen. She'd rather be dead.

'You reckon?' said Ben. 'What does it matter at her age?' He didn't wait for an answer. 'What are her books like?'

'I used to love them,' said Jessica. 'I read them all. There was one called *Nathaniel's Kiss*. I read it in high school and it was just really . . . romantic, I guess.'

'Romantic' was too ineffectual a word to describe the feelings *Nathaniel's Kiss* had provoked in her. She remembered how she'd cried big heaving shuddering sobs, and then she'd kept rereading that last chapter for the pleasure of more crying. In some ways, it felt like Nathaniel was the first man she ever loved.

She couldn't tell Ben that. He never read fiction. He wouldn't understand.

But was that one of the problems in their marriage? That she didn't even bother to try to communicate how she felt about things that were important to her? Or did it not matter? She didn't need to hear him talk about his passion for his car. He could talk about his car with his mates. She could talk about her memories of *Nathaniel's Kiss* with her girlfriends.

Ben took a giant bite of the apple. Jessica couldn't do that anymore, not with her new capped teeth. The dentist wanted her to wear some sort of a mouthguard at night to keep her expensive crowns all safe. It was annoying that the better the stuff you got, the less relaxed you could be about it. It was like the new rug in their hallway. Neither of them could bear to walk on something so astoundingly expensive. They shuffled down the sides and winced when their guests marched straight down the middle in dirty sneakers.

'That smoothie was pretty good,' said Ben, his mouth full of apple. 'But I'm starved. I don't know if my body can cope without pizza for ten days. I don't see why we even have to do that part! What's that got to do with marriage counselling?'

'I *told* you,' said Jessica. 'It's, like, a holistic approach. We have to work on everything: our minds, bodies and spirits.'

'Sounds like a load of –' He cut himself off and walked over to the row of light switches by the wall and started playing with the one that made the ceiling fan work.

He put the fan onto cyclonic speed.

Jessica put a pillow over her face and tried to go for as long as she could without saying, 'Turn it off.' Once, she wouldn't have thought about this. She would have just yelled, 'Oh my God, turn it off, you idiot!' and he would have laughed and kept it on, and she would have tried to turn it off, and he wouldn't have let her, and they would have pretend-wrestled.

Did they laugh more before?

Back when she was working in admin and he was a panel beater working for Pete, back when Ben drove a V8 Commodore that didn't make anyone look twice, and she had B-cup boobs that didn't make anyone look twice either, back when they thought going to a movie and the local Thai restaurant on the same night was *splurging* and when the arrival of the credit card statement each month was, like, really stressful and even once made her cry?

She didn't want to believe it was better before. If it was, then her mother was right, and she couldn't stand it if her mother was right.

Ben turned the fan down to a gentler breeze. Jessica removed the pillow from her face, closed her eyes and felt her heart race with fear of something unnamed and unknown.

It made her think of the vertiginous fear she'd felt the day of the robbery. It was two years ago now that she'd come home from work to discover their ground-floor apartment had been robbed, their possessions strewn everywhere with aggressive, malicious abandon, every drawer open, a black footprint across her white t-shirt, the glint of broken glass.

Ben arrived home just moments later. 'What the hell?'

She didn't know if he immediately thought of his sister, but she did.

Ben's sister, Lucy, had 'mental health issues'. That was the euphemism Ben's lovely, long-suffering mother used. The truth was that Ben's sister was an addict.

Lucy's life was an endless rollercoaster and they all had to take the same ride, over and over, without getting off. Lucy was missing. No-one had heard from her. Lucy had turned up in the middle of the night and trashed the house. Ben's mum had to call the police. They were planning an intervention! But they were going to handle this intervention differently from the last intervention; this time it would work. Lucy was doing well! Lucy was talking about rehab. Lucy was *in* rehab! Lucy was out of rehab. Lucy had been in another car accident. Lucy was pregnant again. Lucy was fucked up and there would never be an end to it, and because Jessica had never known the Lucy of before, the Lucy who was supposedly funny and smart and kind, it was hard not to hate her.

Lucy was the reason for the underlying tension at every event with Ben's family. Would she turn up demanding money or screaming insults or crying crocodile tears because she 'just wanted to be a mum' to the two children she was incapable of bringing up?

Everyone knew Lucy stole. If you went to a barbecue at Ben's place you hid your cash. So it was perfectly natural that Jessica's first thought when she walked into the apartment that day was: *Lucy.*

She'd tried so hard not to say it but she couldn't help it. Just that one word. She wished she could take it back. She hadn't made it sound enough like a question. She'd made it sound like a statement. She wished she'd at least said, 'Lucy?'

She remembered how Ben shook his head. His face was drawn tight with shame.

She had thought, *How do you know it wasn't her?*

But it turned out he was right. The robbery had nothing to do with Lucy. She was on the other side of the country at the time.

So it was just an ordinary happens-to-lots-of-people house robbery. They hadn't lost much because they didn't have much to lose: an old iPad with a cracked screen, a necklace that Ben had given Jessica for her twenty-first. It had a tiny diamond pendant and it had cost Ben something like two months' salary. She'd loved that necklace and still mourned it, even though it had just been a crappy little necklace with a smidge of a diamond, like a *quarter*-carat. The thieves had rejected the rest of Jessica's jewellery box, which she found humiliating. Jessica and Ben had both hated the feeling of knowing that someone had walked through their home, sneering, as if browsing through an unsatisfactory shop.

The insurance company paid out without much fuss, but Ben and Jessica had to pay a five-hundred-dollar excess, which they resented because they hadn't *asked* to be robbed.

It was just an ordinary robbery, except that it ended up changing their lives forever.

'Why are you staring at me like that?' asked Ben. He stood at the end of the bed, looking down at her.

Jessica's gaze came back into focus. 'Like what?'

'Like you're planning to cut off my balls with a cheese knife.'

'What? I wasn't even looking at you. I was *thinking*.'

He kept chewing the remains of his apple and raised an eyebrow. The very first time they ever made eye contact in Mr Munro's maths class he did that: a cool, laconic lift of his left eyebrow. It was *literally* the *hottest* thing she'd seen in her entire life and maybe if he'd raised two eyebrows, instead of one, she wouldn't have fallen in love with him.

'I don't even have a cheese knife,' said Jessica.

He smiled as he threw the apple core into the bin from across the room and picked up their welcome pack.

'We'd better read this, hey?' He ripped open the envelope and papers went flying. Jessica managed to stop herself from grabbing at it and putting it all back in order. She was the one in charge of paperwork. If it were up to Ben they would never file a tax return.

He opened what looked like a covering letter. 'Okay, so this is a "guide map" for our "wellness journey".'

'Ben,' said Jessica, 'this isn't going to work if we don't –'

'I know, I know, I am taking it seriously. I drove down that road, didn't I? Didn't that show my commitment?'

'Oh, *please* don't start on the car again.' She felt like crying.

'I only meant –' His mouth twisted. 'Forget it.'

He scanned the letter and read out loud. '*Welcome to your wellness journey*, yada, yada. *The retreat will begin with a period of silence lasting five days, during which there will be no talking, apart from counselling sessions, no touching, no reading, no writing, no eye contact with other guests or your own companions* – what the?'

'This wasn't mentioned on the website,' said Jessica.

Ben continued to read out loud, '*You may be familiar with the term "monkey brain".*'

He looked up at Jessica. She shrugged, so he kept reading. '*Monkey brain refers to the way your mind swings from thought to thought like a monkey swinging from branch to branch.*' Ben made a sound like a monkey and scratched under his arm to demonstrate.

'Thanks for that.' Jessica felt the tug of a smile. Sometimes they were fine.

Ben read on. '*It takes at least twenty-four hours to silence monkey brain. A period of nourishing silence and reflection settles the mind, body and soul. Our aim will be to discover a beautiful state that Buddhism calls "noble silence".*'

'So we're just going to spend the next five days avoiding eye contact and not talking?' said Jessica. 'Even when we're alone in our room?'

'It's not like we don't have any experience with that,' said Ben.

'Very funny,' said Jessica. 'Give me that.'

She took the letter and read. '*During the silence we request that you walk slowly and mindfully, with intention, heel to toe, about the property, while avoiding eye contact and conversation. If you must communicate with a staff member, please come to reception and follow the instructions on the laminated blue card. There will be guided meditation sessions – both walking and sitting – throughout each day. Please listen for the bells.'*

She put the letter down. 'This is going to be so freaky. We'll have to eat with strangers in total silence.'

'Better than boring small talk, I guess,' said Ben. He looked at her. 'Do you want to do it properly? We could talk here in our room and nobody would ever know.'

Jessica thought about it.

'I think we should do it properly,' she said. 'Don't you? Even if it sounds stupid, we should just follow the rules and do whatever they say.'

'Fine with me,' said Ben. 'As long as they don't tell me to jump off a cliff.' He scratched his neck. 'I don't get what we're going to *do* here.'

'I told you,' said Jessica. 'Meditate. Yoga. Exercise classes.'

'Yeah,' said Ben. 'But in between all that. If we can't talk or watch TV, what will we do?'

'It will be hard without screens,' said Jessica. She thought she was going to miss social media more than coffee.

She looked again at the letter. *'The silence begins when the bell rings three times.'* She looked at the clock in the room. 'We've got half an hour left where we're allowed to talk.'

Or *touch*, she thought.

They looked at each other.

Neither spoke.

'So the silence shouldn't be too hard for us then,' said Ben. Jessica laughed, but Ben didn't smile.

Why weren't they having sex right now? Wasn't that what they once would have done? Without even talking about it?

She should say something. Do something. He was her

husband. She could touch him.

But a tiny fear had trickled into her head late last year and now she couldn't get rid of it. It was something about the way he looked at her, or didn't look at her; a clenching of his jaw.

The thought was this: *He doesn't love me anymore.*

It seemed so ironic that he could fall out of love with her now, when she had never looked so good. Over the last year she had invested a lot of time and money, and a fair amount of pain, in her body. She had done *everything* there was to do: her teeth, her hair, her skin, her lips, her boobs. Everyone said the results were amazing. Her Instagram account was filled with comments like: *You look so HOT, Jessica!* and *You look better and better every time I see you.* The only person without anything positive to say was her own husband, and if he didn't find her attractive now, when she was her very best self, then he must never have found her attractive. He must have been faking it all along. Why did he even marry her?

Touch me, she thought, and in her head it was an anguished wail. *Please, please touch me.*

But all he did was stand up and walk back over to the fruit bowl. 'The mandarins look good.'

chapter eight

Frances

'When did the pain start?'

Frances lay naked on a massage table, a soft white towel draped over her back.

'Everything off and then under this towel,' the massage therapist had barked when Frances arrived at the spa. She was a large woman with a grey buzz cut and the intimidating manner of a prison guard or a hockey coach, not quite the soft-voiced, gentle masseuse Frances had been anticipating. Frances hadn't quite caught her name but she'd been too distracted following instructions to ask her to repeat it.

'About three weeks ago,' said Frances.

The therapist placed warm hands on her back which seemed to be the size of ping-pong bats. Was that possible? Frances lifted her head to see them but the therapist pressed against Frances's shoulder blades so her head fell forward again.

'Did anything in particular set it off?'

'Not anything physical,' said Frances. 'But I did have kind of an emotional shock. I was in this relationship –'

'So no physical injury of any sort,' said the therapist tersely. Clearly she hadn't got the Tranquillum House memo about speaking in a slow hypnotic voice. In fact, she was the opposite: it was like she wanted to get any speaking over and done with as quickly as possible.

'No,' said Frances. 'But I feel like it was definitely connected. I had a shock, you see, because this man I was dating, well, he disappeared and – I remember this very clearly – I was actually phoning the police when I felt this kind of sensation, like I'd been *slammed* –'

'It's probably better if you don't talk,' said the therapist.

'Oh. Is it?' said Frances. *I was about to tell you a very interesting story, scary lady.* She'd told the story a few times now, and she felt that she told it quite well. She was improving it with each telling.

Also, she didn't have long before she had to stop talking for *five days*, and she wasn't sure how she was going to cope with so much silence. She'd only just avoided that terrifying abyss of despair in the car. Silence might tip her over again.

The therapist pressed her giant thumbs on either side of Frances's spine.

'*Ow!*'

'Focus on your breathing.'

Frances breathed in the citrus-scented essential oils and thought about Paul. How it began. How it ended.

Paul Drabble was an American civil engineer she met online. A friend of a friend of a friend. A friendship that turned into something more. Over a six-month period, he sent her flowers and gift baskets and handwritten notes. They talked for hours on the phone. He'd Facetimed with her and said he'd read three of her books and loved them, and he talked expertly about the characters and even quoted his favourite excerpts, and they were all excerpts that made

Frances feel secretly proud. (Sometimes people quoted their favourite lines to her and Frances thought, *Really? I thought that wasn't my best.* And then she felt weirdly annoyed with them.)

He sent her photos of his son, Ari. Frances, who'd never wanted children of her own, fell hard for Ari. He was tall for his age. He loved basketball and wanted to play it professionally. She was going to be Ari's stepmother. She'd read the book *Raising Boys* in preparation and had a number of brief but pleasurable chats with Ari on the phone. He didn't say much, understandably – he was a twelve-year-old boy, after all – but sometimes she made him laugh when they Skyped, and he had a dry little chuckle that melted her heart. Ari's mother – Paul's wife – had died of cancer when Ari was in preschool. So sad, so poignant, so . . . 'convenient?' suggested one of Frances's friends, and Frances had slapped her wrist.

Frances was planning to move from Sydney to Santa Barbara. She had her flights booked. They would need to get married to secure her green card, but she wasn't going to rush into things. If and when it happened, she planned to wear amethyst. Appropriate for a third wedding. Paul had sent her photos of the room in his house that he'd already set up as her writing room. There were empty bookshelves waiting for her books.

When that terrible phone call came in the middle of the night, Paul so distraught he could barely get the words out, crying as he told her that Ari had been in a terrible car accident and there was a problem with the health insurance company and that Ari needed immediate surgery, Frances didn't hesitate. She sent him money. A vast amount of money.

'Sorry, *how* much?' said the young detective who carefully wrote down everything Frances said, his professionalism slipping for just a moment.

That was Paul's only misstep: he underplayed his hand. She would have sent double, triple, quadruple – anything to save Ari.

And then: terrifying silence. She was frantic. She thought Ari must have died. Then she thought Paul had died. No answers to her texts, her voicemail messages, her emails. It was her friend Di who made the first tentative suggestion. 'Don't take this the wrong way, Frances, but is it possible that . . .?' Di didn't even need to finish the sentence. It was as if the knowledge had been lurking away in Frances's subconscious all along, even while she booked non-refundable airfares.

It felt personal, but it wasn't personal. It was just business. 'These people are getting so smart,' the detective had said. 'They're professional and polished and they target women of your age and circumstances.' The sympathy on his handsome young face was excruciating. He saw a desperate old lady.

She wanted to say, 'No, no, I'm not a woman of age and circumstance! I'm me! You're not seeing *me*!' She wanted to tell him that she had never had any trouble meeting men, she had been *pursued* by men all her life, men who truly loved her and men who only wanted to have sex with her, but they were all real men, who wanted her for herself, not con artists who wanted her money. She wanted to tell him that she'd been told on multiple occasions by multiple sources that she was really very good in bed, and her second serve caused consternation on the tennis court, and, although she never cooked, she could bake an excellent lemon meringue pie. She wanted to tell him she was *real*.

The shame she experienced was extraordinary. She had revealed so much of herself to this scammer. How he must have sniggered, even as he somehow responded with sensitivity, humour and perfect spelling. He was a mirage, a narcissistic reflection of herself, saying exactly what she so obviously wanted to hear. She realised weeks after that even his name, 'Paul Drabble', was probably designed to begin the act of seduction by subconsciously reminding her of Margaret Drabble, one of her favourite authors, as she had posted for all to see on social media.

It turned out many other women had been planning lives as Ari's stepmother too.

'There are multiple ladies in the same situation as you,' the detective said.

Ladies. Oh my God, ladies. She couldn't believe she was a lady. That sexless, gentrified word made Frances shudder.

The details of each scam were different but the boy's name was always 'Ari' and he always had a 'car accident' and the distraught phone call always came in the middle of the night. 'Paul Drabble' had multiple names, each with a carefully curated online presence, so that when the *ladies* Googled their suitors – as they always did – they saw exactly what they wanted to see. Of course, he was not the friend of a friend of a friend. Or not in the real-world way. He'd played a long game, setting up a fake Facebook page and pretending an interest in antique restoration furniture, which had got him accepted into a Facebook group run by a university friend's husband. By the time he sent Frances a friend request, she'd seen enough of his (intelligent, witty, concise) comments on her friend's posts to believe him to be a real person in her extended circle.

Frances met up with one of the other women for coffee. The woman showed Frances pictures on her phone of the bedroom she'd created for Ari, complete with *Star Wars* posters on the wall. The posters were actually a little young for Ari – he wasn't into *Star Wars* – but Frances kept that to herself.

The woman was in a far worse state than Frances. Frances

ended up writing her a cheque to help her get back on her feet. Frances's friends spluttered when they heard this. Yes, she gave more cash to yet another stranger, but for Frances it was a way of restoring her pride, taking back control, and fixing some of the trail of destruction left by that man. (She did think a thankyou card from her fellow scam victim might have been nice, but one mustn't give only in expectation of thankyou cards.)

After it was all over, Frances packed away the evidence of her stupidity in a file. All the print-outs of emails where she'd spilled her foolish heart. The cards that accompanied real flowers with fake sentiments. The handwritten letters. She went to shove the folder into her filing cabinet and a sheet of paper sliced open her thumb like the edge of a razor blade. Such a tiny, trite injury and yet it hurt so much.

The therapist's thumbs moved in small, hard circles. A liquid warmth radiated across Frances's lower back. She looked through the hole in the massage table at the floor. She could see the therapist's sneakered feet. Someone had used a sharpie to doodle flowers all over the white plastic toes of her shoes.

'I fell for an internet romance scam,' said Frances. She needed to talk. The therapist would just have to listen. 'I lost a lot of money.'

The therapist said nothing, but at least she didn't order Frances to stop talking again. Her hands kept moving.

'I didn't care so much about the money – well, I *did*, I'd worked hard for that money – but some people lose everything in these kinds of scams whereas I just lost . . . my self-respect, I guess, and . . . my innocence.'

She was babbling now, but she couldn't seem to stop. All she could hear was the therapist's steady breathing.

'I guess I've always just assumed that people are who they say they are, and that ninety-nine per cent of people are good people. I've lived in a bubble. Never been robbed. Never been mugged. Nobody has ever laid a hand on me.'

That wasn't strictly true. Her second husband hit her once. He cried. She didn't. They both knew the marriage was over in that moment. Poor Henry. He was a good man, but they brought out something terrible in each other, like allergic reactions.

Her mind wandered off down the road of her long and complicated relationship history. She'd shared her relationship history with 'Paul Drabble' and he'd shared his. His had sounded so real. It must have had some truth to it? *So says the novelist who makes up relationships for a living. Of course he could have fabricated his relationship history, you idiot.*

She kept talking. Better to talk than to think.

'I honestly thought I was more in love with this man than any other man I'd met in the real world. I was quite deluded. But then again, love is just a trick of the mind, isn't it?'

Just shut up, Frances, she's not interested.

'Anyway, it was all very . . .' Her voice trailed off. 'Embarrassing.'

The therapist was completely silent now. Frances couldn't even hear her breathing. It was like being massaged by a giant-handed ghost. Frances wondered if she was thinking, *I'd never fall for something like that.*

The sharpest knife-point of her humiliation was this: before, if Frances had been asked to pick the sort of person likely to fall for an internet scam, she would have chosen someone like *this* woman, with her bulky body, buzz cut and questionable social skills. Not Frances.

Frances said, 'I'm sorry, I missed your name before.'

'Jan.'

'Do you mind me asking, Jan, are you married . . . in a relationship?'

'Divorced.'

'Me too,' said Frances. 'Twice.'

'But I've just started seeing someone,' offered Jan, as if she couldn't help herself.

'Oh. Great!' Frances's mood lifted. Was there anything better than a new relationship? Her whole career was based on the wonder of new relationships. 'How did you meet?' she asked.

'He breath-tested me,' said Jan, with a laugh in her voice.

The laugh told Frances everything she needed to know. *Jan was newly in love.* Frances's eyes filled with happy tears for her. Romance would never be dead for Frances. Never.

'So . . . he's a policeman?'

'He's a new cop in Jarribong,' said Jan. 'He was bored sitting on the side of the road doing random breath-testing, and we got chatting while he waited for another car to come along. It took two hours.'

Frances tried to imagine Jan chatting for two hours.

'What's his name?' asked Frances.

'Gus,' said Jan.

Frances waited, giving Jan the opportunity to wax lyrical about her new boyfriend. She tried to imagine him for herself. Gus. A local country cop. Broad-shouldered, with a heart of gold. Gus probably owned a dog. A lovable dog. Gus probably whittled. He probably had a tuneful whistle. He probably *whistled* while he *whittled*. Frances was already half in love with Gus herself.

But Jan had gone silent on the subject of Gus.

After a while, Frances kept talking, as if Jan had actually shown interest.

'You know, sometimes I think it was almost worth it, the

money I paid, for the companionship over those six months. For the hope. I should email him, and say, "Look, I know you're a scammer, but I'll pay you to keep pretending to be Paul Drabble."' She paused. 'I would never really do that.'

Silence.

'It's funny, because I'm a romance writer. I create fictional characters for a living, and then I fell for one.'

Still nothing. Jan mustn't be a reader. Maybe she was just embarrassed for Frances. *Wait till I get home and tell Gus about this loser.*

Gus would give a long, low (tuneful) whistle of surprise and sympathy. 'That's what happens in the big smoke, Jan.'

Frances managed to stay silent for a few moments as Jan kneaded her knuckle into a spot on her lower back. It hurt in a glorious, necessary-feeling way.

'Do you work full-time here, Jan?'

'Just casual. When they need me.'

'You like it?'

'It's a job.'

'You're very good at it.'

'Yup.'

'*Extraordinarily* good.'

Jan said nothing and Frances closed her eyes. 'How long have you worked here?' she asked sleepily.

'Only a few months,' said Jan. 'So I'm still a newbie.'

Frances opened her eyes. There was something in Jan's voice. Just a shadow. Was it possible she wasn't quite sold on the Tranquillum House philosophy? Frances considered asking her about the missing contraband, but how would the conversation progress?

'*I think someone went through my bags, Jan.*'

'*Why do you think that, Frances?*'

'*Well, some things were missing.*'

'What sort of things?'

She was too ashamed and too vulnerable without her clothes on to confess.

'What is the director like?' asked Frances, thinking of the reverence with which Yao had looked at that closed door.

Silence.

Frances watched Jan's feet in their chunky sneakers. They didn't move.

Finally, Jan spoke. 'She's very passionate about her work.'

Yao had also said he was *passionate* about his work. It was the theatrical language of movie stars and motivational speakers. Frances would never say she was 'passionate' about her work, although she *was* in fact passionate about her work. If she went too long without writing she lost her mind.

What if she was never published again?

Why would anyone publish her again? She didn't deserve to be published.

Don't think about the review.

'Passion is good,' she said.

'Yup,' said Jan. She chose another spot for knuckle-digging.

'Is she possibly too passionate at times?' asked Frances, trying to understand the point, if any, that Jan was trying to make.

'She cares a lot about the guests here and she's prepared to do . . . whatever it takes . . . to help them.'

'Whatever it takes?' said Frances. 'That sounds –'

Jan's hands moved to Frances's shoulders. 'I need to remind you that the noble silence will begin in just a few moments. Once we hear the third bell we're not allowed to talk.'

Frances felt panicky. She wanted more information before this creepy silence began.

'When you say "whatever it takes" –'

'I only have positive things to say about the staff here,' interrupted Jan. She sounded a little robotic now. 'They have your best interests at heart.'

'This is sounding kind of ominous,' said Frances.

'People achieve great results here,' said Jan.

'Well, that's good.'

'Yup,' said Jan.

'So are you saying that some of their methods are possibly a little . . .' Frances tried to find the right word. She was remembering some of those angry online reviews.

A bell rang once. It reverberated with the melodic authority of a church bell, clear and pure.

Damn it.

'Unorthodox?' continued Frances hurriedly. 'I guess I'm just cautious now, after my experience with that man, that scammer. Once bitten –'

The second bell, even louder than the first, sliced through the middle of her cliché so that it hung foolishly in the air.

'Twice shy,' whispered Frances.

Jan pressed her palms down hard on Frances's shoulder blades as if she were performing CPR and leaned forward so that her breath was warm against Frances's ear.

'Just don't do anything you're not comfortable with. That's all I can say.'

The third bell rang.

chapter nine

Masha

The director of Tranquillum House, Maria Dmitrichenko – Masha to everyone except the tax office – sat alone in her locked office at the top of the house as the third bell rang. Even from all the way up here she could sense the silence fall. It felt like she'd walked into a cave or cathedral: that feeling of release. She bowed her head towards her favourite fingerprint-shaped whorl in the surface of her white oak desk.

She was on her third day of a water-only fast, and fasting always heightened her senses. The window of her office was open and she breathed in great gusts of clean country air. She closed her eyes and remembered how she'd once breathed in all the strange, thrilling scents of this new country: eucalyptus, fresh-cut grass and petrol fumes.

Why was she thinking about this?

It was because her ex-husband had emailed yesterday, for the first time in years. She'd deleted his email, but just seeing his name for even an instant had infiltrated her consciousness, so that now the merest scent of eucalyptus on a breeze was enough to transport her back thirty years to the person she'd once been, someone she could barely remember. And yet she *did* remember everything about that first day, after those endless flights (Moscow, Delhi, Singapore, Melbourne); how she and her husband had looked at each other in the back of that little van, marvelling at all the lights, even in the middle of the street. They'd whispered to each other about the way strangers kept *smiling* at them. It was bizarre the way they did this! So friendly! But then – it was Masha who first noticed this – when they turned their heads, *their smiles shrank to nothing.* Smile, gone. Smile, gone. In Russia, people didn't smile like that. If they smiled at all, they smiled from the heart. That was Masha's first-ever experience of the 'polite smile'. You could see the polite smile as a wonderful or terrible thing. Her ex-husband smiled back. Masha did not.

Nu naher! She did not have time for the past right now. She had a health resort to run! People were depending on her. This was the first time she'd begun a retreat with a period of silence, but she knew already that it was right. The silence would give her guests clarity. It would frighten some of them, they would resist, and people would break the silence, accidentally or deliberately. Couples might whisper in their beds, but that was fine. The silence would set the right tone going forward. Some guests treated this place like summer camp. Middle-aged women got overexcited at not having to cook dinner each night. All that high-pitched chatter. If two men became 'mates', you could be sure rules would be broken.

In the early days, when Masha first opened Tranquillum House to the public, she'd been shocked to discover an order for a family-sized meatlovers pizza being delivered at the back fence. *'Nu shto takoye?'* she shouted, scaring the life out of both the poor delivery boy and the guest. *What's going on here?*

She had learned the funny ways of her guests. Now she took precautions. Security cameras around the property. Regular monitoring. Bags were checked. All for their own good.

She turned sideways in her chair and lifted one leg, pressing her forehead to her shinbone. She occupied her body with the ease of a ten-year-old boy and she liked to say that she *was* only ten years old, because it was coming up to the tenth anniversary of the day it happened. Her cardiac arrest. The day she died and was born again.

If not for that day, she would still be in the corporate world, and she would still be fat and stressed. She had been global operations director for a multinational producer of dairy products. She had been taking Australia's most trusted cheese to the world! (She no longer ate cheese.) She remembered her office, with its views of the Sydney Opera House, and the pleasure she once took in ticking off tasks, formulating policies to streamline procedures, bringing a room full of men to heel. Her life then had been spiritually void, but intellectually stimulating. She especially loved new product development and seeing the company's entire product line laid out on the boardroom table: the lushness of choice, the brightly coloured packaging. In a strange way, it fulfilled the yearning she'd felt as a child when she flicked through illicit shopping catalogues from the West.

But the pleasure she took in her corporate life had been like a polite smile. There was no substance to it. Her mind, body and soul had operated like different divisions of a corporation without a good flow of communication. This nostalgia she felt for her old job was as fraudulent as fond thoughts of her ex-husband. The memories her mind kept throwing up were nothing but computer glitches. She must focus. Nine people were depending on her. Nine perfect strangers who would soon become like family.

She ran her finger down a printout of their names:

Frances Welty
Jessica Chandler
Ben Chandler
Heather Marconi
Napoleon Marconi
Zoe Marconi
Tony Hogburn
Carmel Schneider
Lars Lee

Nine strangers who, right now, were settling into their rooms, exploring the property, nervously reading their information packs, drinking their smoothies, perhaps enjoying their first spa treatments, worrying about what lay ahead.

She loved them already. Their self-consciousness and self-loathing, their manifest lies, their defensive jokes to hide their pain as they cracked and crumbled before her. They were hers for the next ten days, hers to teach and nurture, to shape into the people they could be, should be.

She found the file for the first name on her list.

Frances Welty. Aged fifty-two. The photo she'd submitted showed a woman wearing red lipstick holding a cocktail.

Masha had treated a hundred women like Frances. It was simply a matter of peeling back their layers to reveal the heartache beneath. They longed to be peeled, for someone to be interested enough to peel them. It wasn't hard. They'd been hurt: by husbands and lovers, by children who no longer needed them, by disappointing careers, by life, by death.

They nearly all loathed their bodies. Women and their bodies! The most abusive and toxic of relationships.

Masha had seen women pinch at the flesh of their stomachs with such brutal self-loathing they left bruises. Meanwhile their husbands fondly patted their own much larger stomachs with rueful pride.

These women came to Masha overfed and yet malnourished, addicted to various substances and chemicals, exhausted and stressed and experiencing migraines or muscular pain or digestive issues. They were easy to heal with rest and fresh air, nutritious food and attention. Their eyes brightened. They became expansive and exhilarated as their cheekbones re-emerged. They wouldn't shut up. They left Masha with hugs and tears in their eyes and bright toot-toots of their car horns. They sent heartfelt cards, often with photos enclosed showing how their journeys had continued as they applied Masha's lessons to their day-to-day lives.

But then, two, three, four years later, a good proportion *came back to Tranquillum House*, looking as unhealthy as they'd been at their first visits – or even unhealthier. 'I stopped my morning meditation,' they would say, all wide-eyed and apologetic, but not *that* apologetic; they seemed to think their lapses were natural, cute, to be expected. 'And next thing I was back drinking every day.' 'I lost my job.' 'I got divorced.' 'I had a car accident.' Masha had only reset them temporarily! In times of crisis they returned to their default settings.

That was not good enough. Not for Masha.

This was why the new protocol was essential. There was no need for the strange anxiety that was waking her up in the dark of the night. The reason Masha had been so successful in her corporate career was because she had always been the one prepared to take risks, to think laterally. It was the same here. She tapped her fingertip against the bleary, bloated face of Frances Welty and checked to see which boxes she had selected for what she wanted to achieve over the next ten days: 'stress relief', 'spiritual nourishment' and 'relaxation'. It was interesting that she hadn't ticked 'weight loss'. It must be an oversight. She seemed like the careless sort. No attention to detail. One thing was clear: this woman was crying out for a spiritually transformative experience, and Masha would give it to her.

She opened the next file. Ben and Jessica Chandler.

Their photo showed an attractive young couple sitting on a yacht. They were smiling with their teeth but Masha couldn't see their eyes because of their dark sunglasses. They had ticked the box for couples counselling and Masha was confident she could help. Their problems would be fresh, not calcified after years of arguments and bitterness. The new protocol would be perfect for them.

Next up, Lars Lee. Forty. The photo he'd attached was a glossy corporate headshot. She knew this type of guest very well. He saw attendance at health resorts as a part of his grooming regime, like a haircut or a manicure. He would not try to smuggle in contraband but he would feel that inconvenient rules did not apply to him. His reaction to the new protocol would be interesting.

Carmel Schneider. Thirty-nine. Mother of young children. Divorced. Masha looked at her photo and clucked. She heard her mother's voice: *If a woman doesn't look after herself, her man looks after another woman.* Poor little bunny. Low self-esteem. Carmel had ticked every single box on the list except for 'couples counselling'. Masha felt lovingly towards her for this. *No problem, my lapochka. You will be one of my easy ones.*

Tony Hogburn. Fifty-six. Also divorced. Also here for weight loss. That was the only box he ticked. He would become grumpy and possibly aggressive when his body reacted to the changes in his self-medicating lifestyle. One to monitor.

The next file made her frown.

Could this be her wildcard?

The Marconi family. Napoleon and Heather. Both aged forty-eight. Their daughter, Zoe. Aged twenty.

This was the first time a family group had booked in to do a Tranquillum House retreat. She'd had many couples, mothers and daughters, siblings and friends, but never a family, and the daughter was the youngest guest ever to come.

Why would a perfectly healthy-looking twenty-year-old choose to do a ten-day health retreat with her parents? Eating disorder? That could be it. They all looked underfed to Masha's practised eye. Some sort of strange family dysfunction going on?

Whoever filled in the questionnaire for the family's group booking had ticked only one box: 'stress relief'.

The photo the Marconi family had submitted showed the three of them in front of a Christmas tree. It was clearly a selfie, because they had their heads at funny angles trying to get into the camera frame. They were all smiling but their eyes were flat and empty.

'What happened to you, my lapochki?'

chapter ten

Heather

As soon as the third bell rang, Heather Marconi felt the silence fall, as though a blanket had been gently dropped over Tranquillum House. It was remarkable how palpable it was. She hadn't been especially aware of any ambient noise beforehand.

She had just come out of the bathroom when the bells began to ring, much louder and more commanding than she had anticipated. She had been of two minds as to whether she'd bother to go along with this absurd 'silence' – if they'd wanted a silent retreat they would have booked a silent retreat, thank you very much – but the religious sound of the bells froze her on the spot. Ignoring the silence now felt disrespectful, even in the privacy of their own room.

Her husband sat on an antique sofa in the corner, his finger to his lips like a schoolteacher, because Napoleon *was* a schoolteacher, a beloved schoolteacher in a disadvantaged area, and you couldn't spend twenty-five years teaching geography to recalcitrant boys without bringing home some teacher-like habits.

Heather thought, *Don't shhhh me, darling. I'm not one of your students. I'll talk if I want to talk.* She met his eyes to give him a wink and Napoleon's gaze skittered away as if he had something to hide, but he was always the one with nothing to hide, he was the open bloody book, and the reason he was avoiding her eyes was because the paperwork had specified 'no eye contact' for the next five days and Napoleon would never forget a rule or regulation, even one as pointless and arbitrary as this. What possible good could come of avoiding eye contact between husband and wife? But Napoleon was deeply respectful of road signs and tiny clauses on bureaucratic forms. For him, rules were about politeness and respect and ensuring the survival of a civilised society.

She studied him as he sat in his too-short dressing-gown, his long hairy legs entwined. He had a feminine way of crossing his legs, like a supermodel being interviewed on a talk show. His two shorter, chunkier older brothers gave him hell about the girly way he sat, but he just grinned and gave them the finger.

His hair was still wet from their visit to the hot springs and swim in the pool.

The hot springs were an easy walk from the back of the house, down a generously signposted walking track. There had been nobody else around. They had found the Secret Grotto, a rocky shaded pool just big enough for the three of them to sit in a semicircle and enjoy the views of the valley. Heather and Zoe had listened as Napoleon talked on and on about how the minerals in the water would help their circulation and reduce their stress levels and so on and so forth; she couldn't really remember what he'd said. Napoleon's conversation was like background noise in her life, a radio permanently on talkback, only random phrases making their way into her subconscious. He had obviously been panicked at the thought of five days of silence and had been speaking even faster than usual, without pause, his voice bubbling endlessly, like the frothy, warm, sulphuric-smelling water that bubbled about their bodies.

'Sweetheart, of course I can cope without speaking for five days!' he'd reassured Zoe, who had looked at her father with genuine concern on her beautiful young face. 'If you can cope without your phone and your mother can cope without caffeine, I can cope without conversation!'

Afterwards, the three of them had cooled off in the pool; the relief of the cold blue chlorinated water had been magical after the hot springs. Heather watched Zoe try to race her dad: he swam butterfly, she swam freestyle with a five-second head start. He still won, even though he didn't want to win, but he couldn't get away with pretending to lose like when she was a kid. Then they sat by the pool and Zoe told them a funny story about one of her university tutors that Heather didn't quite get, but she could tell by Zoe's face that it was meant to be funny, so it was easy to laugh. It had been a rare and special moment of happiness. Heather knew they would all three have noted it, and hoped it was a sign of something good.

And now they had to spend the next five days not talking.

Heather felt a burst of powerful irritation – or perhaps it was simply her body demanding a macchiato – because this so-called 'holiday' was not meant to be about suffering. There were undoubtedly multiple other health resorts that offered the same peaceful environment without these draconian deprivations. None of the three of them needed to lose weight. Weight was just not an issue for Heather! She weighed herself every morning at six on the dot and if she ever saw the needle move in the wrong direction she adjusted her diet. Her BMI was in the 'underweight' category, but only by a kilo. She'd always been lean. Zoe sometimes accused Heather of having an eating disorder, just because she was kind of picky about when and what she ate. She didn't put just anything in her mouth – unlike Napoleon, who ate like a vacuum cleaner, hoovering up whatever was around him.

Napoleon stood. He lifted his suitcase onto the bed, unzipped it and removed a beautifully folded t-shirt, a pair of shorts and some underpants. He packed like a soldier whose kit bag would be inspected. He took off his dressing-gown and stood in all his skinny, white, hairy, naked magnificence.

His uncharacteristic silence made him suddenly a stranger.

The muscles on his back moved in unison like an exquisitely engineered machine as he pulled on his t-shirt. Napoleon's height and nerdy demeanour disguised his sexiness.

The first time they had sex, all those years ago, Heather kept thinking to herself, Well, *this* is a surprise, because who knew that a guy like *Napoleon* would have the moves? She'd *liked* him well enough, he was sweet and funny and attentive, but she'd kind of thought sleeping with him would be like doing community service. It was meant to be polite, friendly, 'thanks so much for dinner and the Kevin Costner movie' sex, not mind-blowing sex. She knew Napoleon's memory of their first date was different from hers. His memory was wholesome and sweet and correct, the way the memory of a first date between a future husband and wife should be.

Napoleon zipped up his shorts and buckled his belt. He slid the brown leather through the silver metal clasp with irritatingly quick, efficient moves. He must have felt her eyes upon him, but he didn't look at her; he was so determined to follow these silly rules, no matter what. He was such a good man, so fucking perfect in every fucking way.

The rage hit her with the power and momentum of a

contraction during active labour. There was no escaping it. She saw herself punching his face with a closed fist, crunching his cheekbone, the diamond cluster of her engagement ring breaking his skin, over and over and over and over, blood dripping. The rage wrapped itself around her body, almost lifted her off her feet. She had to grip her toes to the floor to stop herself lunging at Napoleon as he zipped the bag back up and placed it on the floor in the corner of the room where nobody could trip over it.

She focused on a point on the wall where there was a small, island-shaped scratch in the wallpaper and used the variable breathing method she taught mothers to use during the transition phase of labour: pant, pant, *blow*, hee-hee-*hoo*, pant, pant, *blow*.

Napoleon walked across the room and stepped out onto the balcony. He stood with his legs apart and his hands clenching the railing, as if he were on the deck of a lurching ship.

The rage eased, receded, vanished.

Done. She'd got through it again. The oblivious object of her rage bowed his head, exposing his defenceless white neck. He would never know. He'd be horrified and so deeply wounded if he ever knew the violence of her secret thoughts.

Heather felt shaky. Her mouth tasted of bile. It was as though she'd just vomited.

She opened her own suitcase and found shorts and a tank top. Later this afternoon, after the 'meditation', she would need to run. She wouldn't be relaxed after sitting and focusing on her breathing for an hour; she'd be on the verge of madness.

Coming here was a mistake. An expensive mistake. They should have gone to a big anonymous hotel.

She tied the laces on her runners with vicious tugs and

opened her mouth to speak. She was definitely going to speak. This silence was *unnecessary*. They wouldn't speak in the presence of the other guests, but there was no need to maintain this awkward, weird and unhealthy silence in the privacy of their own room.

And what about poor Zoe, alone and silent in the room next door? Heather and Napoleon both panicked if she was alone in her bedroom at home for too long, which was hard because she was twenty years old and needed to study. If there had been no sound for a while one of them would make an excuse to go and check on her. She never complained and she never closed her door. But there were no family suites at Tranquillum House. They'd had no choice but to book her a single room.

She said she was fine, she constantly reassured them she was fine, she was happy; she understood their need to be reassured. But she'd worked so hard this year, much too hard, tapping away grimly on her computer as if a 'media studies' degree were a matter of life and death, and she deserved a break.

Heather looked at the wall above their bed that separated their room from Zoe's and wished she could see straight through it. What was she doing right now? She didn't have her phone. Twenty-year-olds *needed* their phones by their sides at all times. Zoe found it stressful if her battery power dropped below eighty per cent.

They shouldn't be risking their daughter's mental health like this. Zoe didn't sleep alone in a bed until she was ten years old.

Had she *ever* stayed in a hotel room on her own before?

Never. Zoe had been away on holidays with her girl-friends but they would have always shared a room, or so Heather would have thought.

She just broke up with her boyfriend and now she is alone in her room with nothing but her thoughts.

My God. Her heart raced. She knew she was catastrophising. *She is an adult. She's fine.*

Napoleon turned from the balcony, caught her eye and once again dropped his gaze. Heather felt her molars grind. He'd be so disappointed in her if she spoke only five minutes into 'the noble silence'.

Jesus. This was unexpectedly hard. The silence made her thoughts scream. She hadn't realised how much distraction Napoleon provided with his incessant chatter. How ironic if *she* was the one who couldn't handle silence, not him.

They didn't need silence or fasting or detoxification. They just needed a refuge from January. Last January they'd stayed home and that had been a disaster. It was even worse than the year before. It seemed that January was a cruel-eyed, clawed vulture that would terrorise Heather's tiny family forever.

'Maybe we should go away this time,' Napoleon had suggested a few months ago. 'Somewhere peaceful and quiet.'

'Like a monastery,' Zoe had said. Then her eyes brightened. 'Or, I know, a health resort! We'll get Dad's cholesterol down.'

Napoleon's school had offered all the teaching staff free health assessments back in June and Napoleon had been told his cholesterol was high, and his blood pressure was becoming worrisome, and it was great that he exercised, but he needed to make dramatic changes to his diet.

So Heather had Googled 'health resorts'.

Are you in need of significant healing?

That was the opening line on the home page for the Tranquillum House website.

'Yes,' Heather had said quietly to her computer screen. 'Yes, we are.'

It seemed likely that Tranquillum House targeted people of a socioeconomic status a few income levels higher than those of a high-school teacher and a midwife, but their last proper holiday had been years ago, and Napoleon's inheritance from his grandfather had been sitting there in a term deposit. They could afford it. There was nothing else they needed or wanted.

'Are you sure you want to be stuck with your parents at a health resort for ten days?' she'd asked Zoe.

Zoe shrugged, smiled. 'I just want to spend this holiday sleeping. I'm so tired.'

Normal twenty-year-old girls shouldn't be spending that much of their summer break with their parents, but then Zoe wasn't a normal twenty-year-old girl.

Heather had clicked *Book now* and instantly regretted it. It was strange how something could appear so attractive and then, the very moment you committed to it, become wildly unattractive. But it was too late. She'd agreed to the terms and conditions. They could change the time they went, but they couldn't get their money back. The three of them were doing a ten-day 'cleanse' whether they liked it or not.

She'd spent days kicking herself. They didn't need to be 'transformed'. There was nothing wrong with their bodies. Everyone always said the three of them were exercise fanatics! This wasn't the place for the Marconis; it was the place for people like that woman Napoleon had accosted on the stairs. What was her name? *Frances*. You could tell just by looking at her that she filled her life with lunches and facials and her husband's work functions.

She looked vaguely familiar to Heather – probably because Heather knew so many women just like her: wealthy middle-aged women who hadn't worked since before their children were born. There was nothing wrong with those women. Heather *liked* them. She just couldn't be with them for too long without succumbing to rage. They were utterly unscathed by life. The only thing they had to worry about was their bodies, because all that lunching didn't help their figures, so they needed to come to places like this to 'recharge' and to hear the experts tell them the amazing news that if you eat less and move more, you will weigh less and feel better.

Once the silence was over and they were allowed to talk again, Napoleon and Frances would get on like a house on fire. Napoleon would listen with genuine interest as Frances humble-bragged about how her children were studying at Harvard or Oxford or taking a gap year in Europe, where they seemed to be visiting more nightclubs than museums.

Heather wondered idly if she should suggest to Napoleon that he take the opportunity to have an affair while they were here. Perhaps the poor man craved sex, and Frances would be a fine buxom choice.

Heather knew the exact date she'd last had sex with her husband. It was three years ago. If she'd known it was going to be the last time she'd have sex for the rest of her life, she might have bothered to remember the details. She was sure it was good; it generally was good. It just wasn't possible anymore, not for Heather.

She sat on the end of the bed, and Napoleon came and sat down next to her. She could feel the warmth of his body along hers, but their bodies didn't touch, as per the rules.

They waited for Zoe, who was going to knock on their door once she was showered. That was the plan. Then the three of them would wait, *silently*, for the bell and go downstairs together for the first 'guided sitting meditation'.

Zoe was fine. Of course she was fine. She was a good girl. She would do what she said she would do. She always did.

She tried so hard to be everything for them while they tried so hard to pretend that she wasn't their only reason for living.

Heather felt the pierce of grief as sharp as a samurai sword.

She could always hide the rage, but never the grief. It was too visceral. She put her hand to the base of her throat and a tiny, mouse-like sound escaped.

'Just ride it out, sweetheart,' murmured Napoleon. He spoke so quietly it was almost a whisper. Without looking at her, he took her hand, enfolding it in the warmth of his palms, breaking his beloved rules for her.

She clutched at him, her fingers locked into the grooves between his knuckles, like a woman in labour holds her partner's hand as the pain tries to drag her away.

chapter eleven

Frances

The bell rang for the first 'guided sitting meditation' and Frances opened the door of her room at the same time as Ben and Jessica next door. Nobody said anything, which Frances found almost unendurable, and they all avoided eye contact as they walked down the corridor towards the stairs.

Ben wore the same clothes as earlier, while Jessica had changed into skin-tight yoga gear, revealing a figure so magnificent Frances wanted to compliment her on her efforts. It took a lot of commitment and silicone to look that good, and yet the poor kid didn't sashay as she deserved; rather she *scurried*, her shoulders hunched as though she were somewhere out of bounds and trying to escape notice.

Ben, on the other hand, had the stiff, stoic walk of a man being taken off to prison for a crime to which he'd pled guilty. Frances wanted to take them both out to a bar and listen to their life stories while they all ate peanuts and drank sangria.

Why was she even thinking about *sangria*, for heaven's sake? She hadn't drunk sangria in years. It was like her brain kept tossing out random suggestions for every type of food or drink she was going to be denied for the next ten days.

Just ahead of them on the stairs was the chatty giant Napoleon, together with his family. The mother was Heather. *Heather Like Leather.* The daughter was *Not-showy Zoe.* Well done, Frances, you're a genius. Although what was the point of her excellent name-remembering skills? She wasn't at a cocktail party. She wasn't even allowed to look at them.

Napoleon walked in a very odd way, head bowed like a monk, each leg lifted and dropped with agonising slowness, as though he were pretending to be a space-walker. Frances was nonplussed for a moment and then remembered the instructions about mindful walking during the silence. She slowed her pace and saw Jessica flick Ben on the arm to tell him to do the same.

All six of them walked down the stairs in mindful heel-to-toe slow motion, and Frances tried not to notice the absurdity of it. If she started laughing she would become hysterical. She was already quite light-headed from hunger. It had been hours since she licked the KitKat wrapper.

Everyone yielded to Napoleon as the most enthusiastically mindful walker and they all followed him mindfully through the house and then down the stairs to the cool and dark yoga and meditation studio.

Frances took her place on one of the blue mats towards the back of the room and attempted to imitate the posture of the two wellness consultants who sat in the front corners of the room, like exam supervisors, except that their legs were folded like origami, their hands resting on their knees, thumbs and fingers touching, irritating half-smiles on their smooth, tranquil faces.

She noted once again the big television screen and wondered if desperate guests ever crept down in their pyjamas and tried to get a late-night TV fix, although there didn't seem to be a remote anywhere.

As she tried to make herself comfortable she registered a slight but noticeable improvement in her back after her massage. The pain was still there, but it was like one of multiple bolts had been fractionally loosened.

She sniffed. She understood from her long-ago course that meditation was mostly about breathing correctly, and right now she couldn't breathe. People would think of her as the aggravating sniffling lady at the back of the room, and when she inevitably fell asleep she'd suddenly jerk awake after doing one of those loud, snorty snores.

Why hadn't she gone on a *cruise*?

She sighed, and looked around the room for guests she hadn't yet met. To the right of her was a man of about her own age, with a pallid, unhappy face. He sat stolidly on his mat with his legs stuck straight out in front of him, cradling his big, solid belly on his lap as if it were a baby that had been handed to him without his consent. Frances smiled kindly at him. It was nice to see someone here who truly *needed* a health resort.

His eyes met hers.

Wait. No. Please, no. Her stomach lurched. It was the man who had stopped on the side of the road and witnessed her screaming and banging on her horn like a lunatic. It was the man with whom she had freely discussed her menopausal symptoms. *The serial killer on vacation.*

She had not cared what the serial killer thought of her because she was never going to see him again. She had never considered that he might also be checking into Tranquillum House, because he was driving in the opposite direction, *away* from Tranquillum House, *deliberately* misleading her.

This was fine. This was highly embarrassing, but fine. She smiled again, her mouth pulled down in a self-deprecating way to show that she was mildly mortified that she was going to spend the next ten days with him after he'd witnessed her roadside meltdown, but she was a grown-up, he was a grown-up, what the heck.

He sneered at her. He absolutely, most definitely, sneered at her. And then he looked away. Fast.

Frances loathed him. He had been so arrogant on the side of the road, telling her he couldn't let her drive. Was he the police? No. (She felt like they were generally better groomed.) Of course, she would absolutely give the serial killer the *chance* to redeem himself, first impressions could be wrong, she'd read *Pride and Prejudice*, but she rather hoped he would continue to be loathsome for the next ten days. It was invigorating. Probably speeded up the metabolism.

Two more guests came into the room and Frances gave them her full attention. She would befriend them the moment she was allowed to speak. She was excellent at making friends. She felt quite sure that the serial killer was *not* excellent at making friends and she would therefore win.

The first was a woman, whom Frances guessed to be in her mid- to late-thirties, wearing an oversized, brand-new-looking white t-shirt that hung almost to her knees over black leggings, the standard outfit for an average-sized woman who starts a new exercise program and thinks her perfectly normal body should be hidden. Her thick black woolly hair was tied back in a long braid with glinting grey strands and she wore red-rimmed cat's-eye glasses: statement glasses favoured by those who want to appear quirky and intellectual. (Frances had a pair.) The woman had a flustered look about her, as if she'd only just made her bus and she had lots of other places to be today, and might need to leave early.

The flustered lady was followed by an *astonishingly* handsome man with high cheekbones and flashing eyes, who paused at the front of the room, as if he were a movie star walking out onto the set of a chat show to rapturous applause. He was perfectly stubbled, perfectly proportioned and deeply, deservedly, in love with himself.

Frances wanted to laugh out loud at the sight of him. He was too good-looking even to be the tall, dark and handsome hero in one of her books. The only way she could get away with it would be to give him a terminal disease, or a lovely wife. Or possibly both, which would then mean she'd have to find a miracle cure and a kind way to dispose of the lovely wife. Tricky.

He sat himself down on a yoga mat in the easy manner of someone with a daily yoga 'practice'.

The tendons of Frances's neck began to ache from the strain of trying to hold her body so she didn't see the serial killer in her peripheral vision. She rolled her shoulders. Sometimes she exhausted herself.

She turned her head and looked directly at him.

He sat slumped, poking his finger into a hole near the hem of his t-shirt.

She sighed, looked away. He wasn't even worth loathing. Now what?

Now . . . nothing. They were all just sitting here. Waiting. What were they meant to be *doing*?

The desire to interact was an irresistible itch.

Jessica, who sat directly in front of Frances, cleared her throat as if she were about to speak.

Someone else coughed discreetly at the back of the room.

Frances threw in a cough too. Her cough sounded quite bad, actually. She probably had a chest infection. Would they have antibiotics here? Or would they try to cure her with natural supplements? In which case she'd get sicker and sicker and eventually die.

All this coughing and clearing of throats reminded her of being in church. When had she last been in a church? It must have been for a wedding. Some of her friends' children were starting to get married. Girls who wore fuck-me boots in the eighties were now wearing mother-of-the-bride outfits with pretty bolero jackets to conceal their upper arms.

At least at a wedding you could quietly chat to the other guests while you waited for the bride. Compliment your friend on her pretty bolero jacket. This was more like a funeral, although even funerals weren't this silent as people murmured their soft condolences. She was *paying* to be here and it was worse than a *funeral*.

She looked dolefully around the room. There were no nice stained-glass windows to enjoy like in a church. There were no windows or natural light at all. It was almost dungeon-like. She was in a *dungeon* on an isolated property with a group of strangers, at least one of whom was a serial killer. She shivered violently. The air-conditioning was on too high. She thought of the inscription Yao had showed her from the convict stonemasons and wondered if the place might be haunted by their tortured spirits. She'd set a couple of her books in haunted houses. It was helpful for when you wanted your characters to leap into each other's arms.

Napoleon sneezed. A high-pitched shriek of a sneeze, like a dog's yelp.

'Ge*sund*heit!' cried the handsome man.

Frances gasped. He'd broken the noble silence already!

The handsome man clapped his hand to his mouth. His eyes danced. A wave of laughter ballooned in her chest. Oh God, it was like trying not to laugh in class. She saw the handsome man's shoulders shake. He chuckled. She giggled. In a moment she'd be *crying* with laughter and someone would order her to leave the room 'until she could control herself'.

'Namaste. Good afternoon.'

The atmosphere changed instantly as a figure strode into the room, altering the particles of air around her, drawing every eye, bringing the coughs and sneezes and throat-clearing to an instant halt.

The laugher trapped in Frances's chest vanished. The handsome man went still.

'A very warm welcome to Tranquillum House. My name is Masha.'

Masha was an extraordinary-looking woman. A super-model. An Olympic athlete. At least six feet tall, with corpse-white skin and green eyes so striking and huge they were almost alien-like.

In fact, Masha did seem like a different species, a *superior* species, to every other person in the room, even the hand-some man. Her voice was low and deep for a woman, with an attractive accent that made certain syllables shift sideways. Namaste became *nema*ste. The cadence of her speech rolled back and forth between broad Australian and what Frances picked as exotic Russian. Indeed, the woman could easily be a Russian spy. A Russian assassin. Like all the staff, she wore white, except on her it looked less like a uniform and more like a choice: the perfect choice, the only choice.

The muscles on her arms and legs were sculpted in clean, sleek lines. Her hair was bleached platinum and cut so short she'd be able to shake her head, dog-like, when she got out of the shower and be ready to face the day.

As Frances's eyes ran over Masha's exquisitely toned body and compared it to her own, she sank into herself. She was Jabba the Hutt, all pillowy bosom and hips and soft oozing flesh.

Stop it, she told herself. It wasn't like her to indulge in self-loathing.

Yet it would be disingenuous to deny the aesthetic pleasure of Masha's body. Frances had never bought into 'everyone is beautiful', a platitude only women had to be sold, as men could be beautiful or not without feeling as though they weren't really men. This woman, like the handsome man, had a dramatic, almost shocking physical presence. Frances had to talk or write or flirt or joke or in some way *act* before she could make an impact on people around her, otherwise, as she knew from experience, she could stand at a counter in a shop and be ignored forever. No-one could ignore Masha. All she had to do for attention was exist.

For a long, agonising moment Masha surveyed the room, turning her head in a slow arc that took in their cross-legged, silent subservience.

There's something demeaning about this, thought Frances. *We're sitting at her feet like kindergarten kids. We're silent, she speaks.* Also, the rule was no eye contact, and yet Masha appeared to be inviting it. She set the rules so she could break them. *I'm paying for this*, thought Frances. *You work for me, lady.*

Masha met Frances's gaze with warmth and humour. It was as if she and Frances were old friends, and she knew exactly what Frances was thinking and found her adorable for it.

At long last, she spoke again. 'I thank you for your willingness to take part in the noble silence.' I *thenk* you.

She paused.

'I understand that some of you may find this period of silence particularly challenging. I understand, too, that the silence was unexpected. Some of you may be experiencing feelings of frustration and anger right now. You may be thinking: But I didn't sign up for this! I understand, and to you I say this: Those of you who find the silence the most challenging will also find it the most rewarding.'

Mmm, thought Frances. *We'll see about that.*

'Right now you're at the foot of a mountain,' Masha continued, 'and the summit seems impossibly far away, but *I am here to help you reach that summit.* In ten days, you will not be the person you are now. Let me be clear on this, because it's important.'

She paused again. She looked slowly around the room, as if she were satirising a politician. The drama of her delivery was so deliberately hyperbolic it wasn't even funny. It *should* have been funny, yet it wasn't.

Masha repeated, 'In ten days, you will not be the person you are now.'

No-one moved.

Frances felt hope rise in the room like a delicate mist. Oh, to be transformed, to be someone else, to be someone *better.*

'You will leave Tranquillum House feeling happier, healthier, lighter, freer,' said Masha.

Each word felt like a benediction. Happier. Healthier. Lighter. Freer.

'On the last day of your stay with us, you will come to me and you will say this: Masha, you were right! I am not the same person I was. I am healed. I am free of all the negative habits and chemicals and toxins and thoughts that were holding me back. My body and mind are clear. I am changed in ways I could never have imagined.'

What a load of crap, thought Frances, while simultaneously thinking, *Please let it be true.*

She imagined driving home in ten days: pain-free, energised, her head cold cured, her back as flexible as an elastic band, the hurt and humiliation of her romance scam long gone, washed clean! She would walk tall, stand tall.

She would be ready for whatever happened with the new book. The review would have faded to nothing.

(She could actually feel the review right now, like a sharp-edged corn chip stuck in her throat, making it hard to breathe and swallow.)

She might even – and here she felt a burst of childlike anticipation, as if for Christmas Day – be able to zip that amazing Zimmermann dress all the way up again, the one that used to guarantee her compliments (often from other people's husbands, which was always so pleasing).

Perhaps her transformed self would go home and write a thriller or an old-fashioned murder mystery featuring a cast of colourful characters with secrets and a delightfully improbable villain. It might be fun to murder someone with a candlestick or a cup of poisoned tea. She could set it at a *health resort*! The murder weapon could be one of those stretchy green elastic bands she'd seen in the gym. Or she could make it more of a historical health resort where everyone wafted about looking pale and interesting as they recovered from tuberculosis. She could surely throw in a romantic subplot. Who didn't like a romantic subplot?

'There *will* be surprises on this journey,' said Masha. 'Each morning at dawn you will receive your daily schedule, but there will be unexpected detours and plans that change. I know this will be difficult for some of you who hold your lives with tight fists.'

She held up her fists to demonstrate her point and smiled. It was a stunning smile: warm and radiant and sensual. Frances found herself smiling back and looked around the room to see if everyone else was similarly affected. Yes, indeed. Even the serial killer smiled at Masha, although it seemed as if his lips had been forced up only temporarily without his consent, and the moment he got control back he was once again slack-jawed and sullen, pulling at a piece of thread on the fraying edge of his t-shirt.

'Imagine you are a leaf in a stream,' said Masha. 'Relax and enjoy the journey. The stream will carry you this way and that, but it will carry you forward to where you need to go.'

Napoleon nodded thoughtfully.

Frances studied the still, straight backs of Ben and Jessica in front of her, somehow vulnerable in their slim youthfulness, which didn't make sense because they probably didn't say 'oof' each time they stood up from a chair.

Ben turned towards Jessica and opened his mouth as if he were about to break the silence, but he didn't. Jessica moved her hand and the light bounced off an enormous diamond on her finger. Good Lord. How many carats was that thing?

'Before we begin our first guided meditation, I have a story to share,' said Masha. 'Ten years ago, I died.'

Well, that was unexpected. Frances sat a little straighter.

Masha's face became oddly jovial. 'If you don't believe me, ask Yao!'

Frances looked across at Yao, who seemed to be trying not to smile.

'I went into cardiac arrest and I was clinically dead.' Masha's green eyes shone with crazy joy, as if she were describing the best day of her life.

Frances frowned. *Wait, why did you mention Yao? Was he there? Keep your narrative on track, Masha.*

'They call my experience a "near-death experience",' said Masha. 'But I feel that is the wrong terminology because I wasn't just near death, I *was* dead. I experienced death, a privilege for which I am eternally grateful. My experience, my so-called "near-death experience", was ultimately life-changing.'

There were no coughs, no movement in the room. Were people rigid with embarrassment or still with awe?

Here comes the tunnel of light, thought Frances. Hadn't they proved there was a scientific reason for that phenomenon? Yet even as she scoffed, she felt a tingle of goosebumps.

'That day, ten years ago, I temporarily left my body,' said Masha. She said this with casual conviction, as if she didn't expect to be doubted.

Her eyes swept the room. 'There may be doubters among you. You may be thinking, Did she really die? Let me tell you, Yao was one of the paramedics who took care of me that day.'

She nodded at Yao, who nodded back.

'Yao can confirm that my heart did indeed stop. We later developed a friendship and a mutual interest in wellness.'

Yao nodded even more vigorously. Did Frances imagine it, or did the other wellness consultant roll her eyes at that? Professional jealousy? What was her name again? *Delilah*.

What happened to Delilah after she cut off Samson's hair? Frances longed to Google it. How was she going to cope for ten days without instant answers to idle questions?

Masha continued to speak. 'I wish I could tell you much more about my near-death experience, but it is so hard to find the right words, and I'll tell you why – it is simply beyond human comprehension. I don't have the vocabulary for it.'

At least give it a shot. Frances scratched irritably at her forearm, which she understood from a clickbait article to be a symptom of Alzheimer's, although she couldn't be one hundred per cent sure because she couldn't goddamn Google it.

'I can tell you this,' said Masha. 'There is another reality that sits alongside the physical reality. I now know that death is not to be feared.'

Although still best avoided, thought Frances. The more earnest people got, the more flippant she became. It was a flaw.

'Death is simply a matter of leaving behind our earthly bodies.' Masha moved her own earthly body with unearthly grace. She seemed to be demonstrating how one shrugged off a body. 'It is a natural progression, like walking into another room, like leaving the womb.'

She stopped. There was movement at the back of the studio.

Frances turned and saw the youngest person there, Zoe, stand from her cross-legged position in one fluid movement.

'Sorry,' she said in a low mumble.

Frances noticed Zoe's ears were studded with a multitude of earrings in unusual spots Frances didn't even know it was possible to pierce. Her face was pale. She was so exquisite and heartbreaking, just because she was young, or maybe just because Frances was old.

'Excuse me.'

Both her parents looked up at her in alarm, their hands outstretched as if to grab her. Zoe shook her head violently at them.

'Bathrooms are just over there,' said Masha.

'I just need a little . . . air,' said Zoe.

Heather got to her feet. 'I'll come with you.'

'Mum, no, I'm fine,' said Zoe. '*Please*, just let me . . .' She indicated the door.

Everyone watched to see who would prevail.

'I'm sure she is fine,' said Masha decisively. 'Come back when you are ready, Zoe. You are tired after your long journey, that's all.'

Heather surrendered with obvious reluctance and sat back down.

Everyone watched Zoe leave.

The room felt unsettled now, as if Zoe's departure had put things out of balance. Masha breathed in deeply through her nostrils and out through her mouth.

Someone spoke.

'Listen, now this, ah . . . *noble silence* . . . has been broken, could I ask a question?'

It was the serial killer. He spoke belligerently, just like a serial killer, his mouth barely open, so that his words came out in pellets. He was clearly very upset.

Frances saw Masha's eyes widen ever so slightly at this infraction. 'If you feel it's important right now.'

He jutted his chin. 'Did someone go through our bags?'

chapter twelve

Zoe

Zoe stood at the bottom of the stairs outside the heavy oak door of the meditation room, bent double, her hands on her thighs, trying to catch her breath.

Lately she'd been having the occasional mini panic attack. Not proper panic attacks, which she understood to be awful and had people calling for ambulances, just these mini episodes where suddenly out of nowhere she felt like she'd spiked her heart rate in a spin class. It was fine to be puffing and panting when she was doing a spin class, but not when she was sitting cross-legged on the floor doing nothing except listening to a mad woman talk about death.

She wondered if this was how it was for Zach. He used to say that asthma felt like someone had placed ten bricks on his chest.

Zoe put a hand to her chest. No bricks. It wasn't asthma. Just run-of-the-mill panic.

She could always trace back the causes. This time it was hearing Masha's mad thoughts on the wonderfulness of her near-death experience. It had made Zoe remember the poem her Uncle Alessandro had read at her brother's funeral, 'Death Is Nothing at All'. Zoe had started thinking about how much she hated that poem, because it was all lies: her brother had not just gone into another room, he was *gone*, so *gone*, so silent, not a text not a post not a tweet not a word, and next thing she was struggling for breath and all she could think was, *Get out*.

She felt bad about breaking the noble silence, especially after her dad's sneezing had created havoc in the room. The people at this retreat had no idea that those were her dad's most *subdued* sneezes. One of his students had once made a three-minute film called 'Mr Marconi Sneezes' which was just a montage of her dad sneezing at different times with a soundtrack. It had gone a bit viral.

'Did someone go through our bags?' said a man's voice from behind the door.

She'd put money on it being the seedy-looking guy who was nearly as tall as her dad and twice as wide. Zoe couldn't hear the response.

She climbed the narrow stone staircase and shoved hard to open the second heavy door that led back into the main part of the house.

She couldn't disappear for too long because her parents would worry, which wasn't at all suffocating. Ever since Zach died it was as if Zoe's life was in permanent jeopardy and only her parents' secret, ongoing vigilance would save her. Her mum and dad truly believed that if Zoe didn't get the flu shot, if her car brakes weren't checked every six months, if she didn't have a plan for getting home, she would die. It was as simple as that. And when they so casually asked a question like, 'Are you getting an Uber?', their faces averted, their hands busy doing something else, they couldn't disguise the dread beneath their words, and so she didn't brush them off, she didn't walk away when her mother stood next to her and tried to secretly listen to her breathing, even though unlike Zach, who'd had asthma from when he was a child, Zoe had never had asthma in her life. She clamped down hard on her irritation and let them listen to her breathe and gave the answers and constant reassurance they needed.

She wouldn't disappear on them now. She'd just take ten minutes for herself and then she'd sneak back in and hopefully Mad Masha would have got everyone under control by then and they'd all be silently meditating.

There were no staff about as she wandered into the Lavender Room. It was lavishly lavender. There were multiple tall vases stuffed with sprigs of lavender, the soft furnishings and cushions were all in various shades of lavender, and just in case you'd missed the point, *pictures* of lavender adorned the lavender-coloured walls.

Zoe went over to the window which looked straight out onto the rose garden, a rectangle of lush green grass bordered by high hedges, with garden beds of abundant white roses. This was where they would do tai chi at dawn tomorrow morning.

This place was all very nice, if dull – but it was kind of shocking if they really had searched the bags! Luckily Zoe had taken precautions, just in case. She knew how to get alcohol into alcohol-free parties. She'd wrapped up her contraband like a present, using bubble wrap to disguise the wine-bottle shape, complete with a gift tag that said: *Happy Anniversary, Mum and Dad!* She'd checked when she got to the room and the present was untouched in her bag.

On Zach's twenty-first birthday Zoe was going to toast him at midnight with a glass of wine. When she and Zach were born the maths teacher at her dad's school had given them each a bottle of Grange, strange presents for babies.

The bottles were probably meant to be in a temperature-controlled cellar but Zoe's family weren't big on alcohol. The wine had been sitting in the back of the linen cupboard, behind the bath towels, all these years, waiting for their twenty-first birthday. According to the internet, this particular vintage had a 'beautiful limp aspect with a melange of dried fruits and spices and a long, imperious finish'.

Zach would have found that description funny: 'A long, imperious finish.'

Her eyes followed the softly curved silhouette of the blue-green hills along the horizon and she thought of her ex-boyfriend and how hard he'd tried to convince her to join him on a surfing trip to Bali with a group of friends. He couldn't believe it when she insisted it was impossible. 'I have to be with my parents,' she'd told him. 'Any other time, just not January.' In the end he got angry, and then all of a sudden they were taking a break and next thing they were broken up. She'd kind of thought she had loved him.

She banged her forehead gently against the glass of the window. Did he think she *wanted* to be here with her parents? Did he think she wouldn't prefer to be in Bali?

Last January had been terrible, like her parents were burning to death from the inside, their internal organs liquefied while they pretended that everything was just fine.

'Hello there. It's Zoe, isn't it? We met earlier. I'm Frances.'

Zoe turned from the window. It was the strawberry-blonde lady with the bright red lipstick whom her dad had accosted on the stairs. She was adjusting an old-fashioned giant tortoiseshell clip in her hair and she looked flushed in the face.

'Hi,' said Zoe.

'I know we're not meant to be speaking, but I feel like this has turned out to be an unplanned interlude in Masha's noble silence.'

'What's going on down there?'

'It's all got very awkward,' said Frances. She sat down on one of the lavender couches. 'Oh dear, this is one of those swallow-you-up couches.' She shoved two cushions behind her back. 'Ow. My back. Ow.' She wriggled about. 'No. I'm okay. That's better. Well. You know the man, the grumpy-looking one with the hacking cough? Not that I can talk. Don't come too close to me, I don't want to infect you, although I feel like my germs are nicer than his germs. Anyway, he's getting very worked up because apparently he smuggled in a whole *minibar*, by the sound of it, and, well, this is embarrassing, but they took some things from my bag too, and I kind of felt like I should have been supporting the grumpy man. You know, like, that *is* a breach of privacy, you can't do that, we have rights!' She punched a fist in the air.

Zoe sat on the couch opposite her and smiled at the fist-punch.

'But I got embarrassed because I didn't want everyone to know I also brought in contraband that was confiscated, and I know this isn't an episode of *Survivor*, but I didn't want to form an alliance with that man, because he seems so . . . well . . . so I said I needed some air too, which I feel like was one of the bravest things I've ever done.'

'I brought in contraband too,' said Zoe.

'*Did* you?' Frances brightened. 'Did they find it?'

'No, if they searched my bag they missed it. I wrapped it up like a present for my parents.'

'That's genius. What is it?'

'It's a bottle of wine,' said Zoe. 'Really expensive wine. Oh, and a bag of Reese's Peanut Butter Cups. I'm addicted.'

'Yum.' Frances sighed. 'Congratulations. I like your ingenuity.'

'Thank you,' said Zoe.

Frances picked up a cushion and hugged it. 'I'm perfectly capable of going for ten days without a glass of wine, I just . . . well, I don't know, I was being wicked.'

'I don't even like wine,' said Zoe.

'Oh. Did you just want to prove you could beat the system?'

'I brought the wine to toast my brother's twenty-first birthday. It's in a few days. He died three years ago.'

She saw Frances's inevitably stricken face.

'It's okay,' she told her quickly. 'We weren't close.'

People usually looked relieved when she told them that, but Frances's face didn't change at all.

'I'm so sorry,' she said.

'It's fine. Like I said, we really . . . didn't get on.' Zoe tried to clarify it for her. *Don't stress! You're off the hook.*

She remembered her friend Cara, the day after Zach's funeral, saying, 'At least you weren't close.' Cara was really close to her sister.

'What was your brother's name?' asked Frances, as if this were somehow important.

'Zach,' said Zoe, and the name sounded odd and painful in her mouth. She heard a roaring sound in her ears and felt for a moment as if she might faint. 'Zoe and Zach. We were twins. Very cutesy names.'

'I think they're lovely names,' said Frances. 'But if you're twins that means it's your birthday in a few days too.'

Zoe took a sprig of lavender out of a vase and began to shred it. 'Technically. But I don't celebrate on that day anymore. I kind of changed my birthday.'

She'd officially moved her birthday to the eighteenth

of March. It was a nicer date. A cooler, less tempestuous time of year. The eighteenth of March was Grandma Maria's birthday, and Grandma Maria used to say it had never once rained on her birthday and maybe that was true; everyone said they should check the weather records in case it was some sort of phenomenon only Grandma Maria had noticed, but nobody ever got around to it.

Grandma Maria had always said she'd live to one hundred, like her own mother, but she died one month after Zach of a broken heart. Even the doctor said it was a broken heart.

'Zach died the day before our eighteenth birthday,' said Zoe. 'We were meant to be having a "Z" party. I was going as Zoe. Which seemed really funny at the time.'

'Oh, Zoe.' Frances leaned forward. Zoe could tell she wanted to touch her but was stopping herself.

'So that's why I changed it,' said Zoe. 'It's, like, not fair to Mum and Dad to have to celebrate my birthday the day after when they're still totally wrecked from the anniversary. January is really hard for my parents.'

'Of course it would be,' said Frances. Her eyes were bright with sympathy. 'Hard for all of you, I imagine. So you thought it would be good to . . . get away?'

'We just wanted somewhere quiet, and a health resort seemed like a good idea because we're all *really* unhealthy.'

'Are you? You don't look at all unhealthy to me.'

'Well, for a start, I have way too much sugar in my diet,' said Zoe.

'Sugar is the new villain,' said Frances. 'It used to be fat. Then it was carbs. It's hard to keep up.'

'No, but sugar is seriously bad,' said Zoe. It wasn't hard to keep up at all! Everyone knew sugar was terrible for you. 'They've done all this research. I need to withdraw from my sugar addiction.'

'Mmm,' said Frances.

'I eat too much chocolate and I'm addicted to Diet Coke, that's why my skin is so bad.' Zoe put a fingertip to a blind pimple near her lip. She couldn't stop touching it.

'Your skin is *gorgeous*!' Frances gesticulated wildly, probably because she was trying not to look at Zoe's pimple.

Zoe sighed. People should be honest.

'My parents are exercise fanatics, but my dad has a junk-food addiction and Mum basically has an eating disorder.' She reflected. Her mother would not like any aspect of this conversation. 'Please don't tell her I said that. She doesn't really have an eating disorder. She's just kind of weird about food.'

Even before Zach died Zoe's mother had been like that. She couldn't bear to see lavish displays of food, which was a problem, seeing as she'd married a man with a big extended Italian family. Heather suffered from heartburn and stomach cramps and other 'digestive issues' she referred to only obliquely. She never saw food as just food. She always had some fierce emotional response to it. She was *starving* or *bloated* or *craving* something specific and unattainable.

'Anyway, what about you?' she asked Frances. She wanted to shift the focus; she'd revealed far too much about herself and her family to this stranger. 'Why did you decide to do this?'

'Oh, you know: I'm run-down, I've done something to my back, I have a cold I can't seem to shake, I suppose I could do with losing a few kilos . . . just the normal middle-aged stuff.'

'How old are your kids?' asked Zoe.

Frances smiled. 'No kids.'

'Oh.' Zoe was taken aback, worried that she might have made some kind of sexist faux pas. 'Sorry.'

'Don't be sorry.' Frances said. 'It was my choice not to have children. I just never saw myself as a mother. Ever. Even when I was a kid.'

But you're so motherly, thought Zoe.

'No husband either,' said Frances. 'Just two ex-husbands. No boyfriend. I'm very single.'

It was cute the way she said *boy*friend.

'I'm very single too,' said Zoe, and Frances smiled, as if *Zoe* had said something cute.

'I thought I was in love with someone recently but he wasn't who he said he was,' said Frances. 'It turned out to be an internet "romance scam".' She made quote marks with her fingers.

Oh my God, thought Zoe. *How stupid would you have to be?*

'What do you do for a living?' She changed the subject because she was literally going bright red with embarrassment for the woman.

'I write romance novels,' said Frances. 'Or I did. I might be in need of a career change.'

'Romance novels,' repeated Zoe. It was getting worse. She tried to keep her face neutral. Please, God, don't let it be erotica.

'Are you a reader?' asked Frances.

'Sometimes,' said Zoe. Never, ever romance. 'What made you become a romance writer?'

'Well, when I was about fifteen I read *Jane Eyre* and it was a strange, sad time in my life – my dad had just died, and I was hormonal and grieving and just very impression-able. And when I got to that famous line – you know the one: *Reader, I married him* – it just had this profound effect on me. I'd sit in the bath and murmur to myself, "Reader, I married him", and then I'd just sob. It had remarkable staying power. Reader, I married – ooohhh!' She demonstrated herself sobbing dramatically like a teenage girl, hand to her forehead.

Zoe laughed.

Frances said, 'You've read *Jane Eyre*, right?'

'I think I saw the movie once,' said Zoe.

'Ah well,' said Frances sympathetically. 'Anyway, I know that *Reader, I married him* line has become virtually a cliché now it's referenced so often: *Reader, I divorced him. Reader, I murdered him.* But for me, at that time of my life, it was . . . well, profound. I remember being amazed that *four words* could affect me in that way. So I guess I just developed an interest in the power of words. The first romance story I ever wrote was heavily influenced by Charlotte Brontë, except without the madwoman in the attic. My leading man was a heady mix of Mr Rochester and Rob Lowe.'

'Rob Lowe!' said Zoe.

'I had his poster on my wall,' said Frances. 'I can still taste his lips. Very smooth and papery. Matt gloss.'

Zoe giggled. 'I felt the same way about Justin Bieber.'

'There might even be one of my books here,' said Frances. 'There often is in places like this.' She scanned the shelves of paperbacks then smiled, a hint of pride. 'Bingo.'

She stood up, clutching her back, went to one of the shelves and squatted down to pull out a battered-looking chunky paperback. 'There you go.' She handed it to Zoe and sat back down on the couch with a grunt.

'Awesome,' said Zoe. The book looked *terrible*.

It was called *Nathaniel's Kiss* and the picture on the front showed a girl with long, curly, fair hair staring wistfully out to sea. At least it didn't look erotic.

'Anyway, my last book got rejected,' said Frances. 'So I might be looking for a new career soon.'

'Oh,' said Zoe. 'I'm sorry.'

'Well,' said Frances, and she shrugged, gave her a half-smile, her palm up, and Zoe knew what she was trying to say. Zoe's friend Erin thought she wasn't allowed to complain about her life anymore without first prefacing it, 'I know this is nothing compared to what you've been through,' with this solemn, wide-eyed look, and Zoe always said, 'Erin, it's been three years, you're allowed to complain about your life!' And then she nodded along sympathetically while thinking, *You're right, your car needing three new tyres is nothing to complain about.*

'I guess I should go back downstairs,' said Zoe. 'My parents get paranoid if they can't pinpoint my location. I think they'd like to put a tracking device on me.'

Frances sighed. 'I guess I should too.' But she didn't move. She gave Zoe a quizzical look. 'Do *you* think we're all going to be "transformed" by the end of this thing?'

'Not really,' said Zoe. 'What do you think?'

'I don't know,' said Frances. 'I feel like Masha could do anything. She scares the life out of me.'

Zoe laughed and then they both startled at the clamorous sound of a gong being struck repetitively and aggressively from somewhere within the house.

They jumped to their feet and Frances grabbed Zoe's arm. 'Oh God, it's just like boarding school! Do you think we're in trouble? Or maybe there's a fire and we're all evacuating?'

'I think it probably just means the silence is starting again.'

'Yes, you're right. Okay, we'll go back together. I'll go first; I'm older, I'm not scared of her.'

'Yes you are!'

'I know, I am, terrified! Quick, let's go! I'll see you on the other side of the silence.'

'I'll read your book.' Zoe held up the paperback as they left the Lavender Room and headed back downstairs. It was a crazy thing to say, she had no interest in reading a romance book, but whatever, she liked Frances.

'You're not meant to read in the silence.'

'I'm a rebel,' said Zoe. She shoved the book under her top and into the waist of her bike pants. 'I'll be in an alliance with you.'

She was just making a weak joke in reference to Frances's comment earlier about *Survivor*, but Frances stopped in her tracks and turned around with a radiant smile. 'Oh, Zoe, I would *love* to be in alliance with you.'

And all of a sudden it felt like they were.

chapter thirteen

Masha

Two guests, Zoe Marconi and Frances Welty, had excused themselves from the meditation room and not yet come back. The silence had been broken and one guest, Tony Hogburn, was now demanding his money back and threatening to report Tranquillum House to the Department of Consumer Affairs, blah, blah, blah, Masha had heard it all before, while the remaining guests looked on with curiosity or concern.

Masha saw poor Yao shoot her an anxious look. He was a worrier. There was no need for stress. She could handle the childlike tantrums of one unhappy, unhealthy man. Solving unexpected problems energised her. It was one of her strengths.

'I am very happy to give you a full refund.' She fixed Tony with her eyes like a pin through a butterfly. 'You are free to pack your bags and leave immediately. May I suggest you drive yourself to the nearest village, where you will find a fine pub called the Lion's Heart? Their menu includes something called a "Mega Monster Burger" with unlimited fries and soft drink. Does that sound delicious?'

'Sure does,' said Tony truculently.

And yet he didn't get to his feet. Oh, my sweetie pie, you need me. You know you need me. You don't want to be you anymore. Of course you don't. Who would?

He tried to wriggle free of her gaze but she wouldn't let him. 'I understand that you are not happy that we searched your bags, but the terms and conditions of your wellness contract clearly state that we have the right to search luggage and confiscate all contraband.'

'Seriously? Did anyone read that?' Tony looked around the room.

Napoleon raised his hand. His wife, Heather, lifted her eyes to the ceiling.

'It must have been buried in the fine print,' said Tony. His face had turned mottled red, the colour of uncooked steak.

'Growth can be painful,' Masha told him, her voice gentle. He was a child. An enormous sulky child. 'There will be parts of this experience that may be uncomfortable or unpleasant at times. But it's only ten days! The average person lives around twenty-seven thousand days.'

Tony's outburst was actually a serendipitous opportunity to shape all their expectations and mould their future behaviour. She spoke as if only to him, but the message was for them all.

'You are free to leave at any time, Tony. You are not a prisoner! This is a health resort, not a jail!'

A few people chuckled.

'And you are not a child! You can drink what you want to drink, eat what you want to eat. But there is a reason why you came here, and if you choose to stay, I ask you to commit fully to your journey and to put your trust in me and the other staff at Tranquillum House.'

'Yeah, fine, that's . . . I mean, I obviously didn't read

the fine print properly.' Tony scratched hard at the side of his unshaved face and tugged at the fabric of his dreadful hot heavy blue jeans. 'I just didn't appreciate my bags being searched.' The aggression was draining from his voice. Now he sounded embarrassed. His eyes peered out at her from within the prison of his poor, tortured body from which he so desperately needed rescue.

She'd won. She had him. He would be beautiful when she finished with him. They would all be beautiful.

'Are there any more areas of concern before we resume the silence?'

Ben raised his hand. Masha observed his wife flash him a look of horror and move slightly away.

'Um, yeah, I have just one question. Are the cars parked undercover?'

She looked at him for a moment, long enough to help him see the sadness of this deep attachment to his earthly possessions.

He shifted uncomfortably.

'They are parked undercover, Ben. Please don't worry, they are perfectly safe.'

'Okay, but, um, *where* are the cars? I've walked around the property and I just can't see where . . .' As he spoke he removed his cap and briskly rubbed the top of his head.

For the briefest of moments, Masha saw another boy wearing a baseball cap walking towards her, so strange and yet so familiar. She felt the love rise within her chest and she crossed her arms so she could secretly pinch the flesh on her arm, hard enough to hurt, until the vision vanished, and all that was left was here and now and the important tasks that lay ahead.

'As I said, Ben, everyone's cars are perfectly safe.'

He opened his mouth to speak yet again and his wife

hissed something inaudible through her teeth. He closed his mouth.

'So, if everyone is in agreement, I would like to recommence the noble silence and begin our guided meditation. Yao, perhaps you could ring the gong to let our missing guests know we would appreciate their return?'

Yao struck the gong with a mallet, perhaps a little more forcefully than Masha would have done, and within only a few moments Frances and Zoe had returned, their faces apologetic and guilty.

It was clear to Masha that they had been chatting, forming a friendship perhaps, which would need to be monitored. The point of the silence was to prevent this. She smiled benignly at them as they returned to their mats. Zoe's parents sagged with relief.

'Although I will be your guide today,' she said, 'meditation is a *personal* experience. Please release your expectations and open yourself to all possibilities. This is called a guided sitting meditation but that doesn't mean you must sit! Please find the most natural, relaxed position for you. Some of you may like to sit cross-legged. Some of you may like to sit on a chair with your feet flat on the floor. Some of you may prefer to lie down. There are no hard and fast rules here!'

She watched as they chose their positions with self-conscious faces. Frances lay flat on her back. Tony went and sat on a chair, as did Napoleon. The rest remained cross-legged on their mats.

Masha waited until they were all settled. 'Let your eyes drift closed.'

She could sense their fluttering spirits: their anxieties, hopes, dreams and fears. She was so *good* at this. It was a pleasure to excel.

Interviewers would one day ask, 'Were you nervous

when you first introduced the new protocol?' Masha would answer, 'Not at all. We'd done our research. We knew from the beginning it would be a success.' It might be better to admit to a little nervousness. People in this country admired humility. The biggest compliment you could give a successful woman was to describe her as 'humble'.

She looked at her nine guests, all of whom now had their eyes obediently closed as they awaited her instructions. Their destinies were in her hands. She was going to change them not just temporarily, but forever.

'We will begin.'

chapter fourteen

Frances

It was the end of her first day at Tranquillum House and Frances lay in bed, wilfully reading while she drank her 'evening smoothie'. No-one could be expected to give up wine *and* books at the same time.

None of the four novels she'd packed to get her through the next ten days had been confiscated, unlike her wine and chocolate – presumably because books weren't on the 'contraband list' (she would never have come here if so) – but a small slip of paper had been placed inside the front cover of each of them: *A gentle reminder that we recommend no reading during the noble silence.*

What an absolute joke. She didn't know how to go to sleep without reading. It wasn't possible.

The book she was reading now was a debut novel that had received rave reviews. There was a lot of 'buzz' about it. It was described as 'powerful, muscular' and it was written by a man Frances had met at a party last year. The man had been pleasant, shy and bespectacled (not especially muscular), so Frances was trying to forgive him for his lavish descriptions of beautiful corpses. How many more beautiful young women had to die before they could get on with the job of tracking down their murderer? Frances made little 'tch' sounds of disgust.

Now the craggy detective was drunk on single-malt whisky in a smoke-hazed bar and a long-legged girl half his age was whispering into his ear, without inverted commas (this being powerful, literary fiction): I want to fuck you so bad.

Frances, who had reached her limit, threw the book across the room. In your dreams, buddy!

She lay back with her hands clasped across her chest, and reminded herself that her own debut novel featured a piano-playing, poetry-reciting firefighter. It was *cute* that the bespectacled author imagined twenty-something girls ever whispered 'I want to fuck you so bad' into the ears of fifty-something men. She would give the author a consoling little pat on the shoulder next time she saw him at a festival.

Anyway, what did she know? Maybe twenty-something girls did that all the time. She would ask Zoe.

She certainly would not ask Zoe.

She reached for her phone on the bedside table to check the news and the weather for tomorrow.

No phone.

Of course. Well. Fine.

The bed was a luxurious one: a good mattress, the sheets crisp with a high thread count. Her back hurt, but maybe a little less thanks to Jan's giant hands.

She attempted to quieten her 'monkey brain', as per the rules.

In fact, her mind felt stuffed with new faces and new experiences: the long drive here; screaming on the side of the road; the serial killer on vacation (it was that damned book's fault for making her think of serial killers); Ben and Jessica in that car; Yao unexpectedly filling a test tube with her blood; Masha and her near-death experience; chatty Napoleon and his intense wife; lovely young Zoe with her multiple piercings and long, smooth, brown legs, sitting in the Lavender Room telling Frances about her dead brother. That's why Zoe's mother had looked so sad on the stairs. She probably wasn't intense at all. Just sad. The tall, dark and handsome man who'd cried, 'Gesundheit!' and the flustered lady with Frances's glasses.

A lot for one day. Stimulating and distracting. She hadn't had time for any more existential crises, so that was something. She hadn't even thought much about Paul Drabble, apart from when she was telling Jan and Zoe about what had happened. She'd be over her internet scam by the time she left. Over the review. Over everything.

And thin! She'd be so thin! Her stomach rumbled. She was starving. Dinner tonight had been possibly the most excruciating meal of her life.

When she took her place at the long dining room table, she picked up a small card propped in front of her plate:

At Tranquillum House we recommend MINDFUL EATING. Please take small bites of your food. After each mouthful, place your cutlery back on the table, close your eyes and chew for at least fourteen seconds, slowly and pleasurably.

Oh God, she thought. *We're going to be here forever.*

She put down the card and looked up to share a 'can you believe this?' glance with someone. The only ones prepared to meet her eyes were the astonishingly handsome man, who *possibly* winked at her, and Zoe, who definitely grinned, and responded with a look that said, 'I *know*. I can't believe it either.'

Masha wasn't in the dining room, but her presence was felt, like that of a managing director or schoolteacher who could turn up at any moment. Yao and Delilah were there but they didn't sit down to eat with the guests. Instead they stood at the side of the room, at either side of a large candelabrum on an ornate sideboard. The lighting in the room was muted and the candelabrum had three lit candles.

They sat in silence for at least *ten . . . endless . . . minutes* before the meals came out, delivered by a briskly smiling grey-haired lady in a chef's hat. She didn't say a word but nevertheless exuded goodwill. It felt so rude not to thank her. Frances tried to convey warm gratitude with a nod of her head.

Every person at the table received a different meal. Both Heather and Zoe, who sat next to Frances, received delicious-looking *steaks* together with baked potatoes. Frances's meal was a quinoa salad. It was excellent, but in Frances's world she'd call that a 'side', and by the time she'd masticated each mouthful for fourteen seconds it had lost all flavour.

Napoleon, who sat opposite Frances, received some sort of lentil dish. He leaned forward towards the bowl and waved the rising steam towards his nose, enjoying the scent. It was clear the poor man was desperate to chat. Frances would bet that in normal circumstances he would have been discussing the history of the lentil.

The serial killer studied his giant bowl of green salad mournfully before picking up his cutlery and stabbing three cherry tomatoes onto his fork with an air of tragic resignation.

The flustered lady with the quirky glasses received fish, to her apparent delight.

The astonishingly handsome man was assigned chicken and vegetables, which he appeared to find mildly amusing.

Ben received a vegetable curry and finished his meal well before the rest of the table.

Jessica was given a really delicious-looking stir-fry, which was the wrong dish for the poor girl. She spent ages laboriously twirling the long noodles around her fork and then dabbing worriedly at her face with her napkin for splashes of food.

Nobody broke the silence or made eye contact. When Napoleon sneezed again, nobody responded in any way. How quickly people adapted to strange rules and regulations!

Heather ate less than half her steak before putting down her knife and fork with a little puff of irritation. Frances had to restrain herself from leaping on it like a wolf.

Throughout the meal, Yao and Delilah stood silent and unmoving. They were like footmen, except you couldn't snap your fingers and tell them to let Cook know that my lady could do with a larger portion of quinoa, and perhaps a medium-rare sirloin.

The sound of strangers chewing and clinking and scraping their cutlery just about did Frances's head in. Hadn't she once read there was an actual disorder where people suffered real psychological distress at the sound of others eating? There was a name for it. Frances probably had that disorder and had never been diagnosed because you were meant to *talk* while you dined. Something else to remember to Google once she got her phone back.

Eventually they were done, and they all pulled back their chairs and returned to their rooms. You couldn't even say, 'Goodnight! Sleep well!'

Now, as Frances drank the last of her smoothie, she thought about the number of silent insufficient meals ahead of her and considered leaving in the morning.

'No-one leaves early, Frances,' Yao had said today. Well, Frances could be the first. Set a new precedent.

She thought of her massage therapist's whispered warning just before the silence began: *Don't do anything you're not comfortable with.* What did she mean by that? Frances would certainly not do anything she didn't feel comfortable with.

She recalled what Ellen had said when she suggested this place. 'Their approach is really quite unconventional.' Ellen was her friend. She wouldn't send her somewhere *dangerous* . . . would she? Just to lose three kilos? You'd want to lose a lot more than three kilos if they were doing something dangerous. What could it be? Walking across burning coals for enlightenment? Frances would absolutely not do that. She didn't even like walking across hot sand at the beach.

Ellen would have told her if there was walking across hot coals. Ellen was a dear friend.

'I've never trusted that Ellen,' Gillian once said, darkly and knowledgeably, but Gillian was always making dark, knowledgeable comments about people, as if everyone had secret mafia connections that only Gillian knew about.

Frances missed her greatly.

A wave of exhaustion hit her, not surprising after that long drive. She switched off her bedside lamp and fell instantly sound asleep, flat on her back like a sunbaker.

*

A light shone in her face.

Frances woke with a gasp.

'Naturally I knocked,' said Delila[h]
dressing-gown. 'Please? I'll lose my j[ob]
down for it.'

'You will not.'

'I might. Masha wants all the gue[sts]
takes half an hour.'

Lars sighed. He could refuse on pr[inciple]
a first-world, privileged principle he
He was awake now anyway.

He sat up and held out his hand
He slept naked. He could have just
all his glory to make the point that t
when you woke your sleeping gues
night, but he was too well-manner
eyes as he threw back the sheet, alth
quick downward flick. She was only

'Don't forget the silence,' she sai[d]
corridor.

'How could I forget the beautiful
She put her finger to her lips.

*

It was a clear night, the stars were
half-moon illuminated the garden
balmy air was a soft caress against
It was, he had to admit, all very pl

Nine yoga mats had been pla
wearing the Tranquillum House
their heads facing the centre of the
leader Masha sat cross-legged on

Lars saw there was only one emp
to arrive. He wondered if he'd ma

chapter fif

Lars

'What the actual fuck?'

Lars sat up, his heart hammer
end of his bed shining a small to
doing hospital rounds.

He switched on his bedside la

His 'wellness consultant', th
next to his bed holding up the T
gown with one hand. She didn't
and beckoned, as if he would
follow her instructions.

'I'm not going anywhere, s
middle of the night and I like n

Delilah said, 'It's the starlig
the first night. You don't want

Lars lay back in bed and sh
miss it.'

'You'll like it. It's really bea

Lars removed his hand fr
knock before you came into n

dragged from his bed. He never ceased to be amazed by the obedience of people at these places. They allowed themselves to be dipped in mud, wrapped in plastic, starved and deprived, pricked and prodded, all in the name of 'transformation'.

Of course, Lars did too, but he was prepared to draw the line when necessary. For example, he drew the line at enemas. Also, he did not want to ever, ever discuss his bowel movements.

Delilah led Lars to a mat in between the lady who got the giggles when Lars said 'Gesundheit!' earlier and the giant lump of a man who had complained about his contraband being confiscated.

There was something familiar about the big guy with the contraband. It had been hard not to stare at him through dinner. Lars couldn't shake the irritating feeling that he knew him from somewhere, but he couldn't work out where.

Was he one of the husbands? If he was one of the husbands, would he recognise Lars and come after him, like that time he was boarding a plane and a guy in the economy line saw Lars and went nuts? He'd shouted, 'YOU! You're the reason I'm flying cattle class!' Lars had taken extra pleasure in his Perrier-Jouët on that flight (and walked briskly off the plane towards the priority queue at customs). The big guy didn't *look* like one of the husbands, but Lars knew he knew him from somewhere.

He wasn't good with faces. Ray was great with them. Every time they started a new series Lars would sit up on the couch, point at the screen and say, '*Her*! We know her! How do we know her?' Ray normally had it within seconds: '*Breaking Bad*. The girlfriend. Walt let her die. Now shut up.' It was a real skill. On the rare occasions that Lars worked it out before Ray he got very excited and demanded high fives.

Lars lay down on the mat between the big guy and the giggling lady. She reminded Lars of one of Renoir's women – small-faced and round-eyed with curly hair piled on top of her head; creamy-skinned, plump and bosomy, possibly a little vacuous – but he thought they would probably get on. She looked like a fellow hedonist.

'Namaste,' said Masha. 'Thank you for leaving your beds for tonight's starlight meditation. I am grateful to you for your flexibility, for opening your hearts and minds to new experiences. I am proud of you.'

She was *proud* of them. How condescending. She didn't even know them! They were her clients. They were paying for this. And yet Lars felt a sense of satisfaction in the garden, as if everyone wanted Masha to be proud of them.

'The retreat you are about to undertake combines ancient Eastern healing wisdom and herbal treatments with the latest cutting-edge advances in Western medicine. I want you to know that although I am not a practising Buddhist, I have incorporated certain Buddhist philosophies into our practices here.'

Yeah, yeah, East meets West, never heard that before, thought Lars.

'This won't take very long. I'm not going to say much. The stars will do the talking for me. Isn't it funny how we forget to look up at the stars? We scurry about like ants in our day-to-day lives and look, just *look*, what's up above our heads! All your life you look down. It's time to look up, to see the stars!'

Lars looked at the sky emblazoned with stars.

The big guy on his left gave a chesty cough. So did the busty blonde on his right. Jesus. He should be wearing some sort of sanitation mask. If he came back from this thing with a cold, he wouldn't be happy.

Masha said, 'Some of you may have heard of the word *koan*. A koan is a paradox or puzzle that Zen Buddhists use during meditation to help them on their quest towards enlightenment. The most famous one is this: *What is the sound of one hand clapping?*'

Oh Lord. The website had given the impression that this place leaned more towards *luxury* wellness. Lars had a daily yoga and meditation practice, but he preferred his health retreats to avoid too much embarrassing cultural appropriation.

'While you look at the stars tonight I want you to reflect on two koans. The first one is this: *Out of nowhere the mind comes forth.*' Masha paused. 'And the second: *Show me your original face, the one you had before your parents were born.*'

Lars heard the big guy next to him make a wheezy exhalation that caused him to start rolling about coughing.

'Do not struggle to find answers or solutions,' said Masha. 'This is not a quiz, my people!' She chuckled a little.

The woman really was quite a strange mix of charismatic leader and enthusiastic nerd. One moment a guru, the next the newly appointed CEO of a telecommunications company.

'There is no right or wrong answer. Simply look at the stars and reflect without straining for a solution. Just breathe. That's all you need to do. Breathe and watch the stars.'

Lars breathed and watched the stars. He did not think of either of the koans. He thought of Ray, and how, early on in their relationship, Ray had convinced him to go camping with him (never again). They had lain together on a beach, holding hands and looking at the stars, and it had been beautiful, but something had built up and up in Lars's chest until he couldn't take it anymore and he'd jumped up and run into the ocean, *whooping* and tearing off his clothes, pretending he was the type of guy who whooped, the type of guy who didn't think about sharks or the temperature of the ocean in October. He smiled a bit, because he knew he couldn't get away with that now. Ray knew about his shark phobia.

Ray had asked if he could join him on this retreat. Lars couldn't work out his motivation. He'd never wanted to come to one before. Lars did a couple of retreats a year, but Ray always said they sounded hellish. Why did he suddenly want to come along on this one?

Lars thought of Ray's face when he said he'd rather go alone. There was a micro moment when it looked like Lars had slapped him, but then Ray shrugged, smiled and said that was fine, he was going to eat lasagne every night while Lars was gone and watch nothing but sports on TV.

Ray's lifestyle was already squeaky clean and incorporated vegetable juices and smoothies and protein shakes. It wasn't necessary for him to come along to this. Lars needed his time alone.

Did he *want* Lars to feel like shit? Was it somehow related to the text Ray's sister, Sarah, had sent earlier today: *Can you at least think about it?*

She must have sent it without Ray's knowledge. Lars was sure Ray had accepted that his decision about children was final. It wasn't like he hadn't been upfront about his lack of interest in having a family. He had never said otherwise.

'Did I ever say otherwise?' he'd said to Ray, and he'd come close to raising his voice, which was not something he could countenance. He could not be in a relationship with the crassness and indignity of raised voices. It made him shudder to think of it. Ray knew this.

'You never said otherwise,' Ray had responded evenly, and he didn't raise his voice. 'You never misled me. I'm not saying that. I guess I just hoped you might change your mind.'

Sarah, all shiny-eyed and sincere, had offered to help them have a baby. Ray's family were so liberal and lovely and loving. It was fucking annoying.

Lars had recoiled, literally physically recoiled, at the thought. 'God no,' he'd said to Ray and his sister. 'Just . . . no.' He'd felt terrified and suffocated by the thought of all the earnest love he'd have to endure if they had a baby. There would be no escaping it. All those family functions! Ray's mother would never stop crying.

It was not happening. Never. *Out of nowhere the mind comes forth.*

A Zen koan. *Give me strength.*

If Ray really wanted to be a father, should Lars let him go be one with someone else? But wasn't that up to Ray? If Ray couldn't live without children, then he was free to leave. They weren't married. The house was in both their names, but they were both financially secure and sufficiently intelligent people to work all that out. Obviously Lars could handle a fair division of property.

Was it the only way forward? Had their relationship reached an impossible impasse because, either way, one of them had to make an impossible sacrifice? Whose sacrifice was worse?

But Ray had stopped asking! He'd accepted it. Lars felt that Ray wanted something *else* from him. What was it? Permission to leave? He didn't want Ray to leave.

Something tumbled in the sky. A falling star, for God's sake. How had Masha managed that? Lars heard everyone exhale with the wonder of it.

He closed his eyes and all of a sudden it came to him exactly how he knew the big guy on his left and he wished Ray was here so he could tell him, *I got it, Ray, I got it!*

chapter sixteen

Jessica

The author, Frances Welty, who lay on the yoga mat next to Jessica, was fast asleep. She wasn't snoring but Jessica could tell she was asleep by the way she breathed. Jessica considered giving her a gentle nudge with her foot. She'd just missed seeing a falling star.

On reflection, Jessica decided not to bother her. It was the middle of the night. People her age really needed their sleep. If Jessica's mother had a bad night's sleep the bags under her eyes made her literally look like something from a horror movie, though she just laughed when Jessica tried to teach her about concealer. It wasn't *necessary* to look that bad. It was stupid. If Jessica's dad left her for his PA, Jessica's mother would have no-one to blame but herself. Under-eye concealer was invented for a reason.

Jessica rolled her head and looked at Ben on the other side of her. He was staring up at the stars with a glazed expression, as if he were considering those Zen riddles, when really he was probably just counting down the hours until he could get out of here and back behind the wheel of his precious car.

He turned his head and winked at her. It made her heart lift, as if her crush had winked at her in the classroom.

Ben looked back up at the stars and Jessica touched her face with her fingers. She wondered if her skin looked bad without make-up in the moonlight. There had been no time to put on foundation. They were just dragged from their beds. They could have been having sex when that girl came into their bedroom, with just the gentlest knock on their door and without even waiting for them to say, 'Come in,' before she marched on in and shone a light in their eyes.

They hadn't been having sex. Ben had been asleep and Jessica had been lying next to him in the darkness, unable to sleep, missing her phone so badly it felt like she'd had something amputated. When she couldn't sleep at home she simply picked up her phone and scrolled through Instagram and Pinterest until she got tired.

She looked at her scarlet toenails in the moonlight. If she had her phone with her right now she would have photographed her feet, together with Ben's feet, and tagged it #starlightmeditation #healthretreat #learningaboutkoans #wejustsawafallingstar #whatisthesoundofonehandclapping.

That last hashtag would have made her look quite intellectual and spiritual, she thought, which was good, because you had to be careful not to come across as superficial on your socials.

She couldn't shake the feeling that if she didn't record this moment on her phone then it wasn't really happening, it didn't count, it wasn't real life. She knew that was irrational but she couldn't help it. She literally felt *twitchy* without her phone. Obviously she was addicted to it. Still, better than being addicted to heroin, though these days no-one was sure about Ben's sister's most recent drug of choice. She liked to 'mix it up'.

Jessica sometimes wondered if all their problems led back to Ben's sister. She was always there, a big black cloud in their blue sky. Because, apart from Lucy, honestly, what did they have to worry about? Nothing. They should have been as happy as it was possible to be. Where had they gone wrong?

Jessica had been so *careful*, right from day one. What was that stupid thing her mother said? 'Oh, Jessica, darling – this sort of thing can ruin people.'

She said that, all frowny-faced, on what should have been the most spectacular day of Jessica's life. The day that split her life in two.

It was two years ago now. A Monday evening.

Jessica had come home from work in a hurry because she was going to try to make the 6.30 pm spin class. She rushed into the tiny kitchen with its ugly laminate bench-tops to fill her water bottle and there was Ben sitting on the floor, his back up against the dishwasher, his legs splayed, phone held limply in his hand. His face was dead white, his eyes glassy. She got down on the floor next to him, her heart pounding, barely breathing, hardly able to speak. The uppermost thought in her mind was, 'Who? Who?' Her first thought was Lucy, of course. Ben's sister flirted with death on a daily basis. But something told her it wasn't Lucy. He seemed too shocked, and Lucy's death was never going to come as a surprise.

He said, 'Do you remember how Mum sent us that card?'

Jessica's heart contracted because she thought it must have been his mother who had died, and she loved Ben's mum.

'How?' she said. 'How did it happen?' How was it *possible* that Donna had died? She played tennis twice a week. She was healthier and fitter than Jessica. It was probably the stress over Lucy.

'You remember the card she sent?' Ben repeated obliviously. 'Because we were so upset about the robbery?'

Poor Ben. He was obviously mad with grief and for some reason he was clutching on to this memory.

'I remember the card,' she said gently.

It came in the mail. It had a cute puppy on the front with a speech bubble coming out of his mouth, saying, 'Sorry to hear you're feeling low,' and a lottery ticket inside. Donna's message said, *You two deserve some good luck.*

Ben said, 'The ticket won.'

Jessica said, 'What's happened to your mum?'

'Nothing. Mum is fine,' said Ben. 'I haven't told her yet.'

'You haven't told her what?' Jessica's brain couldn't seem to keep up with the words she was hearing and she was suddenly angry. '*Ben.* Has anybody died or not?'

Ben smiled. 'Nobody has died.'

'You're sure?'

'Everybody is in perfect health.'

'Right,' she said. 'Well, good.' As the adrenaline left her body she was suddenly exhausted. She didn't think she could do her spin class now.

'The ticket won. The ticket that Mum gave us after the robbery. That was the lottery office. We won the first division prize. We just won twenty-two million dollars.'

She said tiredly, 'Don't be stupid. We did not.'

He turned to look at her, and his eyes were red and watery and fearful. He said, 'We have.'

If only they'd known in advance: you're going to win the lottery tomorrow. Then they might have acted like proper lottery winners. But it took a long while for it to feel like a fact. Jessica checked and double-checked the numbers on the internet. She called the lottery office back herself to confirm.

It became more real with each phone call they made

to their family and friends, and then they finally started doing the screaming and jumping and crying and laughing expected of lottery winners and invited everyone over to celebrate with the most expensive champagne they could find in the bottle shop.

They toasted those pathetic thieves, because if it wasn't for the robbery they would never have won the lottery!

Ben's mother couldn't get over it. 'It would never even have crossed my mind to buy you a lottery ticket before! That's the first lottery ticket I've ever bought in my life! I had to ask the lady at the newsagent how it worked!' She seemed to want to make sure that no-one forgot that she had bought the ticket. She didn't want a share in the prize (although obviously they ended up giving her money), she just wanted everyone to know of her crucial role in this glorious event.

It was like a better version of their wedding day. Jessica felt special. The centre of attention. She smiled so much her cheeks ached. The money made her instantly more intelligent and beautiful and stylish. People treated her differently because she *was* different. When she looked at her own face in the bathroom mirror that night, she could already see it: she glowed with money. Instant wealth was like the best facial ever.

But even on that first night, even while Ben and his brothers argued drunkenly over which luxury cars to buy, Jessica could sense Ben's fear growing.

'Make sure it doesn't change us,' he slurred, just before they fell asleep that night, and Jessica thought, *What are you talking about? It's already changed us!*

Then there was Jessica's mother, who acted as if the win were a catastrophe.

'You have to be *so* careful, Jessica,' she said. 'This kind of money can send people off the rails.'

It was true that there had been some unexpected diffi-culties with this new life. Some tricky situations they were still trying to unravel. Friendships they'd lost. One family estrangement. Two family estrangements. No. Three.

Ben's cousin, who thought they should have paid off his mortgage. They gave him a car. Jessica thought that was generous! Ben liked his cousin, but he barely saw him before the win. In the end, they *did* pay off his mortgage, but 'the damage had been done'. For God's sake.

Jessica's younger sister. They gave her a *million dollars* but she kept asking for more, more, more. Ben said, 'Just give it to her,' and they did, but then one day Jessica went out to lunch with her and didn't offer to pay the bill, and now they weren't talking. Jessica's heart clenched as she thought about it. She always paid the bill. Always. It was the one time she didn't and, supposedly, that was unforgivable.

Ben's stepdad, because Ben's stepdad was a financial planner and he'd assumed that he'd manage all their finances now that they *had* finances – but Ben thought his stepdad was an idiot and didn't want him near their money, so that was awkward. Ben could have kept his opinions about his stepdad a secret forever if it wasn't for winning the lottery.

And of course, Ben's sister. How could they give her money? How could they not give her money? Ben and his mother had agonised over what to do. They tried to do it all the right way, the careful way. They set up a trust fund. They never gave her cash, but cash was all she wanted. When they bought her a car she sold it within two weeks. She sold anything they bought her. She screamed ugly words at poor Ben: *You rich prick with your fancy car, you won't even help out your own family.* They spent thousands and thousands on expensive rehab programs that Ben's mother had once dreamed about, assuming those exclusive programs would be the answer, if only they had the money. But once they had the money they found out that those weren't the answer. It just went on and on. Ben kept thinking there had to be a solution. Jessica knew there was no solution. Lucy didn't want help.

And it wasn't just their family who thought Ben and Jessica should give them money. Every day they were contacted by long-lost relatives and friends, and friends of friends, asking for 'loans' or a 'helping hand' or wanting Ben and Jessica to support their favourite charity, their local school, their kids' soccer club. Family members they hadn't seen in years got in touch. Family members they didn't know existed got in touch. The requests often had a passive–aggressive edge: 'Ten thousand dollars is probably small change to you but it would mean a *huge* amount to us.'

'Just give it to them.' That was Ben's constant refrain, but sometimes it got Jessica's back up. The *nerve* of these people.

It was bewildering to Jessica that she and Ben fought more about money now that they had an abundance of it. It was impossible to even imagine they'd once felt so upset about the arrival of unexpected bills.

Becoming instantly wealthy was like starting a really stressful, glamorous job for which they had no qualifications or experience, but still, it was a pretty great job. It was hardly something to complain about. There was no need to *ruin* it, as Ben seemed intent on doing.

She sometimes wondered if Ben regretted winning the money. He told her once that he missed working. 'Start your own business then,' she'd said. They could do anything! But he said he couldn't compete with Pete, his old boss. He was like his sister; he didn't want a solution to his problems.

He said that he didn't like their 'snooty new neighbours' and Jessica pointed out that they didn't even know them and offered to invite some of them over for drinks, but Ben looked horrified at the idea. It wasn't like they'd really known their neighbours back at the old flat. Everyone had worked full-time and kept to themselves.

He enjoyed the luxury holidays they took, but even the travel didn't truly make him happy. Jessica remembered a night watching the sun set in Santorini. It was incredible, gorgeous, and she'd just bought a stunning bracelet for herself, and she'd looked across at Ben, who was deep in what seemed like profound thought, and she said, 'What are you thinking about?'

'Lucy,' he answered. 'I remember she used to talk about travelling to the Greek islands.'

It made her want to scream and scream because *they could afford to send Lucy to Santorini* and put her up at a great hotel, but that wasn't possible because Lucy preferred to stick needles in her arms. So fine, let her ruin her own life, but why did she have to ruin their lives as well?

The car was the one thing about the lottery win that made him happy. He didn't really care about any of the other things – not the beautiful house in the best part of Toorak, the concert tickets, the designer labels, the travel. Only the car. His dream car. God, how she hated that car.

Jessica realised with a start that people were standing, straightening their unflattering gowns, suppressing yawns.

She got to her feet and looked at the starry sky one last time, but there were no answers up there.

chapter seventeen

Frances

It was only eight in the morning and Frances was hiking.

It was going to be another hot summer's day, but the temperature at this hour was perfect, the air silky soft on her skin. There was no sound apart from the occasional sweet piercing call of a bellbird and the cracks and rustles of sticks and rocks beneath her feet on the rocky trail.

She felt like she'd been up for *hours*, which in fact she had been.

Today, her first full day at Tranquillum House, had begun before dawn (*before dawn!*) with a firm knock at her bedroom door.

Frances had stumbled out of bed and opened the door to find the corridor empty and a silver tray on the floor, with her morning smoothie and a sealed envelope containing her 'personalised daily schedule'.

She had got back into bed to drink the smoothie with a pillow propped up behind her back while she read her schedule with equal parts pleasure and horror:

DAILY SCHEDULE FOR FRANCES WELTY

Dawn: Tai chi class in the rose garden.

7 am: Breakfast in the dining room. (Please remember to continue to observe the silence.)

8 am: Walking meditation. Meet at the bottom of Tranquillity Hill. (This will be a slow, silent, mindful hike giving you plenty of time to stop and contemplate the magnificent views. Enjoy!)

10 am: One-on-one exercise class. Meet Delilah at the gym.

11 am: Remedial massage with Jan in the spa.

12 noon: Lunch in the dining room.

1 pm: Guided sitting meditation in the yoga and meditation studio.

2–4 pm: FREE TIME.

5 pm: Yoga class in the yoga and meditation studio.

6 pm: Dinner in the dining room.

7–9 pm: FREE TIME.

9 pm: LIGHTS OUT.

Lights out! Was that a suggestion or an order? Frances hadn't been to bed at 9 pm since she was a child.

But then again, maybe she'd be ready for bed by then.

She'd yawned her way through the tai chi class in the rose garden with Yao, silently eaten her first breakfast in the dining room (very good, poached eggs and steamed spinach, although it felt kind of pointless without the essential accompaniment of sourdough toast and a cappuccino) and now here she was with the other guests participating in the 'walking meditation', which was basically a slow uphill hike on a bushland track a short distance away from the house.

The two wellness consultants, Yao and Delilah, were with them. Delilah led the group at the front and Yao was at the back. The pace, set by Delilah, was extremely slow, almost *agonisingly* slow, even for Frances, and if she found it difficult to walk this slowly, she suspected the Marconis – 'exercise fanatics', according to Zoe – were just about losing their minds.

Frances was in the middle of the group, behind Zoe, whose glossy ponytail swung as she walked behind her dad. The serial killer was directly behind Frances, which was not the ideal position for a serial killer, but at least he'd be obliged to kill her in mindful slow motion, so she'd have plenty of time to escape.

At random intervals the group came to a stop, and they then had to stand and gaze silently at some fixed point on the horizon for what felt like an extraordinary length of time.

Frances was all for a leisurely hike with lots of rests to enjoy the view, but at this rate they would never get to the top.

Slowly, slowly, *slowly*, they filed up the hiking trail and slowly, slowly, *slowly*, Frances felt her mind and body adjust to the pace.

Slow was certainly . . . slow . . . but also it was quite . . . lovely.

She considered the pace of her life. The world had begun to move faster and faster over the last decade. People spoke faster, drove faster, walked faster. Everyone was in a rush. Everyone was busy. Everyone demanded their gratification instantly. She'd even begun to notice it in the editing of her books. *Pace!* Jo had begun to snap in her editorial comments, where once she would have written: *Nice!*

It seemed to Frances that readers once had more patience, they were content for the story to take its time, for an occasional chapter to meander pleasurably through a beautiful landscape without anything much happening, except perhaps the exchange of some meaningful eye contact.

The path steepened, but they were walking so slowly that Frances's breathing stayed steady. The trail curved and slivers of views appeared like gifts between the trees. They were getting quite high up now.

Of course, Jo's editing had probably taken on that frenetic tone in response to Frances's declining sales. No doubt Jo could see *the writing on the wall* and that accounted for her increasingly feverish pleas: *Add some intrigue to this chapter. Maybe a red herring to throw the reader off the scent?*

Frances had ignored the comments and let her career peacefully pass away, like an old lady in her sleep. She was an idiot. A deluded fool.

She walked faster. The thought came to her that she might be walking a little too quickly at the exact moment her nose slammed straight into Zoe's shoulder blades.

Zoe had stopped dead. Frances heard her gasp.

Heather had somehow veered off the trail and onto a large rock that overhung the steep side of the hill. The ground fell away directly in front of her. Another step and she would have gone over.

Napoleon had his wife's arm in a fierce grip. Frances couldn't tell if his face was white with anger or fear as his hand closed around her thin upper arm and he hauled her back onto the hiking trail.

Heather didn't thank her husband or smile at him or even meet his eyes. She extricated herself from Napoleon's grasp with an irritated shrug of her shoulder and walked ahead, tugging the sleeve of her threadbare t-shirt straight. Napoleon looked back at Zoe and his chest rose and fell in tandem with his daughter's audibly ragged breathing.

After a moment both father and daughter lowered their heads and continued their slow hike up the trail, as if what Frances had just witnessed had been of no consequence at all.

chapter eighteen

Tony

Tony Hogburn had just returned to his room after yet another hellish experience of a 'guided sitting meditation'. How much more meditation could a man do?

'Breathe in like you're breathing through a straw.' Jesus wept, what a load of absolute horseshit.

He was humiliated to realise that his legs ached from the excruciatingly slow *walking* meditation they'd done this morning. Once upon a time he could have run that trail, no problem at all, as a *warm-up*, and now his legs felt like jelly after walking it at the pace of a hundred-year-old.

He sat on the balcony outside his room and yearned for an ice-cold beer and the feel of an old collie's silky, hard head under his hand. It should have been a mild desire for a beer and a sad ache for a beloved pet, but it felt like a raging thirst in the desert and the deepest of heartaches.

He went to stand up for the two-hundredth time to get relief for this pain from the fridge before remembering for the two-hundredth time that there was no relief to be found. No refrigerator. No pantry. No TV to turn on for a distracting documentary. No internet to surf mindlessly. No dog he could summon with a whistle, just to hear the obedient patter of paws.

Banjo made it to fourteen years old. Good innings for a collie. Tony should have been ready for it, but it seemed he wasn't. In the first week, great gusts of grief hit him whenever he put his key in the lock of his front door. A grief hard enough to buckle his knees. Contemptible. A grown man brought to his knees by a dog.

He'd lost dogs before. Three dogs over the course of his life. It was part of being a dog owner. He didn't get why he was taking Banjo's death so hard. It was six months now, for Christ's sake. Was it possible that he grieved the loss of this damned dog more than any human he'd lost in his lifetime?

Yes, it was possible.

He remembered when the kids were little and the Jack Russell they gave their youngest, Mimi, for her eighth birthday escaped from the backyard and got hit by a car. Mimi had been devastated, crying on Tony's shoulder at the 'funeral'. Tony had cried too, feeling horrible guilt for missing that hole in the fence and sadness for that poor little dumb dog.

His daughter had been such a sweet little thing back then with her soft, round cheeks and pigtails, so easy to love.

Now Mimi was a twenty-six-year-old dental hygienist and she looked just like her mother: skinny, with a pin-like head and a rapid way of talking and walking that exhausted Tony. She was hygienic and busy, Mimi, and maybe not so easy to love, although he did love her. He'd die for his daughter. But sometimes he wouldn't pick up the phone for her. Being a dental hygienist meant that Mimi was used to delivering monologues without fear of interruption. She was closer to her mother than to him. All three kids were.

He hadn't been around enough in their childhood. Next thing they were grown-ups and he sometimes got the feeling that they were doing 'Dad duty' when they called or turned up for a visit. Once, Mimi left a sweet, cooing message on his phone for his birthday, and then right at the end of the message he heard her say in an entirely different tone of voice to someone else, 'Right, that's done, let's go!' as she hung up.

His sons didn't remember his birthday – not that he expected them to remember it; he barely remembered it himself, and he only remembered theirs because Mimi texted him a reminder on the morning of her brothers' birthdays. James lived in Sydney, dating a different girl every month, and his oldest, Will, had married a Dutch girl and moved to Holland. Tony's three granddaughters, whom he only saw in real life every couple of years and Skyped at Christmas, had Dutch accents. They felt entirely unrelated to him. His ex-wife saw them all the time, travelled over there twice a year and stayed for two, three weeks. His oldest grand-daughter excelled at 'Irish dancing'. (Why were they doing *Irish* dancing in *Holland*? Why were they doing Irish dancing at all? No-one else seemed to find this strange. According to his ex-wife, children were doing Irish dancing all around the world. It was good for their 'aerobic fitness' and coordination or something. Tony had seen footage on her phone. His granddaughter wore a *wig* and danced like she had a giant ruler gaffer-taped to her back.)

Tony never expected being a grandfather to be like this: funny-accented little girls talking to him on a screen about things he didn't understand. When he'd thought about being a grandfather, he'd imagined a small sticky trusting hand in his, a slow dawdling walk to the corner shop to buy ice-creams. That never happened, and the corner store wasn't even there anymore, so what the hell was wrong with him?

He stood. He needed something to eat. Thinking of his grandchildren had created a crater of misery in his stomach that could only be filled with carbohydrates. He would make a toasted cheese – *Jesus Christ*. No bread. No cheese. No toaster. 'You might experience something we call "snack anxiety",' his wellness consultant, Delilah, had told him with a gleam in her eyes. 'Don't worry, it will pass.'

He slumped back in his chair and thought back to the day he booked himself into this hellhole. That moment of temporary insanity. His appointment with the GP had been at 11 am. He even remembered the time.

The doctor said, 'Right. Tony.' A beat. 'About those test results.'

Tony must have been holding his breath because he took an involuntary gusty gulp of air. The doctor studied the paperwork for a few moments. He took off his glasses and leaned forward, and there was something in his eyes that reminded Tony of the vet's face when he told him that it was time to let Banjo go.

Tony would never forget the shocking clarity of the moment that followed.

It was like he'd been walking around in a daze for the last twenty years and suddenly he was awake. He remembered how his mind had raced on the drive home. He had been so clear and focused. He needed to act. Fast. He could not spend the short time he had left working and watching TV. But what to do?

So he Googled. 'How to change . . .' Google finished the sentence for him. *How to change my life.* There were a trillion suggestions, from religion to self-help books. That's when he came across an article about health resorts. Tranquillum House was top of the list.

A ten-day cleanse. What could be so hard about that?

He hadn't taken a break in years. He ran a sports marketing consultancy and he'd made one of the few excellent decisions of his life when he hired Pippa as an office manager. She was better than him at basically every aspect of his job.

He would drop some weight. He would get himself together. He would make an action plan. On the drive from the airport he'd felt almost *optimistic*.

If only he hadn't made that stupid last-minute decision to stock up on emergency supplies. He'd already taken the turn-off to Tranquillum House when he did a U-turn and headed back to the nearest town, where he'd seen a drive-through bottle shop. All he'd got was a six-pack of beer (*light* beer) and a bag of chips and some crackers (what the hell was wrong with *crackers*?).

If he hadn't turned around he would never have met Loony Woman on the side of the road. He'd thought she was in some kind of trouble. What other logical reason would there be to sit on the side of the road screaming and banging her horn? When she opened the window and he saw her face, she had looked seriously ill. Was menopause really that bad or was this woman a hypochondriac? Maybe it was that bad. Once he got out of here he'd ask his sister.

Now she appeared perfectly normal and healthy. If he hadn't seen her on the side of the road, he would have picked her as one of those bright-eyed, bushy-tailed 'super mums' that bounded about like labradors when Tony's kids were at school.

He was kind of terrified of her. She'd made him feel like a moron. It brought back a long-buried memory of a humiliating incident from childhood. He'd had a thing for one of his older sister's friends and something happened – he'd said something or done something, he couldn't quite remember – but he knew it was to do with periods and

tampons, something he hadn't understood at the age of thirteen, something innocent and trite that had seemed like the
end of the world at the time.

Now he was fifty-six years old. A grandfather! He'd seen
his wife give birth to their three children. He was beyond
feeling embarrassed by the dark mysteries of a woman's body.
Yet that's how Loony Woman had made him feel.

He stood, agitated, his chair scraping back. There were
two hours of 'free time' to fill before dinner. At home the
hours between work and bed glided by in a haze of beer and
food and television. Now he didn't know where to go. This
room felt too small for him. There were too many cutesy
ornaments. Yesterday he'd turned around and knocked a
vase off a side table, shattering it, causing him to swear so
loudly that whoever was in the room next to his probably
heard. He hoped it wasn't an antique.

He leaned over the balcony and studied the grounds. Two
kangaroos stood in the shade of the house. One of them was
grooming itself, twisting around in a very human way to
scratch. The other one sat still, ears alert; it looked like it was
carved in stone.

He could see the gleaming aquamarine of a huge
kidney-shaped pool. Maybe he'd go for a swim. He couldn't
remember the last time he'd been for a swim. The beach used
to be such a big part of his life when the kids were little. He
took all three to Nippers every Sunday morning for years, to
learn how to be surf-safe. Meanwhile, his three pale-skinned
grandchildren had probably never caught a wave in their sad
little Dutch lives.

He went to his suitcase and pulled out his board shorts,
trying not to think of a stranger's hands rifling through his
clothes, searching for contraband, noting his faded underwear. He needed new clothes.

His ex-wife used to buy all his clothes. He never asked her to buy his clothes, she just did it, and he wasn't interested in clothes, so he got used to it. Then, years later, during the divorce, it appeared that was one of the many, many things she did for which she felt 'taken for granted'. He 'never once said thank you'. Didn't he? Could that be true? Jesus. And if it was true, why wait twenty-two years to mention it? Surely he said thank you. But why not tell him he was being an ungrateful pig *at the time*, so he didn't have to feel like the worst man in the world sitting there in front of that counsellor all those years later? He'd felt so ashamed at that moment he literally couldn't speak. This turned out to be an example of him 'shutting down', 'being emotionally distant', 'not giving a shit' – and on it went until he no longer did give a shit and he was numbly signing the papers.

What was that phrase his wife used to describe him? As if it were funny? 'Amateur human being.' She'd even said it to the counsellor.

A few months after that counselling session it occurred to him that there were various things he'd done in that marriage for which he was pretty sure he'd never been thanked or acknowledged. He took care of everything to do with her car, for example. The amateur human being kept her car filled with petrol. He'd often wondered if she thought it had some sort of self-filling mechanism. He got her car serviced once a year. Did her tax return.

Wasn't it possible they both took each other for granted? Wasn't it possible that taking each other for granted was one of the benefits of marriage?

But it was too late by then.

Now it was five years since the separation and they were the best five years of his ex-wife's life. She was back in touch with her 'true self'. She lived on her own and did evening courses and went on weekends away with a gaggle of bliss-fully divorced women. In fact, they often came to places like this. His ex now had a 'daily meditation practice'. 'How long do you practise before you get it right?' Tony had asked, and she'd rolled her eyes so hard it was a wonder they didn't get stuck there. Whenever she talked to Tony these days she kept stopping to breathe deeply. Come to think of it, she looked like she was breathing through a straw.

Tony pulled up the board shorts.

Jesus Christ.

They must have shrunk badly. He'd probably washed them the wrong way. In cold water. Or hot water. The wrong water. He tugged at the fabric with all his strength and slid the button through the buttonhole.

Done. Except he couldn't breathe.

He coughed and the button pinged free, skittering across the floorboards. He laughed out loud with disbelief and looked down at the huge, hairy bulge of his stomach. It seemed to belong to someone else.

He remembered a different body. A different time. The almighty roar of an ecstatic crowd. The way the sound used to vibrate in his chest. Once there had been no barrier at all between his mind and his body. He thought 'run' and he ran. He thought 'jump' and he jumped.

He rolled down his shorts so that they sat beneath his belly, and thought of his ex-wife, six months pregnant, doing the same thing with an elastic-waisted skirt.

He picked up his room key and put a white bath towel over his shoulder. Were these towels allowed outside? There was probably a clause in the contract about it. Old mate the beanstalk would be able to tell him. Presumably a lawyer. Tony knew all about lawyers.

He left his room. The house was as quiet and still as a

church. He opened the front door and walked out into the afternoon heat and down the paved path that led to the pool.

A woman walked towards him from the opposite direction, wearing a sporty black swimming costume and a sarong tied at her waist. The one with the chunky plait of hair like a horse's tail and brightly coloured cat's-eye glasses. Tony had her pegged: intellectual left-wing feminist. She would write Tony off after five minutes of conversation. Still, he'd rather be ignored by the feminist than interact with Loony Woman.

The path was too narrow for them to pass each other, so Tony stood to one side, which hopefully would not offend her feminist principles, like that time when he'd held open a door for a woman and she'd hissed, 'I can open it myself, thanks.' He'd thought about letting it slam in her face, but he didn't, of course, he just smiled like a gormless goon because not every man was capable of violence towards women, even if they did have the occasional violent thought.

This woman didn't make eye contact, but lifted her hand in thanks as if she were lifting it from the steering wheel of a car to thank him for letting her into his lane, and it was only after she'd gone past him that he realised she was weeping quietly. He sighed. He couldn't stand to see a woman cry.

He watched her go – not a bad figure – then walked on towards the pool, tugging at his shorts to make sure they didn't fall at his feet.

He opened the gate.

For fuck's sake.

Loony Woman was in the pool, bobbing about like a cork.

chapter nineteen

Frances

For heaven's sake, thought Frances. The serial killer.

The mechanisms of the pool gate had bamboozled her for about five minutes but, naturally, he had no problem at all. He lifted the little black knobby thing with one meaty hand and kicked the gate hard with the ball of his foot.

Frances had already had to endure Flustered Glasses powering up and down the pool creating a wake like a speedboat. Now *him*.

The serial killer dropped his bath towel on a deckchair (you were meant to use the stripy blue-and-white towels from reception, but rules didn't apply to him), walked straight to the edge of the pool and, without even bothering to put in his toe to check the temperature, dived straight in. Frances did a sedate breaststroke in the other direction.

Now she was stuck in the pool because she didn't want to get out in front of him. She would have thought she was too old to worry about her body being observed and judged in a swimsuit, but apparently this neurosis began at twelve years old and *never ended*.

The problem was that she wanted to convey strength in all her future interactions with this man, and her soft white body, especially when compared to Masha's Amazonian example, damn her, didn't convey anything much except fifty-two years of good living and a weakness for Lindt chocolate balls. The serial killer would no doubt be the type to rank every woman based on his own personal 'Would I fuck her?' score.

She remembered her first-ever boyfriend of over thirty years ago, who told her he preferred smaller breasts than hers while his hands were *on* her breasts, as if she'd find this interesting, as if *women's body parts were dishes on a menu and men were the goddamned diners.*

This is what she said to that first boyfriend: 'Sorry.'

This was her first boyfriend's benevolent reply: 'That's okay.'

She couldn't blame her upbringing for her pathetic behaviour. When Frances was eight years old, a man patted her mother's bottom as he walked past them on a suburban street. 'Nice arse,' he said in a friendly tone. Frances remembered thinking, *Oh, that's kind of him.* And then she'd watched in shock as her five-foot-nothing mother chased the man to the corner and swung a heavy handbag full of hardback library books at the back of his head.

Right. Enough was enough. She would get out of the pool, at her own pace. She would not rush to grab up her towel to throw over her body.

Wait.

She didn't *want* to get out of the pool! She was here first. Why should she get out just because he was here? She would enjoy her swim and *then* she would get out.

She dived down and swam along the pebbly bottom of the pool, enjoying the dappled light and relishing the ache in her legs from the hike that morning. Yes, this was so lovely and relaxing and she was fine. Her back felt quite good – after her second massage with Jan – and she was definitely a little transformed already. Then, apropos of absolutely nothing, the words of the review slithered snake-like into her mind: *Misogynistic airport trash that leaves a bad taste in your mouth.*

Frances thought of how Zoe had said she would read *Nathaniel's Kiss* just to be nice. The last thing that sad beautiful child needed to read was misogynistic trash. Had Frances accidentally been writing misogynistic trash for the last thirty years? She came to the surface with an undignified gasp for air that sounded like a sob.

The serial killer stood at the opposite side of the pool, breathing hard, his back against the tiles, his arms resting on the paving. He stared straight at her with something like . . . *fear.*

For God's sake, she thought. *I may not be twenty years old, but is my body really so unattractive it actually scares you?*

'Um,' he said out loud. He grimaced. He actually *grimaced*. That's how disgusting he found her.

'What?' said Frances. She squared her shoulders and thought of her mother swinging her handbag like a discus thrower. 'We're not meant to be talking.'

'Um . . . you're . . .' He touched under his nose.

Did he mean, 'You smell'?

She did not smell!

Frances put her fingers to her nose. 'Oh!'

Her nose was bleeding. She'd never had a nosebleed in her life. That review had *given her an actual nosebleed.*

'Thank you,' she said coldly. Both times she'd interacted with this man she had been at a terrible and most mortifying disadvantage.

She tipped her head back and dog paddled towards the steps.

'Head forward,' said the serial killer.

'You're meant to put your head back,' snapped Frances. She waded up the stairs, trying to stop her swimsuit from riding up with one hand while attempting to stem the flow of blood with the other. Great clots of blood slid from her nose into her cupped hand. It was disgusting. Unbelievable. Like she'd been *shot*. She was not good with blood. Not really very good with anything remotely medical. It was one of the reasons why having babies had never appealed to her. She looked up at the blue sky and a wave of nausea hit her.

'I think I'm going to faint,' she said.

'No, you're not,' he said.

'I have low blood pressure,' she said. 'I faint a lot. I could *easily* faint.'

'I've got you,' he said.

She clutched his arm as he helped her out of the pool. He wasn't rough exactly, but there was a detachment to his touch, and a kind of concentrated grunting effort, like he was moving an ungainly piece of furniture through a narrow doorway. A refrigerator, perhaps. It was depressing to be treated like a refrigerator.

The blood continued to gush from her nose. He led her to the deckchair, sat her down, put one towel around her shoulders and the other in front of her nose.

'Firmly pinch the bridge of your nose,' he said. 'Like this.' He pinched her nose and then directed her hand into the same spot. 'That's it. You'll be right. It'll stop.'

'I'm sure you're meant to put your head *back*,' protested Frances.

'It's forward,' he said. 'Otherwise the blood runs down the back of your throat. I'm not wrong on this.'

She gave up. Maybe he was right. He was one of those definite people. Definite people were often annoyingly right about things.

The nausea and dizziness began to ease. She kept pinching her nose and chanced an upward glance. He stood solidly in front of her so she was at eye level with his belly button.

'You okay?' he said. He coughed his phlegmy plague-ridden man cough.

'Yes, thank you,' she said. 'I'm Frances.' She kept one hand on her nose and held out her other hand. He shook it. Her hand disappeared into his.

'Tony,' he said.

'Thanks so much for your help,' she said. He was probably a nice man, even if he had treated her like a refrigerator. 'And you know – for stopping on the road when I was . . .'

He looked pained by the memory.

'I've never had a bleeding nose before,' she told him. 'I don't know what brought it on, although I guess I have had a bad cold. Actually, *you* sound like you've had quite a bad –'

'I might get going,' Tony interrupted her impatiently, aggressively, as if she were an old lady who had accosted him at a bus stop and wouldn't let him get a word in edgewise.

'Places to go, people to see?' said Frances, deeply offended. She'd just been through a *medical crisis*.

Tony met her gaze. His eyes were light brown, almost gold. They brought to mind a small endangered native animal. A bilby, for example.

'No,' he said. 'I just thought I should . . . get dressed for dinner.'

Frances grunted. They had plenty of time before dinner.

There was an awkward moment of silence. He didn't leave.

He cleared his throat. 'I don't know if I'm going to survive this . . . experience.' He touched his stomach. 'It's not really my kind of thing. I didn't expect quite so much hippy-dippy stuff.'

Frances softened, smiled. 'You'll be fine. It's only ten days. Nine to go now.'

'Yeah,' said Tony. He sighed and squinted off at the blue-hazed horizon. 'It *is* beautiful here.'

'It is,' said Frances. 'Peaceful.'

Tony said, 'So you're okay? Keep pinching your nose until it stops.'

'Yup,' said Frances.

She looked down at the scarlet droplets on her towel and found another, cleaner section of fabric to plug her nose.

When she looked up Tony was already walking towards the pool gate. As he lifted his arm to open it, his shorts suddenly slid down to his knees to reveal the entirety of his buttocks.

'Fuck!' he said with deep feeling.

Frances stared. What in the world? The man had tattoos of *bright yellow smiley faces* on both his butt cheeks. It was extraordinary. It was like discovering he was wearing a secret clown suit beneath his clothes.

She ducked her head. A second later she heard the pool gate slam. She looked up and he was gone.

Smiley-face tattoos. How drunk must he have been? It kind of changed her entire view of the man. No longer the arrogant sneering man. He was *Tony*. Tony with smiley face tattoos on his butt.

Tony, the smiley-face-tattoo-butted serial killer?

She chuckled, sniffed, and tasted quite a lot of blood.

chapter twenty

Masha

Another email from him. In just a matter of days. Masha stared at her ex-husband's name on her computer screen. The subject heading of this one read: POZHALUYSTA PROCHTI MASHA.

Please read, Masha.

It was as if he were speaking directly to her. There was an attachment to the email. She heard herself make a noise, a silly, pathetic little squeak, like the sound of someone standing on a child's toy.

She remembered the weight and warmth of his arm across her shoulders as they sat on an awful Soviet-made couch, in a flat that looked identical to their own, except that this one had something extraordinary: a VCR.

If not for that wonderful, terrible VCR, where would she be right now? *Who* would she be? Not here. Not this person. Maybe they would still be together.

She deleted the email then went straight to her deleted items folder and deleted it there too.

This was a crucial moment in her professional life. Focus

was essential. People were depending on her: her guests, her staff. She did not have time for so-called . . . what was that rhyming phrase Delilah used? Blasts from the past. She did not have time for blasts from the past.

And yet her stomach continued to lurch about like the sea. She needed to practise detachment. First, she needed to identify the emotion she was experiencing, observe it, label it, let it go. She looked for a word that could describe how she felt and could only find one from her native language: *toska*. There was no adequate English word to describe the kind of anguished longing she felt for something she could not have and did not even want. Maybe because English-speaking people did not experience that feeling.

What was going on? This was not like her! She stood and went to the exercise mat on the floor of her office and did push-ups until her forehead was covered in sweat.

She returned to her desk, breathing hard, and opened the security program on her computer to check on the location and activities of her guests, her mind focused once again. She had installed CCTV cameras around the property for security reasons, and right now she could see most of her guests.

The young couple walked down the back footpath towards the hot springs. Jessica was in front, her head bowed, Ben a few steps behind, studying the horizon.

The Marconi family appeared to have split up. Napoleon was in the rose garden. He was down on his knees, sniffing a rose. Masha smiled. He was literally stopping to smell the roses.

Meanwhile, his wife was out running. Heather was nearly at the top of Tranquillity Hill. Masha watched for a moment, impressed by her pace on the steep section. Not as fast as Masha, but fast.

Where was the daughter? Masha clicked through grainy

black-and-white images and found her in the gym, lifting weights.

Tony Hogburn was leaving the pool area, where Frances Welty sat on a deckchair, dabbing at her face with a towel.

Lars Lee lay in a hammock in the pergola with some sort of drink he'd obviously persuaded the kitchen staff to give him. He would have used sign language and his good looks. Masha had his number.

No-one else? She clicked through the upstairs corridors and came across a woman wearing a sarong, walking briskly. Carmel Schneider. The other single woman.

Carmel took off her glasses and rubbed her face. Possibly crying?

'Deep breaths,' murmured Masha as Carmel struggled with her room key and banged her fist with frustration against the door.

Eventually, Carmel opened the door and almost fell inside. If only Masha could see what she did once she was in her room. People were so prudish. Yao and Delilah got worked up about legalities. Masha had no interest in seeing the naked bodies of her guests! She simply wanted to gain *knowledge* in order to do her job to the best of her ability.

She would have to rely on audio only. She turned a dial on her screen and keyed in Carmel's room number.

A woman's tear-choked voice emerged loud and clear from Masha's monitor.

'Get a grip. Get a grip. Get a grip.'

chapter twenty-one

Carmel

Carmel stood in her room and slapped her own face. Once. Twice. Three times. The third time she slapped herself so hard her glasses flew off.

She picked them up, went to the bathroom and looked at her flushed cheek in the mirror.

For a moment there, when she was in the pool, swimming her laps, endorphins zipping through her body after that fantastic bushwalk, she'd felt fine, more than fine – she'd felt exultant. It had been years since she'd had time to do laps.

As she swam she gloried in the fact that there was nowhere to be, nothing to do, no-one to worry about. No jazz pick-up or karate drop-off, no homework to supervise, no birthday gifts to buy, no doctors' appointments to book; the endless multitude of teeny-tiny details that made up her life. Each obligation on its own seemed laughably easy. It was the sheer volume that threatened to bury her.

Here, she didn't even have to do her own laundry. Carmel simply had to put her washing outside her door in a little cloth bag and it would be returned to her, laundered and ironed, within twenty-four hours. She'd literally cried with happiness when she read that.

She had set herself a goal of fifty laps of freestyle, faster and faster with each lap. She was going to get so, so fit here! She could almost feel that excess weight falling off her. All she'd ever needed was *time* to exercise and a pantry free of treats. As she swam, she silently chanted in time with her strokes: *I'm so happy, I'm so happy, I'm so happy*, breathe, *I'm so happy, I'm so happy, I'm so happy*, breathe.

But then that tiny voice beneath the exultant chanting, just the faintest whisper, had begun: *I wonder what they're doing now.*

She'd tried to ignore it, chanting louder: *I'm so HAPPY, I'm so HAPPY.*

The voice got louder until it became a shout: *No, but seriously, what do you think they're doing RIGHT NOW?*

That's when she'd felt her sanity come loose. The feeling of panic reminded her of one of those recurring dreams in which she'd lost all four of her daughters in some bizarrely negligent way, such as leaving them on the side of the road, or just forgetting they existed and going out dancing.

She'd tried to calm herself with rational thoughts. Her children were not lost on the side of the road; they were with their father and Sonia, his perfectly lovely new girlfriend, soon to be wife. Carmel knew from the itinerary that today they were in Paris, staying in a 'wonderful' Airbnb flat. Sonia, who 'just loved to travel', had stayed there before. It would be cold, of course, in January, but the kids had new jackets. They were on the trip of a lifetime. They were having a wonderful educational experience while their mother had a wonderful break to 'recharge'.

Their father loved them. Their father's new girlfriend

loved them. 'Sonia said she loves us more than life itself,' Rosie told Carmel after only the *third time* she met the woman, and Carmel said, 'Well, *she* sounds like a total nutcase!' but only in her head. Out loud she said, 'That's so nice!'

It was an amicable divorce. Amicable on Joel's part, anyway. On Carmel's part, it felt like a death no-one acknowledged. He just fell out of love with her, that's all. It must have been so hard for him, living with a woman he no longer loved. He really struggled with it, poor man, but he had to be true to himself.

It happens. It happens a lot. It's essential that the discarded wife remains dignified. She must not wail and weep, except in the shower, when the kids are at school and preschool, and she's alone in the suburbs with all the other weeping, wailing wives. The discarded wife must not be bitchy or unkind about the new and improved wife. She must suck it up but without developing a sour face. It is better for all concerned if she is thin.

Carmel had touched the side and turned to do another lap when she saw that someone had joined her in the pool. The friendly-looking older blonde woman. Carmel almost said, 'Hi,' before remembering the silence and ignoring her.

She kept swimming and thought about how that woman's hair was a similar shade to Sonia's hair. No doubt they both paid handsomely for it.

Carmel's daughter Lulu was fair-haired. Lulu looked entirely unrelated to Carmel, which had never mattered until the day Lulu told her that when Daddy and Sonia took them out to dinner a lady stopped by the table and said to Lulu, 'You've got beautiful hair just like your mummy, haven't you?'

Carmel said, in a high, strained voice, 'Huh, that's funny. Did you tell her that Sonia wasn't your mummy?'

Lulu said that Daddy had said it wasn't necessary to always point out that Sonia wasn't her real mother, and Carmel had said, 'Of course it's necessary, darling, you should point it out *every single time* in your loudest voice,' but only in her head. Out loud she said, 'It's time to clean your teeth, Lulu.'

Remembering this, she'd picked up speed, her arms and legs chopping through the water, harder and harder, faster and faster, but she couldn't sustain it, she wasn't fit enough, she was so unfit, and fat, and lazy, and *disgusting.* And she thought of her four girls on the other side of the world, in Paris, where Carmel had never been, having their hair done by Sonia, and probably sitting still for her, and suddenly she swallowed a giant mouthful of water.

She hopped out of the pool, without making eye contact with the friendly blonde lady, as per the rules, fortunately, because she was crying like a fool, and she cried all the way to her room. There was no way the big man coming down the pathway to the pool hadn't noticed.

'Get a grip,' she said now to her reflection in the mirror.

She wrapped her arms around her body.

She missed her children. It hit her like a sudden fever. She longed for the comfort of their four beautiful little-girl bodies and their heedless, proprietorial use of *her* body: the way they plonked themselves on her lap as if she were a chair, the way they burrowed their hot little heads into her stomach, her breasts. She was always yelping at someone, 'Get *off* me!' When she was with her children, she was needed – essential, in fact: everything relied on her. Someone was always saying, 'Where's Mummy?' 'I'm telling Mum what you just said.' 'Mummmmmy!'

Now she was untethered by obligations, as loose and free as a balloon.

She undid the tie of her swimsuit and let it fall in a heap on the bathroom floor while she studied her naked body in the mirror.

'I'm so sorry. I still care very deeply for you, but we've always valued honesty in our relationship, haven't we?' Joel had said to her a year ago, while he poured her a glass of wine. 'It really hurts me to say this but, the thing is, I'm just not attracted to you anymore.'

He truly thought he was being kind and ethical. He believed himself to be a man who did the right thing. He would never have cheated on her. He simply left her, went straight onto a dating website and replaced her. His conscience was perfectly clear. He'd always liked to keep his possessions well maintained, and if they couldn't be repaired to 'as new' then he updated them.

Carmel lifted her breasts in both hands to where they used to be, when they were 'as new'. She looked at the stretch marks on her wobbly stomach and thought of some sappy Facebook post she'd read about how stretch marks were beautiful because of what they represented, creating new life, blah blah blah. Maybe stretch marks could be considered beautiful if the father of your babies still loved your body.

When Joel asked if he and Sonia could please take the girls on a trip to Europe over the January school holidays – Disneyland in Paris! Skiing in Austria! Ice skating in Rome! – Carmel had said, 'Are you kidding me? You're going on the trip we used to talk about doing? But you're doing it without me?' but only in her head. Out loud she said, 'That sounds like so much fun!' And then she arranged all their passports.

She'd told her sister that she was going to spend the time they were away eating paleo and doing cardio and weights and yoga. The plan was to transform her body.

She didn't want Joel back. All she wanted was for his mouth to drop open when he saw her. She didn't need him to *gape*, although that would be nice. She simply wanted her body to look as good as it was physically possible for her to look, and then maybe, possibly, probably not, but possibly, she herself might check out one of those dating websites where you went to replace your spouse.

'There's not a damned thing wrong with your body. You are *average-sized*, you deluded fool! You are an attractive, intelligent woman, you idiot! You should spend January lying in a hammock and eating cheese,' said Carmel's sister Vanessa, who was furious with Joel and the fat-shaming patriarchy.

Carmel let her breasts drop and put a hand to the curve of her stomach. Average wasn't good enough. Average was too big. Everyone knew that. There was an obesity crisis in this country! She didn't want to fat-shame other people, but she certainly wanted to fat-shame herself because she deserved to be shamed. She used to be two sizes smaller and the reason she was now two sizes larger was not because of her four daughters; it was because she didn't 'take care of herself'. Women were meant to 'take care of themselves'. That's what men said on dating websites: *I'd like a woman who takes care of herself.* They meant: *I want a thin woman.*

And it wasn't like the information wasn't available on *how* to take care of yourself! Everyone knew you simply cut out carbs and sugar and trans fats from your diet! Celebrities generously revealed their secrets. They snacked on a 'handful of nuts' or 'two squares of dark antioxidant-rich chocolate'! They drank a lot of water, stayed out of the sun and took the stairs! It wasn't rocket science! But did Carmel ever take the stairs? No, she didn't.

It was true that she often had the kids with her, and if they walked up too many stairs one of them was liable to run too far ahead while another one sat down and announced that her legs no longer worked, but still, there must have been times when Carmel could have built some 'incidental exercise' into her lifestyle. And yet she hadn't. She neglected her body, she didn't get her hair cut for months on end, her eyebrows were left unplucked, she forgot to shave her legs, and it was no surprise her husband left her, because, as she tried to teach her children, *actions had consequences.*

She thought of the long, sculpted lines of Masha's body.

She imagined *Masha* living Carmel's life, standing at the front door when Joel and Sonia dropped off the girls. Joel wouldn't have left Masha in the first place, but say he did, then Masha's heart wouldn't hammer with pain and humiliation at the sight of her ex-husband and his new girlfriend. Masha wouldn't curve her body around the door at a strange angle as if to hide it from Joel. Masha would stand tall and proud. She wouldn't hunch her body to protect her raw, broken heart.

Her sister said Joel's so-called 'lack of attraction' was Joel's problem, not hers. Her sister said Carmel should learn self-love and texted her links to articles about 'intuitive eating' and 'healthy at any size'. Carmel knew these articles were written by fat people to make fat people feel better about their sad, fat lives.

If she could transform her body, she could transform her life, and she could move on from her failed marriage. That wasn't deluded. That was a fact.

Her sister, who was both wealthy and generous – a most excellent combination – gave Carmel a card for her birthday that said: *Carmel, I don't think you need to lose weight. You're beautiful and Joel is a shallow idiot and you should give ZERO FUCKS what he thinks. But if you're determined to go on a health kick, I want you to do it in style and comfort. I've booked you into*

Tranquillum House for their ten-day cleanse while the kids are away. Enjoy! Ness xx PS And then come home and eat cheese.

Carmel hadn't been that happy to receive a gift since she was a child.

Now she thought of Masha's words: 'In ten days, you will not be the person you are now.' The word 'please' filled her mind. *Please, please, please, let that be true, please, please, please, let me become someone other than this.* She looked at her stupid, dopey, pleading face in the mirror. Her skin was rough and red like an old washerwoman's hands. There was a picket fence of tiny lines neatly indented across her top lip, which was so thin it disappeared when she smiled. The only part of her body that was thin was her top lip. Lips were meant to be plump rosebuds, not mean, thin, disappearing lines.

Oh, Carmel, of course he stopped being attracted to you! What were you thinking? How could he possibly be attracted to someone who looks like you? She lifted her hand to slap her face once more.

There was a gentle knock on the door. Carmel jumped. She pulled on the Tranquillum House dressing-gown and went to open the door.

It was Yao. His head was bowed. He didn't make eye contact or say a word. He held out a small card.

Carmel took it and Yao immediately backed away. She closed the door.

It was a square of thick, creamy cardboard like a wedding invitation. The handwriting was in thick, black, authoritative ink.

Dear Carmel,

Although you are currently scheduled for free time, we ask that you please report immediately to the spa for the Tranquillum House Ultimate Relaxation and Rejuvenation Signature Facial. It's a ninety-minute treatment and will be completed just before dinner. Your therapist is waiting for you.

Yours,

Masha

PS Yao is your assigned wellness consultant, but please know that I will also be doing everything in my power to deliver you the health, healing and happiness you need and deserve.

It was at that moment Carmel Schneider gave herself to Masha with the same voluptuous abandon that novice nuns once surrendered themselves to God.

chapter twenty-two

Yao

It was 9 pm. The guests had all been fed and were safely in their rooms, hopefully sleeping soundly. Yao, Masha and Delilah sat at a round table in the corner of Masha's office with notepads in front of them. They were having their daily staff meeting, at which Yao and Delilah were required to give status updates.

Masha tapped her fingertips on the table. There was always a discernible difference in her demeanour at these meetings. You could see her former corporate identity in the language she chose, the crispness of her speech and the stiffness of her posture. Delilah found it laughable, but Yao, who had never worked in that world, found it charming.

'Right. Next item on the agenda. The silence. Has anyone broken it today?' asked Masha. She seemed brittle. It must be nerves about the new protocol. Yao was nervous himself.

'Lars broke it,' said Delilah. 'He was trying to get out of the daily blood tests. I told him not to be a baby.'

Yao would never say that to a guest. Delilah just said what she was thinking, whereas Yao, *sometimes*, felt just a

192

little . . . fraudulent. Like a performer. For example, he would be helping an ill-mannered guest do a plank and giving them gentle, patient encouragement – 'You've got this!' – while thinking, *You're not even trying, you rude lazy motherfucker.*

'Frances wrote me a note,' said Yao. 'She asked if she could please skip the blood test as she'd had a nosebleed. I told her that was all the more reason to do the test.'

Masha grunted. 'Nobody likes blood tests,' she said. 'I don't like them! I hate needles.' She shuddered. 'When we were applying to come here all those years ago we had to do *many* blood tests: for AIDS, for syphilis. Your government wanted us for our brains but our bodies had to also be perfect. Even our teeth were checked.' She tapped her finger against her white teeth. 'I remember my friend said, "It's like they are choosing a horse!"' Her lip curled at the memory, as if her pride had been hurt. 'But you do what you have to do,' she said, without looking at either of them. It was if she were speaking to someone else not in the room.

Yao looked at Masha's collarbone beneath the straps of her simple white sleeveless top. He had never thought the collarbone to be an especially sensual part of a woman's body until he met Masha.

'Are you in love with this woman or something?' his mother had said to him on the phone, just last week. 'Is that why you work like a dog for her?'

'She's nearly the same age as you, Mum,' Yao told her. 'And I don't work like a dog for her.'

'More like a *puppy*,' Delilah told him. 'You have a crush on her.' They were in bed at the time. Delilah was beautiful and sexually very skilled and he liked her very much, but their hook-ups always felt kind of transactional, even though no money changed hands.

'I'm grateful to her,' Yao said, his hands behind his head as he looked at the ceiling, considering this. 'She saved my life.'

'She didn't save your life. You saved *her* life.'

'My supervisor saved her life,' said Yao. 'I didn't know what the hell I was doing.'

'And now you loooooove her,' said Delilah, putting her bra back on.

'Like a sister,' said Yao.

'Yeah, right,' said Delilah.

'Like a cousin.'

Delilah snorted.

He did care very deeply for Masha. Was that so strange? To love your boss? Surely not so strange when you lived and worked together, and when your boss looked like Masha. She was interesting and stimulating. He found her exotic accent as attractive as her body. He would admit he had a significant crush on her. Perhaps his crush was strange and indicated some flaw in his personality or dysfunctional consequence of his childhood, even though it was just the ordinary, happy childhood of a shy, earnest boy who could get a little too intense about things but mostly slipped under the radar. His parents were softly spoken, humble people who never pushed him. Yao's parents believed in keeping expectations low to avoid disappointment. His father had *said* that out loud once, without irony: 'Expect to fail, Yao, then you will never be disappointed.' That's why Yao found Masha's egotism so refreshing. She was bigger than life. Self-deprecation was something she had never practised and did not understand in other people.

And Masha *had* saved his life.

After her heart attack, she had written letters to both Finn and Yao, thanking them and talking about how her 'near-death experience' had changed her forever. She said that while she floated above them, she had seen the tiny red birthmark on Yao's scalp. She had described it perfectly: strawberry-shaped.

Finn never answered Masha's letter. 'She's a nutter. She didn't need to float above our bloody heads to see your birthmark. She probably saw it when she was sitting at her desk, before she collapsed.'

But Yao was intrigued by her near-death experience. He emailed her, and over the years they kept up a sporadic correspondence. She told him that after she recovered from her heart surgery, she'd given up her 'highly successful' (her words) corporate career and cashed in her company shares to buy a famous historic house in the countryside. She was going to put in a swimming pool and restore the house. Her initial plan had been to start an exclusive bed and breakfast, but as her interest in health had developed, she changed her mind.

She wrote, *Yao, I have transformed my body, my mind, my soul and I want to do the same for others.*

There was an element of grandiosity to her emails he found amusing and endearing, but really she was not especially important to him. Just a grateful ex-patient with a funny turn of phrase.

And then, just after his twenty-fifth birthday, all his dominos toppled: bam, bam, bam. First, his parents announced they were divorcing. They sold the family home and moved into separate apartments. It was confusing and distressing. Then, in the midst of all that drama, his fiancée, Bernadette, broke off their engagement. It came without warning. He thought they were deeply in love. The wedding, reception and honeymoon were booked. How was it possible? It felt like the foundations of his life were collapsing beneath his feet. A break-up wasn't a *tragedy* and yet, to his shame, it felt cataclysmic.

His car got stolen.

He began to suffer from stress-related dermatitis.

Finn moved interstate and the ambulance service transferred Yao to a regional area where he knew no-one, where the call-outs mostly involved violence and drugs. One night a man held a knife to his throat and said, 'If you don't save her I'll slit your throat.' The woman was already dead. When the police came, the man lunged at them with the knife and he was shot. Yao ended up saving *his* life.

He went back to work. Then two days later he woke up just a few minutes before his alarm, as usual, but the moment it went off something catastrophic happened to his brain. He felt it implode. It felt physical. He thought it was a bleed on the brain. He ended up in a psychiatric ward.

'It sounds like you've been under a lot of pressure,' said a doctor with dark shadows under his eyes.

'Nobody died,' said Yao.

'But it feels like they did, doesn't it?'

That was exactly how it felt: like death after death after death. Finn was gone. His fiancée was gone. His family home was gone. Even his *car* was gone.

'We used to call this a nervous breakdown,' said the doctor. 'Now we'd call it a major depressive episode.'

He gave Yao a referral for a psychiatrist and a prescription for antidepressants. 'A well-managed breakdown can turn out to be a good thing,' he told Yao. 'Try to see it as an opportunity. An opportunity to grow and learn about yourself.'

The day after he got home from the hospital he received an email from Masha in which she said that if he ever needed to escape 'the rat race', he was very welcome to visit and try out her new guestrooms.

It felt like a sign.

Your timing is good, I haven't been well, he wrote to her. *I might just come for a few days for a rest.*

He hadn't recognised Masha when he arrived at the house and a goddess in white walked out onto the veranda; a goddess who took him into her arms and said into his ear, 'I will make you well.'

Each time he walked out of Tranquillum House to greet new guests he wanted to create that same experience for them: like the sight of land when you've been lost at sea.

Masha nurtured Yao like a sick bird. She cooked for him and taught him meditation and yoga. They learned tai chi together. They were alone in that house for three months. They didn't have sex but they shared *something*. A journey of some kind. A rejuvenation. During that time his body changed; it hardened and strengthened as his mind healed. He became someone else entirely as he experienced a kind of peace and certainty he'd never known in his life. He shed the old Yao like dead skin.

The old Yao only exercised sporadically and ate too much processed food. The old Yao was a worrier and an insomniac who often woke up in the middle of the night thinking of all the things that *could* have gone wrong in his working day.

The new Yao slept through the night and woke up in the morning refreshed. The new Yao no longer thought obsessively about his fiancée in bed with another man. The new Yao rarely thought of Bernadette at all, and eventually completely eradicated her from his thoughts. The new Yao lived in the moment and was passionate about 'wellness', inspired by Masha's vision for Tranquillum House. Instead of just patching people up, like Yao had done as a paramedic, the plan was to *transform* people, in the same way that he himself had been transformed. It felt like religion, except everything they did was based on science and evidence-based research.

His parents visited separately and told him it was time to return to Sydney and get his life back on track, but within six months of his arrival Masha and Yao opened the doors of Tranquillum House for their first guests. It was a success. And fun. A lot more fun than being a paramedic.

A few days had become five years. Delilah joined the staff four years ago, and together the three of them had all learned so much, constantly refining and improving their retreats. Masha paid generously. It was a dream career.

'Tomorrow, I begin one-on-one counselling sessions,' said Masha. 'I will share my notes with you.'

'Good, because the more we know about each guest, the better,' said Yao.

This particular retreat would set new precedents for the way they did business. It was natural to be nervous.

'I want to learn more about Tony Hogburn's past,' said Delilah. 'There's something about him. I can't put my finger on it.'

'It's going to be fine,' murmured Yao, almost to himself.

Masha reached across the table and grabbed him by the arm, her incredible green eyes ablaze with that energy and passion he found so inspiring.

'It's going to be more than *fine*, Yao,' she said. 'It's going to be beautiful.'

chapter twenty-three

Frances

It was now day four of the retreat.

Frances found she had settled into the gentle rhythm of life at Tranquillum House with surprising ease. She rarely had to make decisions about how to spend her time.

Every morning began with tai chi in the rose garden with Yao. Her schedule always included at least one, some-times *two*, remedial massages with Jan. Some days she had to go to the spa on multiple occasions – if, for example, she was 'assigned' a facial. She did not find this onerous. The facials were divinely scented, dreamlike experiences that left Frances rosy and glowing, with her hair sticking up like the petals of a flower. There were yoga classes in the yoga and meditation studio and walking meditations through the surrounding bushland. The walking meditations got brisker and faster and steeper each day.

In the early evening, when it got cooler, some guests went running with Yao (the Marconi family seemed to do nothing *but* run, even during free time; Frances would sit on her balcony and watch the three of them pelting up

Tranquillity Hill as if they were running for their lives), while others did a 'gentle' exercise class in the rose garden with Delilah. Delilah seemed to have made it her personal mission to get Frances to do push-ups on her toes like a man, and because Frances wasn't allowed to speak, she couldn't say, 'No thank you, I've never seen the point of push-ups.' She now understood that the point of push-ups was to 'work every muscle in her body', which was supposedly a good thing.

Frances meekly allowed Yao to take her blood and check her blood pressure each day, before hopping mutely on the scales so he could record her weight, which she still avoided looking at but which she assumed was *plummeting*, probably in *freefall*, what with all the exercise, and the lack of calories and wine.

The noble silence, which seemed so flimsy and silly in the beginning, so arbitrary and easily breakable, somehow gained in strength and substance as the days passed, like the settling in of a heatwave, and in fact the summer heat had intensified. It was a dry, still heat, bright and white, like the silence itself.

At first, without the distraction of noise and conversation, Frances's thoughts went around and around on a crazy, endless, repetitive loop: Paul Drabble, the money she'd lost, the surprise, the hurt, the anger, the surprise, the hurt, the anger, Paul's son, who was probably not even his son, the book she'd written with delusional love in her heart, which had subsequently been rejected, the career that was possibly over, the review that she should never have read. It wasn't that she'd found any solutions or experienced any earth-shattering revelations, but the act of observing her looping thoughts seemed to slow them down, until at last they came to a complete stop, and she'd found that for moments of time she thought . . . nothing. Nothing at all. Her mind was quite empty. And those moments were lovely.

The other guests were silent, not unwelcome figures in her peripheral vision. It became perfectly normal to ignore people, to not say 'hello' when you found someone else sitting in the hot spring you were visiting but to instead step silently into the bubbling, eggy-scented water with your head averted.

Once, she and the tall, dark and handsome man sat in the Secret Grotto hot spring for what seemed like an eternity together, neither saying a word, both gazing out at the valley views, lost in their private thoughts. Even though they hadn't spoken or even looked at each other, it felt like they'd shared something spiritual.

There had been other pleasant surprises too.

For example, yesterday afternoon, as she had passed Zoe on the stairs, the girl brushed against her and pressed something into the palm of her hand. Frances managed to keep her eyes ahead and not say anything (which was remarkable, as she was very bad at that sort of thing; *both* her ex-husbands had informed her that they could think of no-one who would make a worse spy than her, while they, in spite of their differing personalities, were both apparently eminently qualified to join the CIA at a moment's notice), and when she got to her room she had found a Reese's Peanut Butter Cup in her hand. She had never tasted anything more divine. Apart from Zoe, Frances didn't have much interaction with anyone else. She no longer startled when Napoleon sneezed. She noted that Tony's hacking cough gradually lessened and lessened until it disappeared, and indeed her own cough disappeared around the same time. Her breathing became beautifully clear. Her paper cut vanished and her back pain got better every day. It really was a 'healing journey'.

When she got home she was going to send Ellen an effusive thank-you card for suggesting this place.

According to today's schedule she had a one-on-one counselling session with Masha straight after lunch. Frances had never had any form of *counselling* in her life. She had friends for that. They all counselled each other and it was generally a two-way process. Frances couldn't imagine sitting and telling anyone her problems without then listening to their problems and offering her own sage advice in return. She generally felt that the advice she offered was superior to the advice she received. Other people's problems were so simple; one's own problems tended to be so much more *nuanced*.

But the silence and the heat and the daily massages had all combined to create a peaceful sense of resignation. Masha could 'counsel' Frances if it made her happy.

Frances's lunch that day was a vegetarian curry. She had stopped noticing the sound of everyone chewing and had begun to take the most extraordinary pleasure in her food – extraordinary because she thought she already took quite substantial pleasure in her food! The curry, which she savoured tiny mouthful by tiny mouthful, had a hint of saffron that just about blew her mind. Was saffron always that good? She didn't know, but it felt like a religious experience.

After lunch, while still reflecting on the wonder of saffron, Frances opened the door marked PRIVATE then climbed up two flights of stairs to the princess tower at the top of the house and knocked on the door of Masha's office.

'Come in,' said a voice, a little peremptorily.

Frances entered the room, reminded of visits to the principal's office when she was at boarding school.

Masha was writing something down and she gestured towards the seat in front of her to indicate that Frances should sit while she finished what she was doing.

Her demeanour would normally have made Frances bristle, and she wasn't yet quite so Zen that she didn't note the fact that she had the *right* to bristle. She was the paying guest turning up at the appointed time, thank you very much, not the hired help. But she didn't sigh or clear her throat or wriggle because she was very nearly transformed, definitely thinner, and yesterday she did two push-ups *in a row* on her toes. She'd probably look very similar to Masha quite soon.

A wave of laughter rose in her chest and she distracted herself by studying the room.

She'd love an office like this. If she had an office like this she would probably write a masterpiece without chocolate. There were huge glass windows on all four sides, giving Masha a three-hundred-and-sixty-degree view of the soft, rippling green countryside. It looked like a Renaissance painting from up here.

In the same way that the silence didn't apply to Masha, it seemed that neither did the 'no electronic devices' rule. Masha did not seem averse to the very latest in technology. She had not one but two very smart-looking oversized computer monitors on her desk, as well as a laptop.

Was she surfing the *internet* up here while all her guests digitally detoxed? Frances felt her right hand twitch. She imagined grabbing a mouse, spinning a monitor around to face her, and clicking on a news site. What had happened in the last four days? There could have been a zombie apocalypse or a significant celebrity couple break-up and Frances would have no idea.

She dragged her eyes away from the seductive computer screens and looked instead at the few items on Masha's desk. No photo frames revealing anything personal. There were a few lovely antiques that Frances coveted. Her hand crept out to touch a letter opener. The gold handle had an intricate design with pictures of . . . elephants?

'Careful,' said Masha. 'That letter opener is as sharp as a dagger. You could murder someone with that, Frances.'

Frances's hand flew back as fast as a shoplifter's.

Masha picked up the letter opener and removed it from its sheath. 'It is at least two hundred years old,' she said. She pressed her thumb to the sharp point. 'It has been in my family for a long time.'

Frances made an interested murmur. She wasn't sure if she was allowed to break the silence, and suddenly she was irritated by that.

'I assume the noble silence doesn't apply right now?' she said, and her unused voice sounded strange and unfamiliar to her ears. She'd been so good! She hadn't even talked to *herself* when she was alone in her room, and normally she was very chatty when alone, cheerfully narrating her own actions and engaging in friendly dialogue with inanimate objects. 'Where are you hiding, o peeler of carrots?'

'Ah, you are a person who likes to follow the rules, are you?' Masha rested her chin in both hands and studied her. Her eyes really were a remarkable shade of green.

'Generally,' said Frances.

Masha didn't break eye contact.

'As I'm sure you know, I did have some banned items in my luggage,' said Frances. She was happy with her cool tone, but her face was hot.

'Yes,' said Masha. 'I am aware of that.'

'And I'm still *reading*,' said Frances defiantly.

'Are you?' said Masha.

'Yes,' said Frances.

'Anything good?' Masha replaced the letter opener on her desk.

Frances thought about this. The book was meant to be another murder mystery but the author had introduced far too many characters too early, and so far everyone was still alive and kicking. The pace had slowed. Come on now. Hurry up and kill someone. 'It's quite good,' she told Masha.

'Tell me, Frances,' said Masha. 'Do you *want* to be a different person when you leave here?'

'Well,' said Frances. She picked up a coloured glass ball from Masha's desk. It felt vaguely bad-mannered – you didn't pick up other people's belongings – and yet she couldn't help it. She wanted to feel the cool weight of it in her hand. 'I guess I do.'

'I don't think you do,' said Masha. 'I think you are here for a little rest, and you are quite happy with the way you are now. I think this is all a little bit of joke to you. You prefer not to take things too seriously in your life, yes?' Her accent had deepened.

Frances reminded herself that this woman had no *authority* over her.

'Does it matter if I'm just here for a "little rest"?' Frances put the glass ball back down and pushed it away from her, causing a moment's panic when it began to roll. She stopped it with her fingertips and placed her hands in her lap. This was ridiculous. Why did she feel ashamed? Like a teenager? This was a *health resort*.

Masha didn't answer her question. 'I wonder, do you feel that you've ever been truly *tested* in your life?'

Frances shifted in her seat. 'I've suffered losses,' she said defensively.

Masha flicked her hand. 'Of course you have,' she said. 'You are fifty-two years old. That is not my question.'

'I've been lucky,' said Frances. 'I know I have been very lucky.'

'And you live in the "lucky country".' Masha lifted her arms to encompass the countryside that surrounded them.

'Well, that phrase about us being the lucky country, it's kind of misused.' Frances heard a pedantic tone creep into her voice and she wondered why she was parroting her first husband, Sol, who always felt the need to point this out smugly when someone referred to Australia as being the lucky country. 'The author who wrote that phrase meant to imply that we hadn't earned our prosperity.'

'So Australia is not so lucky?'

'Well, no, we *are,* but . . .' Frances stopped. Was that exactly the point that Masha was trying to make? That Frances hadn't earned her prosperity?

'You never had children,' said Masha, referring to an open file on the desk in front of her. Frances found herself craning to look, as if her file would reveal a secret. Masha only knew she didn't have children because Frances had indicated that when she filled in the booking form. 'Was that decision made by choice? Or was it forced upon you by circumstance?'

'Choice,' said Frances. *This is none of your business, lady.*

She thought of Ari and the PlayStation games he was going to show her when she got to America. Where was Ari now? Or the boy who pretended to be Ari? Was he on the phone to some other woman?

'I see,' said Masha.

Did Masha think she was selfish for not wanting children? It wouldn't be the first time she'd heard that accusation. It had never especially bothered her.

'Do *you* have children?' Frances asked Masha. She was allowed to ask questions. This woman was not her therapist. She probably had no qualifications whatsoever! She leaned forward, curious to know. 'Are you in a relationship?'

'I am not in a relationship and I do not have children,' said Masha. She had become very still. She looked very steadily at Frances – so steadily that Frances couldn't help but wonder if she was lying, although it was impossible to imagine Masha in a relationship. She could never be *half* of any relationship.

'You mentioned losses,' said Masha. 'Tell me about those losses.'

'My father died when I was very young,' said Frances.

'Mine also,' said Masha.

Frances was taken aback by this unasked-for personal revelation.

'I'm sorry,' said Frances. She thought of her last memory of her dad. It had been summer. A Saturday. She was going out to her part-time job as a checkout girl at Target. He was sitting in their living room playing *Hot August Night*, smoking a cigarette, eyes closed and humming along with deep feeling to Neil Diamond, whom he considered to be a genius. Frances kissed him on the forehead. 'See you, darling,' he said, without opening his eyes. For her, the smell of cigarettes was the smell of love. She dated far too many smokers for that reason.

'A lady driving a car didn't stop at a pedestrian crossing,' said Frances. 'The sun was in her eyes. My father was going for a walk.'

'My father was shot in a market by a hitman for the Russian mafia,' said Masha. 'Also an accident. They thought he was someone else.'

'*Seriously?*' Frances tried not to look too avid for more exotic detail.

Masha shrugged. 'My mother said my father had too common a face. Too plain. Like anybody's, like everybody's. She was very angry with him for his plain face.'

Frances didn't know whether to smile. Masha didn't smile, so Frances didn't either.

Frances offered up, 'My mother was angry with my father for going for a walk. For years she said, "It was so hot that day! Why didn't he just stay inside like a normal person? Why did he have to walk everywhere?"'

Masha nodded. Just once.

'My father should not have been at the market,' she said. 'He was a *very* clever man, he had a very senior position for a firm that made vacuum cleaners, but after the fall of the Soviet Union, when inflation went . . .' She made a whistling motion and pointed up. 'Our entire savings, gone! My father's company could not pay him cash. They paid him in vacuum cleaners. So . . . he went to the market to sell the vacuum cleaners. He should not have had to do that. It was beneath him.'

'That's awful,' said Frances.

For a moment it felt as if the giant chasm that separated their different cultures and childhoods and body types could be bridged by the commonality of the loss of their fathers, through terrible chance, and their bitter, grieving mothers. But then Masha sniffed, as if suddenly disgusted by some unmentionable behaviour. She closed the file in front of her. 'Well. It has been nice to chat with you, Frances, to get to know you a little bit.'

She made it sound as if she now knew everything there was to know about Frances.

'How did you end up in Australia?' asked Frances, suddenly desperate for the conversation not to end. She didn't want to go back to the silence now she'd experienced the pleasure of human interaction, and it was fine if Masha didn't want to know more about Frances, but Frances most certainly wanted to know more about her.

'My ex-husband and I applied to different embassies,' said

Masha coldly. 'The US. Canada. Australia. I wanted the US, my husband wanted Canada, but Australia wanted us.'

Frances tried not to take this personally, although she had a feeling that Masha wanted her to take it personally.

Also, ex-husband! They had divorce in common too! But Frances could tell she wouldn't get anywhere trying to exchange divorce stories. There was something about Masha that reminded Frances of a friend from university who had been both deeply egocentric and deeply insecure. The only way to make her open up was with flattery: extremely *careful* flattery. It was like dismantling a bomb. You could accidentally offend them at any time.

'I think it's a very brave thing to do,' said Frances. 'To start a new life in a new country.'

'Well, we did not have to travel the open seas in a rickety boat, if that's what you are thinking. The Australian government paid our airfares. Picked us up at the airport. Paid for our accommodation. You *needed* us. We were both very intelligent people. I had a degree in mathematics. My husband was a talented, world-class scientist.' Her eyes looked back into a past Frances longed to see. 'Extremely talented.'

The way she said 'extremely talented' didn't make her sound like a divorced wife. She sounded like a widow.

'We're lucky you came then,' said Frances humbly, on behalf of the Australian people.

'Yes. You are. Very lucky,' said Masha. She leaned forward, her face suddenly alight. 'I'll tell you why we came! Because of a VCR. It all starts with the VCR. And now nobody even has a VCR! Technology . . .'

'The VCR?' said Frances.

'Our neighbours in the flat next to ours got one. Nobody could afford such a thing. They inherited money from a relative who died in Siberia. These neighbours were good friends of ours and they asked us over to see movies.' Her gaze became unfocused, once again remembering.

Frances didn't move; she didn't want Masha to stop this sudden sharing of confidences. It was like when your uptight boss goes to the pub with you and loosens up over a drink and suddenly starts chatting to you like you're an equal.

'It was a window into another world. Into a capitalist world. It all seemed so different, so amazing, so . . . *abundant*.' Masha smiled dreamily. 'Dirty Dancing, Desperately Seeking Susan, The Breakfast Club – not that many, because the movies were insanely expensive, so people had to swap them. The voices were all done by the same person holding his nose to disguise his voice because it was illegal.' She held her nose and spoke in a nasal voice to demonstrate.

'If it wasn't for that VCR, for those movies, we might not have worked so hard to leave. It was not easy to leave.'

'Did the reality live up to your expectations?' asked Frances, thinking of the glossy, highly coloured world of eighties films and how bland suburban Sydney would feel when she and friends emerged blinking from the cinemas. 'Was it as wonderful as in the movies?'

'It was as wonderful,' said Masha. She picked up the glass ball that Frances had put down and held it in the flat palm of her hand as if daring it to roll. It stayed completely still. 'And it was not.'

She put the ball back down decisively. Suddenly she seemed to remember her superior status. Like when your boss remembers you have to work together the next day.

'So, Frances, tomorrow we will officially break the silence and you will get to know the other guests.'

'I'm looking forward –'

'Enjoy your evening meal because there will be no meals served at all tomorrow. Your first light fast will begin.'

She held out her hand in such a way that Frances found herself automatically rising to her feet.

'Have you done much fasting before?' Masha looked up at her. She said 'fasting' as if it were an exotic, delightful practice, like belly dancing.

'Not really,' admitted Frances. 'But it's just a *light* fast, right?

Masha smiled radiantly. 'You may find tomorrow a little testing, Frances.'

chapter twenty-four

Carmel

'You have already lost some weight, I see.' Masha opened Carmel's file to begin her counselling session.

'*Have* I?' said Carmel. She felt like she'd won a prize. 'How much?'

Masha ignored the question. She ran her finger down a sheet of paper in the file.

'I thought I might have lost some – but I wasn't sure.' Carmel heard her unused voice tremble with pleasure. She hadn't dared to hope. It seemed that Yao deliberately stood in such a way that she couldn't see that dreaded number on the scales each day.

She put a hand to her stomach. She had suspected it was getting flatter, her clothes looser! She'd been secretly touching her stomach, like when she was pregnant for the first time. This retreat was just like that euphoric time: the feeling that her body was changing in new and miraculous ways.

'I guess I'll probably lose even more when we start the fast tomorrow?' Carmel wanted to demonstrate her enthusiasm and commitment to the retreat. She would do whatever it took.

Masha said nothing. She closed Carmel's file and balanced her chin on her folded hands.

Carmel said, 'I hope it's not just fluid loss. They say that in the first few days of a diet you mostly just lose fluid.'

Masha still said nothing.

'I know the meals here are all calorie-controlled. I guess the challenge will be maintaining my weight loss when I go home. I'd be really grateful for any nutrition advice you can give me going forward. Maybe a recipe plan?'

'You do not need a recipe plan,' said Masha. 'You are intelligent woman. You know what to do to lose weight, if that's what you want. You are not especially fat. You are not especially thin. You want to be thinner. That is your choice. I find this not so interesting.'

'Oh,' said Carmel. 'Sorry.'

'Tell me something about yourself that is not related to your weight,' said Masha.

'Well, I have four daughters,' said Carmel. She smiled at the thought of them. 'They're aged ten, eight, seven and five.'

'I know this already. You are a mother,' said Masha. 'Tell me something else.'

'My husband left me. He has a new girlfriend now. So that's been —'

Masha waved that away irritably, as if it were of no relevance. 'Something else.'

'There *is* nothing else right now,' said Carmel. 'There's no time for anything else. I'm just a normal busy mum. An overweight, stressed-out, suburban mum.' As she spoke she scanned Masha's desk for family photos. She must not have children. If she did, she would know how motherhood swallowed you up whole. 'I work part-time,' she tried to explain. 'I have an elderly mother who is not well. I am always tired. Always, always tired.'

Masha sighed, as if Carmel were not behaving.

'I know I need to work more exercise into my schedule?' offered Carmel. Was that what she wanted to hear?

'Yes,' said Masha. 'Yes, you do. But I find this also not so interesting.'

'When the kids are older I'll have more time to –'

'Tell me about when you were schoolgirl,' interrupted Masha. 'What were you like? Smart? Top of class? Bottom of class? Naughty? Loud? Shy?'

'I was mostly near the top of the class,' said Carmel. Always. 'Not naughty. Not shy. Not loud.' She thought about it. 'Although, I *could* be very loud. If I felt strongly about something.'

She remembered a heated argument with a teacher who wrote 'the thunder boomed, the lightening flashed' on the blackboard. Carmel stood up to correct the teacher's spelling of 'lightning'. The teacher didn't believe her. Carmel wouldn't back down, even when the teacher yelled at her. She was all-powerful when she knew without doubt that she was in the right. But how often did you know for sure that you were right? Hardly ever.

'Interesting,' said Masha. 'Because right now you do not seem like a very loud person.'

'You should see me in the morning when I yell at my kids,' said Carmel.

'Why have I not seen this "loud" Carmel? Where is she?'

'Um – we're not allowed to speak?'

'That is a good point. But see – even then, when you made a very valid point, you said it like a question. You put this questioning sound at the end of your sentences.

Like this? Your voice goes up? Like you are not really sure? Of everything you say?'

Carmel squirmed at Masha's imitation of her speech patterns. Was that really how she sounded?

'And your walk,' said Masha. 'That is the other thing: I don't like the way you walk.'

'You don't *like* the way I *walk*?' spluttered Carmel. Wasn't that kind of rude?

Masha stood and came out from behind her desk. 'This is how you walk right now.' She rounded her shoulders, dropped her chin and did a scurrying kind of sidestep across the room. 'Like you are hoping no-one sees you. Why do you do that?'

'I don't think I exactly –'

'Yes, you do.' Masha sat back down. 'I don't think you always walked like this. I think once you walked properly. Do you want your daughters to walk like you walk?' It was obviously a rhetorical question. 'You are a woman in the prime of your life! You should march into a room with your head held high! Like you are walking onto a stage, a battlefield!'

Carmel stared. 'I'll try?' she said. She coughed, and remembered to turn it into a statement. 'I will try. I will try to do that.'

Masha smiled. 'Good. At first it will feel strange. You will have to fake it. But then you will remember. You will think, Oh, that's right, this is how I talk, this is how I walk. This is me, Carmel.' She knocked her closed fist against her heart. 'This is who I am.'

She leaned forward and lowered her voice. 'I will tell you a secret.' Her eyes danced. 'You will look thinner if you walk like that!'

Carmel smiled back. Was she joking?

'Everything will become clearer over the next few days,' said Masha, with a gesture that made Carmel stand up quickly, as if she'd outstayed her welcome.

Masha pulled a notepad towards her and began to write something down.

Carmel hovered. She tried to put her shoulders back. 'Could you just tell me how much weight I've lost so far?'

Masha didn't look up. 'Close the door behind you.'

chapter twenty-five

Masha

Masha studied the large man who sat on the other side of her desk, his feet planted solidly on the floor, his hands curled in meaty fists on his thighs, as if he were a prisoner hoping for parole.

Masha remembered how Delilah had implied there was something unusual or secretive about Tony Hogburn. Masha did not agree. The man was not especially complex. He seemed to her to be a simple, grumpy fellow. He had lost weight already. Men who drank a lot of beer always did lose weight when they stopped, whereas women like Carmel, who had much less weight to lose, took much longer. In truth, Carmel hadn't lost any weight at all, but there was no benefit in Carmel hearing that.

'How did you come across Tranquillum House, Tony?' Masha asked him.

'I Googled "How to change your life",' said Tony.

'Ah,' said Masha. As an experiment, she sat back, crossed her legs, and waited for his eyes to travel down her body, which they did, of course (the man was not dead yet), but not for very long. 'Why do you want to change your life?'

'Well, Masha, life is short.' His gaze moved past hers to the window behind her head. Masha noted that he seemed much calmer and more confident now than when he had complained about his contraband being confiscated. The positive effects of Tranquillum House! 'I didn't want to waste the time I had left.'

He looked back at her. 'I like your office. It's like you're on top of the world up here. I get claustrophobic down in that yoga studio.'

'So how do you hope to change your life?'

'I just want to get healthier and fitter,' said Tony. 'Drop some weight.'

Men often used that phrase: 'drop some weight'. They said it without shame or emotion, as if the weight were an object they could easily put down when they chose. Women said they needed to 'lose weight', with their eyes down, as if the extra weight was part of them, a terrible sin they'd committed.

'I used to be very fit. I should have done this sooner. I really regret . . .' Tony stopped, cleared his throat, as if he'd said more than he wanted.

'What do you regret?' asked Masha.

'It's not anything I've done. It's more everything I *haven't* done. I've just kind of moped about for twenty years.'

It took a fraction of a second to translate the English word 'moped' – a word she didn't hear much.

'Twenty years is a long time to *mope*,' said Masha. Foolish man. She herself had never moped. Not once. Moping was for the weak.

'I kind of got into the habit of it,' said Tony. 'Not sure how to stop.'

She waited to hear what he would say next. Women liked to be asked questions about themselves but with men it was better to be patient, to be silent and see what eventuated.

She waited. The minutes passed. She was considering giving up when Tony shifted in his chair.

'Your near-death experience,' he said, without looking at her. 'You said you no longer feared death, or something like that?'

'That's right,' said Masha. She studied him, wondering about his interest in this subject. 'I no longer fear it. It was beautiful. People think death is like falling asleep but for me it was like waking up.'

'A tunnel?' said Tony. 'Is that what you saw? A tunnel of light?'

'Not a tunnel.' She paused, considered changing the subject and putting the focus back on him. She had already revealed too much of her personal life earlier to that Frances Welty, with her bouncy hair and red lipstick, nearly knocking Masha's glass ball off the desk, like a child, asking her greedy, nosy questions, making Masha forget her position.

It was hard to believe Frances was exactly the same age as Masha. She reminded Masha of a little girl in her second-grade class. A plump, pretty, vain little girl who always had a pocket filled with Vzletnaya candies. People like Frances lived candy-filled lives.

But she did not feel that Tony had lived a candy-filled life. 'It was not a tunnel, it was a lake,' she told him. 'A great lake of shimmering coloured light.'

She had never told a guest this before. She had told Yao about it, but not Delilah. As Tony ran a hand over his unshaven jaw, considering her words, Masha saw again that incredible lake of colour: scarlet, turquoise, lemon. She hadn't just seen that lake, she had experienced it with all her senses: she had breathed it, heard it, smelled it, tasted it.

'Did you see . . . loved ones?' asked Tony.

'No,' lied Masha, even as she saw an image of a young man walking towards her through the lake of light, colour streaming off him like water.

Such an ordinary but exquisite young man. He wore a baseball cap, like so many young men did. He took it off and scratched his head. She had only ever seen him as her baby, her beautiful fat-cheeked toothless baby, but she knew immediately that this was her son, this was the man he would have and should have become, and all that love was still within her, as fresh and powerful and shocking as it had been when she'd held him for the first time. She did not know if it had been a precious gift or a cruel punishment to have experienced that love again. Perhaps it was both.

She saw her son for what could have been a lifetime, or what could have been a few seconds. She had no concept of time. And then he was gone, and she floated near her office ceiling, above the two men working on her lifeless body. She could see a button on the floor where they had ripped open her silk shirt. She could see one of her legs splayed at a strange angle, as if she'd landed there after falling from a great height. She could see the top of another young man's head, the white part in his dark hair revealing a tiny strawberry-shaped birthmark, the dampness of his forehead as he sent electrical pulses through her body, and somehow she felt everything he felt: his fear, his focus.

Her next conscious memory had been the following day. She was back in the drab confines of her body and a tall beautiful nurse was saying, 'Hello there, sleeping beauty!' It was like being returned to jail.

Except it wasn't a nurse. This woman was the doctor who had performed her heart surgery: a quadruple bypass. In the years to come Masha often considered how her life would have been different if her heart surgeon had looked like the vast majority of heart surgeons. Her prejudices would have made her dismiss everything he had to say, no matter the accuracy. She would have put him in the same category as the grey-haired men who worked for her. She knew better than all of them. But this woman made Masha snap to attention. She felt strangely proud of her. She too was a woman at the top of her profession in a man's world, and she was *tall*; it somehow mattered that she was tall like Masha. So Masha listened attentively as she talked about reducing her risk factors when it came to diet and exercise and smoking, and she listened when the doctor said, 'Don't let your heart be a casualty of your head.' She wanted Masha to understand that her state of mind was just as important as the state of her body. 'When I was on the wards in my first term of cardiac surgery we had something called the "beard sign",' she said. 'Meaning that if one of our male patients was so miserable he couldn't even be bothered to shave, his chances of recovery were not as good. You must take care of your whole self, Masha.' Masha shaved her legs the very next day for the first time in years. She went to the cardiac rehabilitation exercise program suggested by the doctor, determined to top the class. She *attacked* the challenge of her health and her heart in the same way that she had once attacked challenges at work, and naturally she over-achieved beyond all expectations. 'Good God,' said the surgeon when Masha went to her for her first check-up.

She had never once moped. She re-created herself. She did it for the tall attractive doctor. She did it for the young man in the lake.

'My sister also had a near-death experience,' said Tony. 'A horseriding accident. After her accident, she changed. Her career. Everything about her life. She got right into *gardening.*' He gave Masha an uneasy look. 'I didn't like it.'

'You don't like gardening?' said Masha, teasing a little.

He gave her a half-smile, and she saw a flash of a more attractive man.

'I think I just didn't want my sister to change,' he said. 'It felt like she'd become a stranger. Maybe it felt like she'd experienced something I couldn't understand.'

'People are frightened of what they don't understand,' said Masha. 'I never believed in life after death before that. Now I do. And I live a better life because of it.'

'Right,' said Tony. 'Yeah.'

Again Masha waited.

'Anyway . . .' Tony exhaled and patted his thighs, as if he were done. Masha would get nothing else of interest out of him. It did not matter. The next twenty-four hours would tell her so much more about this man. He would learn things he did not know about himself.

A glorious sense of calm settled upon her as she watched him leave the room, hitching up his pants with one hand. Those last remnants of doubt were gone. Maybe it was because of the thoughts of her son.

The risks were calculated. The risks were justified.

No-one ever ascended a mountain without risk.

chapter twenty-six

Napoleon

It was dawn at Tranquillum House. The fifth day of the retreat.

Napoleon parted the wild horse's mane three times both sides.

He enjoyed the soft swooping moves of tai chi, and this was one of his favourite moves, although he heard his knees crunch like a tyre on gravel as he bent his legs. His physio said it was nothing to worry about: people Napoleon's age crunched. It was just middle-aged cartilage.

Yao led this morning's class in the rose garden, quietly and calmly naming each move for the nine guests who stood in a semicircle around him, all wearing their green Tranquillum House dressing-gowns. People seemed to be wearing the robes more often than not now. On the horizon behind Yao, two hot-air balloons ascended so slowly above the vine-yards it looked like a painting. Napoleon and Heather had done that once, on a romantic weekend away: wine-tasting, antique shops; multiple lives ago, before children.

It was interesting: when you have children you think

your life has changed forever, and it's true, to an extent, but it's nothing compared to how your life changes after you lose a child.

When Masha, an extraordinarily fit and healthy-looking woman, clearly passionate about what she did (his wife mistrusted passion and Zoe was still young enough to find it embarrassing, but Napoleon found it admirable), had spoken on the first day about how this experience would change them 'in ways they could never have imagined', Napoleon, once a believer in self-improvement, had felt an unusual sensation of bitter cynicism. He and his family had already been transformed in ways they could never have imagined. All they needed was peace and quiet, and certainly an improvement in their diets.

While I admire and salute your passion, Masha, we do not seek or desire further transformation.

'The white crane spreads its wings,' said Yao, and everyone moved in graceful unison with him. It was quite beautiful to see.

Napoleon, who stood at the back, as always (he'd learned to stand at the back of every audience once he hit six foot three), watched his wife and daughter lift their arms together. They both bit their bottom lips like chipmunks when they concentrated.

He heard the knees of the guy next to him crunch too, which was pleasing, because Napoleon guessed he was at least a decade younger than him. Even Napoleon could see this guy was notably handsome. He looked at Heather to see if she was maybe checking out the good-looking guy, but her eyes were opaque, like a doll's eyes; as usual, she was somewhere deep and sad within herself.

Heather was broken.

She had always been fragile. Like a piece of delicate china.

Early on in their relationship, he thought she was feisty, funny, a tough chick, athletic and capable, the sort of girl you could take to the football or camping, and he was right, she *was* exactly that type of girl. She was into her sport, she loved camping and she was never high-maintenance or needy. The opposite: she found it hard to admit she needed anyone or anything. When they first started going out, she once broke her toe trying to move a bookshelf on her own, when Napoleon was on his way over and could have lifted that piece of plywood junk with one hand. But no, she had to do it herself.

The fragility beneath that feisty demeanour came out slowly, in odd ways: a peculiar attitude towards certain foods that may have just been a sensitive stomach, but may have been something more; an inability to make eye contact if an argument got too emotional or to say 'I love you' without bracing her chin, as if she were preparing to be punched. He'd thought, romantically, that he could keep her funny, fragile little heart protected, like a tiny bird in the palm of his hand. He'd thought, full of love and testosterone, that he would protect his woman from bad men and heavy furniture and upsetting food.

When he first met her odd, detached parents he under-stood that Heather had grown up starved of love, and when you're starved of something you should receive in abundance, you never quite trust it. Heather's parents weren't abusive, but they were just chilly enough to make you shiver. Napoleon became excessively loving in their presence, as if he could somehow *make* them love his wife the way she should be loved. 'Doesn't Heather look great in this dress?' he'd say. 'Did Heather tell you she came top in her midwifery exams?' Until one day Heather mouthed the words: *Stop it*. So he stopped it, but he still touched her more than usual whenever they visited her family, desperate to convey through his touch: *You are loved, you are loved, you are so, so loved.*

He'd been too young and happy to know that love wasn't enough; too young to know all the ways that life could break you.

Their son's death broke her.

Maybe a son's death broke any mother.

The anniversary was tomorrow. Napoleon sensed its dark, malignant shadow. It was irrational to feel frightened of a day. It was just a sad day, a day they were never going to forget anyway. He reminded himself that this was normal. People felt like this on anniversaries. He'd felt this same impending sense of doom last year. Almost as if it were going to happen again, as if this were a story he'd read before and he knew what lay ahead.

He'd hoped that doing this retreat might make him feel calmer about the approach of the anniversary. It was a marvellous house, so peaceful and, yes, 'tranquil', and the staff seemed kind and caring. Yet Napoleon felt skittish. At dinner last night his right leg had begun to tremble uncontrollably. He'd had to put a hand on his thigh to still it. Was it just the anniversary? Or the silence?

Probably the silence. He didn't like having all this time with only his thoughts, his memories and regrets.

The sun rose higher in the sky as the Tranquillum House guests moved in unison with Yao.

Napoleon caught a glimpse of the profile of the big chunky guy who had tried to smuggle in the contraband. It had seemed like he might be a troublemaker, and Napoleon had kept his teacher's eye on him, but he appeared to have settled down, like one of those students you thought was going to be your nemesis for the whole year but then turned out to be a good kid. There was something about this guy's profile that reminded Napoleon of somebody or something from his past. An actor from some old TV show he used to enjoy as a child, perhaps? It felt like a good memory, there was something pleasant about the feelings he invoked, but Napoleon couldn't put his finger on it.

Somewhere in the distance a whipbird called. He loved the sound of the whipbird: that long, musical crack of the whip that was so much a part of the Australian landscape you had to leave the country to realise how much you missed it, how it settled your soul.

'Repulse the monkey,' said Yao.

Napoleon repulsed the monkey and remembered three years ago: this day, this time. The day before.

It was around this time three years ago that Napoleon was making love to his sleepy wife for the last time in their marriage. (He assumed it was the last time, although he hadn't given up entirely. He would know if she was ever ready. All it would take would be a look. He understood. Sex felt cheap now, tawdry and tacky. But he'd still be up for some cheap, tawdry sex.) She'd fallen asleep again – she used to love her sleep back then – and Napoleon had quietly left the house and headed for the bay. He kept the surf ski on the roof rack of his car throughout the long summer holiday. When he came back, Zach was eating breakfast at the sink, shirtless – he was always shirtless – hair sticking up in tufts. He looked up, grinned at his father, and said, 'No milk,' meaning he'd drunk it all. He said that he might come with Napoleon for a paddle the next day. After that Napoleon worked for a few hours in the garden and cleaned the pool, and Zach went to the beach with his friend Chris, and then Napoleon fell asleep on the couch, and the girls went out – Heather to work, Zoe to a party. When Zach came home, Napoleon did ribs on the barbecue for the two of them, and afterwards they had a swim in the pool and talked about the Australian Open, and Serena's chances, and conspiracy theories (Zach liked conspiracy theories) and how Chris had told Zach he wanted to go into gastroenterology. Zach was gobsmacked by the bizarre specificity of Chris's career plans because Zach didn't even know what he wanted to do *tomorrow*, let alone for the rest of his life, and Napoleon told him that was fine, there was plenty of time to settle on a career, and these days no-one had just one career anyway (he absolutely told him it was fine; he'd double-checked his memory about a thousand times), and then they played table tennis in honour of the tennis, best of three, Napoleon won two, and then they watched a movie, *The Royal Tenenbaums*. They both loved the movie. They laughed a lot. They stayed up too late watching the movie. That's why Napoleon was tired the next morning. That's why he hit the snooze button on his phone.

It was a split-second decision he would regret until the day he died.

Napoleon knew everything about that day because he'd examined his memories over and over, like a homicide detective combing through the evidence. Over and over he saw it: his hand reaching for the phone, his thumb on the snooze button. Over and over he saw the other life, where he made a different decision, the right decision, the decision he normally made, where he didn't hit snooze, where he turned off the alarm and got out of bed.

'Grasp the bird's tail,' said Yao.

It was Heather who found Zach.

The sound of his wife's scream that morning was like no sound he'd ever heard before.

His memory of running up the stairs: it seemed like it took a lifetime, like running through mud, like something from a dream.

Zach had used his new belt to make the noose.

It was a brown leather belt from R.M. Williams that Heather had bought him for Christmas, only a few weeks earlier. It cost ninety-nine dollars, which was ridiculous. 'Expensive belt,' Napoleon had said to Heather when she showed it to him. He remembered fishing the receipt from the plastic bag, raising his eyebrows. She shrugged. Zach had admired it once. She overspent every Christmas.

You broke your mother, mate.

The kid did not leave a note or a text. He did not choose to explain his actions.

'Carry the tiger over the mountain,' said Yao, who was a young man, maybe only ten years older than Zach. Zach could have worked somewhere like this. He could have grown his hair long. He would have looked good with one of those beards they all had these days. He could have lived a fantastic life. So many opportunities. He had the brains, the looks, the facial hair. He was good with his hands. He could have done a trade! He could have done law or medicine or architecture. He could have travelled. He could have done drugs. Why didn't he just do drugs? How wonderful to have a son who made bad choices but not irreversible bad choices; a kid who did drugs, who *dealt* drugs even, who got arrested, who went off the rails. Napoleon could have got him back on the rails.

Zach never even owned his own car. Why would you choose to die before you knew the pleasure, the spectacular pleasure, of owning your own car?

Apparently, that young bloke in front of him drove a *Lamborghini*.

Zach had chosen to turn his back on this beautiful world of whipbirds and Lamborghinis, long-legged girls and hamburgers with the lot. He chose to take a gift from his mother and use it as a murder weapon.

That was a bad choice, son. It was the wrong thing to do. It was a really bad choice.

He heard a sound and realised it was him. Zoe turned to look at him. He tried to smile at her reassuringly. *I'm fine, Zoe, just yelling at your brother.* His eyes blurred.

'Needle at the bottom of the sea,' said Yao.

My boy. My boy. My boy.

He was not broken. He would never stop grieving for Zach, but he had made a decision in the week after the funeral. *He must not break.* It was his job to heal, to be there for his wife and his daughter, to get through this. So he studied the literature, he bought books online and read every word, he downloaded podcasts, he Googled the research. He attended the Tuesday night Survivors of Suicide group as faithfully as his mother once went to Sunday mass, and now he ran the group. (Heather and Zoe thought he talked too much, but that was only in social situations. On Tuesday nights he hardly spoke a word; he listened and he listened on his fold-out chair and did not flinch while a tsunami of pain crashed all around him.) He gave speeches to parent groups and schools and did radio interviews and edited an online newsletter and helped with fundraising.

'It's his new hobby.' He'd overheard Heather say that on the phone one night to someone, he never found out to whom because he never mentioned it, but he never forgot it, or the bitter tone; it sounded close to hatred. It hurt because it was both a malicious lie and the shameful truth.

He could find hatred in his heart for her, too, if he went looking for it. The secret of a happy marriage was not to go looking for it.

He saw his wife's thin arms curved up towards the sun to 'master its life force' and his heart filled with painful tenderness for her. She could not heal and she refused to even try. She never went to the support group except for that one time. She did not want to hear from other parents who had lost sons because she believed Zach was superior to their stupid sons. Napoleon thought Zach was superior to their stupid sons too, but he still found solace in giving back to this community he had never asked to join.

'The white crane spreads its wings.'

Sometimes there are no signs.

That's what he told the newly grieving parents at the Tuesday night group. He told them there was research to suggest that teenage suicide was often the consequence of an impulsive decision. Many had suicidal thoughts for only eight hours before their attempts. Some idiotic kids put as little as *five minutes' thought* into their catastrophic choice.

He did not tell them other things he had learned from his research, such as that suicide survivors often reported that their first thought after they'd swallowed the pills, after they'd jumped, after they'd cut, was a version of: *My God, what have I done?!* He did not tell them that many survivors of suicide are transformed by their experience and go on to live happy lives, sometimes with little psychiatric intervention. He didn't tell them that if the decision to take their lives was in some way thwarted, if the means was removed, their suicidal thoughts often disappeared with time and never returned. He didn't tell them how Britain's national suicide rate dropped by a third when coal gas was phased out, because once people no longer had the option to impulsively stick their head in the oven, there was time for their dark and dreadful impulses to pass. He didn't think it was helpful for parents to know just how much bad luck was involved in the loss of their children; that perhaps all they'd needed was a well-timed interruption, a phone call, a distraction.

But Napoleon knew it, because that was Zach. *Impulsive.* The absolute definition of impulsive. He never thought things through. He never thought of the consequences of his actions. He lived in the moment, as you were meant to do. He practised mindfulness. No yesterday. No tomorrow. Just now. *I feel this now, so I will do this now.*

If you chase the waves along the beach your new runners will get wet and they will stay wet for the rest of the day. If you run about outside when the pollen count is high (even though we told you to stay indoors), you will have an asthma attack. If you give up your life, you won't get it back, kid, it's gone.

'Zach, you've got to think!' Napoleon used to yell at him.

That's why Napoleon knew without a doubt that if he'd got up at the time he'd originally planned, if he hadn't pressed the snooze button on his alarm that morning, if he'd knocked on Zach's door and said, 'Come paddling with me,' then right now he'd have a wife who wasn't broken and a daughter who still sang in the shower and a son about to celebrate his twenty-first birthday.

Napoleon was meant to be the one who knew and understood boys. He had a drawer full of cards and letters from the boys he'd taught over the years, and their parents, all telling him how very special he was, how much he'd contributed to their lives, that they would never forget him, that he'd pulled them back from some terrible brink, a wrong path, that they'd be eternally grateful to their wonderful teacher, Mr Marconi.

Yet he'd somehow failed his own boy. The only boy in the world who mattered.

For a year he'd searched for answers. He'd talked to every friend, every teammate, every teacher, every coach. None of them had answers. There was nothing more to know.

'Fan through the back,' said Yao.

Napoleon fanned through the back and felt his muscles stretch and the sun warm on his face as he tasted the sea from the tears that ran heedlessly down his face.

But he wasn't broken.

chapter twenty-seven

Zoe

Zoe saw the tears slide down her father's face and wondered if he knew he was crying. Her dad cried a lot without seeming to realise he was doing it, like a scratch he didn't know was bleeding, as if his body excreted grief without his knowledge.

'Touch the sky,' said Yao.

Zoe followed the graceful arc of Yao's arms and turned now in her mother's direction, and saw the deep crevices in her mother's face and heard once more the sound of her mother's scream that awful morning. Like the scream of an animal caught in a trap. A scream that tore straight through Zoe's life like a razor blade.

Tomorrow it would be three years. Would it ever get any easier for her parents? Because it sure didn't look like it was getting any easier. There was no use hoping that once they got through this next anniversary, things would get better, because she'd thought that the last two anniversaries. She knew that when they went back home it would all be just the same.

It felt like her parents were sick with a terrible, incurable disease that ravaged their bodies. It felt like they'd been assaulted. As if someone had come after them with a baseball bat. She had not realised that grief was so physical. Before Zach died, she thought grief happened in your head. She didn't know that your whole body ached with it, that it screwed up your digestive system, your menstrual cycle, your sleep patterns, your skin. You wouldn't wish it on your worst enemy.

Sometimes it felt like Zoe was just *waiting out* her life now, enduring it, ticking off events and days and months and years, as if she just had to get herself through something unspecified and then things would be better, except she never got through it and it never got better and she would never forgive him. His death was the ultimate 'fuck you'.

'At least you weren't close,' said her friend Cara in her head.

At least we weren't close. At least we weren't close. At least we weren't close.

chapter twenty-eight

Heather

Heather didn't see Napoleon's tears as they did tai chi.

She was remembering something that had happened last week, after a long, exhausting night shift when she'd helped to deliver two baby boys.

It was impossible not to think of Zach every time she held another newborn baby boy and stared into those sad wise eyes. All babies had that same wise look, as if they'd just come from another realm where they'd learned some beautiful truth they couldn't share. Every day brought an endless stream of new life.

Heather had gone to get her coffee from the hospital cafe after her shift and run into a familiar face from the past. There was no time to turn away and pretend she hadn't seen. She recognised her instantly. One of the soccer mums. Before Zach gave it up. Lisa Somebody. A friendly, bubbly lady. It had been years. Lisa Somebody's face lit up when she saw Heather. *Oh, I know you!* And then, as so often happened, a moment later her face fell, as she remembered what she'd heard on the grapevine. You could virtually read her thoughts: *Oh fuck, she's that mother, but no time to look away!*

Some people crossed the street to get away from her. She'd seen them do it. Some people recoiled. They literally recoiled, as if what had happened to Heather's family was vile and shameful. This woman was one of the brave ones. She didn't duck or hide or pretend.

'I was so sorry to hear about Zach,' she said. She even said his name without lowering her voice.

'Thank you,' said Heather, longing for coffee. She looked at the boy standing next to her on crutches. 'This must be . . . Justin?' The name came to her on a flood of memories of shivering Saturday mornings on the soccer field, and suddenly, without warning, the anger exploded in her chest, and this kid, this living, stupid kid, was her target.

'I remember you,' she hissed at him. 'You were the kid who never passed to Zach!'

He stared at her with blank, slack-jawed horror.

'You never passed to Zach! Why didn't you pass?' Heather turned to Lisa. 'You should have made him pass!' Her voice rose beyond the bounds of what was acceptable in a public place.

Most people would have made their excuses and scurried away. Some people might have retaliated. *Your dead son doesn't give you the right to be rude.* But this Lisa, this woman Heather barely knew, a woman who (Heather now remembered) had once taken Zoe home to her place and fed her lunch after Zach had an asthma attack on the field, just looked at Heather steadily and sadly and said, 'You're right, Heather, I should have made him pass.'

And then Justin, who had been *nine years old* when he played with Zach, had spoken up in his deep young man's voice and said, 'Zach was a great striker, Mrs Marconi.

I should have passed to him more. I used to be really bad at passing the ball.'

The generosity, the kindness, the maturity that young man showed that day. Heather had looked at his face – the freckles on his nose, the tiny black whiskers around his young boy's mouth – and seen the grotesque face of her son on the last day of his life.

'I'm so sorry,' she'd said, weak and trembling with regret, and she'd left without making further eye contact with either of them, without picking up her coffee. Yet again she'd turned the anger that should have been directed only at herself on someone else.

'Snake creeps through the grass,' said Yao.

She saw herself sitting alone in Zach's room, her hand opening the drawer of his bedside cabinet. Heather was the snake that crept through the grass.

chapter twenty-nine

Frances

It was nearly 3 pm as Frances made her way, with some eager-ness, downstairs to the meditation studio for the breaking of the silence. She hadn't eaten anything solid since the night before and she was very hungry. When the breakfast and midday bells had rung today, Frances had gone to the dining room to find a row of smoothies set out on the sideboard, labelled by name. Frances had found hers, and tried to drink it slowly and mindfully, but it was gone before she knew it, and her stomach had begun to rumble, loudly and embarrassingly.

She was not really starving, but she was yearning; not so much for food, but for the ritual of food. Maybe if she'd been at home, running around doing errands, it would be easy to skip a few meals (not that she ever did, she'd always had difficulty comprehending the phrase 'I forgot to eat lunch'), but here, especially during the silence, meals were crucial to break up the day.

She'd tried to distract herself by reading in the hammock but her book had taken an outlandish turn which she couldn't handle on an empty stomach.

Her spirits lifted when she walked into the studio. The lights had been turned off and the room was illuminated by clusters of flickering candles. It was cool down here, some sort of essential oil burner was pumping out a heady mist, and spine-tingling music was being piped through invisible speakers.

Frances always appreciated a little effort when it came to ambience. She noted low camp-like beds had been set out around the sides of the room, with blankets and pillows. Headphones and eye masks were laid out on the pillows, with water bottles alongside, like business-class seats thoughtfully arranged for a long-haul flight.

Masha, Yao and Delilah sat cross-legged in the middle of the room, along with the three members of the Marconi family and the tall, dark and handsome man.

'Welcome, please join the circle,' Masha said as more people filed into the room behind Frances.

Masha wore a long, white, sleeveless satin and lace dress somewhere between a wedding dress and a nightgown. She'd made up her eyes so that they were even more prominent. Yao and Delilah, extremely attractive young people, looked almost ordinary and washed-out next to this celestial being.

Within a few moments, everyone was there. Frances was seated with Heather on one side, and young Ben on the other. She wondered how Ben was feeling. Probably missing his car. She studied his tanned, hairy leg in the candlelight – not in a sexual way, thank the Lord, just in a kind of fascinated way, because all this silent mindful meditating over the last few days made everything fascinating. Each individual hair on Ben's leg was like a *tiny tree* in a *dear little forest* –

Ben cleared his throat and shifted his leg. Frances straightened and met the eyes of the tall, dark and handsome man seated on the opposite side of the circle. He sat straight-backed and solemn, yet somehow in a manner that conveyed he wasn't taking any of this too seriously. She automatically went to look away but he held her gaze and winked. Frances winked back and he looked startled. She was a terrible winker; she found it hard to close only one eye and had been told that her attempt looked like an extraordinary facial spasm.

'And so we come to the end of our noble silence,' said Masha. She grinned and punched the air. 'We did it!'

Nobody said a word, but there was a gentle murmur of sound: exhalations, the shifting of bodies and half-chuckles of acknowledgement.

'I'd like us to now slowly reintroduce conversation and eye contact,' said Masha. 'We shall each take a turn to introduce ourselves and speak for just a few moments about whatever comes to mind: perhaps why you chose to come to Tranquillum House, what you're enjoying most about your experience so far and what you've found most challenging. Are you dying for a cappuccino or glass of sauvignon blanc? I get it! Share your pain with the group! Are you missing a loved one? Tell us about that! Or maybe you'd just prefer to deliver straight-up facts: your age, your occupation, your hobbies, your star sign.'

Masha smiled her extraordinary smile and everyone smiled back.

'Or recite a line of poetry, if you like,' she continued. 'It doesn't matter what you say. Simply enjoy the experience of speaking, connecting, and making eye contact with your fellow guests.'

People cleared their throats, adjusted their posture and stroked their hair in preparation for public speaking.

'While we get to know each other, Yao and Delilah will distribute your afternoon smoothies,' said Masha.

Such was Masha's charismatic charm that Frances hadn't even noticed Yao and Delilah stand up. Now they began to glide about the room distributing tall glasses. This afternoon's smoothies were all the same emerald-green colour. *Spinach?* thought Frances with alarm, but when she took hers and had a sip she tasted apple, honeydew melon and pear, with undertones of moss and bark. It brought to mind a walk by a babbling brook in a dappled green forest. She tossed it back like tequila.

'Why don't you go first, Frances?' said Masha.

'Oh. Okay. Well, I'm Frances. Hi.' She put down her empty glass, dipped her head and licked her teeth for lipstick. She realised she was automatically adopting her professional public-speaking persona: warm, humble, gracious, but a little stand-offish in order to repel any huggers in the signing line.

'I came to Tranquillum House because I was kind of in a bad way: my health, my personal life, my career.' She allowed her gaze to travel the circle. It felt strangely intimate, looking everyone in the eye again. 'I write romance books for a living and my last one got rejected. I also got badly burned in an internet romance scam. So.'

Why was she telling them all about the scam? Blab, blab, blab.

Tony looked steadily back at her. He had more stubble than before, and his face seemed more defined. Men always lost weight so easily, the fuckers. She faltered a little. Was he sneering again? Or was he just . . . looking at her?

'So the first five days have been good!' All at once she was desperate to talk. She didn't care if she gave them 'too much information'. The words spilled from her mouth. It was like that greedy feeling of sitting down to an excellent meal when you were very hungry and after the first mouthful you were suddenly shovelling food into your mouth like a machine.

'I enjoyed the silence more than I thought I would, it did seem to calm my thoughts. In addition to being rejected I was very upset about this really very nasty review, I was thinking about it obsessively in the beginning, but I'm not even thinking about it at all now, so that's good, and, well, I miss coffee and champagne and the internet and . . .' *Shut up, Frances.* 'And, you know, all the normal luxuries of normal life.'

She sat back, her face warm.

'I'll go next,' said the tall, dark and handsome man. 'I'm Lars. I'm a health-retreat junkie. I indulge and atone, indulge and atone. It works for me.'

Frances looked at his chiselled cheekbones and golden-toned skin. *It certainly does work for you, lovely Lars.*

'I'm a family lawyer, so I need to drink a lot of wine after work.' He paused as if to allow time for his audience to laugh, but no-one did.

'I always do a retreat in January because February is my busiest time of year. The phone starts ringing the day the new school year starts. You know, Mum and Dad realise they can't spend another summer together.'

'Oh dear,' said Napoleon sombrely.

'As for Tranquillum House, I love the food, love the location and I'm doing fine. I don't miss anything much except for my Netflix account.' He lifted his smoothie glass as if it were a cocktail and toasted the room.

Flustered Glasses lady spoke up next, although she was noticeably less flustered than she had been the first day.

'I'm Carmel. I'm here to lose weight. Obviously.'

Frances sighed. What did she mean, *obviously*? Carmel was thinner than her.

'I love everything about this place,' said Carmel. '*Everything.*' She looked at Masha with a degree of intensity that was unsettling. She lifted her smoothie glass and drank deeply.

Jessica spoke up next, eagerly, as if she couldn't wait for her turn. 'So, my name is Jessica.'

She sat cross-legged, her hands placed on her knees like a kid in a school photo, and Frances could see the cute little girl she had been not all that long ago, before she succumbed to the temptation of all those cosmetic procedures.

'We came here because we've been having really very serious troubles with our marriage.'

'We don't need to tell everyone that,' muttered Ben into his chest.

'No but, babe, you know what? You were right when you said I'm too obsessed with appearances.' She turned to look at him intently. 'You were *right*, babe!' Her voice skidded up to an uncomfortably high pitch.

'Yeah, but . . . Okay, Jesus.' Ben subsided. Frances could see the back of his neck turning red.

'We were heading for a *divorce*,' continued Jessica, with touching earnestness, as if the word 'divorce' would be shocking to all.

'I can give you my card,' said Lars.

Jessica ignored him. 'This noble silence has been really good for me, really great, really *clarifying*.' She turned to Masha. 'It's, like, I had so much noise in my head before I came here. I was, like, obsessed with social media, I admit it. I just had this constant chitchat going on.' She opened and closed her hand next to her ear to demonstrate. 'And now I see everything more clearly. It all started with the money. We won the lottery, you see, and everything changed and it really fucked us up.'

'You won the lottery?' said Carmel. 'I've never known anybody who won the lottery.'

'We were actually going to keep that kind of . . . shush shush,' said Jessica. She pressed her fingertip to her lips. 'But we changed our mind.'

'Did we?' said Ben.

'How much did you win?' asked Lars, and then he immediately held up his palm. 'Inappropriate! Don't answer that! None of my business.'

'How did you find out you'd won?' asked Frances. 'Tell us the story.' She wanted the story of the moment their lives changed forever.

'I'm so glad to hear that the silence has given you clarity, Jessica,' Masha interrupted before the conversation could take a turn towards this exit. She had a remarkable ability to ignore what didn't interest her. 'Who else?'

Ben spoke up. 'Yeah. I'm Ben. Jessica's husband. Jessica covered why we're here. I'm fine. The silence has been fine. The food is better than I expected. I'm not sure what we're achieving, but it's all good. I guess I miss my new car.'

'What sort of car, mate?' asked Tony.

'Lamborghini,' said Ben, tender-eyed, as if he'd been asked the name of his newborn son.

Tony smiled. It was the first time Frances had seen him smile and it was the most unexpected, apple-cheeked smile. It entirely transformed his face. It was like a baby's smile. His eyes disappeared into a mass of wrinkles. 'No wonder you miss it,' he said.

'If I won the lottery I always thought I'd get a Bugatti,' mused Lars.

Ben shook his head. 'Overrated.'

'*Overrated* he says! The most stunning car in the world is *overrated*!'

'If I ever won the lottery I'd get a cute little red Ferrari,' offered Zoe.

'Yeah, well the Ferrari is —'

Masha cut off the sports car conversation. 'Who haven't we heard from yet? Tony?'

'You all know me as the desperado who tried to bring in the contraband,' said Tony. He smiled again. 'Here for weight loss. I miss beer, pizza, ribs with plum sauce, wedges with sour cream, family-sized chocolate bars — you get the picture.' His initial enthusiasm waned and he lowered his eyes, clearly keen for everyone to stop looking at him.

'Thank you,' he said formally, to the floor.

Frances didn't believe him. There was more to his decision to come here than just weight loss.

Napoleon raised his hand.

'Go ahead, Napoleon,' said Masha.

He lifted his chin and recited. *'It matters not how strait the gate, How charged with punishments the scroll, I am the master of my fate, I am the captain of my soul.'* His eyes gleamed in the shadows from the candlelight. 'That's, ah, from Nelson Mandela's favourite poem, "Invictus".' He looked uncertain for a moment. 'You said we could recite poetry.'

'Absolutely I did,' said Masha warmly. 'I love the sentiment.'

'Yes, well, it just came into my head. I'm a high-school teacher. The kids like to hear that they are masters of their own fates, although . . .' He laughed a strange sort of a laugh. Heather, who sat next to him, placed a gentle hand over his jiggling kneecap. He didn't seem to notice it. 'Tomorrow is the third anniversary of our son's death. That's why we're here. He took his own life, so that's how *my* kid chose to be master of his own fate.'

The room became very still, as if, for just a moment, they all held their breath. The tiny gold flames on the candles trembled.

Frances compressed her lips so no words would escape. She felt as if all feelings were too big and unwieldy for her body, as if she might burst into tears or burst out laughing, as if she might say something overly sentimental or intimate. It was like she'd drunk too much in an inappropriate setting, a business meeting with publishing executives.

'I'm so sorry for your loss, Napoleon,' said Masha and she reached out her hand as if she wanted to touch Napoleon, but he was too far away. 'So very sorry.'

'Why thank you, Masha,' said Napoleon chattily.

If Frances didn't know better she would have thought *he* was drunk. Had he got stuck into Zoe's smuggled wine? Was he having a nervous breakdown? Or was this just a natural response to the breaking of the silence?

Zoe looked at her father, her forehead creased like that of an elderly woman, and Frances tried to imagine the missing boy who should have been sitting next to her. *Oh, Zoe,* thought Frances. She had suspected it might have been suicide when Zoe didn't say how he died. Her friend Lily, who used to write beautiful historical romances, had lost her husband ten years ago and all she had told people was that 'Neil died unexpectedly' and everyone understood what that meant. Lily hadn't written since.

'Who else would like –'

But Napoleon interrupted Masha. 'Got it!' he cried. 'I know who you are!' he said to Tony. 'It's been driving me mad. Heather, darling, do you see who it is?' Napoleon turned to his wife.

Heather looked up from the empty smoothie glass she'd been studying. 'No.'

'I know who he is,' said Lars proudly. 'I worked it out on the very first day.'

Frances looked at Tony, who was looking awkwardly down at his glass with an expression of discomfort, but not confusion, as if he knew what they were all talking about. Who *was* he? A *famous* serial killer?

'Heather!' cried Napoleon. 'You know him! I promise you know him!'

'From . . . school? Work?' Heather shook her head. 'I don't . . .' .

'I'll give you a clue.' Napoleon chanted, '*We are the Navy Blues!*'

Heather studied Tony. Her face cleared. 'Smiley Hogburn!'

Napoleon pointed at Heather as if she'd correctly guessed his charade. 'Exactly! It's Smiley Hogburn!' Then he seemed to doubt himself. 'Aren't you?'

Tony looked strained. 'Years ago I was,' he said. 'Thirty kilos ago.'

'But Smiley Hogburn played for Carlton,' said Jessica. '*I'm* a Carlton supporter! Aren't you, like, a total legend?' She said it like there must have been a mix-up.

'It was probably before you were born,' said Tony.

'Carlton is a *football* team, right?' whispered Frances to Ben. She was very ignorant of anything to do with sport; a friend once told her it was like she'd lived her whole life in a bunker.

'Yep,' said Ben. 'Aussie Rules.'

'That's the jumping one?'

Ben chortled. 'They do jump, yeah.'

Smiley Hogburn, thought Frances. There *was* something blurrily familiar about that name. She felt her perception of Tony shift. He was a man who used to be someone, like Frances used to be someone. They had that in common. Although Frances's career was slowly fading away, whereas presumably Tony's had ended officially, probably with an injury of some sort – all that jumping! – and he was no longer leaping about the football field.

'I knew you were Smiley Hogburn!' said Lars again. He seemed to be looking for some sort of recognition that he wasn't getting. 'I'm not normally good with faces but I worked out who you were straight away.'

'Did you have to finish up playing because of a sporting injury?' asked Frances. She felt that was quite a knowledgeable, empathetic question to ask a sportsperson. It was probably something to do with *ligaments*.

Tony looked mildly amused. 'I had multiple injuries.'

'Oh,' said Frances. 'I'm sorry to hear that.'

'Two knee reconstructions, hip replacement . . .' Tony seemed to be doing a sad assessment of his body. He sighed. 'Chronic ankle issues.'

'Were you called Smiley Hogburn because you *did* smile a lot, or because you *didn't*?' asked Zoe.

'Because I did smile a lot,' said Tony, unsmilingly. 'I was kind of a simple guy back then. Happy-go-lucky.'

'*Were* you?' said Frances, unable to hide her surprise.

'I was,' said Tony. He smiled at her. He seemed to find her funny.

'Weren't you the one with the smiley face tattoos on your butt?' said Lars.

'I've seen them!' cried Frances before she could help herself.

'Have you now?' said Lars suggestively.

'*Frances*,' said Tony, and he put a finger to his lips as if they had something to hide. Wait! Was he flirting with her?

'Oh no, not in *that* way,' said Frances. She looked nervously at Masha. 'I saw them accidentally.'

'My brother used to have your poster in his bedroom!'

It was Delilah, breaking ranks and speaking like a human being. 'The one where you're jumping six feet in the air and the other player is pulling down your shorts and you can see your tattoos! Hilarious!'

'Fancy that. We have a famous athlete in our midst.' There was an edge to Masha's voice. Maybe she wanted to be the only athlete in their midst.

'Former athlete,' Tony corrected her. 'It was a long time ago.'

'So . . . who haven't we heard from yet?' said Masha, clearly keen to change the subject.

'Post-sport depression,' said Napoleon. 'Is that what you've got? I've read about it. It affects a lot of elite sports-people. You've got to focus on your mental health, Tony . . . Smiley . . . Tony – I hope you don't mind if I call you Smiley – you really do, because depression is an *insidious* –'

'Who's next?' interrupted Masha.

'I'll go next,' said Zoe. 'I'm Zoe.'

She seemed to gather her thoughts. Or was she nervous? *Oh, sweetheart.*

'As Dad already said, we decided to come to Tranquillum House because we can't stand to be at home in January, because that's where my brother hung himself.'

Masha made a strange startled sound and pressed her hand to her mouth. It was the first time Frances had observed Masha show any sign of weakness. Even when she spoke about her father, for whom she clearly grieved, she'd still been controlled.

Frances watched Masha swallow convulsively for a few seconds, as if she were choking, but then she regained her composure and carried on listening to Zoe, although her eyes looked a little watery, as if she really had just choked on something.

Zoe looked at the ceiling. The circle of people seemed to tilt towards her with the weight of their useless sympathy.

'Oh wait, Dad probably didn't say that Zach hung himself, but if you were wondering, like, what was his *method of choice*, that was it! It's popular.'

She smiled and rocked in tiny circles. The silver studs along her ears gleamed.

'One of his friends said that was so "brave" of Zach – to choose that way to kill himself. Instead of pills. Like he'd been bungee jumping. God!' She blew out a puff of air and her hair lifted from her forehead.

'*Anyway*, once we became, like, total experts on suicide, we stopped telling people how he did it. Because of suicide contagion. Suicide is really contagious. My parents were terrified I'd catch it too. Like chicken pox. Ha ha. I never caught it though.'

'Zoe?' said Napoleon. 'Darling, maybe that's enough.'

'We weren't close,' said Zoe to the group. She looked at her hands and said it again. 'Like, sometimes people think because we were twins we were really close, but we went to different schools. We had different interests. Different *values*.'

'Zoe,' said her mother. 'Maybe now is not the –'

'He got up really early that morning.' Zoe ignored her mother. She fiddled with one of the many earrings in her earlobe. Her empty smoothie glass lay on its side against her thigh. 'He hardly ever got up early. He took out the recycling bin, because it was his turn, and then he went back upstairs and killed himself.' She sighed, as if she were bored. 'We took it in turns to take out the bins. I don't know if he was making some kind of point by doing that. It really pissed me off. Like, thanks so much for that, Zach, good on you, that makes up for you killing yourself.'

'Zoe?' said Heather sharply.

Zoe turned in her mother's direction, but very slowly, as if she had a stiff back. 'What?'

Heather took the smoothie glass and placed it upright on the floor, out of the way. She leaned towards her daughter and brushed a lock of hair out of Zoe's eyes.

'Something is not quite . . .' Heather's gaze travelled around the circle of people. 'Not quite right.'

She turned to Masha. She said, 'Have you been medicating us?'

chapter thirty

Masha

Focus. Only. On your breathing. Focus. Only. On your breathing.
Masha was fine, perfectly fine, she was under control. For a moment there, when Zoe said what she said, Masha had very nearly lost her focus completely; time slipped. But now she was back, her breathing steady, she was in control.

This information about the brother should have come out in her one-on-one counselling sessions with the Marconi family. They had all freely said they were here for the anniversary of his death, but none had mentioned he took his own life. Masha should have seen through their evasive behaviour. It was not like her to miss this. She was extremely perceptive. They had deliberately misled her and as a result she had been unprepared. She had felt *blindsided*.

And now this question from Heather: 'Have you been medicating us?'

Before Heather spoke, Masha had been observing the group, watching their mannerisms become freer, their pupils dilate and tongues loosen. They were clearly losing their inhibitions, speaking fluidly, with refreshing honesty.

Some, like Napoleon, fidgeted, whereas others, like Frances, were very still. Some were flushed, others pale.

Right now, Heather was both: pasty white with hectic spots of colour on her cheeks.

'Have you?' she demanded. 'Have you been medicating us?'

'In a manner of speaking,' said Masha calmly.

Heather's question was not ideal and not anticipated, although perhaps it should have been, because Heather was a midwife, the only one of the guests, as far as Masha knew, with any medical expertise. But Masha would handle this.

'What do you mean, "in a manner of speaking"?'

Masha did not like Heather's tone. Snappy. Disrespectful.

'Well, *medicating* implies . . .' Masha searched for the right words. 'A dulling of the senses. What we're doing here is *heightening* the senses.'

'You need to tell us exactly what you've been giving us! Right now!' Heather moved up onto her knees, as if she were ready to leap to her feet. Masha was reminded of a ferocious little dog. One she'd quite like to kick.

'Hang on, what's going on here?' said Napoleon to Heather.

Masha flashed a look at Yao and Delilah: *Be ready if needed*. They gave her barely perceptible nods, both gripping the discreet medical pouches they had clipped around their waists.

This was not how it was supposed to go.

chapter thirty-one

Lars

In his long history of health resorts Lars had experienced some bizarre and unusual practices, but this was a first. It was ironic because one of the side benefits of coming here was to cut *down* on his recreational drug use.

'It's called micro-dosing and it's perfectly safe,' said their esteemed leader, who, as always, sat cross-legged and straight-backed, her incredible long white legs so entwined that sometimes Lars got distracted trying to work out where each leg started and ended.

'There are multiple benefits: higher levels of creativity, increased focus, heightened spiritual awareness, improved relationships – I could go on and on. Basically, you function just a little better than a normal person. The doses are about a tenth of a normal dose of LSD.'

'Wait . . . what?' asked Frances. She laughed uncertainly, as if she'd heard a joke she didn't quite get. Lars liked her already. 'Sorry. You're not saying that *we've* been taking *LSD*?'

Lars saw most of his fellow guests were staring at Masha with dull incomprehension. This was surely too conservative a crowd to cope with a revelation about drugs, even taking into account the popularity of cocaine in the suburbs. Lars himself dabbled with coke, ecstasy and pot, but never LSD.

'As I said, it's called micro-dosing,' said Masha.

'It's called spiking our smoothies with a hallucinogenic drug,' snapped Heather.

Heather. Before today, Lars would never have picked Heather as her name. It was far too soft a name for this skinny, tanned woman with quadriceps that looked like machine parts and a permanent pained squint as if she were peering straight into the sun. Every time Lars had looked at her during the silence, he'd imagined pressing his thumbs to the point between her eyebrows and saying, 'Chill.' Now he felt bad about feeling aggravated, because she'd lost her son. The woman was allowed to frown.

'It's called outrageous,' continued Heather. She wasn't squinting now. Her eyes were ablaze with fury.

'I don't quite understand,' said her adorably addled husband, a long celery stick of a man, so dorky he was cool. His name was *Napoleon*, which just added to his marvellousness.

Lars didn't think he was high. He'd been feeling great, but he generally did feel good on any sort of cleanse. Perhaps the doses were too small to affect him, or he'd built up a tolerance. He surreptitiously ran a finger around the edge of his smoothie glass and licked it. He thought about how, on the first day, he'd drunk his smoothie and said to Delilah, 'This is so good. What's *in* this stuff?' and Delilah had said, 'We'll give you the recipes when you leave.' Lars had been imagining the recipes would specify the number of teaspoons of chia, not how many milligrams of LSD.

'But . . . but . . . we're here to detoxify!' said Frances to Masha. 'You're saying we've cut out caffeine and replaced it with *acid*?'

Tony, aka Smiley Hogburn, said, 'I can't believe you confiscated my beer and now you've given me drugs. I've never taken drugs!'

'You don't think alcohol is a drug?' said Masha. 'LSD has been ranked one-tenth as harmful as alcohol! What do you think of that?'

'I guess LSD has no calories,' said Carmel. It was easy to remember her name because Lars had a friend called Carmel who was also boringly convinced she was fat. Carmel's glasses sat crookedly on her face but she didn't seem aware of it. She had been mooching about for the last five days with that recently-kicked-in-the-face look Lars knew so well from his clients. The one that ignited a deep burn of rage in his belly; the rage that had fuelled his entire career. He'd put a million bucks on her husband having left her for a trophy wife.

'Does LSD also speed up the metabolism?' Carmel asked hopefully. 'I really feel like my metabolism might be speeding up. I've never had drugs either, but I'm completely fine with this. I have total respect for you and your methods, Masha.'

Getting thin won't help you feel better, honey. Take the fuckwit to the cleaners. Lars would talk to her later. See who represented her.

'I can't believe you've been giving my underage daughter LSD,' said Heather.

'I'm not underage, Mum,' said Zoe. 'I'm feeling pretty good right now; better than I've felt in a while. They're only micro-doses. It's all good.'

'It's not all good!' her mother sighed. 'For Christ's sake.'

Napoleon spoke earnestly. 'Masha, listen, I had a terrible experience with drugs when I was a teenager. It was a "bad trip", as they say. One of the worst experiences of my life and I always told my kids that's when I swore off drugs forever. So I appreciate what you're saying, but I'm not taking anything.'

'My God, Napoleon, you've already *taken* it!' said Heather through gritted teeth. 'Are you not listening?'

'This is bullshit,' said the lottery-winner kid. What was his name again? A good, wholesome, straight-boy name. What was it? The kid trembled with so much suppressed rage it looked like he was having a seizure and he spoke through clenched teeth. '*I did not choose this.*'

His young wife spoke up. 'Ben is, like, full-on anti-drugs.'

Ben, thought Lars. That was it. Ben and his cosmetically enhanced wife was . . . *Jessica*. Ben and Jessica. No chance those two had a pre-nup, and now there was significant money at stake if the marriage fell apart. They'd be the type to lose it all to their lawyers.

'He doesn't even like taking aspirin,' said Jessica. 'His sister is an addict. A proper addict. This is not good.' She put her hand on her husband's shoulder. 'I don't see how this is going to help our marriage. I'm not feeling very happy about this either. Not happy at all.'

Her poor little Barbie doll face did look very unhappy. Lars felt something unfurl in his chest: a deep, rich welling of sympathy for poor Jessica. Poor, poor little plastic Jessica. Confused little rich girl. All that money and no idea how to spend it, except on cosmetic procedures that were doing her no favours.

'I understand your fear,' said Masha. 'You've been brainwashed because of the misinformation spread by governments.'

'I have not been *brainwashed*,' said Ben. 'I have *seen* it for myself.'

'Yes, but those are street drugs, Ben,' said Masha. 'The problem with street drugs is you can't control the content or dosage.'

'I cannot believe this.' Ben got to his feet.

'LSD has actually been used very successfully to treat drug addiction,' said Masha. 'Your sister could benefit from it. In the right setting.'

Ben smacked his hands to his face. 'Unbelievable.'

Masha said, 'Do you know, there was a great man. His name was *Steve Jobs*.'

Lars, who had been expecting her to say the Dalai Lama, snickered.

'I always admired him greatly,' said Masha.

'Not sure why you took all our iPhones away then,' muttered Tony.

'Do you know what Steve Jobs said? He said that taking LSD was one of the most important, profound experiences of his life.'

'Oh, well then,' said Lars, greatly amused. 'If Steve Jobs said we should all take LSD, then we really should!'

Masha shook her head sadly at them, as if they were misguided but lovable children. 'The side effects of psyche-delic drugs are *minimal*. Respected researchers at Ivy League universities are doing clinical trials as we speak! The results have been excellent! Micro-dosing has allowed you to focus on your meditation and yoga practices over the last week, as well as alleviating the withdrawal symptoms you would otherwise have suffered by cutting out far more dangerous substances, like alcohol and sugar.'

'Yes, but, Masha . . .' said Heather. She sounded calmer than before. She splayed her fingers on both hands as if she were waiting for a fresh manicure to dry. 'The effects I'm feeling right now, the effects I suspect we are now all begin-ning to feel, that has to be more than just a micro-dose.'

Masha smiled at Heather, as if she couldn't be happier with her. 'Oh, Heather,' she said. 'You are a smart lady.'

'That last smoothie was different,' said Heather. 'Wasn't it?'

'You are right, Heather,' said Masha. 'I was about to explain this but you keep racing me to the punch!' She corrected the phrase almost instantly. '*Beating* me to the punch!' Her strong white teeth gleamed in the candlelight. It was hard to tell if it was a smile or a grimace.

'What's happening now is the next step in a rigorously planned and executed new protocol.' She looked around the room, giving everyone tiny nods, as if dispensing affirmative answers to their unspoken questions. *Yes, yes, yes*, she seemed to be saying. 'You are about to embark on a *truly* transformative experience. We've never done this before at Tranquillum House and we're all so excited about it. You are the first nine guests to have this extraordinary opportunity.'

A glorious sense of well-being spread like honey throughout Lars's body.

'For most of you, your last smoothie contains both a dosage of LSD and a liquid form of psilocybin, a naturally occurring substance found in certain mushrooms.'

'*Magic mushrooms*,' said Tony with disgust.

'Oh my goodness,' said Frances. 'It's like I'm back doing my arts degree again.'

Lars was so happy he'd chosen Tranquillum House for this cleanse. What a truly wonderful place. How innovative and cutting edge.

'But that's what caused my bad experience,' said Napoleon. 'My bad trip. It was a magic mushroom.'

'We won't let that happen, Napoleon,' said Masha. 'We are trained medical professionals and we're here to help and guide you. The drugs you have taken have been tested to ensure they are in their purest form.'

Lovely, top-quality, pure drugs, thought Lars dreamily.

'It's called guided psychedelic therapy,' said Masha. 'As your ego dissolves you will access a higher level of consciousness. A curtain will be drawn back and you will see the world in a way you've never seen it before.'

Lars had a friend who had travelled for days in the Amazon to take part in an Ayahuasca ceremony, where he'd vomited repeatedly and been eaten alive by bugs in his search for enlightenment. This was delightfully civilised in comparison. Five-star enlightenment!

'What a load of bullshit,' said Tony.

'But I lost my mind,' said Napoleon. 'I honestly lost my mind, and I did not like losing my mind.'

'That's because you weren't in a safe, secure environment. The experts call it "set and setting",' said Masha. 'For a positive experience you need the right mindset and a controlled environment like we've created here today.' She gestured about the room. 'Yao, Delilah and I are here to guide you and keep you safe.'

'You know you're going to get sued for this,' said Heather serenely.

Masha smiled at her tenderly. 'In a moment, I'm going to ask you to move to one of the stretchers, where you may lie down and enjoy what I can assure you will be a truly transcendent experience.'

'And what if we don't want this experience?' said Tony.

'I think we're all strapped into the spaceship now.' Lars nudged Tony's big beefy shoulder with his own. 'All you can do is sit back and enjoy the ride. I find your smile very charming, by the way.'

'Oh, so do I!' said Frances. 'I love his smile! It's like his whole head kind of crumples up like a . . . like a . . . crumpled tissue.'

'Jesus,' said Tony.

'You yourself are very handsome,' said Frances to Lars. 'Devastatingly handsome, in fact.'

Lars always felt fondly towards people who were unequivo-
cal in their acknowledgement of his looks.

'That's kind of you,' he said modestly. 'I can't take credit
for it. I come from a long line of devastatingly handsome
men.'

'I feel like giving us drugs without our permission must
be against the law,' said Jessica.

Of course it's against the law, you twit, thought Lars.

'Please don't call me a twit,' said Jessica.

Lars's blood ran cold. She could read his mind and she
was extraordinarily wealthy. She now had the capacity to
take over the world for her own nefarious purposes.

'We're here for couples counselling,' said Jessica to Masha.
'We paid for couples counselling. This is all just pointless for
us.'

'This will have a profound impact on your marriage,' said
Masha. 'You and Ben won't be separated on your journey.
You will sit together and experience this as a couple.' Masha
indicated one of the clusters of cushions in the corner. 'Your
smoothies contained a different formula from everyone
else's. We studied the research carefully and we found that
MDMA was the best –'

'Ecstasy,' snapped Heather. 'She means ecstasy. She's
given you a *party drug*. Unbelievable. Kids die every year
after taking ecstasy tablets, but don't let that bother you.'

'You're being kind of a downer about all this, Mum,' said
Zoe.

'Let's go,' said Ben to Jessica. He held out his hand to his
wife and looked at Masha. 'We're leaving.'

'Just . . . hold on.' Jessica didn't take his hand.

'Again, when used in a controlled environment, MDMA
is perfectly safe. It has been trialled for prescription psychotherapy with great success to treat PTSD, social anxiety and

for couples therapy!' said Masha. 'There has never been a single death or even a single adverse reaction to a clinically administered dose of MDMA.'

'This is not a clinical setting!' cried Heather.

Masha ignored her. 'MDMA is an empathogen. It produces feelings of empathy and openness.'

'It *is* a very nice experience, you guys,' said Lars lovingly.

Masha gave him a disapproving look. 'But this is not about dancing all night at a club. This is *guided therapy*. You will find, Ben and Jessica, that you become more sensitive to feelings and more accepting of each other's views. You're about to communicate in a way you've probably never communicated before.'

'Consent,' said Napoleon. 'I feel like that's what's missing here. I feel like . . . I'm pretty sure . . .' He held up a finger. 'I read the paperwork very carefully, and I feel certain we did not consent to this.'

'No, we fucking did not,' said Tony.

Jessica stuck one of her long, fake fingernails in her mouth and chewed.

Careful, thought Lars. *Those things look sharp.*

'What things look sharp?' Jessica frowned at Lars, and then turned to Ben. 'Maybe we should give it a go?'

Ben, who was still on his feet, shook his head, his eyes fixed on a far-off horizon only he could see. 'I did not choose this,' he said again. 'Drugs are dangerous. Drugs are *bad*. Drugs *ruin lives*.'

'I know, babe,' said Jessica, looking up at him. 'But maybe we should just go with it?'

'I think you two should go for it,' said Lars. 'I've seen a lot of bad marriages, but I think your marriage has . . .' There was a fine word he needed to finish his fine sentence but it had escaped his brain.

The word swooped about between Jessica and Ben like a frisky butterfly before it landed, quivering, on Tony's hand. Lars leaned forward and read it.

'*Potential!*' he said. 'I think your marriage has potential.'

Time slowed, and then snapped back to normal pace.

Delilah stood right in front of him. She'd teleported herself, the clever minx.

'It's time to lie down now, Lars,' said Delilah. Teleporting was a handy skill that Lars would like to develop. He would order *Teleporting for Dummies*. He felt like that was the kind of witticism his new friend Frances would appreciate, but he saw that Frances was with Yao, lying down on one of the stretchers, trustingly lifting her head as Yao placed a mask over her eyes.

'Up you get.' Delilah offered her hand. Lars was momentarily transfixed by a thick, lustrous curl of black hair that fell over her shoulder. He studied it for an hour and then he took her hand.

'I know all about bad marriages,' Lars explained as he let her haul him to his feet. Delilah was as strong and powerful as Wonder Woman and she also strongly resembled Wonder Woman. She was quite wondrous in many ways, although he would not let her near his hair.

'Let's talk about that more in a moment,' said Delilah, as she led him to a stretcher. 'We can explore it during your guided therapy.'

'No thank you, sweetheart, I've already done years of therapy,' said Lars. 'There is nothing I don't already know about my psyche.'

He thought of all those fat files crammed with pages of handwritten words about the Great Mysteries of Lars, which could in reality be summed up in a few paltry paragraphs.

When Lars was ten his father left his mother for a woman

called *Gwen*. There may have been nice Gwens in the world, but Lars doubted it. His mother was screwed in the financial settlement. Now Lars spent his days eviscerating wealthy men who left their wives: an endless, pointless revenge fantasy against his long-dead father, a job which he found emotionally and financially satisfying.

He was a control freak because he'd lost control of his life when he was a kid, and weird about money because he'd grown up with none, and he wasn't sufficiently *vulnerable* in his relationships because . . . he didn't want to be vulnerable. He loved Ray, but there was a part of himself he withheld, because Ray had had a happy, functional childhood, and it seemed Lars subconsciously wanted to punch him in the face for having the happy childhood that Lars didn't get. That was it. Nothing more to know, nothing more to learn. A few years ago Lars had swapped therapy for health resorts, and Ray took up cycling and got skinny and obsessed like all city cyclists. Life was good.

'You haven't done this sort of therapy,' said Delilah.

'No thank you,' said Lars firmly and politely. 'I'll just take the trip.'

Lars lay down and got himself comfortable. Big Tony, Smiley Hogburn, lay on the stretcher next to his. Masha kneeled by his side, tucking him in with swift sure movements like he was a giant, grizzled baby. Lars met Tony's eyes just before Masha covered them with a mask. It was like looking into the terrified eyes of a prisoner. Poor Tony. *Just relax and enjoy it, big man.*

Delilah leaned in close to Lars, her breath warm and sweet. 'I'm going to leave you for a moment, but I'll be back to check in on you and to talk about whatever is on your mind.'

'There's nothing on my mind,' said Lars. 'Don't you touch my hair while I'm asleep, Delilah.'

'Very funny. I've never heard that joke before. Masha and Yao are here too. You're not on your own. You're in safe hands, Lars. If there is anything you need, just ask.'

'That's sweet,' said Lars.

Delilah put the mask over his eyes and headphones over his ears.

'Look for the stars,' said Delilah.

Classical music cascaded from the headphones directly into his brain. He could hear each note separately, in its entirety, with absolute purity. It was extraordinary.

A little boy with dark hair and a dirty face said to Lars, 'Come with me. I've got something to show you.'

'No thanks, buddy,' said Lars. 'I'm busy right now.'

He recognised this little kid. It was his boyhood self, little Lars, trying to give him a message.

'Please,' said the little boy, and he took Lars's hand. 'I've got something I need to show you.'

'Maybe later,' said Lars, pulling his hand free. 'I'm busy right now. You go play.'

Remember this, he thought. *Remember it all*. He would tell Ray all about it when he got home. Ray would be interested. He was always interested in everything that happened to Lars. His face so earnest and open and hopeful.

Ray didn't want to *take* anything from him. All Ray wanted was his love.

For a moment that simple thought was everything, it hung there suspended in his consciousness, the answer to every question, the key to every lock, but then his mind exploded into a billion purple petals.

chapter thirty-two

Zoe

Zoe's dad was refusing to lie down and put on his head-phones, and those were the *rules*, but her dad didn't want to follow them and that was the first time in Zoe's life that she had ever seen her dad break the rules and it was so funny and awesome.

Zoe carefully pressed each of her fingertips against her thumbs as she watched Masha try to convince her dad to lie down. Her mum was shouting: 'Illegal . . . Unconscionable! . . . Appalling!'

She was a savage little spitball of rage. It was cute. What did Zach used to say when Mum got mad? 'Mum's being a savage cabbage.'

She closed her eyes. *Mum is being such a savage cabbage right now.*

Thought you weren't talking to me. His voice was clear as a bell in her ear.

I'm not. I hate you. I can't stand you.

Yeah. I can't stand you either. Why do you keep telling people we weren't close?

Because we weren't. Before you died, we hadn't talked in, like, a month.

Because you were being a bitch.

No, because you were being a total loser.

Fuck off.

You fuck off. I downloaded your Shakespearean Insult Generator.

I know you did. It's funny, right? Do you like it? You pribbling half-faced harpy.

And I broke your electric guitar.

I saw that. You threw it across the room. You spleeny milk-livered lewdster.

I'm so angry with you.

I know.

You did it on purpose. To get back at me. To win.

Yeah, no. I can't even remember what we were arguing about.

I miss you every single day, Zach. Every single day.

I know.

I'll never be a normal person ever again. You took that away from me. You made me ABNORMAL and it's lonely being abnormal.

You were already kind of abnormal.

Very funny.

I think the parents want us over there.

What?

Zoe opened her eyes and the yoga studio was a million miles wide and her mum and dad were tiny specks in the distance, beckoning to her. 'Come sit with us.'

chapter thirty-three

Frances

Frances felt the soft, frosty tickle of snowflakes on her face as she and her friend Gillian flew across a star-studded sky in a sleigh drawn by white horses.

A pile of books filled her lap. They were all the books she'd ever written, including foreign language editions. The books were open at the top like cereal boxes. Frances dipped her hand into each book and pulled out great handfuls of words to scatter across the sky.

'Got one!' said Sol, from the back of the sleigh, where he and Henry sat smoking cigarettes and killing off unnecessary adjectives with catapults.

'Leave them be,' said Frances snappily.

'Let's get all those adverbs too!' said Sol happily.

'Even the rhyming ones?' asked Henry affably.

'That's an imperfect rhyme,' pointed out Frances.

'They're just words, Frances,' said Gillian.

'So profound, Gillian,' said Sol.

'Shut up, Sol,' said Gillian.

'She never liked you,' Frances told Sol.

Sol said, 'That sort of woman always secretly wants an alpha male.'

Frances smiled fondly at him. Egotist but sexy as hell. 'You were my first-ever husband.'

'I was your first-ever husband,' agreed Sol. 'And you were my second-ever wife.'

'Second wives are so young and pretty,' said Frances. 'I liked being a second wife.'

'By the by, Gillian kissed me once,' said Henry. 'At someone's thirtieth birthday party.'

'She was drunk,' said Frances. 'Don't get a big head about it.'

'I was drunk,' agreed Gillian. 'I felt bad about that until the day I died.'

'Henry, you were my second husband,' said Frances. 'But I was your *first* wife. Therefore not as pretty.'

Gillian said, 'Why do you keep identifying your husbands?'

'Readers get impatient if they have trouble working out which character is which,' explained Frances. 'You've got to help them out. None of us is getting any younger.'

'Except this isn't a book,' said Gillian.

'I think you'll find it is,' said Frances. 'I'm the protagonist, obviously.'

'I feel like that tall Russian lady is giving you a run for your money,' said Gillian.

'She is not,' said Frances. 'It's all about me. I'm just not sure of my love interest yet.'

'Oh my God, it's so obvious,' said Gillian. 'Blind Freddy could pick it.' She shouted at the sky, 'You knew it from day one, right?'

'Gillian! Did you just try to break the fourth wall?' Frances was shocked.

'I did not,' said Gillian, but she looked guilty. 'I'm sure no-one noticed.'

'How tacky,' said Frances. 'How very gimmicky.'

She dared to look up and the stars were a million darting eyes on the look out for rule-breaking in her story: sexism, ageism, racism, tokenism, ableism, plagiarism, cultural appropriation, fat-shaming, body-shaming, slut-shaming, vegetarian-shaming, real-estate-agent-shaming. The voice of the Almighty Internet boomed from the sky: *Shame on you!*

Frances hung her head. 'It's just a story,' she whispered.

'That's what I'm trying to tell you,' said Gillian.

An endless gossamer-like sentence embroidered with jewel-like metaphors, far too many clauses and meaning so obscure it had to be profound wrapped itself around Frances's neck, but it really didn't suit her, so she wrenched it off and flung it into space, where it floated free until at last a shy author on his way to a festival to accept a prize grabbed it from the sky and used it to gag one of his beautiful corpses. It looked lovely on her. Grey-bearded critics applauded with relief, grateful it hadn't ended up in a beach read.

'Will younger readers even recognise the term "Blind Freddy"?' asked Jo, who floated alongside Frances doing a line edit. She sat astride a giant lead pencil. 'Could it be ableist?'

'What's interesting is that I'm a fictional character,' said her internet scammer from the back of the sleigh, where he sat between Henry and Sol, his arms around their shoulders. 'Yet she loved me more than either of you.'

'You're nothing but a scam,' said Sol. 'She never even met you, let alone fucked you, cocksucker!'

'!!!!' cried Jo.

'I agree. Delete,' advised Gillian. 'My mother reads your books.'

'As her loving ex-husbands, it's our duty to beat you to a pulp,' said Henry to Paul Drabble. 'Scram, scam.'

'Life is nothing but a scam,' said Gillian. 'It's all just a giant illusion.'

'Scram, scam,' chuckled Sol. 'Good one.'

He and Henry fist-bumped.

'You're both far too old for fist-bumping,' sighed Frances, but her ex-husbands were busy bonding. She always knew they'd like each other if they ever met. She should have invited them both to her fiftieth.

She realised that Paul Drabble had vanished, as easy as that. There was no pain in the empty space he'd left behind. It turned out he'd meant nothing at all. Not a thing.

'He was just a credit on my bank balance,' she told Gillian.

'Debit, you idiot,' said Gillian.

'Debit, credit,' said Frances. 'Whatever. I am completely over him.'

'I was the one who meant something,' said a child's voice. It was Ari, Paul Drabble's son.

Frances didn't turn around. She could not look at him.

'I thought I was going to be his mother,' she said to Gillian. 'It's the only time in my life I even considered being a mother.'

'I know,' said Gillian.

'So embarrassing,' whispered Frances. 'I am so deeply embarrassed.'

'It's a loss, Frances,' said Gillian. 'You're allowed to grieve your loss even if it's embarrassing.'

The snow fell silently for days as Frances grieved her loss of an imaginary boy and Gillian sat beside her, head bowed in sympathy, until they were frozen, snow-covered figures.

'What about my dad?' asked Frances in the spring, when the snow melted, butterflies danced and bees buzzed. 'Why isn't he here on my trip? I'm the one writing this thing, Gillian, not you. Let's get Dad on board.'

'I'm here,' said her dad from the back of the sleigh.

He was alone, wearing the khaki safari suit he wore for Christmas lunch 1973, captured forever in the framed photo on her writing desk. She reached back and took his hand. 'Hello, Dad.'

'You were always so crazy about the boys.' Her dad shook his head. Frances smelled his Old Spice aftershave.

'You died when I was too young,' said Frances. 'That's why I made such bad choices in men. I was trying to replace you.'

'Cliché?' asked Jo from astride her lead pencil, which was bucking like a horse. '*Whoa*, boy!'

'Stop editing me,' said Frances to Jo. 'You're retired. Go look after your grandchildren.'

'Don't even pretend you have unresolved daddy issues – you do not,' said Gillian. 'Take responsibility.'

Frances pinched Gillian on the arm.

'Ouch!' said Gillian.

'Sorry. I didn't think it would hurt. It's not like any of this is real,' said Frances. 'It's just a story I'm making up as I go along.'

'Speaking of which, I always thought your plots could be better structured,' said Gillian. 'The same goes for your life. All this chopping and changing of husbands. Maybe you could think about planning ahead for the final chapters. I never had the courage to say that when I was alive.'

'You actually did say that when you were alive,' said Frances. 'More than once, as a matter of fact.'

'You're always acting like you're the heroine of one of your own novels. You just fall into the arms of the next man the narrator puts in front of you.'

'You told me that too!'

'Did I?' said Gillian. 'That was impolite of me.'

'I always thought so,' said Frances.

'I could have been kinder,' said Gillian. 'I may have been on the spectrum.'

'Don't think you're getting any more character development now you're dead,' said Frances. 'You're done. Let's focus on *my* character development.'

'You're easy: you're the princess,' said Gillian. 'The passive princess waiting for yet another prince.'

'I could kill the emu,' said Frances.

'Well, we'll see, won't we, Frances? We'll see if you can kill the emu.'

'Maybe.' Frances watched the emu, alive again, but still incapable of flight, run across the star-studded sky. 'I really miss you, Gillian.'

'Thanks,' said Gillian. 'I would say I missed you too, but that would not strictly be true as I'm actually in a constant state of bliss.'

'I'm not surprised. It's so beautiful,' said Frances. 'It's kind of like the northern lights, isn't it?'

'It's always there,' said Gillian.

'What is? The northern lights? They are not always there. Ellen paid a fortune and didn't see a thing.'

'This, Frances. This beauty. Just on the other side. You just have to be quiet. Stay still. Stop talking. Stop wanting. Just be. You'll hear it, or feel it. Close your eyes and you'll see it.'

'Interesting,' said Frances. 'Did I tell you about my review?'

'Frances, *forget* the review!'

Gosh. Gillian sounded quite cranky for someone who didn't have anything to do except lie back and enjoy the exquisite beauty of the afterlife.

chapter thirty-four

Yao

'Where are you now, Frances?' asked Yao.

He sat on the floor next to her stretcher, and removed her headphones so she could hear him.

'I'm in a story, Yao,' said Frances. He couldn't see her eyes because of the mask, but her face was animated. 'I'm writing the story and I'm *in* the story. It's quite a nice story. I've got a kind of magic realism vibe going, which is new for me. I like it! Nothing needs to make sense.'

'Okay,' said Yao. 'Who else is in the story with you?'

'My friend Gillian. She died. In her sleep, when she was forty-nine. It's called Sudden Adult Death Syndrome. I thought it was just for babies. I didn't even know it was possible.'

'Does Gillian have anything to say to you?'

'Not really. I told her about the review.'

'Frances, *forget* the review!'

It wasn't professional but Yao couldn't hide his frustration. Frances kept talking on and on about the review. Shouldn't authors be used to bad reviews? Wasn't it just an occupational hazard?

Try being a paramedic. See how you go when a psycho husband holds a knife to your throat while you're trying to save his wife's life, which you can't save, because she's already dead. Try that, Frances.

Frances pushed up her mask and looked at Yao. Her hair stuck up comically, as if she'd just got out of bed.

'I'll have the seafood linguine. Thank you so much.' She snapped an imaginary menu shut, pulled her mask back over her eyes and began to hum 'Amazing Grace'.

Yao checked her pulse and thought of a long-ago night after a university party when he'd looked after a drunk girl in someone's bedroom. Yao listened to her incoherent, slurred rambling for hours and made sure she didn't choke on her vomit, before he finally fell asleep and woke up at dawn to her face inches away from his, and her sick-sweet breath in his nostrils. 'Get out,' she said.

'I never touched you,' Yao told her. 'Nothing happened.'

'Get the fuck out,' she said.

He felt like he *had* taken advantage of her, raped an unconscious girl. It didn't matter that he would never do such a thing, that he wanted to make a career out of healing; at that moment he was the representative for his gender and he had to cop it on the chin for all their sins.

Guiding Frances on her psychedelic therapeutic journey was nothing like looking after a drunk girl. And yet . . . it kind of felt like looking after a drunk girl.

'I haven't had sex in so long,' said Frances. White spittle gathered at the corner of her mouth.

Yao felt a little ill. 'That's too bad,' he said.

He looked over at Masha, who sat with Ben and Jessica, their three shadows enormous on the wall. Masha nodded as the couple spoke. It seemed like their therapy was going well. Delilah was talking to Lars, who had sat up from his stretcher and was chatting calmly with her, as if they were both guests at a party.

All his patients were fine. He had a crash cart on stand-by. They were all being monitored. There was nothing to worry about, and yet it was so strange because, right now, all his senses were screaming one inexplicable word: *Run*.

chapter thirty-five

Tony

Tony ran across an endless field of emerald green carrying an oddly shaped football that weighed as much as three bricks. His arms ached. Footballs weren't normally that heavy.

Banjo ran along beside him, he was a puppy again, bounding along with the same joyful abandon as a toddler, getting in between Tony's legs, tail wagging.

Tony understood that if he wanted to be happy again, he simply needed to kick this strange misshapen football through the goal. The football represented everything he hated about himself: all his mistakes, his regrets and his shame.

'Sit!' he said to Banjo.

Banjo sat. His big brown eyes looked up at Tony trustingly.

'Stay,' he said.

Banjo stayed. His tail whooshed back and forth across the grass.

Tony saw the white goalposts rise like skyscrapers above him.

He lifted his foot, made contact. The ball sailed in a perfect arc across a clear blue sky. He knew immediately it was good. That rollercoaster feeling in his stomach. There was nothing better. Better than sex. It had been so long.

The crowd roared as the ball went straight through the middle of the goalposts and the euphoria blasted like rocket fuel through his body as he leaped high in the sky, one fist raised like a superhero.

chapter thirty-six

Carmel

Carmel sat on a plush velvet couch in a snooty fashion shop specialising in the latest designer bodies.

Carmel wasn't wearing a body. It was so wonderful and relaxing not wearing a body. No thighs. No stomach. No bum. No biceps. No triceps. No cellulite. No crow's feet. No frown marks. No caesarean scar. No sun damage. No fine lines. No seven signs of ageing. No dry hair. No frizzy hair. No grey hair. Nothing to wax or colour or condition. Nothing to lengthen or flatten, conceal or disguise.

She was just Carmel, without her body.

Show me your original face, the one you had before your parents were born.

Her little girls sat either side of her on the couch, waiting for her to choose a new body. They were all quietly reading age-appropriate quality chapter books and eating freshly cut fruit. No devices. No sugary snacks. No arguing. Carmel was the best mother in the history of mothering.

'Let's find you a divine new body for your divine new

life,' said Masha, who was the manager of the shop. She was dressed as a Disney princess.

Masha ran her finger along a rack filled with different bodies on hangers. 'No, no, maybe . . . oh, now *this* one is nice!' She draped the body over one arm. 'This would look lovely on you. It's very fashionable, and such a flattering shape!'

It was Sonia's body. Her sleek blonde hair. Her trim waist.

'I don't like the ankles,' said Carmel. 'I prefer a more finely tapered ankle. Also, my husband's new girlfriend has that exact same body.'

'We don't want that one then!' said Masha. She hung it back up and selected another one from the rack. 'How about this one? So striking. You'll turn heads wearing this one.'

It was Masha's body.

'It's amazing, but honestly, I don't think I can carry it off,' said Carmel. 'It's kind of too dramatic for me.'

Her daughter Lulu put down her book. She had peach smeared around her mouth. Carmel went to wipe it away but then she remembered she had no fingers. Fingers were useful.

'That's your body there, Mummy,' said Lulu, and she pointed at Carmel's body sagging on a doorhandle, without even a hanger.

'That's my old body, darling,' said Carmel. 'Mummy needs a new one.'

'It's yours.' Lulu was implacable as always.

Masha held up Carmel's old body. 'It does look very comfortable,' she said.

'Could we at least take it in a few inches?' said Carmel.

'Of course we can.' Masha smiled at her. 'We'll make it beautiful. Here. Try it on.'

Carmel sighed and put back on her old body.

'It really suits you,' said Masha. 'Just some minor adjustments.'

'I quite like the ankles,' admitted Carmel. 'What do you think, girls?'

Her daughters threw themselves at her. Carmel marvelled at the blue veins in her hands as she cupped her daughters' heads, the thump of her heart and the strength of her arms as she hefted a little girl on each hip.

'I'll take it,' she said.

'You're going to love your body,' said Masha.

chapter thirty-seven

Masha

My God, it is all going incredibly well, thought Masha. The therapy was working exactly as the research said it would. Carmel Schneider had just made a breakthrough in relation to her body-image issues. There had been a moment where for some reason she kept trying to take her clothes off, but Masha had put a stop to that and she'd just had a very good conversation with her about body acceptance.

The triumph was as tangible as a trophy, solid and gleaming gold in Masha's hands.

chapter thirty-eight

Napoleon

Napoleon sat with his back against a wall of the studio, watching the floor breathe in and out with the rapid, heart-breaking vulnerability of a sleeping baby.

This happened last time, he reminded himself. It was just an optical illusion. Walls and floors did not breathe. And so what if they did breathe? What was so bad about that?

The walls of that seedy smoky club had breathed too, and he'd become convinced he was trapped within an amoeba hurtling through space. It had made perfect sense at the time. The amoeba had swallowed him whole like the whale swallowed Jonah and he was stuck in that amoeba for a thousand years.

Twenty years old and he was so sure his brain had been fried, and he took such pride in his brain, and the only way to comfort himself in the bleak days that followed was by chanting: *Never again, never again, never again.*

And yet here he was, trapped once more.

I'm not in an amoeba, he told himself. *I'm at a health resort. They have given me drugs without my permission and I'm just going to have to wait this out.*

At least he was in this very pleasant, nice-smelling, candle-lit studio, not that packed bar with all those looming faces.

He held hands with his girls. Heather's hand in his left. Zoe's in his right. Napoleon had refused to lie down on one of those stretchers or put on the mask and headphones. He knew the only way to keep a good firm grip of his mind was to sit upright with his eyes open.

Masha pretended she was fine with that, but Napoleon knew she was annoyed that they weren't following the correct procedure for 'optimum results'.

Napoleon recognised the moment she made the decision not to push the issue. It was like he could read her mind. *Pick your battles*, she thought. Napoleon had to pick his battles with his students. He was good at picking his battles. He used to do the same with the kids.

'Pick your battles,' he said softly. 'Pick them carefully.'

'I know which battle I'm picking – I will not rest until that woman is behind bars,' said Heather. She was watching Masha move about the room, chatting to her guests, placing the back of her hand against their foreheads.

'Look at her, sashaying about as if she's fucking Florence Nightingale,' said Heather. 'Psychedelic therapy, my foot.'

Napoleon wondered if there was some sort of professional jealousy going on here.

'Can you see the walls breathing?' he asked, to take her mind off things.

'It's just the effects of the drugs,' said Heather.

'Well, I know that, darling,' said Napoleon. 'I just wondered if you were experiencing the same effects.'

'I can see the walls breathing, Dad,' said Zoe. 'They look like fish. It's awesome. Are you seeing the colours?' She glided her hands back and forth as if through water.

'I am!' marvelled Napoleon. 'It's like phosphorescence.'

'Great. A nice druggy dad-and-daughter bonding experience,' said Heather.

Napoleon noted that she was in a very bad mood.

'Zach would think this was hilarious,' said Zoe. 'All of us getting high together.'

'He's here actually,' said Napoleon. 'Hi, Zach.'

'Hey, Dad.' It didn't even seem that remarkable that Zach was sitting right in front of him, wearing shorts and no shirt. The kid never wore a shirt. It just felt like everything was right again, the way it used to feel, the four of them hanging out together, taking each other's existences for granted, just being a family, a run-of-the-mill family.

'Do you see him?' said Napoleon.

'Yes,' said Zoe.

'I see him too,' said Heather, her voice full of tears.

'Your turn to take out the recycling, Zach,' said Zoe.

Zach gave his sister the finger and Napoleon laughed out loud.

chapter thirty-nine

Frances

Frances sat up on her stretcher, pushed back her headphones and pulled her eye mask down around her neck.

'Thank you,' she said to Delilah, who sat next to her, smiling at her in a way that could be called condescending, as a matter of a fact. 'That was lovely. Quite an experience. I feel like I learned a great deal. How much do I owe you?'

'I don't think you're done yet,' said Delilah.

Frances looked around the room.

Lars and Tony were on stretchers next to each other. Tony's head lolled to one side, his feet splayed in a V shape. Meanwhile, Lars's profile looked like that of a Grecian god and his feet were neatly crossed at the ankles, as if he were napping on a train while listening to a podcast.

Ben and Jessica were in a corner of the room kissing like young lovers who have just discovered kissing and have all the time in the world. Their hands moved over each other's bodies with slow, passionate reverence.

'Goodness,' said Frances. '*That* looks like fun.'

She continued to survey the room.

Carmel lay on her stretcher, her thick black hair spread like seaweed around her head. She held up her hands and wiggled her fingers as if she were trying to see them through her eye mask.

Napoleon, Heather and Zoe sat in a row with their backs against the wall, like young travellers stranded at an airport. There was a boy sitting in front of them. He stuck his finger up at Zoe.

'Who is that boy?' said Frances. 'The boy without the shirt?'

'There is no boy,' said Delilah. She reached for Frances's headphones.

'He's laughing,' said Frances. She tried and failed to grab at Delilah's arm to stop her pulling the eye mask back over her eyes. 'I think I'll go say hello.'

'Stay with me, Frances,' said Delilah.

chapter forty

Heather

Heather focused on her breathing. She was determined to keep a tiny part of her brain safe and sober and in charge of monitoring the effects of the psilocybin and LSD; one brightly lit office window in a dark office tower.

She knew, for example, that in reality her son rotted beneath the earth; he was not really there with them. And yet he seemed so real, and when she reached out to touch his arm, it was his flesh: firm and smooth and tanned. He tanned easily and he was hopeless about putting on sunscreen, even though she nagged.

'Don't go, Zach.' Napoleon jerked upright and reached out his hands.

'He's not going, Dad,' said Zoe. She pointed. 'He's still right there.'

'My boy,' sobbed Napoleon. His body convulsed. 'He's *gone*.' His sobs were guttural, uncontrolled. 'My boy, my boy, my boy.'

'Stop that,' said Heather. This was not the place, not the time.

It was the drugs. Not everyone reacted the same way to drugs. Some labouring mothers got plastered on just one whiff of nitrous oxide. Others screamed at Heather that it wasn't working.

Napoleon had always been susceptible. He couldn't even cope with coffee. One long black and you'd think he'd taken speed. An over-the-counter painkiller could send him loopy. The only time he ever had a general anaesthetic, which was for a knee reconstruction the year before Zach died, he'd had a bad reaction when he came out of it and scared a poor young nurse to death by supposedly 'speaking in tongues' about the Garden of Eden, although it wasn't clear how she understood what he was saying if he was *speaking in tongues*. 'She must be fluent in tongues,' Zach had said, and Zoe had laughed so much, and there was no greater pleasure in Heather's life than watching her children make each other laugh.

Watch your husband, she thought. *Monitor him.* She narrowed her eyes and clenched her jaw to maintain focus, but she felt herself drift hopelessly, inevitably away on a sea of memories.

She is walking down the street pushing her two babies in a big double stroller and every single old lady stops to make a comment and Heather is never going to make it to the shops.

She is a little girl staring at her mother's stomach wishing she could make a baby grow in there so that she can have a brother or sister but the wishing doesn't work, wishing never works, and when she grows up she will never have an only child, a lonely only.

She is opening the door of her son's bedroom because she's going to do a load of washing and she may as well scrape up some of the layer of clothes on his floor and her whole body resists what she is seeing and she thinks, I'm doing a load of washing, don't do this, Zach, I want to do laundry, I want to keep this life, please, please let me keep this life, but she hears herself screaming because she knows it's too late, there is nothing to be done, the life of one second ago is gone.

She is at her son's funeral and her daughter is delivering a eulogy, and afterwards people keep touching Heather, so much touching, everyone wants to paw at her, it is repulsive, and they are all saying, Oh, you must be so proud, Zoe spoke so beautifully, as if it's fucking school speech night not her son's funeral, and can't you see my daughter is alone now, how can she live without her brother, she never even existed without him, and who cares if she spoke beautifully, she can't even stand, her father is holding her upright, my daughter can't even walk.

She is watching Zoe take her first steps at only eleven months, and Zach, who has never even considered such a thing, is shocked, he can hardly believe it, he is sitting on the carpet with his little plump legs stuck out in front of him and he is looking up at his sister with big astonished eyes and you can see he is thinking, What is she DOING? and she and Napoleon are laughing so hard, and maybe wishes do come true because this is family, this is what she never had, never knew, never dreamed, this is a moment so perfect and funny and this is her life now, just a string of perfect, funny moments one after the other, like a string of beads that will go on forever.

Except that it won't.

She is alone in Zach's bedroom crying, and she thinks that Napoleon and Zoe are somewhere in the house crying too, all alone crying in separate rooms, and she thinks families are probably meant to grieve together but they aren't doing it right, and to distract herself she goes through Zach's drawers for the hundredth time, even though she knows there is nothing to find, no note, no explanation, she knows exactly what she will find – except that this time, she does find something.

She was back.

Napoleon still rocked and sobbed.

Had she been gone for a second or an hour or a year? She didn't know.

'How are the Marconi family feeling right now?' Masha sat in front of them. 'Could this perhaps be a good opportunity for a family therapy session about your loss?'

Masha had multiple arms and multiple legs but Heather refused to acknowledge her multiple limbs because it was not real, people simply did not have that many limbs. Heather had never once delivered a baby with that many limbs. She was not falling for it.

'When you say it's your fault, Napoleon, are you referring to Zach?' asked Masha, all faux concern.

Heather heard herself hiss, 'Jesus fucking Christ.'

Heather was a snake with a long forked tongue that could whip from her mouth and pierce Masha's skin, shooting venom through her veins, poisoning her, the same way Masha had poisoned Heather's family. 'Don't you dare talk about our son! You know nothing about our son.'

'My fault, my fault, my fault.' Napoleon banged his head against the wall. He was in danger of concussing himself.

Heather gathered up all her mental strength to focus her mind and crawled around to face Napoleon on her hands and knees. She grabbed his head between her hands. She could feel his ears against her palms, the warmth of his stubbled skin.

'Listen to me,' she said in the loud, carrying voice she used to cut through the screams of a woman in labour.

Napoleon's eyes rolled about, bulging and veined with blood, like a frightened horse.

'I pressed snooze on my alarm,' he said. He repeated it over and over. 'I pressed snooze on my alarm. I pressed snooze on my alarm.'

'I know you did,' said Heather. 'You've told me so many

times, darling, but it wouldn't have made a difference.'

'It wasn't your fault, Dad,' said Zoe, her lonely only, and it seemed to Heather that she spoke very much like a zombie, not a university student, and that her young, beautiful mind was already fried like an egg, sizzled to a crisp. 'It was my fault.'

'Good,' said Masha. The Poisoner. 'This is so good! You are all speaking from your hearts.'

Heather turned and screamed in her face. 'Fuck off!'

A pellet of Heather's spittle flew in a slow arc from her mouth and hit the target of Masha's eye.

Masha smiled. She wiped her eye. 'Excellent. Release all that rage, Heather. Let it all out.' She stood, and her multiple limbs drifted about her like an octopus's tentacles. 'I will be back momentarily.'

Heather turned back to her family. 'Listen,' she said. 'Listen to me.'

Napoleon and Zoe made eye contact with her. They were all three in a temporary air pocket of clarity. It wouldn't last. Heather had to speak fast. She opened her mouth and began to tug an endless tapeworm from deep down in her throat, and it was making her gag and vomit, but there was relief in it too, because at last she was wrenching it free from her body.

chapter forty-one

Zoe

The walls no longer breathed. The colours were fading. Zoe felt like she was sobering up. It was like that feeling at the end of a party when you walked out of a stuffy room into the night air and your mind cleared.

'Zach was on medication,' said Zoe's mother. 'For his asthma.'

Why did that matter? Zoe could tell that her mother thought she was sharing something momentous here, but she had learned that what was momentous to your parents was often not that momentous to you, and what was momentous to you was often not that momentous to your parents.

'I like to call it Zachariah's Theory of Momentous-ity,' said Zach, who was still there with them.

'Don't tell me your theories. I'm all alone, taking care of the parents,' said Zoe. 'And it's an onerous responsibility, thou fuckwit, because they are both cray-cray.'

'I know, I'm sorry, thou mangled pox-marked clack dish,' said Zach.

'I need you to concentrate, Zoe,' said her mother.

'I know he was on medication for his asthma,' said her dad. 'A preventative. So what?'

'One of the side effects can be depression and suicidal thoughts,' said Heather. 'I told you the specialist wanted to prescribe it to him and you said, "Are there any side effects?" and I said . . . I said . . . "No."'

The regret dragged at her face like claw marks.

'You said no,' repeated Zoe's father.

'I said no,' said her mother. Her eyes were pleading for forgiveness. 'I'm so sorry.'

A cliff face of momentous-ity loomed in front of Zoe.

'I hadn't even read the leaflet in the box,' said her mother. 'I knew Dr Chang was the best, I knew he wouldn't prescribe anything with dangerous side effects, I trusted him, so I just said, "No. It's all fine. I've checked." But I lied to you, Napoleon, I lied.'

Zoe's dad blinked.

After a while, he said slowly, 'I would have trusted him too.'

'You would have read the leaflet. You would have gone through it so carefully, reading every word, asking me questions, driving me crazy. I'm the one with the medical training but I didn't even read it. I thought I was so busy at that time. I don't know what I thought I was so busy doing.' Her mother rubbed her hands down her cheeks as if she were trying to smear herself away. 'I read the leaflet about six months after he died. I found it in his bedroom drawer.'

'Well, darling, it wouldn't have made any difference,' said her dad dully. 'We needed to get the asthma under control.'

'But if we'd known depression was a possibility we would have monitored him,' said Zoe's mother. She looked desperate to make him understand the full breadth of her guilt. '*You* would have, Napoleon, I know you would have!'

'There were no signs,' said her dad. 'Sometimes there are no signs. No signs at all. He was perfectly happy.'

'There were signs,' said Zoe.

Her parents turned to her, and their faces were like those clown faces at an amusement park, turning back and forth, mouths agape, waiting for the ball to drop.

'I knew he was upset about something.'

She remembered walking by his bedroom and registering the fact that Zach was lying on his bed but he wasn't looking at his phone or listening to music or reading, he was just *lying there*, and that was not Zach. Zach didn't just lie on his bed and stare at the ceiling.

'I thought something was going on at school,' she told her parents. 'But I was angry with him. We weren't talking. I didn't want to be the first one to talk.' Zoe closed her eyes so she could not see the disappointment and pain on her parents' faces. She whispered, 'It was a competition to see who would be the first one to talk.'

'Oh, Zoe, sweetheart,' said her mother from far, far away. 'It's not your fault. You know it's not your fault.'

'I was going to talk on our birthday,' said Zoe. 'I was going to say, "Happy birthday, loser."'

'Oh, Zoe, you stupid-head,' said Zach.

He put his arm around her. They never hugged. They weren't that sort of brother and sister. Sometimes when they passed each other in the hallway they randomly shoved each other for no reason at all. Like, hard enough to hurt. But now he was hugging her, and talking in her ear, and it was him, it was Zach, it was absolutely him, he smelled of that stupid Lynx body wash which he said he used ironically but he totally used because he believed the ads about how it made the girls think you were hotter.

Zach pulled her close and whispered in her ear. 'It was nothing to do with you. I didn't do it to get at you.' He gripped her arm to make sure she got his point. '*I wasn't me.*'

chapter forty-two

Napoleon

He would do anything for his girls, anything, so he took the dreadful, heavy secrets they'd been carrying and he saw the relief with which they handed them over, and now he had his own secret, because he would never tell them how angry their secrets made him, never ever, never ever ever.

The walls continued to pulsate as his wife and daughter held his hands and he knew this nightmare would last an eternity.

chapter forty-three

Masha

Ben and Jessica sat cross-legged on cushions facing each other. Their hands gripped each other's forearms as if they were on a narrow beam and trying to maintain their balance. It was glorious to see. Ben spoke directly from his heart and Jessica listened, transfixed by his every word.

Masha guided only when necessary. The MDMA was doing exactly what it was meant to do: dissolving barriers. They could have spent *months* in therapy to get to this point. This was an instant shortcut.

'I miss your face,' Ben said to Jessica. 'Your beautiful face. I don't recognise you. I don't recognise us or anything about our lives. I miss our old flat. I miss my job. I miss the friends we lost because of this. But most of all I miss your face.'

His words were crisp and clear. There was no slurring. No equivocation.

'Good,' said Masha. 'Wonderful. Jessica, what do you want to say?'

'I think that Ben is body-shaming,' said Jessica. 'I'm still me. I'm still *Jessica*. I'm still in here! So what if I look a bit different? This is the fashion. It's just fashion. It's not important!'

'It's important to me,' said Ben. 'It feels like you took something precious and fucked it up.'

'But I feel beautiful,' said Jessica. 'I feel like I was ugly before and now I'm beautiful.' She stretched her arms above her head like a ballerina. 'The question is: who gets to decide if I'm beautiful or not? Me? You? The internet?'

Right now, she did look beautiful.

Ben considered for a moment.

'It's your face,' he said. 'So I guess you should decide.'

'But wait! Beauty is . . .' Jessica pointed at her eye. She began to laugh. 'Beauty is *in the eye of the beholder.*'

She and Ben laughed and laughed. They clutched each other, repeating 'beauty is in the *eye* of the beholder' over and over, and Masha smiled at them uncertainly. Why was that funny? Perhaps it was an inside joke. She began to feel impatient.

At long last they stopped laughing and Jessica sat up and touched her lower lip. 'Look. Fair call. I might have over-done it on the lips last time.'

'I liked your lips before,' said Ben. 'I thought you had beautiful lips.'

'Yeah, I get it, Ben,' said Jessica.

'I liked our life before,' said Ben.

'It was a shitty little life,' said Jessica. 'An ordinary shitty little life.'

'I don't think it was shitty,' said Ben.

'I feel like you love your car more than me,' said Jessica. 'I'm jealous of your car. *I* was the one who scratched it. That was me. Because I feel like your car is a slutty girl having an affair with my husband, and so I scratched her slutty face.'

'Wow,' said Ben. He put both hands to the top of his head.

'*Wow.* That is . . . wow. I can't believe you did that.' He didn't sound angry. Just amazed.

'I *love* the money,' said Jessica. 'I love being rich. But I wish we could just be rich and still be us.'

'The money,' said Ben slowly, 'is like a dog.'

'Mmm,' said Jessica.

'A great big out-of-control pet dog.'

'Yeah,' said Jessica. 'Yeah. That's right.' She paused. 'Why is it like a dog?'

'So, it's like we got a dog, and it's the dog we always wanted, we dreamed of this dog, this dog is our dream dog, but it's changed everything about our lives. It's, like, really distracting, it barks all through the night wanting our attention, it won't let us sleep, we can't do *anything* without taking the dog into account. We have to walk it, and feed it, and worry about it, and . . .' He scrunched up his face, working it out. 'See, the problem with this dog is that it *bites*. It bites us, and it bites our friends and family; it's got a really vicious streak, this dog.'

'But we still love it,' said Jessica. 'We love the dog.'

'We do, but I think we should give the dog away,' said Ben. 'I think it's not the right dog for us.'

'We could get a labradoodle,' said Jessica. 'Labradoodles are so cute.'

Masha reminded herself that Jessica was very young.

'I think Ben is using the dog as a . . . story to explain how the lottery win has impacted your lives,' she said. 'A metaphor, that is.' The word metaphor came to her a fraction later than she would have liked.

'Yeah,' said Jessica. She gave Masha a sly, shrewd look and tapped her nose with her forefinger. 'If we're going to get a dog we should get it before the baby comes.'

'What baby?' said Masha.

'What baby?' said Ben.

'I'm pregnant,' said Jessica.

'You are?' said Ben. 'But that's awesome!'

Masha reeled. 'But you never –'

'You gave my pregnant wife drugs,' said Ben to Masha.

'Yeah, I kind of feel really angry about that,' said Jessica to Masha. 'Like, I think you should go to jail for a very long time for this.'

chapter forty-four

Heather

Heather woke but did not open her eyes.

She was lying on her side, on something thin and soft, her hands pillowed beneath her head.

Her body clock told her it was morning. Maybe around 7 am, she would have guessed.

She was no longer high. Her mind felt clear. She was in the yoga and meditation studio at Tranquillum House and today was the anniversary of Zach's death.

After years of nausea she'd vomited up her secret and now she felt shaky, strange and empty, but also better. She felt *cleansed*, which, funnily enough, was exactly what Tranquillum House had promised. Heather would have to write them a glowing testimonial: *I feel so much better after my time at Tranquillum House! I especially enjoyed 'tripping' with my husband and daughter.*

Obviously they would leave this place immediately. They would not eat or drink anything provided by Masha. They would go straight to their rooms, pack, get in the car and leave. Perhaps they would go to a cafe in the nearest town and order a big fried breakfast in Zach's honour.

Heather wanted to spend this year's anniversary alone with her family talking about Zach, and tomorrow, she wanted to somehow mark her children's twenty-first birthday in a way that wasn't about shame or grief, or everyone pretending to forget that this was Zoe's birthday too. Napoleon had been saying it for so long: we have to separate Zach from the way he chose to end his life. There was so much more to Zach than his suicide. One memory should not eclipse all the other memories. But she hadn't listened. She had somehow thought that his unhappiness that one day nullified everything else that he did in his life.

Now, all at once, she knew that Napoleon was right. Today they would mark the anniversary of his death by pooling their best memories of his eighteen years of life, and the grief would be unbearable, but Heather knew better than anyone that the unbearable could be borne. For the last three years she'd been grieving Zach's suicide. Now it was finally time to grieve his loss. The loss of a beautiful, silly, smart, impetuous boy.

She hoped that his sister would cope today. All that rubbish about 'not being close' to Zach. Heather's heart ached for her. The child adored her brother. They were ten years old before they stopped creeping into each other's beds at night when they had nightmares. Heather would need to tell her over and over that it wasn't her fault. It was Heather's failure alone. Her failure to notice her son's change in behaviour and her failure to give anyone, *including Zach himself*, a reason to look for it.

And at some point today they would report the madwoman's actions to the police.

Heather opened her eyes and saw that she was lying on a yoga mat, face to face with her sleeping daughter. She was still asleep, her eyelids fluttering. Heather was close enough to feel Zoe's breath on her face. She put her hand to her cheek.

chapter forty-five

Frances

Frances pulled the headphones from her head. They got caught in her hair. She tugged them free, her eyes still shut.

She was on a flight. The only time she fell asleep wearing headphones was on a flight.

She could hear the sound of far-off construction. A drill. A jackhammer. A digger. Some such thing. It was an intermittent mechanical roar. A lawnmower? A leaf blower. She lay on her side, drew the blanket up over her shoulders, and tried to make herself sink back into deep, delicious sleep. But no, there was the sound again, pulling her inexorably up, up, up, and it wasn't a machine, it was the sound of a man snoring.

Had she got drunk and slept with a stranger last night? Good Lord, surely not. It had been decades. She didn't feel any of the symptoms of a hangover, or the shame of a seedy sexual encounter. Her mind felt clear and bright, as if it had been pressure-cleaned.

Her memory clicked into place in one solid block.

She was in the yoga and meditation studio at Tranquillum

House, and yesterday she'd drunk a delicious smoothie containing hallucinogenic drugs resulting in an extremely beautiful, remarkably vivid dream that had lasted forever, about Gillian and her dad and her ex-husbands, with many symbols and visual metaphors which she looked forward to interpreting. Yao, and sometimes Delilah, and sometimes Masha, had kept interrupting her lovely dream, asking irritating questions and trying to steer her in certain directions. Frances had ignored them; she was having too much fun, and they were aggravating her. She sensed that after a while they gave up on her.

She'd been in space.

She'd been an *ant*.

Also a butterfly!

She'd been on a sleigh ride with Gillian across a stunning starlit sky, and more, much more.

It was like waking up the first morning back home in your own bed after a long international holiday to multiple exotic locations.

She opened her eyes to darkness and remembered her eye mask. The sound of snoring got even louder as she pulled it off. Her eyes didn't feel gritty or blurry. Everything was in crisp colour. She could see the vaulted stone ceiling above her. Rows of downlights. They were all switched on.

She sat up and looked around.

The man snoring was Lars. He lay on the stretcher next to hers, flat on his back, still wearing his eye mask, a blanket pulled up to his chin, his mouth wide open. His body twitched in tandem with each snore. It was pleasing to hear someone so good-looking with such a loud, unpleasant snore. It kind of redressed the balance.

Frances reached over with her bare foot and gave his leg a gentle shove. Henry was a snorer. Once, towards the end of the marriage, he was wearing shorts, and he'd looked down and said confusedly, 'I don't know why I'm always getting these bruises right here on my calf. It's like I keep bumping into something.' *My right foot*, thought Frances. She felt terrible about that right up until their last day together when they fought over the division of cutlery.

She scanned the room.

Tony – she would not be calling him 'Smiley' – had just sat up on his stretcher. It looked like he had a headache by the way he rested his forehead in his hands.

Carmel was also upright and was attempting to comb her fingers through her black, frizzy hair, which stood out in a wild halo around her head.

She met Frances's eye. 'Bathroom?' she mouthed, although she'd been in the studio as often as Frances.

Frances pointed to the toilets at the back of the cellar and Carmel got to her feet, staggering a little.

Ben and Jessica sat shoulder to shoulder against a wall, drinking bottled water.

Heather and Zoe lay face to face where they had fallen asleep on a yoga mat. Heather was absently caressing Zoe's hair.

'Need water?' Napoleon crouched down with difficulty on his long legs in front of Frances and offered her a bottle of water. 'I'm assuming it's not spiked with drugs,' he said. 'I guess if we're worried we could just drink from the tap, although they could do something to the water supply if they really wanted.'

'Thank you.' Frances accepted the water, suddenly desperate for it, and drank nearly the whole bottle in one go. 'Just what I needed,' she said.

'I guess it's a good sign that they left us with water,' said Napoleon. He straightened. 'They haven't completely abandoned us.'

'What do you mean?' asked Frances. She stretched luxuriously. She was *really* looking forward to breakfast.

'We're locked in,' said Napoleon apologetically, as if he were the one responsible. 'There doesn't seem to be a way out.'

chapter forty-six

Carmel

'I'm sure this is all just part of the process,' said Carmel. She didn't know why everyone looked so worried. 'They're not going to leave us down here for much longer. It's all fine.'

The time, according to Napoleon, the only one among them with a watch, was coming up to 2 pm, and they had still not heard from any of the staff at Tranquillum House. They had been down here for close to twenty-four hours now.

They all sat in a circle similar to the one from the previous day, when they'd introduced themselves. Everyone looked exhausted and grimy. The men needed shaves. Carmel was desperate to clean her teeth, but she wasn't especially hungry, even though she hadn't eaten for coming up to *forty-eight hours*, so that was kind of wonderful. If appetite suppression was one of the side effects of last night's perfectly enjoyable drug experience, then she was all for it.

Each of them had confirmed for themselves that the only access point to the room was the heavy oak door at the bottom of the stairs, and that the door was undeniably, irrefutably locked with what looked to be a brand-new gold security keypad next to the doorhandle. Presumably there was a code that would unlock the door, but multiple combinations of numbers had been attempted with no success.

Frances had suggested that the code might be the same as the one given at the front gate of Tranquillum House.

Napoleon said he'd already thought of that but had no memory of the number.

Carmel had no memory of it either. She'd been crying when she arrived at Tranquillum House, suddenly struck by a memory from her honeymoon when they'd stayed at a hotel with a similar-looking intercom. It seemed stupid now. Her honeymoon hadn't been *that* great. She'd got a terrible UTI.

Ben thought he remembered the access code for the front gate, but if he did, the number didn't work.

Tony thought he remembered too, although he remembered one digit differently to Ben, but that number didn't work either.

Carmel suggested the phone number for Tranquillum House, which for some reason she was able to recite, but they had no luck with that.

Frances wondered if the code was related to the letters of the alphabet. They tried various words: Tranquillum. Cleanse. Masha.

Nothing worked.

Zoe wondered if it was meant to be a kind of a game. An 'escape room'. She told them there was a bizarre craze where people *allowed* themselves to be locked up in a room for the pleasure of trying to work out how to escape. Zoe had been to one before. She said it was great fun, with multiple clues concealed in what looked like normal objects. For example, Zoe and her friends had to find and assemble the parts of a torch that had been hidden around the room. The torch could then be used to shine a light on a secret message in the back of a wardrobe with further instructions. A timer counted down the minutes on a wall and Zoe said they got out just seconds before the timer went off.

But if this was an escape-room game it seemed it was a very tricky one. The yoga studio was virtually empty. There were towels, yoga mats, stretcher beds, water bottles, headphones, eye masks and burnt-out candles from the night before, and that was it. There were no bookshelves with messages in books. No pictures on the wall. There was nothing that could feasibly represent a clue.

There were no windows that could be smashed in either the men's or the women's toilets. No manholes, no air-conditioning ducts.

'It's like we're trapped in a *dungeon*,' said Frances, which Carmel thought was melodramatic, but then the woman wrote romantic fiction for a living so you had to allow for an overactive imagination.

Eventually, they'd sat back down, dispirited and dishevelled.

'Yes, this is all just part of the process,' said Heather to Carmel. 'Spiking our drinks with illegal drugs, locking us up and so on and so forth. Nothing to worry about, it's all fine.'

She was using a very sarcastic, familiar tone for someone Carmel had only just met.

'I'm just saying we should trust the process.' Carmel tried to remain reasonable.

'You're as deluded as her,' said Heather.

So that was definitely rude. Carmel reminded herself that Heather had lost her son. She spoke evenly. 'I know we're all tired and stressed, but there's no need to get personal.'

'This *is* personal!' shouted Heather.

'Sweetheart,' said Napoleon. 'Don't.' The gentle way he scolded his wife made Carmel's heart ache.

'Do you have children, Carmel?' asked Heather in a more civilised tone.

'I have four little girls,' said Carmel carefully.

'Well, how would you feel if someone gave your children drugs?'

It was true that she wouldn't want a single drug to cross their precious lips. 'My children are very little. Obviously Masha would never —'

'Do you have any idea of the serious long-term health consequences we could all be facing?' interrupted Heather.

'I feel worse than I've ever felt in my entire life,' said Jessica.

'There you go,' said Heather with satisfaction.

'Well, I feel *better* than I've ever felt in my entire life,' said Carmel. It wasn't entirely true, there was the teeth situation, but she did feel quite good. Her mind was filled with images she hadn't yet had a chance to interpret, as if she'd just spent a day at some incredible immersive art exhibit.

'I feel pretty good so far,' admitted Frances.

'I do have a significant headache,' said Lars.

'Yeah, me too,' said Tony.

'I feel like I might be down a dress size.' Carmel pulled at the loose waistband of her leggings. She frowned, trying to remember some important revelation she'd come to last night about her body. It didn't matter . . . it did matter . . . it was the only one she had? Somehow it didn't seem quite so profound and transcendent a revelation when she tried to pin it down with ordinary words. 'Although I'm not trying to change my body *completely*. I'm just here to get healthy.'

'Healthy?!' Heather banged her palm against her forehead. 'This place has gone way beyond bloody dieting!'

'Mum.' Zoe put her hand on her mother's knee. 'Nobody died. We're all still here. Just . . . please, relax.'

'Relax?!' Heather took Zoe's hand in hers and shook it. '*You* could have died! Any one of us could have died! If there was anyone with underlying mental health issues that could have been exacerbated, or heart issues! Your dad has high blood pressure! He should never have been given drugs.'

'People probably think you're the one with mental health issues,' murmured Zoe.

'That's not helping,' said Napoleon.

'Can't we just pick the lock on the door?' said Frances, and she looked hopefully at Tony.

'Why are you looking at me? Do I look like I have a lot of break-and-enter experience?' he said.

'Sorry,' said Frances. Carmel could see her point. Tony *did* look like someone who might have dabbled in a bit of breaking-and-entering in his youth.

'We could try. We'd need something to pick it with,' said Ben. He patted himself down and came up with nothing.

'I'm sure there's no need to panic just yet,' said Napoleon.

'It's obviously a kind of problem-solving exercise and eventually she'll realise that we can't solve it.' Lars yawned, then lay down on a yoga mat and shielded his eyes with his arm.

'I think they're watching us in here,' said Jessica. She pointed to a corner of the ceiling. 'Isn't that a camera up there?'

They all looked up at the tiny security camera with a flashing red light above the blank television screen.

'Yao told me they had some kind of security intercom system,' said Frances.

'Me too,' said Carmel. 'On the first day.'

It felt like a hundred years ago.

Heather leaped to her feet and addressed the camera. 'You let us out immediately!' she shrieked. 'We did not come here to spend the anniversary of our son's death *locked in a room with strangers*!'

Carmel flinched. She had forgotten the anniversary was *today*. The woman was allowed to snap and snarl as much as she wanted.

There was silence. Nothing happened.

Heather stamped her foot. 'I can't believe we're *paying* for this.'

Napoleon stood and pulled Heather into his arms. 'It doesn't matter where we are today,' he said.

'It does,' Heather cried quietly into his shirt. Suddenly she seemed diminished, all the rage gone, just a tiny, sad, traumatised mother.

'Shhh,' said Napoleon.

She was saying something over and over and it took a moment for Carmel to distinguish the words: 'I'm sorry, I'm sorry, I'm sorry.'

'It's okay,' said Napoleon. 'We're fine. Everything is fine.'

Everyone looked away from what seemed like an unbearably private moment. Zoe avoided looking at her parents also. She went to a corner of the room, put one palm against a wall, stood on one leg and held her ankle in the other hand, doing a yoga class for one.

Carmel looked at the blank screen of the television, suddenly desperate to be far, far away from this family's pain, which so dwarfed her own. She felt a sharp stab of homesickness. Her home was beautiful. She recalled this as if it were brand-new information. Not a mansion by any means, but a comfortable, sunshine-filled family home, even when it had been trashed by four little girls. She'd been the one to renovate it, to make it beautiful. People said she had 'an eye'. When she got home she would remember to enjoy it.

'I might see if I can kick that door down,' said Tony.

'*Great* idea,' said Carmel. People were always kicking down doors in the movies. It seemed quite simple.

'I'll do it,' said Ben.

'Or I'll ram it.' Tony limbered up, rolling his shoulders.

'*I'll* ram it,' said Ben.

'The door opens inwards,' said Lars.

There was a pause. 'Does that matter?' asked Frances.

'Think about it, Frances,' said Lars.

Tony looked deflated. 'Let's try to pick the lock then.' He put his fingertips to his forehead and breathed deeply. 'I'm starting to feel a little . . . claustrophobic. I want to get out of here.'

So did Carmel.

chapter forty-seven

Frances

They collected everything they could find that would work as a possible lock pick: one hairclip, one belt buckle, one bracelet. It was Frances's bracelet and she had nothing else to contribute except ignorant enthusiasm, so she stayed out of the way and the lock-picking committee became Ben, Jessica, Napoleon, Tony and Carmel. They seemed to be enjoying themselves destroying her bracelet and discussing exactly what was needed: 'teeth to push the pins out' or some such thing.

She went instead to talk to Zoe, who sat in the corner of the room, hugging her knees.

'You okay?' Frances asked, sitting down next to her and putting a tentative hand on the curve of her back.

Zoe lifted her head and smiled. Her eyes were clear. She looked lovely. Not like someone who had spent the previous night tripping. 'I'm fine. How was your . . . experience last night?'

Frances lowered her voice. 'I don't approve of what Masha did, outrageous et cetera, your mother is right, drugs are bad, illegal, wrong, just say no and all that . . . but I have to admit, I'm with Steve Jobs: it was one of the most fantastic experiences of my life. What about you?'

'There were good and bad parts,' said Zoe. 'I saw Zach. We all saw Zach. You know . . . hallucinated him, we didn't really see him.'

'I thought I saw him too,' said Frances without thinking. Zoe turned her head.

'I saw a boy,' said Frances. 'With you and your mum and dad.'

'You saw Zach?' Zoe's face lit up.

'Sorry,' said Frances. 'I hope you don't think that's disrespectful. Obviously, I never knew your brother. It was just my imagination, creating his image.'

'It's fine,' said Zoe. 'I like that you saw him. You would have liked him. He would have talked to you. He talked to anyone.' She stopped. 'I don't mean that in a bad way –'

'I know what you're saying.' Frances smiled.

'He was interested in everyone,' said Zoe. 'He was like Dad. Chatty. He would have asked you about, I don't know, the publishing industry. He was the biggest nerd. He liked watching documentaries. Listening to these obscure podcasts. He was fascinated by the world. That's why . . .' Her voice broke. 'That's why I could never believe he'd choose to give it up.'

She banged her chin against her propped-up knees. 'When he died we weren't talking. We hadn't been talking for, like, weeks. We used to have these really big screaming arguments over . . . lots of things: the bathroom, the television, the charger. It all seems stupid now.'

'That's what siblings do,' said Frances, seeing a flash of her own sister's pursed lips.

'We had this thing where if the fight got really bad we'd

stop talking to each other and it was like a competition to see who would talk first, and the person who talked first was *kind of* saying sorry without saying sorry, if you know what I mean, so I didn't want to be the one to talk first.' She looked at Frances as if she were telling her something truly terrible.

'I used to have a very similar arrangement with my first ex-husband,' said Frances.

'But I could tell there was something not quite right with him,' said Zoe. 'That week. I could tell. But I didn't ask him. I didn't say anything. I just ignored him.'

Frances kept her face neutral. There was no point saying, *You mustn't feel responsible.* Of course she felt responsible. Denying her regret would be like denying her loss.

'I'm so sorry, darling.' She wanted to envelop the child in a big, probably unwelcome hug but she settled for placing a hand on her shoulder.

Zoe looked over at her mother. 'I've been so angry with him. It felt like he did it on *purpose* just to make me feel bad forever, and I couldn't forgive him for that. It just felt like the meanest, cruellest thing he'd ever done to me. But last night . . . this sounds stupid, but last night, it felt like we talked again.'

'I know,' said Frances. 'I talked to my friend Gillian, who died last year. And my dad. It felt different from a dream. It felt so vivid. It felt realer than real life, to be honest.'

'Do you think maybe we really *did* see them?' There was so much tremulous hope in Zoe's face.

'Maybe,' lied Frances.

'It's just, I was thinking how Masha said that after her near-death experience she realised there was this other reality, and I just thought . . . maybe we sort of accessed it.'

'Maybe,' said Frances again. She didn't believe in alternate realities. She believed in the transcendent power of love, memory and imagination. 'Anything is possible.'

Zoe lowered her voice so much that Frances had to lean in close to hear. 'I feel like I've got him back now, in a weird sort of way. Like I could text him if I wanted.'

'Ah,' said Frances.

'I don't mean I *will* text him,' said Zoe.

'No,' said Frances. 'Of course not. I understand what you're saying. You feel like you're not fighting anymore.'

'Yeah,' said Zoe. 'We made up. I used to always be so relieved when we made up.'

They sat in silence for a few comfortable minutes and watched the lock pickers crouched down next to the door.

'By the way, I forgot to tell you: I read your book during the silence,' said Zoe. 'I loved it.'

'You loved it?' said Frances. 'Really? It's fine if it wasn't your cup of tea.'

'Frances,' said Zoe firmly, 'it was my cup of tea. I *loved* it.'

'Oh,' said Frances. Her eyes stung, because she could see that Zoe was telling the truth. 'Thank you.'

chapter forty-eight

Zoe

She lied. The book was so, so sappy.

She had finished it yesterday morning (there was nothing else to do here), and it was fine, she kept turning the pages, but you knew from the very beginning that the girl would end up with the guy, even though they hated each other at first, and that there would be trials and tribulations but it would all work out fine in the end, so what was the actual point of reading it? There was one part where the girl fainted into the guy's arms, which, like, was romantic or whatever, but did anyone ever really faint in real life? And if they did, was anyone ever really there to conveniently catch them?

Also, where was the *sex*? It took, like, three hundred pages to get to the first kiss, and the book was called *Nathaniel's Kiss*.

Zoe preferred books about international espionage.

'I thought it was a fantastic book,' she told Frances, perfectly poker-faced. *Your country is depending on you, Zoe.*

'Maybe you're still high,' said Frances.

Zoe laughed. Maybe she was. 'I don't think so.'

She couldn't believe she'd got high with her *parents*. That had been the freakiest part of the whole experience. The fact that her mum and dad were there with her. *Whoa*, she kept thinking. *There's Mum. Whoa. There's Dad.* Worlds collided with volcanic sparks and supersonic booms.

She felt like she could spend the rest of her life remembering everything that happened last night. Or it could all disappear. Either way was possible.

But one thing that wouldn't change when she left here was her mother's revelation.

She and her mother had barely spoken to each other this morning. Right now she was doing sit-ups, although Zoe noticed that she was doing them with less . . . *aggression* than usual. In fact, as Zoe watched, she stopped and lay flat on her back with her hands on her stomach, staring at the ceiling.

All these years Zoe had longed for someone to blame other than herself. After Zach died, she'd been through all of his technology: his phone, his email accounts, his social media. She *wanted* to find evidence that he'd been bullied, that there was something going on in his life which was nothing to do with her that could explain his decision. But there was nothing. Her dad had done it too. He'd met up with every single one of Zach's friends, interviewing them, trying to understand. But nobody understood. All his friends were devastated, as baffled as his family.

Now it seemed possible that there was nothing going on in the outside world. It was all in his head. It was the effects of the asthma medication making him temporarily lose his mind.

Maybe. She would never know for sure.

Her mother's revelation didn't exonerate Zoe, but it did give her someone with whom to share the blame. For just a moment, she allowed herself the pleasure of hating her mother. Her mother should not have let him take those stupid tablets. Her mother should have read that leaflet *like a responsible mother*. Like a mother with medical training.

But then she remembered the sound of her mother's scream that morning and she knew she could never truly blame her.

It had been so wrong, and almost *childish* of her mother to keep this a secret, but that very childishness made Zoe feel better. For the first time ever, she saw her mother as just a girl: a girl like her who made mistakes, who screwed things up, who was just making it all up as she went along.

Yes, her mum should have read the leaflet about the side effects, just like Zoe should have gone into her brother's bedroom when she saw him lying on his bed. She should have walked into his room, sat on the end of his bed, grabbed his gigantic foot, given it a shake, and said, 'What's wrong with you, loser?'

Maybe he would have told her, and if he *had* told her, and if he'd made it seem serious enough, she would have gone to her dad and said, 'Fix it,' and her dad would have fixed it. She looked at her dad, the only innocent one in their family, on his hands and knees peering at the lock. He'd get them out of here. He could fix anything given the opportunity. He just hadn't been given the opportunity to fix Zach.

It wasn't okay, it would never be okay, but it felt like hard knots in her stomach were loosening and she wasn't resisting. Other times when she'd started to feel better, when she'd found herself laughing or even looking forward to something, she had immediately pulled herself up. She had felt as though getting better would be forgetting him, betraying him, but now it seemed like there might be a way to remember not just the times they fought, but also the times they laughed so hard their faces hurt, to remember the times they stopped talking, but also the times they talked, about anything and everything, to remember the secrets they kept from each other but also the secrets they shared.

Zoe studied Frances's profile as she too watched the group of lock pickers. Frances looked younger today, without all that bright red lipstick she wore every day even when she was doing an exercise class. It was like she thought her red lipstick was a piece of clothing she couldn't be seen without.

Zoe felt all at once as if she *was* Frances, a middle-aged lady who wrote books about romance but fell for a romance scam; and she was her dad, who cried all the time without even knowing he did it, on his knees now trying to pick a lock; and she was her mum, so angry with the world but mostly with herself for the mistakes she'd made; and she was the hot guy who won the lottery but didn't seem that happy about it; and she was his wife with the incredible body; and she was the gorgeous gay divorce lawyer; and she was the lady who thought she was fat; and she was the man who used to smile and play football. She was all of them, and she was Zoe.

Wow. Maybe she *was* still high.

'It means a lot to me that you liked my book,' said Frances, turning to face her, eyes shiny. It was sweet. It seemed like Zoe's opinion really mattered to her.

Well done, kid, said Zach. *Thou droning, dog-hearted dewberry.*

Zach was still there. He wasn't going anywhere. He was going to stick around while she finished uni and travelled and got a job and got married and got old. Just because he chose death didn't mean Zoe couldn't choose life. He was still there in her heart and her memory, and he was going to stay beside her, keeping her company right until the end.

chapter forty-nine

Ben

They got nowhere trying to pick the lock. Ben could tell straight away that it wasn't going to work. They didn't have the right tools and the locking mechanism was newly installed. There was some swearing and tetchy remarks: 'You try it then!'

People kept coming up with suggestions for the security code, but that red light kept flashing its mean little *fuck you* rejection signal. Ben hated that red light.

He reckoned even his friend Jake, a locksmith, wouldn't be able to do it. He'd once asked Jake if he could pick any lock anywhere. 'With the right tools,' Jake had answered.

They didn't have the right tools.

Finally, Ben gave up. He left Carmel and the older men, Napoleon and Tony, to their useless endeavours and went and sat up against a wall with Jessica, who sat chewing on her false fingernails. She looked at him and smiled tentatively. Her lips were dry and chapped. They had kissed forever last night, in front of people. Sometimes Masha had been there, sitting right next to them, and they just kept right on kissing, like two horny teenagers on public transport.

But it had felt different from being a horny teenager because there was no end goal. He wasn't doing the kissing just to get to the sex. The kissing was the point. Ben felt like he could have done it forever. It wasn't like sloppy drunken kissing, it was hyperreal, like every part of his body had been involved. He couldn't pretend he'd hated his first experience of drugs. It had been incredible. Was this what his sister destroyed her life for?

Would Ben steal in order to experience that again?

He thought about it. No. He still didn't want to do it again, thank God. So he wasn't an addict from that one time he tried drugs.

His mother had been telling him that ever since he was ten years old, her face haggard with worry over his sister. 'It only takes once, Ben, only once, and your life is ruined.' He heard it over and over, like a bedtime story. The story was about how the beautiful princess, his sister, got taken away by the evil monster of drugs. 'You must never ever, never ever, never ever,' his mother would say, holding his arm so tight it hurt and looking at him with such terrified intensity he always wanted to look away, but he had to maintain eye contact because if he looked away she would start the *never ever, never ever, never ever* chant again.

He didn't need his mother to tell him that drugs ruined your life. The evidence was right there in front of his eyes. He was only ten when it started, and Lucy was five years older, but he still remembered the old Lucy, the first Lucy, the real Lucy who got taken away. The real Lucy played soccer and she was really good. She sat at the dinner table and ate her dinner and said stuff that made sense and laughed when something was *funny*, not for hours at a time at nothing, and if she lost her temper it was normal anger, not the anger that turned her eyes red and mean, like a demon's eyes. She didn't steal, she didn't break things and she didn't bring home skinny, rat-faced boys with matching red demon eyes. He didn't need to be told never ever, never ever. He knew what the monster did.

Ben's poor mother would have a panic attack if she heard he'd been given drugs.

'It's okay, Ben,' said Jessica quietly, as if she'd read his mind. 'You're not an addict now.'

'I know that.' He put his hand over hers and wondered if maybe the couples counselling had worked. Although, if so, why didn't he feel more elated? Maybe it was the crash after the high. That's what got people addicted. The highs were so great, and the lows were so shit in comparison that you'd risk doing anything to get back to the high.

He and Jessica had talked. He remembered that. They'd talked about so much. About everything. Maybe more than they'd ever talked in their entire relationship. They talked about the money. He remembered he'd told her he didn't like the way she'd changed her face and her body. It was strange, because that had seemed like such a big deal before, like the biggest deal ever, and now it seemed like absolutely nothing. Why had it mattered so much? So he didn't like her puffy new lips. Why was that the end of the world?

And the car. She'd been the one who scratched the car. That didn't seem to matter much either now. It was like those smoothies had sucked all the air out of their arguments, and now they were all wrinkled and deflated and kind of embarrassing. Like they'd both been making a whole lot of fuss about nothing.

There was something else they'd talked about too. Something he thought might have been more significant. He'd remember it in a moment.

Jessica pulled out her shirt and sniffed her cleavage. 'I stink. I'm going to try and have a sponge bath at the bathroom sink.'

'Okay,' he said.

'I need to wash my face,' said Jessica. She ran a hand over her cheek.

'Okay,' said Ben. He glanced at her. 'Not a single person in this room will care if you're not wearing make-up.'

'There will be a single person who cares,' said Jessica, as she got to her feet. 'Me. *I* care.' But she didn't seem angry.

He watched her walk towards the bathrooms.

Are we fixed? Do we have the right tools now?

He wanted a Bacon & Egg McMuffin. He wanted to be at work with the guys listening to FM radio, making cars beautiful again. He was going back to work when they got home. He didn't care if they didn't need the money; he needed the work.

How much longer would they be left down here? He had to see *sky*. Even when he was working, he never spent a full day without going outside to eat his lunch.

He remembered a TV show he'd seen about a guy in jail who might have been wrongfully convicted and how he told his mother that he hadn't seen the moon in seven years. Ben experienced a full body chill when he heard that. That poor, poor schmuck.

'Hey. Mind if I sit here?'

It was Zoe, the girl who was here with her parents.

She sat down next to him.

When he'd seen her over the last few days he'd wondered why someone of her age, who was obviously fit and sporty, would choose to come to a place like this. Now he knew.

'I'm sorry about your brother,' he said.

She glanced at him. 'Thank you.' She pulled on her ponytail. 'I'm sorry about your sister.'

'How do you know about my sister?' asked Ben.

'Your wife mentioned it – when we heard about what was in the smoothies yesterday. She said she was an addict.'

'Right,' said Ben. 'I forgot that.'

'It must be hard,' said Zoe. She flexed her toes.

'It's hard for Jessica,' said Ben. 'It's like she has to keep hearing the same old story. She never knew Lucy before the drugs, so to her, she's just a messed-up junkie.'

'You never really get anyone else's family,' said Zoe. 'I broke up with my boyfriend because he wanted to go to Bali this week, and I said I couldn't go anywhere, I had to be with my parents for the anniversary of my brother's death. He was, like, "So are you going to have to spend that week in January with your parents *for the rest of your whole life?*" And I said . . . "Uh, *yeah.*"'

'He sounds like kind of a jerk,' said Ben.

'It's hard to pick the jerks,' said Zoe.

'I bet your brother would have picked him for a jerk,' said Ben, because it wasn't hard for a guy to pick the jerks, but then he wanted to kick himself. Was that an insensitive thing to say on the anniversary? And maybe her brother wasn't the type to be on the lookout for his sister.

But Zoe smiled. 'Probably.'

'What was your brother like?' asked Ben.

'He liked science fiction and conspiracy theories and politics and music that no-one had ever heard of,' said Zoe. 'He was never boring. We disagreed on basically everything there is to disagree on.' For a horrible moment he thought she might cry, but she didn't.

She said, 'What was your sister like? Before the drugs? Or beneath the drugs?'

'Beneath the drugs,' repeated Ben. He thought about it: *Lucy beneath the drugs.* 'She used to be the funniest person

I knew. Sometimes she still is. She's still a person. People treat addicts like they're not real people anymore but she's still . . . she's still a person.'

Zoe nodded, just once, almost businesslike, as if she heard what he said and she got it.

'My dad just wanted to cut her off,' said Ben. 'Have nothing more to do with her. Pretend like . . . she never existed. He said it was a matter of self-preservation.'

'How did that work out for him?' asked Zoe.

'It worked out great for him,' said Ben. 'He left. Mum and Dad got a divorce. He doesn't even ask about Lucy when I see him.'

'I guess everyone has, like, different ways of coping with stuff,' said Zoe. 'After Zach died, my father wanted to talk about him all the time and my mother couldn't bear to say his name, so . . .'

They sat in silence for a few moments.

'What do you think is going on here?' asked Zoe.

'I don't know,' said Ben. 'I really don't know.'

He watched Jessica walk out of the bathroom. She looked across at Ben and smiled, a bit self-consciously. It would be because she wasn't wearing make-up. These days he hardly ever saw her without that gunk plastered all over her face.

He looked at his wife and he knew that he loved her, but at the same time a thought occurred to him. All that kissing wasn't reconnecting. It was saying goodbye.

chapter fifty

Frances

Nobody came. The hours passed as slowly as if they were passengers stuck on a plane not moving from the tarmac.

Everyone kept returning to the keypad and trying out random combinations of numbers over and over.

Frances tried the alphabet code with multiple words: LSD, Psychedelic (hard to spell). Unlock. Open. Key. Health.

That red light flashed again and again and it started to feel personal.

Moods began to fluctuate in odd and unexpected ways.

Heather became quiet and withdrawn, her limbs floppy. She went to a corner of the room, put three yoga mats on top of each other, curled up on her side and fell asleep.

Lars sang. Endlessly. He had a deep, melodic voice, but he changed from song to song as if someone was turning a dial looking for a particular radio station.

Eventually Tony said abruptly, 'Christ Almighty, put a sock in it, mate,' and Lars looked startled, and stopped in the middle of 'Lucy in the Sky with Diamonds', as if he hadn't realised he'd been singing for all that time.

Carmel made an irregular *kwock* sound by clicking her tongue and Frances challenged herself to see how long she could put up with it. She was up to thirty-two *kwocks* when Lars said, 'How long do you intend to keep that up for?'

Some people exercised. Jessica and Zoe practised yoga poses together. Ben did an extraordinary number of push-ups, and finally stopped, breathing heavily, drenched in sweat.

'You should conserve your energy,' suggested Napoleon mildly. 'While we're fasting.'

Fasting didn't feel like the right word to Frances. Fasting implied an element of choice.

Napoleon didn't speak as much as Frances would have expected. She had thought from their first meeting that he was a talker, but he was quiet and contemplative, frowning at his watch and then glancing up at the camera on the ceiling with a quizzical look, as if to say, '*Really?*'

'What if something has happened to them?' said Frances eventually. 'What if they've all been murdered or kidnapped or fallen ill?'

'They've locked us in,' said Lars. 'So it seems like they planned this.'

'Maybe they did plan it, but it was just meant to be for an hour or so,' said Frances. 'And *then* something terrible happened to them.'

'If that's the case, we'll be found eventually,' said Napoleon. 'Our friends and families will notice when we don't return from the retreat.'

'So we could be here for another, what, four, five days?' said Frances.

'We'll be so thin,' said Carmel.

'I might lose my mind,' said Ben, and his voice sounded shaky, as if it were already happening.

'At least we have running water,' said Napoleon. 'And bathrooms. It could be worse.'

'It could be better,' said Tony. 'Room service would help.'

'I *love* room service,' said Frances.

'Room service and a movie,' sighed Tony.

They locked eyes and Frances looked away first because she was accidentally imagining herself in a hotel room with him. Those tattoos on his butt as he came out of the shower. That *smile*.

She gave herself a mental slap across the cheek, and thought of her dad sighing, 'You were always so crazy about the boys.' Fifty-two years old and still no sense. Just because they both liked room service didn't mean they were compatible. What would they talk about while they ate their room service? Football?

'We'll offer them *money*,' said Jessica suddenly. 'To let us out! Everyone has a price, right?'

'How much?' said Ben. 'A million? Two million?'

'Steady on,' said Lars.

'They're not going to let you out on a promise,' said Tony, but Jessica had already walked to the middle of the room and was addressing the camera.

'We're prepared to pay a fee to get out of here, Masha!' She jammed her fists into her waist. 'Money is no issue for us. We've got no shortage of cash. Honestly, we're happy to pay for . . . ah . . . an upgrade. We want to skip this part of the program, thanks, and we're happy to pay a penalty.' She looked around the room uncomfortably. 'For everyone, that is. We'll cover the cost for everyone to get out.'

Nothing happened.

'I don't think Masha is motivated by money,' said Napoleon quietly.

Frances thought, *What does motivate her?*

She remembered her counselling session and the way Masha's eyes had lit up when she spoke of how the VCR had once been a window into another world, but presumably movies no longer interested her. She had definitely wanted Frances to know that Australia needed her brains. Approval? Admiration? Was that it?

Or was it love? Was it that simple? She just wanted love, like everyone did. But some people had such a peculiar way of manifesting that need.

'We don't even know if they're watching us,' said Lars. 'Maybe they've all got their feet up somewhere and they're watching *Orange Is the New Black*.'

'We did not pay for shared accommodation!' Jessica jabbed her finger up at the camera. 'I'm not sleeping in here again tonight! We paid for a double room and I want to be back in my room! I'm hungry, I'm tired!' She lifted up a strand of her hair and smelled it. 'And I need to wash my hair right now!'

'Oh my God.' Ben put both his hands on his temples. He ran about in a comical half-circle. 'I just remembered what you said! You're pregnant! You said last night you were pregnant!'

'Oh yeah,' said Jessica, turning to her husband. 'I forgot.'

chapter fifty-one

Delilah

'She's not pregnant.' Yao's face was pasty with panic. 'She is absolutely not pregnant.'

Delilah, Masha and Yao were in Masha's office, watching the live CCTV footage of their guests in the meditation room.

'I would never have allowed a pregnant woman to take those substances,' said Yao. 'Never.'

'So why does she keep saying she is?' asked Masha.

They'd been here for hours. Masha and Yao stood and paced as they watched, but Delilah had finally sat down in Masha's chair.

Delilah was tired and hungry and kind of over it. Maybe she was kind of over being a wellness consultant. Four years now and the guests were all starting to blend together. They were all so self-absorbed, and sometimes she felt like she was a minor character in a story about everyone except her.

Over the years only a handful of guests had ever asked Delilah a single question about herself. Which, fine, the guests didn't have to talk to her at all if they didn't want, but they all assumed she would be so fascinated by *them*! The things they told her: about their marriages, their sex lives, their bowels! If she had to hear another story about someone's irritable bowel syndrome, she would slash her wrists.

And then there were the complaints that came thick and fast: the softness of their pillows, the temperature of their rooms, the *weather*, like she could control the weather.

It was nice when people seemed to truly believe they were 'transformed' at the end of a retreat, but Delilah wasn't quite as evangelical about this whole transformation business as Masha and Yao.

Yes, she enjoyed yoga, her core strength was excellent, she had a six pack and she liked having a six pack, meditation was relaxing, mindfulness was great, and she had no problem introducing drugs into the equation, that made life interesting, and sure, it might give people some insights into their psyches, although, honestly, most of their psyches didn't seem that, you know, *complex*. This wasn't God's work. This was a health resort.

Delilah was skilled at giving the impression she cared as much as Masha and Yao. She could talk the talk, walk the walk. God, she'd done it with dairy products when she was Masha's executive PA. *Yes, yes, I'm just passionate about yoghurt.* Then after Masha's heart attack she'd left dairy and done it with *insurance*. All those years working as a PA had been great training to be a wellness consultant: nod and smile and agree and make things happen behind the scenes and don't ask questions unless absolutely necessary. Masha paid well. Delilah had nearly reached her savings goal. She was going to travel for a year.

'I did pregnancy tests for all the women,' said Yao. 'Even the older women. She's not pregnant.'

'So why did she say she was?' asked Masha again.

'I don't know,' said Yao. He was very upset. Almost in tears.

'So she can sue us for giving her drugs,' said Delilah.

'She doesn't need money.' Masha gestured at the screen. 'Like she said, money is no issue.'

Delilah shrugged and sighed. 'Maybe she just wants to make a point, like: "What if I *was* pregnant and you gave me drugs!"'

'She's not pregnant,' said Yao again.

'She doesn't know we know that,' said Delilah. 'And her husband's sister is an addict so, you know, they're really anti-drugs. Pity we didn't know that.'

Masha swung around. 'But they should be happy, their therapy went so well! They kissed!'

'That's because they were high,' said Delilah. Sometimes Masha had a bizarre innocence to her. Did she really think the kissing between those two *meant* something?

'They kissed for a very long time,' said Masha to Delilah.

'Yes,' said Delilah. 'That's what happens when you take ecstasy. That's why they call it the love drug.'

The first time Delilah took ecstasy she kissed Ryan, her boyfriend at the time, for over two hours straight, and it was incredible kissing, the best kissing of her entire life to date, but it didn't mean she wanted to *marry* the pompous British twat with his tight purple shirts. It was just kissing.

'It wasn't just the drug,' said Masha. 'I led them to many important breakthroughs.'

'Mmm,' said Delilah.

Like all of Delilah's bosses ever, Masha was a total narcissist. Delilah found it hilarious when Masha spoke so solemnly to guests about the 'dissolving of the ego', as if her giant-sized ego could ever be dissolved. Over the last few years, Delilah had observed Masha's ego flourish, nurtured by the guests who hung on her every word and the doglike devotion of Yao.

'I have a gift for this,' she said, straight-faced, when, really, what the hell would Masha know about relationships? In all these years Delilah had never known her to be in one. Delilah couldn't tell if she was straight or gay or bi or just had no sexual orientation whatsoever.

'I thought they would be more positive at this stage of their journeys,' said Masha. 'More *grateful*.'

Delilah exchanged a look with Yao. Wow. That was *almost* an acknowledgement of a mistake. At the very least it was the acknowledgement of a moment of doubt.

Yao looked terrified, as if his whole world were falling apart. The dude was obsessed with Masha, probably in love with her. Delilah couldn't tell if his interest was sexual; it was more like the way a super-fan behaves around a rock star, as if he couldn't quite believe he was allowed in the same room as her.

'It will all be fine,' said Masha to Yao. 'We just need to carefully consider how we proceed.'

'We should feed them,' said Delilah. She knew this from her waitressing days. Get some complimentary garlic bread out to the table. Stuff them with carbs and they'll stop complaining about the long wait on their mains.

'It hasn't even been forty-eight hours yet!' said Masha. 'They all knew the retreat would include fasting.'

'Yes, but they *didn't* know it would include LSD,' said Delilah. 'Or being locked up.'

She thought that Masha had badly overestimated her guests' commitment to transformation. When people said they came to Tranquillum House to be 'enlightened', what they really meant was 'skinnier'.

Anyway, as far as Delilah could see no-one in that room

looked particularly *transformed*. There was no way in hell Heather Marconi was coming out of that room and giving them a five-star review on TripAdvisor.

Masha, being Masha, had never doubted that this new protocol was going to be a success. She had no concerns about the issue of consent. She said it was too risky to ask for it because the ones who most needed help would be the ones most likely to refuse. The glorious ends would justify the means. No-one would complain once they experienced their personal transformations!

'Let's keep our focus on solutions,' said Masha now, as she contemplated her guests moving about their temporary prison. She didn't even look that tired.

Delilah remembered a night more than ten years earlier, when she was working as Masha's PA. Someone had discovered a major error in their analysis for the budget they were presenting to the board of directors the following day. Masha had worked thirty hours straight, right through the night, without stopping, to rectify the error. Delilah had stayed in the office with her, but she'd had a couple of power naps to keep herself going. The presentation was a triumph.

Six months later Masha had her heart attack.

Five years after that, when Delilah had honestly kind of forgotten Masha's existence, she called to ask Delilah if she'd like to train as a wellness consultant at a health resort she was starting up.

Masha liked to tell guests that they would hear about Delilah's supposed 'wellness journey', but they never heard about it because there was no wellness journey. Delilah resigned from her job as PA for the chief executive douchebag at an insurance company. Her wellness journey was basically a train ride from Central Station to Jarribong.

'I think we should let them out,' said Yao. 'They were meant to be out by now.'

'We have to be ready to adapt,' said Masha. 'I told you both that at the beginning. For dramatic results, you need dramatic action. I know this is uncomfortable for them, but that's the only way people *change*. They have water. They have shelter. We are taking them out of their comfort zone, that's all. That's when growth occurs.'

'I'm just not sure that this is right,' fretted Yao.

'Turn up the audio,' said Masha.

'Obviously we're obligated to report this to the police as soon as we're out,' said a woman.

'Who's that?' said Masha.

'Frances,' said Yao, his eyes on the screen. Frances had her back to them. She was talking to Lars.

'*Frances!*' said Masha. 'She loved her experience. She seemed to get so much out of it!'

Lars was saying, 'Morally obligated. Legally obligated. We've got a duty of care. They'll kill someone eventually if we don't.'

'I don't know if I'd want them to do actual jail time,' said Frances. 'I think their intentions were good.'

'Right now, I'm deprived of my liberty, Frances,' said Lars. 'I'm not too worried if someone does a little jail time for this.'

'Oh God.' Yao moaned into his knuckles. 'It's a disaster. They're not even . . . trying!'

'It's not a disaster,' said Masha. 'They'll work it out. It's just taking a little longer than we expected.'

'They don't seem any different after the therapy,' said Yao. 'They just seem so . . . angry.'

Delilah suppressed a sigh. *It's called a hangover, you fools.*

She said, 'Would anyone like a green tea?'

'Thank you, Delilah, that's very thoughtful,' said Masha gratefully, and she touched Delilah on the arm and smiled that soul-warming smile.

Even before, when Masha didn't look anything like a goddess, when she was just a frumpy high-level executive who was really good at her job, she had charisma. You wanted to please her. Delilah had worked harder for Masha than she'd ever worked for anyone, but now it was time to close this chapter in her life.

Clearly the police were going to be involved. Delilah had been the one to access the drugs on the dark web, a process she had enjoyed and a new skill to add to her CV along with PowerPoint. She thought her actions probably wouldn't be enough for her to go to jail, but they might be, and she felt like she wouldn't enjoy jail.

Part of her had known all along it was going to come to this. There was a kind of inevitability to it, from the moment Masha had first handed her the book about psychedelic therapy and said, 'This is going to revolutionise the way we do business.' Delilah remembered thinking, *This won't end well.* But she'd been feeling bored for a while. Experimenting with drugs was interesting and she'd kind of wanted to see the train wreck.

They micro-dosed guests' smoothies for over a year without ill-effects. People had no idea. They believed it was the organic food and meditation that caused them to feel so great. They rebooked because they wanted to feel that great again.

Then Masha decided she wanted to do more than micro-dosing. She wanted to do something 'revolutionary'. She wanted to 'push the envelope'. She said they would be changing the course of history. Yao had argued. He didn't want to change the course of history. He just wanted to 'help people'. Masha said this would be helping people in a way that would truly change their lives forever.

The clincher had been when he'd tried the psychedelic therapy himself with Masha as his guide. Delilah hadn't been there – it was her weekend off – but when she saw Yao next he had an even crazier, more obsessive blaze in his eyes than before, and he was quoting from the research as if it was the research that had changed his mind, when it was just the power of hallucinogenic drugs and the power of Masha.

Obviously Delilah tried the psychedelic therapy too. Her experience had been awesome, but she wasn't stupid enough to think any of those feelings or so-called 'revelations' were *real*. They were just drugs. She'd done magic mushrooms before. It was like mistaking lust for love, or thinking that the sentimental feelings you got when you heard a certain song were genuine. Get real. Those feelings were *manufactured*.

When Yao had gone on and on about what he'd supposedly *learned* from his psychedelic therapy she kind of wanted to slap him. It was just another example of how that sweet, stupid boy was addicted to Masha. He was a lost cause. Nothing was ever going to change there.

Delilah didn't go to the kitchen to make green tea. She went straight to her room and collected her ID. Everything else about this particular life – the white uniforms, the sandalwood scent, her yoga mat – she left behind.

Ever since she'd joined the workforce, she'd known this about herself: she was, at heart, a PA. The smoother of the way. Like a butler or a lady-in-waiting. Someone seen and not heard. She wasn't the captain of this ship and she sure as hell wasn't going down with it.

Within five minutes she was behind the wheel of Ben's

Lamborghini, driving towards the nearby regional airport, where she would take the next available flight, wherever it was going.

The car drove like a dream.

chapter fifty-two

Jessica

'How far along are you?' asked Heather from her position in the corner of the room. She sat up and rubbed her knuckles so hard into the sockets of her eyes that Jessica winced. You needed to be careful with the delicate skin around your eyes.

'Um, let's see. Two days,' answered Jessica. She put a hand to her stomach.

'Two *days*?' said Carmel. 'Do you mean your period is two days late?'

'No, I'm not late yet,' said Jessica.

'So you haven't done a test?'

'No,' said Jessica. Jeez. What was with the Spanish Inquisition? 'How could I?'

This was so weird, all of them standing around in this small room like they were at an office party, but they were talking about her periods.

'So you might not be pregnant?' asked Ben. Jessica couldn't tell if his shoulders dropped with relief or disappointment.

'I am,' said Jessica.

'What makes you think so?' asked Carmel.

'I just know,' said Jessica. 'I could tell. As soon as it happened.'

'You mean you knew at the moment of *conception*?' said Carmel. Jessica saw her exchange a look with Heather, as if to say: *Can you believe this shit?* Older women could be so condescending.

'Well, you know, some mothers do say they could tell they were pregnant at the moment of conception,' said Heather kindly. 'Maybe she is.'

'I bet a lot of women think they "know" and then it turns out they're wrong,' said Carmel.

'What's the big deal?' said Jessica. Why did this strange fuzzy-haired woman sound so angry with her? 'I mean, I know, we weren't meant to be touching during the silence.' She glanced up at the silent dark eye of the camera watching them. 'We weren't meant to be taking drugs either.'

The sex had happened in the dark on their second night at the retreat. Not a word spoken. It was all blind, silent touch, and it had been raw and real, and afterwards she lay awake and felt a wave of peace wash over her, because if their marriage was over, so be it, but now there was going to be a baby, and even if they didn't love each other anymore, the baby was created from a moment of love.

'But wait, she's on the pill,' said Ben to Heather and Carmel, as if Jessica weren't even there. 'Can that happen?'

'Only abstinence is one hundred per cent effective, but if she's . . .' Heather looked at Jessica. 'If you've been taking the pill every day, at the same time, it's probably unlikely that you're pregnant.'

Jessica sighed. 'I went off the pill two months ago.'

'Ah,' said Heather.

'Without telling me,' said Ben. 'You went off the pill without telling me.'

'Uh-oh,' said Lars quietly.

'You didn't mention this last night,' said Ben. 'When we were "speaking from our hearts".'

He sarcastically quoted Masha, his face stone-hard, and Jessica thought about last night, and how their words had flowed like water. But she hadn't told him last night about going off the pill. She'd still kept secrets even when she was high. Because she'd known it was a betrayal.

She *should* have said it last night, when his face was all soft and she felt like they were two halves of one person. She'd felt like that was a beautiful truth the drugs had helped her discover, but it had been a beautiful lie.

'Yeah,' said Jessica. She lifted her chin and remembered the kissing and how, as they'd kissed, a single thought had blinked on and off like a neon sign in her head: *We're okay. We're okay. We're okay.*

But they weren't okay. Nothing she'd thought last night had been real. It was all just drugs. Drugs *lied*. Drugs fucked you up. She and Ben knew that better than anyone. Sometimes Ben's mother sat and cried over the pictures of Lucy before she fell for the lies of drugs. Now that was a 'transformation'.

'Don't waste your money on this stupid retreat,' Jessica's own mother had said before they came here. 'Give all that money to charity and go back to *work*. Then your marriage will be just fine. You'll have something to talk about at the end of the day.'

Her mother seriously thought Jessica could go back and work in that shitkicker job when she now earned more in bank interest in just one month than she used to earn in a whole year. Jessica couldn't make her mother understand that once you had that much money you were changed forever. You were worth more. You were better than that.

You couldn't go *back*, because you could never see yourself that way again. Rationally, she knew it was just dumb luck that had got her rich, but deep, deep down an insistent voice in her head told her: *I deserve this, I was meant for this, I AM this person, I was always this person.*

'Oh dear. Take it from someone who knows: getting pregnant is not the best way to try to save a marriage,' said Carmel.

'Well, thanks, but I wasn't trying to save my marriage,' said Jessica.

'What were you trying to do, Jess?' asked Ben quietly, and for a moment it was like last night, just the two of them together in their little boat floating down a river of ecstasy.

'I wanted a baby,' said Jessica.

She was going to document her journey on Instagram. Sideways shots of her 'baby bump'. A stylish gender reveal party. Blue or pink balloons would fly out of a box. Hopefully pink. People would put heart emojis in the comments.

'I was scared you'd say no,' she told Ben. 'I thought if we were going to break up I'd better hurry up and get pregnant.'

'Why would I say no? We always said we'd have children,' said Ben.

'Yes, I know, but that was before we started to have . . . issues,' said Jessica. She couldn't have borne to hear him say, 'Are you kidding? Us?'

'So this baby isn't anything to do with me,' said Ben. 'You assumed we were breaking up and wanted to have a baby on your own?'

'Of course it's to do with you,' said Jessica. 'I only wanted your baby.'

She could see him soften, but then, idiotically, without thinking, she said, 'You're the father. You can see it whenever you want.'

'I can see it whenever I want!' exploded Ben. You would think she'd said the worst thing in the world. 'Gee. Thanks.'

'No, I didn't mean – I just meant, *God*.'

Their words no longer flowed like water. Now their conversations stopped and started in hard little jabs.

'It's probably premature to be sorting out access visits,' said Lars.

'I doubt she's even pregnant,' said Carmel.

'I *am* pregnant,' insisted Jessica. 'I just hope these drugs haven't hurt the baby.'

'You won't be the first or the last to have got drunk or high in the very early days of pregnancy,' said Heather. 'I'm a midwife, and the things some mothers have admitted to me, especially when the partners have left the room! If you *are* pregnant, there's a good chance your baby will be fine.'

'So much for being the anti-drug crusader, Mum,' said Zoe.

'Well, there's nothing to be done now,' said Heather under her breath, although Jessica could hear her perfectly well.

'I've been taking folate tablets,' Jessica told her.

'That's great,' said Heather.

'Yep, so great: folate, a little LSD and some ecstasy,' said Ben bitterly. 'The perfect start to life.'

'Don't worry about it, she's probably not even pregnant,' said Carmel in a low voice.

'What is your fucking *problem*?' Jessica's voice rose to an embarrassingly high pitch. She knew she shouldn't be swearing and showing her emotions like this, but she felt suddenly very upset.

'Hey now,' said Napoleon soothingly.

Frances, the romance author, plonked herself down and went bright *red* in the face, as if she'd never heard the f-word in her life.

'Sorry,' said Carmel. She lowered her head. 'It's probably just envy.'

'Envy? You're, like, jealous of *me*?' said Jessica. Wasn't this woman too old to feel jealous? 'Why?'

'Well . . .' Carmel laughed a little.

The money, thought Jessica. *She's jealous of the money.* It had taken her a while to realise that people of any age, people she considered grown-ups, of her parents' generation, who you would think wouldn't care that much about money because their lives were virtually done, could still be jealous and weird about it.

'Well, you're thin and beautiful,' said Carmel. 'I know it's embarrassing to admit this at my age – I've got four beautiful daughters, I should be way beyond this – but my husband left me for a . . .'

'Bimbo?' suggested Lars.

'Sadly not. She's got a PhD,' said Carmel.

'Oh, honey, you can still be a bimbo with a PhD,' said Lars. 'Who represented you? I assume you're still in the family home?'

'It's fine. Thank you. I'm not complaining about the settlement.' She stopped and looked at Jessica. 'You know what? I'm probably jealous of you being pregnant.'

'Haven't you got four children?' said Lars. 'That seems like more than enough.'

'I don't want any more children,' said Carmel. 'I just want to go back in time to when everything was beginning. Pregnancies are the ultimate *beginnings*.' She put a hand to her stomach. 'I always felt beautiful when I was pregnant, although I must admit my hair looked preposterous. I've got all this thick black Romanian hair, so when I was pregnant, it went wild.'

'Wait, why did it go wild?' asked Jessica. She was not

prepared for her hair to go wild, thank you very much. Surely there was a shampoo and conditioner to fix that.

'Your hair stops falling out when you're pregnant,' said Heather. 'So it gets thicker.' She touched her own hair. 'I loved my hair when I was pregnant.'

'I'm sure you *are* pregnant, Jessica,' said Carmel. 'And I'm sorry.' She paused. 'Congratulations.'

'Thank you,' said Jessica. Maybe she wasn't pregnant. Maybe she'd just made a fool of herself in front of these people. She looked at Ben. He was studying his bare feet as if they had the answer. He had huge feet. Would their baby have huge feet too? Could they really be parents together? They weren't too young. They could afford a baby. They could afford a dozen babies. Why did it seem unimaginable?

Tony had gone to the bathroom and come back with a damp towel that he wordlessly handed to Frances. She pressed it to her forehead. She was sweating.

'Are you not well, Frances?' asked Carmel.

Everyone looked at Frances.

'No,' said Frances. She waved a languid hand in front of her face. 'Just . . . you know how you talked about how much you liked beginnings? I've got my own personal *ending* going on here.'

'Ah,' said Heather, as if that made perfect sense to her. 'Don't think of it as an ending. Think of it as a beginning.'

Carmel said, 'When I was a teenager, my mother used to wear this badge that said, "They're not hot flushes, they're power surges." I was absolutely *mortified* by it.'

The three of them laughed that self-satisfied, middle-aged-woman laugh that made you want to stay young forever.

chapter fifty-three

Frances

'You alright?'

Tony sat on the floor next to Frances, in that uncomfortable way men sat on the ground at picnics, as if they were looking for somewhere to stow their legs.

'I'm okay,' said Frances. She pressed the damp towel to her forehead as the wave of heat continued to engulf her. She felt strangely sanguine, even though she was locked in a room with strangers and having a hot flush. 'Thanks for the towel.'

She studied him. His face was pale and there were beads of sweat across his forehead too. 'Are *you* okay?'

He patted his forehead. 'Just a bit claustrophobic.'

'You mean like properly claustrophobic? Not just *I really want to get out of here* claustrophobic?' Frances let the towel drop to her lap.

Tony tried to bend his knees up towards his chest, gave up, and stretched them out again. 'I'm mildly claustrophobic. It's not that big a deal. I didn't like being down here even before we were locked in.'

'Right then, I need to distract you,' said Frances. 'Take your mind off it.'

'Go right ahead,' said Tony. He smiled a half-version of his full-on smile.

'So . . .' said Frances. She thought about what Napoleon had said yesterday before their smoothies had their full effect. 'Did you suffer from that "post-sports depression" when you gave up football?'

'That's a really sparkling topic of conversation to hit off with,' said Tony.

'Sorry,' said Frances. 'I'm not at my best. Also, I'm interested. My career might be kind of ending right now.'

Tony grimaced. 'Well. They say that a sports star dies twice. The first time is when they retire.'

'And was it like a death?' asked Frances. It would feel like a death if she had to stop writing.

'Well, yeah, kind of.' He picked up a half-melted candle and pulled off a chunk of wax. 'Not to be dramatic about it, but the game was all I knew for all those years, it's who I was. I was a kid straight out of school when I started playing professionally. My ex-wife would say I was still a kid when I finished. She used to say it stunted me. She had this phrase she'd picked up somewhere: professional sportsperson, amateur human being.' He put the candle back on the floor and flicked away the piece of wax with his fingertips. 'She used to repeat it every time I . . . demonstrated my amateur approach to life.'

There was a hurt look in his eyes that belied his light humorous tone. Frances decided his ex-wife was a witch.

'Also, I wasn't ready to finish up. I thought I had one season left in me, but my right knee thought otherwise.' He pulled up one leg and pointed at the offending knee.

'Stupid right knee,' said Frances.

'Yeah, I was pissed off with it.' Tony massaged his knee. 'A sports doctor friend told me that retiring is like coming off cocaine; your body is used to all those feel-good chemicals: serotonin, dopamine, and – *bam* – suddenly they're gone and your body has to readjust.'

'I don't think I've ever experienced those feel-good chemicals doing exercise,' admitted Frances. She picked up the candle he'd discarded and dug her thumbnail into the soft wax near the wick.

'You probably have,' said Tony. 'Doing certain types of exercise.' He paused.

She blinked. Wait. Was that *innuendo*?

He continued talking. Maybe she'd got it wrong.

'You probably find this laughable but there were some games where we were all where we were meant to be and we all did what we were meant to do, and it all just came together, like a piece of music or poetry or . . . I don't know . . .' He met her eyes and winced, as if preparing himself for derision. 'Sometimes it felt transcendent. Like drugs. It really did.'

'That's not laughable,' said Frances. 'That makes me want to take up AFL.'

He gave a deep appreciative chuckle.

'My ex-wife used to say that all I ever thought about was the game. It probably wasn't much fun being married to me.'

'Oh, I'm sure it was,' said Frances without thinking, and caught herself staring at his massive shoulders. She changed the subject hurriedly. 'So what did you do after you stopped playing? How did you re-create yourself?'

'I set up a sports marketing consultancy,' said Tony. 'It's done well – you know, for a business run by an amateur human being. I thought I was doing better than a lot of my teammates. Some of them really fucked up – I mean . . . stuffed up their lives.'

'I feel like fucked up is the correct phrase to use there,' said Frances.

He gave her his full 'Smiley' grin. It really was the funniest smile.

'You're kind of annihilating that candle,' he said.

She looked guiltily at the mess of wax in her lap. 'You started it.' She brushed the wax onto the floor. 'Go on. So you set up this consultancy.'

'I had one friend who said to me, "Don't you hate the way that everyone only wants to talk about who you *used to be*?" but I honestly never minded that. I liked it when people recognised me; I never mind talking about the man I used to be. But anyway . . . late last year I started to get these symptoms, this incredible fatigue, I just felt something was wrong, even before I got on Dr Google.'

Frances felt herself go cold. She was at an age where people in her circle didn't imagine serious illnesses, they got them. 'And . . .?'

'So, I took myself off to my GP, and he ran a lot of tests, and I could tell he was taking it seriously, and I said, "Are you thinking pancreatic cancer?" Because that's what I was thinking – that's how I lost my dad, and I know it runs in families. And the GP just gave me this look – I've known him for years – and he said, "I'm covering all bases."'

Oh, damn it to hell.

'It was just before Christmas, and he called me in to give me the results. He pulled out the file and, afterwards, I realised I had these words in my head, and I was saying them to myself, and it just . . . shocked the life out of me that I would think that.'

'What words?' asked Frances.

'I was thinking, *Let it be terminal.*'

Frances blanched. 'And . . . but . . . is it?'

'Oh, I'm fine,' said Tony. 'Nothing wrong with me, except that I obviously don't have a healthy lifestyle.'

Frances exhaled. She hoped not excessively. 'Well, thank goodness.'

'But it shook me up – that I would think that, that I would *hope* for a terminal diagnosis. I thought, *Mate, how fucked up is your head?*'

'Yeah, that's bad,' said Frances. She felt energised in that bossy female way that she knew drove men crazy, but there was really nothing you could do about it once you felt that sense of righteousness surge through you, because they were such idiots. 'So, right, you've got to get this fixed. You need –'

He held up his hand. 'I've got it under control.'

'It's really very bad that you thought that!'

'I *know* it is. That's why I'm here.'

'So you probably need –'

He put his finger to his lips. 'Shhh.'

'Therapy!' she got in quickly.

'Shhh.'

'And –'

'Zip it.'

Frances zipped it. She held the wet towel to her face to hide her smile. At least he wasn't thinking about his claustrophobia now.

'Tell me about this bastard who scammed you,' said Tony. 'And then tell me where he lives.'

chapter fifty-four

Yao

'What's wrong with this one now? Is she sick? Why is she dabbing at her face like that?'

Masha's accent, usually just a flavour, sounded more pronounced than usual to Yao. Yao's parents were the same. They sounded extra Chinese when they were stressed about their internet service or health.

He should call his parents. 'You are wasting your life with this woman!' his mother had said the last time they talked.

'Yao?' said Masha. She had sat down in the chair vacated by Delilah and was looking up at him, her big green eyes so worried and vulnerable. She was rarely vulnerable. It was exquisite torture to see her so.

'Frances is menopausal,' said Yao.

Masha shuddered. 'Is she?'

Yao knew Masha was a similar age to Frances, also in her fifties, but she was presumably not experiencing any symptoms of menopause. Masha was a puzzle Yao could never quite solve. She enjoyed discussing the most intimate intricacies of the digestive system, she had no shame when it came to nudity (why would she?) and often walked about naked when there were no guests on the property, but the word 'menopause' caused her to shudder, as if something so distasteful could never happen to her.

Yao looked at the back of Masha's neck and saw a small inflamed lump: a mosquito bite. It was strange to see any form of blemish on her beautiful body.

She reached back with her hand and scratched it.

'You're making it bleed,' he said. He put his hand over hers.

She waved him away irritably.

'Delilah is taking a long time,' he said.

'Delilah is gone,' said Masha, her eyes on the screen.

'Yes, she went to get you tea,' said Yao.

'No, she is gone,' said Masha. 'She's not coming back.'

'What are you talking about?'

Masha sighed. She looked up at him. 'Have you not worked it out yet? Delilah looks after Delilah.' She turned back to the screen. 'You can go too, if you like. I will take responsibility for it all. The new protocol was my idea, my decision.'

She could never have applied the new protocol without his medical expertise. If anyone should pay, it was Yao.

'I'm not going anywhere,' he said. 'No matter what happens.'

Over a year ago now, Masha had come across an article about micro-dosing in Silicon Valley. White-collar professionals were using micro-doses of LSD to increase their productivity, alertness and creativity. Micro-dosing was also being used with some success to treat mental illnesses like anxiety and depression.

Masha was fascinated in her typical Masha way. Yao loved her sudden wild enthusiasms and the fearless way she strode into unfamiliar territory. She tracked down the person who wrote that first article and phoned him. That's what led to her learning about psychedelic therapy, where people were given 'full doses' of psychedelic drugs. Within a very short time, she became obsessed. She ordered books online. She made more phone calls to experts all around the world.

This was the answer, she said. This was what would take them to the next level. Psychedelic therapy, she said, was *the magic shortcut to enlightenment.* Scans showed that the brain activity of someone who had taken psilocybin bore striking similarities to the brain of an experienced meditator during deep meditation.

At first, Yao had just laughed in disbelief. He had no interest. When he was a paramedic he had seen the terrible impact of illegal drugs. The man who had held a knife to his throat had been suffering the psychotic effects of crystal meth. Yao had treated junkies. They were not a good advertisement for the wonderful effects of drugs.

But Masha chipped away at him, day by day.

'You're not listening. This is nothing like that,' she said. 'Would you not use penicillin because of heroin?'

'Penicillin does not affect brain chemistry.'

'Okay then, what about antidepressants? Antipsychotics?'

That low, persuasive, accented voice in his ear, those green eyes fixed on his, that body, that beautiful hold she had over him.

'At least study the research,' she said.

So he did. He learned about the government-approved clinical trials of psychedelic drugs being used to help ease the anxiety of patients with terminal cancer. The results were overwhelmingly positive. So, too, were similar trials with war veterans suffering PTSD.

Yao became curious and intrigued. Eventually he agreed

to try the therapy himself.

Delilah got the supplies on the dark web, including the drug-testing kits. Yao did all the testing.

He and Delilah both agreed to be the guinea pigs. Masha would be the psychedelic therapist. She herself, because of her medical history, could not do the therapy, but that was fine because she had already had transcendent experiences through her meditation and her famous near-death experience.

The psychedelic therapy had been, as Masha promised, transformative.

Even if medicating the guests turned out to be a mistake, he would never regret that.

It started with a journey down a tunnel that was possibly a waterslide (but the water was not wet, which was a brilliant idea) that ultimately spat him out in a cinema, where he sat on a red velvet seat and ate buttery popcorn while he watched as his whole life was played back to him, frame by frame, from the moment of his birth, right through school and university, up until the moment he arrived at Tranquillum House, except that he didn't just watch it happen, he re-experienced every incident, every failure, every success, and this time around he'd understood *everything*.

He understood that he'd loved Bernadette, his fiancée, more than she'd ever loved him and that she was never going to be the right woman for him. He understood that his parents had never been suited to each other either. He understood that he had the wrong personality to be a paramedic. (He was depleted, rather than energised, by bursts of adrenaline.)

Most significant of all, he learned that his phobia about mistakes had begun when he was a child.

It was an incident he was sure he had never heard about from his parents or remembered before, but under the influence of psychedelic drugs he re-experienced it in vivid detail.

He was no more than two or three years old, in the kitchen of their old house. His mother briefly left the room and he thought to himself, *I know! I'll help do the stirring*, and he'd carefully pulled a chair over to the stove, and he was so pleased with himself that he'd worked out this smart solution. He'd climbed up on the chair and he was about to reach out to the bubbling saucepan when his mother came back into the kitchen and *shouted* at him, so loudly, and his heart leapt out of his chest and he fell from the chair into endless space and his mother caught him, and shook him so hard his teeth chattered. He understood at last that he had internalised his mother's terror at *her* mistake, not his.

Delilah, who refused to reveal much about her own experiences, had been unimpressed by Yao's revelations. 'So it's your mother's fault you're a nervous nellie? Because she saved you from being scalded? What a terrible mother. No wonder you're so *damaged*, Yao.'

Yao ignored her. Sometimes Delilah seemed angry with him. He did not know why and he didn't care, because the day after his psychedelic therapy he woke dizzy with a new freedom: the freedom to make mistakes.

Perhaps this was his first mistake.

He looked at the screen showing nine people who did not look to be transformed in any way. They looked tired, agitated and angry. They were meant to be out by now, beginning the next stage of their 'rebirth'.

The 'code-breaker puzzle' should have taken an hour at most. It was meant to be a fun, stimulating group activity to help them bond as a group. Back in Masha's corporate days, she'd once been on a team-building retreat where they'd done a similar exercise and everyone had loved it. She said that people had come out of the room laughing and high-fiving each other.

Masha said she had come up with something sophisticated, subtle and symbolic that would integrate perfectly with their psychedelic experiences. ('Never afraid to blow her own trumpet, is she?' Delilah had said to Yao. Yao had put it down to jealousy. What woman wouldn't be jealous of Masha?)

Yao had worried that it was perhaps *too* subtle, but what did it matter? The code-breaking wasn't integral to their transformations. If the guests couldn't break the code within the hour, they would let them out and lead them straight to the dining room for platters of fresh fruit and organic, sugar-free hot chocolate for breakfast. Yao had been looking forward to that part, imagining how everyone's faces would light up as he, Masha and Delilah triumphantly entered the dining room, plates aloft. People would clap, he'd thought.

Yao had eaten a nectarine after his own psychedelic therapy session, and he could still remember the sensation of his teeth sinking into that sweet flesh.

Once they'd eaten, the group was to share what they'd learned through their experiences. After that, beautiful hardbound journals would be handed out, so that everyone could write down how they planned to integrate what they'd learned about themselves into their lives back home.

But nothing was going according to plan.

It felt like it had first gone off track with Heather's unexpected question, 'Have you been medicating us?', which meant that Masha's presentation of the treatment had begun on a defensive note, although she'd responded brilliantly, even under attack. People had got so angry, as if they truly believed something sinister was going on, when this was all for their benefit.

Yao had checked and rechecked the dosages, the possible side effects, the guests' medical histories, their daily blood tests.

There should have been only positive outcomes. He had checked everyone's vital signs throughout the night. Nothing had gone wrong. There had been no unexpected side effects. Napoleon had become agitated, but Yao had given him a dose of lorazepam and he'd calmed down.

It was true that the therapy side of it, from Yao's perspective at least, had been a little clunky. There was a disappointing banality to some of the insights the guests experienced, especially when compared to his own transcendent revelations. But Masha had been thrilled. After all the guests had fallen asleep, she'd locked the door of the meditation studio, flushed with success.

They had not imagined this.

As the time had passed, both Yao and Delilah had begun to say, 'I think we should let them out. Or give them a clue.'

But Masha was convinced that they would work it out. 'This is essential to their *rebirthing*,' she'd said. 'They need to fight their way out like a baby squeezes its way out of the birth canal.'

Delilah had made a small sound like a cough or a snort.

'We have given them so many hints,' Masha kept saying. 'Surely they are not so stupid.'

The problem was that the longer they left them locked up, the hungrier and angrier and stupider they got.

'Even if they do work it out,' said Yao now, 'I think their primary emotion will still be anger.'

'You may be right,' said Masha. She shrugged. 'We may need to be more creative going forward. Let us see what happens.'

Yao saw himself on that chair, his small, pudgy hand reaching for the pot of boiling water.

'Look!' said Masha. She pointed at the screen. '*Finally*. We have progress.'

chapter fifty-five

Frances

Frances and Tony sat next to each other in companionable silence. Most people were sitting now, except for Napoleon, who paced constantly. No-one was attempting to decode the security lock of the cellar door.

Someone hummed 'Twinkle, Twinkle, Little Star'. Frances thought it was Napoleon. She sang the words in her head along with him: *Up above the world so high, Like a diamond in the sky.*

She thought of the night of the starlight meditation and her sleigh ride across the starry sky with Gillian. Lars had been singing 'Lucy in the Sky with Diamonds' before. That was the song that had been playing when she first lay down on the stretcher.

She mentally listed the other songs that had played through the headphones.

'Vincent'.

'When You Wish Upon a Star'.

Beethoven's 'Moonlight Sonata'.

They all related to stars or the sky or the moon.

What had Masha said last night? Something like: *All your life, you've been looking down. You have to look up.*

'I think we're meant to look up,' she said. She got to her feet.

'What?' Lars propped himself up on his elbows. 'Look up where?'

'All the songs were about stars and the moon and the sky,' she said. 'And Masha said that we have to look up.'

The younger ones caught on first. Zoe, Ben and Jessica leaped to their feet and began to walk around the room, craning their necks to study the vaulted stone ceiling with curved wooden rafters. The older ones followed more slowly and warily.

'What do you think we're looking for?' asked Napoleon.

'I don't know,' said Frances.

After a moment, she said sadly, 'Maybe I'm wrong.'

'*There!*' Heather pointed. 'See? Do you see?'

'I see it!' said Jessica.

Frances followed her gaze. 'I don't actually see anything,' she said. 'My eyesight is terrible.'

'It's a sticker,' said Tony. 'A sticker of a gold star.'

'What good is a sticker?' asked Carmel.

'There's something above the sticker on the rafter there,' said Zoe.

'It's a package,' said Napoleon.

'I still can't see it,' said Frances.

'It's wrapped up in brown paper.' Heather took Frances's hand and pointed it up to the ceiling, trying to get her to look in the right direction. 'It's jammed into the little triangle where the two rafters meet, camouflaged against the wood.'

'Oh yes, I see it,' said Frances, although she didn't.

'Okay, so let's get it down,' said Jessica to Ben. 'Lift me up onto your shoulders.'

'I'm not lifting you up, you're pregnant,' said Ben. 'You're possibly pregnant.'

'Lift *me* up, Dad,' said Zoe to her father. 'You're the tallest.'

'I don't think we'd get enough height.' Napoleon tilted his head back, considering the distance. 'Even if you stood on my shoulders you wouldn't reach it.'

'The obvious thing to do is throw something up to knock it down,' said Lars.

'I'll jump up and knock it down,' said Tony. He looked up at the rafter with a gleam in his eye. 'I just need a couple of you guys to give me leverage.'

'You cannot possibly jump that high,' said Frances.

'I got the mark of the year three times in a row,' said Tony.

'I don't know what "the mark of the year" means, but that's impossible,' said Frances. It was like a joke to think of someone jumping that high. 'You'll injure yourself.'

Tony looked at her. 'Have you ever watched a game of Aussie Rules in your life, Frances?'

'I understand that you leap about energetically –'

'Seriously,' said Lars. 'We just need to throw something up there, dislodge it from the rafters.'

'We *leap about*,' repeated Tony as if to himself. 'We *leap about energetically.*'

'It's *very* impressive leaping,' said Frances. She remembered how she'd made the mistake of scoffing when Henry had started talking about how he wanted to learn to hang-glide at the age of fifty. All her friends had shaken their heads. *Oh, Frances, you never tell a man in the middle of a midlife crisis that he can't do something.* Henry did three months of hang-gliding lessons and suffered a chronic hip injury before he felt he'd proved his point.

'My highest mark ever was close to twelve feet.' Tony looked up at the rafter. 'I can reach that, no problem.'

'Off the back of that Collingwood player, right?' said Heather. 'Jimmy Moyes? Napoleon and I were at that game.'

Napoleon recited, '. . . *the leap into heaven, into fame, into legend – then the fall back to earth (guernseyed Icarus) to the whistle's shrill tweet.*'

'Is that a poem about football?' asked Frances.

'It is, Frances,' said Napoleon in a teacherly way. 'It's called "The High Mark" by Bruce Dawe. It's about how the mark is the manifestation of the human aspiration to fly.'

'It's really lovely,' said Frances.

'Oh my God, could we leave the poetry and the football and maybe just focus on getting out of here?' said Lars, as he picked up an empty water bottle, aimed it like a javelin and threw it up towards the ceiling. It hit the rafter and bounced back again.

'I'll get that parcel,' said Tony, and his chest swelled and his shoulders went back like a superhero emerging from a telephone box.

chapter fifty-six

Yao

'What are they *doing*?' asked Masha.

'I think Tony is going to try to launch off their backs like he's in a game of football,' said Yao worriedly.

'That's crazy,' said Masha. 'He's too heavy! He will hurt them!'

'They're hungry and tired,' said Yao. 'They're not thinking straight.'

'It's so obvious what they should do,' said Masha.

'Yes,' said Yao. Lars had the right idea.

'Why are they not building a simple human pyramid?' said Masha.

Yao looked at her to see if she was serious.

'They are just not that smart,' said Masha. 'This is the problem we face, Yao. They are not smart people.'

chapter fifty-seven

Frances

Napoleon and Ben had positioned themselves beneath the rafter, their heads lowered, their bodies tensed.

'Should we jump at the same time?' suggested Napoleon. 'Give you more height?'

'No,' said Tony. 'Just stand still.'

'I don't think this is such a good idea,' said Carmel.

'It's a ludicrous idea,' said Lars.

'Now that you mention it . . .' began Heather, but it was too late.

Tony ran from the doorway at full pace.

He leaped up vertically, one knee dug into Napoleon's back, the other into Ben's shoulder. For a fraction of a second, Frances saw the young man within the old. The athlete he'd once been was there in the length of his body and the resolve in his eyes.

He got up there! Impossibly high! He was going to do it! What a *hero*! One hand slapped the rafter, but then he crashed to the floor on his side with an almighty thud. Napoleon and Ben staggered in opposite directions, muffling curses.

'That wasn't at all predictable,' sighed Lars.

Tony sat up cradling one elbow, his face as white as toothpaste.

Frances got onto her knees next to him, to be supportive, even though her knees crunched. 'Are you okay?'

'I'm fine,' he said through gritted teeth. 'I think I just dislocated my shoulder.'

Frances's stomach turned at the sight of his shoulder protruding at a strange, distressing angle.

'Don't move it,' said Heather.

'No,' said Tony. 'I need to move it. It's going to pop back in when I move it.'

He moved his arm. There was an audible pop.

Frances toppled in a dead faint straight into his lap.

chapter fifty-eight

Zoe

Zoe's poor dad clutched his back where he'd just borne the entire weight of one Smiley Hogburn. She was kind of surprised that her mother had allowed that little exercise to go ahead. Maybe it was the drugs, or her crazy fury over the drugs, or maybe it was just that she and her dad were star-struck by meeting an AFL legend.

'Sorry, everyone,' said Tony. 'Last night I dreamed I was playing again. This felt . . . this felt like it would be easy.' He gently patted poor Frances on the cheek. 'Wake up, lady writer.'

Frances sat up self-consciously from Tony's lap and pressed a single fingertip to the centre of her forehead. She looked around her. 'Did we get the package down?'

'Not quite,' said Zoe's dad, who never wanted anyone to feel like a failure. 'Very close!'

Zoe looked around for something to throw up at the rafter. She picked up a three-quarters-full bottle of water, held it in the palm of her hand and took aim.

She hit the package straight on. It fell into Ben's hands.

'Nice shot.' He handed it to her.

'Thanks,' she said.

'Open it,' instructed Jessica, as if Zoe had been intending to just look at it for a while.

The package had that firm, soft consistency of something encased in bubble wrap. She fumbled with the masking tape and tore at the brown paper.

'Careful,' said her mother. 'It might be breakable.'

Zoe pulled at the tape on the bubble wrap and was reminded of opening a birthday gift, surrounded by people at a party, all eyes on her and Zach. Tomorrow was their twenty-first birthday. It might be time to reclaim it. She thought that maybe, once they got back to Melbourne, she would tell her parents that she wanted to go to La Fattoria for pizza to celebrate her twenty-first. It felt suddenly as if it might be possible to do some of the things they'd stopped doing after Zach died. It wouldn't be the same without him, it would never be the same, but it felt possible. She would still take off the olives and leave them along the edge of her plate for Zach.

And now she really, really felt like pizza. Her mouth watered at the thought of pepperoni. She would never take pepperoni for granted again.

She unrolled the bubble wrap. Inside was a small hand-painted wooden doll of a little girl wearing a scarf around her head and an apron around her waist. She had red circles on her cheeks and quizzically angled eyebrows. She seemed to be saying to Zoe, 'Uh, hello?'

Zoe turned it around and held it upside down.

'It's a Russian doll,' said her mother.

'Oh, right.' Zoe twisted the top and bottom halves of the doll in opposite directions to reveal the smaller doll inside.

She handed the halves to her mother, and opened the next doll.

Within moments there was a row of five dolls of increasingly smaller sizes on the floor between them.

'Wait, is that the last one?' said Carmel. 'It's empty. Normally there is a tiny final doll that you can't open.'

'No message?' said Frances. 'I thought the security code would be inside the last one!'

'So what the hell does that mean then?' said Ben.

'I don't know.' Zoe tried to suppress a yawn. She was all at once exhausted. She longed for her own bed, for her phone, for pizza, for all this to be over.

'Okay, this is really starting to piss me off now,' said Lars.

chapter fifty-nine

Masha

Masha saw Yao's smile of relief fade from his face as he watched the screen.

'But wait, why isn't the code in the doll?' He turned to Masha. 'The plan was to put the security code in the doll!'

Masha lifted up the last tiny doll from where it sat on her keyboard and held it between her fingertips. 'Yes, you're right, that was the original plan.'

'So . . . but why isn't it there?' Yao's eyebrows were drawn together just like those of the doll.

'I had an epiphany,' said Masha. 'While I was meditating. Suddenly I knew what needed to be done in order for them to achieve true transformation after their psychedelic experiences. This – what is happening to these nine people right now – is quite literally a koan. It is a koan *in practice*.' He must surely see the brilliance of it.

Yao stared at her without comprehension.

'A koan is a paradox that leads to enlightenment!' said Masha. 'A koan demonstrates the inadequacy of their logical thinking!'

'I know what a koan is,' said Yao slowly.

'Once they surrender and accept that there is no solution, well then, they will be free. That is the central paradox of this koan,' said Masha. *The solution is no solution.*'

'The solution is no solution,' repeated Yao.

'Exactly. Do you remember this koan? A master who lived as a hermit on a mountain was asked by a man, "What is the way?" and the master said, "What a fine mountain this is." The man felt frustrated. He said, "I am not asking you about the mountain, but about the way!" The master said, "So long as you cannot go beyond the mountain, my son, you cannot reach the way."'

'So in this case the mountain is . . . the security door?'

'Take detailed notes,' said Masha impatiently. She pointed at the screen and at his notepad. 'Don't forget. This is very important for the book we will write.'

'They've been in there for too long,' said Yao. 'They're hungry and tired. They are going to lose their minds.'

'*Exactly,*' said Masha. She herself had not eaten now for more days than she could remember and she had not slept since the night before the therapy sessions. She touched Yao lightly in the centre of his chest with her finger. She knew the power of her touch on him. She had not yet fully exploited that power but she would if necessary. '*Exactly.* They must lose their minds! You know this. The self is an illusion. The self does not exist.'

'Sure, okay,' said Yao. 'But, Masha –'

'They must *surrender,*' said Masha.

'I think they're going to report us to the police,' said Yao.

Masha laughed. 'Remember the Rumi quote, Yao. *Out beyond the idea of wrongdoing and right doing there is a field. I'll meet you there.* Isn't that beautiful?'

'I don't think the justice system is interested in fields,' said Yao.

'We can't give up on them, Yao.' Masha gestured at the screen. 'They have all come so far.'

'So how long are you planning on keeping them locked up?' Yao's voice sounded thin and strained, as if he'd become an old man.

'That's not the right question,' said Masha tenderly, her eyes on the computer monitor as some of the guests gathered around the door to the studio. They were taking it in turns to punch in different combinations of numbers. Lars punched the door with his fist like a spoiled child.

'I think I should let them out now,' said Yao.

'They must open that door themselves,' she said.

'They can't,' said Yao.

'They can,' said Masha.

She thought about the sunny Australian lives these people had been handed at birth. They had only ever known supermarket shelves that overflowed with choice. They had never seen an empty grocery store with nothing but boxes of Indian tea. They did not *need* attributes like ingenuity or resourcefulness. The clock struck five and they turned off their computers and went to the beach because they did not have a hundred university-educated candidates all too willing to take their job off their hands.

'Oh yes, I did that for U2 tickets once,' an Australian woman at Masha's work had said when Masha described the horrendous queues that lasted for days at the embassies and how she and her husband took turns to wait, and Masha had said, 'Yes, very much the same.'

She remembered how, when they were right in the middle of the application process, her husband received a card in the mail to report to the KGB office.

'It will be fine,' her husband said. 'Do not worry.'

It was like he was already an Australian, the phrase 'no worries' built into his psyche before he even knew the words, but in the Soviet era people had received those cards and never come back.

When Masha dropped him off outside that tall, grey building he kissed her and said, 'Go home,' but she didn't go home; she sat in that car for five hours, the simmering terror in her heart misting up the windows, and she would never forget the relief that detonated through her body when she saw him walking down the street towards her, grinning like a boy on an Australian beach.

Only a few months later she and her husband stood at the airport with American dollars hidden in their socks while a sneering customs office upturned the entire contents of their carefully packed suitcases, because they were traitors betraying their country by leaving, and her grandmother's necklace broke and beads scattered like pieces of her heart.

Only those who have feared they will lose everything feel true gratitude for their lucky lives.

'We must terrify them,' she told Yao. 'That is what they need.'

'Terrify them?' said Yao. His voice quavered. He was probably tired and hungry himself. 'I don't think we should terrify our guests.'

Masha stood. He looked up at her; like her child, like her lover. She could feel the unbreakable spiritual connection between them. He would never defy her.

'Tonight will be their dark night of the soul,' she said.

'Dark night of the soul?'

'A dark night of the soul is essential for rapid spiritual progress,' said Masha. 'You've had your own dark night of the soul. I've had mine. We need to break them before we can make them whole again. You know this, Yao.'

She saw the flicker of doubt in his eyes. She stepped closer to him, so close that they were almost touching.

'Tomorrow they will be reborn,' she said.

'I just don't know —'

Masha stepped closer still and for the merest fraction of a second she let her eyes drop to his lips. Let the darling boy think the impossible was possible.

'We are doing something extraordinary for these people, Yao,' said Masha.

'I'm going to let them out,' said Yao, but there was no conviction in his voice.

'No,' said Masha. She lifted her hand tenderly to his neck, careful not to reveal the silvery glint of the syringe. 'No, you're not.'

chapter sixty

Frances

Frances twirled an empty water bottle on her finger, round and round, until it flew off and skittered across the floor.

'Stop that,' said Carmel severely, and Frances could tell that was the voice Carmel used when one of her little girls was being annoying.

'Sorry,' she said at the same time as Carmel said, 'Sorry.'

It was, according to Napoleon's watch, 9 pm. They had been in here now for just over thirty hours. They hadn't eaten for over forty-eight hours.

People had begun complaining of headaches, light-headedness, fatigue and nausea. Waves of irritability swept the room at intervals. People bickered, then apologised, then snapped again. Voices quivered with emotion and skidded into hysterical laughter. Some people drifted off to sleep and then woke with a loud gasp. Napoleon was the only one who stayed consistently calm. It felt like he was their unofficially appointed leader, even though he wasn't issuing any instructions.

'Don't drink too much water,' Heather had told Frances

when she'd seen her returning from the bathroom after filling her water bottle yet again. 'Only drink when you're thirsty. You can die from drinking too much water because you flush out all the salt in your system. You can go into cardiac arrest.'

'Okay,' said Frances resignedly. 'Thank you.' She'd thought drinking lots of water would stave off the hunger pangs, although she wasn't as hungry as she thought she would be. The desire for food had peaked just before they'd found the useless Russian doll package and then gradually begun to wane until it became more abstract; she felt like she needed *something*, but food didn't seem to be the answer.

Her friend Ellen was a fan of intermittent fasting and she'd told Frances that she always experienced feelings of euphoria. Frances didn't feel euphoric, but her mind felt scrubbed clean, clear and bright. Was that the drugs or the fasting?

Whatever it was, the clarity was an illusion, because she was having difficulty differentiating what had and hadn't happened since she'd got here. Did she dream of her nose-bleed in the pool? She hadn't really seen her dad last night, had she? Of course she hadn't. Yet the memory of talking with her father felt more vivid than her memory of the nose-bleed in the pool.

How could that be?

Time slowed.

And slowed.

Slowed.

To.

A.

Point.

That.

Was.

So.

Slow.

It.

Was.

Unsustainable.

Soon time would stop, literally stop, and they would all be trapped in a single moment forever. That didn't seem too fantastical a thought after last night's smoothie experience, when time had elongated and contracted, over and over, like a piece of elastic being stretched and released.

There was a long, heated discussion about when and if they should turn the lights out.

It had not occurred to Frances that there was no natural light down here. It was Napoleon who'd figured it out; he'd been the one to find the light switch this morning when he woke up. He said he'd crawled around the room on his hands and knees and run his hands around the walls until he found it. When he flicked the switch to demonstrate for them, the room was plunged into a thick, impenetrable darkness that felt like death.

Frances voted for the lights to go off at midnight. She wanted to sleep: sleeping would pass the time, and she knew she'd never sleep with those blazing downlights. Others thought that they shouldn't risk sleeping; they should be 'ready to take action'.

'Who knows what they're planning next?' Jessica shot a hostile look at the camera. At some point she had scrubbed off all her make-up. She looked ten years younger, younger even than Zoe; too young to be pregnant, too young to be wealthy. Without the make-up, the cosmetic enhancements looked like acne: a teenage blight that would pass when she grew up.

'I don't think anything sinister is going to happen in the middle of the night,' Carmel said.

'We were woken up for the starlight meditation,' said Heather. 'It's entirely possible.'

'I liked the starlight meditation,' said Carmel.

Heather sighed. 'Carmel, you really need to kind of reframe your thinking about what's going on here.'

'I vote for lights off,' said Frances in a low voice. Napoleon had showed them where the microphones were installed in the corners of the room. He'd told them all, in whispers, that if they wanted to share something they didn't want heard they should sit in the centre of the room with their backs to the camera and keep their voices as low as possible. 'I think we should give Masha the impression of total *acceptance*.'

'I agree,' whispered Zoe. 'She's exactly like my year eleven maths teacher. You always had to let her think she'd won.'

'I'd prefer lights on,' said Tony. 'We're at a disadvantage if we can't see.'

In the end, there were more in favour of 'lights on'.

So here they all sat. Lights on. Occasional low murmurs of conversation like you'd hear in a library or a doctor's waiting room.

Long periods of silence.

Frances's body kept twitching and then she would remember that there was no book to pick up, no movie to switch on or bedside lamp to switch off. Sometimes she'd be almost on her feet, before she realised that the decisive thing she was planning on doing was *leaving the room*. Her subconscious refused to accept her incarceration.

Carmel came and sat next to Frances. 'Do you think we've gone into ketosis yet?' she asked.

'What's ketosis?' asked Frances. She knew perfectly well what it was.

'It's where your body starts to burn fat because —'

'You don't need to lose weight,' interrupted Frances. She tried not to snap, but she had not been thinking about food and now she was.

'I used to be thinner,' said Carmel. She stretched her perfectly normal legs out in front of her.

'We all used to be thinner,' sighed Frances.

'Last night I hallucinated that I didn't have a body,' said Carmel. 'I feel like there was maybe a message my subconscious was trying to give me.'

'It's so obscure. What could that message *possibly* be?' mused Frances.

Carmel laughed. 'I know.' She grabbed the flesh on her stomach and squeezed. 'I'm stuck in this cycle of self-loathing.'

'What did you do before you had children?' asked Frances. She wanted to know if there was more to Carmel than just hating her body and having four children. Early in Frances's career, a friend had complained that the mothers in her books were too one-dimensional and Frances had thought secretly, *Don't they only have one dimension?* She'd tried to give them more depth after that. She even gave them the leading roles, although it was hard to know where to put the children while their mothers were falling in love. When her editorial notes came back Jo had written all over the margins, *Who is looking after the kids?* Frances had to go back through the manuscript and make babysitting arrangements. It was annoying.

'Private equity,' said Carmel.

Goodness. Frances wouldn't have picked that. She wasn't even quite sure what it *meant*. How were they going to find a middle ground between private equity and romance?

'Did you . . . like it?' Surely that was safe.

'Loved it,' said Carmel. '*Loved* it. It was a long time ago now, of course. Now, I've got a part-time, entry-level job which is basically just data entry to try to keep the cash coming in. But back then I was kind of a high-flyer, or on my way to becoming one. I worked long hours, I'd get up at five every day and swim laps before work, and I ate whatever the hell I wanted, and I found women who talked about their weight excruciatingly boring.'

Frances smiled.

'I *know.* And then I got married and had kids and I got totally swallowed up by this "Mum" persona. We were only meant to have two, but my husband wanted a son, so we kept trying, and I ended up with four girls – and then, out of the blue, my husband said he wasn't attracted to me anymore and he left.'

Frances said nothing for a moment as she considered the particular cruelty of this kind of all-too-common midlife break-up and how it crushed a woman's self-worth. 'Were you still attracted to *him*?'

Carmel thought about it. 'Some days.' She put her thumb to the empty spot on her ring finger. 'I still loved him. I know I did, because some days I'd think, Oh, what a relief, I still love him, it would be so inconvenient if I didn't love him.'

Frances thought of all the things she could say: You'll meet someone else. You don't need a man to complete you. Your body does not define you. You need to fall in love with you. Let's talk about something other than men, Carmel, before we fail the Bechdel test.

She said, 'You know what? I think you are most *definitely* in ketosis.'

Carmel smiled, and at that moment the room went dark.

chapter sixty-one

Napoleon

'Who turned the lights out?'

It was his angriest teacher voice; the one that got even the worst-behaved boy in a class to sit down and shut up. They had agreed the lights would stay on.

'Not me.'

'Not me.'

'Not me.'

The voices came from all around the room.

The darkness was so complete Napoleon instantly lost all sense of up and down. He held out his hands in front of him blindly, like he'd done this morning.

'Is that you?' It was Heather's voice. She had been sitting next to him. He felt her hand take his.

'Yes. Where's Zoe?'

'I'm here, Dad.' Her voice came from the other side of the room.

'None of us was near the light switch,' said Tony.

Napoleon felt the rapid beat of his heart and took pleasure in his fear. It was a respite from the grey feeling that

384

descended upon him the moment he woke up this morning. A thick fog had spread its soft fingers throughout his brain, his heart, his body, weighing him down so that it was an effort to speak, to lift his head, to walk. He was trying to pretend he was fine. He was fighting the fog with all his strength, trying to behave normally, to trick himself into getting better. It might be temporary. It might be just for today. Like a hangover. Tomorrow, perhaps, he would wake up and be himself again.

'Maybe Masha is telling us it's time to go to sleep now.' It was Frances. He recognised her light, dry voice in the darkness. Before last night Napoleon would have said that he and Frances had similar personalities, in that they shared a certain base level of optimism, but not now. Now all his hope had drained away, it had seeped out of him and evaporated like sweat, leaving him empty and spent.

'I'm not tired,' said Lars. Or maybe Ben.

'This is fucked.' That was Ben. Or maybe Lars.

'I think Masha is about to do something,' said Jessica, he was pretty sure. She sounded more intelligent when you couldn't see her face.

There was a moment of silence. Napoleon kept waiting for his eyes to adjust but they didn't. No figures emerged. The dark seemed to get darker.

'It's a bit creepy,' said Zoe, with a tremor in her voice, and Napoleon and Heather both moved reflexively, as if they could make their way through the darkness to get to her.

'It's just dark. We're all here. You're safe.' That was definitely Smiley Hogburn, comforting Zoe.

Napoleon wished he could tell someone that he'd kind of played football with Smiley Hogburn. He realised the person he wished he could tell was himself, the self who no longer existed.

The darkness settled.

It *was* creepy.

'Maybe Lars should sing,' said Frances.

'At last some appreciation for my talent,' said Lars.

'We should all sing,' said Carmel.

'No thanks,' said Jessica.

'You and me, Carmel,' said Lars.

He began to sing 'I Can See Clearly Now' and Carmel joined in. She could sing beautifully. What a surprise to hear her voice rise in the darkness like that, holding the melody with such grace. How people could surprise you.

Napoleon had thought when he woke this morning that the feeling that permeated his body must be anger, because he had the right to be incandescent with anger at his wife for what she had concealed from him, and what she had chosen to finally reveal in the most nightmarish of settings, as his mind had struggled to separate ghastly fiction from reality – although now he thought he was free of the drugs, he did not have any doubt about what had and hadn't really happened. He'd dreamed of Zach, but he hadn't dreamed Heather's revelation.

He didn't remember asking her about the side effects of the asthma medication and yet he could imagine exactly how she would have replied: with unconcealed impatience, because *she* was the one in their family in charge of all decisions relating to health. Heather had the medical training, he was the teacher. He was in charge of homework. She was in charge of medication. She took pride in not questioning his decisions about education, although he would *happily* have been questioned by her, he was always eager for a debate, but she just wanted to get things ticked off the list. She liked to think of herself as the efficient, no-nonsense one in their relationship. The one who got things done.

Well, look what you got done, Heather.

She was right when she said that, given the opportunity, he would have read the leaflet that came with the medication, and yes, Napoleon would have monitored Zach, and he would have *told* him. He would have said, 'This might affect your mood, Zach, you need to watch out for it and let me know,' and Zach would have rolled his eyes and said, 'I never get any of those side effects, Dad.'

He could have, he would have, he should have, he might have saved him.

Every day for three years Napoleon had woken up each morning and thought, *Why?* And Heather knew why, or could take an educated guess at *one possibility* of why, and she had deliberately denied him the comfort of her knowledge, because of her guilt. Did she not trust his love? Did she think he would have blamed her, left her?

Not only that, they had an obligation to make this *known*, to let the authorities know that this had happened. My God, there could be other children dying. They needed to make the community aware that those side effects should be taken seriously. It was incredibly selfish of Heather to have kept this to herself, to have protected herself at the risk of others. He would call Dr Chang as soon as he got out of here.

And Zoe. His darling girl. The only one to see that something wasn't right because she knew Zach best. All she'd needed to say was: 'Dad, something is wrong with Zach,' and Napoleon would have acted because he knew how dangerous a boy's feelings could be.

He could have, he would have, he should have, he might have saved him.

They'd had *conversations* about depression around the dinner table. Napoleon knew all the conversations you were meant to have with your kids, and he made sure they had those conversations: don't give out your personal details on the internet, never get in the car with a driver who has been drinking, call us at any time of the night, tell us how you feel, tell us if you are being bullied, we can fix things, we promise we can fix things.

Am I angry? He had been asking himself that question all day, wondering if the fog was just anger masquerading as something else, but the feeling that had infiltrated all the cells of his body was something far more and something far less than anger. It was a dull nothingness with the weight and texture of wet cement.

As he sat there lost in the darkness, listening to Carmel sing, as Lars lowered his voice and let her take the song, it occurred to him: *Maybe this was how Zach felt.*

Whether the asthma medication caused it, or whether it was teenage hormones run amok, or a combination of both, maybe this was how it felt: like his mind, body and soul were shrouded in grey fog. Like there was not much point to anything at all. Like you could act and look exactly the same on the outside but on the inside everything was different.

Oh, mate, you were just a kid, and I'm a man, and it's been less than a day, and already I just want it to end.

He saw his son's face. The first rough graze of stubble, the curve of his eyelashes when he looked down, avoiding eye contact. He could never meet his father's eyes when he'd done something wrong. He hated to be in trouble and the poor kid was always in trouble. Zoe was smarter. She could twist her narrative to make it appear she'd done the right thing.

It looked like girls were controlled by their feelings, but the opposite was true. Girls had excellent control of their feelings. They spun them around like batons: *Now I'm crying! Now I'm laughing! Who knows what I'll do next! Not you!* A boy's emotions were like baseball bats that blindsided him.

At that moment, that morning, three years ago, Zach didn't make a bad choice. He made what to him must have felt like the only choice. What else could you do when you felt like this? It was like asking those people in the burning towers not to jump. What else could you do if you couldn't breathe? You would do anything to breathe. Anything at all. Of course you jump. Of course you do.

He saw his boy looking at him with eyes pleading for understanding.

Zach was such a good kid. Of course Napoleon did not accept or condone the kid's decision – it was the wrong decision, it was a stupid decision, the worst decision – but for the first time ever, he felt he might understand how he came to make it.

He imagined taking him onto his lap the way he'd once done when he was a little boy, holding him close, whispering into his ear:

You're not in trouble, Zach. I'm so sorry for yelling at you. I understand now, son. You're not in trouble, mate.

You're not in trouble.

You're not in trouble.

'Napoleon?' said Heather. He was squeezing her hand too tightly. He loosened his grip.

A black-and-white image flickered on the screen above their heads. Carmel broke off her singing.

'What the hell?' said Lars.

Masha's voice boomed at a volume that made Napoleon's ears throb. Her face filled the screen. She smiled at them, radiant with love. 'Good evening, my sweetie pies, my lapochki.'

'My God,' said Heather under her breath.

chapter sixty-two

Frances

She's mad. She's crazy. She's nuts. She's unhinged.

It had all been a joke before. What Frances really meant was that Masha was odd, alternative, intense, excessively tall and exotic and different in every way from Frances. She hadn't truly questioned Masha's state of mind. Part of her had wondered if Masha was a genius. Didn't all geniuses seem mad to mere mortals?

Even the drugs hadn't truly concerned her. The fact was that if Masha had asked, 'Would you like to try this smoothie laced with LSD?' Frances might have said, 'Sure, why not?' She would have been impressed by all the talk about 'research', comforted by Yao's background as a paramedic and intrigued by the possibility of a transcendent experience, and she would have been especially susceptible if someone else had said yes first. (As a teenager, her mother had once said to her, 'If all your friends jumped off a cliff, would you jump too?' Frances had answered, without guile, 'Of course.')

But now, sitting here in the dark, watching Masha's image on the screen, it was clear: Masha was not quite right. Her green eyes shone with an evangelical fervour that would not respond to logic or sense.

'Congratulations to all of you!' she said. 'I am so pleased with your progress. You have all come so *far* from day one!' She clasped her hands together like an actress accepting an Oscar. 'Your journeys are nearly complete.'

The screen lit up the room in ghostly patches of light so that Frances could see everyone's faces as they all stared up at Masha.

'You need to let us out of here!' shouted Jessica.

'Can she hear us?' asked Carmel uncertainly.

'No need to shout, Jessica. Hello there, Carmel. I can see you, I can hear you,' said Masha. 'The magic of technology. Isn't it amazing!'

Her eyes looked off-centre at the camera. It made it easier not to succumb to her madness.

'I was so happy when you solved the escape puzzle and found the matryoshka,' said Masha.

'But we didn't solve it!' said Frances. She was personally offended by this. 'We're still *here*. There was no damned code in the doll.'

'Exactly,' said Masha. '*Exactly*.'

'What?' said Frances.

'You worked as a team, though not quite to the extent I'd hoped. I assumed you would build a human pyramid to reach the doll — all of you! — rather than playing football.' Her lip lifted in a sneer on the word 'football'. Frances felt defensive of Tony.

'When I was at school in Serov, many years ago, we made a human pyramid that was quite remarkable, I have never forgotten it.' Her eyes lost their focus, and then she snapped back. 'Anyway, that does not matter, you got there in the end, you found the doll and here we are.'

'The doll told us nothing,' said Jessica. 'It was empty.'

'That's right, Jessica,' said Masha patiently, as if to a small child who does not understand the way the world works.

'She's not making any sense,' muttered Ben.

'What I'd find truly transformative right now is a long hot shower,' said Lars. He smiled up at Masha with the full force of his gorgeous face. It was like he was holding a glowing lightsaber up to the screen. Frances would bet that smile had opened many doors before.

But not this one. Masha just smiled back. It was an epic battle of beauty and charisma.

Lars held on for as long as he could before he surrendered. His smile vanished. 'For God's sake, I just want to get out of here, Masha.'

'Ah, Lars,' said Masha. 'You need to remember what Buddha said: "Nothing is forever except change."'

'This already feels like forever, Masha.'

Masha chuckled. 'I know you like your solitude, Lars. It is hard to find yourself having to interact with strangers all day long, yes?'

'Everyone is very nice,' said Lars. 'That's not really the point.'

'We just want to go back to our rooms,' said Heather. She sounded quite meek and reasonable. 'The psychedelic therapy was wonderful, thank you, but –'

'It was wonderful, was it? You have changed your tune then, Heather!' A fine thread of aggression ran through Masha's words. 'I hope you speak from the heart. I heard talk of reporting me to the police! I must confess that was hurtful to me.'

'I was upset,' said Heather. 'As you know, today is the anniversary of my son's death. I wasn't thinking straight. Now I understand.' She looked up at the screen with what appeared to be complete acquiescence. It was inspiring to see. 'We *all* understand,' continued Heather. 'We're so grateful for what you've done for us. We would never have had this opportunity in our normal lives. But now we'd just like to go back to our rooms and enjoy the rest of the retreat.'

Frances tried to put herself in Masha's position. It came to her that Masha considered herself an artist and, like any artist, she craved praise. She simply wanted recognition, respect, five-star reviews, gratitude.

'I think I speak for all of us when I say this has been an *incredible* experience,' she began.

But she was interrupted by Tony.

'Is that Yao behind you?' He was on his feet, his eyes on the screen. 'Is he alright?'

'Yao is here, yes,' said Masha.

She moved to one side of her computer screen and gestured graciously like a model on a game indicating the prize.

The prize was Yao.

He was slumped forward in Masha's chair, asleep or unconscious on Masha's desk, one cheek squashed flat, while his arms formed a semicircle around his head.

'Is he breathing? What's wrong with him?' Heather also stood and moved to a position beneath the television screen. She dropped the fake acquiescent tone. 'What has he taken? What have you given him?'

'Is he alive?' asked Frances in panic.

'He is just napping,' said Masha. 'He is so tired. He has been up all night, working hard for you!'

She caressed Yao's hair, and pointed at something they couldn't see on his scalp.

'That is Yao's birthmark. I saw it during my near-death experience.' She smiled back at the camera and Frances shivered. 'That is when I came face to face with my own mortality in the most remarkable and wonderful way.' Her eyes shone. 'This evening, you too will face your mortality. Sadly, I can't give you the privilege of looking death *directly* in the eyes, but I can give you a glance, a glimpse! An unforgettable glimpse that will . . .' She searched for the right word and found it with obvious satisfaction. 'That will *amalgamate* all of your experiences so far: the silence, the psychedelic therapy, the escape puzzle.'

'He doesn't look like he's napping,' said Heather. 'Have you given him something?'

'Ah, Heather,' said Masha. 'You are practically a doctor, aren't you? But I can assure you, Yao is simply napping!'

'Where is Delilah?' asked Ben.

'Delilah is no longer with us,' said Masha.

'What do you mean "no longer with us"?' said Ben. 'What does that mean?'

'She has left us,' said Masha airily.

'Of her own *accord*?' asked Frances.

She thought about the other Tranquillum House staff: the lovely smiley chef who brought out the food; *Jan*, with her miraculous healing hands. Where were they, while the guests were locked up and Yao lay unconscious on Masha's desk?

'I need you all to listen carefully,' said Masha, ignoring Frances's question about Delilah. She moved to the front of the camera again so that Yao's body was concealed. 'We are now going to play a fun *icebreaker*!'

'I feel like the ice is well and truly broken, Masha,' said Lars.

'Buddha said that we must "radiate boundless love towards the entire world", and that's what this exercise is all about. It's about love. It's about passion. It's about getting to know each other,' said Masha. 'I call it: "Death Sentence!"'

She looked at them expectantly, as if waiting for an enthusiastic eruption of questions and comments.

Nobody moved.

'You like the name?' said Masha, lowering her head and lifting her eyes in a way that could almost be considered flirtatious.

'I do not like the name,' said Napoleon.

'Ah, Napoleon, I like *you*. You are an honest man. Now, let me explain how this activity works,' said Masha. 'Imagine this: You have all of you been sentenced to death! You are on death row! Maybe that would have been a better name? Death Row.' She frowned. 'I think that is better. We will call it "Death Row".'

Carmel began to weep softly. Frances put her hand on her arm.

'So how does this game Death Row work? Let me explain. If you are sentenced to death, what happens? You need someone to argue on your behalf, don't you? To argue for clemency, for a stay of execution. Obviously that person is your . . .' Masha raised encouraging eyebrows.

'Lawyer,' finished Jessica.

'Yes!' cried Masha. 'Your lawyer who defends you! The person who says to the judge, "No, this person does not deserve to die! This is a good person, Your Honour! An upstanding member of the community with so much to offer!" You see what I'm saying? So, you are all lawyers and you each have a client. You understand?'

Nobody spoke.

'I have assigned your clients. Let me read out the names to you.'

She held up a piece of notepaper and read out: 'Frances defends Lars. Lars defends Ben.' She looked up at them. 'You're listening? I will only say this once.'

'We're listening,' said Napoleon.

'Heather defends Frances, Tony defends Carmel, Carmel defends Zoe, Zoe defends Jessica, Jessica defends Heather, Ben defends Napoleon and . . .' she took an exaggerated breath '. . . Napoleon defends Tony! Whew! That's all of you!' She looked up from the paper. 'Do you all know you are defending?'

Nobody answered. They all looked dumbly back at the screen.

'Tony, who are you defending?' asked Masha.

'Carmel,' said Tony evenly.

'And Zoe, what about you?'

'I'm defending Jessica,' said Zoe. 'I don't really understand what crime she's committed.'

'The crime is not relevant. We've all committed crimes, Zoe,' said Masha. 'I think you know that. No-one is innocent.'

'You're a psychotic –'

'So presumably you are the judge, Masha?' Napoleon spoke loudly over the top of his wife.

'That's right! I will be the judge!' said Masha. 'You will each have just five minutes to defend your client. It's not long – but it's long enough. Don't waste time with waffle! Make sure that every word packs a punch.' She curled her hand into a fist.

'You will have the night to prepare. Presentations will be at dawn. You must ask yourself, *Why does my client deserve to live?*'

'Because *everyone* deserves to live,' said Tony.

'But why your client in particular? Let's say there is only one parachute left! Only one place left in the lifeboat! Why should your client take that parachute over someone else?' said Masha.

'Then it's women and children first,' said Tony.

'But what if you are all the same gender? All the same age? Who lives? Who dies?' said Masha.

'Is the game called "Last Parachute" now?' said Lars, his face hard with bitter mockery. 'So we're all going to sit around and discuss ethical dilemmas like first-year philosophy students while Yao lies there comatose on your desk? Wonderful, this is all just so transformative.'

'Careful,' said Tony under his breath.

'This is an important *exercise!*' shouted Masha. The tendons on her neck were rigid with rage.

Frances felt sick. She was going to lose this game. She always performed poorly in these kinds of 'activities' and now her 'client', Lars, had already got the judge offside.

Ben spoke up in a placatory manner. 'So, could you just explain, please, Masha, what happens if — according to you, our judge — we *don't* successfully defend our clients?'

Masha breathed in deeply through her nostrils. 'Well, obviously we don't *generally* execute our guests! That's not good for business!' She laughed gaily.

'So this is all just . . . hypothetical?' said Ben.

'That's enough questions!' screamed Masha so loudly that Carmel took a step back and landed quite hard on Frances's toe.

'This is totally ludic—' began Heather. Napoleon grabbed her arm.

'We're all going to take part in the exercise, Masha,' he said loudly. 'It sounds very . . . stimulating.'

Masha nodded graciously. 'Good. You're going to find it transformative, Napoleon. You really are. Now, I must give you light for this enlightening exercise!' She reached out her hand and the lights came back on, causing everyone to blink and stare dazedly at each other.

'Once we've defended our "clients", will you let us out?' asked Carmel, rubbing her eyes, her voice hoarse.

'You're asking the wrong questions, Carmel,' said Masha. 'Only *you* can set yourself free. Remember, I talked to you just a few days ago about impermanence. Nothing lasts forever. Do not cling to happiness *or* suffering.'

'I just really want to go home right now,' said Carmel.

Masha clucked sympathetically. 'Spiritual awakenings are rarely easy, Carmel.'

Frances raised a hand. 'I need a pen. I can't prepare a presentation if I can't write it down!' She patted the empty pockets of her sweatpants. 'I have nothing to write with!'

Masha behaved as if Frances hadn't spoken. 'Now, my sweetie pies, I wish you the best of luck. I shall be back at dawn. Remember to focus your thoughts. Ask the right questions of your clients, and listen with your heart. Convince me why each of *you* deserves to live.'

She looked fondly at Yao if he were her sleeping child, patted his head and then looked back at the screen. 'Let me leave you with these words: "Ardently do today what must be done. Who knows? Tomorrow death comes." The Buddha.' She put her hands together in prayer and lowered her head. 'Namaste.'

chapter sixty-three

Lars

The guests of Tranquillum House stood in a huddled, whispering group in the centre of the studio, their heads bent, like a cluster of banished smokers outside their office on a chilly day. Lars could smell acrid sweat and stale breath. Ben and Jessica held hands. Carmel and Frances both chewed at their fingernails. Tony tugged aggressively at his bottom lip, as if he could somehow contort his mouth into providing the correct answers, while Zoe kneaded her stomach and studied her feet and her parents both studied her.

'I'm sure Yao is fine, don't you think? And Delilah? There is no way Masha would really hurt anyone,' said Frances. 'No way in the world. She sees herself as a healer.'

Lars could tell Frances was trying to convince herself. The longer they were in here the more stripped back she got. Her red lipstick was gone and her blonde hair, which had been in a bouncy circa 1995 ponytail, was now slicked back against her head. Lars liked Frances, but she wasn't the lawyer he would have retained, given a choice, if he were on death row. He didn't know who he would have chosen out of this motley lot. He wasn't sure how much it really mattered. Masha was going to do what she was going to do.

'We just need to make it look as if we're going along with the madness,' he said to the group.

'I agree,' said Napoleon. 'We have to play along and take the first opportunity we can to find a way out of here.'

'I believed in her,' said Carmel sadly. 'I believed in this.' She indicated her surroundings. 'I thought I was being transformed.'

'So I'm representing you,' said Frances to Lars anxiously. 'We need to talk. God, I would do anything for a *pen*.'

'Well, supposedly I'm representing you, Frances, in this grotesque . . . *game*,' sighed Heather. 'So I guess we need to talk too.'

'Okay, yes, yes, but just let me talk to my client first,' said Frances, breathing fast. She put a hand to her chest to try to calm herself. Lars smiled at her. She would be the sort to play a game of charades with endearing seriousness and little skill, as if it were a matter of life and death, and now that it truly might be a matter of life and death (surely not!), she was in danger of hyperventilating.

'Let's go have a chat, Frances,' said Lars soothingly. 'And then you can go convince Heather why you should live.'

'This is pathetic,' said Heather as they split up into pairs.

'We're an odd number,' said Napoleon. 'I'll wait for my turn.' He lowered his voice even further. 'I'll just keep looking around for a way out of here.' He wandered off, his hands shoved in the pockets of his dad shorts.

Lars and Frances went to sit in a corner.

'Right.' Frances sat cross-legged in front of Lars. She frowned intensely. 'Tell me *everything* about your life, your relationships, your family.'

'Tell her I'm a philanthropist, I do a lot of things for the community, volunteer work . . .'

'Do you?' interrupted Frances.

'You write fiction!' said Lars. 'Let's just make it up! It doesn't actually matter what you say as long as it looks like we're going along with the exercise.'

Frances shook her head. 'That woman might be crazy, but she can smell insincerity a mile off. I am going along with the exercise and I'm doing it properly. You tell me everything, Lars, right now. I'm not kidding.'

Lars groaned. He ran his fingers through his hair. 'I help women,' he said. 'I only represent women in divorce cases.'

'Seriously?' said Frances. 'Isn't that discriminatory?'

'I get my clients by word of mouth,' said Lars. 'They all know each other, these types of women, they play tennis together.'

'So you only represent wealthy women?' said Frances.

'I'm not doing it for *love*,' said Lars. 'I make good money. I just make sure a certain type of man pays a fair price for his sins.'

Frances tapped her thumbnail against her front teeth like an imaginary pen. 'Are you in a relationship?'

'Yes,' said Lars. 'We've been together for fifteen years. His name is Ray and he would probably prefer I wasn't "sentenced to death".'

He felt a sudden burst of longing for Ray and for home, for music and the sizzle of garlic, for Sunday mornings. He was done with health resorts. When he got out of here he was going to book a holiday for him and Ray, a gastronomic tour of Europe. The man had got too skinny. His eyes looked huge in his face. All that obsessive bike riding. Legs spinning in a blur, up and down the hills of Sydney, faster and faster, trying to get those endorphins flooding his body, trying to forget that he was in a relationship where he gave more than he got.

'He's a good person,' said Lars, and he was surprised to find himself close to tears, because it occurred to him that if he were to die, Ray would be snatched up like a too-good-to-be-true deal at the supermarket, and someone else could very easily love him the way he deserved to be loved.

'Poor Ray,' murmured Frances, as if she knew what he was thinking.

'Why do you say that?' said Lars.

'Oh, it's just you're so good-looking. I was briefly in love with a handsome man in my youth and it was awful, and you're just . . .' she gestured at him '. . . ridiculous.'

'That's kind of offensive,' said Lars. There was a lot of prejudice against people who looked like him. People had no idea.

'Yeah, yeah, get over it,' said Frances. 'So . . . no kids?'

'No kids,' said Lars. 'Ray wants children. I don't.'

'I never wanted children either,' said Frances.

Lars thought of Ray's mother at Ray's thirty-fifth birthday last month. As usual she'd had 'one too many glasses of champagne', which meant she'd had two glasses. 'Can't you let him have *one* baby, Lars? Just one itsy-bitsy baby? You wouldn't have to lift a finger, I promise.'

'Did your psychedelic therapy give you any special insights into your life?' asked Frances. 'Masha would probably like it if I mentioned that.'

Lars thought about last night. Some parts had been spectacular. At one point, he realised he could *see* the music coming through his headphones in waves of iridescent colour. He and Masha had talked, but he didn't think there had been any particular insights. He'd told her at length about the colour of the music and he felt like she might have got bored, which he'd found insulting because he'd been speaking very eloquently and poetically.

He didn't think he'd told Masha about the little boy who kept appearing in his hallucinations last night. She would have liked that.

He knew that the dark-haired, dirty-faced kid who kept grabbing Lars's hand was there to remind Lars of something significant and traumatic from his childhood, one of those formative memories that therapists were always so excited about dredging up.

He had refused to go with the young Lars. 'I'm busy,' he kept telling him, as he lay back down on a beach to enjoy the colours of the music. 'Ask someone else.'

I don't care what my subconscious is trying to tell me, thanks anyway.

At one point in the night he got into a conversation with Delilah that didn't feel therapeutic, more like shooting the breeze; in fact, he was pretty sure he could feel a sea breeze while they chatted.

Delilah said, 'You're just like me, Lars. You don't give a shit, do you? You just don't care.'

Did she have a cigarette in her hand at that point? Surely not.

'What do you mean?' Lars had said lazily.

'You know what I mean,' Delilah said. She'd sounded so sure of herself, as if she knew Lars better than he knew himself.

Frances banged her knuckles in rapid motion against her cheekbones.

'Stop hitting yourself,' said Lars.

Frances dropped her hand. 'I've never represented anyone in court before,' she said.

'This isn't court,' he said. 'This is just a silly game.'

He looked over at Jessica, supposedly pregnant.

'Tell Masha that my partner and I are planning to have a baby,' he said flippantly.

'We can't lie,' said Frances. She was clearly exasperated with him, poor woman.

The expression on her face made him think of Ray when Lars had done something to annoy or frustrate him. The compressed lips. The resigned slump of his shoulders. Those disappointed eyes.

He remembered the impish face of that little boy from last night and realised with a start that it wasn't his younger self at all. The kid had hazel eyes. *Ray's* eyes. Ray and his sister and mother all had the same eyes. Eyes that made Lars want to close his own because of all that terrifying love and trust and loyalty.

'Tell Masha if I don't live I'll take out a wrongful death lawsuit against her,' Lars told Frances. 'I'll win. I guarantee you I'll win.'

'What?' Frances frowned. 'That doesn't even make sense!'

'None of this makes sense,' said Lars. 'None of it.'

He saw again the dark-haired little boy with the hazel eyes, felt the tug of his hand and heard his insistent voice: *I've got something to show you.*

chapter sixty-four

Jessica

Jessica and Zoe sat opposite each other, cross-legged, on a yoga mat, as if they were about to do a joint Pilates exercise.

Jessica would have given anything to be in a Pilates class right now. Even the cheap one she did before they won the money, in that draughty community hall, with all the local mums.

'Do you think this is, I don't know, serious?' Zoe's eyes darted over to her parents and back. Jessica couldn't help but notice Zoe had great natural eyebrows.

'Ah, yeah, I kind of do,' Jessica answered. 'I feel like Masha is, like, totally capable of anything. She seems very unstable.' She tried to control her breathing. The fear kept rising and then receding in her stomach, like bouts of nausea on an amusement park ride.

'She wouldn't really, like, *execute* anyone, of course,' said Zoe, smiling fiercely, as if determined to show she was making a joke.

'Of course not,' said Jessica, but how did she know what this woman could do? She'd given them drugs without their consent, and who knew what she'd done to Yao and Delilah. 'It's an exercise, that's all, to make us think. It's just a really stupid exercise.'

'I'm worried my mother might antagonise Masha. She's not taking it seriously enough.' Zoe shot a look at Heather.

'Don't worry, I'll do a really good job defending her,' said Jessica. 'Your mother is a *midwife*. She helps bring new life into the world. Also, I was on the debating team. First speaker.' *Jessica is a conscientious student*. That was the comment she used to see most often on her report cards.

'And I'll do a good job defending you!' Zoe sat up straighter, with the air of a fellow conscientious student. 'So, okay, I thought, first of all, I should obviously mention your pregnancy, right? You can't execute a pregnant woman. That would be against some convention or something, right?'

'That's true,' said Jessica doubtfully, although she wasn't sure why she felt doubtful. Was it because the pregnancy wasn't confirmed? Because it seemed like that was exploiting a loophole? She only deserved to live because her innocent child deserved to live?

And if she wasn't pregnant, why *should* she live? Just because she really *wanted* to live? Because her parents loved her? Because she knew her sister loved her too, even if they were currently estranged? Because her Instagram followers often said she 'made their day'? Because last financial year her charitable donations were higher than what had once been her annual income?

'When we won the money, we really tried to, you know, not be *selfish*,' she told Zoe. 'To share it, to give to charity.' She ran her fingers through her hair like a comb and lowered her voice. 'But we didn't give it *all* away.'

'No-one would expect that,' said Zoe. 'It was your prize.'

'That's one thing I miss about our old life,' admitted Jessica. 'Before we got rich we didn't ever have to think about whether we were "good" people, because we didn't have time to be good. We were just paying the bills, getting by, living our lives. It was kind of easier.' She winced. 'That makes it sound like I'm complaining and I promise you I'm not.'

'I've read about lottery winners who go on crazy spending sprees and their relationships end and they lose the lot and end up on the dole,' said Zoe.

'I know!' said Jessica. 'When we won, I did a lot of research about lottery winners. So I, like, knew the pitfalls.'

'I reckon you've done a good job of it,' said Zoe.

'Thank you,' said Jessica gratefully, because sometimes she had longed for someone to give her a good mark for how well she'd handled the prize money.

She'd tried so hard to be a well-behaved lottery winner. To invest properly, to share appropriately, to get tax advice, to go to posh fundraiser balls where terrifyingly elegant people sipped French champagne while they bid obscene amounts of money on obscure items at charity auctions: 'All for a good cause, ladies and gentlemen!' She thought of Ben tugging at his bow tie, muttering, 'Who the fuck *are* these people?'

Should she have spent more at those charity balls? Less? Not gone at all? Sent a cheque? What would have made her a better person, more deserving of life right now?

If this had happened before the win, what would Zoe have said? Jessica deserves to live because she works really hard at her boring-as-batshit job and she's never even flown business class in her life, let alone first class, so what sort of life is that?

The money defined her now. She didn't even know who she was before the money.

'Ben didn't want to make any decisions except for which car to buy,' she told Jessica. 'He didn't want anything to change . . . and that's just not possible.'

She touched her lips and looked down at her boobs, which were objectively awesome.

Would her defence case be better if she didn't look like this? If she hadn't spent so much money on her body?

'Why would you *want* to look like one of those dreadful Kardashians?' her mother had once asked her.

Because Jessica thought those dreadful Kardashians were stunning. It was her prerogative to think so. Before the money Ben had drooled over images of luxury cars and Jessica had drooled over pictures of models and reality stars that were maybe photoshopped, but she didn't care. He got his car, she got her body. Why was her new body more superficial than his new car?

'Sorry.' She looked back up at Zoe, and remembered that this girl's brother had committed suicide. Zoe had probably never met anyone as superficial as Jessica in her life. 'None of that helps you build my case, does it? Why should this girl live? Oh, because she tried really hard when she won the lottery.'

Zoe didn't smile but gave Jessica a very serious, focused look. 'Don't worry, I can put a good spin on this.'

She looked up at the television screen where Masha's face had loomed. 'What do you think will happen next? After we've played her stupid game?'

'I don't know,' said Jessica honestly. 'It feels like anything could happen.'

chapter sixty-five

Masha

Masha collected a cushion from the Lavender Room. Yao made no sound as she lifted his head from her desk and slid the cushion beneath his cheek. His fluttering eyelids were not fully closed, revealing the shimmery slivers of his eyes.

She remembered adjusting a blanket around a small sleeping form. It felt like a memory that belonged to someone else, although she knew it was hers. The memory had no texture to it, no smell or colour; it was like the scenes from the security cameras around the building.

That was not correct. She could give the memory colour and texture if she so chose.

The blanket was yellow. The smell was No More Tears baby shampoo. The sound was the tinkling tune of the Brahms lullaby as a mobile with dangling toys turned in slow circles. The touch was of soft warm skin beneath her fingertips.

But she did not choose to remember that right at this moment.

She switched off the monitor so she could no longer see

or hear her guests. She needed a break from them. The pitch of their voices was like fingernails on a blackboard.

The sedative she'd given Yao was one they'd prepared in case a guest had a bad reaction to yesterday's smoothies and became so violent or agitated as to be a danger to themselves or others. Masha understood that Yao would sleep for a few restful hours and then he'd be fine. It was Yao himself who had taught both Masha and Delilah how to administer the injection in the event of an emergency.

This had not been planned, but it had become clear to her that Yao's loss of confidence in the protocol was a serious liability. He needed to be temporarily removed from the strategic decision-making process. She'd needed to act fast and she had, in the same way that she had once culled non-performing staff or even entire divisions. Her ability to make swift decisions and execute those decisions in the face of change had been one of her strengths throughout her working life. *Agility.* That's what it was. She was both metaphorically and literally agile.

But once Yao slept, she felt oddly alone. She missed him. She missed Delilah too. Without Yao or Delilah here there was no-one to mentor, no-one observing her actions, no-one to whom she needed to explain herself. It was strange. She had lived alone for large chunks of her life. When she was renovating Tranquillum House and creating and refining the personal development plan that resulted in her incredible physical and spiritual transformation, she had spent months at a time without seeing a soul, and she had not felt the loss of company at all. But her life was different now. She was rarely alone. There were always people in the house: her staff, her guests. This reliance on people was a weakness. She needed to work on that. She was a work in progress.

Nothing stays the same.

It was a hypothetical exercise she had set for the guests, but their fear needed to be real. She had not seen enough fear. She had seen cynicism and doubt. These people were disrespectful. Ungrateful. Quite unintelligent, to be frank.

Those drugs weren't cheap. They had cut into her profit margins. She had been prepared to take less profit for their benefit. Dear Yao had worked so hard to ensure the correct dosages for each guest. There had been many late nights getting this right!

The new protocol was meant to be Masha's career pivot. She was ready to be part of a bigger world again. She missed the public recognition she had enjoyed in her corporate life: the profiles in business magazines, the invitations to deliver keynote addresses. She wanted to publish articles and deliver speeches at conferences and events. She had already put the word out about a potential book deal. The response had been positive. *Personal transformation is a topic of perennial interest*, wrote one publisher. *Keep us posted.*

Masha had enjoyed the thought of her previous colleagues seeing her reincarnation. They would probably not recognise her at first, and then they would respond with awe and envy. She had escaped the rat race and look what she had achieved. There would be magazine profiles and television interviews. She planned to employ a publicist. She certainly intended to mention Yao in the acknowledgements of her book and would even consider promoting him to a more senior position at Tranquillum House while she was busy on the speaking circuit.

Masha's glittering, glorious future lay ahead and these ungrateful dolts stood in the way of it. Masha had anticipated year-long waiting lists after the news of their success got out. Prices would have to rise to reflect the demand. These people had been offered this incredible program for a bargain-basement price and they did nothing but moan.

They thought they were hungry! Had they ever known true hunger? Had they ever lined up *for more than five minutes* to buy basic food supplies?

Masha considered the blank computer monitor and thought about turning it back on, but she didn't want to see them right now. She was too angry with them. That Heather Marconi was so disrespectful. Masha did not like her.

If any one of them had a brain, they could be out of that room right now and on their way to the police to make their complaints about how *poorly* they had been treated, when the truth was they had been lovingly nurtured.

Masha took a key from her top drawer and unlocked the cupboard beneath her desk.

For a moment she sat and studied the contents. Her mouth filled with saliva. She lunged forward and grabbed a bag of Doritos and a jar of salsa. The bag was fat and smooth and crackled in her hand.

She remembered the woman who would come home late at night from the office after working a sixteen-hour day and sit in a dark room in front of the television to mindlessly eat Doritos and salsa. That had been Masha's evening meal. She had not cared about her body. Her body meant nothing. She just bought bigger and bigger-sized clothes when she noticed. All she cared about was work. She smoked and did no exercise. As that doctor had said, she was a heart attack or a stroke waiting to happen.

She opened the pack and breathed in the scents of fake cheese and salt. Her mouth watered. Her stomach churned with self-disgust. It had been over a year since she had last indulged in this depraved, disgusting act. This was all because of her ungrateful guests.

Last time she ate Doritos it had also been a guest's

fault. He had put a one-star review on TripAdvisor about Tranquillum House and written a litany of lies. He said they had bed bugs. He posted a photo of the bites. There were no bed bugs. He made it all up because Masha told him on the last day that he was a candidate for a heart attack or a stroke unless he continued to change his lifestyle when he got back home. She knew this because she *recognised* him as the person she had once been. Yet she offended him by using the word 'fat'. He *was* fat. Why the surprise? Wasn't that why he came here?

Masha put the first Dorito on her tongue and her whole body trembled with the chemical reaction it invoked. She knew exactly how many calories she was about to consume and how much exercise she was going to need to do to burn them off. (Alternatively, she could vomit.)

She crunched the Dorito between her teeth and opened the jar of salsa with one hard twist of her wrist. Once she had weak, useless arms that would have struggled to open this jar. That sad fat woman in front of the television used to swear and tap away at the lid with a spoon, trying to loosen it.

In the life before that, there had been a man for opening jars. She used to call for her husband sharply like he was a servant, and he would open the jar, smile and touch her. He was always touching her. Every single day for years and years she was touched.

But that was someone else. It had been decades now since she was touched with love.

She thought briefly of Yao's hand tonight touching hers, and she took another Dorito from the pack and scooped out the red, glistening salsa.

Yao made a tiny sound like a child. His cheeks were flushed. He looked like a feverish baby.

Masha put the back of her hand to his forehead and held it there for a moment. He did feel hot.

She shoved the Dorito in her mouth and began to eat faster and faster, yellow crumbs falling all over her desk and her dress, as she allowed herself to remember the last day of that life of so long ago.

It was a Sunday. Her ex-husband was out being a 'laid-back' Australian. Australians liked to call themselves 'laid-back', as if that were a good thing. He had accepted an invitation from his work colleagues to play a game where they shot each other with balls of paint. It would be 'fun' and a 'lot of laughs'.

Yes, it sounded very laid-back: running around shooting each other. The other wives were going but Masha stayed home with the baby. She had nothing in common with those women, and they dressed so badly it made her depressed and homesick. Masha was a working mother. She had work to do. She was ten times smarter than all the men at the company where she worked, but she had to work ten times harder for the recognition she deserved.

She was too tall. Sometimes her colleagues pretended not to understand her and sometimes she could tell they really didn't understand, even though she spoke better English than them. She didn't appreciate their humour – she never laughed on time – and they didn't appreciate hers. When she made a joke, often a very funny, sophisticated, intelligent joke, they stared at her with confused, blank faces.

At home she had many friends, but here she experienced a strange kind of shyness. It made her angry and resentful to feel that way, because back home she would never have been called shy. She held herself stiffly because she could not stand to be laughed at, and here there was always the possibility that she might misunderstand or be misunderstood. Her husband didn't care when that happened. He found it funny.

He had fearlessly dived straight into the social scene before he knew the rules, and people loved him. Masha was proud of him for that, although also a little envious.

Once, Masha and her husband were invited to her boss's home for what Masha assumed was a dinner party. She dressed very nicely, very sexy, high heels and a dress. Every single woman but Masha wore jeans.

The invitation said 'Bring your own meat'. Masha confidently told her husband: 'No, no, that is a joke! An Australian joke. Not very funny but most definitely a joke.' They would not make the embarrassing mistake of taking it seriously.

But it was not a joke. The women in jeans carried plastic shopping bags looped over their hands. The bags contained packages of uncooked meat. Just enough for two. Two steaks. Four sausages. Masha could not believe her eyes.

Her husband was quick. He slapped his hand to his forehead. 'Oh no, we left our meat at home!' he told the host.

'No worries,' said the host. 'We've got plenty to spare.'

So generous of him to spare a little meat for the guests he'd invited to his home.

The moment they walked through the front door women and men split into different groups as if they were banned from talking to each other. The men stood around a barbecue overcooking the meat for what seemed like hours. The food was inedible. There were no chairs. People sat anywhere. Three women sat on a *retaining wall*.

After that day, Masha decided not to concern herself with establishing a social circle in Sydney. What was the point? She had an eleven-month-old baby and a demanding full-time job and a husband. Her life was busy and satisfying and she was truly happy, happier than she'd ever been in her life. It was gratifying to have a baby so clearly superior to other babies in terms of both beauty and intelligence. This was an objective fact. Her husband agreed. Sometimes she felt sorry for other mothers when they saw her baby, sitting so dignified and upright in his stroller, his fair hair shining in the sun (so many other babies were bald, like old men), his little head swivelling from side to side as he observed the world with his big green eyes. When he found something funny, as he often did (he got that from his father), he chuckled, right from his belly, surprisingly deep, and everyone in hearing distance had to laugh too, and at that moment, as Masha exchanged smiles with those around her, real smiles, not polite smiles, she wasn't isolated at all; she was a Sydneysider, a mother out with her child.

That Sunday, she had nearly finished her work when the baby woke up. He no longer cried when he woke up. Instead he made a musical 'aaaah' sound, as if he was playing with his voice. He let the sound go up and down, up and down. He was as happily tone deaf as his father singing as he stirred a pot on the stove.

At one point he called out, 'Ma-ma! Ma-ma!' He was so smart. Many children of that age did not have a single word in their vocabulary.

'I'm coming, my lapochka!' she called back. She only needed five minutes more and she would be done.

He became quiet again. She finished what she was doing. It took less than five minutes. Maybe four.

'Did you get tired of waiting for me, little bunny?' she said as she opened the door of his bedroom. She thought he might have fallen back asleep.

He was already dead.

He'd strangled himself playing with a long white cord from the window blind. It was not an uncommon accident, she later learned. Other women had seen what she saw that day. Their trembling fingers had untangled their precious babies.

These days there were warning tags on blind cords. Masha always saw them when she walked into a room, even from very far away.

Her husband said it was an accident and there was nothing to forgive as he stood at the hospital wearing the paint-splattered overalls from his game. She remembered the fine spray of blue dots across his jaw, like blue rain.

She remembered also one strange moment when she had looked at the strangers all around her and wanted her mother, a woman who had never really liked Masha, let alone loved her, and who would provide no comfort. Yet, for just one moment in her grief, Masha had craved her presence.

She refused her husband's forgiveness. Her son called for her and she did not go to him. It was unacceptable.

She let her husband go. She insisted he find another life and he did eventually, although it took much, much longer than Masha wanted. It was such a relief when he was gone, when she no longer had to experience the pain of seeing the face that so resembled that of their beautiful son.

Although she refused to read the emails he sent and wanted to know nothing about him, she accidentally discovered many years ago, when she came across a man in a food court who was still friends with her husband, a man who was there on the day they shot the balls of paint, that her husband was healthy and happy, that he had married an Australian girl and had three sons.

Masha hoped that he still sang when he cooked. She thought that he probably did. In her research, she had read of the hedonic treadmill theory, which said that people returned to a certain pre-set level of happiness regardless of what happened to them, whether it was very good or very bad. Her husband had been a simple, happy man whereas Masha was a complex, unhappy woman.

Masha's son would have been twenty-eight this August. She probably would have had a difficult relationship with him if he had lived. They probably would have fought like Masha had once fought with her mother. Instead he would always be her singing, chuckling baby and a beautiful young man wearing a baseball cap walking towards her through a lake of colour.

She should have been allowed to stay with him.

Masha looked at the empty bag of Doritos. Her fingertips were stained yellow the way her father's had once been stained by nicotine. She ran the heels of her hands over her mouth, and turned the monitor back on to observe her guests.

They were all awake, she saw. They sat in small groups, chatting, in that laid-back Australian way. They were too relaxed. This was no dark night of the soul. It could have been a barbecue. These people did not truly believe they were facing death sentences.

Never once had a member of staff defied her the way these people were defying her.

The screen of her monitor pulsed as if it were alive. Was there some sort of malfunction? She put her finger to it and felt it quiver like a dying fish.

She was momentarily confused before she remembered she had earlier taken seventy-five milligrams of LSD to improve her decision-making and mental clarity. This was simply a hallucination. She needed to relax and allow her brain to find all the right connections.

She looked around the room and noticed a vacuum cleaner sitting quietly in the corner of her office. It was not pulsating. It was quite real. She had just not noticed it before. The cleaners must have left it. They had excellent cleaners here. She only recruited and employed the best. It was important to maintain quality standards at all levels of your business.

There was something so familiar about the vacuum cleaner.

'*Oh!*' she said, for her father was picking up the vacuum cleaner, clumsily, with both hands. It was such a cumbersome thing. He walked towards the door with it.

'*No, no, no!*' she screamed. '*Papochka!* Put it down! Do not go!'

But he looked back at her sadly and smiled, and he was gone and no man would ever love her the way her father had loved her.

He was not real. She knew this. It was very easy to see what was real and what was not. Her mind was very sharp, sharp enough to differentiate.

She closed her eyes.

Her baby's voice was calling for her. *No. Not real.*

She opened her eyes and he was crawling across her office floor, babbling nonsense to himself.

She closed her eyes quickly. *No. Not real.*

She opened her eyes. A cigarette would calm her.

She opened her secret cupboard once more and removed an unopened packet of cigarettes and a lighter. The geometry of the pack enthralled her. Each of its four mathematically aligned angles was so pleasing.

She opened the pack, removed a cigarette and rolled its cylindrical shape back and forth between her fingertips. The lighter was orange, a colour of such depth and beauty it astonished her.

She ran her thumb across the tiny rough-edged wheel of the lighter. A gold flame burst forth, instantly and obediently.

She let it go and did it again.

The lighter was a miniature factory producing perfect flames on demand. There was such beauty in the efficient production of goods and services.

A thought of crystalline clarity: Masha should forget the wellness industry completely and return to the corporate world. Forget pivoting. She should *jump*. It would simply be a matter of reactivating her LinkedIn account and within a very short time she would be headhunted, fielding offers.

The boy in the baseball cap sat on the other side of her desk, dripping puddles of iridescent colour all over her floor.

'What do you think?' she asked him. 'Should I do that?'

He didn't speak, but she could tell he thought it was a good idea.

No more entitled, ungrateful *guests*. She would once again conduct multiple departments of a company like an orchestra: accounting, payroll, sales and marketing – it was all coming back to her, the glorious unassailable solidity of a documented reporting structure with her name at the top. She would micro-dose daily to optimise her productivity. Ideally her staff would do the same, although the people in HR would have all sorts of objections.

She had begun a new life when she emigrated, when her son died, and again when her heart stopped. She could do it again.

Sell this property and buy an apartment in the city.

Or . . .

She studied the tiny, flickering flame. The answer was right there.

chapter sixty-six

Ben

'So, Napoleon, I've got you,' said Ben, walking next to the older man as he strode up and down the length of the cellar. 'I mean, I'm defending you.'

He felt like he should call him Mr Marconi or Sir. He had that teacher-ish manner. The sort of teacher you still wanted to impress even after you'd left school and bumped into him at the shops looking startlingly short. Not that he could imagine Napoleon ever looking short.

'Thank you, Ben,' said Napoleon, as if Ben had been given a choice.

'So, okay,' said Ben. He rubbed his stomach. He had never been so hungry in his life. 'I guess it's pretty simple why you deserve a stay of execution. You're a husband and a father, and, well, I hope it's okay to include this in my speech – but your wife and daughter have already lost enough, haven't they? They couldn't lose you too.'

'You can say that if you like.' Napoleon smiled sadly. 'That's true.'

'And you're a teacher,' said Ben. 'So kids depend on you.'

'They do. Yep.' Napoleon rapped his knuckles on the brickwork. Ben had seen him do this a hundred times since they'd been down here, as if he were hoping that he'd find a loose brick that would give them a way out. Ben knew it was hopeless. There was no way out of here except that door.

'Anything else I should say?' asked Ben, and his voice cracked. When he'd had to deliver the toast at Pete's wedding he thought he might pass out. And now it was his job to defend this man's *life*?

Napoleon turned away from the wall and looked at Ben. 'Mate, I don't think it matters what you say. I wouldn't take it too seriously.' He clapped him on the shoulder. 'I think we need to take *Masha* seriously, but not the game itself.'

'You've got yourself a dud defence lawyer here,' confessed Ben. 'I got lucky. Lars is defending me and he's *appeared* in court.'

When Lars had his 'meeting' with Ben, he only asked two or three quick questions before he said, 'How about this?' And then he launched into an eloquent speech, like something on *television*, all about how Ben was a morally upstanding young man on the very cusp of adulthood, about to become a father, deeply committed to his marriage, with so much to give to his wife, his family, his *community* and so on and so forth. It all just flowed out, without a single 'um' or 'ah'.

'Think that will do the trick?' he asked at the end.

'Sure,' marvelled Ben.

And then Lars had gone off to the bathroom to fix his hair in preparation for his 'appearance'.

'I get so terrified of public speaking, I can't even breathe,' Ben told Napoleon.

'Do you know the only difference between fear and excitement is the exhalation?' asked Napoleon. 'When you're afraid you hold the air in the top part of the lungs. You need to exhale. Like this. *Ahhhhh.*' He put his hand to his chest and demonstrated with a long, slow breath out. 'Like that sound people make after a firework explodes. *Ahhhhh.*'

Ben did it with him. '*Ahhhhh.*'

'That's it,' said Napoleon. 'Tell you what – I'll go first. I'm defending Tony, so I'll bore Masha to death speaking about his football career. I plan to do a run-down of every game he played. That'll show her.' He stopped at the beam near the inscribed brick in the wall. 'You saw this?'

'The convict graffiti?' Delilah had shown it to them on their first tour of the house. Ben and Jessica hadn't really been that interested.

Napoleon grinned. 'Fascinating, eh? I read up on the history of this place before we came. These brothers eventually got their tickets of leave and ended up becoming very respectable, highly sought-after stonemasons. Far more successful than they would have been back home in England. They've got thousands of descendants in this area. When they were sentenced to be transported to Australia I bet they were devastated. They probably felt like it was the end of the world. But it turned out to be the making of them. The lowest point of your life can lead to the highest. I just find that so . . .' For a moment he looked profoundly sad. 'Interesting.'

Ben didn't know why he suddenly felt in danger of crying. It must be hunger. It occurred to him that when he got home he owed his dad a visit. Just because his dad had given up on Lucy didn't mean Ben should give up on him.

Ben put his fingers to the inscription. He thought about how everyone said it was such fantastic luck that he and Jessica won the lottery, but sometimes it didn't feel that way.

He looked over at Jessica. Was he really going to be a dad himself? How could he advise a kid on how to live his life when he hadn't yet worked it out himself?

'Remember the exhale, mate,' said Napoleon. 'Just breathe out the fear.'

chapter sixty-seven

Heather

'I'm quite a good friend,' said Frances to Heather. 'You could mention that.' She chewed a fingernail. 'I remember birthdays.'

'I'm hopeless at birthdays,' said Heather. In reality she was hopeless at friends, and after Zach died she could see no point to them at all. Friends were an indulgence.

Frances winced. 'I did totally forget a good friend's birthday this year, but that was because I was caught up in this internet scam and I was so distracted that day, and then it got to midnight, and I thought, Oh my God, *Monica*! but it was too late to text, so —'

'What about your family?' Heather interrupted, before she heard this Monica's life story. She found Frances to be quite flaky. 'Do you have family?'

Heather looked over Frances's shoulder at her own family. Zoe was sitting with Jessica, their heads bowed close, as if they were two friends sharing secrets. Napoleon and Ben walked as they talked, Ben listening intently and nodding respectfully like he was one of Napoleon's best students.

She didn't know what was going on with Napoleon right now. It was like an imposter was doing an excellent job performing the role of Napoleon. He was saying and doing all the right things and nearly getting away with it, but there was something just not quite right.

'Yes,' said Frances. 'I have family.' She looked uncertain. 'I guess I'm not that close to my immediate family. My father died and my mother remarried and moved overseas. The south of France. I have a sister, but she has a lot on her plate. Their day-to-day lives wouldn't be impacted that much if I was gone.'

'Of course their lives would be impacted,' said Heather.

'Well . . .' Frances gave the blank screen a nervous look. 'I'm not saying they'd dance on my grave.'

Heather looked at her, surprised. The woman looked genuinely frightened. 'You do know you're not really on death row, don't you? This is just a stupid power game for that maniac.'

'Shhh,' hissed Frances. 'She could be listening.'

'I don't care,' said Heather recklessly. 'I'm not scared of her.'

'I kind of think you *should* be.' Frances shot another uneasy look at the screen.

'It's fine, I'm going to play along,' said Heather, to comfort the poor woman. 'I don't think you should be executed.'

'Thanks so much,' said Frances.

'So what else should I say?'

'Appeal to her ego,' said Frances. 'Start out by saying that it's true that Frances's life didn't mean all that much until this point, but now she has done this retreat, she has been rehabilitated.'

'Rehabilitated,' said Heather.

'That's right.' Frances was as jittery as a junkie. 'Make

sure you use the word "rehabilitated". I think she'll like that. Make it clear that I've seen the error of my self-indulgent ways. I'm going to exercise. Eat clean. No more preservatives. I'm going to *set goals.*'

'*Good morning, my sweetie pies!*'

Masha's voice boomed through the room as her image flickered to life once more on the screen.

Frances gasped and swore, clutching Heather's arm.

'It is time!' cried Masha. She took a long, deep drag of a cigarette and blew the smoke out the side of her mouth. 'It is time to play Death Sentence. Wait. We're not calling it that, are we? It is time to play Death Row. A much better name! Who thought of that name?'

'But it's not time yet!' Napoleon looked at his watch.

Heather stared at the screen. Masha was *smoking.* She didn't know why she was so surprised after everything else that had happened, but it was shocking and distressing, like seeing a nun lifting her habit to reveal suspenders.

'You're smoking!' accused Jessica.

Masha laughed and took another deep drag. 'I am smoking, Jessica. Occasionally, in times of stress, I smoke.'

'You're high,' said Ben tiredly, sadly, and Heather could hear in his voice the years of resigned disappointment suffered by an addict's relative. Ben was right. Masha's eyes were glassy, and her posture was strange and stiff, as if her head wasn't attached to her body and she was worried it would roll off.

Masha held up an empty smoothie glass. 'I have taken steps to reach a higher level of consciousness.'

'Is Yao okay?' asked Heather. She tried to keep her tone respectful, even though her throat burned with hatred. 'Could we please see Yao?'

The screen of the camera seemed to be angled differently

from the previous time. Masha stood in front of a window in what looked like her office, although it was dark outside, so it was impossible to tell for sure.

'He is not your concern right now,' said Masha. 'It is time for you to present your cases for your clients. Will they live? Will they die? This is such a stimulating and thought-provoking exercise, I think.'

'It's only 3 am, Masha!' Napoleon tapped the face of his watch. 'It's not dawn. You said we'd do this at dawn.'

Masha lunged at the screen and pointed her cigarette at him. 'Guests should not wear watches during retreats!'

Napoleon reeled back. He held up his wrist. 'I've been wearing it the whole time. Nobody said I couldn't wear a watch.'

'The watch should have been handed in with the other devices! Who was your wellness consultant?'

'It's my fault, Masha. I take responsibility for this.' He unbuckled his watch.

'It was Yao, wasn't it?' screamed Masha. She looked demonic. Her scream reverberated through the room. Flecks of her saliva dotted the screen.

'Jesus Christ,' said Tony quietly.

Zoe came to stand next to Heather and took her hand, something she hadn't done since she was a very little girl. It felt like no-one breathed.

Heather squeezed Zoe's hand and, for the first time since they'd been trapped down here, she experienced true dread.

She thought of those times throughout her working life when the atmosphere in a labour ward went from focused to hyper-focused, because a mother's or a baby's life hung in the balance and every member of staff in that room knew the next decision made had to be the right one. Except in this case she had no training or experience to fall back upon. She longed to *act*, but she was impotent, and the overwhelming powerlessness reminded her of those nightmarish moments when she found Zach, her fingers looking for a pulse she already knew she wouldn't find.

'I am *very* disappointed in Yao!' raged Masha. 'That was an unacceptable mistake! I shall make sure HR knows! A note will go on his file. He will receive a formal letter of warning.'

Napoleon held up his watch by the strap and showed it to Masha. 'I'm taking it off.'

Zoe squeezed Heather's hand convulsively.

'I'm sorry. It was my fault,' said Napoleon in the slow careful tone of someone placating a crazed gunman. 'I'm going to destroy it.' He dropped the watch to the ground and went to put his foot over it.

Masha switched tone. 'Oh, stop being so dramatic, Napoleon, you could cut your foot!' She waved her cigarette about gaily, as if she were in animated conversation at a party, a glass of wine in the other hand.

Heather heard Zoe take a shaky breath and the thought of her daughter's fear made her want to hurt this madwoman.

'I am not the sort to become too obsessive about bureaucratic rules. I am flexible! I am big picture!' Masha took a long drag of her cigarette. 'On the Myers–Briggs personality test I am the Commander! I think you will not be surprised to hear that.'

'This is not good.' Lars peered up at the screen through splayed fingertips.

'She's off with the fairies,' murmured Tony.

'Nothing is forever,' said Masha irrelevantly. 'Remember that. It's important. Now, who will be presenting first?' She looked around as if searching for something. 'Does everyone have coffee? Not yet? Don't worry. Delilah will have it all under control.'

She smiled and held out her arms as if she were sitting at the head of a conference table.

Heather shuddered with a sudden sense of overwhelming fear. *She's hallucinating.*

At that moment Masha's attention was caught by the cigarette between her fingers. Minutes passed and she continued to stare at the cigarette.

'What's she *doing*?' whispered Carmel.

'It's the LSD,' said Lars in a low voice. 'She can't believe she's never noticed the innate beauty of the cigarette.'

Finally, Masha looked up. 'Who is presenting first?' she asked calmly. She flicked the ash from her cigarette onto a windowsill.

'I will,' said Tony.

'Tony! Excellent,' said Masha. 'Who are you defending?'

'Carmel,' said Tony. He gestured at Carmel, who made a strange, awkward movement, as if she couldn't decide whether to curtsey or hide behind Lars.

'Go ahead, Tony.'

Tony cleared his throat. He stood with his hands clasped and looked respectfully up at the screen. 'I'm representing Carmel Schneider today. Carmel is thirty-nine years old, divorced, with four young daughters. She is their primary caregiver. She is also very close to her older sister, Vanessa, and her parents, Mary and Raymond.'

Masha looked bored. She sniffed.

Tony's voice trembled. 'Carmel's mother, Mary, is not in good health and Carmel normally takes her to her doctors' appointments. Carmel says that she's just an ordinary person, doing the best she can, but I think anyone bringing up four little girls on her own is pretty special.' He pulled nervously at the collar of his t-shirt as if he were adjusting a tie. 'Carmel also volunteers at her local library teaching English to refugees. She does this once a week. She's been doing this since she was eighteen, which I think is very impressive.' He clasped his hands in front of him. 'Thank you.'

Masha yawned theatrically. 'Is that it?'

Tony lost his temper. 'For Christ's sake, she's a young mother! What else do you want to hear? Obviously she doesn't deserve to die.'

'But where is your USP?' said Masha.

'USP?' asked Tony blankly.

'You've forgotten the basics, Tony! What is your unique selling proposition? What makes Carmel unique and special?'

'Well,' said Tony desperately, 'she is very special because . . .'

'I also wonder why you did not begin with a basic analysis of strengths, weaknesses, opportunities and threats? It's not rocket science, people! And visual aids! I see no visual aids! A simple PowerPoint slideshow would have helped support your arguments.'

Heather made eye contact with Napoleon: *What do we do?* She saw the confusion and fear on his face and that made her panic grow, because if Napoleon had no answers, they were in trouble. She thought of those times in hospital emergency waiting rooms with Zach when they realised they were dealing with a numbskull of a triage nurse, how they would exchange looks over Zach's head, and how they both knew exactly what to do and say to act as advocates for their child. But they had never dealt with this dizzying lack of logic.

'I'm sorry,' said Tony humbly. 'Obviously, PowerPoint would have helped support my argument. Yes.'

'Sorry doesn't cut it!' snarled Masha.

'Could I go next?' A loud voice cut unexpectedly through Masha's.

Heather saw with a start that it was Carmel, her chin lifted, her eyes unflinching.

'I've prepared a *strategic analysis* on behalf of Zoe Marconi, and what we should be doing, ah, going forward, and I'd really like your buy-in on this, Masha.'

Masha's face smoothed. She lifted a hand. 'Go ahead, Carmel.'

Carmel strode to the centre of the room and straightened an imaginary suit jacket, even though she was wearing leggings and a pink singlet top emblazoned with the sequinned word HAWAII. 'I know you wanted me to really drill down on this, Masha, and think outside the box.'

It was hard to reconcile this woman of such confidence with the Carmel who had just a few hours earlier begged so pathetically to go home. Now you could practically see her power suit. Was she an *actress*? Or was she calling on the memory of a previous profession? Whatever it was, it was impressive.

'Absolutely.' Masha made a brisk chopping motion with the side of her hand. '*This* is more like it. We need to push the envelope. This is very impressive, Carmel.'

It could almost be amusing if it weren't so terrifying.

'The way I see it, we've got a real window of opportunity here to leverage Zoe's core competencies,' said Carmel, 'and achieve, ah . . . best-practice solutions.'

'Oh well *done*,' whispered Frances.

'That's right.' Masha nodded. 'We should always be aiming for best practice.'

It was bizarre to see how well she responded to this meaningless corporate-speak, like a baby responds to the sound of its mother's voice.

'The question is this,' said Masha shrewdly. 'Does it align with our corporate values?'

'Exactly,' said Carmel. 'And once we have all our ducks in a row, we need to ask this: is it scalable?'

'Is it?' said Masha.

'*Exactly*,' said Carmel. 'So what we're looking for is . . .' She faltered.

'Synergies,' murmured Lars.

'Synergies!' said Carmel with relief.

'Synergies,' repeated Masha dreamily, as if she were saying, 'Paris in spring.'

'So to sum up, we need a synergistic solution that dovetails –'

'I've heard all I need to hear,' said Masha briskly. 'Action that please, Carmel.'

'Will do,' said Carmel.

Masha stubbed out her cigarette on the windowsill behind her. She leaned back against the window. 'Welcome to Tranquillum House.'

Oh dear God, thought Heather. *We've lost her again.*

Masha smiled. No-one smiled back. Heather saw that every face in the room was slack with exhaustion and despair, like the face of a woman who has innocently prepared a 'natural birth plan', created a playlist, and who, after thirty hours of labour, is told that she must now have an emergency caesarean.

Masha said, 'I promise you this: in ten days, you will not be the person you are now.'

'Fuck,' said Jessica. 'Fuck, fuck, fuck.'

'It's just the drugs,' said Lars. 'She doesn't know what she's saying.'

'That's not the problem,' said Ben. 'She doesn't know what she's *doing*.'

Masha lowered her head and put her fingertips to the neckline of her dress.

'We will all do push-ups now,' she said. 'Push-ups are the perfect functional integrated resistance exercise. It's the only exercise that works every single muscle in your body. Twenty push-ups! Now!'

No-one moved.

'Why do you ignore me?' Masha jabbed a finger at the screen. 'Push-ups! Now! Or I will be forced to take action!'

What action could she possibly take? But they didn't wait to find out. They dropped to the floor like soldiers.

Heather tried to lift and lower her tired, hungry body in a parallel line as Masha counted out loud, 'One, two, three! Drop those hips! No Harbour Bridges!'

Was she still in her hallucinogenic state, where she seemingly believed they all worked for her? Did she plan to kill them all? Heather felt a sudden wild panic. She'd brought her daughter to this place. Zoe's life could rest in the hands of this mad, drug-affected woman.

She looked around her. Frances did girl push-ups on her knees. Jessica cried as she, too, gave up and went from her toes to her knees. Tony, the former athlete, dripped sweat as he did perfect form push-ups at twice the speed of almost everyone else, in spite of having just popped his shoulder. Heather noted that her own darling husband kept pace.

'Eighteen, nineteen, twenty! Relax! Excellent!'

Heather collapsed onto her stomach and looked up. Masha had pressed her face so close to the screen that all they could see was a magnified image of her nose, mouth and chin.

'I'm just wondering,' said the disembodied mouth. 'Can you smell it yet?'

It was Napoleon who answered in the calm, gentle voice he would use for a toddler. 'Smell what, Masha?'

'The smoke.'

chapter sixty-eight

Tony

The screen turned to static but Masha's voice continued to ring through the room.

'Deep transformation is possible but you must *detach from your beliefs and assumptions!*'

'I *can* smell smoke,' said Zoe, her face white.

'That's right, Zoe, you can smell smoke, for this house, my house, is burning to the ground as we speak,' said Masha. 'Possessions mean nothing! Will you rise from the ashes? Remember, Buddha says, "No-one saves us but ourselves"!'

'Look,' whispered Frances.

Wisps of black smoke drifted sinuously beneath the locked heavy oak door.

'Let us out!' Jessica screamed so loudly her voice turned hoarse. 'Can you hear me, Masha? You let us out right now!'

The screen turned black.

Masha's absence was now as terrifying as her presence had been.

'We need to block that doorway,' said Tony, but Heather and Napoleon were way ahead of him, returning from the

435

bathrooms carrying dripping wet towels that they were rolling into tight cylinders, as if this was their job, as if they'd been expecting exactly this situation.

As they got to the door the volume of smoke increased suddenly and frighteningly, pouring into the room like water. People began to cough. Tony's chest tightened.

'Everybody get back!' shouted Napoleon, as he and Heather shoved the rolled-up towels between the door and the floor, forming a tight seal.

The low level of claustrophobia Tony had been experiencing ever since they first discovered the locked door threatened to turn into full-blown panic. He felt his breathing become ragged. Oh God, he was going to lose it in front of all these people. He had no job to do. He couldn't even put the towels at the door because Heather and Napoleon were already doing it. He couldn't help. He couldn't kick down that door because it opened inwards. He couldn't fight anyone. He couldn't do a damned thing.

He coughed so violently his eyes filled with tears.

Frances grabbed his hand and pulled. 'Get away from the door.'

He let her pull him back. She didn't let go of his hand. He didn't let go of hers.

Everyone huddled at the point in the room furthest away from the door.

Napoleon and Heather came and stood with them, their eyes already bloodshot from smoke. Napoleon pulled Zoe close to him and she buried her face in his shirt. 'The door didn't feel hot,' he said. 'That's a good sign.'

'I think I can hear it,' said Carmel. 'I can hear the fire.'

They all went quiet. It sounded at first like heavy settled rain, but it wasn't rain; it was the unmistakable crackle of flames.

Something heavy and huge crashed to the ground above

them. A wall? There was a dramatic whoosh of air, like wind in a storm, and then the flames grew louder.

Jessica made a sound.

'Are we all going to die down here?' asked Zoe. She looked up at her father with disbelief. 'Is she seriously going to let us die?'

'Certainly not,' said Napoleon, with such matter-of-fact, grown-up assurance Tony wanted to believe Napoleon had special knowledge, except that Tony was a grown-up too, and he knew better.

'We'll all put wet towels over our heads and faces to protect us from smoke inhalation,' said Heather. 'Then we'll just wait this thing out.'

She sounded as calm and assured as her husband. Maybe Tony would be the same if one of his kids or grandkids were here.

He thought of his children. They would grieve for him. Yes of course his children would grieve for him. They wouldn't be ready to lose him, even though he didn't see them that often these days. This knowledge felt like a surprise, as if he'd spent the last few years pretending his children didn't love him, when he knew they loved their dad, for Christ's sake. He knew that. Late last year, Will forgot about the time difference and rang in the middle of the night from Holland to tell him about his latest promotion at work. 'Sorry,' he said. 'I wanted to tell you first.' Thirty years old and he still wanted his dad's praise. According to Mimi, James was always posting pictures from Tony's foot-ball career online. 'He shows off about you,' Mimi said, rolling her eyes. 'Exploits your fame to pick up girls.' Then there was Mimi herself, his baby, bustling about his house, setting things right. Every time she broke up with another dickhead she turned up at his house to 'give him a hand'. She couldn't lose her dad right now, when she was still dating dickheads.

He wasn't ready to die. Fifty-six years wasn't long enough. His life felt suddenly incredibly rich and abundant with possibility. He wanted to repaint the house, get another dog, a puppy; it wouldn't be betraying Banjo to get a puppy. He always got another puppy in the end. He wanted to go to the beach, eat a big breakfast at the cafe down the road while he read the paper, listen to music – it was like he'd forgotten music existed! He wanted to travel to Holland and see his granddaughter perform in one of those stupid Irish dancing competitions.

He looked at Carmel, who he had written off as a kooky intellectual because of her glasses. He'd asked her how she came to teach English to refugees and she explained that her dad was a refugee from Romania back in the fifties and a next-door neighbour took it upon herself to teach him English. 'My dad didn't have any aptitude for languages,' said Carmel. 'And he's very impatient when he feels insecure. It would have been a tough slog. So my sister and I both teach English as a second language now. To honour Auntie Pat.'

Who the fuck did Tony honour? Who the fuck did Tony help out? He didn't even give back to the sport that had given him so much joy. Mimi had been at him for ages to coach a local team of kids. 'You might even enjoy it,' she said. Why had he been so against the idea? Now he couldn't think of anything more wonderful than standing on a field in the sunlight teaching kids to see the music and poetry of football.

He met the frightened eyes of the woman whose hand he still held. She was as nutty as a fruitcake, talked too much, had clearly never seen an AFL game in her life. She wrote romance books for a living. Tony hadn't read a novel since high school. They had nothing in common.

He didn't want to die.

He wanted to take her out for a drink.

chapter sixty-nine

Frances

The nine guests huddled in the furthest corner of the yoga and meditation studio, wet towels draped over their heads and shoulders, while Tranquillum House burned to the ground.

Frances listened to the sound of the hungry flames and wondered if the crash she'd just heard was that beautiful staircase. She remembered how Yao had said on that first day, 'We won't sink, Frances!' and imagined ripples of fire consuming that beautiful wood.

'Our Father, who art in heaven, hallowed be thy name,' murmured Jessica into her knees, over and over. 'Our Father, who art in heaven, hallowed be thy name.'

Frances wouldn't have picked Jessica as a believer, but maybe she wasn't, because she couldn't seem to get any further than 'hallowed be thy name'.

Frances, who had been brought up Anglican but lost religion sometime back in the late eighties, thought it might not be good manners to pray for deliverance right now, when she hadn't even said thank you for so long. God might have appreciated a thankyou card over the years.

Thank you for that long, hot, sex-filled summer in Europe with Sol.

Thank you for that first year of my marriage to Henry which, to be honest, God, was one of the happiest of my life.

Thank you for a career that has given me virtually nothing but pleasure and I'm sorry for all that fuss about the review. I'm sure that reviewer is one of God's children too.

Thank you for my health, you've been quite generous in that regard, and it was rude of me to make such a fuss over a bad cold.

Thank you for friends who are more like family.

Thank you for my dad, even though you took him a little early.

Thank you for Bellinis and all champagne cocktails.

Sorry for complaining about a paper cut while others suffered atrocities. Although, to be frank, that's why I gave up believing in you – that whole paper cuts for some versus atrocities for others thing.

Carmel cried into her wet towel and jumped at the sound of yet another crash.

Frances imagined the balcony of her room hanging at an angle and then smashing to the ground in a shower of embers.

She imagined billows of black smoke illuminated by fiery light against a summer night's sky.

'The smoke in here isn't getting any worse,' she said to Carmel, to be comforting. 'Napoleon and Heather did a good job with the towels.'

She could still smell and taste smoke, but it was true, it wasn't getting any worse.

'We might be fine,' said Frances tentatively.

'We will be fine,' said Napoleon. He sat between his wife and daughter, holding their hands. 'It's all going to be fine.'

He spoke with such assurance and Frances wished she hadn't caught sight of his face as he readjusted the wet towel, because it was filled with despair.

It's coming for us, she thought. *It's coming for us and there is nowhere to hide.*

She remembered Masha saying, 'I wonder, do you feel that you've ever been truly *tested* in your life?'

Jessica lifted her head from her knees and spoke in a muffled voice through her towel. 'She never even heard all our presentations.'

It was cute the way she still wanted to see logic in Masha's actions. She would have been the kid who couldn't stand it when the teacher forgot to do the quiz that had been promised.

'Do you think Yao is still alive?' asked Zoe.

chapter seventy

Yao

Yao dreamed of Finn.

Finn was very keen that Yao wake up.

'Wake up,' he said insistently. He banged together a pair of cymbals. He blasted a horn in Yao's ear. 'Mate, you really need to wake up to yourself.'

Yao returned to consciousness while Finn receded. He felt the imprint of something soft and scratchy against his cheek. He lifted his head. There was a cushion on Masha's desk. He remembered the feeling of the needle in his neck. The surprise of it, because that was not a decision he could respect.

He heard the sound of something burning. He smelled smoke.

He lifted his head, turned around and saw her, smoking a cigarette, looking out the window.

She turned to face him and smiled. She looked sad and emotional, but resigned, like his fiancée when she broke off their engagement.

Masha said, 'Hello, Yao.'

Yao knew it was over, and he knew he'd never love anyone ever again quite the way he loved this strange woman.

His voice rasped in his throat. 'What have you done?'

chapter seventy-one

Frances

Still it went on. The burning. The crashing.

Frances's fear peaked and then plateaued. Her heart rate slowed. A great tiredness swept over her.

She had always wondered how she would feel if her life was in mortal danger. What would she do if her plane began to plummet towards earth? If a crazed gunman put the barrel to her head? If she was ever truly tested? Now she knew: she wouldn't believe it. She would keep thinking right until the last word that her story would never stop, because there could be no story without her. Things would keep happening to her. It was impossible to truly believe that there would be a final page.

Another crash. Carmel startled again.

'Wait a moment,' said Lars sharply. 'That sound – it's the *same* sound as before. It's exactly the same.'

Frances looked at him. She didn't understand.

Napoleon sat up straighter. He removed the towel from his face.

Jessica said, 'There's a pattern, isn't there? I *knew* there was a pattern. Crackle, whoosh, small bang, crackle, crackle, crackle, huge scary bang.'

Frances said, 'I'm sorry, I don't get it.'

'It's on a loop,' said Tony.

'You mean it's a recording?' said Ben. 'We're listening to a recording?'

Frances couldn't get her head around it. 'There's no fire?' She could *see* the fire clearly in her head.

'But we saw smoke, we smelled smoke,' said Heather. 'Where there's smoke, there's fire.'

'Maybe it's a controlled fire,' said Zoe. 'She wants us to think we're in danger.'

'So this is her way of making us look death in the face,' said Tony.

'I *knew* she wouldn't let us die,' said Carmel.

Lars threw the wet cloth on the floor and went to stand in front of the screen. 'Well done, Masha,' he shouted. 'You've successfully scared us all half to death and we'll never be the same again. Could we please go back to our rooms now?'

Nothing.

'You can't keep us in here forever, Masha,' said Lars. 'What's that mantra you keep repeating? Nothing lasts forever.' He smiled ruefully and pushed his damp hair back from his forehead. 'We feel like we've been down here forever.'

Nothing lasts forever, thought Frances. Masha had made a point of saying that so many times. *Nothing lasts forever. Nothing lasts forever.*

She remembered how she'd told Masha there was no code in the doll and Masha had answered, 'Exactly.'

Frances said now, 'When was the last time someone tried the door?'

'I honestly think we've tried every possible code combination there could be,' said Napoleon.

'I don't mean the code,' said Frances. 'I mean the doorhandle. When was the last time someone tried the doorhandle?'

chapter seventy-two

Yao

'Did you sleep well?' asked Masha. She took a drag of her cigarette.

Yao ran a diagnostic eye over her: dilated pupils, sheen of sweat on her forehead, fidgeting.

'Did you have a smoothie?' he asked. He lifted an empty Doritos packet from Masha's desk, shook it and watched the yellow crumbs fall. If she'd eaten *Doritos*, she had to be in an altered state. The Doritos were more shocking than the cigarette.

'I did.' Masha exhaled smoke and smiled at him. 'The smoothie was delicious and I have been experiencing many remarkable insights.'

He'd never seen her smoke. She made smoking look beautiful. Yao had never smoked and now he wanted to try it. It looked natural and sensual, the smoke curling languidly from her fingers.

He remembered the first time he met her, ten years ago in that big office, and how she'd smelled of cigarette smoke.

Yao looked at the computer screen on her desk. A clip of a burning two-storey house. An eave crashed to the ground.

'You sedated me,' said Yao. He ran his tongue around his dry mouth. He felt dull-witted with shock. He couldn't quite comprehend that she had done this.

'Yes, I did,' said Masha. 'I had no choice.'

The sky outside the window began to lighten.

'The guests?' asked Yao. 'Are they still down there?'

Masha shrugged moodily. 'I don't know. I am sick of them. I am sick of this industry.' She took another drag of her cigarette and brightened. 'I've made a decision! I'm going back to FMCG.'

'FMCG?' asked Yao.

'Fast-moving consumer goods,' said Masha.

'Like toothpaste?' said Yao.

'Exactly like toothpaste. Would you like to come and work with me?'

'What? *No.*' He stared at her. She was still Masha, she still had that extraordinary body, still wore that extraordinary dress, and yet he could feel her power over him slipping away as he watched her morphing back into the corporate executive she'd once been. How was that possible? He felt as betrayed as if a lover had admitted infidelity. This wasn't just a job for him, it was his life, his home, it was virtually his *religion*, and now she wanted to leave it all behind to go and sell *toothpaste*? Wasn't toothpaste part of the ordinary world they had turned their backs on?

She didn't mean it. It had to be the smoothie talking. This was not an example of a transcendental insight. With her medical history, she should not have had the smoothie, but now she had, she should be lying down, with her headphones on, and then Yao could *guide* her psychedelic experience away from toothpaste.

But right now he had nine guests to worry about.

He looked away from her and turned off the burning house footage on the computer. He clicked onto the security program that showed the yoga and meditation studio.

There was no-one there. Crumpled towels lay all over the floor of the deserted room.

'They're out,' said Yao. 'How did they escape?'

Masha sniffed. 'They finally worked it out. The door has been unlocked for hours.'

chapter seventy-three

Carmel

All the men insisted on walking ahead of the women up the stairs from the yoga and meditation studio, ready to slay lions or wellness consultants offering smoothies. It was kind and gentlemanly and Carmel appreciated it, and felt glad not to be a man, but it seemed their chivalry was unnecessary. The house was silent and empty.

Carmel still couldn't believe there was no fire. The images in her head had been so real. She had thought she wouldn't see her children again.

'Surely it won't just *open*,' Heather had said when they all stood at the door and Napoleon put his hand on the handle, insisting they all *stay back, stay back, stay back* . . .

It opened, as if it had never been locked at all, to reveal a steel rubbish bin sitting directly outside the door.

Napoleon tilted it forward and showed them the contents. There were burnt fragments of newspaper at the bottom and a pile of melted misshapen plastic water bottles on top. There were still a few glowing red embers left, but that was all that remained of the towering inferno they had all imagined.

They wandered as a group into the empty dining room and looked at the long table where they'd shared their silent meals. Grey morning light filled the room. Magpies warbled and a kookaburra laughed its liquid laugh. The dawn chorus had never sounded so lyrical. Life felt exquisitely ordinary.

'We should find a phone,' said Heather. 'Call the police.'

'We should just leave,' said Ben. 'Find our cars and get the hell out of here.'

Nobody did anything.

Carmel pulled out a chair and sat down, her elbows on the table. She felt the same shocked sense of ecstatic relief as she had just after giving birth. All that shouting of instructions. All that fear. All that fuss. Over and out.

'Do you think anyone is here in the house at all?'

'Wait. Someone is coming,' said Lars.

Footsteps approached down the hallway.

'Good *morning*!' It was Yao. He carried a huge platter of tropical fruit. He looked tired, but otherwise in perfect health. 'Please take your seats. We have a delicious breakfast prepared for you!' He placed the platter on the table.

Wow, thought Carmel. *He's going to pretend everything is normal.*

Zoe burst into tears. 'We thought you were dead!'

Yao's smile wavered. 'Dead? Why would you think I was dead?'

'You looked pretty out of it, mate,' said Tony.

'We had to play a game called "Death Row,"' Frances told him, from an armchair by the door. She looked just like one of Carmel's daughters telling tales about her sibling. 'It was a horrible game . . .' Her voice trailed off.

Yao straightened a bunch of purple grapes that was slipping off the side of the platter. He frowned.

Carmel took up the slack. 'We had to pretend to be

lawyers.' She remembered that exhilarating moment when she'd spouted all that meaningless jargon that was nevertheless so meaningful to Masha. It had been terrifying but also wonderful. Like a fairground ride that had flipped her upside down and then round and round. 'We had to argue for a stay of execution. I defended . . . Zoe.'

As she spoke she realised how farcical it sounded. It was so obviously all just a game. Why had they taken it so seriously? If they told the police about it, they would surely just laugh.

'And then she never even let us *complete* the activity,' complained Jessica.

'Yes, I was quite looking forward to my turn,' said Frances.

'You were not,' said Heather.

Carmel took a single grape from the fruit platter, even though she didn't feel especially hungry. She must have gone beyond hunger. She bit straight through the centre of the grape. *Oh my God*, she thought, as the juice exploded in her mouth. She shuddered with gratitude. It was like all the cells of her body reacted to this tiny sustenance. She felt like she was close to some amazingly complex yet breathtakingly simple revelation about the true precious beauty of food. Food wasn't the enemy. Food gave her life.

'I know some of last night's activities might have seemed . . . unusual,' said Yao. He was a little hoarse but you had to admire him. He was continuing to play his violin as the *Titanic* sank beneath the sea. 'But everything that happened was designed for your personal growth.'

'Cut the shit, Yao,' said Lars. 'You must know it's all over. We can't let anyone else go through what we went through last night.'

'We have to close you down, mate,' said Tony.

'That boss of yours has to go straight to a secure psychiatric ward,' said Heather.

'I will not be going to any *ward*,' said Masha.

Carmel's heart leaped in her chest.

Masha stood in the doorway of the dining room wearing a Hillary Clinton-style red pantsuit that looked ten years out of date and three sizes too big for her. 'I'm going back to work.'

'She's still flying high as a kite,' said Ben.

'Masha,' said Yao despairingly. 'I thought you were resting.'

'You all look so well!' Masha studied the group. 'Much thinner. Much healthier. I'm sure you are all happy with your results!'

Heather made a derisive sound. 'We're thrilled, Masha, we're just thrilled with our results. This has been so relaxing.'

Masha's nostrils flared. 'Don't use that sarcastic tone! You report to me. I have authority to –'

'Not this again,' said Heather. 'You're my boss, are you? We all work for you? We've all got to do a PowerPoint presentation now or what . . . you *execute* us?' She imitated Masha's accent.

'That's not helpful, my love,' said Napoleon.

'I know all about you, Heather,' said Masha slowly. 'I was there last night. I heard your secrets. You told me everything. You tell me I gave drugs to your daughter, I am such a terrible person to do this, even though I did it to help you and your family. Well, you tell me this: *what drugs did you allow your son to take?*'

Masha's fists were clenched. She held something tightly in her right hand. Carmel couldn't see it what it was.

'What sort of a mother are you?' Masha asked Heather. There was a strange, powerful animosity between these two women that Carmel didn't understand.

'That's enough,' said Napoleon.

Yao moved across the room towards Masha, as Heather responded to her comment with a peal of scornful laughter. She said, 'I'm a better mother than you would ever be.'

Masha roared like an animal. She leaped at Heather, a silver dagger held high, ready to plunge into her neck.

Napoleon jumped in front of his wife and Yao jumped in front of Masha at the exact moment Frances stood from her chair, grabbed the candelabrum from the sideboard and swung it wildly at Masha's head.

Masha fell instantly. She lay at Frances's feet without moving.

'Oh God,' said Frances. The candelabrum hung in her hand. She looked up at everyone, her face filled with horror. 'Have I killed her?'

chapter seventy-four

Frances

Afterwards Frances would try to work through her decision-making process, but she never could. It was like her brain short-circuited.

She saw the two-hundred-year-old letter opener in Masha's hand.

Careful. That letter opener is as sharp as a dagger. You could murder someone with that, Frances.

She saw Masha lunge for Heather.

She felt the unexpected heaviness of the candelabrum in her hand.

And next thing Masha was lying at her feet, and Frances had her hands in the air like a criminal because a large policeman was pointing a gun directly at her and saying, 'Don't move, please!'

The well-mannered cop was Gus, Jan the massage thera-pist's boyfriend, and he was just as lovely as Frances had imagined him to be, especially once he put his gun away. Gus did not charge Frances with the murder of Masha, because Masha was not dead. After just a few terrifying moments, she sat up, a hand to the back of her head, and told Frances she was fired, effective immediately.

Jan, wearing a summer dress, was with Gus, looking flushed and excited at the events that had transpired at her workplace. Apparently, she and Gus had been chatting (in the middle of the night; from their glances, Frances deduced it was a post-coital chat) and Gus mentioned that at the end of his shift he'd pulled over a girl who was speeding in a yellow Lamborghini. It was immediately obvious to Jan from Gus's description that this girl could only be Delilah, and as it seemed unlikely that there could be two yellow Lamborghinis in the area, and it therefore looked like Delilah might have stolen a guest's car, and as Jan was already suspicious about the fact that nearly all the Tranquillum House staff had been asked to leave during the middle of a retreat (which the chef told her had never happened before), she had convinced Gus to drive straight to the house with her to check things out.

'She's probably concussed,' said Yao, after examining his boss. 'Or it might be that she's still tripping.'

Gus said that he wouldn't be charging Frances with assault because there were multiple witnesses who all confirmed that her quick actions had most likely saved Heather's life, although Frances knew that Heather might have been Masha's target but the only ones in danger were Napoleon, who had pushed Heather aside, and Yao, who had placed himself directly in front of Masha.

Heather said, 'Thank you, Frances.' She put a hand to the side of her neck and considered the potential murder weapon. 'That could have been quite nasty.'

Heather refused to acknowledge Masha at all, right up until when the ambulance arrived and took Masha to the local hospital. 'Thank you for visiting! Please remember to rate your stay with us on TripAdvisor!' she cried out merrily, as the two blue-uniformed paramedics led her away.

More local police officers turned up, and then, once Gus and his friends discovered the large quantities of illegal drugs on the premises, a second group arrived, and these ones had harder eyes and shinier shoes, and they weren't quite as interested in the extraneous details as Gus was.

Yao was taken away in a police car to make a statement.

Before he left, he turned to them all and said simply, 'I'm very sorry.'

He looked sad and defeated and ashamed, like a teenage boy who has had a party get out of control while his parents are away.

Ben's Lamborghini was found in the car park of the regional airport two hours' drive away. It was supposedly not damaged, although Ben would see about that. Delilah had not yet been located.

There was a lot of tedious paperwork. Everyone had to give long separate statements to the police about the events that had transpired over the last week.

It was hard sometimes to give a logical account of what happened. Frances could sense their scepticism.

'So you thought you were locked up?'

'We *were* locked up.'

'But then you just opened the door and left?'

'Well, you see, we'd stopped trying the handle,' said Frances. 'I think that was the point Masha was trying to make: that sometimes the answer is right there in front of you.'

'I see,' said the police officer. You could tell from his face that he didn't see at all and that *he* sure as hell wouldn't have got himself locked in that room. 'And you thought there was a fire.'

'There was smoke,' said Frances, her mouth full of mango,

the golden flesh as fresh and sweet as a summer morning. 'And the sounds of a fire.'

'Which in reality was a YouTube clip of a house burning down played over an intercom,' said the cop without inflection.

'It was very convincing,' said Frances unconvincingly.

'I'm sure it was,' said the cop. You could see it was taking all his willpower not to roll his eyes. 'You have . . .' He pointed at her face.

Frances wiped her sticky chin. 'Thanks. Don't you just love summer fruit?'

'Not really a fan.'

'Not a fan of *fruit*?'

Lars, the only member of the group with any legal expertise, tried to ensure everyone stayed on message.

'We were tricked. We had no idea there were drugs on the premises,' he said loud enough for everyone to hear as he was led off for his interview. 'We were not told what those smoothies contained.'

'I had no idea there were drugs on the premises,' said Frances again. 'I was tricked. I was not told what those smoothies contained.'

'Yeah, I know,' said the policeman. He gave up trying and rolled his eyes. 'None of you did.' He closed his notebook. 'I'll let you get back to your mango.'

One of the local cops recognised Tony and drove back home to get a Carlton shirt for him to sign, and got quite teary about it.

Finally, as the long day began to draw to a close, and the drugs were removed as evidence, they were all told that they were free to leave, as long as they made themselves available for any future questioning.

'We're free to leave, but are we free to *stay*?' Frances

asked Gus, the last police officer there. It was too late in the day to drive six hours back home.

Gus said he didn't see why not, as it was no longer an active crime scene. No-one had died and the drugs were gone and they were technically still paying guests. He seemed to be working through the legalities in his mind, reassuring himself of his decision. Jan gave everyone a ten-minute mini massage to release tension. She said they might want to get themselves checked out at the local hospital but no-one felt inclined to do so, especially as that was where Masha had been taken. Tony said his shoulder was perfectly fine.

'Is this what you meant when you said don't do anything you're not comfortable with?' Frances asked Jan when it was her turn for a massage.

Poor Jan was horrified. 'I meant don't do burpees or jumping lunges!' she said, as her practised fingers performed their magic on Frances's shoulders. 'Burpees are terrible for anyone with back issues and you've got to have really stable knees before you do a jumping lunge.' She shook her head. 'If I'd suspected anything like this I would have informed the police immediately.' She looked adoringly at Gus. 'I would have informed Gus.'

'Does he whistle?' asked Frances, following her gaze.

Apparently he didn't whistle or whittle, but was still just about perfect.

Once Gus and Jan had left, the nine of them went into the kitchen to prepare something for their dinner. They were euphoric with freedom as they flung open cupboards, and there was a moment of awed silence as they all stood in front of the massive stainless steel refrigerator and saw the abundance of food it contained: steak, chicken, fish, vegetables, eggs.

'Today is my twenty-first birthday,' announced Zoe.

They all turned to look at her.

'It's also Zach's birthday.' She took a deep shaky breath. 'It's *our* birthday today.'

Her parents moved to stand on either side of her.

'I think we might need a little glass of wine with our dinner,' said Frances.

'We need music,' said Ben.

'We need a cake,' said Carmel. She rolled up her sleeves. 'I'm a master baker of birthday cakes.'

'I can make pizza,' said Tony. 'If there's flour, I can make pizza dough.'

'*Can* you?' said Frances.

'I can,' he said, and he smiled.

Zoe retrieved the bottle of wine she'd smuggled in from her bedroom, and Frances searched the house until she found a goldmine of presumably uncollected contraband brought in by previous guests, including six bottles of wine, some of which looked quite good, in a small room behind the reception desk. Ben found their mobile phones, and they reconnected with the world, and discovered not all that much had happened in the last week: a sporting scandal that only Tony and Napoleon found scandalous, the break-up of a Kardashian marriage that only Jessica and Zoe found relevant, and a natural disaster where the only fatalities involved those who flagrantly ignored warnings, so, you know. Ben used his phone to play music and took on the responsibility of DJ, accepting requests across generations and genres.

Everyone got drunk on wine and food. Jessica grilled perfect medium-rare steaks. Tony twirled pizza dough. Frances acted as sous chef to whoever needed her. Carmel made an incredible cake and became flushed and beautiful at all the praise that was heaped upon her. A surprising number of people danced and a surprising number of people cried.

Lars could *not* dance. At all. It was delightful to watch.

'Are you doing it on *purpose*?' asked Frances.

'Why do people always ask that?' said Lars.

Tony could dance. Very well. He told them that back in the day he and some other players had done ballet classes as part of their training. 'Helped build up my hamstrings,' he explained as Frances and Carmel clutched each other and giggled helplessly at the thought of Tony in a tutu. He responded by executing a perfect pirouette.

Frances had never been in a relationship with a man who could pirouette or make pizza dough. That was just something interesting to note and not a reason to let Tony kiss her. She knew he wanted to kiss her. The feeling of being at a party with a man who wanted to kiss her, but had not yet done so, was exactly as good as the first time she experienced it, at the age of fifteen, at Natalie's sixteenth birthday party. It heightened everything. Just like a hallucinogenic drug.

They toasted Zoe and Zach.

'I didn't want twins,' said Heather, holding up her glass of red wine. 'When the doctor told me it was twins, I'm not going to lie, I said a four-letter word.'

'Well, that's a great start, Mum,' said Zoe.

'I'm a midwife,' said Heather, ignoring her. 'I knew the risks of a twin pregnancy. But it turned out the pregnancy didn't give me any trouble at all. I had a natural birth. Of course, they gave me a lot of trouble once they were out in the world!'

She looked at Napoleon. He took her hand.

'Those first few months were hard, but then, I don't know, I think we got them into a routine when they were about six months old, and I remember, after I finally got a good night's sleep, I woke up looked at them and thought, Well, you two are pretty special.

'They always took it in turns to do things first. Zach was born first but Zoe walked first. Zach ran first.' Her words faded a little. She went to take a sip of wine and then remembered she hadn't finished her toast. 'Zoe got her driver's licence first, which, as you can imagine, made Zach crazy.'

She stopped again. 'The fights! You would not believe the fights they had! They'd be wanting to kill each other and I'd put them in separate rooms, but within five minutes they'd be back together again, playing and giggling.'

Frances realised that Heather was giving the exact speech she would have given if Zach hadn't died: an ordinary, proud mum speech in a backyard, with the younger generations rolling their eyes and the older generation brushing away tears.

She held up her glass. 'To Zoe and Zach: the smartest, funniest, most beautiful kids in the world. Your dad and I love you.'

Everyone held up their glasses and said after her, 'To Zoe and Zach.'

Napoleon and Zoe didn't do a toast.

Instead, Napoleon lit the candles on Carmel's cake, and they all sang 'Happy Birthday' and Zoe blew out the candles and no-one said, 'Make a wish,' because every single person in that room was wishing the same thing. Frances could see him so clearly, the boy who should have been there, sitting shoulder to shoulder with Zoe, jostling with her to blow out the candles, their lives ahead of them.

After plates were handed around with the (excellent) cake, Zoe demanded that Ben play a song that Frances didn't recognise, and Ben played it, and he and Jessica and Zoe danced together.

There were promises to keep in touch. People friended and followed each other. Jessica set up a WhatsApp group on their phones and joined them all.

Carmel was the first one to succumb to exhaustion and say, 'Goodnight.' Everyone was leaving for home the next morning. Those who were from interstate had changed their flights and transfers to the next day. Carmel was from Adelaide, and the Marconi family and Tony were from Melbourne. Tony was the only interstate guest who had hired a rental car, and he was going to drive Ben and Jessica to pick up their car from where it had been abandoned by Delilah. Lars and Frances, the only guests from Sydney, had declared their intentions to sleep late and have a lazy breakfast before heading off.

Frances somehow already knew that everything was going to feel different in the morning.

They would all feel the tug of their old lives. She'd been on group package holidays and cruises before. She knew the process. The further away they got from Tranquillum House, the more they would think, 'Wait, what was that all about? I have nothing in common with those people!' It would all begin to feel like a dream. 'Did I really do a Hawaiian dance by the pool?' 'Did I really attempt to do a charade of the Kama Sutra just so my team would win?' 'Did I really take illegal drugs and get locked up with strangers?'

At last there was just Frances and Tony, alone at the long table, drinking a final glass of wine.

Tony held up the bottle. 'Refill?'

Frances looked at her glass, considered. 'No, thank you.'

He went to refill his own glass, changed his mind and put the bottle back down.

'I must be transformed,' said Frances. 'Normally I'd say yes.'

'Me too,' said Tony.

He got that decisive, focused, *I'm going in* look men got on their faces when they'd decided it was time to kiss you.

Frances thought of that first kiss at Natalie's sixteenth birthday party, how incredible and glorious it was, and how that was the boy who ended up telling her that he preferred smaller breasts. She thought of Gillian telling her to stop acting like the heroine of one of her own novels. Tony lived in Melbourne and was no doubt very settled in his life there. She thought of how often she'd moved for a man, how she'd been prepared to pack up her life and move to America for a man who didn't even exist.

She thought of Masha asking, 'Do you want to be a different person when you leave here?'

She said to Tony, 'Normally, I'd say yes.'

chapter seventy-five

One week later

'So, I'm not pregnant,' said Jessica. 'Never was pregnant. It was all in my head.'

Ben looked up from the couch. He picked up the remote and turned off *Top Gear*.

'Okay,' he said.

She came and sat down next to him and put her hand on his knee and for a moment they sat in silence and didn't say a word, but somehow they both knew what it meant.

If she'd been pregnant, they would have stayed together. There was enough love left to stay together for a baby.

But she wasn't pregnant, and there wasn't enough love left to try again, or for anything else, except an inevitable, amicable divorce.

Two weeks later

The house smelled of gingerbread and caramel and butter. Carmel had cooked all her daughters' favourite foods for their homecoming.

She heard the sound of the car pulling into the driveway and went to the door.

The car doors flew open and out tumbled her four little girls. They knocked her to her knees with their embraces. She buried her nose in their hair, the crooks of their arms. They burrowed into her and instantly began to fight over her like she was a favourite stuffed toy.

Lizzie got elbowed in the eye by one of her sisters and wailed. Lulu screamed at Allie, 'Let me have a turn hugging Mummy! You're taking *all* of her!' Sadie grabbed at Carmel's hair and tugged, bringing tears of pain to her eyes.

'Let your mother stand up!' snapped Joel. He never did well on long-haul flights. 'For Christ's sake.'

Carmel managed to stagger to her feet.

Lulu said fiercely, 'I am never ever leaving you again, Mummy.'

Joel snapped, 'Lulu! Don't be so ungrateful. You just had the holiday of a lifetime.'

'No need to get cross with her,' said Sonia. 'We're all tired.'

Watching her ex-husband's new girlfriend criticise him reminded Carmel of the euphoria she'd experienced after drinking that drug-laced smoothie.

'Go inside, girls,' said Carmel. 'There are treats.'

The girls ran.

'You look *great*,' said Sonia, who looked grey-faced and jet-lagged.

'Thanks,' said Carmel. 'I've had a really nice break.'

'Have you lost *weight*?' asked Sonia.

'I don't know,' said Carmel. She honestly didn't know. It no longer seemed important.

'Well, I don't know what it is, but you just look

transformed, you really do,' said Sonia warmly. 'Your skin looks great, your hair . . . everything.'

Carmel thought, *Damn it, I'm going to become your friend, aren't I?*

She realised that Joel wouldn't even notice any difference in her. You never changed your appearance for men, you changed it for other women, because they were the ones carefully tracking each other's weight and skin tone along with their own; they were the ones trapped with you on the ridiculous appearance obsession merry-go-round that they couldn't or wouldn't get off. Even if she'd been a perfectly toned and manicured gym junkie, Joel would still have left her. His 'lack of attraction' had nothing to do with her. He didn't leave her for something better, but for something new.

Joel said, 'We got seated right near the toilets on the flight home. Bang, bang, bang, went the door all night. I never slept at all.'

'Unacceptable,' said Carmel.

'I know,' said Joel. 'I tried to get us upgraded on points, but no luck.'

Carmel registered the upward lift of Sonia's eyes. Yes, definitely friends.

'So, I've been thinking it might be good if you could help with some of the chauffeuring around to after-school activities this year,' said Carmel to Joel. 'I wore myself out trying to do everything on my own last year and I want to keep up this new exercise routine I've got going.'

'Of course,' said Sonia. 'We're co-parents!'

'My mouth feels disgusting,' muttered Joel. 'I think it's the dehydration.'

'Send me their schedules,' said Sonia. 'We'll get it all worked out. Or, if you want, we could have a coffee together, talk it through?' She looked nervous, as if she'd overstepped.

'That sounds good,' said Carmel.

'I set my own hours, so I can be really flexible,' said Sonia. The enthusiasm bubbled up in her voice. 'I'd *love* to help out with their ballet, any time. I always dreamed of having a little girl and doing her hair for ballet and, well, as you know, I can't have children of my own, so I'm never –'

'You can't have children?' interrupted Carmel.

'I'm sorry, I thought you knew that,' said Sonia, with a sideways glance at Joel, who was busy running his finger around the inside of his mouth.

'I didn't know that,' said Carmel. 'I'm sorry.'

'Oh, it's fine, I've fully accepted it,' said Sonia, with a second glance at Joel that told Carmel it was *not* fine for Sonia, but it was just great for Joel. 'But that's why I'd love to help with ballet. Unless you want to keep that for yourself, of course.'

'You're very welcome to take them to ballet,' said Carmel, who was *not* a ballet mum and could never manage those sleek ballet buns to the satisfaction of her daughters or their teacher, Miss Amber.

'Really?' Sonia clasped her hands as if she'd been given the most precious gift, and the joyous gratitude in her eyes made Carmel want to cry with gratitude too. The girls weren't going to have to be confused by the arrival of a half-sibling and Carmel was going to get out of all things ballet. Miss Amber would love Sonia. Sonia would *volunteer* to help out doing hair and make-up at the concerts. Carmel was permanently off the hook.

Later today Carmel would tell Lulu to never *ever* correct anyone who said how much she looked like her mummy when she was out with Sonia.

'I'll research the best calendar-sharing apps.' Sonia took out her phone from her handbag and tapped herself a note.

Carmel experienced another burst of euphoria. She might have lost a husband, but she'd got herself a *wife*. An efficient, energetic young wife. What a bargain. What an upgrade.

She'd be there for poor Sonia when, in ten years or so, Joel decided he was due for *his* next upgrade.

'Can we talk about ballet another time?' said Joel. 'Because right now, I really need to get home for a shower.' He made a movement towards his car.

'We need to say goodbye to the girls!' said Sonia.

'Of course,' sighed Joel. It seemed like it had been a long holiday.

'Was it paleo?' Sonia whispered to Carmel, as they headed inside the house. 'Five:two? Eighteen:six?'

'Health resort,' said Carmel. 'Very trippy place. It changed my life.'

Three weeks later

'You're panting,' said Jo to Frances.

'I've been doing push-ups,' said Frances, facedown on her living room floor, the phone to her ear. 'Push-ups work every muscle in your body.'

'You have not been doing push-ups,' scoffed Jo. 'Oh my God, I haven't interrupted you *in flagrante delicto*?'

Only Frances's former editor could both pronounce and *spell* 'in flagrante delicto'.

'I guess I should be flattered that you think I'm more likely to be having sex at eleven in the morning than doing push-ups.' Frances sat up into a cross-legged position.

She'd lost three kilos at Tranquillum House and put them straight back on once she was home, but she was trying to incorporate a little more exercise, a little less chocolate, a little more mindful breathing and a little less wine into her lifestyle. She was feeling pretty good. The whites of her eyes were most definitely whiter, according to her friend Ellen, who had been shocked to hear about Frances's experiences.

'When I said their approach was unconventional, I meant the personalised meals!' she cried. 'I didn't mean LSD!' She thought about it, and then said wistfully, 'I would have loved to try LSD.'

'How's retirement?' Frances asked Jo.

'I'm going back to work,' said Jo. 'Work is easier. Everyone thinks I have nothing to do all day. My siblings think I should take full responsibility for our elderly parents. My children think I should take care of their children. I love my grandchildren, but day care was invented for a reason.'

'I knew you were too young to retire,' said Frances as she tried to touch her nose to her knee. Stretching was so important.

'I'm starting my own imprint,' said Jo.

'*Are* you?' said Frances. She sat up straight. A tiny burst of hope. 'Congratulations.'

'Naturally I've read the new novel, and naturally I love it,' said Jo. 'Before I think about making an offer, I just wondered how you'd feel about incorporating a little blood-shed? Potentially even a murder. Just the one.'

'Murder!' said Frances. 'I don't know if I've got it in me.'

'Oh, Frances,' said Jo. 'You've got plenty of murderous impulses lurking away in that romantic old heart of yours.'

'Have I?' said Frances. She narrowed her eyes. Maybe she did.

Four weeks later

Lars didn't know he was going to say it until he said it.

Since he'd been back home the dirty-faced little dark-haired boy with Ray's hazel eyes kept materialising just as he drifted off to sleep, and suddenly, irritatingly, he'd be wide awake with the exact same thought in his head, like a brand-new revelation every time: the kid didn't want to show him something terrible from his past. *He wanted to show him something wonderful in his future.*

What a load of nonsense, he kept telling himself. I'm not a different person. That was just drugs. I've taken drugs before. That was a hallucination, not a goddamn epiphany.

But now Ray stood at the pantry putting away groceries, all those protein shakes, and Lars heard the words coming out of his mouth: 'I've been thinking about the baby idea.'

He saw Ray's hand stop. A can of tinned tomatoes poised midair. He didn't say a word. He didn't move or turn around.

'Maybe we could give it a shot,' Lars said. '*Maybe.*' He felt sick. If Ray turned around right now, if he threw his arms around him, if he looked at him with all that love and happiness and need in his eyes, Lars would vomit, he would definitely vomit.

But Ray knew him too well.

He didn't turn around. He slowly put the can of tomatoes down. 'Okay,' he said, as if it were neither here nor there to him.

'We'll talk about it later,' said Lars, with a firm knuckle rap on the granite benchtop, which kind of hurt.

'Yep,' said Ray.

A little while later, when Lars came back into the house to retrieve his sunglasses after saying he was going out to the shops, he heard the unmistakable sound of a six-foot man jumping up and down on the spot while *shrieking* into the phone to someone who was presumably his sister: 'Oh my *God,* oh my *God,* you're never going to believe what just happened!'

Lars stopped for a moment, his sunglasses in his hand, and smiled, before he headed back outside into the sunshine.

Five weeks later

There was a documentary about the history of Australian Rules football on TV. Frances watched the whole thing. It was actually fascinating.

She called Tony. 'I just watched a whole hour of television about your sport!'

'Frances?' He sounded like he was puffing.

'I've just been doing push-ups,' he said.

'I can do ten in a row now,' said Frances. 'How many can you do?'

'A hundred,' said Tony.

'Show-off,' said Frances.

Six weeks later

Napoleon sat in the waiting room of a psychiatrist he'd been referred to by his GP. It had taken him six weeks to get the first available appointment. *That's the mental health crisis problem right there,* he thought.

Since returning from Tranquillum House, he'd been surviving: teaching, cooking, talking to his wife and daughter, running his support group. It was amazing to him that everyone treated him as if he were just the same.

It reminded him of the blocked-ears feeling after a flight, except all his senses, not just his hearing, felt muted. His voice seemed to echo in his ears. The sky was leached of colour. He did nothing that he wasn't obliged to do because the effort of existence exhausted him. He slept whenever he could. Getting up each morning was like moving his limbs through thick mud.

'Everything okay?' Heather sometimes said to him.

'All good,' said Napoleon.

Heather was different after their time at Tranquillum House. Not happier exactly, but calmer. She had joined a tai chi class in the park down the road. She was the only one under the age of seventy. Heather had never been the sort of woman to have girlfriends, but for some reason she fitted right in to this elderly circle.

'They make me laugh,' she said. 'And they don't demand anything from me.'

'What are you talking about?' said Zoe. 'They demand lots of you!' It was true that Heather seemed to be spending a lot of time driving her elderly new friends to and fro from doctors' appointments and picking up prescriptions for them.

Zoe had a new part-time job. She seemed busy and distracted with her university course. Napoleon kept a careful eye on her, but she was good, she was fine. One morning, a week or so after they'd got back from the retreat, he stopped by her bathroom door and overheard a beautiful sound he hadn't heard in three years: his daughter singing off-key in the shower.

'Mr Marconi?' said a short blonde woman who reminded him a little of Frances Welty. 'I'm Allison.'

She ushered him into her office and motioned to a chair on the opposite side of a coffee table with a book about English gardens and a box of aloe vera scented tissues.

Napoleon didn't wait for the niceties. He had no time to lose.

He told her about Zach. He told her about the drugs he was given at Tranquillum House and how, ever since then, he'd been struggling with what he believed to be depression. He told her that his GP had offered him antidepressants, and he probably did need antidepressants, but he knew sometimes it was hard to get the dosage right, it wasn't an exact science, he understood and appreciated this, he had done the research, he knew all the brand names, all the side effects, he'd put together his own spreadsheet if she was interested in taking a look, and he knew that sometimes, during that initial period, patients didn't get better, they got worse, they suffered suicidal thoughts, and he knew this because he knew people who had lost family members in that way, and he also knew that he overreacted to drugs, he knew this about himself, and maybe his son had the same sensitivity, he didn't know, and he was sure that those people at that health resort meant well, and maybe this depression had been going to happen anyway, but he felt that he was possibly the one person in that room who should never, ever have been given that smoothie.

And then, limp with exhaustion, he said, 'Allison, I am terrified that I will . . .'

She didn't ask him to finish the sentence.

She reached across the coffee table and put her hand on his arm. 'We're a team now, Napoleon. You and me, we're a team, and we're going to work out a strategy and we are going to beat this, okay?'

She looked at him with all the passion and intensity of his old football coach. 'We're going to beat it. We're going to win.'

Two months later

Frances and Tony were taking a walk, nine hundred kilometres apart, in different states.

They'd got into the habit of keeping each other company as they went for walks around their respective neighbourhoods.

At first they'd walked with their mobile phones pressed to their ears, but then Tony's daughter, Mimi, had said they should use headphones, and now their ears no longer ached when they finished and they could walk for even longer.

'Are you on your steep bit yet?' asked Tony.

'I am,' said Frances. 'But listen to my breathing! I'm not puffing at all.'

'You're an elite athlete,' said Tony. 'Have you murdered anyone yet?'

'Yep,' said Frances. 'Did it yesterday. Murdered my first character ever. He totally deserved it.'

'Did you enjoy it? Hello, Bear.'

Bear was a chocolate labrador that Tony often passed on his walks. Tony didn't know Bear's owner's name, but he always said hello to Bear.

Tony told her about his upcoming trip to Holland to see his son and grandchildren.

'I've never been to Holland,' said Frances.

'Haven't you?' said Tony. 'I've only been once. I'm hoping it's not going to be as cold as last time I went.'

'I've never been to Holland,' said Frances again.

There was a long pause. Frances stopped on the side of the street and smiled at a lady wearing a straw hat, watering her garden.

Tony said, 'Would you like to come to Holland with me, Frances?'

'Yes,' said Frances. 'Yes, I would.'

Their first kiss was in the Qantas lounge.

Three months later

Heather sat on the end of her bed and rubbed lotion into her dry legs, as Napoleon set the alarm on his phone for the next day.

He'd been seeing a psychiatrist, and he seemed to be doing well, but he didn't talk much about what went on in those sessions.

She watched as he put the phone on the bedside table.

'I think that you need to shout at me,' she said.

'What?' He looked up at her, startled. 'No, I don't.'

'After the retreat, we've never properly talked about it again – the asthma medication.'

'I wrote all those letters. It's on the record.' Of course, Napoleon had done the right thing. He'd found the right contacts through Dr Chang. He'd documented it all. There was never any intent to sue but he needed to make sure that what happened was on the public record. He'd written to the authorities, to the pharmaceutical company: *My son, Zachary Marconi, took his own life after being prescribed* . . .

'I know,' said Heather. 'But you never said anything about . . . what I did.'

'You are not to blame for Zach's suicide,' said Napoleon.

'I don't want you to *blame* me,' said Heather. 'But I just feel like you're allowed to be angry with me. You're allowed to be angry with Zoe, too, but you're not going to shout at Zoe –'

'*No*, I do not want to shout at Zoe.' He looked horrified at the thought.

'But you can shout at me. If you like?' She looked up at him, where he stood by the side of the bed, his brow furrowed in pain as if he'd just that instant stubbed his toe.

'Absolutely not,' he said, in his pompous schoolteacher voice. 'That's ridiculous. That achieves nothing. You lost your son.'

'Maybe I need you to be angry with me.'

'You do not,' said Napoleon. 'That's . . . sick.' He turned away from her. 'Stop this.'

'Please.' She got up on her knees on to the bed so she could look him in the eyes. 'Napoleon?' she said.

She thought about the home she grew up in, where nobody ever yelled or laughed or cried or screamed or expressed a single feeling, except for a mild desire for a cup of tea.

'Please?'

'Stop this nonsense,' he said through clenched teeth. 'Stop it.'

'Shout at me.'

'No,' he said. 'I will not. What next? Should I hit you too?'

'You'd never hit me in a million years. But I'm your wife, Napoleon, you're allowed to be angry with me.'

It was like she saw the anger shoot through him, from his feet to the top of his head. It flooded his face. It made his whole body tremble.

'You should have checked on the fucking side effects, Heather! Is that what you want to hear?' His voice rose on an ascending scale until he was shouting as loud as she'd ever heard him shout, louder even than when Zach, at nine years old, old enough to know better, nearly ran in front of a car to chase a ball, a ball he'd been told to leave behind, and Napoleon shouted 'STOP!' so loudly that every single person in that car park stopped.

Heather's heart raced as Napoleon held his hands on either side of her shoulders and shook them violently, as if he were shaking her hard enough to make her teeth rattle, except he didn't touch her.

'Does that make you happy? Is that what you wanted to hear? Yes, I am angry because when I asked you about side effects for a medication you were giving my child *you should have checked*!'

'I should have checked,' she said quietly.

He grabbed his phone from the bedside table. 'And I shouldn't have pressed snooze on this fucking piece-of-shit phone!'

He threw it against the wall.

Heather saw tiny shards of glass fly.

For a long beat neither of them said anything. She watched his chest rise and fall. She watched the anger leave him.

He sank onto the bed, facing away from her, put his face into his hands and spoke in a hoarse, heartbroken voice with only pain and regret left, so softly it was barely above a whisper, 'And our daughter should have told us there was something wrong with her brother.'

'She should have told us,' agreed Heather, and she laid her cheek against his back and waited for both their hearts to resume their normal pace.

He said something else but she didn't catch it. 'What?'

He said it again. 'And that's all we'll ever know.'

'Yes,' said Heather.

'And it will never, ever be enough,' said Napoleon.

'No,' said Heather. 'No, it won't be.'

★

That night Heather slept deeply and dreamlessly for seven hours straight, something she hadn't done since Zach died, and when she woke she found herself moving across the invisible, un-crossable expanse that had separated her and Napoleon for the last three years, as if it had never been there in the first place. She had made some bad decisions in her life, but saying yes to a freakishly tall, nerdy boy's polite invitation to see a 'well-reviewed film called Dances With Wolves' was not one of them.

You're not meant to think of your children when you make love. Sexuality between married parents is for behind closed doors. And yet, that morning, as Napoleon took her so tenderly into his arms, she thought of her family of four, of both her children, of the baby boy who would never become a man, and the baby girl who was a woman now, and the powerful currents of love that would always run between them: husband and wife, father and son, mother and son, father and daughter, mother and daughter, brother and sister. So much love that came about because she said yes to a movie invitation.

And then she thought of nothing at all, because that nerdy boy still had the moves.

One year later

Ben and his mother had imagined it so many times that he thought they would surely be prepared when it finally happened, but they weren't.

Lucy died of an overdose during one of her good periods, which is often the way, just when everyone thought that maybe this time she was going to make it. Lucy had started an interior design course. She was driving her kids to school.

She'd been to a *parent–teacher night* for her eldest son, which was unprecedented. She had her eyes on the future.

Ben's mother found her. She said she looked strangely peaceful, like a little girl having a nap, or a thirty-year-old who gave up battling the monster that just refused to let her be.

Ben thought first about ringing Jessica. They were on very good terms, although he still squirmed with embarrassment when he thought about the post she'd put on Instagram 'announcing' their split, as if they were a celebrity couple who owed it to their public to let them know the true story before the media began hounding them. She wrote: *We'll always be best friends but we've decided the time has come to lovingly separate.*

Right now, Jessica was in the middle of auditioning for the next season of *The Bachelor*. She said it wasn't so much that she wanted to find love, and she doubted she would, but it would be great for her 'profile' and it would guarantee her so many thousand more Instagram followers. He couldn't laugh too much because she was an 'ambassador' for multiple charities and her Instagram account was filled with photos of glamorous lunches and balls and breakfasts that she and a new group of society friends were so 'honoured' to have organised.

Ben was back working with Pete. The guys gave him a hard time in the beginning – 'You short of a buck, mate?' – but eventually they gave up and forgot he was rich. Ben still had the car, and a nice house, but he'd put a lot of his money into a foundation run by his mother to help support families of addicts.

Lars helped them split their assets without vitriol and without going to court. That was one thing they'd gained from their retreat at Tranquillum House: meeting a great family lawyer.

Ben didn't ring Jessica to tell her about Lucy straight away. He couldn't bear to hear the lack of surprise in her voice. Instead, he dialled Zoe's number. They'd become online friends and occasional texters since the retreat but they'd never actually talked on the phone.

'Hello, Ben,' she said cheerfully. 'How are you?'

'I'm calling —' He found he couldn't speak. He tried to remember to exhale.

Her tone changed. 'Is it your sister?' she said. 'Is it Lucy?'

She was there at the funeral. His eyes kept seeking her out.

chapter seventy-six

Five years later

Yao wouldn't normally have turned on daytime television, but he had just returned home from a stressful time at playgroup where his two-year-old daughter had sunk her teeth into the arm of another child and then thrown back her head and laughed like a vampire. It had been both embarrassing and terrifying.

'Oh yes, you were a biter,' his mother told him on the phone. 'She gets it from you.' She said this with some satisfaction, as if the propensity to bite was a wonderful trait to pass on to your children.

Yao put his daughter down for a nap and pointed a stern finger at her. 'Never do that again.'

She pointed a sterner finger back up at him. 'Never do that again.'

Then she lay down, plugged her thumb in her mouth and closed her eyes. He could still see her dimple, which meant she was just pretending to be asleep, hardly able to suppress her hilarity.

He stood there for a few moments, marvelling at her

dimple and the roundness of her baby cheeks, marvelling as he so often did that he had been parachuted into another life, a brand-new life as a stay-at-home dad in the suburbs.

He had received a fourteen-month suspended jail sentence after pleading guilty for his role in the events at Tranquillum House. Masha had insisted to police that she must take sole responsibility for the new protocol they'd attempted to introduce and that her employees were nothing more than oblivious, obedient halfwits. She said she was the one who mixed the smoothies, which was true, but Yao had been right there with her, checking and double-checking dosages. Yao's mother said if she'd been the judge, he would have gone to prison. Both his parents had been so angry. They could not comprehend his actions. Most days, Yao could not comprehend them himself. It had all seemed so reasonable at the time. The prestigious researchers! The journal papers!

'That woman had you in a trance,' his mother said.

His mother vehemently denied that the incident he'd remembered during his psychedelic therapy ever happened.

'Never,' she said. 'I would never leave you alone in a kitchen with something boiling on the stove. Do you think I'm stupid? Would you do that with your child? You had better not!'

She said that Yao's fear of mistakes came from no-one but himself. 'You were *born* like that!' she told him. 'We tried so hard to make you understand that mistakes do not matter. We told you again and again that you should not try so hard to be perfect, it did not matter if you made a mistake. Sometimes we purposely made mistakes so you would see that everyone made them. Your father used to deliberately drop things, bump into walls. I said to him, "That's a bit much." But he seemed to enjoy it.'

Yao wondered then if he'd been misinterpreting his

parents his whole life. When they talked about keeping expectations low to avoid disappointment, it wasn't because they didn't believe in dreams. It was because they were trying to protect him. Also, his father was not as clumsy as he had thought.

★

Delilah did not face court, because no-one could ever track her down. Yao thought idly of her at times and wondered where she was; if she was on some remote island, restoring a boat, like the escaped prisoner in his favourite movie, *The Shawshank Redemption*. ('That's every single man in the world's favourite movie,' one of the mothers at playgroup had told him once. She knew because she'd tried internet dating.) But Yao suspected that it was more likely Delilah had disappeared into an urban environment and was working again as a PA. Sometimes he still thought of that skirt she wore, a thousand years ago, when she worked for Masha.

Yao was disqualified from working as a paramedic or anything in the health industry. After he left Tranquillum House and the charges were settled, he had moved into a one-bedroom apartment in a location virtually equidistant to the locations of his parents' homes, and he ended up getting a job as a translator of Chinese legal documents. It was dull, laborious work but it paid the bills.

One day he got a call. Afterwards, he wondered if a phone call that is going to change your life has a portentous ringtone, because when he heard that ring, as he sat alone, eating his sad dinner for one, he experienced the most remarkable full-body shiver of presentiment.

It was Bernadette, his ex-fiancée, calling to say hi. She'd been thinking about him. She'd been thinking about him a lot.

Sometimes your life changes so slowly and imperceptibly that you don't notice it at all, until one day you wake up and think: *How did I get here?* But other times life changes in an instant, with a lightning stroke of good or bad luck, with glorious or tragic consequences. You win the lottery. You step out onto a pedestrian crossing at the wrong time. You get a phone call from a lost love at exactly the right time. And suddenly your life takes a violent swerve in an entirely new direction.

They were married within the year and his wife got pregnant immediately. It made sense for her to go back to work and for Yao to stay home with the baby while he continued doing his translation work, which now seemed interesting and stimulating.

Once he knew his daughter wasn't faking sleep anymore, he went into the living room, sank down on the couch and turned on the TV. He would treat himself to twenty minutes of rubbish television to soothe himself from the stress of the biting incident, and then he'd get in an hour of work before it was time to think about dinner.

The remote slipped from his hand.

He whispered, '*Masha.*'

*

'*Masha,*' said a man on the other side of the same city, a spanner in his hands. He didn't normally watch daytime television either, but he had come over to do a few jobs around his daughter-in-law's house, as his son was good with numbers but not much else.

'Do you know her?' His daughter-in-law lifted the baby girl she'd been breastfeeding while she watched TV onto her shoulder and patted her back.

'She looks like someone I used to know,' said the man, carefully not looking at his daughter-in-law because he did not want to see her breasts, and also because he could not tear his eyes from his ex-wife.

Masha looked so beautiful. Her hair was dark brown with bits of blonde, shoulder-length, and she wore a dress of all different shades of green that made her eyes look like emeralds.

The man sat on the couch next to his daughter-in-law and she glanced at him curiously but didn't say anything else. They watched the interview together.

Masha had written a book. It was about a ten-day personal development program that incorporated psychedelic drugs, being locked in a room with strangers and undergoing an innovative kind of therapy that involved facing fears and solving riddles.

'Surely people aren't falling for this,' murmured his daughter-in-law.

'Now, obviously these drugs you mention are illegal,' said the interviewer.

'Unfortunately, yes,' said Masha. 'But that will not be the case forever.'

'And I understand you did jail time for supplying illegal drugs while attempting to test out this program.'

The man clenched the spanner he still held in his lap. *Jail time?*

'I did,' said Masha. 'But I will never regret that time. It was very important to me.' She lifted her chin. 'My time behind bars was a *transformative experience*. I learned so much, and I explain all my experiences in this book, which is available now, in all good bookstores.' She picked up the book and held it in front of her face.

The interviewer cleared her throat. 'Masha, what do you

say about the rumours that people have been attending these courses you offer, held in different secret locations across the country, and that you are, in point of fact, offering LSD and other hallucinogenic drugs to your attendees?'

'That is absolutely untrue,' said Masha. 'I unequivocally deny it.'

'So you are not running these programs in secret locations?'

'I am running very unique, tailored, incredibly effective personal development programs to small, select groups of people, but there is nothing illegal going on, I can assure you of that.'

'I hear there is a waiting list,' said the interviewer. 'And that people are paying quite hefty fees to attend.'

'There is a waiting list,' said Masha. 'People should visit my website if they would like to go on the list, or call the toll-free number I believe is appearing on the screen right now. There is a special offer for those who call within the next twenty-four hours.'

'If there is nothing illegal going on, I wonder why the locations are kept secret and change on a regular basis,' said the interviewer. She looked at Masha expectantly.

'Was that a question?' asked Masha, with a seductive smile straight at the camera.

'What a *nutter*,' said the man's daughter-in-law. 'I bet she's making millions.' She stood, and held out the baby to her father-in-law. 'Will you hold her? I'll make us some tea.'

The man moved the spanner off his lap and took his granddaughter. His daughter-in-law left the room.

Masha was talking about something called 'holotropic breathwork', which she said was 'psychedelic therapy without the psychedelics'.

'That's where you breathe fast to get high, right?' said the interviewer, rather rudely and sceptically.

'It is a much more complex, sophisticated process than that,' said Masha.

An image appeared on the screen of Masha at some kind of conference centre, striding about a stage with a tiny microphone attached to her ear, while an auditorium packed with people looked on with rapt attention.

The man held the baby up and spoke in his native tongue into her ear. 'That crazy woman is your grandmother.'

★

He remembered the day their second son was born, only three months after they lost their firstborn so tragically.

'He is yours.' Masha had refused to look at the baby. Her averted face, her sweat-soaked hair flat against her forehead, could have been carved from marble. 'Not mine.'

A nurse at the hospital said, 'Mum will come around.' It was the grief. She was still in shock, probably. Such a terrible thing to go through, losing her son when she was six months pregnant with her second. That nurse did not know his wife's strength. She did not know Masha.

Masha discharged herself from the hospital. She said she was going straight back to work, that very day, and she would send money. She would make enough money in her job so that her husband could take care of the new baby, but she wanted nothing to do with him.

She spoke very calmly, as if this were a business arrangement, and she only lost her temper once, when the man fell to his knees and clutched her and begged her to let them be a family again. Masha screamed into his face, over and over, 'I am not a mother! Can you not understand this? I am not a mother!'

So he let her go. What else could he do? She did exactly what she said she would and sent money, more and more each year, as her career became more successful.

He sent her photos. She never acknowledged them. He wondered if she even looked at them and he thought that maybe she did not. She was a woman with the strength to move mountains. She was a woman as weak as a child.

He remarried two years later. His son called his Australian wife 'Mummy' and spoke with an Australian accent, and they had two more sons and lived an Australian life in this lucky country. They played cricket on the beach on Christmas Day. They had a swimming pool in their backyard and his sons caught the bus home and on hot summer days they ran straight through the house, tearing off their clothes, and jumped into the pool in their undies. They had a large circle of friends, some of whom dropped by their house without phoning first. His second wife grew up in a small country town, and her accent was from 'the bush', broad and thick and slow, her favourite phrase was 'no big deal' and he loved her, but there had been occasions over the years when he would be standing in his backyard at the barbecue, turning steaks, a beer in his hand, cicadas screaming, a kookaburra laughing, the splash of water, the smell of bug spray, the early evening sun still hot on his neck, and without warning Masha's face would appear in his mind, her nostrils flared, her beautiful green eyes blazing with superiority and contempt but also childlike confusion: *These people! They are so strange!*

For many years he had given up communicating with Masha. He didn't bother to send photos of their son's wedding, but five years ago, when their first grandchild was born and he was awash with the fierce, all-consuming love of a new grandparent, he had emailed again, attaching photos of the baby, with the subject heading: PLEASE READ,

MASHA. He wrote that it was fine that she chose not to be a mother, he understood, but now, if she wanted, she could be a grandmother and wasn't that wonderful? There was no reply.

He looked now at his granddaughter. He thought he could see something of Masha in the shape of her eyes. He held the baby with one arm and extracted his phone from his pocket with the other, and snapped a photo of her exquisite, sleeping face.

He wouldn't give up. One day Masha would answer. One day she would weaken, or find the strength, and she would answer.

He knew her better than anyone.

One day she would.

chapter seventy-seven

Reader, she didn't marry him, but he moved to Sydney for her and they lived together, and Tony was there beside her during the resurgence of her career, when Frances's first foray into 'romantic suspense' turned out to be a surprise hit. (A surprise to everyone except Jo, who called her up the day after she delivered the revised manuscript and said, in a very un-grandmotherly tone, 'You fucking nailed it.')

Frances was also a surprise hit with Tony's grandchildren in Holland, who called her 'Grandma Frances', and Tony credited Frances with the family's decision to move back to Sydney, which was entirely unwarranted, as his son Will had got a transfer, nothing to do with her. But she was besotted with his grandkids – her grandkids – and all of her friends said that was just so *typical* of Frances, to skip the hard yards and go straight to the good part, where you got to love them and spoil them and hand them back.

But they forgave her.

chapter seventy-eight

Of course, not everyone gets a happy ending, or even the chance of one. Life doesn't work like that. Case in point: Helen Ihnat, the reviewer of Frances's novel *What the Heart Wants*, lost her entire life savings in a mortifying, high-profile cryptocurrency scam and lived in a state of quite profound unhappiness for the rest of her days.

But as she despised neatly tied-up happy endings, she was fine with that.

chapter seventy-nine

Oh, reader, of course she married him eventually. You've met her. She waited until her sixtieth birthday. She wore turquoise. She had eleven bridesmaids, none of whom was under the age of forty-five, thirteen flower girls and one page boy, a toddler just learning to walk, who clutched a Matchbox car in each of his tiny fists. His name was Zach.

Every chair at the reception was tied up with a giant white satin bow at the back.

It was the most beautiful, ridiculous wedding you've ever seen.

Acknowledgements

As always there are so many people to thank for their support with this book. Thank you to my talented editors who worked so hard to make *Nine Perfect Strangers* so much better in so many significant ways: Georgia Douglas, Cate Paterson, Amy Einhorn, Maxine Hitchcock, Ali Lavau and Hilary Reynolds.

Thank you to Elina Reddy for giving so generously of her time to help me develop the character of Masha. Elina is not only a wonderful artist but has the ability to paint such vivid pictures with her words. Maria (Masha) Dmitrichenko was the winning bidder at a Starlight Children's Foundation charity event to have a character in one of my books named after her and I thank her for the use of her name.

Thank you to Dr Nikki Stamp for answering my questions. She is one of only a handful of female heart surgeons in Australia and the dialogue I gave Masha's heart surgeon came straight from her fascinating book, *Can You Die of a Broken Heart?*

Thank you to Kat Lukash and Praveen Naidoo for help with my Russian and my football, to Lucie Johnson for sharing health resort stories and to my brother-in-law Rob Ostric, for the expression on his face when I asked how he would feel about driving a Lamborghini down an unsealed road. Thank you to my sister Fiona for instantly answering my texts demanding information. Thank you to my charming fellow guests at the Golden Door health resort for a lovely week where I saw the sun rise, which was very pleasing, although I feel no particular need to see it do so again.

Thank you to my agents: Fiona Inglis and Ben Stevenson in Sydney, Faye Bender in New York, Jonathan Lloyd and Kate Cooper in London and Jerry Kalajian in LA. Thank you to my publicists for your patience and for all that you do: Tracey Cheetham in Sydney, Gaby Young in London and Marlena Bittner in New York. Thank you also to Conor Mintzer, Nancy Trypuc and Katie Bowden.

Thank you to Adam for helping me create Tranquillum House, for stopping to answer strange random questions at intervals throughout the day, for waking me with coffee, for looking after me and for always being on my side. Thank you to George and Anna for being beautiful and for helpfully pointing out the swearwords whenever you saw my manuscript open on the screen. Thank you to my mother, Diane Moriarty, for help with proof-reading and for being the sort of mother who would thankfully *never* move to the south of France.

Writing can be a lonely job so I want to thank some of my 'colleagues' in the business. Thank you to my sisters and fellow writers Jaclyn Moriarty and Nicola Moriarty, and thank you to my friends and fellow writers Dianne Blacklock, Ber Carroll, Jojo Moyes and Marian Keyes. Thank you to the talented Caroline Lee for your wonderful narration of my audio books.

Thank you to Nicole Kidman, Per Saari and Bruna Papandrea for their extraordinary faith in this book before they'd read a single word.

Thank you to my readers. Like Frances, I have the loveliest readers in the world and every day I'm grateful to you.

I've dedicated this book to my sister Kati, and to my father, Bernie Moriarty, because they have always been so strong and brave and funny in the face of adversity and because I suspect even on their bad days they could do more push-ups than Masha.

★

The following books were useful to me in my research: *No Time to Say Goodbye: Surviving The Suicide of a Loved One* by Carla Fine, *Acid Test: LSD, Ecstasy and the Power to Heal* by Tom Shroder, *Therapy with Substance: Psycholytic Psychotherapy in the Twenty First Century* by Dr Friederike Meckel Fischer, and *The Doors of Perception* by Aldous Huxley.

★

If you or anyone you know is suffering from depression, call Lifeline on 13 11 14, beyondblue on 1800 22 4636, or Kids Helpline on 1800 55 1800.

Liane Moriarty
Big Little Lies

'I guess it started with the mothers.'
'It was all just a terrible misunderstanding.'
'I'll tell you exactly why it happened.'

Pirriwee Public's annual school Trivia Night has ended in
a shocking riot. A parent is dead. Was it murder, a tragic
accident . . . or something else entirely?

Big Little Lies is a funny, heartbreaking, challenging story of
ex-husbands and second wives, new friendships, old betrayals
and schoolyard politics.

No. 1 *New York Times* bestselling author Liane Moriarty turns her
unique gaze on the dangerous little lies we tell ourselves every day
and what really goes on behind closed suburban doors.

*'Let me be clear. This is not a circus. This is a murder
investigation.'*

'It draws out lashings of dark humour, and ultimately drama . . .
although the style and emotional register are quite different,
Moriarty's ability to mine suburban anxieties in a compelling
way calls to mind Tsiolkas' *The Slap*.'
SATURDAY AGE

'The secrets burrowed in this seemingly placid small town . . . are
so suburban noir they would make David Lynch clap with
glee . . . A fantastically nimble writer, so sure-footed that the book
leaps between dark and light seamlessly; even the big reveal in the
final pages feels earned and genuinely shocking.'
ENTERTAINMENT WEEKLY

Liane Moriarty
The Husband's Secret

Cecilia Fitzpatrick, devoted mother and successful Tupperware consultant, has found a letter from her husband.

'To be opened only in the event of my death'

But Cecilia's husband isn't dead, he's on a business trip. And when she questions him about the letter on the phone, Cecilia senses something she hasn't experienced before. John-Paul is lying.

We all have secrets. But not like this . . .

'Intelligent and funny with a good strong plot and an intriguing premise' *SATURDAY AGE*

'Amid three intertwined storylines and terrific plot twists Moriarty presents a nuanced and moving portrait of the meaning of love, both marital and familial' *USA TODAY*

'One of the Top Ten Books of the Year' *PEOPLE MAGAZINE*

'Emotionally astute, immensely smart . . . destined for critical accolades and a big-screen adaptation' *ENTERTAINMENT WEEKLY*

'A bold and daring novel, layered and morally challenging' *RICHARD AND JUDY BOOKCLUB REVIEW*

Liane Moriarty
The Hypnotist's Love Story

As a hypnotherapist, Ellen O'Farrell is fascinated by what makes people tick. So when she falls in love with Patrick, the fact that he has a stalker doesn't faze her in the slightest. If anything it intrigues her, and the more she hears about Saskia, the more she wants to meet this woman. But what Ellen doesn't know is that they've already met . . .

Saskia has been posing as one of Ellen's clients. Unable to let go of the life she so abruptly lost, she wants to know everything about the woman who took her place.

But it's not only Saskia who doesn't know when to stop: Ellen also has to ask herself what lines she's prepared to cross to get the happy ending she's always wanted.

'A compelling love triangle . . . romance with an edge . . . the latest triumph . . . What lifts this tale to another plane is the level of empathy that runs through the narrative.' *AUSTRALIAN WOMEN'S WEEKLY* BOOK OF THE MONTH

'Superb in technique . . . All of her novels set themselves extremely difficult tasks . . . The novel blends elements of crime, horror and love story . . .' *SUNDAY AGE*

'A warmly humorous, gently poignant, ultimately comforting tale of frustration and redemption . . . Moriarty writes with both a frisky wit and a generosity of spirit that's truly disarming . . . It will make you feel warm all over.' *USA TODAY*

Liane Moriarty
What Alice Forgot

When Alice Love surfaces from a strange dream to find she's
been injured in a gym, her first concern is for her unborn baby.
She's desperate to see her husband, Nick, who she knows will be
worried about her.

But Alice isn't pregnant. And Nick isn't rushing to her bedside.
She is a mother of three going through a bitter divorce.

Alice has lost ten years of her life – and she wants them back.

'A bittersweet tale by a gifted writer, whose light touch doesn't stop
her exploring darker themes, such as infertility and the sad erosion
of a once radiant love.' *AUSTRALIAN WOMEN'S WEEKLY*
BOOK OF THE MONTH

'What [Moriarty] writes are acute social comedies of the feminine,
where the domestic is more political than cosy . . . Technically this
premise is a challenge, which Moriarty makes appear effortless . . .
Great stuff.' *THE AGE*

'A thought-provoking story that explores family dynamics with
intelligence, wit and sensitivity but without any sentimentality.'
COURIER-MAIL

'An intriguing exploration of how people change . . . Alice's
amnesia is skilfully used and like a detective, she must piece
together the details of a life she cannot remember.' *SUN-HERALD*

Liane Moriarty
The Last Anniversary

Sophie Honeywell always wondered if Thomas Gordon was the one that got away. When she turned down his proposal three years ago, she broke his heart. Now that Sophie is single, longing for a baby and nearly 40, he's starting to look a lot more attractive . . .

Sophie is just as shocked as Thomas when his Aunt Connie leaves Sophie her beautiful house on Scribbly Gum Island. This tiny island is home to the famous 'Munro Baby Mystery' – a seventy-year-old unsolved crime.

Sophie soon discovers that nearly everyone on the island has a secret, and the biggest secret of all, the truth behind the Munro Baby Mystery, is set to explode on an extraordinary night that will test a marriage, a family and a friendship – the Last Anniversary.

'A stunner several shades darker than typical chick lit . . . Moriarty's prose turns from funny through poignant to frightening in an artful snap.' *PUBLISHERS WEEKLY*

'Intriguing mystery-cum-drama . . . things nearly fall apart before coming together in this endearing story that, like life, is a mix of the sad, the happy, the absurd and the magical.' *AUSTRALIAN WOMEN'S WEEKLY* BOOK OF THE MONTH

'A brave author who takes a risk to write about subjects not often found in this genre . . . This is a great read.' *GOOD READING*

Liane Moriarty
Three Wishes

The Kettle triplets have had a mortifying public mishap. Their noisy, champagne-soaked birthday dinner has come to an abrupt end following a violent argument and an emergency dash to the hospital.

So who started it this time? Was it angry, hurt Cat, still recovering from the 'Night of the Spaghetti'? Or Lyn, who at least on the outside seems to have everything under control. Or maybe it was the unpredictable Gemma, the sister who can't keep a secret, except the most important one of all . . .

'In this non-stop narrative, siblings rival each other, break up and make up. Moriarty is good at social observation, mixing high drama with low comedy and moments of genuine poignancy.'
SUNDAY AGE

'Funny, wry, touching . . . the drama is raw and real. Each of the beautifully drawn characters is so vividly alive, their triumph becomes your own, you choke a bit when bad things happen and want to throw rocks at anyone who hurts them.'
AUSTRALIAN WOMEN'S WEEKLY
BOOK OF THE MONTH

'I appreciated how she didn't produce any last-minute sugarcoating out of the hat. I really did believe in the strength of the characters to pull through: in fact, it made me believe in the resilience of the human race!' MARIAN KEYES